FC 17th

RECEIVED

FEB 2 3 2006

By_____

BROOKLAND

Emily Barton

FARRAR · STRAUS · GIROUX   New York

BROOKLAND

Farrar, Straus and Giroux
19 Union Square West, New York 10003

A portion of this work was originally published, in slightly different form, in *Conjunctions*.

Grateful acknowledgment is made to the following for permission to reprint previously published material: Haiku used as epigraph, from *The Essential Haiku: Versions of Bashō, Buson, and Issa*, edited and with an introduction by Robert Hass. Introduction and selection copyright © 1994 by Robert Hass. Unless otherwise noted, all translations copyright © 1994 by Robert Hass. Reprinted by permission of HarperCollins Publishers.

Library of Congress Cataloging-in-Publication Data
Barton, Emily, 1969–
    Brookland / Emily Barton.— 1st ed.
      p. cm.
    ISBN-13: 978-0-374-11690-3 (alk. paper)
    ISBN-10: 0-374-11690-3 (alk. paper)
    1. New York (State)—History—1775–1865—Fiction. 2. Women— New York— (State)—Fiction. 3. Brooklyn (New York, N.Y.)—Fiction. 4. Sisters—Fiction. I. Title.

PS3552.A7685B76 2006
813'.54—dc22

2005016269

Designed by Jonathan D. Lippincott

www.fsgbooks.com

1 3 5 7 9 10 8 6 4 2

Frontispiece: Illustration of the "Flying Pendent Lever Bridge" from Thomas Pope's *Treatise on Bridge Architecture*, New-York, 1811. Courtesy of Lehigh University Digital Library

FOR JEROME DOUGLAS BARTON

Chrysanthemum growers—
You are the slaves
    of chrysanthemums!
        —*Yosa Buson*
        (translated by Robert Hass)

BROOKLAND

IHPETONGA

A t the close of the workday on Thursday the twenty-fourth of January, 1822, Prue Winship sat down at the large desk in the countinghouse of Winship Daughters Gin to write a letter to her daughter, Recompense. The power train had been sprung free of the windmill for the night, and the machines of the distillery sat quiet, the embers of its great fires still smoldering. Prue could hear the low horn of the steam ferry as it approached the Brooklyn landing. Her sister, Tem, with whom she ran the distillery, had retired an hour since to the Liberty Tavern, and had said she'd be home for supper; their overseer, Isaiah Horsfield, had gone home to his family. He'd left a stack of papers on his section of the desk, and would no doubt see to them first thing in the morning.

Prue's husband and fourteen-year-old son awaited her return, but she did not wish to put off writing the letter another day. In honor of Prue's fiftieth birthday, her daughter had sent her a lavish gift: a magnificent paisley shawl Recompense's father-in-law had brought back from a journey to Kashmir. Prue had opened the packet the evening before, and had delighted in the shawl's softness and its jewel-like shades of blue and green. When she'd wrapped it around herself in the kitchen, her son, Matty, had clapped in admiration and proclaimed her "the very queen of the Gypsies." Tem had shaken her head.

Prue might have dispatched her thanks in a quick note, had Recompense not enclosed a letter with the parcel. After wishing her mother a happy birthday, she had written the good news that she was with child.

Should no ill befall her, she expected to deliver in the autumn. In light of this disclosure, and of the obvious adulthood it bestowed on its bestower, Recompense asked her mother to tell her about the bridgeworks, which she knew had caused her parents both happiness and misfortune, but about whose history she knew little. Recompense had never, until that moment, gathered herself to ask either of her parents about that chapter in their lives. The distillery had consumed most of her mother's time and energy, and Recompense had always feared importuning her with questions that might spoil her for business. As for Recompense's father, he was too good-natured and self-effacing to be much of a storyteller, and she found it difficult to cast him in her imagination as an actor in any sort of drama. Yet she wished to know the story of the bridge, if her mother had the time and inclination to entrust it to her.

Prue was discomfited by the request. She had always loved her daughter, but had given most of her adult life to keeping Winship Daughters Gin solvent enough to repay the high cost of insurance and her own significant debts. The distillery was the legacy her father had bequeathed her, and she had slaved to make it profitable enough to pass on to her own son and daughter. The children themselves had been, she admitted now, of secondary importance. And after placid Recompense had declined a third time to be trained in the family business, Prue had felt herself powerfully betrayed, and had wondered, with a flash of a coldheartedness she had not experienced in some time, if she would ever again have use for such a daughter. Jonas Sutler, the son of a man in the whaling trade at Hudson, had come soon after to ask for Recompense's hand; and as her husband had given his warm consent, Prue had sat wondering why anyone would want such an unadventurous creature and why she herself was too hard-hearted to feel any of the emotions appropriate to the occasion. Yet when the August wedding day had arrived, Prue had felt a terrible, wrenching ache at the thought of her daughter leaving. She'd wished she could say she had never known such an ache before, but its pain had been so poignant because of its familiarity. It had reminded her in an instant of every loss she had ever suffered; and as Mr. and Mrs. Jonas Sutler had departed for their wedding tour of the Upper Hudson, Prue had stood on the landing of the New Ferry and wept into her husband's coat.

Prue had struck up the correspondence to ease the intolerable pain of having a little-valued daughter vanish from sight. She herself had once passed the town of Hudson by boat, but not knowing she would ever wish to envision the particulars of its streets, she had committed nothing but its vaguest outline to memory. Now she peppered her daughter with questions, and learned the Sutlers had a tall house bounded by a fence, with a garden that continued to produce cabbage and chrysanthemums well into October. The household employed three Irish servants. Jonas had grown up in educated society, and the wives and sisters of his cousins and childhood friends were lively conversationalists, zealots for good books, the manumission of the few remaining local slaves, and politics. Yet for all this, Recompense confessed to missing Brooklyn, with its old Dutch houses scattered across the landscape despite a newly laid grid of regular streets. She was homesick; in addition to which she was spending the longest evenings of the year propped up on a sofa and trying to keep down salt biscuits and tea. Prue realized it was only natural her daughter should seek out the missing pieces of her family history. And though she herself had taken pains to conceal the story of the bridge-works all this time—one evasion leading to the next until at last she had lost sight of the original reason for her reticence—her love for her far-off daughter, and her compunction at having ignored her before she'd moved away, made Prue believe she could change her course. It was thus that on the first full day of the sixth decade of her life, Prue Winship thanked her daughter for the beautiful shawl, expressed her delight at the prospect of a grandchild, and commenced in a roundabout way telling the story Recompense wished to hear. The correspondence would hold them both in its thrall the remainder of that winter and spring.

"There is much to tell you," she wrote,

though of course if you were here I would brush off your questions and return to my gin as ever I have done. But distance changes much;— I have missed you with a pain very like that of yearning for the dead since you've been gone. And you were a decade since old enough to hear the whole of it. I would like to think only my busyness in the distillery has kept me from relating it, but this is not so. My silence on this matter has been partly due to bad character; which I hope at this late date I can emend.

You ask for the story of the bridgeworks, but if I am to give you not

only the history of that matter but its justifications, I must begin by
relating a metaphysickal crime I long ago committed against my sister
Pearl. I laid a curse upon her when I was still a child. Perhaps you will
think it peculiar of me to recall such a fancy now; but that tale itself
unfolds from my twin obsessions, with Mannahata & with Death; and
all three must stand in some wise as the founders of the bridge. To
relate the story properly, dear one, I shall begin there.

I was born in January of 1772 and Pearl in July of 1778, which gave
me six and one half years to grow accustomed to being my parents' only
child. This was more time than you had before Matty came along, but
you must surely know what a long span it seemed. My parents, Matthias
and Roxana Winship, were an odd lot. As I may not have hitherto told
you, my father had escaped the seminary at Cambridge to jump on the
Eliza Dymphna in Boston Harbour, and he set sail for the West Indies,
slaves, and rum. To the chagrin of his father, a dissenting minister,
Matty Winship,—your grandfather, that is,—realized what the colonies
lacked was good, native-brewed *strong drink*, produced on a large scale;
so he took his next passage to England & there apprenticed himself to a
rectifier of distilled spirits. Eight years later he returned with a receipt
for an excellent and most alcoholick geneva, and with my sharp-tongued
mother, Roxana Parker (also a refugee from dissenting parents), in tow.
They settled here in Brookland, where stood a derelict windmill, as old
Mr. Joralemon had tried his inexpert hand at distilling once before, only
to burn his operation to the ground. Here on the East River, Father
reason'd, would also be easy shipping for the forthcoming gin. Father
had no license to distill liquor,—none was granted at that era, as the
Crown's policy was to keep the colonies dependent on the mother
country for finished goods,—but he resolved from the start to pay the
inspectors handsomely; & there was no man among them so loyal he
could not be tempted by a small gift of money and a monthly allotment
of good gin. This, of course, until the colonies engaged in open
rebellion, at which time the manufacture of goods in defiance of royal
decree became an act both lucrative *and* patriotickal.

Because he'd not been born to the business of distilling, in those
first years my father often asked my mother's advice on the savour of
the finished product (this though she knew little about gin, though she
did have her fair measure of sense); as a result of which, in my early

childhood I was largely left to do as I pleased, so long as I kept within the bounds of our stone fence. I was forbidden to wander the distillery lest my hand be smashed in the herb press, and forbidden to run out in the road lest, Mother told me, some officer with wrist frills try to offer me a pear. I had only a hazy notion what the war meant beyond the movement of troops, the building & toppling of forts, and the occasional fusillade of artillery fire, which sent the slaves & housewives running to gather the children indoors and left me quaking with fear for my Daddy, who would not leave the distillery to come up the hill and check on us until the gunfire had subsided. I saw men both in uniform and ordinary cloaths limping about town with bandages on & leaning on crutches; and there was a sad autumnal funeral in which the children of the Sands family bawled their eyes dry because they'd lost their father in the fighting. As their mother had died the previous year, they were hastily removed to their grandparents' property east of Bergen's Hill, a location which at that time seemed so far distant, I feared I would never see them more. Thus I gathered early on that soldiers, even those who dressed neatly, were not to be trusted, though the local boys seemed to find them congenial company. I was also denied free access to our kitchen, but only because our slave, Johanna, was blind and half deaf with age, and likely to stumble over me or set me on fire. She was a gruff old woman; you would'n't have liked her. All these rules were my mother's, by the bye; it had been Father's original notion to fit me out with a pint-sized firearm and set me loose upon the neighbourhood;— which, when he suggested it (rather, I should add, to my pleasure), resulted in my mother huffing up the front stairs to reappear only well past sunset with her lips pursed shut. Johanna, meanwhile, tisked and muttered much of the afternoon, which gave me to understand she could hear well enough, were the topick sufficiently juicy.

Because of this lack of direction I was often lonely and bored; but it was my solace the long leg of our fence ran along the crest of Clover Hill, uninterrupted that quarter mile. I paced its length in all kinds of weather, looking north-westward across our manufactory, the port, and the river, to the great city on the far shore. Just past dawn and right before dusk, when no fires were lit at our distillery or the Schermerhorn ropewalk, I could see clearly all the way to Mannahata.

As I'm sure you well remember from your own childhood, the

booming straits was a feast for the eye of a watchful girl. There were no
steamboats then; everything on the river was powered by wind or by
oar. Packets from the far continents discharged drab passengers along
with barrels and bright fruits. Losee van Nostrand plied the only
ferryboat between his landing and Fly Market, loudly crying, —Over!
each time he returned. Pointy-tipped wherries and flat-bottomed dories
wove among the hulking ships, and in winter dodged the flotillas of ice
that hugged both shores. When barges set out for New-York, they hung
low in the water with timber, vegetables, rope, or my father's gin; and
when they returned they rode high & empty on the grey waves.

I could see best by standing atop the tumbledown fence, though I
could do so only when safely beyond your grandmother's purview.
—*Mannahata!* I'd whisper to the city, straining ever northward against
her dense forest, and —*Scheyichibi!* to the green hummocks of Jersey,
stretched out before me in a broad, flat band. —*Ihpetonga!* I'd think
passionately, feeling the resonating power of the rocky Heights on
which I stood as I called it by its ancient name. The natives of the place
had been driven east into Nassau and Suffolk generations before my
parents had arrived (though, on occasion, I dug one of their
arrowheads, or a wampum shell, or a shard of pot from the soil of our
yard), but I still liked to let their words roll round my mouth, like
smooth river stones. These were clearly the names by which the places
knew themselves. I felt them respond to my call, however quietly I
voiced it; and I half expected the ground to tremble and send forth
some spirit, either to squash me like a bug or to do my bidding.

I kept an eye trained ever on New-York, to learn what I could of
that foreign place. The spire of her largest church rose higher than her
trees, and her three- and four-story buildings,—veritable *exaltations* of
window glass,—stood ranked up each morning to reflect the rising sun
and the broad dome of sky. Yet the windows never opened, and I could
neither see nor imagine families stacked one atop the other within. The
bluffs of Clover Hill sang with birds and nickering horses, but no sound
but the booming of ships' guns came from across the river. The scents
of ripe corn, horse dung, & my father's juniper berries tickled my nose
in summer, but though the westerly wind blew fierce, New-York had no
smell but brine. All the life I could see was of people and horses in the
immediate vicinity of the docks. Some other child would have thought

nothing of these circumstances, but it was by these signs,—fueled, I
admit, by that same natively dark imagination that later jumped to
conclude, whenever you or Matty were tardy for supper, that you'd been
drown'd in the millpond or run down by the stage; and woefully
unchecked by parental intervention,—that I came to believe the Isle of
Mannahata was, in fact, the City of the Dead. Once I had chanced upon
this notion,—which another might have tossed out, but which I, made
nervous by the sights & sounds of the war & by my mother's weird
rules governing my ingress and egress, determined could be nothing but
the dark truth the world strove to hide from children,—everything I saw
across the water added to New-York's sepulchral mystery. All those
goods that travelled thither were offerings to appease the shades; and it
was a grim but necessary duty my father fulfilled when he loaded his
barge with libations. That he bore the task so lightly & returned each
time with the same blithe expression on his brow, I took for the mark of
his good character and valour.

It did not help that your dry-witted grandparents spoke often of the
Other Side, that life to which each of us was doomed or blessed,
according to his merits, to go when this one expired. (I was too young
to understand these references as sarcastickal, or to know I was living in
a house of non-believers, who'd named me as much to mark their
freedom from the strictures under which they'd been raised as because
they thought it pretty.) *Viz.*, my father once said, through the fug of
tobacco smoke that surrounded him of an evening, —Let's sleep late on
Sunday, Roxy. The hell with church.

I shouted, —Hooray! as Domine Syrtis spoke half the time in
Dutch, some of the time in German, and muttered the rest, which made
my skin itch as if I'd rolled in poison sumac.

—Mind your tongue, Reverend, Mother answered, with her
particular roll of the *R*s and a flare of the nostrils she often directed at
him. Like yours and mine, her hair was russet as a winter apple and
kinked as a piglet's tail, and it rendered her already extravagant
expressions even more so. The humour of his epithet was lost upon me,
as it was only later, and by driblets, I learned of his escape from
godliness. —If she says that in front of Johanna, she'll get her mouth
warshed.

I looked to see what Johanna was doing. She'd fallen asleep in the rocking chair by the hearth, her silver head thrown back, her pulse flickering in the velvety patch of cream-in-the-coffee skin beneath her jawbone. —Not my Prue, Father answered. She knows one only says the hell with church in *pitickular* company. She knows it's our secret. He puffed on his pipe and widened his grey eyes at me encouragingly.

But I was mighty confused, & had a fleeting realization that if I'd been born to the Livingstons across the way, my life would have been duller, but I'd likely have understood, in such situations, what was wanted of me. —But I should'n't give a tinker's damn if Johanna heard me say the hell with church, I told them. Would'n't it be a miracle if she heard annithing?

—Hey, now, Johanna is my dearest friend. You see? Mother asked, trying in vain to purse her lips; but she and Father were both laughing. She leaned over & kissed him full on the mouth. Matty Winship, you'll have some talking to do when you reach t'Other Side, that's all I'll say.

—It depends what part of the place I hope to inhabit. The Devil'll have me in his quarter, no questions asked.

—You'll change your tune if he comes for ye tomorrow, she countered.

—Well, if he does, I'll shout for your help straightaway. He pulled her down into his lap, and kissed the side of her throat, where I knew the skin was particularly soft. Roxy, you could talk the Devil out of his best cloven shoes.

—Daddy, I said, you're not going to the Devil, are you?

They both laughed at me. —Not if the domine can help it. But we'll show him, wo'n't we, who'll be more welcome in Satan's house? That is, if Satan even *has* a house; which I sorely doubt.

As an adult, I recognize the foregoing as, first off, the banter of two people in love, and second, of two people with no earthly notion how their words might influence the mind of a suggestible child. At the time, I could be nothing but shocked & terrified. These were, after all, the two most important of the dozen adult persons who made up the known world, and I took what they said for uninflected truth. In one breath, Father had condemned the domine and his church to Hell, and in the next claimed no such place existed; and I further deduced not only that my father's death was nigh, but that both my parents were doomed to punishment for thinking this such a laughing matter. I did not believe I could express my foreboding without eliciting their scorn, so I betook myself to my room,—which, when later I came to share it with my sisters, would seem strait enough, but at the time was a vast savanna on which my fears might frolick,—and there worried that every tap of a branch against the windowpane was the bony fingers of Death, come knocking. I kept watch most of the night, and shivered each time I heard the wind, the clatter of carriage wheels, or soldiers out singing their sad barroom songs on the Ferry Road.

You may wonder it never occurred to me New-York might constitute not another realm but another place of habitation; I can tell you only, it did not. Death was everywhere, and the natural direction in which my mind turned. As you must recall from your own girlhood, our yard was littered in all seasons with the half-et corpses of birds, attacked by who knew what neighbourhood predators. On one occasion, I watched a dead squirrel sink in upon itself day by day, & slowly reveal its armature of chalky bone. I learned of my mother that when a woman grew large with child, then appeared about town slender, sad-eyed, and unencumbered, it meant her baby had gone straight from her womb to the churchyard, instead of stopping at the cradle prepared for it; and I heard Cornelis Luquer's shrieks rise up from the noisy river when his brother Nicolaas was drowned in a boating accident. His father, also called Nicolaas, enlisted the aid of the New-York & Brookland fishermen, who dredged the river with nets until the small, red-headed body of Mr. Luquer's namesake was found. It seemed I saw the dead as often as I saw the living: their mandibles bound to their skulls with strips of linen, their hands slack, their skin oaty as dishwater whether they'd been soldiers or widows, mothers or children, struck down by illness, injury, mishap, or age. Domine Syrtis mumbled over them and consigned them to the soil; beyond that, no one would entrust me with any but the vaguest explanation of where they went, once they'd cast off from these shores.

No, dear Recompense, I do not know how I could have done anything but what I did, which was to set myself with renewed vigour to uncover what part of the Other Side I regarded, across the water, that I might know if, with a suitable measure of trembling awe, I'd be able to spy my Daddy, once he went there for keeps. That I could'n't tell what I look'd at,—whether it was Heaven or the other place,—disquieted me, and I briefly nursed the awful suspicion that my parents had been correct, and all the dead, both good & evil, went to the same destination. But no theology I'd heard of supported such a theory. To entertain it felt as if I stood on the edge of a precipice, and I could not reckon how far I might plummet, therefrom. No, it had to be one or the other; and if Heaven was as free from want as the domine described it, then the New-Yorkers' insatiable need of gin & fruit meant they were living in Hell. I could not guess where God resided, but I figured dead sinners slipped down to van Nostrand's landing in the dark of night, paid off their grim ferryman in shells, boarded his Indian *canoo*, and made their whispering progress across the water. If I could muster the courage to wander out alone one night, I would see it with my own eyes.

While the mouse-brown Livingston daughters set traps for chipmunks & coddled their dolls, I stood watch on the fence each time my father set out on a barge to deliver his wares. He could not understand why I'd hug him so fiercely before he left, and he'd return home, inevitably, that same afternoon, with the scent of fried food and pipe smoke in his hair, and something stowed in his pocket for me;— some sweet, or fruit, or picture pamphlet. These gifts undid me, so great was my desire for them, and so equally great my fear of his truck with the shades. When I'd look at the peach with tears in my eyes, he'd rumple my hair, call me a *silly little goat,* and head over to the pump to wash. Any gift that was not perishable, I took to my room, where I lifted up the one loose plank on the floor, just as you did,—I know you thought without my knowledge,—when you were a girl; and tucked it in for safekeeping.

I observed the busy wharves of New-York with care. I reasoned the damned must have been travelling thither from everywhere around, the *wampum* grounds to the east and Pavonia to the west; why else should they have needed everything in such vast quantities? This convocation of the accursed also surely explained why so many ships were sunk in Henry Hudson's River and up at Hell Gate, and children like Nicolaas swept off in the current of our own tidal straits. It only stood to reason that those eternally condemned would seek to churn up our waters; and this was the first thing made me think we wanted a bridge from here to there. If the living were blind to the spirit boats, they were much imperiled by them; & while I did not suppose one could cajole the dead

to use some other mode of transport, it did seem possible to get my
father, on his delivery trips, up out of harm's way. If he could cross by
bridge, I reckoned, he could avoid the danger of the water, and perhaps
simply fling the goods over to the Other Side, never leaving so much as
a hair or a footprint in the Land of the Shades. I could not think how
he'd get past having to take their money.

There were precious few bridges in Brookland, then as now,—none
of any magnitude in the colonies. Had I known enough of the topick to
study the bridges of the mother country, I'd have learned that a
structure of a hundred feet in length was considered a prodigious span.
I was no more than five years of age, but I resolved in my childish way
to learn what I could of building, to store up against future use. I began
following your grandfather around his distillery, asking him to explain
the functions of the stills, liquor-backs, chutes, gears, drive belts, &
machines. He complied, with a bemused grin on his broad countenance,
though the doggedness with which I'd determined to learn these things
obviously unnerved him.

Had my parents asked what troubled me, I'd have told them, and all
the vapours would have been dispelled; but they did not ask. For
reasons of friendship & a perverse understanding of loyalty, my mother
refused to hire any other help while Johanna yet lived; and as Johanna
was next to no assistance to her, the sheer work of the house kept her
grim-faced & busy the day long. Managing our household also seemed
to cost my mother an inordinate lot of fret. Mrs. Livingston, after all,
had *two* daughters, yet still found time to hang over the open top of her
Dutch door when a neighbour passed by with gossip. Mother spared
herself no such luxury and did not appear to have any such friends, and
I sensed she had neither time for nor interest in my moods. Father,
more ample in all directions, brought home ribands and books from Fly
Market, and would lean back in his chair & spin me yarns that would
have banished the shades from some other girl; and he ever addressed
me with a smile whose import, I knew, was to coax me to do likewise.
Yet his efforts did not strike their mark. I remain'd fixed on my own line
of thought until, at last, I must have become impossible to abide, for
Mother scrubbed me with a brush and brought me to the domine for
counsel. She did'n't tell me why, but I was'n't stupid: I could guess.

When we arrived, the rectory stank of pickled herring. The domine, his chin hidden behind his tall collar, exhaled it on his breath. My mother described my melancholia with expressive gestures of the hands. I sat on my own fingers, lest they fly out to cover my nose. The domine worried his thatchy beard, & said, —Well, *mein Schmetterling*, leaning toward me. I sat tighter on my hands. It was his habit, when not muttering in Dutch, to pepper his conversation thus with German. In later years I unkindly thought he did this to show any who might be unsure on this point that he was university educated, but at the time, it was my simple misfortune to be either mystified or irked by his every turn of phrase. He was Brookland's only minister, so even the child of atheists could not escape him, but I wished he could be less a fishy old dodderer and, if naught else, a stern avenger like my Pappy, the Reverend Mr. Elihu Juster Winship, whom I'd met the previous autumn.

My father, set at long last on making amends with him, had taken me north to Massachusetts Colony, through fields and tracts of woodland that smelled sharply of fallen leaves. We'd passed what seemed hundreds of encampments of soldiers, ours and the Crown's, along the way. Their tents would cluster in a field like a flock of geese come down for the night; and on two occasions Father had stopped to bestow casks of gin on ragged battalions of the Continental Army, who'd given such ululations of thanks I'd gripped tight to my father's leg & steeled myself against being scalped. To Father's surprise, I'd liked my grim old Pappy well enough, preaching and all. Your great-grandfather's sermons were so stingy of human affection they'd shriveled his lips to a permanent pucker, as if he had an unripe persimmon forever upon his tongue; yet he had a great deal of rhetoric at his command. If his orations were full to overflowing with hellfire, at least they were'n't dull as a snowstorm Sunday: They made a child stand up straight. I feared the perdition to which he claimed I & my dark humour were headed, but I almost liked the thrill of contemplating where my ultimate destination might be. Daddy, meanwhile, was full of tales about him,—how he'd raised his children with nary a toy but a worn-out boot, to which Father referred with alternating affection and disgust, calling it *Bootie*; the result of which, I deduced, was that he'd grown into a man who could not refuse a measure of port, and who, though engaged in a grubby business, was known for his attention to the cut of his clothes.

But I should return to Domine Syrtis, who'd been speaking all this while, and whose fat servant, Jannetje, had deposited a plate of warm aniseed *koekjes* in front of me, though she surely knew I had not been brought in for good behaviour.

—*Und so, mein Schmetterling,* Syrtis was saying. To mask the smell of his breath, I ate the *koekjes* quickly, barely swallowing one before inserting the next. —I do not blame your Mamma for fearing all that care upon your brow. But I daresay, Mrs. Winship, he tittered, if a child be born with morbid preoccupations, so much the less work for the Church, later on! He was still chirruping at his own fine sense of humour.

My mother raised her thin eyebrows. —You think it well she should be so glum? You think it healthy? I choked on an oversized mouthful, and instead of patting my back, she slapped my wrist when I reached for another *koekje.*

—Prudence is a good, God-fearing child, he said. He smiled, showing me his yellow teeth. I tried to smile back as I worked the dry meal in my mouth. Jannetje, more empathetick than my mother, gave me a mug of cool cider. He went on —If you seek a course of action, I suggest instruction in needlework. Busy hands will keep her from despond!

Mother thanked him, thanked Jannetje, and drew me so quickly from the rectory, a hail of crumbs sprang from my lap to the floor. She rarely pulled me so, though I saw other mothers do it; and when I looked up at her, I could see her brown eyes were slick with sadness or anger. —I'm sorry I ate so quickly, I offered. As this did not make her slacken her pace, I told her I would'n't mind learning to knit.

—Please! she replied, & tossed a stray frizzled curl off her face.

Two of the King's men, currying their horses in front of the Livingston house, whistled to us as we passed, and one doffed his cap to my mother. I was too young to understand the politicks of the rebellion, but knew that my parents, unlike many of the neighbours (whom Daddy said were either too Dutch or too apathetick to care), sided with the revolutionaries. My parents were popular with His Majesty's troops anyway, as they supplied to Joe Loosely's tavern,—known then alternately for its location as the Ferry Tavern, for its construction as the Old Stone, and for its beautifully painted sign as the King's Arms,— a gin rumoured to be as tasty as any across the sea, and guaranteed to wallop its consumer. If I awakened before my parents, I sometimes winced to find a rabbit or grouse hanging by its legs from our *stoep* beams; a gift from the Fourth Prince of Wales, who took their guns out for late-night carousing. Mother nodded curtly to the soldiers, as if they were interrupting her thoughts, and continued on in silence until we reached the head of Joralemon's Lane. Then, bending down to me, she said, in an evener tone, —He's never been sad a day in his life, and he's foolish to think it's so simple. That's all.

She led me down through the ravine & brought me into the brewhouse, where the agitators were making a great din of the mashing, and told Father that Domine Syrtis had pronounced me hopeless; and that it was her opinion the only remedy for my melancholick spirits would be a younger sibling; and presently, she broke down in tears, audible even above the slosh & whine of the machines. While the workers looked on uncomfortably, Father packed me off into the yard, but I knew why she was crying: Infant after infant had quit her womb, unfinished. I had learned this from Johanna, who had, I thought, intimated the fœtuses might have chosen to return to God because they were unwilling to call such a gloom box as me Sis.

Yet my mother's tears worked some alchemy, for that very winter, Pearl took root inside her. They did not tell me until I had long since deduced her imminence; and in my grief at being, as I saw it, first ignored, then displaced in their affections by some newcomer, I felt flashes of scalding hatred for the unborn child, and could not douse that inner flame.

How it shames me to tell this to my own daughter! Particularly as I recall your joy at the birth of your younger brother. I have long shrouded all this from you, as if, by keeping my distance, I could prevent your curiosity. We both see now, it is not so. And if it is possible I can diminish your love for me by these admissions,—well, I shall pray it is not possible & press on.

I tried to anticipate the baby's arrival. I carried my doll, Nell,—for whom I'd never much cared,—everywhere with me, cradled in my arms; but when no one was looking, I pinch'd a hammer and nails from the cooper's shed, lifted Nell's yarn hair, and honed my skills on her wooden skull; though the very fact I wished to do so filled me with shame. When I paced along the crest of Brookland's Heights, battered Nell in hand, I raged less against the interloper than against my own mortifying rage. My inner voice cried out to God,—knowing full well my parents did not believe in Him,—to help me, or to strike me for my sin; or, if He did not exist, to let my parents themselves rescue me from it; and one spring afternoon, in a whisper, begged Him to smite the usurper before it drew breath. Immediately I tried to take back what I'd thought, but my prayer had already sailed out, on a puff of smoke from the stillhouse, over the river. There it settled in some New-York treetop & grew.

For as it happened, no prayer was answered but that one. My sister was born with a terrible defect to her vocal cords: Even when she emerged from the womb, she could emit no sound but a rasping sigh, such as a person makes choking on a fishbone. Had I dropped her into a boiling pot, she could not have turned an angrier red than when she eked out this exhalation. She would not take the breast. Johanna, who, though confined by infirmity to the house, ordinarily sat peeling potatoes or letting down my hems, now rocked my sister day and night. She sang her tuneless lullabies, in Dutch, English, and some tongue of her own devising, and tried to coax the baby to suck from a washrag a spoonful of our mother's milk sweetened with maple sugar. When I was not out anxiously walking the fence, I sat by her & dandled Nell, as if this could nullify my dark deed. But though Johanna's eyes were blurred with cataract, she could see me clear enough.

—It's your fault for cursing her, she said, as usual a bit too loudly, and with that odd lilt her voice had from having grown up speaking Dutch.

I checked to make certain my parents were beyond earshot, but did not respond.

Johanna cocked her head to the side. —I know you're there, Prue.

—I did'n't curse anybody, I said lamely.

—Did the Devil come and do that work on Nell's head, then?

It was true: Nell was nearly as bad off as the baby. I was considering burying her, next new moon, in the yard.

—I know what you've done, Johanna went on, her voice lowering. I wondered what had possessed her to poke her fingers around Nell's skull. She leaned in close to me, her milk-filmed eyes on the ceiling and the sloe-eyed bundle against her chest. —And the Lord knows, too.

This babe is hardly longer for the world than those that come before. And I know who prayed that it be so. She transferred the baby into one arm, and took the other palm to her temple. She said —*Krijg de tyfus.* You make my head ache.

A wellspring of tears bubbled up behind my nose. The baby frightened and disgusted me, but my prayers had mostly been for a change of heart I only now,—too late!—experienced, and for my parents to mind me, which would not happen now they had an ailing infant. I thought if my sister died, my mother might never look at me more. Waves of guilt crashed over me for having prayed to send a critter no larger than a loaf of bread yonder in the sloggy bottom of a *canoo.* She flailed her spindly arms as if to illustrate her helplessness.

I ran upstairs to confess to my mother, but she was in bed, as she had been since the birth, knitting a frilled infant's jacket. She did not look up, though she must have seen or heard me at the threshold; in those days, it seemed she only surfaced from beneath her thoughts for my father. Seeing her so intent on the jacket, which I felt sure would never be worn, made my nose and throat burn the more, so I ran outdoors to find my father; but I saw only the hired men out tasseling the Indian corn and picking cherries in the orchard, some workers shooting dice in the mill yard, & the Hessian soldiers from upferry, out practicing their drills in their spit-shined boots. I went up to the summit of Clover Hill, therefore, to brood by the fence. The onion grass was growing plentifully, and I pulled some up to eat the hot roots; but I found my mouth so full of tears, I could not enjoy them.

For, dear Recompense, my father could argue with Dr. de Bouton until Judgment Day,—and he did argue with him of an evening, until they were both near insensate with liquor; and he once rode all the way across Mr. Boerum's estate to fetch Mrs. Friedlander, who could only stroke the poor infant's bald head and prescribe her a tincture of slippery elm,—but I knew the cause of my sister's deformity, and was stunned by the magnitude of the wrong I'd committed. My parents had told me their parents' God was a blackguard, and Pappy had impressed on me that his Lord was terrible fierce; but if this God of his and the domine's could turn so capriciously on an infant, His heart was even darker than my own. I was sick with unhappiness. I dreaded pulling the covers from my face each morning, for fear my features would some day be revealed as deformed as my nature. I still found my sister uncanny, but could not imagine her being ferried across the straits to live for all eternity in dun brown New-York. Who would tend her, so small and frail? I thought the Other Side must contain some safeguard against such an eventuality: some cold, grim orphanage in which she might lie listlessly about with the stillborn and those taken by the pertussis & diphtheria before being baptized, damned forever through no fault of their own. Our brothers and sisters might be there also, but each would feel himself in a private hell, as none had lived long enough to earn a voice or a name; they would have no means by which to recognize one another.

And so I prayed God to spare her. I prayed she be able to stand with me in the dooryard, the salt breeze on our cheeks, & eat the spicy roots of onion grass. I did not bother to ask for a lusty voice or a long life for her;—now young Nicolaas Luquer'd been drowned, and I knew how many babies went down in the churchyard unnamed, I knew it was no use, begging. The bargain I sought to strike with God was, if He would let her live three or four summers more, He could do with her as He pleased.

It seems as impossible to me as it must to you the Creator would do business on such terms, but again I found my prayer answered. That very day, my sister began to suck more greedily at Johanna's milk-soaked rag; the next, she accepted some of Mrs. Friedlander's tincture, and later took the breast. Though she'd shriveled to a sack of saffron skin and chicken bones, she began to fatten; and her complexion soon faded to a cherry blossom pink. She sprouted some wisps of dark hair. My father resumed the careful superintention of his grain and distillery, & Dr. de Bouton returned to his usual, solitary tippling. I missed having him around the house; I had been fascinated by the bushy black brows beneath his snow-white hair, and had liked watching them move as he spoke. At summer's end, my sister was brought into the church and christened. I never learned by what means my parents chose her name, but I think they must have meant to call her,—with a different sort of irony than that with which they'd named me, or else reverting in those dark days to the faith & fear of their childhoods, with no ironickal import whatsoever,—our *Pearl* of great price, our kingdom of Heaven.

So you see, in my imagination my sister was always tied to the world beyond, in a way your Aunt Temperance,—born the next summer, and named, as I had been, according to your grandfather's queer sense of humour,—never could be. From the moment she arrived, Tem could call for my attention as surely as if she were a mosquito in the bedroom; but each time Pearl whistled (an otherwise rude habit for which she early showed proficiency, and which she imbued with uncommon grace) or opened her mouth in a rasping laugh, she reminded me by how fine a thread she was moored to this world, by how narrow a margin I had escaped punishment for my sin. You will learn soon enough how otherworldly a thing a small child can be,—if you do not remember this about your brother because of the strapping fellow he's become,—but Pearl's affliction made her doubly so. Remember, too, that her very existence had spelled the end to my childhood freedoms. As Pearl could not shout out when in danger or pain, she was never trusted to her own devices as I had been. Thus, while Tem babbled to herself and banged on pots, I followed Pearl as another child might follow a push toy, as she rolled & lurched about the house. She came to like onion grass as much as I did, but if she accompanied me outdoors to dig it up, I could not stand idly by dreaming, lest some accident befall her there at the edge of the bluff. She showed stealth in hunting down the eggs of the fractious hen who laid outside her box, and was of great assistance in chasing the motley-patterned, six-toed kittens who roamed our yard; but I could not have explained to her how when I caught them, I was entranced by the way their hearts beat fast within their delicate ribs, or how I wished I could cut one open, to lay bare the clockwork within. (—Never fear; I desisted.)

I learned my letters & numbers and the rudiments of natural philosophy of my father, & begged him to teach me to distill, which he said I could not learn, being female. I had desultory shouted lessons in sewing and cookery from Johanna. I roughhoused with Ben and Isaiah, the sons of my father's overseer, Israel Horsfield. Father's cooper, Scipio Jones, taught me to make up a paste of whiting and linseed oil,—after I pled with him, having seen Mrs. Livingston's men do likewise when re-fixing her old glass to new window sashes,—to fill the holes in Nell's head. This gave her bruised scalp enough solidity to support more yarn hair, and Scipio praised her beauty lavishly. I straightaway attached myself to the cooperage, whose staves could be used for all manner of miniature building projects, now I had returned my stolen hammer. When my father sent a wagon down to Luquer's mill to retrieve the day's yeast and ground grain and to leave off the spent wash to fatten Mrs. Luquer's pigs, I would ride down to the pond, where oysters then grew as large as the span of my two hands. One of the men would prize them open for Cornelis and me, so we might slurp the sweet, springy flesh off the shells. Interesting things were, then as now, wont to wash up in the logs of the millrace's trash rack, and old Nicolaas Luquer,—who died when you were yet small,—would lay them out to dry on the rack's small pitched roof, for the delight of his children. When I arrived in my father's wagon, he would sometimes take me down by the plashing water wheel, and we would squat together on that low roof, marveling over a bloated single shoe or a rusted hinge. He would show me these treasures with conspiratorial glee, as if Cornelis & Jens were nowhere near so temperamentally well suited as I to appreciate the curious bounty our river brought him.

But again, I digress; or realize, rather, I am growing old, and have begun to fear my memories of Brookland & my childhood,—which are among my dearest possessions,—will dissipate along with my breath and spirit when my bones are laid in the confines of the grave. I shall leave you half a thriving manufactory; but how I wish I could also bequeath you that vanished world and the people you have never known, who were so dear to me.

You see! You promise a grandchild to a gloomy old woman whose heart has ever seemed to you devoted singularly to business, and in an instant she waxes sentimental. You asked of my bridge, your father's bridge, and here I sit, telling you a whole novel's worth of Johanna & Nell & Pearl. Perhaps I should say, in conclusion upon those topicks,—for this letter, at least,—that my sisters kept my hands busy, and, as the domine had promised, this kept me if not altogether clear of the Slough of Despond, then walking a small elevated berm around its periphery. While I believe my melancholick humour continued to vex my mother, I was never again marched out to the rectory.

Forgive me for going on at such length about my self. I reckon you, who've always been so modest, will consider there is rather too much *I* in this letter; yet I also reckon you'll pardon me the transgression. It is, after all, a sin born of a worser one,—the sin of silence on many subjects most central to the formation of my character and our family. I hope it suffices to redress the wrong now; & the bridge,—I shall arrive there shortly.

I am full of questions for you, if you feel inclined to answer them: How do you get on with Jonas, having seen him now every day of the past six months? How well do you like a house with servants? Have you come to think Father & me odd for keeping house so minimally? You have much to tell.

Please write as soon as you may. We all miss you keenly; your father has constructed quite a noble phantasy of your life in Hudson, in the absence of detail regarding the true facts. For the nonce, if he has not gone up to the Liberty Tavern to join Aunt Tem, he must wonder where I am,—it has long since grown dark. I await your word, if I have overspoke or if this missive has pleased you. The latter, I pray,—

Yours ever,
Yr loving Mother

Two

THE ICE BRIDGE OF 1782

P rue remembered the day on which she'd learned New York was simply New York. The realization hit her as a clapper strikes the side of a bell—the result, she believed, of her diligence at her lessons and her responsibility for her sisters. She was coming, by degrees, to comprehend the logic of science, arithmetic, and grammar; and her studies and duties provided ever more solid ground upon which her thinking might found itself. One warm morning in the autumn of 1781, she glanced up from the retaining wall separating the mill yard from the straits, and noticed old Mr. Remsen loading a herd of goats onto a barge tethered at his dock. The animals' hooves beat a tattoo on the wooden ramp, and they bleated accusingly as Remsen herded them down, saying, "That's enough, that's enough. It's not like you'd have any better a time of it here in Brookland." He raised a hand to Prue when he saw her; she waved back. Two of his slaves pushed off from the wharf, and Prue continued to hear the goats' yells and complaints until they were well into the river. She crossed her arms and watched the barge's slow progress across the water. When it arrived at the other side, the slaves laid the plank to the dock, and Remsen commenced the considerably more difficult task of driving the animals up it. As Prue looked on, she had the most prosaic of realizations—*Oh, they keep livestock there*—but this fact, which she had surely always known if she'd but bothered to remark it, was enough to startle her out of the delusion she'd labored under for years. *And if they keep livestock*, she reasoned, *they must be as ordinary as we Brooklanders.* She might have stood there marveling all morning had Israel Horsfield not leaned out the countinghouse window, put his fingers to the corners of his mouth, and whistled to her. She hoped he was calling her in to learn something of bookkeeping; but this never happened. He simply waved—content, no doubt, to have put a stop to her woolgathering—and ducked back inside to his work.

General Cornwallis had recently surrendered to the Continental Army; to Matty Winship, at least, the colonies' eventual independence seemed secure. A peace had not yet been declared, however, and some of the king's troops still lingered in Brooklyn. The Winships, the Looselys, and Tony and Tobias Philpot, who owned the Sign of the Twin Tankards, an alehouse a quarter mile down the Jamaica Turnpike, made a good profit from the presence of lonely, half-idle soldiers on guard duty; and they did the occupying army such a service in providing them the solace of liquor, they had no men quartered on them. But Prue's father's other friends had long been grumbling about the horses, livestock, firewood, and produce the troops commandeered, the game they poached, and the fields they ruined with their tent staves. The Livingstons, Hickses, and Cortelyous still had the Fourth Prince of Wales garrisoned on their land, and they were tired of the disruption and the expense. Mrs. Cortelyou believed their living in such close proximity bred pestilence, and Mrs. Livingston further worried for the welfare of her daughters, Patience and Rachael. To Prue they were dull as the domine's sermons, but their mother clearly considered them vibrant enough to catch an officer's eye, and she clucked around them like a broody hen. Even the Philpots' upstairs whores had begun to gripe about their constant duties and ailments, though if Prue's mother had known she had anything to do with them, she'd have tried to chain her to Johanna's chair. Brooklyn's forests had been denuded of all but their sapling trees, and the general mood had grown so dark, Prue sometimes wondered if her own spirits were not more subdued than her toddling sisters' simply because she was older. Perhaps somberness accrued to one as did longer legs and better pronunciation. This seemed true of Isaiah Horsfield, six months Prue's junior: The great blue eyes on his pointy Horsfield face were growing more thoughtful by the day. That his eight-year-old brother, Ben, still insisted on playing a marauding pirate and brandishing his knife in every game of frigate did not necessarily contradict Prue's theory. She expected his flaxen curls to straighten and go brown as his brother's had done, and his mood to turn color likewise.

To her surprise, however, she awakened one morning in January 1782 to whoops and hollers rising from the river. She could pick out the clear sopranos of both Horsfield brothers calling, "Hoyay, hoyay! Lo-*seee*!" but many of the other happy voices were unmistakably adult. The bedroom Prue shared with her sisters faced eastward, away from the river, but their two dark heads immediately popped up and pressed against the window. Tem began to scratch at the jewels on the glass.

"What's that?" she asked Pearl. She was not yet three, and the question sounded more like "Whuzzat?" Pearl understood her; she pulled the corners of her lips down and began to wipe persistently at the cleared space with her sleeve. Through the dewy opening, Prue saw their father running, in his nightclothes and with his boots on, over the frozen grass. "Daddy!" Tem shouted, slapping the window. Her palm made a dull knock he couldn't hear. Both Tem and Pearl had their small, dark eyes set closer to their noses than was the norm, which Prue thought made their expressions look comical as they turned to her for explanation.

"Well, I don't know," she said. One or both of them had wet their bed in the night, and Prue turned back their fragrant eiderdown to dry. "Could be it's a shipwreck, or someone feared drowned. Could be a fire."

"Quit frightening 'em," their mother called up from the kitchen, her voice gravelly as if she'd slept ill. Prue sometimes thought Pearl's preternatural hearing was partial compensation for her lack of speech; but she knew it was something Pearl had acquired from their mother, as were the sharp eyes. Downstairs, Roxana cleared her throat and said something more quietly to Johanna, who replied with a vigorous "Mmm-hmm."

Prue was certain they were talking about her. "Off with the nightgowns," she said to her sisters.

"Fire," Tem said, as if it sounded like fun. Fires were, indeed, among the more entertaining events in the village. All the fathers, and slaves of both sexes, ran out with their leather buckets; and if the fire could not be contained, the bells at the distillery pealed out an alarum. This alerted the New Yorkers' volunteer fire company to climb aboard their great floating engine and row it lumberingly across. While Prue hoped no one's house was burning, she agreed with Tem it would be a treat to see the engine. It had seemed monstrous to her when she'd thought New York the land of the shades, but now she could watch with fascination as it pumped water through its hose, making a most satisfactory racket.

Tem and Pearl battled their gowns off over their heads and stood before Prue, their bright, swaybacked bodies topped with fine black hair sticking out in all directions and crackling with static. She pulled on their smocks and worked their arms through. They both tried to wedge their feet into the incorrect shoes. Before Prue could dress herself, Matty Winship came banging through the kitchen door.

"Frozen," he said, stamping his feet. "Clear across. And there was one more egg." Prue heard it clack dully into the wooden egg bowl.

"Clear across, Reverend?" Roxana asked. "You're exaggerating. It was but halfway frozen yesterday, and that hasn't happened since—"

The rest of her words, however, were cut off by the artillery of Tem's and Pearl's small wooden-soled shoes clattering down the stairs. Their father growled, and picked up a child; Prue could hear from the giggling it was Tem. "My little piss-pants," he called her, and kissed her loudly. She laughed some more.

"You'll spoil them," Roxana said, without much force.

Prue was proud of her ability to go up and down stairs without waking the dead, and did not arrive until her father had a daughter on each shoulder and Johanna was cracking eggs by feel into the skillet.

"Boilt," Tem shouted. *"Boilt!"*

"*Jezus*, I hear you, Major General," Johanna grumbled, and kept one egg back for the pot.

"You," Father said to Prue. His cheeks and chin were marked with stubble, spotted, unlike his hair, with gray. He was already well laden with girls, so Prue didn't imagine he'd come tickling. "When shall it be your tenth birthday?"

"Wednesday next."

"Well, your gift has come early. What have you asked me for till my ears rang, and never received?"

"To learn distilling?" Prue asked.

Her father shifted Pearl's weight to get a better grip on her. "Beyond that."

Prue had to think a moment to arrive at an answer. She had never, in truth, asked for much else; her late adventures with God had given her the impression it was best to keep one's mouth shut. "To go to New York with you, on the barge?" she asked.

"Indeed," he answered. "But it'll be better than a gin barge. We are not only going to New York today—we shall walk there over an ice bridge."

"Oh!" Prue cried, imagining a frigid structure had somehow been erected overnight. She could not help jumping into the air, noisy shoes and all. "Oh!"

" 'Oh, oh'; that's enough," Roxana said, and cleared her throat again. She spat into her palms to smooth down Tem's and Pearl's hair. She had some difficulty reaching the girls—aloft as they were on their father's shoulders, and squirming to try to escape her—and this obviously displeased her.

"No, Roxy, I'd worry if she wasn't excited," Matty opined. "Did you hear that shouting come off the river just now?"

Prue nodded.

"That was Losee and a handful of neighbors who couldn't row home after market yestereve. This morning, they walked across. Losee had his arms up and pumping, as if his dog had won a fight."

Prue was still trying to imagine who'd had the time to cut and stack all the ice, but Johanna, parceling the eggs into bowls with moderate accuracy, said, "Dangerous, walkin' across rivers. Don't you remember when that little Luquer drowned?" Tem's egg slithered over her toast.

"Nicolaas Luquer fell off a boat," Prue said.

Johanna felt for the table and put down Tem's bowl.

"He *fell off a boat*."

"But didn't one of the Sands daughters plummet through the ice of the millpond?" Roxana asked.

"Christ, yes, a lifetime ago," Matty said. "Must you mention it in front of the gells? It was a warm day, and it was the millpond. Today's cold enough to freeze a witch's—"

Roxana whistled sharply at him through her teeth as she reached over to swat him. He shook his head in annoyance, but Pearl smiled. No doubt, Prue thought, she liked it when someone else communicated as she did.

"It's bloody bitter outside," Matty went on, putting Tem down, "and the whole river's frozen. Believe me, the men who walked across this morning read the ice as carefully as the ancients read entrails."

Roxana sniffed, and hoisted Pearl free of her father's arms to place her on her chair. She said, "Let them eat before their eggs get cold."

Prue had heard of the North River freezing, up by Kingston, but never of any such happening in her own, more southern clime. Until the previous day, the river had only been frozen to about a hundred yards from shore; the men had dragged gin and timber out on sleds, and had loaded the goods onto barges at the edge of the ice. Prue could smell her eggs beckoning, but all she could think of was the fathers of the neighborhood. She pictured them wrapped ("like *Esquimaux*," she wrote Recompense) in skins and furs, and gathered on the far bank, in the sad light of five in the morning, looking eastward to their homes and the dawn. She could imagine them consulting in low voices with their slaves. The person who'd taken the first step must have considered himself brave, but after that, they must all have felt themselves on holiday.

Matty Winship said, "The gells won't see the like again for years. Roxy, come. We'll wrap 'em up tight against the cold."

"Eat your egg," Roxana said, tapping lightly at the back of Tem's hand. "Good thing Losee's home safe. Mrs. van N. must've had a fright yesterevening when he didn't return."

Tem poked her finger into the yolk to break it, then smeared it down Pearl's hair. Pearl turned to Tem with a look of shock on her face, and opened her mouth in what would have been a piteous yowl had she been her sister; as it was, she merely hissed. Almost as soon as the egg was smeared, Roxana slapped Tem smartly on the cheek. Tem, of course, began to bawl; and Johanna limped off, muttering, to prod at the fire.

After the tearful breakfast, Roxana bound her daughters up so tightly in mufflers, Prue thought she might choke; but as if to make up for this, her father hoisted her onto his broad back and carried her all the way down to the river. The juniper bushes sat plump, fragrant, and dusted with snow in the otherwise bare dooryard. Johanna had refused to accompany them, but Prue wasn't certain she'd understood the invitation. At that time, Joralemon's Lane, which ran south of the distillery from the top of Clover Hill to the Shore Road—and which Prue thought, with mild indignation, ought to be called Winship's Lane, as no Joralemon had lived on the property in years—was only a rocky, rutted path snaking down the bottom of the ravine, so Prue was jogged along on her father's back. The sails of the windmill, halfway down the hill between the house and the works, barely turned in the still, cold air, and the bright flag of the nascent republic drooped from its tall pole. The freeze meant the waterwheels of the mill and the rope manufactory could not turn; and as no traffic could move, either, the river was quieter than Prue had ever known it. Both the gin works and the ropewalk were on holiday, so none of the fires were burning, to smoke up the view. A few of Winship Gin's slaves were out behind the retaining wall in the frozen dirt yard, smoking their cheroots and calling out greetings to the bright-eyed New Yorkers as they arrived. "Get to work!" Matty called to them, but most smiled at him and waved to the girls. Prue imagined Israel Horsfield had already been down to tell the men work was canceled for the day, and had probably paid off a boy or two to stand on the road and alert any late-morning stragglers. In confirmation of her theory, one of the men—a free Negro named Elliott Fortune, her father's fermenting master, who was friendly toward Prue—blew his employer a farting sound in reply.

The ice was unlike that of the millpond, so meticulously swept clean for skating: This ice was a bumpy, dull gray, and dirty with ash, twigs, trapped fish, and bits of the week's papers. As Matty stepped onto it, with Prue still on his back, Prue half expected it to give way and groan; Roxana drew in her breath sharply and pulled both toddlers up short by their hands. Matty cast her a dismissive glance over the shoulder and continued out onto the ice. "Look, Roxy," he said, "half the persons of our acquaintance are out and don't seem to be coming to any harm."

Prue noticed the ice was also supporting dozens of people she didn't recognize, and with no more danger than an occasional loss of one's footing. A group of the Schermerhorn slaves, released from the rope manufactory for the morning, stood in a circle clapping and blowing into their hands while one man jumped with all his might, as if it were possible to break through. One of His Majesty's brigs was frozen just offshore, her sailors sliding along on the brackish ice. They hallooed and whistled as people passed, and one called out, "Hey, Matthias Winship—get back to your place and make the gin!"

"Never you fear, sir," Matty called back. Prue beamed with pride to be thus aloft on his shoulders. "It's a year in the casks before its minute in your tankards. I'm sure it's your hope as well as mine you'll all be home by then."

"Amen," the sailor said quietly, but sound carried well in the crisp atmosphere. He spat over his shoulder for emphasis.

"What's it do in the casks?" Prue asked.

"It steeps like tea." He let her down to the ground, where she slipped on the tricksy surface, eliciting his laughter. Tem got a running start and came skidding on top of her, hooting with joy. Pearl, who was trying to skate in her shoes, arrived more slowly; but the Horsfield boys were never far off from a commotion and came to jump on the pile like piglets, with Ben, as usual, in the lead.

"Careful of the little 'uns, Isaiah," Roxana said, but her tone suggested she didn't think there was much to be done about rowdy Horsfields. Their blond sister, Maggie, was Pearl's age and apparently under the boys' supervision, but she hung back from the fracas as if such entertainment were beneath her dignity.

A few dozen yards out onto the ice stood Simon Dufresne's Black Peg, as she was known, with a large tray suspended from her neck. Roxana had always evaded Prue's questions about Peg, but Johanna had taken her aside to whisper that Peg had begun her life as Simon's father's kitchen slave. After the father's death, Simon had freed her, out of love. Now, though the domine would have nothing to do with them, nor some of the villagers, either, they lived together as man and wife, an arrangement which made Johanna shake her head and smile, but which she would not further explain. Dufresne was the only farmer in the neighborhood who paid wages to all his men, as a result of which, Prue's father had told her, his family did not live so comfortably as Prue's own. "Hot pears, nice hot pears!" Peg cried. She was tall, and the fringed red ends of her muffler streamed down her back. "Piping hot! Get 'em while they're hot! Hot pears for a penny!" Tem shot up like a rocket at Peg's cry, and bit Ben hard on the exposed skin of his wrist when he tried to wrestle her back into the pile.

"You get 'im, Temmy!" their father shouted to her. She roared at Ben in reply, then ran off toward Peg.

Roxana said, "Don't encourage her," then shouted out to Ben, "Are you all right?" But he was already up, trying to keep Isaiah from arriving first.

When Prue dusted herself off and went over to her father for money, he was saying to their mother, "She may be the littlest, but damme if she doesn't spit fire." Roxana didn't look appeased. He fished a sixpence from his pocket and gave it to Prue, saying, "For the Horsfields as well. Check she didn't draw blood." Prue noticed the concern with which her mother was watching Ben shake out his injured wrist, then ran off, slipping, to catch up with the other children.

Even as she held her goal of a hot pear in mind, Prue realized what a wonder it was to be able to run across the East River. The buildings that so fascinated her were drawing nearer, and she couldn't wait to see them up close. She might have taken a certain grim satisfaction had a spirit canoe gone skidding across the ice; but she found reassurance in seeing nothing but ordinary rowboats lately abandoned by their owners near the New York shore, their oars hanging back in their locks.

The Horsfield boys were high as Peg's shoulder and clamoring for sweets, but Peg shooed them away so that Pearl, skating methodically across on her shoes and whistling a pleading trill, might have first pick. It was one way or the other with Pearl: Half the neighbors treated her as if she were a changeling, but those who didn't seemed to like her attentive air and were willing to wait for her signs. "That's a good girl," Peg encouraged her, kneeling so Pearl might have a better view. Pearl picked the pear most evenly glazed in molasses; directly Tem grabbed another, almost without looking.

"Daddy gave me enough for all of us," Prue said to Ben, who reached under her cap to tug on her earlobe in thanks. Her heart leapt at his weird gesture; she understood it to differ from the aggression Tem wreaked upon her. At least, it felt sweeter. As he took his hand away, she grabbed his wrist, and saw that although there were still red tooth marks in the skin, Tem hadn't drawn blood. He pulled away and shouted for his pear, once more shaking the bitten hand. Persnickety Maggie frowned at the selection of sweets still available to her, and lastly Prue turned over the sixpence and took her own, dripping warm molasses on the paper and her mitten.

"Thank you, Prudie. Now, eat that up," Peg said to Pearl, who had her whole face buried in the fruit and molasses running down the yoke of her coat. "Good girl." Then Peg winked at Prue and called out, "Fresh hot pears!" to a group from New York skidding past.

The children walked along more sedately then, sucking on their pears and the sheepy fibers of their mittens. When Prue turned to see where her parents were, they were walking gloved hand in gloved hand. Her mother's face, so recently clouded with worry over Ben and the sturdiness of the ice, was bright, if not from pleasure, then at least from the brisk weather. When Prue turned forward again, she drew in a breath of delight, for before her were the sights she'd dreamed of all her life, even larger and more vivid than she'd imagined. When she'd peered at Manhattan previously, she'd looked down from the top of Clover Hill; but now she was looking up, and the warehouses along the waterfront loomed over her. As the party drew nearer New York, the ice grew ever more thickly littered with trapped boats. ("Little shallops and sleak periaguas were left where they lay," Prue wrote to Recompense, "with buckets & lengths of rope strewn in their hulls. Groups of boys approach'd them with obvious curiosity, but either found nothing worth pilfering or else desisted in the clear view of such multitudes.") Some distance north, Prue thought she saw Losee's flat-bottomed ferryboat, tethered to what looked to be the market wharf and in no danger from the huge freighter that rested nearby. There were also more mongers on the New York side—an old man selling chestnuts from a kettle fire, and a blind woman shaking a tankard for pennies in exchange for paper twists of popcorn from a basket at her feet. Two slaves were out making music with a mandolin and a Jew's harp; and some New Yorkers were trying their wooden-bladed skates on the bumpy, uncongenial ice.

"Hold, Prue," her father called from behind her. She stopped to wait for them, and the rest of the children slowed around her as if they were a school of fish. As he drew nearer, Matty asked Isaiah, "Where're your folks? Do they know you've gone off?"

"They know. I'm in charge," Isaiah replied, his somber face indicating he could be trusted.

Matty put his gloved hand on Prue's shoulder. "And you; is New York as you thought it would be?"

"I'm not sure," Prue replied. She hadn't thought it would seem so marvelous to step up off the water onto a wooden dock as solid and lichen-stained as any in Brooklyn. "I'm not sure what I thought." How workaday New York appeared when she saw it face to face! The height of the warehouses was awe-inspiring, but their windows rippled just as old glass did in Brooklyn, and the buildings were clad in the same weathered shingles and Holland brick. Women of all shapes and ages were hurrying past with dirt on their hems and pigeons in their baskets, and men went by on business, their furrowed brows intent on not remarking the change in the view. The children had climbed up into a market about the size of Brooklyn's, but with more permanent-looking wooden stalls. Prue smelled the familiar odors of blood, fish, chickens, and hay. There were bonfires in this market and out in the street; people were huddled around them for warmth. "Where are we?" she asked her father.

He crouched down beside her; a horse and calash whipped past. "This is Old Market, where poorer folk do their shopping," he said. Some of the king's soldiers were passing around a wineskin. "The Fly Market is on up the way," Matty continued, inclining his head northward, in the direction of the bustle. "That's where the ferry lands, and where the real truck is done."

"Why do they call it Fly Market?" Isaiah asked. Ben added, "Indeed; that's disgusting."

"I don't know," Matty answered them. "Imagine it's something Dutch."

Roxana was also crouched down, trying to remove molasses from Tem's mittens with spit and a handkerchief. Tem looked around at the people bustling past, while Pearl whistled a titmouse's chipper call and stalked after Maggie Horsfield, who made herself blind and deaf to her.

"I'd like to see it," Prue said, though in truth there was nothing she didn't want to see.

"I'll show you everything I can while we're here." Matty went around to them all, taking the decimated pear cores and tossing them in the gutter. Ben had eaten all of his, swallowing the seeds. "At the very least, Fly Market, the taverns I serve, and the bank, in which I keep your future fortune."

The way Roxana blew air out her nostrils made it seem *fortune* was an exaggeration. "We'll head home before they all tire out," she said. "We can't very well carry six of them." Prue saw then that her mother's cheer was superficial; it had not erased the sad lines at the corners of her eyes.

"Ben and I can carry ourselves," Isaiah said. "And I can carry Maggie."

His sister shot away from him, as if this were a punishment.

"Shall we, then?" Matty asked.

"To Fly Market!" Ben cried. He grabbed Isaiah in a playful stranglehold, unseating his hat, and Isaiah struggled to throw him off. Ben sometimes reminded Prue of a setter pup—good-spirited, but somewhat lacking in sense. Still, she wouldn't turn up her nose if her father brought a puppy home from the market instead of a book. Ben dragged Isaiah on, both of them yelping, and took the lead. Prue picked up Isaiah's hat, and Pearl, having given up on Maggie, whistled a tune to herself and slipped her sticky mitten in Prue's free hand. Matty put his arm around Roxana's shoulders.

"What do you think, Roxy?" he asked quietly. "A boy'd be fine."

Prue pricked up her ears. "I've enough to do with the three little beasties," Roxana answered. "Those Horsfields'll burn their father's house down, mark me."

"But a boy—to carry on the business."

"We've already tried. Three is enough. Maybe if the one wasn't tainted."

Prue pointed out to Pearl a white horse trotting past, its rider with a plume in his hat. Pearl continued to whistle and nodded her head with what looked like interest, but Prue knew she'd heard every word. The Horsfield boys sped ahead.

"Mmm," Matty said. Prue may have been a week shy of ten years old, but she could hear he wasn't finished on the topic.

"Let's catch up with them," she told Pearl, and began to run. Tem grabbed her other hand and the hat, and they galloped on until they were a few paces shy of the boys. Maggie was crying at being left behind, and Prue thought she caught Pearl smiling about it. None of the children knew where they were going, but Ben stopped at every street corner to look back to Matty Winship for guidance. Then he'd set off at a run again, dragging Isaiah with him, skirting around the bonfires and dodging the traffic and other pedestrians. In this fashion, perhaps a quarter hour later, they arrived at a much larger market, its wooden stalls thronged with Thursday shoppers despite the miracle of the weather. Prue was delighted to see such a crowd, though surprised to see so few black faces among the white. ("They only farm a good ways north of the market," her father told her the next day. "They've less of a need for slaves.") As

Prue looked out to the water, she saw it was indeed Losee's dull green boat tethered to the wharf, where he'd left it the evening before.

"Fly Market!" Ben said, his blue eyes casting greedily around. "Iz, do you have any money?"

Prue picked Pearl up so she might see better, and exclaimed with interest whenever her sister pointed or whistled at some attractive dainty. There was so much for sale here, Prue wondered why she saw Mrs. van Nostrand at market every week, buying Brooklyn meat and cheese like anyone else; her husband could have brought home delicacies of every order for the asking. Prue's own father could have done the same, and she wondered why he didn't. The children wove among the stalls and saw smoked meats, eggs the pale colors of spring flowers, entire stalls full of cheese, bolts of fabric to rival any in Mrs. Tilley's store, and row upon row of books. Prue could imagine her father perusing them and asking the bookseller questions. Pearl was heavy, but Prue did not want to put her down; when she could rest her eyes from the visual wealth around her, Pearl watched her elder sister with an expression of love and trust far exceeding what Prue felt she'd earned. She imagined Pearl would someday outgrow this admiration, but as long as it persisted, Prue would do all she could to encourage it. Over the top of a low bookshelf, Prue saw Ben and Isaiah reading something, and she caught Isaiah's eye. "Did you know there could be so many goods in one place?" she asked.

He sucked on his lower lip while he thought it through. "I didn't know there could be so many *people* in one place. Nor so many marvelous things. Show her the book, Ben." Ben held up a detailed illustration on waterproofing from a shipbuilding book. At the engraving's left, two workmen were uncoiling rope from a cauldron of pitch; at its right, they were wedging the rope into a seam on a rowboat's hull.

"Careful, now," the bookseller called, "I saw those filthy mittens you stowed in your pocket."

Ben shot Isaiah an angry glance as he put the book back down.

At the inland side of the market, Joe Loosely and his wife hove into view, looking as dazed by the sights as Prue herself felt. Matty Winship and Joe Loosely were good friends, and as they clapped each other on the shoulder, Prue noticed how of a type they were: both solidly built, with friendly features and chestnut hair. (Mr. Loosely was less well endowed in this regard.) Prue's sharp-featured mother could not less have resembled Mrs. Loosely, who came of Dutch stock, but they greeted each other warmly. Prue shifted Pearl so her weight might rest on the other arm, and Pearl gave a contented hiss as she nestled in.

"Not at the tavern?" Matty asked. "Seems it'd be a banner day for business."

Mrs. Loosely nodded what appeared to be her rueful agreement, and Joe said, "It is, indeed. But even an innkeeper's entitled to a holiday. Is it not so, Annetje?"

"I'm not so sure," she said, but she was already distracted by Maggie. As the Looselys had no children, they made a pleasant fuss over their small neighbors, dirty hands and all.

"The men are looking after the place. It's only for a few hours," Joe said. "And quite the miracle."

"Indeed," Matty said, though Prue was certain he did not ascribe the frozen river to God.

"Makes a man realize what a fine thing it'd be to have a bridge. We could saunter across to Fly Market on a Sunday stroll."

"In all the time we could spare from the tavern," Annetje Loosely said, with an arch tone Prue could tell was only half in jest.

"Have you been showing the kids the town?" Joe asked, resting his hand on Tem's head as if she were a newel post. Tem squirmed, but could have gotten free if she'd wanted to. "How'd you get charge of all these Horsfields?"

"Simple accretion," Matty Winship replied.

"Isaiah's in charge," Ben offered. "And Mr. Winship's only shown us the market."

"Then let's take 'em to City Hall," Joe said. He looked around a moment before deciding on a direction and setting out that way with Tem. "D'ye know, Miss Temmy, that New York is important enough to have its own seat of government? Not a little farming town like our Breuckelen." He gave the name a hearty Dutch pronunciation that made his wife laugh. Tem did not appear to care, and began to look peeved about the hand on her head. The streets themselves entranced Prue—she loved the way the buildings massed up as high as the rocky bluffs on either side of Joralemon's Lane. Ben and Isaiah ran and shouted as usual, but Prue felt an unexpected calm descend on her as she contemplated the majesty of her surroundings and the perfect ordinariness of the people she passed.

"Hey, Matty?" she heard Joe continue, though his voice did not dispel her reverie. "I've been thinking what to do about my sign."

"Well, you can't take it down," his wife said. "The whole neighborhood would miss it." The Looselys' sign depicted the king's arms in vivid color and detail, and was popularly counted one of the best works of art in Brooklyn.

"But I can't display it, either, as things stand. I wonder if Matty Winship might not employ his prodigious sign-makin' skills to render the thing more patriotical?"

"I'll think on it," Prue's father said, and reached over to take Pearl from her arms, as if he'd intuited how heavy the child had grown. Just then, a litter of screaming piglets went running across the street, with a slave boy in hot pursuit; but even the pigs and the laughter they engendered could not draw Prue entirely from her thoughts. She enjoyed seeing the grandeur of the City Hall, and New York's big brown church, which seemed as magnificent as a cathedral compared to Brooklyn's low-ceilinged meetinghouse. She loved walking over the smooth, triangular common, and could imagine how lush it would be when the grass was green and the lilac hedges were in bloom. Her father pointed out the heavy iron bars over the door to the Bank of New-York—meant, Prue gathered, to assure people their money was safe inside. There were people everywhere in Manhattan, ten or a hundred times as many as in Brooklyn; but all she could really think was how plain this place was, and how wonderfully so. Had anyone present known how she'd misled herself with her childhood lucubrations, she might have died of embarrassment on the spot; but no one did. As she walked that day, she was attuned to her family and friends, but more deeply so to the city itself, and to the ebullient life coursing through its streets.

When Roxana called out, "The Sign of the Crossed Keys—Matty, we should feed them before they faint," Prue was startled to realize how hungry she'd grown. She also noticed Tem tugging at her sleeve, and picked her up, though Tem immediately pushed both hands against her shoulder to try to get free.

"How can you even remember the place?" Matty asked Roxana.

She made a small plosive sound and shook her head. "It was where

we ate after we signed the papers for the property," she said. "I wouldn't
soon forget."

Prue liked the huge placard depicting crossed keys.

Mrs. Loosely herded the children down the steps as if they were
sheep.

"Whuzzis?" Tem asked, looking bothered.

Prue said, "I think we're having dinner here." She knew Mrs. Loosely
served food at the Ferry Tavern, but mostly to bachelors like Dr. de Bouton and the brothers Hicks. Prue had picked at a smoked fish on her father's plate there while idly listening to the adults discuss the news, but
she had never eaten a meal away from her own table. Maggie appeared
spooked by the steps leading down to the basement doorway and turned
her face toward Isaiah's coat; and once they were indoors, the din that re-
verberated from the vaulted brick ceiling startled Prue's ears. All around,
men of business were tucking into their chops as if nothing unusual were
taking place outdoors. Most of them were dressed neatly, but none, she
thought, so well as her father, who wore a clean collar and cuffs and a
blue cravat though he was only wandering around with his family. Prue
almost laughed to think she might ever have imagined such an establishment existing in the Land of the Shades; and her father, seeing the fleeting smile, brushed at her cheek to encourage it.

Joe spoke to a woman in a red apron, who led them to a large table
near the rear and returned mere moments later with a heaping basket of
fried oysters and clams, a pitcher of cider, and a bouquet of wooden
mugs.

As the Horsfield boys grabbed for their food, Prue thought briefly of
Persephone, who had eaten the pomegranate seeds in Hell and ever after
been bound to the place. But the clams were sweet as sugar and the cider
more alcoholic than that her mother served; there was no good argument
against eating in a New York inn.

"Why're you so quiet?" Ben asked her.

She flinched a little, shy to have been caught. Roxana answered for
her: "Because she's a dark-minded critter; you know that, Ben." This
made Prue want to slump down on her bench, but she could see that
both her mother and Ben were still smiling and that her father had put
his arm around her mother's shoulders. They remained mysterious,

though Prue felt she had learned a good deal about the world outside Brooklyn that day.

By the time the meal was through, the afternoon was already settling in toward evening; a shadow covered the whole side of the street. Tem was drooping, and Roxana slung her over her shoulder like a washrag. Prue could see her mother working up some reproach for her father, but before she could voice it, he said, "We'll get them home quick as we can."

"Shame for such a day to end," Joe Loosely said. "It'll be a long time before we have another holiday."

Mrs. Loosely picked up Maggie, who had refused to eat any lunch and still looked disgruntled. Pearl got to perch on her father's shoulders; while Ben and Isaiah, as promised, moved under their own power. Prue felt relieved to find them tired enough to walk along without any shoving or games. After a few minutes weaving through traffic on the busy streets, even the adults fell quiet, and the Looselys ended up walking somewhat ahead of the rest of the party. Ben began directing Isaiah to collect mementos from the journey: a discarded newssheet, some gray New York pebbles, an apple pilfered from a cart. As they stepped out onto the surface of the water, Prue marveled at how natural it now seemed to walk over the surface of a frozen river. This was how quickly one's view could change.

"Roxy?" Matty said softly.

Prue moved away from the group as if in search of something for Ben's collection, so she might keep her parents in view and continue to listen. Her mother raised her thin eyebrows in reply.

"If we aren't—if we don't try for a boy, we shall have to train one of the girls to run the distillery."

She dropped her head to one side, as if releasing water from her ear. "I don't know," she said. "I suppose it wouldn't be the worst thing."

"Not Pearlie, of course, and Tem's too little yet to know what she'll be good for. But Prue."

Roxana caught Prue's eye and raised her chin to indicate she shouldn't be so nosy. "It's a serious business. Do you suppose you could manage, Prue?"

Prue glanced at the boys, who were lost in their endeavor. Her heart almost leapt from her body at the thought of being trained to the distillery. This was the thing she most coveted. The machines, and the mysteries of the business, seemed such a worthwhile and practical pursuit compared to wondering where the dead resided; and she'd be able to spend whole days and years in her father's company. "I imagine I could," she said. Then, fearing her mother would see the eagerness in her eyes and refuse her, she headed back toward the boys and pushed hard on Ben's slender back. She had no real desire to fight with him—and indeed, she grew sorry she'd started anything when he pulled her to her knees—but she didn't know what else to do with her enthusiasm.

Her father said to her mother, "I know it's what she wants. She might prove to have a talent for it."

"She might," her mother replied more quietly. But Prue's ears were attuned to her even as Ben reached under her coat to tickle her ribs. "She wouldn't make a mistake lightly."

"Hey, hey," Isaiah said, and pulled Ben off. They were both laughing. Prue was far more interested in her parents than in the boys, but she thanked Isaiah anyway.

"We'll see," Matty said. "Perhaps in the spring." Prue thought she could hear in his voice the hope he might still, somehow, get a son. "Matthias Winship and Daughter," he said, as if to see if it wanted alteration.

Matthias Winship & Daughter. It rang like a church bell; and though they might eventually have to append a final *s* for Tem, there were years to come in which it could be Prue's private demesne. She would have repeated the name in her mind indefinitely had Ben not called out, "Look!" Her gaze followed where his finger pointed, and she saw her beloved bluffs of Ihpetonga, tinged pink against the darkening sky. "That's our house, Iz!"

Prue could make out a squat white structure near the ferry landing, and some Horsfield family sheets and britches hanging stiffly on their line. Their mother had died the previous year, and the washerwoman never quite seemed to get abreast of all their laundry. "Doesn't look like much from here, does it?" she asked.

Isaiah, holding on to Ben, said, "Easy."

There, farther south, were the sails of her father's windmill, motionless in the still air and small as a doll's arms. In the rosy light, the black crags—from whose slopes most of the cypress had been harvested to make casks for the gin—looked neither majestic nor fearsome, but simply dull. She could make out the name of the establishment—*Matth' Winship, Distiller & Rectifier of First-Quality Gin*—beckoning to her in tall letters from one of the storehouses whose broad side faced the river. The cherry orchard was a cluster of bare twigs, and the Winship house, among the more prominent in the village, was a brown clump, like a bird's nest.

"Your place doesn't look like much, either, does it?" asked Ben.

"No."

Far off to the right, she could just make out the Luquer Mill, and beyond it, the dark mouth of the bay and the blurred trees of the Governor's Island. How fine it would be to have a bridge.

"So what do you say, Prue?" her father asked. "Shall we give it a go?"

Already the light had gone more blue, and the sandy buildings of Winship Gin looked as if they'd been deserted for decades.

"I'd like to," she said, not looking at him. "I think we should. Let's change the sign."

Two stray dogs gamboled past; when one went down spinning, the other skittered around it and barked. Matty Winship said, "That's my girl," but his enthusiasm did not sound genuine.

Joe Loosely clapped his gloved hands. "She'll make a fine distiller, Matty Winship. But you must paint my sign first. A deal's a deal."

"I can do yours immediately, in the cooper's shed," Matty answered. "The side of my warehouse'll have to wait till she proves her mettle at making liquor."

Prue was still young enough to feel spring might take eons to arrive, but she knew the manufactory needed undergo no visible change for her to begin her work there. Tem was fast asleep on their mother's shoulder, as Maggie was on Mrs. Loosely's, and Pearl would not have cared much about the conversation even if she'd understood it; the Horsfield boys were by now far ahead of her, chasing after the dogs. In this joy, she realized, as in the self-devised torments she'd suffered all those years, she was alone. Yet there was magic in this isolation. She was to be initiated into the mysteries.

They arrived home before dark, all spent. The Looselys escorted the Horsfield children home, and Tem and Pearl woke up when they entered the warm house, and were eager to tell Johanna of their travels. Pearl's frantic whistling couldn't reach Johanna, who nodded absently at Tem's exclamations as she stirred the pot. While Tem shouted about the market and the food, Prue began to undress her, to get at her soggy diaper. Tem kept trying to push her off, but at last held her smock up to help.

"Did you not even go out to see it?" Prue shouted to Johanna. "It was remarkable."

Johanna cast a glance over her shoulder, not quite in the direction of Prue's voice. "Don't you know I've seen enough already in this lifetime? No need to gape at anything more. You'll see, when you're a dried-up old woman such as I."

"Oh, please, Johanna," Prue's mother said. "It's your own fault you missed something wonderful. It's not the fault of your age." But willfully or not, Johanna did not hear her; and she doled out their soup without saying another word.

In the middle of the night, Prue was awakened by a strange sound, a moaning as if some large creature lay wounded. At first the noise frightened her, but she saw her sisters slept through it; and as she listened, she realized it must be the ice of the river breaking to allow the tidal current to continue in its usual course. A heavy rain was drumming on the roof; the temperature must have risen since nightfall. While Prue sat up in her bed, the river groaned and made a long series of cracking sounds akin to an old barn crumbling. In a short while, however, this subsided to the sound of rushing water that so underlay Prue's every thought, she couldn't generally hear it unless she listened for it. At some point, she must have fallen asleep. In the morning, there was no trace of there ever having been an ice bridge, and the distillery and ropewalk were bustling earlier than usual, as if to atone for the previous day's "Saint Monday." As she dressed her sisters, Prue wondered if she might have imagined the whole affair.

But her doubt could not persist, for her father brought the sign from the king's arms down to Scipio Jones's cooperage that very afternoon. Matty worked on it at odd moments over the course of the next week, and Israel Horsfield said her father would let none but Scipio advise him on it, and locked the shed when neither of them was there to guard it. Prue harangued Israel with questions, but could get no answer from him; so she began to pull at Scipio's cuffs, and even tried offering him some smoked pilchards as a bribe, at high cost to the fabric of her pocket. He brushed her off, however, saying, "You'll enjoy it more if you let it be a surprise."

The night before Prue's birthday, her father was out late, drinking, she assumed, with Losee and Joe; but, as it turned out, he'd been hanging the new sign, and had waited till most of the village had gone to sleep so it might come as a true surprise. Her tenth birthday, then, turned out to be another day of hubbub in the village, for everyone was either tickled by or angry about what her father had done. To the bottom of the shield, he had appended a crescent-shaped piece of wood on which he'd written, in bold white letters, *Jos. Loosely' Liberty Tavern*; and the beautiful rendition of the king's arms now depended from still another placard, depicting an eagle of liberty swooping down to snatch up the escutcheon in its sharp beak. Prue saw the brigadier general of the Hessians come pat her father on the back and laugh about this minor act of insurrection, though of everyone in Brooklyn, he should have been the most upset by it. She did not think she'd ever understand the reasons or motives for the war, but her faith in her father was nearly infinite.

That Sabbath evening, a balladeer came to town, and the Winships took their children to the Twin Tankards, as many families did, to hear the song. The balladeers were often disreputable-looking characters, with scruffy hair or gaps in their teeth; but they arrived almost as frequently as the New York papers and sang about the war and news in other towns, providing a good evening's entertainment. This singer wore a patch over one eye, which caused Pearl to hide her face in fear of him; but to Prue's delight, he sang not of battle, murder, or the ordinary perfidies, but of the freezing of the North and East Rivers, which he claimed was all the news, from Massachusetts to the Carolinas.

Three

THE DISTILLERY

That very week, despite her father's lingering doubts, Prue's training at the distillery began.

Her mother's chief fear was that her hair would catch in a drive belt, so instead of dressing it, as she had always done, in two fuzzy auburn braids, she wound it onto the back of Prue's head and fixed it with a comb. Prue was pleased when she saw herself in the looking glass. The coiffure wasn't more flattering than the former one, but it made her look eleven or twelve, which she counted as progress. Roxana was also concerned lest some article of Prue's attire snag in the machinery, so she bought some sturdy gray linen from Mrs. Tilley and had Johanna make Prue a pair of close-fitting knee britches, such as boys wore. Johanna had to feel every stitch with her fingers, but her sewing was still expert, and the britches came out well enough. They fastened beneath the knee with tortoiseshell buttons, for whose fanciness Ben teased Prue, though he did not seem to mind the britches themselves. Between these and the new hairstyle, Prue no longer fully resembled a girl, and she knew this would be even more pronounced when the cobbler finished her long work boots. But she told herself she had never been popular with the Livingstons, the most feminine girls in the neighborhood. It was impossible to risk losing the regard of those who'd never held her in any; and Ben would no doubt value her more highly now that her clothes allowed her to run more quickly and fight like a boy.

Prue's father didn't worry about her hair or her clothing, having, as he did, at least some native faith in her common sense. Prue intuited, however, his concern about her aptness for the task she was undertaking. She was quick at writing and arithmetic, but she knew the prospect of teaching her the art and science of distilling daunted him, not only because of her sex. Even before she began her training, she understood the business was complex: There were raw materials to acquire and wastes to dispose of, machines to be kept in good order and on strict schedules of time and temperature, a few score men, of varying abilities, to be fed and clothed if they were slaves, and properly directed, kept off the bottle, and paid their wages if free; and there was the product itself, which sold only because it was of the finest quality. "But I'll tell you what the real trouble is," he told her the day they began. He sat down on his chair in the countinghouse, so their eyes might be on a level. "The process is sufficiently arcane, even now I sometimes find myself surprised it transmutes grain into alcohol and not into gold."

"I won't be dismayed," Prue said, though when he spoke in terms of alchemy, she was.

He smiled at her with his lips pressed tight. "That's my girl," he said.

She nodded. She wasn't certain he meant this as a compliment.

"Good. If it suits you, I'd like to begin with the process itself, of distilling and rectifying spirits. Although it's the more complicated aspect of what you'll have to learn, I assume if you understand it, you'll apprehend the business side of things more easily. If not, we can always train up that little Izzy Horsfield. He'll make a good manager, mark me."

"He always seems worried about something," Prue said.

"Exactly my point. For your part, it's enough if you can make gin."

She inhaled a deep breath, took a sip of the coffee she was drinking despite its bitter taste, now she was a working person, and, wondering if she'd been wrong to volunteer for this task, followed her father down the open stairs to the mill yard.

Prue had always thought the buildings of the distillery were arranged in the most pleasing and symmetrical fashion possible, though now they did not look especially welcoming. The brewhouse, in which the distilling process began, sat at the southern end of the property, where Joralemon's Lane joined the Shore Road and raw materials might be most easily delivered. As the gin progressed through the stages of its manufacture, it traveled from building to building and tank to tank, heading northward toward the ropewalk and the ferry. The four long, narrow buildings in which most of the work was done—the brewhouse, cooling house, stillhouse, and rectifying house—were clustered away from the water, toward the foot of Clover Hill, to decrease the danger of flooding; and between the buildings and the straits was the hard-packed sand of the mill yard, in which the workers took rest and exercise, and in the center of which stood the countinghouse. Matty Winship and Israel Horsfield kept their paper-strewn office on the second story, and reached it via the outdoor staircase, against whose weathered planks their boots resounded whenever they went up or down. The office had windows on all four sides, so they might look out on any part of the works while seeing to other business. The ground floor was an empty room, swept clean weekly by a slave named Owen; there was thus always a suitable space in which to address the workers and give the wage-earners their pay, regardless of the weather. (Prue knew neither the ropewalk nor the sawmill nor the gristmill had an assembly room; but her father had once told her he'd been treated like a pig as a journeyman, and had rankled under the indignity. "Mind, I don't provide 'em with French cravats or silken hose," he'd said, "but they do as they're told without grumbling if they can warm their hands by the stove of a winter afternoon.") At the northern waterfront edge of the property stood the casking house and storehouses, and those other buildings whose function supported, but was not integral to, the whole endeavor of making liquor: the cooperage, smithy, stables, slave quarters, privies, and cook shed. Past these, Matty Winship owned a stretch of open strand between his works and the Schermerhorn rope manufactory. If ever his business boomed enough to warrant it, he could expand northward.

From her visits to the manufactory, Prue had gathered the making of gin was hot, noisy, fragrant, and complicated, but she did not know how much so until her father led her down into the mill yard that morning. He began by asking her, "You know that I grow barley?"

"And Indian corn, vegetables, and juniper." She loved when the men hauled up kelp from the straits to fertilize the fields. It had a familiar, almost human stink.

He waved good morning to John Putnam, the brewhouse's foreman, who was hurrying past with a sheaf of papers in one hand. "Good. I grow barley for the gin, but not nearly enough to supply the works entire;

and I'm no malter, either. I buy the remainder of my grain from Mr. Remsen and Mr. Cortelyou, and from a fellow in Nassau County, when the local supply won't suffice. Mr. Cortelyou has made his fortune selling malted barley to me and to the Longacre Brewery, up in Queen's County. And it all goes down to the Luquer Mill to be ground. You know why it comes and goes in wagons?"

Some men were shouting outside the stillhouse, but her father didn't seem concerned. Prue had lost her train of thought in watching them, and didn't know the answer.

"So it doesn't get wet on a barge, monkey. Come, you've got a fine noggin there. Let's put it to use."

He opened the barn-sized door to the brewhouse, and Prue could feel the rumble of the great machines thrumming in her feet and her rib cage. At one end of the room, fires were lit beneath three copper cauldrons, each large enough, Prue thought, to hold a small outbuilding; and the moment the door was shut again, she began to sweat in her tall, heavy boots. Men were shouting to one another as they scrambled over the ramps and ladders surrounding the wooden mash tuns in the room's center; she had no idea how they could hear one another above the din. The agitators inside the first two tuns made a violent racket as they turned, and when boiling water spilled from the cauldrons down the chute to the third tun, it was loud as the river after a hard rain. Leather drive belts whirred and clattered over their wooden drums.

Her father leaned down close to her ear. "You know why it's called the mash room?" he asked her.

She craned her lips up toward his face. "Because they're mashing grain in there," she said.

"And you know why that's done?"

Prue thought a moment before giving her answer; she was anxious to get everything right. "To extract the sugar from it."

"Yes," he said. "We pump the water to the cauldrons from the liquor-back, which collects groundwater a good distance from the taint of salt in the straits. When it's good and hot, it spills into the tuns, as you just saw, there to be mashed for three hours. The fires beneath are just warm enough to keep things goin'."

Four men went running up the ramp to the third tun with paddles in their hands to prevent clotted grain from sticking in the agitators. They all had the necks of their shirts unbuttoned and their sleeves rolled up past their elbows.

"Are you ready to help?" Matty asked.

Prue was somewhat frightened by the noise and bustle but excited to be part of it, too. "Perhaps this first time, I can simply watch," she said.

"Nah." He gave her a courage-inducing rub on the arm, and she stumbled against him from its force. "You're going to be a distiller. You want to know simply by the smell how the wort is coming along."

So up the ramp to the first tun they went. The men made room; and a young fellow, whose florid mustache was already drooping in the steam from the tun, cracked a smile at Prue and said to her father, "You think she'll manage it, Mr. Winship?"

Matty took the man's paddle and gave it to Prue. "She's the best I've got, Mr. Southey. She'll have to."

Even above the din of the drive train and the moving agitator, she could hear the commentary this provoked. She wanted to run down the ramp and up the hill and take Pearlie for a walk; and she wanted to stay put and prove them wrong.

The lip of the tun stood shoulder high to a girl, and each spiked agitator within was twice as long as she. Prue had had no inkling how dangerous this process could be. If she fell in, she could easily drown, if her skull was not smashed instantly by the thrust of the agitating arm. She put the paddle's butt end on the ground and leaned into it as if it were a staff while she contemplated the roiling mess of the mashing. Her father leaned down beside her.

"Don't be afraid of it," he said, "and don't take it for granted, either. Whatever you do, don't go in. If the paddle drops, shout out. There's a warning bell over there"—he pointed to the northeast corner of the room, where a bell hung with its rope wound neatly around a cleat—"and the nearest man will ring it. As soon as he hears it, the windmill keeper disconnects the crown gear from the drive shaft, and the whole manufactory shuts down. It may seem a lot of fuss for a paddle, but it'll keep a whole batch of wort from ruination by splinters, and probably save your arm besides."

To have her arm caught thus seemed a fair repayment for what she'd done to Pearl. Prue determined to put this thought out of her mind.

He taught her to watch the rhythm of the agitator, so she might put her paddle in and stir the mash without threat of injury, and she worked all morning alongside Mr. Southey, who seemed eager to catch her out in a fault. The sweat streamed down her face and arms and the channel between her shoulder blades. Her palms were rubbed raw, and her arms burned with exhaustion, but she determined she'd work as well as a man if it broke her. When the bell rang for lunch, she wished she could ask her father to carry her to the countinghouse, but she clung to her pride; and once there, devoured her bread and cheese as greedily as would a coyote. She could hardly believe his collar hadn't wilted after a morning of such arduous work.

Prue spent a month in the brewhouse, sometimes accompanied by her father, more often working side by side with the men while her father saw to other business. The work brought out a deep, semipermanent flush in her cheeks, sinews in her arms, and calluses in her palms, but though Ben teased her about it, she could see he was jealous he had to spend his mornings in the domine's school. She began to notice subtle differences in the scent of the wort—the way it smelled light and sweet, like honeysuckle nectar, when the mashing began, but nearly approached the odor of young beer when it was ready to move on. That first month, she had no real idea where it went when the mashers had done with it. One man would disconnect the agitator from the drive train, and another tripped a switch that opened a large, screened valve in the bottom of the tun. The wort went cascading downward, who knew where, leaving the mash behind. Soon a second batch of boiling water would be let into the tank, so the mash might be reused for another, slower mashing. After this second mashing, the spent grains would be brought up in buckets, loaded onto a wagon, and sent out for the nourishment of Mrs. Luquer's pigs. Then came the enjoyable task of scrubbing down the tun, for which purpose the men let ladders down into it. Prue always volunteered to go inside, and often thought of Jack and the Beanstalk while she did the work, as if the tun might turn out to be some giant's butter churn.

By March, her father thought her knowledge of the brewhouse sufficiently advanced to move forward. "And I think she's an inch taller, too," he told Roxana one Monday morning over breakfast.

"I'll be sorry to leave the mash room, for all the hard work," Prue added. "I do love the smell of the wort."

Roxana flared her nostrils at her eldest daughter, but was too busy wiping porridge from Tem's face to reply.

"I've been amazed how much variation there is, from one mashing to the next," Prue continued, though she knew better than to prod her mother so.

"As if I haven't heard enough about wort in my lifetime?" Roxana said. "About wort and feints and gin?" Tem still refused to place her porridge spoon square in her mouth, and her mother took it from her and forced it in. "Christ, Reverend, while you're training her, you might teach her to raise less tedious subjects at table."

Prue was hurt by her mother's rebuke, but Tem shoved her wooden bowl to the floor and began howling, and there would be no further discussion. Prue could not decipher the glimmer in Pearl's black eyes as she sat primly eating her oats.

"Your mother's ill humor notwithstanding, it's a good-luck day for you," Matty told Prue as they walked down the lane. Indeed, it was a balmy March morning that could lull a body into believing winter wouldn't last until May. "The next stage of the distilling process is considerably less work—a perfect job for a little woolgatherer like ye."

Prue smarted under the epithet, but knew it was true. Pearl was her own odd case, but though Tem was still well shy of her third birthday, Prue could already see she'd never bog herself down with reflection. It was Prue's own intrinsic nature, not everyone's, to wonder and brood. "I didn't mean to anger her," she said.

"No, you didn't," her father replied, providing little solace.

That morning, he took Prue down to see where the wort traveled when it left the tuns—deep into the brewhouse's cellar, into a cast-iron cistern called the under-back. The under-back's chamber was dank and noisy, as the power train kept two pumps whirring constantly to dispatch groundwater back to the sea, and the stone walls magnified their sound. The wort came cascading down the chute into the cistern, and a second set of pumps worked to draw it up and over to the cooling floor in the next building. A gruff, taciturn man called Hank Rapalje presided over this operation; his job was to check from time to time that all the pumps were functioning correctly. His skin had acquired a subterranean pallor, and Prue stayed as far from him as possible during her weeks under his tutelage, as he gave off a musty odor that reminded her of Johanna.

By contrast, the cooling house seemed like paradise. One climbed a short set of open stairs to reach it, as it was elevated on stilts, some eight feet off the ground. The cooling floor was a shallow tank into which the wort was pumped from the under-back. This tank was as wide and broad as the room it occupied—twenty feet long by fifty across—and paved in cast-iron sheets to make it impervious to water. The room's pretty gambrel roof was supported by great unfinished beams, and its walls could open almost entirely to the breezes by a series of curtains and doors. A scant distance above the cooling floor's surface hung a latticework of planks resembling the top crust of a pie; and a balcony hung higher up the entrance wall, so the cooling house's foreman might stand aloft for a better view. Six men were ambling along the planks when Prue and Matty first entered, all holding paddles shorter than those in the brewhouse. Only two of the men looked to be slaves. The place was warm and smelled like rising dough, and a balmy breeze wafted in through the long, open walls.

"Quite the place, isn't it?" Matty said.

Prue only then noticed she had, indeed, been daydreaming. "What's the work to be done here?" she asked.

"You'll like it," he said, and took down a paddle from the wall and handed it to her. It was much lighter than the one she'd used in the mash room. "And it's perfect weather in which to learn it—it's less idyllic in December. D'ye smell the bready smell of the wort?"

Prue nodded her head.

"That's well and good, but if it ferments too quickly, we've got beer instead of spirits—and we can't turn a profit on beer. So the cooling men walk about the planks and stir. In that way, the wort at the tank's bottom is continually brought up to the top, where it can be cooled and freshened by the breezes."

"That's all the work?"

"That, picking out any debris that happens in, and helping wayward birds find their way back outdoors before they soil the goods with their excrement. And like the tuns, the thing has to be scrubbed down after each few batches to keep the product clean. How d'ye think you'll do?"

"Very well, thank you," Prue said.

"Then I'll leave you to enjoy yourself. Follow Mr. van Voorhees's instructions, if he has any to give you." Here a slightly built fellow raised his hand from across the room. "Mr. Horsfield or I'll be back to fetch you for lunch."

The cooling floor seemed incontrovertible proof there was a merciful God in Heaven. How else, Prue reasoned as she took up her paddle and began to walk and stir, could she explain work such as this existing in the world? It would leave her the entire day to dream. She held the paddle by its end and gingerly let it down to touch bottom; the tank, as it turned out, was less than two feet deep. One of the slaves laughed when he saw her do it. "Not so frightening, is it?" he asked her.

"No, not at all."

She would be able to amble along lost in her thoughts, with no danger whatsoever if she happened to fall in. The men with whom she'd be working also looked cleaner and more refined than Mr. Rapalje. She wagered they'd smell better as well.

"What's he, training ye up to manage the cooling floor when I'm a grizzled old man?" van Voorhees asked when they passed each other on the boards. "That's a nice bit of work for a girl."

"No," she said, and drew herself up to her full height. She was learning to brace herself against people's usual reaction to her undertaking. "He's training me to run the works entire."

He smiled and nodded, perhaps insinuating he'd already known what Prue was doing and believed she was bound to fail. She reminded herself not to take offense. This had been the response of the brewers as well, but she'd done a good enough job to keep them quiet.

Prue learned the business of cooling within the hour—the work was to wander and stir. Midmorning, a bossy jay flew in the west wall and Prue whistled and flapped her arms to shoo it out; van Voorhees told her that in autumn, there would also be leaves to remove. This was all, however. A batch of wort took most of a morning or afternoon to cool, and when it was ready, the men used their paddles to direct it toward a series of chutes near the north wall. Thence it descended to the fermenting-backs, which were housed belowground, exactly as the under-back had been. There, van Voorhees told her, the fermenting master introduced yeast to ferment the wares in a controlled fashion.

Prue would gladly have remained in the cooling house a year, and felt glad her father hadn't removed her the very next morning, by which time she'd learned all there was to know. When, after a few weeks, she stood looking at the countinghouse floor and told him she'd imbibed all the lessons the cooling house had to offer, he lifted her chin and countered, "You're a diligent thing, but you're a child yet, too. A little more time enjoying yourself won't harm ye."

"Thank you," Prue said.

From across the desk, Israel Horsfield said, "Don't spoil her, now."

"I won't," Matty answered. "She earns her keep." He let her walk the boards of the cooling house a few weeks longer.

In April, while the papers reported Ben Franklin was in Paris negotiating the peace, Prue moved on to help the fermenting master, the freeman Elliott Fortune, measure yeast and time the wort's ripening. News from the larger world interested her—she could not help hearing about it, either directly from her father or out on the streets—but Prue was far more concerned with learning to keep her eye on the clock, though she soon began to be able to judge her product's readiness by odor and taste. (The liquid that entered the fermenting-backs as wort left them as wash, which was pumped through pipes up to the stillhouse's copper wash-stills.) Matty Winship came down every few days to challenge her knowledge of the subject, but each time, he agreed with Mr. Fortune she was learning well, and might soon be able to manage a batch on her own.

Prue stayed in the fermenting room longer than she had in the other areas of the distillery; though the place itself was gloomy, she found Mr. Fortune congenial, and they agreed the process of making wash was as delicate and important as any she would need to learn to become a distiller. Near the end of May, however, he pronounced her ready to move on, and her father again came to oversee her personally. She had not known enough to value such supervision when she'd begun her training that winter; but now she knew how much else he had to attend to, and considered herself lucky when she could command his time and attention.

"Now, this'll be a fine spring for you," he told her, as he walked her around the periphery of the stillhouse, with its four great copper stills all shining and burbling, crowned with snaking copper tubes that reminded Prue of her own hair. "This is the real business of distilling, and the part that'll make or break ye. If you can't get proof spirit out of that wash, you might as well throw up your hands and jump in the river; because river water's worth as much as the product will be. Do you think you can pay close attention and master it?"

Prue said, "I do." She had learned, in a few months at the distillery, that even when her confidence in herself wasn't strong, she could sooner or later make good on a promise by diligence.

"Hmm," he said, "I've almost begun to think so myself. But it's no use raising my hopes; it's not everyone can be a distiller. It's here in the stillhouse, you know, the alchemy begins."

Talk of alchemy continued to make Prue nervous, but she found even the most equivocal expression of her father's faith gratifying.

Each wash-still, she learned, had a thermometer attached to its side, because the heat of its contents was of paramount importance. "The men tend the still fires with great care, because the interior temperature must remain at all times above one hundred eighty and below two hundred twelve degrees Fahrenheit. For what happens at two hundred twelve?"

"Water forms blisters, and boils," Prue said dutifully. She hoped none of the men was listening to her catechism; in truth, they all seemed too absorbed in their work to notice her.

"Quite so. At two hundred thirteen degrees, all the wash would go bubbling up the pipes, and we be left begging for alms on the streets. But at two hundred eleven, the alcohol in the still vaporizes, without producing steam. Those alcoholical vapors ascend from the still into the copper worm," he said, pointing to the snaky tube overhead on the nearest wash-still, "and the worm makes its way down the inside of this tank."

Here he led her to a wooden tub as big as a mash tun. Water was splashing noisily in through its top, and equally loudly out through its bottom, into a chute in the floor. "This is called the worm tub," Matty told her, "and the water that surrounds the worm is constantly refreshed direct from the river. The alcoholical contents of the worm are thus kept cool, and as a result, the vapors within condense into liquid."

Here Prue's mind began to wander—she knew nothing of condensation except as it affected a jug of cool water or her house's window glass; she couldn't say why it should become liquid. But watching the noisy worm tub, a question arose to draw her back from her peregrinations. "Where does the water go from the bottom?"

"The warm refuse from the bottom of the tub travels down the pipes and out to splash over our waterwheel, which provides ancillary power for the pumps here and in the rectifying house, as we're far from the windmill, and a waterwheel's easier to manage than a whole 'nother mill." He watched her a moment to see if she'd understood, and went on, " 'Ancillary'—"

"I know," she said, "I remember. It's Latin, from *ancilla*, a servant."

"Christ a'mighty. Your mother said the Latin wouldn't stick."

Prue felt awkward about her father's compliments, chiefly because she knew his doubts about her would be confirmed if ever she bungled a task. Whatever good opinion he had of her also seemed fragile because she knew it would vanish if he learned what she'd done to Pearl. As a result, she often dreamed up scenarios in which he uncovered her secret through stealth, or in which she herself accidentally revealed it. These fantasies made her skin creep, but she could not force herself to leave them off.

The condensed alcoholic vapors went by the name of low-wine. From the worm, it flowed into low-wine receiving-backs and was brought back up again to the spirit stills, where it was redistilled to increase its potency. "If any of the low-wine acquires a foul odor during the second distillation, we call it feints and give it up for lost, letting it run off into the river. The spirit proper, however, spills into its own receiving-backs in the cellar, and there Mr. Horsfield and I test the batches to bring them up to a standard strength. Until they reach it, we keep sending them back for further distillation; and one never knows how many trips through the spirit still will make a batch perfect. Sometimes only one additional distillation is required, sometimes three. And when it's strong enough—twenty times stronger than gin—we mix it down with spring water and call it proof spirit."

"So when do you make the gin?" Prue asked.

"In its own due time," Matty answered. "But what gives gin its particular taste happens in the rectifying stills; what we're making here has no real taste nor smell a'tall." She must have looked vexed, because he patted her on the head and said, "Never you fear—I'll do my best to teach you. But each thing in its turn. Manning the stills is a tricky business, and a great deal can go wrong in the worm. I'll learn you that, and then, God help us both, we'll get on to rectifying. Perhaps by the time you're twelve."

Prue's eyes widened—she hoped not to have to spend a solid year and a half in this hot, noisy room. Then, too, she was fixing to spend her entire life here; she might as well get used to it.

"I'm only ribbing you," he said. "You won't surprise me if you move on to rectifying soon enough; you've been a quick study thus far. But for now, you work here."

Prue remained in the stillhouse through the summer, and indeed found distilling more complicated than the processes she had hitherto attempted. The art of keeping the fires at the correct temperature—which sometimes involved reaching briskly in with tongs to roll a flaming log, as big as she, out onto the tile hearth—required one to overcome one's natural aversion to fire, and she wondered if she'd ever master it. Being anywhere near the fires was misery, and made the beating sun outdoors seem almost a relief. Stills were finical: If the heat was to distribute evenly around their bases, the whole affair had to be shut down and polished every fourth workday. The worm sprang leaks, it seemed, as often as it worked properly, breeding lazy speculation while someone climbed into the empty tub with a lantern, searching for a hole the size of a pin; and the flannel at the worm's base, meant to trap any foul-smelling oils released by the process of condensation, frequently clogged the apparatus entire. Prue found the work frustrating, however, for a more basic reason: Having spent six months in uninterrupted study of the distillery, she was beginning to have opinions about how things should be done. If she voiced them to her father, he'd hear her out; but in his absence, the men would wince as if she were imbecilic or speaking in French, then awkwardly return to their work. She had no doubt it was difficult for grown men to listen to a half-grown girl; but she knew her vision to be as clear as anyone's around her. She resigned herself to keeping her opinions private until she grew taller.

The rewards of all this work were threefold. First, in late July, her father began taking her down to the receiving-backs and instructing her in how proof spirit's potency was judged, both by objective measurement and by the way it burned the tongue. Prue delighted in any aspect of her appointed profession that smacked of science; and Israel Horsfield shook his head over Prue's glee the first time she introduced the hydrometer into its small glass vessel to measure the spirit's specific gravity.

"She'll be a regular Galileo Galilei," he told Matty, scratching his pointy chin.

"Do you know what you've got there?" Matty asked Prue.

Prue examined the new instrument, bobbing in the vessel. "Looks like twelve thirteenths the weight of water," she said, though she didn't understand precisely why the instrument should be calibrated in this way. "That's proof spirit, is it not?"

"Absolutely," Matty said. "But it's not off by a tenth of a point? Because it makes a difference here." He examined the vessel himself, and pronounced her assessment sound. "I'll be damned, Israel, but she's as meticulous as we are." To Prue he said, "So we give it the second test. Remove the hydrometer, and take a wee sup from that vessel—but mind you, it burns, so no more than a drop to your tongue."

Prue felt flush with having read the hydrometer correctly, and tilted the beaker into her mouth. Her sinuses at once filled with fire, and the next moment, she was spluttering, with tears and mucus running down her face. Both her father and Israel Horsfield were laughing at her.

"Next time you'll know," her father said, and brought her up, choking, into the mill yard and out to the pump for water.

But the day after this humiliation came her second reward: the new sign announcing the distillery's name. Scipio Jones whitewashed the words that had previously graced the side of the storehouse, but her own father climbed up the ladder to trace the outlines for the new letters, which Scipio then painted over the course of the next few days. Her father may yet have regretted his lack of a son, but Prue felt stirred when she first saw the black letters, shadowed in gray, gleaming out toward the port for all to see. Henceforward, those traveling across from Manhattan would see *Matth^s Winship & Daught^r, Distillers & Rectifyers of 1st-Quality Gin*, and Prue felt sober and proud, knowing that everyone in Brooklyn and New York now knew a studious girl was learning to make spirits.

Prue's third reward was to be allowed to learn rectifying. She knew this was the place her father's art shone, and the part of the process he most feared she might be unable to master. "I don't mean to belittle you by saying it," he told her as he led her into the rectifying house—a building smaller than the stillhouse, yet similarly equipped with stills, and dominated by a looming iron hulk of a machine, with its great flat jaws yawning open—"but the truth is, when I was an apprentice, there were four others besides me, and none of them ever got the knack of it enough to start a place of 'is own. Everything you've learned until now is important, but it's all for naught if the rectifying goes afoul." Prue wondered why it had to be that everything could be ruined at each stage of the process; and she continued to stare at the gaping mouth of the machine. The men were piling up wood for a fire. "That's the press, little goat, the thing your mother most fears. Promise me you won't lose a finger in it; she'll never let either of us forget it."

"I promise," Prue said, but the press looked fierce.

"If you learn it right, rectifying'll be your great joy here," he said. She could not tell if he intended this to placate or frighten her. "There's no other task requires such knowledge and mastery, nor none that gives a man such pride in his work at day's end. From an odorless spirit, a gifted rectifier makes a product that delights the senses and buoys up the heart. Isn't that a fine thing?" She was too nervous and confused to answer. "That's all right, piglet," he said, and worked his fingers into her tightly bound hair. "You'll see."

By means of this hydraulic press, he extracted the pungent essence of juniper as well as various other berries and herbs. Their first day in the rectifying room, he showed her how the press worked—how he wiped down the lower surface, laid the herbs to be extracted on it, and used his whole body weight to depress the lever and bring down the top jaw. Prue was amazed a single man could operate a machine of such gargantuan size; Matty explained the workings of the hydraulic mechanism to her, and showed her the place where the water dripped out from the hinges. The essence of the material—in this case, lavender plucked from their garden—trickled into a small vessel at the side of the machine, in an amount Prue thought disproportional to the quantity of herbs they'd placed in it. After unlatching and lifting the jaw, Matty once again wiped off the pressing surface, and let Prue help him work the lever on the next batch.

"And attar of lavender goes into gin?" she asked, trying to enjoy the sweet fragrance wafting into the room, and trying to dwell less on the danger of the work.

"Can do, but it needn't," he said. She knew her eyes must have widened, for he went on, "I'd think by now you wouldn't be surprised to find it all so complicated. There's no fixed receipt for gin, love, not in general. For Winship gin, I've my own certain way, but I still make the slightest adjustments from one batch to the next. It's the great pleasure of the work, and the place a gin man proves 'is mettle."

Prue was shocked to know this whole manufactory was devoted to making a product whose recipe was no more precise than that for bean soup; and for the first time she sincerely doubted her fitness for the business. She could follow instructions well enough; but the idea of having to invent them anew for each day's gin discouraged her. "What goes in it, then?" she asked.

"The all-important juniper, of course." The Winships cultivated the evergreen bushes in their dooryard as other families tended roses. The sharp scent of the berries, ripening year-round, was so much a part of Prue's olfactory landscape she noticed its absence wherever else she went about town. "But one can flavor the liquor with a myriad of other spices and sweets. I've used orris, angelica, lemon peel, cardamom, coriander; and the master I studied under used everything from sweet basil to China tea. But that was in England, of course; there wasn't any tea tax there."

"Soon enough we shan't be taxed any longer," Prue offered.

Her father began wiping down the press once more. "Not by the Crown; but mark well, wherever there's a government, an honest man has fees to pay. And you will, too, if you become a distiller."

Prue did not care for that "if."

That day, she watched him work and smelled the various extracts he produced; and later in the week made some of her own, with his help with the lever. She came to understand how a gifted rectifier introduced these sundry essences in novel and harmonious proportion to the final distillation of spirit, such that their individual properties would be less evident than the balance of the whole. The product had to be recognizable to the palate and nose, have a taste that stamped it as *Winship* gin, a thing a man would willingly plunk down his wages for when beer could be had at half the cost.

So into the autumn of 1782, Prue spent whole mornings roaming Brooklyn and asking if she might pick spices from her neighbors' gardens, or begging specimens of rarer varieties from Mrs. Friedlander. She knew this behavior—even more than her knee britches—made Mrs. Livingston click her tongue. She could not operate the press without assistance, but one of the slaves would help her crush whatever leaves and berries she acquired. And under her father's tutelage, she learned to taste and smell her herbs indoors and out, in the hot stillhouse and down by the cool river, by themselves on a fresh palate and in combination with other herbs and food. Her father brought her a small ledger from New York, and to its lined pages she entrusted inexpert drawings of plants, along with detailed notes on their tastes and interrelationships. Each week, she brought this book to her father for review; and though he chuckled over her sometimes zealous choice of adjectives ("The lemon balm was 'sprightly,' was it? I'll take your word, missy"), he seemed pleased, overall, to find her palate educable and her attention not yet flagging. He began to speak so often of her progress to the family that Roxana's eyes would glaze over when ginger and cinnamon came up at table.

"Might you teach her to cook and bake in the off hours?" she asked him one evening. "It'd prove a far sight more practical; and I daresay she already knows her spices better than I do."

Matty laughed. Tem, meanwhile, had finished her meal, and began marching around the kitchen, hollering commands to invisible workers. She had never been to the distillery, so she'd copped most of her phrases from what she'd overheard on the wharves. Though Prue thought she herself should have had enough poise to disregard her sister, Tem's mimicry nettled her.

At the end of November 1782, a preliminary peace treaty was at last signed at Paris. Word did not reach Brooklyn until late December. The war had lasted all Prue's sentient life, and she realized that although she'd known it would someday come to an end, and had hoped with her father it would come to this one, she had always half considered it a permanent fixture, like a house. It would take some while, the men speculated down at Loosely's tavern, for the Crown to pack up its troops and send them home; so the Cortelyous had time left to grumble about pocked fields and poached pheasant, and the Winships might yet earn a tidy profit from the soldiers' love of the barroom. No one knew how long the occupying forces would remain, but to celebrate, Matty Winship put in an order for a doll-sized rectifying still, to be made to order at the English foundry from which all the original equipment had come. He had a talent for drawing, and when he explained the manner in which he thought she might practice her future art upon a gallon of spirit at a time, and showed her his delicate pencil sketch, she thought him as good as an Old Master. When the still arrived in early spring, she began to use it exactly as he had described, while the fires of the rectifying house roared and spat all around.

Prue had been using her new still a few weeks when Congress declared the official end to the war; and soon after came the order for those soldiers garrisoned in Brooklyn to return home across the sea. Those few remaining Loyalist families who had not yet left New York voluntarily began to pack up their homes to move to Canada; Prue saw how awkwardly they were treated at Mrs. Tilley's or on the street. She had imagined there would be general jubilation, but there was little; the process of making peace had dragged on so, most of the neighbors seemed weary. After all the complaints the occupying forces had engendered, Prue had thought the Livingstons and Cortelyous would rejoice to see them go. But the soldiers had been in Brooklyn a long time, which made their parting bittersweet. White women and Negresses were suddenly to be seen crying in the streets—the mistresses and whores, many of them holding babies, or with small children clustering around their skirts and shrieking for their papas. Prue asked her mother and Johanna what would become of them, but found them both, conveniently, stone deaf. Many of the neighborhood boys, including Ben, were also heartbroken at the prospect of the troops' departure.

"There won't be any more quoits, or shooting lessons, or card games for money," he complained to Prue as the neighborhood children watched some of the enlisted men tie up their bedrolls with hempen twine. Ben had his hands tucked under his armpits as if for warmth, though it was a balmy spring day.

"But it's a good thing they'll finally go," Isaiah told her. "And I, for one, shan't miss the gambling."

"Because you've been too much of a girl to take part in it," Ben said.

"Because I've been stalwart in the face of temptation," Isaiah corrected him, "which we shall all be better off without."

"I should knock you senseless for saying that," Ben said, but he kept his arms folded and his eyes on the soldiers.

Later in the week, the officers hitched their carts to the farmers' horses, and went in clusters down to the waterfront, where they waited with long faces to begin their journey home. When at last they were all

gone, Prue could see the full extent to which they'd devastated the landscape of Brooklyn—hewed down the forests, furrowed the fields with
trenches, eaten up most of the livestock, and riddled the sides of barns
with holes from their countless drunken games of darts—and the quiet
that reigned in the village at night seemed unnatural.

When Prue wrote to Recompense about that period, she described it
thus:

A few prisoners had survived the fœtid English prison ships in
Wallabout Bay and were set free, but most succumbed soon thereafter
to putrefaction or despair. A score of the natives of Brookland,
Bedford Corners, Flat Bush, & Midwout were found among the dead,
but only one Brooklander was recovered among the living:—Ivo
Joralemon, a grandson of the farmer who'd sold my father his land. I
had only a vague recollection of Ivo as a quiet, slender boy in the years
before the war, but he came home skinny as a hoppergrass & seemingly
more aged than his parents, with one leg so gangrenous, Dr. de Bouton
had to amputate it. The Joralemon house stood close by our own, to the
opposite side of the Ferry Road; and when Ivo's cries pealed out across
the countryside, my own leg could feel the pain in sympathy, & I gritted
my teeth till at last he must have fallen unconscious. I should not have
been surprised had people heard his shouts all the way to New-York,
where I half imagined his soul would soon be bound. Ivo Joralemon
recover'd from the surgery, but limped around town hunched over his
crutches, and never again spoke. The Livingston daughters joked he
would marry Pearl. I pretended not to hear them.

My parents, the Looselys, & the Philpots had profited from the war,
but the rest of the village was hard hit. When I took breaks from my
work at the distillery, I sometimes saw fathers in their best suits of
cloaths, standing together in threes or fours on van Nostrand's landing. I
was not close enough to read their expressions, but their postures were
glum; and I knew they were going to beg the bank for new mortgages
on their properties, or for leniency on the terms of their current liens.
Joe Loosely, who during the war had run his auctions only sporadically,
now advertised one almost every week. On any given Saturday, the
hammer rang on his block as carefully husbanded stores of lumber &
seeds sold for pennies. Even the cost of a hired laundrywoman had

grown prohibitive, and my father & Joe Loosely were the only men in Brookland who still had clean linen on workdays. All the other men wore starched collars out on Sunday, then grew progressively sootier till the Saturday next. One could tell in an instant who was too poor to have his razor ground.

And yet Brookland as a whole did not succumb, as I had thought it might do, to melancholy. Many families,—the Joralemons, Remsens, Rapaljes, & Cortelyous,—had lived on the land under Dutch rule, and their ancestors had weathered the change when the English arrived; they rebuilt after the long occupation with what must surely have been the same doggedness & faith. The King's officers had purchased the far western portion of Mr. Remsen's fields,—the area whose boundary everyone in the village knew to be pounded by the waves,—for a cemetery; & now, instead of crops, their dead were planted there in neat rows. Some of the westernmost were almost immediately unburied by the tide, but the rest slumbered peacefully. After a decent interval, Mr. Remsen returned the field to the cultivation of asparagus, and the resulting shoots are still counted the most succulent in King's County. (Do you shudder, dear Recompense, to hear what you have et?) As farms were parceled off on the auction block, some new arrivals bought up land for the Friends' meeting a short distance out the Jamaica Turnpike. From the way the men had long griped about the ravages of the war, it had seemed to me my village must be doomed; but appearances spoke otherwise.

And for me, the pleasures of working with herbs, concocting recipes, & trying them upon my father's sensitive tongue were legion. My mother's attention yet wandered when I spoke of my progress and discoveries, but my father could no longer doubt my aptitude for the business, & he rewarded this with high praise. I held on to this knowledge when I approach'd him to ask if my next task might be to learn the workings of the mill's machinery.

—What, you want to know how the drive train works? he asked. He could not disguise the condescension in his voice. —You've already learned how to *make gin.* It's a far sight more than anyone thought I could teach a girl.

I felt smaller than my years, but I made my self hold my shoulders square. —I know how the drive train works, I said, looking out the countinghouse window toward the wharf, as if the direction of my gaze could lessen the strength of my impertinence. —The crown wheel hooks into the lantern pinion, and it sets the whole thing spinning.

My father went over to the shelf & poured him self a nip of the wares. It was early for this; he ordinarily waited until operations were complete for the day.

—If I'm to run it some day, sha'n't I have to know the mechanicks of everything?

He drank his cup down, and placed it carefully on the desk he shared with Israel Horsfield. —I suppose. But it might be thirty years from now.

—Even so, I said.

He shook his head at me & said, —Gears an' drive belts it shall be, then. But I warn you, I'm condemning you to a life of spinsterhood. No man in 'is right mind will share his bed with a woman knows so much of machines.

I faced my father as bravely as I could. At that time I did'n't care about marriage. I could see plain enough what it had made of my mother;—but I could not dream of saying such a thing before him.

Reading this, Recompense thought how well her mother's knowledge of machines had served her; and smiled to see how incorrect her grandfather had been. The world contained at least one man who, looking around a village of girls trained in the domestic arts, preferred the distiller. Now that she was so far from home, Recompense thought perhaps she did, too. She curled deeper into the smooth cushions of the divan, and did her best to picture the machinery her mother spoke of, truly to apprehend, for the first time in her life, how her mother's manufactory worked.

Four

PEARL'S SIN

P rue spent four years studying her father's trade—the first two perfecting the manufacture of the product itself while learning the intricacies of the manufactory's machines, and the second two training to run the business: learning the proper methods to care for the buildings and equipment, design and inspect casks, keep books, deliver goods, dun the company's debtors, and distribute payroll while persuading the paid workers to take only a fraction of their due in wares. She seldom found herself at leisure, and when she did was often bone-tired or foggy-headed, but she was still resolved to study what she could of engineering. She learned that in the year of Tem's birth, a bridge constructed entirely of cast iron had been built in Shropshire, and she pleaded with the Fly Market bookseller to order a volume detailing its methods. He scowled at her, and her father browsed the shelves elsewhere, as if to minimize his connection to her, but eventually she gave over her thirty-seven and a half pence and folded the bookman's promissory note into her pocket. When the book arrived an age later, Prue applied herself to its diagrams of stress and strain until her mind ached.

"You'll ruin your eyes," her mother scolded in passing.

"Leave her be," her father counseled, though Prue knew he neither approved nor disapproved of her fancy. It was a solace Cornelis Luquer also took an interest in the physical world. They could share their books and discuss their way through whatever seemed unclear.

At ten years old, Prue had thought it a marvel to travel to New York City and ponder her late misconceptions about the place. At fourteen, when Congress was sitting in that city while it awaited a more permanent home, Prue's head was full of belts and batches, but she still thought about bridging the East River. It would ensure easy shipping of gin in winter, after all; she continued to dream about it when she stood gazing out over the straits. She brooded on the terrible thing she had done to Pearl, the one truly mean-spirited action of her life thus far, and still worried someone in her family would learn her secret. Though she no longer had as much time as she'd had in childhood to ruminate on death, she remained anxious it would come for her father or her sisters, to whom she grew daily more attached. Where once New York had seemed a sacred destination, she now made deliveries there in all kinds of weather, and had twice been pitched into the cold, salty water en route. She knew the streets on which a small pedestrian was likely to be run down, and those on which she could buy candy; she knew her father's customers by name. She accompanied him regularly to the gloomy bank. Over time, his banker—Timothy Stover, who had the carriage and voice of a Quaker but lacked the sober manner—came to answer her questions as carefully as her father's.

When she had begun her training, her sisters had been too small to be tutored in much besides kneading wads of dough and embroidering with huge needles and yarn. Though Johanna by then had spent half her day in bed with headache and the rest in her chair, working her lips and muttering, her face had lit up as if Jesus Himself had appeared in the room whenever Pearl had brought her handiwork for inspection. Johanna would slide her palsied fingers over the fabric with pleasure and deliberation; and when she'd descried whatever Pearl had made thereon—usually a series of stabs and lunges intended to represent flowers, trees, or the inevitable cat—she'd praise Pearl lavishly for it. Pearl must have sensed it was Johanna who'd nursed her in her fragile infancy, for she loved her out of proportion to the old woman's personal merits. Prue's praise, or their parents', was welcome enough, but Johanna's approbation made her bounce up and down as if she needed to use the pot. Prue knew she had no right to feel jealous; she was, after all, down at the manufactory all day, while Pearl spent hours in Johanna's company. Still, Pearl's glee irked her. Had Johanna possessed her sight, she would not have known what she looked upon.

"You can't tell what it is," Prue protested on one occasion.

Pearl crossed her black eyes at her, while Johanna merely lifted and shook her chin.

"You can't tell what that is!" Prue shouted.

"I can, indeed," Johanna squawked in return. " 'Tis a barn cat, is it not, Pearlie?"

Pearl stroked Johanna's wrinkled cheek in reply.

Johanna placed the piece of linen—which resembled nothing so much as bare winter branches—on her lap and stroked it. "Remember when you tried to knit a muffler, when you were hardly older than she, Prudence Winship? *Jezus Christus*, you may as well have tried to knit a sheep. *Jezus*, have mercy on her soul!"

Pearl laughed, her throat clicking quietly. Some of the neighbor children thought this sound eerie, but it fell easy on the family ears.

Prue tried to imagine what Ben would do in such a situation, but realized he was too blithe to get himself into such a corner in the first place. She stalked outside, determined to pull her jealousy out by the roots but feeling an ounce of coldhearted pleasure, meanwhile, that no one ever complimented Tem's sloppy needlework or lumpy porridge. Prue disliked that as soon as Tem was big enough, she would also be trained at the distillery; Prue wanted to keep its secrets as her own, and would have told no one her hope that, as Tem hadn't yet shown an aptitude for anything, she would also prove second best at making gin. Prue went over to the chicken coop to see if any of the hens had laid; and though they clucked as if she was a nuisance, they let her take three eggs.

Prue cupped them gently in her two hands, as she had no apron or skirt to gather up for a basket. It should have been enough, she reasoned, that Tem and Pearl had ferreted out their dark eyes and straight black hair from some dim corner of the cosmos; Tem was the prettier of the two, but they both had an enviable regularity of feature. Put another way, it seemed fair that if Prue herself was to have to make do with a head of kinky curls and a face that would never quite hang together, she should also be allowed more responsibility and entrusted with more arcane knowledge.

As she brought the eggs back in, she realized that Tem, while not marked by the same gloom that colored her own mind, was tainted in her own way: She was ever enthusiastic at the beginning of an inquiry, but her interest flagged once the subject became known to her. This struck Prue as potentially a more insidious defect than mere dark-mindedness, with which, after all, their mother had still managed to marry, bear three living children, and make a life for herself. Tem's first day reading was full of struggle and delight, but when she discovered the days to follow would be equally strenuous, she began to slouch into the posture of a comma, her small head, to all appearances, too heavy for her spine to bear. She beamed with satisfaction when she learned to write her capitals, yet behaved as if it were a personal affront that she must also learn her minuscules. Prue thought she might pitch out of her chair when the topic of cursive script arose. Tem had no intrinsic talent for numbers, nor for any of the tasks that kept a household in order. Were she entrusted with the tinderbox, she couldn't make the flint catch. Pearl, by contrast, could strike a spark as well as her parents, and deliver it safe into the hearth without causing a moment's worry. Seeing that she liked the responsibility, Matty brought her a small silver tinderbox from New York and afforded it a place of honor on the mantel. Meanwhile, if Tem was even sent to poke a fire, it sputtered; if she was asked to dust a room, she would leave cobwebs in the corners and clouds of hair beneath the rug.

At the age of six, however, Tem seemed to know she could make up for her near-universal want of useful skill by cultivating her native sociability. It was clear to Prue her father was popular in the neighborhood as much because of the spirit he was born with as the spirit he distilled; and Tem had obviously chosen to emulate him in this regard. Her capacity to mimic was unrivaled in Prue's experience; she could tremble in perfect synchronization with Johanna's seemingly random fits of palsy, turn her gaze inward exactly as their mother did, and throw back at Prue the slight catch in her voice when she was afraid of something, thus nearly bringing her to her knees with embarrassment. In emulating their father, Tem learned to look the distillery workers—even the slaves—in the eye, call them by "Mr." and their surnames, and commit to memory the names of their children, though they would never be brought by to play. She learned to walk down the street with her head held high and a smile on her lips, no matter how many gaps her departing milk teeth had left in her grin. She learned to whistle nearly as well as Pearl did. None of these talents could immediately be shown as handy as if, for example, she'd proven masterful at sums or had an unusual gift for language, but she clearly wasn't stupid.

It was no surprise Pearl should turn out to be more studious. On the day Prue had explained to her what writing was, and what were its uses, she may yet have been, as their father called her, a "little piss-pants," but she'd opened her mouth and bawled with happiness. She'd understood writing would free her from isolation, and had taken up the study thereof with a fierce dedication. Her diligence sobered Prue. Unlike Tem, Pearl would finish an evening's lessons, then ask for more; and since the age of five, she had been able to write clearly enough on a slate for her words to be intelligible to people outside the family. As soon as she'd learned to express herself thus with any specificity, some of the pantomimes she'd thitherto used to assuage her desires became unnecessary, and from a distance she appeared a more ordinary child, except for her size; she was unusually slight, and Tem had shot up past her while they were still in diapers. (Prue wondered if this, too, might not somehow be her own fault.) Up close, anyone could see from the expression with which she listened that she was a bright child, a quick study. Pearl showed herself so capable of numeric manipulation, Prue had to turn her tutoring over to their father when Pearl was only seven. The patterns she began to devise for the ornamentation of pillow slips and napkins were proclaimed by those neighbors who still spoke of the Pierreponts (who early in the war had been exiled, as vociferous Loyalists, to the barrens of New Jersey, leaving their huge white house vacant) to be fine as any that family had brought from France. Anything that existed in nature she could draw with pencil or needle; and when nature ceased to provide sufficient inspiration, Prue and her father began bringing books unlike any they'd previously acquired home from their journeys westward. The library upon which he'd educated Prue had released its secrets only upon perusal of dense blocks of text, but for Pearl he bought *The Cyclopædia of Natural Wonders* and *A Compendium of the Beauties of Art*. The illustrations in these books were etched in more shades of gray than the water of the East River contained, and they were veiled behind sheets of tissue that crackled to the touch and hinted at intricacies they only half concealed. In this way, Prue and Pearl learned, by firelight, the flora and fauna of Europe, the Americas, and the Indies, the magnificent buildings of the Egyptians and the Chinese, the many-limbed gods of the Hindus, and the heroic paintings of Italy. Tem would sometimes glance at the plates, but if their parents would let her go out, she was happier rolling hoops and tossing quoits with the Luquer boys, doing imitations for them of pious Patience Livingston, whose jaw practically never moved when she spoke, or gathering huckleberries from the side of the road. It didn't matter to Tem that the laundrywoman cursed her each Monday for coming home with grass or berry stains on her clothes. Books were not her pleasure—being out with people was; and if she devoted her learning to games, she was learning how to win them with moderate frequency. She made no apologies for her predilections, and announced them so adamantly, the adults made little effort to control her.

Prue's sisters were as unlike in temperament as in interests. Tem was accustomed to being the center of attention in groups of children, and to earning their approbation through her mimicry; but she would prickle the moment she perceived a slight. Pearl, by contrast, possessed a workmanlike good cheer, which at the time Prue thought almost miraculous, given the hardships of her existence, but which she later came to remark in others who kept company with misfortune. Pearl seemed to have been born understanding how a neighbor's unease could be disarmed with a forthright smile, and how pity could be brushed off likewise. As a result, when children squabbled in the market, their mothers would hold Pearl up as an example. "You'd not hear Miss Pearlie crying about it!" was often barked at a sniveling child; along with, "Be thankful you're better off than that blighted little Winship, God bless 'er." These scoldings had two effects: first, to make the berated child dislike Pearl, and second, to mortify Prue. Pearl, who should have been bothered by the neighbors' example-making, bore it lightly, bowing her pretty head, and making sly remarks on her slate about the perpetrators once the sisters were past their purview. (*Lees't I don't have the Blight of a Foul Temper lyk her Daught*^r, she commented once, in response to something Mrs. Livingston had said; and about Mrs. Remsen, she one day simply wrote, *Cow.*)

Prue held out hope Tem's inattention would prevent her wanting to come into the distillery; but the thrill of all the people and bustle clearly outweighed the difficult work the place would require of her. Her parents began discussing the possibility in the summer of 1788, when Tem had recently turned nine years old. Pearl was busy sketching the banner Matty would have his men carry in a forthcoming parade to support New

York's ratification of the Constitution. Prue found the verse Pearl had come up with,

> *Broklands Distillers,*
> *Prowd & true,*
> *Stand with Publius,*
> *As shld you.*

rather limping, but the two workers she'd drawn flanking a cask of gin were true as life.

"One's enough in the business," Roxana argued. She was wrapped in a shawl though it was warm outside, and feeding Johanna porridge from a bowl as if she were an infant. "Pearl'll live with us always, but Tem we might manage to marry off."

Pearl flared her nostrils from over her sketch, but Roxana was too busy with Johanna's supper to notice. Johanna smacked her lips and closed her eyes after each bite, as if she could conceive of no better meal than this. Prue was confused by the scene: sad, afraid, and at one level relieved to see Johanna brought so low, and jealous to see her mother caring for her so artlessly.

Matty said, "I think we ought to let the girl decide. It's only fair." He looked squarely across the table at Tem, who was trying to draw a horse with a piece of charcoal. "What do you think, missy? You want to join your elder sister in the distillery?"

"Sure I do," she said, without glancing up from her drawing.

Prue felt her temper simmering, but managed to hold steady. "Do you realize how hard the work is?" she asked Tem, trying to prevent her annoyance leaking into her voice. "Do you realize how much studying you'll have to do?"

"It's a different kind of studying," Tem replied. "I shan't have to sit still for it."

Roxana looked peevishly at Tem, whom she had little notion how to manage. Matty, meanwhile, was laughing, and leaned across the table to pat Prue on the cheek. "She'll be a different sort of apprentice than you were, won't she?"

"I suppose."

When Tem gave up on her drawing, Pearl put down her pencil, seized

Tem's charcoal, and drew an actual horse on top of the fat goatlike creature on the page. Later in the week, Tem and Prue marched proudly beside their father in the huge, noisy parade. Pearl was a mere spectator,
holding Israel Horsfield's hand; and the boisterous crowds along Broad-
way were so dense, Prue thought it was impossible her sister could have
seen much. But that evening Pearl recounted the sights and sounds in
great detail, and claimed thoroughly to have enjoyed her trip across the
busy river on the barge. *& w. so menny in Support, shurly our Lawmakrs will let
us join the Fedural Union?* she wrote.

"We can hope," Matty told her.

I am certin they will.

Matty shook his head and laughed when, later in the month, the papers proved his small daughter correct. Support for the Constitution had
been far from universal, but at last the State of New York had given its
consent.

Matty and Roxana decided Tem would be brought into the distillery
that September, when the neighborhood boys went back to school after
harvest. Roxana had her hands full looking after Johanna, who was
spending more and more time in bed, though Dr. de Bouton could deduce no cause but old age for her headaches. (He left her with some
packets of white powder to be dissolved in water and sipped when the
pains struck. Prue licked her finger and dipped it in one when no one was
looking, and thought it tasted like ordinary kitchen soda.) Pearl would
henceforward have to look after herself. Prue, meanwhile, was furious
that she, who'd wanted to learn distilling with her whole heart and
showed a true aptitude for natural philosophy, had not been allowed to
begin studying until the age of ten. If only, she thought, she still believed
in the Other Side and could fantasize sending Tem to the orphanage. If
only, instead of pledging herself so single-mindedly to herbs and rectifying, she had given even a shred of her attention to God, who might help
her through this crisis, which no one in her family seemed to understand.
But how could she approach Him? If she asked her parents for guidance
in this regard, they'd scoff at her; Johanna believed, but if it were possible to make her understand a question, there would be no eliciting information without also summoning forth her scorn, rage, and
prognostications of hellfire. The domine still bored Prue, and she felt too

awkward to ask guidance of the Friends. She did, at least, think she could find a few minutes in each workday to sit down by the water on the retaining wall and ponder her dilemma. The workers about the mill yard would wave to her, but she knew how to brush them off; and it was a relief to let her mind rest briefly while her father's slaves heaved casks of gin onto barges, and up on the Schermerhorns' wharf they loaded gigantic spools of rope. She observed how steadily Losee rowed his ferry across the straits. Weeks went by, and although she spent most of her free moments thus in fair and foul weather, she could not ascertain how to open a pathway of communication with the Infinite. She knew it was a difficult question, however, and told herself she shouldn't mind if the answer took its time arriving.

In the meanwhile, Tem was being outfitted for her work, and the pleasure she took in her new, boyish clothes made Prue's teeth itch. Tem had harangued their mother with requests for a leather vest, such as craftsmen wore, until at last Roxana had relented. Prue and her father had gone down to the tanner past the Luquer Mill the next morning and brought back a small, supple, dark brown length; Roxana had taken it to the seamstress the following day, though as she'd left the house, she'd complained quietly but audibly about having to leave Johanna alone in the house. Pearl had volunteered to stay behind, but the whole situation had left a sour taste in Prue's mouth, both because no other slave in Brooklyn was treated better than the children of the family and because her parents seemed not to mind Tem's peacockery at all. The afternoon Roxana brought the vest home from the seamstress, Tem put it on with her knee britches and high boots and paraded around the kitchen as happily as the rooster strutted around the yard. "Do I look a picture?" she asked, with an unconcern for the question's propriety that nearly sent Prue over the rafters. "I wish we had a big looking glass, like the Livingstons'. I want to see how I look."

"You look fine," Prue said. She noticed Pearl stabbing rather more forcefully than was necessary at her needlework.

Their mother said, "I need to rest," and walked toward the stairs. "Wake me when it's time to start supper."

"It hardly matters what you look like," Prue said. She began to brush down her boots of the day's caked dust. "You'll be working."

"I disagree," Tem said. "I know the men watch to see what you do and how you do it. Daughter of the proprietor, and all that." She picked her two long pigtails up in the air. "I think I should cut my hair, to complete the picture."

"*Och God,*" Johanna muttered from the corner. Her eyes were closed and she had her palm to her brow.

Pearl quickly wrote, *How is't she c" only heer us when we're contemplating Mischief?* and held it up to Prue.

Johanna, who seemed to know nothing of the interjection, went on, "You'll not hear the end of it."

Tem said, "If I'm to work like a boy, I would have hair like a boy. And so should you," she added, nodding her head toward Prue.

"Then bring me the scissors," Prue said.

You shall not? Pearl wrote.

"I shall, unless you want to do it."

Pearl's small face darkened. Johanna continued muttering in Dutch and rocked her chair to and fro.

Tem handed Prue the scissors, point-end first. "To here," she said, indicating her collarbone. She drew up a chair, sat on it with her back to Prue, and untied her ribbons.

Prue looked inquiringly at Pearl, who still appeared vexed, but placed her slate and needlework on the chair. When Pearl took the scissors, they seemed large in her hand.

Tem's hair was fine and straight, except where the ribbons had kinked it, and it cut as easily as muslin. As the hair fell to her feet, Pearl began to laugh her quiet laugh. "Shh," Prue told her.

Tem said, "I needed a haircut," and the last few tendrils snaked to the floor. Pearl had cut on a slight diagonal, and gave the scissors back to Prue to straighten out the line. Prue was amazed at how satisfying it felt to feel the hair come free. When she'd finished, she wiped the stray bits from the back of Tem's vest and said, "All done. Let's have a look at you."

Tem stood and turned to face her sisters. Her hair hung in a lank curtain to her nape, exactly as Isaiah's did, and seemed to end abruptly, as if the missing length would always suggest its absence. Pearl was hissing delightedly, and covered her mouth with both hands. In a moment, Prue's eyes grew accustomed to Tem's new appearance, which forced her to admit the shorter hair somehow made her pretty sister even prettier. "What's'a matter?" Tem asked.

"Nothing," Prue said. "I think you'll like it."

Tem went upstairs to look in their small glass, shouted "Hoyay!" and vaulted down the steps on her return. From bed, Roxana called out, "Can't you leave me in peace for an hour?" Tem kissed her sisters on their cheeks. "I love it," she said.

Pearl bowed, her face red. Prue said, "Sit down. I'll put your tails back in."

For what might have been the first time in her life, she sat obediently. Johanna was still stewing in her chair, which creaked over the floorboards as she swore beneath her breath; Pearl was still laughing. When Prue tied the ribbons back in, Tem's pigtails stuck out slightly, resembling paintbrushes.

At that moment, Matty came in from the distillery, banging his boots against the doorsill to clean them. Tem ran to present herself in her new guise as distillery worker. "Holy Christ," he said, and looked to see who'd done it. The scissors sat unclaimed on the table. He wiped his palm across his mouth, then stifled a laugh. "Which one of you did it?"

Tem said, "Pearl did."

Pearl grabbed her slate and quickly wrote, *Prue help'd.*

"She did, did she?" He took one of Tem's pigtails in each hand, and pulled on them to tilt her face upward. He shook his head at her. "I'll have my work cut out for me when it's you who's sixteen." He patted Tem's cheek, said, "Hello, Johanna," and went up the back stairs.

Some sort of a row ensued, but when her parents appeared half an hour later, Prue thought she heard a trace of her mother's old humor when she commented, to no one in particular, "There's punishment on the Other Side for these kinds of transgressions. That's all I'll say."

This was the first instance in which Prue caught sight of Pearl's deep strain of waywardness. Until then, she had thought her middle sister as good as gold, perhaps as the result of her own execrable actions against her. Prue was mollified to think Pearl might, after all, be merely human, and she herself free from blame. She kept an eye upon Pearl, to see when and how her perversity might again show forth.

Its next appearance came in November, when much of the talk from Mrs. Tilley's to the mill yard centered on Congress's decision to make

New York the official, if temporary, center of the new nation's government. "Does it mean we'll see Mr. Franklin and Mr. Jefferson when we
go to the bank?" Prue asked Israel Horsfield.

He shook his head equivocally. "It's possible, of course, but I don't
suppose it's likely. They'll be busy men, with a great deal of lawmaking to
accomplish."

"Still," Prue said, "they'll have to eat."

"And drink. Believe me, we're counting upon it."

Gossip also dwelled on the influx of emigrants from France. It would
be another year before that far-off country exploded in turmoil; but as
rats are the first to sniff out a ship's imminent demise, some workmen
must have had the premonition that all was not right. Brooklyn's recovery
from the devastation of the late war had also, to Prue's surprise, been ro-
bust; it was a good time for a man to come try his fortunes in King's
County. By November, a number of émigrés had arrived in Brooklyn
with nervous expressions and beautiful clothes. Providentially, the Hicks
brothers had that very summer decided to parcel off a portion of their
sizable farm into city lots, upon which a tradesman or shopkeeper might
build a home. They were calling the spot Olympia, as if it were not
merely a few new streets in an old village. There had been no Frenchmen
in Brooklyn since the Pierreponts had been exiled during the war, but at
the time Tem came into the distillery, Prue began hearing colorful French
curses in the saw pit out past the Twin Tankards and over the rising posts
and beams of Olympia's homes. The whine of the van Vechten sawmill,
a few hundred yards north of the ferry, pierced the neighborhood air far
more regularly than theretofore; and Prue watched the progress of all the
new buildings with interest, when she could spare the time from her
work. She was busier now than she'd previously been, for in addition to
helping her father in the usual ways, she was helping him train Tem. As
Prue had suspected, Tem showed interest in learning any new thing the
distillery might present her, but her attention flagged during the weeks
necessary to acquire a particular skill. When Tem grew bored she also
grew irritable. Prue found the autumn long and trying.

The immigrants meanwhile opened forges and a chandlery, a dry-
goods shop down by the tannery and the Luquer Mill, a farrier's, and
even a perfumery, dealing in flower waters and aromatic oils, which Prue
haunted under the pretense of educating her nose. Soon enough, some

of the Frenchmen had purchased a plot from the Cortelyous—north of the ferry in the direction of Wallabout Bay, but close by Olympia—and begun to erect a church of their own. Domine Syrtis was by then an ancient man who shuffled around his house in a dressing gown; he had requested a replacement from Amsterdam, and apparently even in private did not deny the need for a new house of worship. The French church, which opened that autumn, began to draw a good crowd on the Sabbath, which Matty Winship remarked to Tem and Prue with some surprise. "I thought we were all heathens," he said, leading them along the low catwalks above the fragrant, steaming wort.

"Will we have to go?" Tem asked. Prue wished she'd phrased the question differently; she herself was curious about the new church.

"Never fear. Your mother wouldn't have it."

Tem reached her paddle down into the wort and splashed it around, releasing billows of steam.

"Easy, easy," their father said. "You must be gentle with it. As with your mother. I don't know if Pearlie's worn her down or if it's Johanna's frailty, but she tolerates less than she used to."

"I'm gentle," Prue said.

"I know."

"And she needn't care for Johanna the way she does," Tem said. "No one else in Brookland treats their slaves like royalty."

"That's enough from you," he said. "Your mother loves Johanna. When she arrived in this country, she knew no one but me, and when we bought Johanna of Mr. Remsen, she found her first and only friend. That's enough said against her." He crouched down to pick a brown oak leaf from the tank, and said no more.

It wasn't long before those believers who'd been raised outside the Dutch church thought if a motley bunch of Catholics could get up the money, so could they; and a limping Mr. Whitcombe who lived down by Gowanus Creek took out a subscription for a Congregational assembly. Prue thought no one would contribute to his venture. Ben had told her that whenever Mr. Whitcombe rode to town, he passed by the ruins of the Cobbleskill Fort, which was haunted; so he must have had some truck with the dark forces. Prue also thought it about as likely her father would contribute as that he would sell one of his daughters. She was only sixteen, however, and underestimated the power of convention. Joe

Loosely convinced Matty it would be uncivil for a family of the Winships' prominence not to contribute at least a small sum, though Roxana's eyes flashed fire when she heard of her husband's donation. Thereafter, Matty professed a tepid interest in the progress of the new church and rectory, out near the end of Buckbee's Alley, where it abutted the Jamaica Turnpike. He packed a picnic one day and took his three daughters up there, on the theory Tem and Prue should use every available opportunity to observe construction, as the distillery would one day need to be expanded. Pearl had no need to go, but disliked being left behind. While Tem ruminated over her bacon sandwich, Pearl wrote questions on her slate, erasing with her sleeve when the need arose, so that by midafternoon, the fabric was caked hard with dust. That evening, Prue spread Mrs. Friedlander's calendula salve on Pearl's forearm to relieve the prickly rash the chalk dust had raised.

The minister, from the same institution that had failed to convert Matthias Winship, never arrived. Word soon came from Boston that this Reverend Mr. Crowley had been thrown by a spooked horse only a week after receiving his calling, and had subsequently died of internal bleeding. On hearing the news, Roxana said, "It's a sign from the Laird. Now we'll never have to go." But Prue felt a yearning for the church. She hoped it would be less grim than her grandfather's, which she remembered all these years later; but part of her thought, if she was as dire a sinner as she had always suspected herself, and as Pappy had called her, it might be best to learn how to amend her behavior.

Mr. Whitcombe apparently wrote back to Boston right away to request a replacement; and was informed, in due time, that a newly minted Reverend Mr. William Severn would arrive in Brooklyn as soon as he could tie up his father's estate. "More tragedy," Roxana commented, shaking her head. "It's what churches bring."

In November, while loafing out by the retaining wall with both her sisters, Prue chanced to hear Losee cry, "Over!"

She looked out to see him hunched over his oars and approaching his pier, with a gray-haired passenger and a number of crates sinking his boat low in the water. Tem was chewing on a sliver of birch bark, and Pearl was barefoot in the sloppy sand on the far side of the wall, her feet and lips pale blue, starting to search for mussels for their supper. They both looked expectantly to Prue, as if it were hers to give permission to run up to the ferry.

"Give me the bucket," she said. "Where are your shoes?"

Pearl lifted her hands in ignorance and slung the bucket, empty but for her neatly folded jersey, over one shoulder.

"If you aren't too cold, it'll be fine."

Pearl nodded.

Tem and Prue were wearing their work britches; Prue assumed Pearl's bare blue feet would attract no more attention than this. She disliked taking her out in public when she did not have her slate at hand, but if they waited, the commotion would blow over without them. They went up along the Shore Road, Pearl's feet at first leaving damp half-moons of footprint.

Losee, meanwhile, was shouting for wheelbarrows and, when the Winship sisters arrived, was as red-faced as a steamed lobster. A couple of Joe Loosely's stable boys were standing by with the barrows almost dangling from their lazy hands.

"Next time, I'll charge you double fare for all that rotten detritus," Losee was saying. "And you'll have to pay Loosely's boys, they don't work for free. *Godverdomme!*" A waiting passenger handed down a cup of water from the bucket. Losee said, "Thank you," took a sip, and splashed the rest over his inflamed face. The passenger in the boat recoiled slightly, with an expression as if he had a dried pea in his shoe.

"With all due respect, sir, there will not be a next time," he said. His overcoat was threadbare, and he was wrapped nearly to his knees in a patched russet muffler. "Had anyone bothered to tell me Brookland did not adjoin New York, I should not have betaken myself to the latter."

"No one bothers to say what's common knowledge. Unload, boys."

"He don' wanna pay," said the smaller of them.

"I shall compensate you fairly."

"A man can't take the stage to a place can only be reached by water," Losee added.

A crowd was gathering, so the Winship sisters slipped up the open stairs to the dock. The children of the neighborhood had a sixth sense for unrest, and the end of the Ferry Road was clotted with young Luquers, van Suetendaels, Cortelyous, and Livingstons. Ben and Maggie

Horsfield clambered up the stairs right behind their friends; and a pod of speckled harbor seals heaved themselves onto the nearby black rocks, their whiskered faces glistening as if with interest as they wagged their heads.

"Where are we taking these?" the small boy said. He staggered under the weight of the first heavy crate.

"To the parsonage."

Losee broke out in a grin. "The new minister, have we? I'm sorry, then, I was so taciturn while I rowed you over; but it's hard work, you know, hauling such a load."

"Indeed. Careful with that, there are plates inside," he said to the larger boy. The minister held out one hand to Losee and removed his hat briefly with the other. "I am William Severn. Am I to assume you are a member of my congregation?"

Losee shook with him but said, "No, sir. Reformed Dutch."

"Ah."

"You know, your church isn't finished."

As Prue watched him, she could see he wasn't such an old man as at first she'd thought him. His hair had perhaps gone gray from some shock, but it framed a youthful face. He might have been handsome, if not for the undershot chin. "Are you certain?"

Losee hoisted himself out of the boat, and put a hand down for the minister. "Only one church going up. The house is done."

The minister climbed up as if unaccustomed to boats. Losee, by contrast, always looked strange on dry land, so hunched and powerful were his shoulders and bowed his legs from decades in the confines of his dory.

Mr. Severn said, "I closed up my late father's home with all due haste to come serve the people of this town."

Mrs. Tilley moved toward him from the edge of the crowd. "Reverend Mr. Severn," she said, "I'm Adeline Tilley. I own the shop up on the turnpike."

"Pleased to meet you," he said, still looking cross.

"We're pleased you've arrived; and we are so sorry for the delay in the church." She twisted her apron nervously in her hands. The plain Livingston daughters, Patience and Rachael, giggled; they were surely thinking, as Prue was, that Mrs. Tilley hoped to snare the young minister for her daughter. "I don't know how, but we shall find a place for you to preach this Sunday."

"That's kind of you," he said. As he tried to step through the crowd toward her, the wheel of one of the barrows caught between the planks of the dock, and the two crates it carried pitched onto the ground. "Dammit!" cried the boy who'd been wheeling it. The crates' nailed tops burst open, and as if they'd spewed forth candy, the younger children all surged forward, shouting, to inspect what was spilling out—an assortment of books, plates, kitchen utensils, and smaller articles, all packed in wood shavings. Tem and Pearl were subsumed in the melee in an instant.

"Hey!" called Losee. "That's enough, you little rag pickers!" But they continued to dig and exclaim. Joe Loosely came outdoors to see what the commotion was, and leaned against the stone wall of his tavern to pack his pipe.

Ben approached Prue, with his hands guiltily in his pockets. "Both your sisters in there?" he asked.

She said, "Yes."

"Mine is, too."

"Where's Isaiah?"

Ben shrugged his shoulders. "You know him, he doesn't like a squabble."

Prue glanced anxiously back toward the fray. "Do you think we should get them out?"

"Undoubtedly. But you know, Pearl never has any fun."

Prue had never considered Pearl's plight thus, but immediately realized he was correct. "I suppose she can't cause much harm."

Losee and Mrs. Tilley began pulling the kids away. "Who is this— Maggie Horsfield? You should be ashamed of yourself! Rummaging in the possessions of your new minister. Where's your— Ben! Take this child home."

Maggie said, "Sorry, Mrs. Tilley," with an inflection that suggested she called her something rude behind her back. Ben beckoned to Maggie, and she walked glumly out toward him.

Either her desertion spurred a more general one or the children had determined there was nothing titillating among Mr. Severn's household goods, for Losee and Mrs. Tilley at last succeeded in clearing them. Pearl's face lit up with a toothy grin. She stopped halfway back to pick a splinter from her foot. "Serves you right," Prue told her, but without much spirit. Pearl looked at her sister quizzically, aware of her equivocation. She pulled her bucket up over her arm again and pushed her wispy fringe back from her brow.

Mr. Severn's possessions were strewn as if an animal had rooted through them, the books and trinkets spilled alongside a trampled tablecloth, a lady's fan, a timeworn wooden bowl. Prue had not known the particulars of a life could look so sad as they did, tumbled on the dock of a foreign town. The minister was blinking as if to hold back tears, and Prue was suddenly ashamed of herself for allowing her sisters to behave as they had. Mr. Severn knelt uncomfortably, as if his knees pained him, and began to dust down his possessions and return them to their crates. Mrs. Tilley crouched just as clumsily; and even Losee, next to whom the new minister resembled a sapling, stooped to rectify the wrong, his face still rosy.

Prue expected the guilty children to run off, but they were as transfixed as she by the sight of three grown people working together so somberly. In the distillery, men grunted as they heaved loads, and shouted encouragement and taunts to one another; it was likewise with any labor she'd witnessed in the streets. These three worked in a silence that made the splashing of the day's calm river seem garrulous. One of the seals barked on the rocks, and others joined it in chorus. When the boxes were reloaded, with the boards that had so tenuously held them shut laid in alongside them, Joe walked down to his stable hands and said, "Take the minister's things up Buckbee's Alley. Be cautious of the ruts in the road, and unload as he asks into the house. You'll accept no gratuity for your service."

"It is not the lads' fault," Severn said.

Joe shook his large head. Prue was accustomed to seeing him drinking with her father; this dark expression was unusual but must have made clear to the new minister that Joe Loosely could be taken at his word. The crowd parted to let the wheelbarrows pass, and Mr. Severn wrapped his muffler tighter around his throat before following, his head bowed as if he could thus hide his blush. The boys steered up the paved center of the Ferry Road, and the rest of the neighborhood remained rooted to the dock. Prue caught Jens Luquer's eye, but he quickly turned away, engrossed in the scratching of his nose, as he, too, ought to have been in the distillery. Patience Livingston, who spent her leisure time sewing homely garments for the poor, and who peered down her nose at children who wasted their free hours on pleasure, pulled her shawl up the back of her neck and ducked out toward the street. Ben said, "I'll take Mags home before she gets in trouble," and, with a palm on her back, steered her toward their homestead.

Prue said good-bye to him; her sisters didn't acknowledge Maggie's departure. "Come," she said, giving a tug to one of Tem's short braids. "The mash tuns are to be cleaned today, and Johanna will wonder what's become of Pearl's mussels."

"Do I have to do it? My bones ache," Tem said.

"You do. I'm sorry."

She muttered, "I'm sure Johanna hasn't even noticed she's gone."

Some of the Schermerhorns' workers were out on break from the ropewalk, and three of Mr. Remsen's slaves had his dinghy belly-up for repair on what was still called Butcher's Wharf, though Prue had never known a butcher to work there. She thought they had all surely seen the scuffle at the landing and were sending the Winship daughters their disapprobation. Pieter Schermerhorn opened the French door from his office to his balcony and stepped out for air; as if nothing unusual had happened, he waved to the girls as they approached.

"Hi, Mr. Schermerhorn," Tem called out.

"Hello, Miss Temmy," he replied. "Shouldn't you be at work?" He winked at them. "Where are Miss Pearl's shoes?"

"Don't know, sir," Tem said, and began to giggle as soon as they'd passed him.

They all knew he envied their father; he was a bachelor, sharing the rope manufactory and his home with his widowed cousin, Wilhelmus, and between them they could not scrounge up even so much as a daughter or niece to whom to leave the thriving walk. At the distillery gate, Pearl pointed up toward their backyard privy and excused herself; Tem and Prue went to the brewhouse to find their father and finish their day's work. He and a dozen men were deep inside and bent over the first two mash tuns, scrubbing.

"Hi, Daddy," Prue said.

He peered up from the great vat and wiped his sweaty cheek against his shoulder. "Long break," he said, but he smiled at them. If he'd been indoors all that while, he wouldn't have heard of their adventure.

"We'll come in."

"We're nearly done, miss," said someone deep in the yawning tub.

Tem cried, "Woo-hoo!"

"Mind your manners, there. You've both done good work today. Go up and wash," their father said. "See if your mother wants any help."

Tem was watching Prue as they went outside, but Prue didn't want to risk saying anything. The fires were still roaring in the stillhouse. "Should we tell them about what happened?" Tem asked as they started toward the hill.

"I don't know yet."

Pearl was down in the shallows, with her skirt drawn through her legs and tucked into her apron band. She was searching for mussels, and she beckoned frantically to her sisters. "We should help her," Prue said.

"I don't want to pick mussels," Tem said. "I'm exhausted."

"Oh, come," Prue said, and tried to lift her up, but Tem bore down and made herself heavy. Prue began tickling her, and kept tickling until she fell, yelping, on the hard-packed sand. Then Prue pulled Tem's boots off, and began running with them down toward the water. Tem quickly caught her, and brought her down; and when they'd tired themselves out, they helped Pearl with the mussels. Pearl looked annoyed by their antics, or perhaps, Prue thought, she was troubled by what she'd done that afternoon. If so, it would serve her right; on the theory her lot was difficult enough, their parents rarely scolded her, but Prue was glad if participation in a scavenging mob made a mark on her conscience.

Johanna was napping by the fire when they returned to the house, her mouth a gash of large yellow teeth and the spaces where teeth had formerly been. "See?" Tem whispered. "She didn't even notice you were gone."

Pearl appeared unconvinced. She placed the mussel bucket by the table, and took another bucket out to the pump for water in which to boil them. Prue brought up two fistfuls of parsnips from the cellar. When the door banged shut behind her, Johanna awakened, rocking upright in her chair and gripping her dress above her heart. "Who's that?" she asked.

Her eyes were, by then, completely filmed over with cataract, for which Dr. de Bouton could do nothing. It made them gleam like opals. Prue thought something looked strange about Johanna's face, but assumed it was a trick of the firelight.

"It's Prue," Prue said. As Johanna still look frightened, she shouted, "Prue! Preparing supper!"

"God in Den Haag!"

Prue placed a wooden bowl on the table to catch the parsnip peelings. Pearl brought the water in and dumped it into the cauldron. She took the paring knife rather brusquely from Prue. "Hey," Prue said.

But Pearl was cross about something. With the knife still in hand, she made a wringing gesture, which Prue took to mean she was to leave her with the parsnips and go wash.

"I was thinking of frying them in butter," Prue said.

Pearl nodded as she began to pare. The skins flew in an expert arc into the bowl.

Tem went out wandering the minute their supper was cleared from the table; and Prue thought she herself would never have been allowed out after dark, at nine years old.

When the dishes were done, Prue went upstairs to retrieve the book she was reading, and Pearl followed close behind her. *May I shew you something?* she wrote, touching Prue's arm before holding the slate out to her.

Prue sat down on her bed, her index finger folded into the book.

Pearl tucked the slate into her waistband and pocketed her chalk, crouched down beneath the table under the eaves, and began to pry up the nails holding the loose plank to the floor. The hole held the sisters' few treasures: rounded bits of sea glass, shells, buttons scavenged from the British officers, and Nell, now that both Tem and Pearl considered themselves too old to play with her. From the hole Pearl brought up a slender, leather-bound volume, with golden lettering on its spine: *Les chefs-d'oeuvres d'art français, Tome I.*

"Pearl," Prue said. She hadn't seen this book before, and knew it was ill-gotten. She put her own reading down and took it from her. Unlike the penny editions she and her father often chose, this book had marbled endpapers, and the edges of the pages were gilt. Its text was dense, apparently in French, but here and there were steel engravings as finely detailed as any Prue had seen, of fat nudes, and heroic figures, scantily clad, in poses of action. She could not help giggling over it. "Great God, Pearl, where'd you get this?"

Pearl winced but looked at her sister hopefully, as if she might somehow expiate the sin.

Prue handed it back to her. She felt the very roots of her hair tingle with the intoxicating idea Pearl had done something bad, and with the fear it was somehow her own fault, both for inaugurating Pearl's life with a curse and for not calling her back from the fray at the landing. "You shall have to give it back, then."

Pearl shook her head no.

"Pearl—"

She drew out her chalk and slate. *I'd have to say I stole it.*

"Well, you did steal it. You must return it."

Pearl looked at Prue as if it were impossible she should thus be scolding her. *He'll be so angry,—Moth' & Fath',—*

"Of course they'll be angry," Prue interrupted. She meant to keep her temper, but her voice was starting to rise. "All the more reason—"

Pearl quickly erased with her sleeve. "Shh!" she hissed. It was one of the only sounds she could make, occurring, as it did, not by action of the vocal cords but between the tongue and teeth.

But it was too late. "What's that?" Roxana called up the stairs. She was halfway up before Pearl could fit the book back into its hole, and when she stepped into the room, Pearl was crouched guiltily in the corner. "What are you doing?" Roxana asked. She looked to Prue. "What's she doing?"

Prue was accustomed to reporting on Tem. Pearl had never been on the wrong side of this arrangement, but of course knew of it, and glared at her. Prue wondered if her mother had even known about the hole. She continued to look at both girls.

"Give it here, then," Roxana said, as if they'd stood stalemated for hours. She knelt down, her knees popping, and extended her hand.

Pearl gave the book over, then sat looking up from beneath her fringe, her eyes round as saucers. Roxana flipped the book back and forth and frowned at it. "Your father didn't buy this for you, I take it?"

Pearl had left her slate on the bed. Instead of passing it to her, Prue said, "It fell out from the new minister's things."

Roxana flipped it over again. "Matty?" she called into the hallway. "Can you come up?"

"Just a moment," Matty said. Prue could hear him depositing his pipe on the hob and his newssheet on the chair.

Roxana met him at the top of the stairs with the book. "Reverend, Prue says the new minister lost it somehow, and Pearlie picked it up. I didn't even know he'd arrived."

Matty Winship was in his house shoes, but even so, the two large steps he took to enter the girls' room were fearsome. "You were part of that mob?" he asked Pearl, his tone restrained but obviously displeased.

Prue held Pearl's slate out to her, but she neither took it nor made any other sign of response. "She—"

"I'm speaking to Pearl," Matty said. "Answer me."

Pearl retreated farther beneath the table.

"Answer me!"

"She doesn't have her slate," Prue said, and continued to hold it out to her.

"She doesn't need a damned slate to nod," he said. He grabbed Pearl's upper arm and pulled her out to the middle of the room. Whether or not he'd actually hurt her, she was twisting violently from him, and exhaled a long, rasping breath that must have been a shriek. "Answer me, damn you!" He wrenched her around and slapped her cheek. Her small face froze in surprise.

"Matty—" Roxana said.

He held up his palm to her in warning. "No. I did not raise them to— Christ! Answer me, Pearl: Did you swarm the minister?" He shook her. "Did you pick like a scavenger through his goods?"

She continued to twist away from him and was, by then, howling almost silently and had begun to cry. Prue had never imagined he could handle one of his daughters so roughly; she could see his behavior confused Pearl as much as frightened her. Prue tried to think of something to say that might induce him to let her sister go, but her mind was blank.

"It is too much, Pearl. Do you hear me?" he yelled. His voice was beginning to go hoarse. "Too much!" All of a sudden he released Pearl's arm. She crumpled away from him, and held her hand over the spot he'd gripped. "I have never once raised a hand to you, not *once*, because I have never known a sadness such as I felt at your birth."

"Matty," Roxana said again.

"No, Roxy." Prue realized her father was not hoarse at all—he, too, had begun to cry. "You have no idea how much your trouble pains me," he said to Pearl. "If I were a religious man, I'd have been on my knees every day of your life, praying God to make your lot otherwise. But Pearl, if there were a God, could He have done this to you? No. No God would let little children be maimed. No God would give you a life in which you'll never be free to leave this house or have a family of your own."

Prue could hardly believe her father had said all this aloud, and wished he might retract it. She thought her mother's blank expression indicated similar disbelief, though it might also have been shock that Matty Winship, the household's only blithe spirit, had lost his temper. Prue coaxed Pearl into her lap. Tem would have spilled out in all directions, but Pearl still fit snugly, nursing her upper arm.

Matty wiped his nose on his sleeve. "I'm sorry, Pearlie. It's nor here nor there, is it? This is your lot. Tem and Prue will carry on at the manufactory, and they love you. They'll look after you."

Roxana sighed and sat down wearily on Prue's bed.

"It's only the truth, Roxy."

"She's ten years old."

He once again gruffly wiped his nose. "So, very well. I cannot give you an easy life, nor meaningful work, as I can give your sisters. What matters most to me, then, is that you should grow to be a good person."

"She is good," Prue said.

"Good enough to steal from a man who's just buried his father and come to live among strangers?"

Pearl flailed in her sister's arms. Prue first tried to contain her, then realized she was grabbing for the slate, which Prue reached down from the bed and handed to her. Pearl took it, and heaved a sob. *I'm sory*, she wrote, though the chalk skipped over the spot where a tear had fallen.

"It was a gross incivility, Pearl. And what for?" He took the beautiful book from Roxana and opened to a page. "This book isn't any better than those I bring you, though it's prettier bound. I give you the best I can. You don't even read French."

Prue heard Tem walking softly up the stairs, unlike the usual way she clambered. She must have sensed something amiss.

"There's nothing for it but to march you up to the minister to make your apologies."

Pearl sat bolt upright and wiped her slate. *No*, she wrote.

"No?"

"We can do it for her," Roxana said.

He turned to his wife with his lips parted in amazement. "What good would come of that? She'll apologize herself."

Pearl wrote, *UNFAIR*, and held the slate out before her, her head turned to one side as if, by not seeing him, she could render herself deaf to his command.

Matty shook his head no. "You may agree to go peacefully in the morning, or I shall drag you there right now. But you will go."

Pearl held up her word again, and Matty let out an exhausted breath before grabbing her out of Prue's lap. The slate slipped from her hands.

"Put your shoes on," he said. Prue had never seen his face so mirthless. He tried to force Pearl's feet into a pair of clogs by the door, but she hissed and spat, wriggling in his grasp like a trapped fox. Half her hair had come loose from her braids and hung around her like the strings of an old black mop.

"Those are Tem's," Prue said. Tem herself was standing, weirdly quiet, out in the hall. She was still in her work boots, with her loose-fitting coat unbuttoned over the leather vest. "They won't fit her."

"I don't care if they're Louis Philippe's. Put them on."

Pearl was bawling by now, but she put her feet in the shoes, which were too large for her. With the book in hand, their father marched her from the room. The shoes rang like a volley of gunshots across the hall and down the stairs, and both Tem and Prue winced when they heard Pearl stumble on the bottom step. Matty cursed under his breath as he pulled on his boots; then the door slammed shut behind them. Tem stood unusually still. Their mother reached a hand up to the nape of her own neck and closed her eyes. "I am so sorry you witnessed that," she said.

Prue was uncertain what to say; if it would be worse to ask her to explain what had transpired or to let it pass. She watched her mother rub the base of her own skull.

After what seemed an age passed, she straightened up, and Prue could see from the glaze over her eyes how exhausted she was. She looked at

Tem as if she hadn't noticed her previously. "Where were you?" she asked, her tone too flat to convey any accusation.

"Down at the Remsens'."

Roxana nodded, as if this were where Tem ought to have been after dark. "Why don't you both wash your hands and come sit by the fire with me till Daddy and Pearl come home."

Prue said, "You should lie down."

Roxana smiled as she sometimes did when she was sad—the corners of her lips dropped, but the expression was more tender than a frown. "I'll rest in the parlor. But I'll have to speak to your father when he returns." She reached over and rubbed the spot between Prue's bony shoulder blades, as if she were a baby in need of soothing. Then she patted her and made her way toward the stairs.

The girls still had water in their pitcher from the morning. Tem sat without even fidgeting while Prue rinsed her face. Tem gave her a towel and asked, "What happened?"

Prue sat down beside her. "Pearl pinched a book from the minister's things."

Tem's mouth became a delighted *O.*

"Nay, don't," Prue said.

"I know it isn't funny, but I'm glad, for once, she got to do something rotten."

"I am, too," Prue whispered. She was also still disturbed by the scene she'd witnessed. At long last she took her volume of Vasari downstairs.

Despite the rumpus, Johanna was snoring in her room off the kitchen. Pearl's sleek mottled cat stood coiled up facing a corner, its tail switching behind it. Roxana was in the parlor, with her stocking feet up on the arm of the divan. Such a scene—in which there were no games to play—would ordinarily have made Tem shout out in complaint, but she took up her father's newssheet and tried to apply herself to it.

The clock cycled through more than an hour before the kitchen door opened and shut. Prue knew it would have been polite to remain reading, but she had not learned a thing about Simone Martini, though she'd dutifully turned her pages; and her mother and sister also sprang up to crowd through the hallway to the kitchen. Pearl was so pale she looked almost gray, but their father had neatened her hair. She stood looking at the floor until her cat came and rubbed against her leg. Tears filled her eyes at once. She picked the cat up and carried it upstairs, its yellow eyes over her shoulder reflecting the firelight as she ascended. Matty poured himself a dram of gin, drank it in silence by the fire, and said, "He wasn't angry."

Roxana blinked and sat down.

"He took one look at her and saw what misery she'd suffered. Must have thought me an ogre. He seems kind; perhaps he was a bit of a scoundrel as a lad. I volunteered her to help him set up house, or whatever such a little creature might do, but he declined."

"Sounds like a decent fellow," Roxana said. Prue couldn't detect even a ripple of sarcasm in her tone.

"Yes, I think so. I hope you won't mind, but I offered him our assembly room for his church." He poured himself a second cupful, and before he drank it, handed it to Prue. "Aniseed."

Prue smelled it and stuck her tongue in. She was beginning not merely to appreciate gin, but to like it. "It's good when it tastes like licorice."

"Yes."

"Why'd you do that?" Roxana asked. As her husband did not respond, she added, "I assume he accepted."

Matty nodded. Prue gave him back his cup.

"Hmm," Roxana said, and again took her fingers to the back of her neck.

Matty shrugged his broad shoulders. "He's a good man, Roxy, and someone owed him a bit of kindness after what he suffered this morning. Besides, it was the assembly room or Whitcombe's barn; and I can't suppose even you hate the church enough to ask a man to preach among cattle. I certainly don't."

So, against Roxana's silent disapproval, Mr. Severn preached the Gospel under the roof of a nonbeliever that Sunday, as he would continue to do until the following March, when the church's roof would at last be in place, and the plaster upon the lath. That week it was the scandal of the town that the Winships did not bother to take their daughters to church even when the services were in their own backyard; but Matty told the girls not to listen to gossip. He said, "We don't have to pretend we're aught but what we are, to do a fellow a good turn." He could not have known how much Prue yearned to sit on those makeshift benches and pray to God and Mr. Severn to forgive her and Pearl for their various sins.

Pearl held her grudge all the next day and refused to look any of her family in the eye. Johanna, idly burning their breakfast, had either been aware of the histrionics the night before or could smell Pearl's sulking; for she commented, "*Och God*, just like her sister, just like Prue," to all who passed. Prue heard her say it to her mother as Roxana grabbed two of Prue's ugly pot holders and removed the ruined oatmeal to the compost.

Prue watched her from the doorway as she left the pot out by the well to cool and later be scrubbed. "Don't worry," she said. Her voice carried in the crisp morning air. "She no longer knows what she says."

But Prue knew what Johanna meant, and still hoped the rest of them would never discover it. Her mother and Johanna were such good friends, she could not imagine Johanna had kept her secret all this time; yet her mother had never mentioned it. Pearl's ears had certainly pricked up just then, but it was clear she was spoiling for a fight. Prue now saw there truly was something odd about Johanna's face—a purplish swelling, as of a large bruise, where her cap was pushed askew near her left temple. On any other morning she would have mentioned it straightaway.

More than her father's uncustomary wrath, what had vexed Prue about the previous evening's incident was to have seen Pearl reduced so swiftly to a near-animal state. When her slate was not at hand, she was, Prue realized, hardly better able to express herself than a dog. And although Prue had never before thought much about the way the right forearm of Pearl's every dress was caked slick with chalk dust, this now saddened her. She went up late that afternoon to Mrs. Tilley to inquire if something might be purchased to aid her sister. Gray-haired Mr. Severn was standing by with a list of provisions in hand and his ragged muffler wrapped tight around his throat. He smiled bashfully at Prue when she entered, and motioned for her to conduct her business first. Prue walked to the counter, and the minister turned back to examining the dry goods. She kept her eye on him. Mrs. Tilley appeared most interested in how the minister discomfited Prue; but on request, she brought down a catalogue of goods that featured a small silver note case on a chain. Pearl could wear this around her neck, with its wooden pencil holding fast the clasp, yet have her hands free like an ordinary person. "What would it cost?" Prue asked.

"Four pounds, and I'm sure worth every shilling."

Prue whistled through her teeth, and when she saw Mrs. Tilley's expression, recollected this was not acceptable practice outside the Winship home and distillery. "Sakes," she said, and felt herself blushing. "I'll have to ask my father." The pencils wouldn't last Pearl long, either; she would have to buy a bushel of them.

"No," Mr. Severn said. He came closer to her and fumbled in his pocket for his purse. "Please. It would be my pleasure."

Mrs. Tilley now looked even more annoyed, Prue presumed because she was considering her own daughter's prospects. "Mr. Severn," she said sternly. "Don't you think our distiller can better afford such an expenditure than you?"

"Without doubt," he replied. He took out two pounds sterling and laid them with care on the counter. "But my heart goes out to the girl. It is a terrible lot, to be so isolated. This is all I have, for now, but perhaps you'll allow me to place the rest on credit—"

Prue said, "I can't—"

"I owe your father a debt of gratitude, Miss Winship, for giving a home to my church. If he would come, I could repay him in spiritual tender, but I cannot force his conscience." He tugged the muffler away from his throat; it must have been stifling hot, and looked itchy. "Please, Prudence."

No one ever called her by her full name, and it buzzed in her ears. She said, "Thank you very much, Mr. Severn."

When she left, with the receipt for the case in her pocket, he followed her outside and shut the jingling door behind them. "May I have a word?" he asked. He hunched down in his shoulders to make himself more her size.

Prue nodded. Mrs. Tilley was watching with interest through the glass panes in the door.

He said, "Your shopkeeper is a good woman, but one can say nothing in front of her without having it broadcast like grass seed over all the town." He had coaxed a smile from her, and nodded as if pleased. "When the case arrives, do you tell Pearl it came from me. She seemed in such torment when your father brought her to my house, and if she won't look me in the eye, I see no other way to apologize."

"I will, sir. But I feel it is unequal payment."

He drew his chin deeper under the muffler.

"That is, I feel we should do something for you as well." She looked him over. What could such a person need? He had a home and a hired woman; he would have a wife soon enough, if either Mrs. Tilley or Mrs. Livingston had her way. "I'm not a very good knitter—my father is training me for the distillery, as you may know—"

"Yes, it's quite the topic—"

"But I could offer to make you a new muffler, as your old one—as your old one appears to be much worn."

He put his hand up to his throat as if to ask if this threadbare thing was that to which she referred. "This? Oh," he said. "No. I couldn't part with it. My late mother knitted it for me."

"I'm sorry," Prue said, both because she was sorry he'd lost his mother and because she was sorry she'd made the gaffe. "I didn't mean to—"

"I understand," he said.

"Pearl is a very good knitter," she offered, though she wanted to kick herself for doing so. "And she works wonders with an embroidery needle."

He nodded. "Well. If ever she forgives me for having been the cause of her dishonor, perhaps she'll tell me about it herself." He looked back through the door's six small panes to Mrs. Tilley, who was dusting her shelves with unusual vigor. "I should finish my business here," he said.

Prue said, "Thank you again," and as she walked back toward the Ferry Road, felt the eyes of the neighborhood upon her.

The note case arrived after the New Year; it was larger and heavier than Prue had imagined, but would still provide Pearl a degree of freedom she had theretofore lacked. Mrs. Tilley looked tart when Prue wrapped it in her handkerchief to bring it home. Pearl's whole face lit up when she opened it; and though Prue saw her parents wonder whence the money for the object had come, they had the decency not to ask until later, in private. Pearl put the case around her throat immediately and was never again, in all her days, seen to go so much as from one room to the next without it.

Prue waited until she had Pearl alone by the back fence to tell her the case's provenance. Pearl drew her lips in to think about it. She was not yet adept with the contraption, and took a moment to free the pencil from its hasp and turn the book in the correct direction to write. *Becaus he pity'd me?* she wrote.

"I think he rather regretted how Father treated you," Prue said.

Pearl continued to chew on her lower lip. *Y' th'un should never have spoken.*

Prue could not respond to this. She wished she had not so elicited her father's rage, but knew she'd been correct about the stolen book. "He said if you'd forgive him, he'd like to see some of your needlework."

Pearl raised her thin eyebrows, in perfect imitation of their mother. She flipped to a clean page. *What' e think I stoal it for?*

"What do you mean?"

Patterns. She glanced back toward the house, then wrote, *You want to go to the church, do'n't you?*

Prue was unnerved by the person watching her—a child who looked much younger than her years, yet stood staring at her with steady black eyes. It was no use hiding things from her; her parents would pass on someday, but Pearl was forever. "Very much," she said. "I have always wanted to. Since before you were born."

I, too, wish to go.

"I'll take you, then, this Sunday."

Tem'll poak fun at me.

"We shan't tell her."

Pearl closed her book and patted it where it hung above her belly. She swayed a little as she walked back to the house.

That Sunday, Prue had her father's keys hidden in her pocket when she offered to take Pearl out for a walk. They stood by the back fence and watched as those neighbors of English descent filed down the lane to the mill yard and entered the assembly room. When the door shut, Prue drew Pearl out into Joralemon's Lane, and they hurried down against the stiff wind rising from the river. At the distillery gate, Prue paused and said, "It's too cold to walk up barefoot, but we'll have to be very quiet."

Pearl turned up her collar and kept walking, casting a disparaging glance over her shoulder at her sister as she went.

As she placed her hand on the plain banister, Prue glanced into the room. The benches were arranged so the parishioners had their backs to the door and the outdoor stairs. Prue recognized Mr. Severn—facing them at the far end of the room—from his gray hair and bashful posture, but through the ripples of the window glass, and as she was moving, she could not see if he had seen them. She wanted to hide her face, as if this could prevent her from being recognized.

She had never before noticed the sound of the countinghouse lock, but it clicked and shuffled as she turned the key. Pearl was staring at it as if she could will it to be silent. At last the door gave and let them in. Prue wished the parish would strike up a hymn, but all she could hear was Mr. Severn's muffled voice coming up through the floorboards and the occasional creak of someone moving below.

She shut the door behind them and went to take Pearl's coat, but Pearl shook her head no; they could see the plumes of their breath, and there would be no lighting the stove without giving themselves away. Prue did, however, lean down to remove her shoes, and she helped Pearl out of hers while she was there. She placed them on the rough floorboards as gently as she would have laid down a baby.

Mr. Severn was difficult to hear from the far side of the room; so, with infinite care, they crossed the cold floor in their stocking feet, skirting the great desk and the stove with its kettle on top. Prue knew Mr. Severn was standing, with his Bible and some papers on a stool, at the far northern end of the assembly room. The windows above where he stood were behind the paper-strewn desk and looked out on the rectifying room, casking room, storehouses, and ropewalk. Their father had left two of their mother's coffee cups, filthy with stains and grounds, on the bookshelf beneath the window. The sisters sat down on the floor and turned their backs to the shelf. They were so nearly atop where Mr. Severn stood, Prue could feel the reverberation of his voice before she could make out the text of what he was saying.

She knew nothing of church. She had understood little in her childhood visits to the domine, and since then had been given no Bible, no catechism, no lessons in doctrine. She heard nothing familiar but the quaver in the voice of the shy, good man beneath her. She knew nothing but the way her heart called out to God, unheard by any but Pearl. She saw Pearl had closed her eyes to listen, and she did the same.

Through the baffling of the floorboards, Mr. Severn's voice sounded intimate, as if he were alone and simply musing aloud. ". . . on the subject of our relationships of temper and feeling to our fellow men," he was saying.

Prue did not follow, but she trusted she would.

" 'Ye have heard that it hath been said, "Thou shalt love thy neighbor, and hate thine enemy." ' The Gospel of Matthew says this on the principle, I suppose, that half a loaf is better than no bread."

To Prue's surprise, the congregation laughed. She and Pearl both opened their eyes. The pews creaked as people must have leaned forward to hear him better.

"People fulfill the last of the maxim without taking much pains about the first," he went on. His voice had gained a little strength, a little melody. "The art of hatred is quite thoroughly developed among mankind; it is one of those graces that do not need much nourishing. But the art of loving one's neighbor is a different one, inasmuch as most people are not altogether lovely."

Here, too, a few people tittered in agreement. Pearl worked open the top button of her coat and began fishing for her book as he went on. "Anyone can love that which is intrinsically lovely, but nobody, without God's grace in his soul, can love one who is not to some extent lovely. It is mother-love where one loves unlovely things, for a babe is not lovely. It is nothing at first; it is all yet to be: But the mother discerns wonderful things in the child. There is a love that can love beauty, and nothing else; there is a love that can love excellence, and nothing else; there is a love that can love a being that is without excellence or beauty, and love him into it. It is divine love that here I mean. I will read you the next verse. Men and women, you are in danger of losing your souls on this verse more than on any other part of the whole Bible. More people make shipwreck on this passage of Scripture than on any other. The whole shore along here is thick with wrecks."

Pearl touched her sister's sleeve. Prue looked over to see she had written: *Is this what we've been missing all along, w. ye Domine?*

"No," Prue whispered.

Then he's good, Pearl wrote on a new page.

The people beneath were silent, and Prue could hear his pages rustling. " 'I say unto you,' " he read, his voice growing fuller by the moment, " 'love your enemies.'

" 'Oh yes,' say many, 'if they confess, if they acknowledge their wrongs, I will forgive them, and love them.' Well, let us read on.

" 'Bless them that curse you,'—and *while* they are cursing you—'do good to them that hate you,'—and whose hatred is burning like fire—'and pray for them which spitefully use you, and persecute you; that ye may be the children of your Father, which is in Heaven'; for that," he said, "that is the spirit which is to make you the children of God. 'For he maketh his sun to rise on the evil and on the good,' on liars, on thieves, on murderers, on those who betray their families and friends; for though they are benighted and corrupt, yet are they not human beings, who have eternity before them? If God does not hold out hope to them, who will? And if God does not love them, who shall? '—and sendeth rain on the just as the unjust.' "

Pearl had let the book drop down on its chain, but she was holding tight to the pencil in her small hand. Prue could picture Severn's face before her, his brown eyes bright with emotion. She wondered if it was possible to love a man on such short acquaintance.

"If all farmers had rain according to their personal merits," he continued, "there would be queer farming abroad." Again, people laughed. Prue thought, if Pappy was looking down from Heaven, he was considering ways to punish this infidel. "But God sends rain on the just and the unjust, because by nature as well as by spiritual grace He seeks perpetually to win men, through gratitude, to service and to love.

" 'For if ye love them which love you,' " he read, " 'what reward have ye?'

"Why, that is commerce, exchange, shilling for shilling. Anybody can do that.

" 'Do not even the publicans the same? And if ye salute your brethren only,'—that is, if you greet only those that belong to your church, or think as you think, or act as you act—'do not even the publicans so? Be ye therefore perfect, as your Father which is in Heaven is perfect.'

"And how is that?" he continued. Could he feel her there, above him? Could he feel the glow of holy love awakening in her breast? "It is by the temper of divine benevolence. No man is a Christian because he is a professor of religion. No man is a Christian because he loves to go to church, or read his Bible, or say his prayers. No man is a Christian who has not the spirit of Christ; and the spirit of Christ is a spirit of beneficence. If you are tenderhearted, if you are gentle, if you are kind, if you are slow to anger, if you are easy to forgive, if you love your enemies, and even those that spitefully use you and persecute you, then you have Christ's spirit, and you belong to God's family, and you will someday, not long from now, be raised up with Him in bliss. Let us rise."

And there was a rustle of skirts and shoes, and the benches creaking below. Pearl was shaking her head no. "What?" Prue asked.

I shu'n't have done it, Pearl wrote.

"It's done," Prue whispered. The warbling notes of a hymn began to rise up through the floorboards. "You'll make up for it some other way."

Prue and Pearl remained in the countinghouse, safely beneath the level of the windows, until they heard the last parishioner shut the assembly room door. In almost any other family, Prue thought, a visit to church would be considered either salutary or a plain necessity; only in theirs was it a transgression. She felt giddy with her secret, and could see Pearl did as well. They kept it to themselves all week and returned the following Sunday, and week after week thereafter. Looking back as an adult, Prue knew her parents must have suspected their destination, given the regularity of their disappearances; but at the time, she felt safely swaddled in her secret, protected by it from anything unpleasant about the world or her own character. She felt Mr. Severn was opening up the heavens for her.

Late that winter, when the river was frozen halfway across, Johanna's bruise hardened into an egg-shaped cyst with tentacles that snaked off toward her nose and up into her hair. Prue believed she had seen the growth forming all that while beneath Johanna's white muslin cap, but at last it protruded unmistakably. The morning Prue's mother first saw it, she questioned Johanna about it, but Johanna would give no answer but to draw her shawl closer around her shoulders and shake her head. Roxana ran out for Dr. de Bouton. It was a bright, bitter Saturday morning; Roxana opened and shut the door quickly, but still let in a fine spray of glittering snow. When she returned, she reported in a low tone that de Bouton's servant had had to rouse him from bed. Prue and Pearl had taken over the preparation of breakfast in her absence, and she had nothing to do but pace the kitchen floor. "How could we not have known?" she asked of no one in particular as they waited for the doctor to finish his examination. The fire popped and settled.

Prue kept silent. She knew she ought to have spoken up in the autumn, when first she'd seen the bruise; but she could not undo what was done.

The doctor took his time with Johanna, who answered his questions in her loud, cracked voice. When at last de Bouton emerged, he closed

Johanna's door softly behind him. His woolly hair was standing on end; Roxana had allowed him no time to comb it, and he appeared not to have slept the night before. "Should you go upstairs?" he asked Pearl. Pearl gripped on to Prue's hand, as if this could prevent her exile.

"Let them hear whatever you have to say," their father said. Tem was fastening the buttons of her work vest as if nothing were amiss.

De Bouton looked down at his boots before turning to Matty. "Your woman has developed a lesion to the brain. I know not how long it festered there before appearing, but from its form I deduce it is cancerous in nature, and not some more benign growth."

Roxana raised her hands to her mouth and walked to the window.

"Can such a tumor be removed?" Matty asked. Prue knew de Bouton had excised a growth from the breast of one of the van Vechten daughters, who still lived and breathed, though she was ever in poor health.

The doctor took a breath and stifled a cough. "Perhaps in some cases, yes. But I fear that both its location and Johanna's advanced age make its removal unadvisable. I fear, quite simply, that I should kill her in attempting to effect a cure." Prue heard her mother crying behind her, but felt she could not move with Pearl gripped on so tight. Prue's fingers began to go numb. "I am sorry, Mrs. Winship," he continued. "I know she is dear to you, that you have treated her more kindly than many a servant, let alone a slave."

"Indeed," Roxana said quietly.

"What may we do to ease her suffering?" Matty asked.

Dr. de Bouton shook his head. "There is little to be done. Cool compresses, the medicine I have given you for headache, clear broth."

"Very well," Matty said. He slipped some coins from his pocket into de Bouton's palm. "We are all sorry to have disturbed you so early."

Dr. de Bouton bowed to Roxana before letting himself out into the biting cold.

It was a workday; both Tem and Prue were dressed and ready for the fermenting room, in whose operations Tem was at the time being trained. Pearl at last let go of Prue's hand and ran to their mother. Matty went to them and put his arms around them both. To Prue he said, "This is terrible news. Will you be able to perform your work today?"

Prue felt a chill flicker up her spine; she could not deduce the correct answer. "Yes, sir. I suppose so."

"Good, then. Go tell Mr. Horsfield what has transpired, and that I shall be down as soon as I am able. Then off to Mr. Fortune with you. You, too, lambkin," he said to Tem.

Tem caught Prue's eye, then looked pointedly to the pot that still bubbled over the fire. Prue shook her head no, took their coats from their hooks, and led her sister out the front way to avoid the knot by the kitchen door.

"A fine morning it'll be without any breakfast," Tem grumbled.

The air was so cold, Prue felt it weighing against her chest. "We'll manage." The doctor had left the gate open, and Prue pulled it to. The girls started down the ravine in silence. Some of their father's workers were also late, and hurried past to arrive at the distillery before them.

"Will Johanna die, then?" Tem asked after a moment.

"I believe so."

Tem exhaled a vast plume of breath. "I can't imagine it."

"Perhaps we shall keep her awhile longer yet," Prue said, though in her guilty heart she knew she half wished they would not.

She sent Tem straight down to Mr. Fortune, and herself went to the countinghouse to speak to Mr. Horsfield. As she climbed the open stairs, she could not help the thrill that coursed through her body. The next day, she would follow this same route to hear Mr. Severn's sermon; and surely his words would, however unwittingly, build a shelter in which she might take refuge from her guilt and fear.

Five

JOHANNA

In the second year of Tem's apprenticeship, the distillery outgrew its bounds. Matty Winship did not know whom to thank for his good fortune—the swarms of new immigrants, now escaping the bloodshed in France, who had to spend for everything they desired; the federal government, newly installed in Manhattan and thirsty for gin; or simply all those who'd suffered the privations of the war and now loosened their purse strings in the general atmosphere of prosperity—but he did not think he'd be able to meet demand for his liquor two years down the pike. On hearing the news, Tem began strutting around, certain her own contribution had played some pivotal role in this success. Prue, by contrast, couldn't sleep for two nights, so vivid were her fantasies of customers whose gin had not arrived coming to pound on their door. By the Friday of the week, she was so tired, objects seemed to wiggle when she stared at them, and when she caught a glimpse of herself in the mirror, she resembled a raccoon. Israel Horsfield called her out from the brewhouse midmorning, and took her up to the countinghouse to talk. He was a tall, slim man with angular features, and as kind as she knew he was, Prue worried he planned to chastise her.

"What've I done?" she asked as they entered the office.

He had a tight grin on his face that disturbed her more than a frown would have, but he said nothing. He closed the door behind them, and took his seat at the great desk. As her seat was beside his, she took Tem's, across the table. Out the window, she could see men unloading empty casks from two barges.

"What've I done, Mr. Horsfield?" she repeated.

"Nothing, Prue," he said. "Your father's a bit worried about you, though."

"Why so?"

His grin relaxed and broadened, and he more closely resembled Ben. "You've been looking wan of late. He's concerned—well, it's a difficult subject to raise, which is why it's somehow fallen to me; but we're all concerned you may have lost your heart somewhere."

"My heart?" she asked. She wondered if he meant Ben or Mr. Severn, and her cheeks began to prickle with warmth. "No, sir. I can't sleep for worrying about the orders we won't be able to fill."

Israel closed his eyes and raised his palm to his head. "Should have known. You're just like your mother, a'en't you?" Prue wasn't flattered. "I'll make you a coffee," he said. "You could use it."

"Thank you," she said, and went back to looking out the window. She tried to count the casks and failed. She heard Israel banging grounds from the pot into the slop bucket.

"Prudie Winship, it means business is good. You should be pleased. Do you know what your father plans to do?"

She knew it meant something was wrong with her that her first thought was to imagine bleary-eyed workers toiling through the night. On this idea's heels came a more logical possibility: "Expand the works?"

He set the pot down on the stove. "Exactly so. Let me show you." He riffled through the loose papers on the desk and extracted a sheet covered with boxes and squiggles representing the distillery and the river. He placed it before Prue and leaned down over her shoulder. "Your father believes we can cut the end wall clear from each of the buildings"—here he took up a pencil and indicated this—"build them out longer, and move those farthest down the production line north, toward the ropewalk. It'll require quite a bit of horsepower, but we'll be able to save some of the foundations, which were what required the most work when we built the distillery."

Prue thought about watching the laborers dig the cellar pit for the rectory, and didn't recall it requiring more work than any other task. Israel sat down beside her, in her father's chair. "With such sandy ground, you see," he went on, "it's hard to keep a building plumb. The ropewalk sinks more than an inch a year in its northwest corner, which is why you always see the workmen out shoring it up. When your father and I built these buildings, we drove piles as deep as we could into the sand and lay great, flat foundation stones atop them, solid enough for the buildings to rest upon. They've held up well; we'll use the same method. Will you help us draw up the plan?"

"I can't draw," Prue said.

"Mmm." Israel looked at his sketch of the distillery. "Nor can I. But it'll look better once your father puts his hand to it. In the meanwhile, you can help us decide by what degree we should increase each stage of production. It's a tricky issue, as it involves not only the space but the machinery, men, and the time it takes to work each part of the process." The coffee had begun to boil, and he removed it from the stove and poured it out. "One thing more, Prue."

She took the cup and broke off some sugar, keeping her eyes on him.

"If a certain young man of our acquaintance ever does aught to make you look so pale, I'll beat him senseless."

Prue smiled, despite her exhaustion. The gentle way Israel was watching her showed her he knew he'd hit the mark, but she felt less discomfited by this than she had a moment before. She was also pleased at the prospect of redesigning the works; she loved having a problem to think through.

Her father had filed away the measurements of all the buildings twenty years before, but Israel borrowed the carpenter's Gunter's chain, and he and Prue stalked the property, deciding exactly how far each house could extend without the whole works encroaching upon the rope-walk. Israel ordered new foundation stones from a quarry up in Wilbur that could ship the stones down along the Hudson. When Tem discovered that Prue had been released indefinitely from her ordinary labor, she pouted and yelled as if she might thus be excused from her studies; but their father was firm and made her keep on in the casking house, no matter how unpleasant she made herself to the foreman. Ben and Isaiah gave themselves leave to quit Mr. Severn's school—from which, they argued, they would both graduate anyway, come spring—and volunteered themselves for any opportunity to assist in the measuring. Israel Horsfield was furious with them when first he saw them loose in the middle of the day, but Isaiah assured him the study of building would serve him at least as well as the Lucretius with which Mr. Severn was torturing them. After two days, Israel himself wrote Mr. Severn asking for his sons to be excused while business demanded it. Cornelis Luquer cursed his apprenticeship at the grain mill—but for learning his father's business, he would have been free to participate in the first engineering project of any size in the neighborhood, and he complained to Prue of his jealousy at every turn.

For two weeks, Prue, Ben, and Isaiah argued with their fathers over the best spacing of the buildings for ease of production, and over the best method for constructing walkways above the various production rooms. Prue's own design—for simple balconies, with railings to prevent mishap—won the day, and looked well enough indeed when her father worked up a detailed drawing, including all the measurements necessary to build them. Ben and Isaiah wanted to stay on and assist in the ditch-digging and carpentry, but when the plans were complete and the workers apprised of them, Prue's friends were sent back to school.

At that time, in the spring of 1790, the distillery employed nearly sixty men and had four horses in its stables. No one part of the manufactory could function while the others lay dormant, and Roxana Winship began predicting ruin before the work even began. But it had been Tem's idea—Prue wished it had been her own—to increase production before the works shut down so the storehouses would be full when the building commenced; and with so many laborers, the digging and construction proceeded quickly. Prue and Tem learned how heavy even a spadeful of sand could be by the end of a day, and the kind of concentration two men needed not to injure each other with a double-handled saw; and their industry was matched by the workers', each of whom, slaves included, had been promised a pound sterling if the work was completed by summer. When the foundation stones arrived by barge from Wilbur, Matty Winship and Israel Horsfield bartered with farmers from Red Hook to Wallabout for the loan of their oxen; and Prue thrilled at the commotion when six teams of the snorting beasts labored to drag the huge slabs over logs laid down on the sand. Matty Winship had ordered the new cauldrons and stills from England before the work began, and had men building the new mash tuns before the brewhouse was even complete. By the time the rectifying room was under way, he was calling on the Remsens and Cortelyous to find out how much grain he could buy of them, and at what cost. Before it arrived, he advertised in the New

York papers for more men; "For, dammit," he told Prue, as they stood atop two ladders, fastening a leather drive belt around one of the new drums, "before I die, I shall see you have more than a hundred *employés* to supervise."

"But you aren't going to die," she said. Both the leather and the lumber still smelled fresh and sweet.

He made a plosive sound of disdain through his lips. "Of course I shall, Prue. So will you. All we can both hope is that it'll happen a good ways in the future. And I imagine it will. If Death fancied our house, after all, he'd long since have come for Johanna." They were ten feet apart, but he could see her face and added, "Don't look so glum, now. I thought I'd have done with that expression when I let you come work with me."

"You did," she said. "You shall." She tried to remind herself of her pride in her walkways, which were sturdy if not beautiful. But work well done could not prevent her from wondering what would happen if her father fell off the ladder right then.

He did not wait to complete the new storehouses before resuming production; if the liquor had to go into the assembly hall, this would be only for a short while, and the distillery fell further behind on its orders each day that passed. Twenty men would keep on building, but the second Monday in June, the brewhouse would reopen. In celebration of the event, Matty brought a cask of the previous year's wares out into the yard one afternoon, tapped it, and gave every worker his dram. Prue saw the four lazy boys in Joe Loosely's employ slip into the line, and felt tempted to warn her father; but when it came their turn, he gave each of them a wink with his sup of gin, and sent him back up to the ferry.

Ben and Isaiah left off their studies again for a few hours, to view the completed work and take part in the festivities. "You've grown taller from the work," Isaiah told Prue.

"Meatier, too," Ben said.

Prue swatted at him, but Ben was already running into the brewhouse, where he began clambering up the side of a new tun. "Ho!" he called as he looked over the top. "It's as big as the Luquers' swimming hole! Can I go in?"

"Don't," Prue said. "We'll have to drop a ladder in to get you back out." She wanted to add that, at seventeen, he ought to have been able to comport himself better.

He commenced galloping around the platform at the tun's perimeter. She was sure he'd pitch into the tank or to the ground and break his neck.

Isaiah walked more gravely around and between the giant tuns. "The whole operation's stark admirable," he said. "And you were correct about the walkways. They've come out well."

"Thank you."

Ben stopped and sat down, his legs dangling over the platform's edge. "Has Pearlie seen this?"

"No."

"Why not?" he asked. "She'd be interested. Let me go get her," he offered, and was about to jump off the edge of the platform to the ground when Prue called, "Don't! Use the ramp." He sneered at her, but did as she said.

Prue herself ran up Joralemon's Lane, and found the house quiet and her mother staring at the grain in the wood of the kitchen table, her eyes red. She did not look up when Prue pulled the door closed by its latch.

"Mum?" Prue asked. "Will you come down and see what we've done at the works?" When her mother didn't respond, she asked, "What's the matter?"

Roxana sighed, lifting her collarbones halfway to her chin. "Johanna fares poorly," she whispered. "Pearl is sitting by her."

Prue walked softly into Johanna's bedroom and noticed, for the first time, a sweet stench, like attar of violets. Pearl looked up from her chair by the bedside. Johanna's breath rasped like a wood plane, and she was pawing in her sleep at the gruesome tumor, close by the spot she had always touched when Tem or Prue vexed her. Pearl fixed her needle in her embroidery and looked anxiously up at her sister's face.

Prue did not know what to say. After a moment Pearl opened her pad and wrote, *I'm worrit'd about her. Surely this is her Last End?*

Prue watched Johanna's breast rise and fall. "I'm not certain, Pearl; she's looked dreadful before and pulled through. We should call for the doctor." Prue left the door open behind her as she returned to the kitchen. "If you come down to the distillery with me, you'll be halfway to Dr. de Bouton's. He'll come."

Roxana continued to look at the table. "You've never liked Johanna." Prue did not know how to answer her. Roxana closed her eyes a moment and licked her lips. "Your father got on well in this village from the start, but the womenfolk of Brookland have never had much to do with me. I'm not like them, I suppose." She smiled wanly, Prue thought to let her know it was no use denying it. "Johanna has never asked me to be other than what I am. It pains me to contemplate losing her."

Prue could not help thinking Johanna was a slave and had had little choice in the matter; she could befriend or antagonize her mistress, but not escape her. But Prue said only, "We'll fetch the doctor for her. Please come see what we've done, down at the works."

Roxana continued to give her the sad half smile. "Your father's proud."

Pearl came in from the sickroom with her tambour frame in one hand.

"Come tour the new buildings," Prue said.

Pearl put the embroidery on the table and wrote, *W^th Jo^a unwell?*

"A brief tour."

Moth^r coming?

"I don't think so," Prue said.

Pearl frowned and wrote a note to her mother. Prue looked over her sister's shoulder, and saw the note said, *Come it^s importint to her.*

"And to Father and Tem," Prue added.

"What of Johanna?" their mother asked.

Pearl wrote, *She wo'n't stir & we'll be back immediatly.*

Roxana stood as if it cost her some effort, and tucked a loose wisp of hair behind her ear. Then she smiled at her daughters in earnest.

Down below, many of the men had gone back to work on the storehouses, but the foremen were still standing around with their cups, and Ben and Isaiah were among them. Matty's face lit up when he saw his wife. "Hoy, Roxy," he said, and put his arm out for her.

She leaned her head toward his shoulder. "Johanna's ill," she said.

"How so?"

"Abed and breathing poorly. I'm on my way to fetch de Bouton."

He nodded, but the news did not appear to have dispelled his good mood.

"Quite a lot you've done here," Roxana said.

Pearl bent and straightened her knees a few times in eagerness to get on with her visit.

"Poor thing," said John Putnam, the brewmaster. "Wish I had a sweet for ye."

Pearl kept bouncing as if she hadn't heard him, but the expression of delight had hardened on her features.

"I'll show her around," Ben said, pouncing on her from behind. She pitched forward happily; she was tiny for twelve years old, and no one ever roughhoused her.

"There's so much to show you," Matty said, and kissed Roxana's forehead.

She didn't shrug free of him, but neither did she soften into his embrace, as Prue had often seen her do. "Delightful," she said. "I'll be delighted to know what's been keeping you from home all these months. If, indeed, this manufactory be the culprit."

One of the foremen whistled through his teeth, and Ben whisked Pearl off toward the brewhouse. "It is," Prue said, and watched her mother color.

"You don't even know what I speak of," she said.

"I can see by her countenance she does," Matty said, and laughed to himself. "Come. You need to fetch the doctor and it's high time Prue and I got back to work. Let's have our look round and be through."

When they arrived at the new cooling house, Pearl drew in her breath in delight. She stepped out onto the lattice of planks and strode to the middle of the room. "It is lovely, isn't it?" Prue said.

Pearl could scarcely communicate when far away from people, but she nodded her head yes.

"Of course she likes it," Matty said. "She's an eye for beauty, don't you, Pearlie?"

But Pearl was off toward the great open windows, watching the traffic on the river go by and whistling one of the tunes she'd heard the French laborers sing up by the ferry. Prue wondered how Pearl could never have seen the cooling floor before, but, of course, Pearl was no more allowed to wander the distillery than the streets. It was too dangerous for a girl who couldn't be heard if any ill befell her.

After showing them the works, Matty kissed his wife and small daughter good-bye, and Roxana led Pearl up the Shore Road to fetch Dr. de Bouton. When Tem and Prue came home from the distillery that evening, they found their mother in Johanna's chair, with her hands in her hair. "What's wrong?" Prue asked.

"De Bouton was insensible with drink," she said.

Tem went up the stairs as if she hadn't heard this.

"Did you go for Philpot?" Prue asked.

"He's not really a doctor," Roxana said.

"But he's better than none." As her mother did not reply, Prue walked back outdoors and up toward the Jamaica Turnpike to fetch him. As she skirted Simon Dufresne's wagon and another bearing the day's last load of lumber down from the van Vechten sawmill, she thought how odd it must feel to give way to extreme old age. She had watched Domine Syrtis dodder until one day he could do so no more; a similar anticlimax had punctuated the life of old Mrs. Joralemon. This natural death, in which the organism simply wore out, struck Prue as stranger than the scourge of disease. The typhus had borne off Mrs. Horsfield two years after Maggie had been born, a death the whole village had mourned. Her demise had been swift, and painful because unexpected; but Prue could not understand why people hoped to be overtaken by some creeping deformity of body or mind. True, there would be no great surprise, as in suddenly finding oneself stricken with a fatal ailment. Yet the knowledge of one's own imminent decease seemed more frightening to Prue. Then again, she had felt certain all day Johanna was no longer cognizant; and hoped she would remain so when Dr. Philpot came, for otherwise she would berate him with charges of quackery. Johanna's mother, Elsa de Peyster, was said to have been a wise woman of even greater skill than Mrs. Friedlander; and when she'd still had her wits partway about her, Johanna had always condescended to anyone who'd claimed knowledge of healing.

Dr. Tobias Philpot, in addition to keeping the Twin Tankards with his brother, Antony, was a purveyor of patent medicine. He seemed a nocturnal creature, with a sleepy gaze and an eternal growth of purplish stubble on his cheeks and chin. At that hour of the afternoon, he was in the quiet barroom, wiping down the tables with a rag. The only customer was a well-dressed Negro Prue didn't recognize—perhaps a traveler, staying upstairs—who barely looked up from his schnitzel when she entered. Dr. Philpot did, and said, "Prue Winship," as if she was a pleasant surprise. "We never see you, except when the singers come."

"Good afternoon."

"Tony was just saying he wished we'd see more of your father." Dr. Philpot had a low, pleasant voice, and took his time choosing his words. Though everyone said his medical training had been of the most perfunctory kind, she imagined his calm manner provided comfort in times of distress. "Such a jolly man. He understands there's no enmity, on our side? If we had a license for hard liquor, his gin would be our first choice. Or your gin, I should say."

Prue said, "You're kind; but I think he knows. It's simply that Joe is one of his dearest friends. He drinks there, when he isn't drinking at home." Joe Loosely exerted the same monetary influence over the state regulators Matty Winship had when his business had been beholden to the Crown; Joe paid them off handsomely, and in return, his was the only establishment selling gin and brandy anywhere near the ferry. Brooklyn was not yet an incorporated village, and with no elected officials of its own, there was nobody to whom an alehouse-keeper like Tony Philpot might apply for redress. Winship gin could be had in Midwood and Bushwick, but it was the Philpots' ill fortune to be too close to Joe. "I'll tell him to stop in soon."

The customer took a long pull at his ale. Prue knew he was listening.

Tobias Philpot dunked the rag in his bucket and wrung it out with care. "Anything I can do for you this afternoon? Tone's made some coffee, and if you like, we've some of Peg Dufresne's jam and biscuits."

"Thank you," Prue said, "no." Tony and Tobias had no womenfolk; but while the Hicks brothers had gone greedy and mean after a few decades in each other's company, the Philpots, like the Schermerhorns, had become solicitous of women and children. "I've actually come to ask you to examine our serving woman. She's doing poorly."

"Your slave, Johanna?"

Prue nodded.

"Had quite a tongue on her, in her day. When your father bought her of old Mr. Remsen, the whole village said only a stranger would be so gullible."

"She would still have the tongue, could she speak."

"Well, it served all of us right, for minding other people's business." He winced as he finished wiping down the table. "Lived with her all your life; you must be quite fond." Prue tried to think up a reply, but he wasn't looking at her. "De Bouton has told me she's a cancer on her brow. Is it for this you've come?"

Prue nodded again. He pulled out a chair at the damp table, inviting her to sit, but she said, "Thank you, but I really should get back."

"Why didn't you go for de Bouton?" he asked, without malice.

Prue said, "He's stone drunk, sir."

Dr. Philpot shook his great, jowly head. "Sometimes I think, when I reach my end, there'll be payment to be made for this business I'm in. Will there be anything more?" he asked his lone customer.

As the man was chewing, he simply shook his head no.

Dr. Philpot walked out of the barroom and into the hall, and craned his head up the stairs. "Tone? Can you see to the customer? I've a medical visit to pay."

"Coming," Tony said from somewhere upstairs.

Dr. Philpot returned, Prue thought nearly as slowly as if he were walking through water. "I'll do what I can," he said. "Of course I can make no promises."

Prue said, "We're grateful you can come at all."

From behind the counter he brought forth two of his brown bottles, with wax seals over the stoppers, and testimonials in small type. With his usual languor he placed them on the counter, then held an empty jug under one of his taps. "Some ale for your father," he said.

"Thank you. He'll like that."

He stoppered it and pushed all three bottles forward on the counter. Prue reached for her pocket, but he held forth his stubby hand and said, "Please. We'll see what I can do."

He took his time packing his wooden case, and ran his hand across his jaw, already shadowed with his evening beard, before heaving the box aloft. Prue hurried to open the door for him. Out in the barn, he took great care in saddling his fat black horse, and he secured the medical box to her back. Prue wanted to exhort him to make haste, but also remembered there was likely little he could do for Johanna. "Will you ride?" he asked Prue, still holding the horse by the reins.

The horse, Bonnie, shook her head, but Prue didn't take it amiss. "Won't you?"

"I often walk her," he said. "I think she finds me a bit heavy; but you'll suit her fine."

He held the gentle mare still while Prue mounted, and he led the horse by the reins as they ambled downriver together. Mrs. Livingston's roses were blooming, and perfumed the evening air.

At the Winship house, Dr. Philpot spoke in soothing tones to Johanna, despite that she could not hear him. He drew his breath in across his teeth when he saw the tumor—it had grown large and solid as an egg, its tentacles more numerous and as sturdy as twigs—and at the sound of his dismay, Roxana left the room and walked out into the dooryard. Prue and Pearl remained in Johanna's cramped chamber with Dr. Philpot and Johanna, who had not even opened her eyes upon examination.

"It must pain her," he said. Prue thought he was speaking to himself. "Does she still take liquids?" he asked Prue.

"From time to time."

He nodded and bent down to unhitch his case. "Give her hourly a spoonful of my Eugenic Water. I doubt she'll be with you long; but this will help ease her pain." He put the bottles on the night table and handed her the jug of ale. "As I said, for your father."

"Thank you. How much do we owe you?"

"Never mind for now. Send him in when he's the time."

Prue led him to the door, and saw that the sun was setting in great rolls of pink clouds over Manhattan. Bonnie, tethered to the post, was eating clover. Prue's mother was pacing, out by the well, and wringing her hands in her apron. The scent of the ripening berries on the juniper bushes was pungent and sweet. Prue had no idea what was keeping her father. She went back into the house and found Pearl reading the label on one of the bottles.

"What's in Eugenic Water?" Prue asked.

Pearl opened her case and wrote, *Lawdanum & Moonshine.* She sighed, and Prue thought she understood more than Maggie Horsfield, for all Maggie's pretensions of superiority. It was clear from the set of her shoulders and the steadiness of her gaze she knew the bottle contained no cure.

Prue administered the first dose of the nostrum but felt her stomach lurch when she did so; there was something awful in the greedy way Johanna's tongue sought out the medicine when the rest of her was letting go by degrees. Pearl agreed to give the medicine from then on. She did not seem to flinch at either death's proximity or the stench in the room.

When Johanna passed a week later, Roxana wept as if she'd lost a child. Matty comforted her and put her to bed, then came down to find his three daughters sitting in the parlor, wide awake but doing nothing. The windows were open, admitting gnats and a warm breeze. Pearl was curled up on the divan with her cat in her arms; Tem looked as if she understood something somber had occurred but wasn't certain exactly what. Prue simply held still, afraid if she moved she might explode with guilt. "No," her father told her, as he sat on the arm of her chair and reached up to rub her scalp, "don't look so low. It's a great sadness Johanna will no longer be with us, but you girls loved her well, and did your best to help her in her last days. You brought Dr. Philpot, don't forget."

Prue wanted to accept his benediction, but as usual thought he understood little of what troubled her. At a gross level, she felt responsible for the existence of Johanna's tumor in the first place, as it had been Prue who'd first made Johanna's head ache with worry over Pearl, and in exactly that spot. Underlying this, she felt some relief no longer to have to watch the poor woman dying; and beneath it all lay that which she could tell no one: the solace of knowing Johanna would now take her secret with her into the dirt of the Reformed Dutch churchyard, if indeed she had kept it all these years. Prue knew that even to think this was a betrayal of the same order as having cursed her sister in the first place; nevertheless, she breathed more easily than she had in all her days. In the eyes of the rest of her family, she was a sober, diligent, hardworking girl; only Johanna had seen the depths of her vileness. And to know such a person was gone from this world—vanished as surely as if her body had been taken up into the clouds—was freeing. To whom could she confess such a confidence? Not her sisters, nor her parents, nor even Ben and Isaiah. She wanted none of them to know she thought such reprehensible thoughts. She was a grown woman of eighteen, trained to run a distillery; she ought to have been more practical-minded.

There were no specific customs in Brooklyn regarding the funerals of slaves. Many of the inhabitants kept slaves for kitchen work if not for the fields, but there was talk in the barrooms of a gradual manumission; and though Prue could not see how her father could run his manufactory at profit entirely on paid labor, she knew he planned to do so someday. When one of the Rapaljes' slaves had died, they'd buried her decently but without show, and in a similar act of conscience had hired paid help to replace her. Roxana insisted that Johanna had been as much a member of their family as anyone and deserved a full funeral. "I'd sooner lie down in the grave beside her than allow her to be buried with no more dignity than a pet dog," she said with a vehemence that unsettled Prue. Roxana had the new domine, who hadn't known Johanna by name, conduct a service, and afterward invited all the neighbors and the distillery's workers back to the house for cider and seed cake. Prue put on her one brown dress for this occasion, and it constricted and chafed against her, though not nearly so much as did her discomfort about her sin. Then, too, she noticed she was not the only sinner in the room. There was Dr. de Bouton, reeking of liquor in the afternoon, and Henry Hicks and Mr. Patchen, neither of whom had a kind word for anyone. The neighbors were gluttonous in their consumption, and the men went out of the house, seriatim, to spit tobacco. Maggie Horsfield must have been as displeasing to God's sight as Prue, for the way she stepped aside to admire the curtains when Pearl drew near her. Isaiah and Ben closed ranks in front of Maggie, as if to shield her from Pearl's view. Though they had long since reached their full height, they hadn't filled out at all; and their narrow faces, the image of their father's, clearly showed their shame. Ben tossed Pearl a sugared nut, which she caught and popped sheepishly into her mouth. Prue wondered if this was sufficient apology for Maggie, who now stood with her back to the room, examining the still life Pearl had embroidered using cast-off strands of the family's hair. It was a weird object—less because of the hair than because of the lifelike accuracy with which she'd depicted twigs and dried leaves—and Prue could imagine Maggie giving an unflattering account of it to whomever she counted among her friends.

In what the neighborhood considered a rare act of generosity, the Hicks brothers sent over their mulatto cook, Abiah Browne, to help with the cleaning the next day. She was no older than Prue, and prettier, with a head of chestnut curls that fell in orderly spirals from beneath her woolen kerchief. She watched with curiosity as Prue fastened her knee britches and pulled on her heavy boots. While Prue, Tem, and their father worked at the distillery that day, Abiah cleaned the house of footprints and spilled beer and threw all Johanna's linens outdoors to await the washerwoman. (Pearl reported her horror at the scent of putrefaction.) She moved Johanna's bedstead into the kitchen, and attacked even the ceiling of the sickroom with soap and water, by means of a washrag wrapped around the business end of a broom. When Prue returned home from work, Abiah was eating some buttered peas at the kitchen table, and the whole house smelled pleasant and damp. "It must have been a lot of work," Prue said.

Abiah finished chewing and said, "It's all right."

Prue went into Johanna's room. The scent of soap was strong, but she wondered if she only imagined the odor of decay still lingered beneath it. The room had always been small, and for some reason looked smaller now that it was denuded of personal effects.

"Do you feel her in there?" Abiah asked.

Prue felt a tingle in her spine. "Excuse me?"

"Everyone says she was a seer, like her mother. I felt eyes on me, the whole while I was in there."

"My sister Pearl's, perhaps."

Abiah shook her head no. "It's no worry. They didn't feel malign." She took a long drink of water. "I put your supper on, and it should be ready soon; but there are more peas, if you'd like, in the meanwhile." She tipped her head toward a skillet on the hob.

Prue said, "Thank you," and took a wooden spoon to move the peas to a bowl. They smelled green and sweet. As she sat down at the table, she noticed all the sticky spots had been scrubbed clean, as they had not been for some while. She felt a physical sense of relief at not having to watch where she placed her elbows. "It's lovely to have the place so neat. Johanna had been unwell a long time, and my mother doesn't care much for housekeeping."

Abiah pushed the crock of butter to her across the table. "Well, if your parents ever seek a replacement, ask them to come calling."

"Don't you like working for the Hickses?"

Abiah shrugged her shoulders. "I like it fine. But your family's temperament seems more pleasant."

Prue nodded, and deduced from Abiah's comment that her mother had remained abed all day. If she'd been down, Abiah would have found her work more trying.

After Abiah had gone home and the family had retired to the parlor, Prue went back into Johanna's room. The grate had been swept clean, but because of its proximity to the kitchen, the room was still hot. The ropes creaked on the mattress when Prue sat down. Could it be, she wondered, that Johanna sat beside her, or was in their backyard or drifting around Fly Market? It could not be; she reminded herself it was childish to think it might. Still, she could not convince herself any of these possibilities was more distressing than the possibility that so unique a human soul could vanish, leaving nothing behind her but an ivory hair comb and two dresses to be given to the poor.

Six

MR. SEVERN'S VISIT

March 1st

Dearest Recompense,

Very well; I see you do not yet fully understand that of which I write. What could have been more natural, than to have lost my heart to such a man? You did not know me then; & I was exactly the girl to be smitten with him. I was surrounded by people each hour of the day and night, yet counted myself lonely;—he too had a certain solitariness in the very way he comported himself. He was young, and though he was not handsome he had his peculiar beauty. He had been kind to my sister Pearl,—on whose behalf I was ever watchful for a slight,—and had also shewn kindness to my self. & his preaching gave me my first true taste of religion, and opened my eyes to the possibility of a God who had mercy on sinners.

When his church moved to its permanent home, I was crestfallen, for we could no longer sneak in, as the sermons were not on our own property & there was no longer an upstairs. It seem'd an unlikely pass for two girls of good family to be in, not to know how to manage to get themselves religion. (Or perhaps in other quarters the young folk were fired up with holy fervour; but Brookland was a village of people young & old who visited church on Sunday, then pretended it did not exist till the following week.) Yet your Aunt Pearl & I did work it over, as carefully as if it were a chicken bone & we intent on sucking off the last tender bits of meat. The crux of the problem was: We both wished to spend time in Mr. Severn's company, for differing purposes, but I at least did not wish to tell her what mine was. Hers, I assumed, was simple, in that she desired to expiate her guilt over the theft. It was providential for me in this instance that Pearl was not allowed to wander at will, for the same reason she'd never seen the cooling house until I brought her: For if a carriage came barreling toward her, how could she alert its driver to her peril? After a few Sabbaths without our secret church, she simply requested I take her to him, to make good on the promise about the needlework.

Later that very week I escorted her to the small, bare rectory, and sat tongue-tied by at table while Mr. Severn encouraged Pearl to tell him of her talents & interests. He waited with a kindly smile for her written replies, and it was in watching the manner in which he watched her I first came to understand she was as beautiful as Tem. Thitherto I had thought my appreciation of her came of the peculiar admixture of love & guilt I bore her, but Mr. Severn's eyes danced when he looked upon her. She may have been the runt of the litter, I surmised, but she was a pretty runt all the same. Pearl was obviously intoxicated by his attention, and wielded her pencil proudly each time she replied to him. I wondered if our minister saw her eager writing as I did, as the mark of her difference from the rest of us.

He invited us to visit him as often as we pleased, and a curious narrative began to unfold: which was, we truly became friends. His interest in Pearl was not of the sort she usually elicited,—that people felt pity for the poor mute,—but rather, he took real pleasure in her curiosity & in her observations of the world around her. He spoke to me furthermore as a peer. Until that time it had not occurred to me how I had been creeping up on adulthood; but for all his grey hairs, and th'important work he had come to perform in our community, Mr. Severn was not so much older than I. He was in need of friendship, intellectual companionship, & someone with whom to argue on points of his theology. Pearl and I were both unequal to this last task, yet enjoyed his disquisitions on the subject. I felt it an honour,—which I wanted to trumpet to Patience Livingston, out of sheer spite,—that he asked me to call him by his nickname, *Will*; and I did not think this at all odd of him.

It was on a rainy evening in his first spring among us Will Severn came to call on my parents. He carried a dog-eared volume of Pappy's sermons as testament to his admiration for the old man, then long since passed on. He knocked on the front door, as no one ever did, & consequently we all gathered in the parlour with quizzical expressions on our faces to see who had come. He held up the tattered volume while unwinding himself from the seemingly endless length of his shabby scarf. —I only had occasion to hear him preach thrice, he said, once greetings were exchanged, but his sermons were formidable. They called me to follow in his path.

Mr. Severn's boots meanwhile were puddling our floor, & Pearl went to the kitchen and brought back a towel. Mother appeared peevish, her lips pursed tight,—but I could not tell if this resulted from the puddle or the man's very presence. Or rather, I could not see how she could find the man himself disagreeable, but understood his churchiness might have offended her. I was pleased that as it was a Sunday, my father was wearing his best blue coat & a silken weskit. Church or no church, it was his day of rest, and he looked as respectable a paterfamilias as I could have hoped.

Father said, —They drove me from the church entire, but Prue rather liked th'old fire & brimstone, did'n't ye, gell? He did'n't await my reply before adding, —Show'm what a good little hostess you are, love; bring the man a drink.

—I'll get it! Tem shouted. She was so eager to be thought a distiller.

—Yes, I said, Pappy's preaching did impress itself upon my memory.

—*Pappy*, Will Severn repeated, smiling at me. —I can hardly imagine the Reverend Mr. Elihu Juster Winship responding to such an appellation. What a slab of New-England granite he was!

—Here 'tis, Tem said. She'd brought a pitcher of gin and two short glasses. I thought she looked unnaturally pretty in her day shirt and work britches, with her short hair loose; but I would've given my left eye to be wearing a simple plaid dress such as Pearl had on & sopping up his puddle from the floor.

Father took the pitcher from Tem & said to Mr. Severn, —You do'n't know the half of it. Girls, take his cloak. Will you join me, sir, in a nip o' the wares?

—Oh, I could'n't, sir, I do'n't partake of spirits.

—Now, come, Father said, I offer it in hospitality.

I took Mr. Severn's cloak, hat, & muffler to hang on the little-used hook by the front door. They all stank of the rain, but my knees nearly buckled at inhaling the scent that underlay them, of his sweat and of the cedar chest in which he stored his clothes.

—Besides, that's not any ole spirits, Tem offered. 'Tis gin of our *own mannifacture*.

—And indeed, Father added, this pitickular batch is my daughter Prue's making.

—In that case, he said, & took his cup and sat down upon the divan with it, in a manner indicating that sitting on a divan holding a cup of liquor was not the custom in Massachusetts.

We all follow'd round to sit & there were not enough chairs, so Pearl pulled up a footstool to sit at my feet. Mother kept an eye on the Reverend's dripping cloak. He took a hearty sup of the gin and spluttered. We girls all laughed at him;—Pearl & I out of fondness, and Tem, I felt sure, because she was already unbeknownst to our father tippling in the storehouses after hours, precisely, she said, to avoid such outbursts. —My, he said, it does bite.

Tem said, —That's a strong one Prue made. I think she rectified it *four times*.

Mother said, —Do'n't be a louse, Temmy; bring the man some water.

Tem sprang up & Mr. Severn said, —It's very good gin, Miss Winship.

I felt my cheeks go pink. He cleared his throat a few times, and took a good draught of the water Tem brought & handed him with a smart little curtsy. —Mr. Winship, he said when he had recovered himself, I must tell you again how grateful I was all those months you allowed me to use your property to hold my worship meetings.

—No need. 'Tis any decent fellow would'a done the same.

Mother gave each of them a dark look.

—I have met any number of decent fellows since arriving in Brookland, and none other offered me a comfortable place for my church. But this is why I've come: because I see you are good folk, and wish your family might join us, of a Sunday.

Here Father raised his glass to the man, and drank it down in one neat swallow. —I do'n't mean to give offense, he said, but I spoke plain when I told you my father had drove me from the church. Roxana's family did her the same turn, by dint of treating her too strict. We're non-believers through & through, and we've raised these little pups of ours the same.

—No, Mr. Severn said. Your daughters have a hunger for the life of the spirit.

Could I have made my thoughts leap directly across into his thinker at that moment, without use of the intermediary,—as well as *audible to my parents*,—vehicle of speech, I would gladly have done so. Barring such cognitive powers, I merely glared at him, & assumed Pearl to be doing the same. He must have caught our meaning, for in an instant he went red as a beet, though he still looked at me imploringly.

—They do? Father asked. Which of them do you mean, pray?

—Oh, all of them, sir, Mr. Severn said, and turn'd his shy gaze to our father. If I was not mistaken, he was beginning to perspire. —Three such lovely daughters;—it simply seems wrong to deny them the comforts of an understanding of God & the uses of a virtuous life.

—About the latter part I cannot disagree with you, Father said, and I am doing my best to educate them in that regard. It is only on the former we diverge.

Pearl meanwhile was writing something on her book, then held it up over her shoulder, such that only I could read it. It said, *Do b'leeve he*ˢ *Sweet on you.*

—Shht, I scolded her, before I realized I'd done so aloud. All their eyes turned to me, & I knew not what to say to explain myself. —I cannot speak for Tem and Pearl, I ventured, but I do sometimes wish I understood more thoroughly why people believe, who do believe.

I too, Pearl wrote, thankfully on a fresh sheet.

—*Och God*, Mother said, exactly as Johanna would have done. She was shaking her head.

Father drew his lips between his teeth. I thought his expression did not bode well. After a moment he said, —Well, why did'n't you say so, monkey? He gave a strained and somewhat ominous laugh here, I thought for Mr. Severn's benefit. —I did'n't press you into service at the distillery, you know; you've always done as you wished. (I thought as he said this it was not so;—I had fought to be trained in the making of gin, & had had to prove myself against his skepticism. Still I understood this performance was for Mr. Severn & not for me, so I kept mum.) If it's sermonizing you hanker for, I suppose you may go and get some without coming to any lasting harm; only,—and you'll excuse my saying so, Mr. S.,—do'n't say I did'n't warn ye. If it's church you want, church you shall have, but I wager you'll find it terrible dull and chiefly wrong-headed besides. Again, Mr. S., beg your pardon.

—No offense taken, Will said, though how he could fail to be discomfited by the foregoing escaped me.

—And you, Temmy? Father asked.

—I'll not go, she said, but I never did,—

Here Pearl reached over and clouted her sharply on the knee.

Tem said, —Ow! but said nothing further, which was surely Pearl's intention in thwacking her.

Mr. Severn was still scarlet. Father said, —Perhaps they could in some way profit by your instruction, sir. Perhaps you could learn 'em to sit still, at least, better 'n I have done.

—Oh, he said. But my school is only for boys,—

Mother said, —I'm certain he meant that metaphorickal-wise.

Pearl wrote a new note & held it up for each of us to see in turn. It read, *We shall look forward to heering a Sermon. We shall come on Sunday.*

—I believe you'll regret it, Father said.

With his eyes cast down, Mr. Severn added, —At nine, then.

He remained talking with us another hour. The whole while, I felt torn between delight in his presence & desire to see him leave, lest he tell our parents some other thing we did not want them to know. It redounded to his credit with me, he had not taken that first opportunity to inform them about our visits.

So it was thus Pearl & I began to go, with our parents' grudging and bewildered consent, to church. I felt awkward & ugly when I put on my one dress, but too afraid of my parents' teasing to ask for a new one; likewise, the first time we took our seat in one of the rearmost pews, the eyes of half the village spun round to look at us, & I did not like their expressions. Every countenance seemed to bear the message, *There's plain Prue Winship, sweet on the minister & come to get him to pay court.* A few seem'd to add, *Plenty of money, too, for all her peculiarity. She'll get what she wants.* After that first Sunday, however, Ben contrived to come sit beside

me, and held my hand tightly in his. This was no more proper than the
sin of which my neighbours' glances correctly accused me, but I felt
glad of his friendship all the same.

My dear, I am begun to think, if instead of writing you these letters,
I were to put my pen to some topick of broad social interest, I might
manage to submit a column weekly to the *Long-Island Courier*. I enjoy the
writing, & it is some comfort to know that if for years I have been short
in my replies to you, I may now redress that wrong, and learn you some
of what you wish to know. But the answers I receive from you divulge
little, except your interest in furthering the story along. You have ever
been impressionable, and I know a new city, a new husband, and a babe
within do not go unremark'd in your mind & heart. I realize I may not
have altogether earned the right to be your confidante, but I would
gladly be so, if I may.

So. I shall proceed, but first I await yr word—

Faithful^y

PW

Seven

ROXANA

V isitors stopping by the Winship household after Johanna's death might have surmised, from the house's condition, Roxana's spirits had finally picked up. No housekeeping could change that the house was old, Dutch, and dreary, but in her cleaning after the funeral Abiah Browne had scrubbed the windows with newssheets and vinegar. Later in the week she returned to begin training a trumpet vine Matty had transplanted from the Horsfields' yard to grow over the long-neglected trellis. Against Roxana's wishes, Matty went to Jacob and Henry Hicks and asked if they'd be willing to share Abiah's services a few days per week. As they were not, he took Abiah aside and offered her substantially larger wages than the Hicks brothers paid her. She gave her former employers a few days to advertise for a replacement, then tied her possessions in a bundle and walked downriver to the Winship house.

When Roxana saw her, she wept. She had been keeping Johanna's room almost as a shrine, and not allowing the girls in; she could not tolerate the notion of a new person moving into the place her friend had occupied. Abiah stared at the floor while Roxana ranted at her, and sat down at the table when Roxana ran upstairs and shut her door. Pearl came up and wrote a note intended to comfort her, and thus discovered Abiah couldn't read. As if Prue did not have sufficient responsibilities already, Matty set her to teach Abiah in the evenings, "As," he said, "it will be a hardship for Pearl if she cannot communicate with her."

Pearl missed Johanna, and sometimes cried for her; but she did her best to welcome Abiah with an open heart, despite that the two could barely communicate. Abiah was young and mild-tempered, and seemed like springtime itself compared to their mother's gloom.

Roxana suffered no malady either Dr. de Bouton or Dr. Philpot could diagnose, only the despondency that had afflicted her in bouts as long as Prue could remember. Dr. de Bouton counseled that time would help heal her; Dr. Philpot recommended small doses of his Eugenic Water, to ease her toward the oblivion she seemed to desire. Roxana preferred the second prescription, and soon had her husband or her daughters walking up to the Twin Tankards for a bottle of the elixir on a regular basis. She would ask Abiah for nothing.

Roxana's grief was genuine, and Prue could imagine how low she herself would feel if Ben were to die, or Mr. Severn; yet as the weeks and months wore on, her mother's misery began to grate upon her. "I don't understand," she told her one night, as they stood together drying dishes at the sideboard. "We all grieve for Johanna," Prue for more complicated reasons than any of her kin could know, "but she was old and ill. Her time had come."

Roxana sniffed at her in exasperation. "You'll see when you get older, Prue. You form attachments to people—you grow to love them—and sooner or later you lose them all. Your parents, your friends; you might think you'll be able to keep your children a spell, but if my womb offers any forecast for yours, you'll lose half of them, too, by and by. Even if you have the good fortune to live into your decrepitude, you die and leave all you loved behind you."

This was unsettling to a girl of nineteen. It also raised her dander. "All those circumstances cause sadness, I know. But she was an old woman. She was a slave, not your child—you may have loved her, but you also *bought* her of Mr. Remsen."

Roxana glared at her with her lips shut tight. They had begun to sprout wrinkles at their corners from so often holding this expression. "You're a coldhearted creature," she said, then refused to speak to Prue the rest of the evening.

Prue had a hundred reasons to find this infuriating, chiefly that at one level her mother was right: Prue had cursed her infant sister and hated the family's frail old slave, and now could muster no sympathy for her own mother's grief. But she could not lash out at her; it would have been unfair, when her mother's spirits were so depressed. Abiah, who already had opinions about the affairs of the household, concurred. One morning, after a row that had sent Roxana weeping to her bedroom, Abiah took Prue aside and whispered, "You say Philpot and de Bouton don't know what to do. But has your father brought in Mrs. Friedlander?" As a result, Prue walked out across Boerum's Hill that morning though the expedition would make her late to work, and brought the old woman back with her. Mrs. Friedlander smoothed Roxana's brow and left Abiah with the dried petals of a red flower with no English name, to be steeped twice daily into a tisane. No one saw any improvement result from the medication, but the family remained hopeful it would work given time.

Despite Abiah's industriousness, a pall fell over the Winship house—in part from legitimate grief and in part from Roxana's distortion of it. Though the family did not discuss it, those who could began to spend less time at home. For Tem, little changed, as she had always preferred to be out in the company of the Luquer or Remsen children. But where Matty had formerly retired to the tavern one evening in three or four, he now began a regular program of kissing his daughters after supper, going upstairs to kiss his wife, and leaving to drink with Joe Loosely. He told his family all the most thoughtful men of the neighborhood—himself, Israel Horsfield, Joe Loosely, Nicolaas Luquer, old Mr. Boerum, Dr. de Bouton, and Theunis van Vechten, who was Brooklyn's sawyer by trade, but had always fancied himself a bit of a natural philosopher—had "formed a Junto, for the discussion of subjects of merit, based on that model society for debate founded by the estimable Mr. Benjamin Franklin."

"What's a subject of merit?" Tem asked. Her tone did not indicate real interest.

"Something like the affairs of France. We shall begin, however, with something closer to home—the necessity of and difficulties militating against bridging the East River. There's a proposal been put forth by an Englishman, name of Thomas Telford. Heard of him, Prue?"

Prue nodded. She hesitated to express her eagerness to learn of the project and see the design. Her mother's scorn for her fascination with the distillery had done nothing to temper her enthusiasms, but had taught Prue to keep the outward signs thereof in check. "He's a famous man, Daddy—a county surveyor by trade, I believe. He built a masonry bridge a few years since, well known for its harmonious proportion."

"Hmm," Matty said. He seemed more interested in his roast and potatoes. "You know more of it than Joe, and he's the one who's set up the Junto."

"May I join in the discussion?" Prue asked.

"No, lambkin, it's a club: men only."

"But I—"

"I know," her father said. "You're as versed as any of us on the question. You know the difficulty the sand poses, and the breadth of the span, and the need to build high enough to admit tall ships. But I won't have my daughter spouting opinions in a smoky barroom."

Prue did, at least, convince him to take good note of what he heard at the Junto and relay it back to her; but his report the next morning disappointed her. "It won't do," he told her as they walked down the lane to begin the day's labor. His face looked swollen from too much drinking or not enough sleep, and his black hat wanted blocking. "We're none of us a bridge architect, of course, but Telford's plan wouldn't clear the water by a sufficient distance to admit the masts of an oceangoing vessel. He's proposed a sort of drawbridge for the river's center, but it's not sensible."

Prue had never considered a drawbridge, and her mind was already spinning out the possibility. "Why so?"

"Our ports'd lose half their custom if the straits could only be navigated by one ship at a time; and he estimates the time to raise and lower the thing at two hours, despite an ingenious block and tackle system and using oxen for the brunt of the work. A terrible plan; though beautifully, persuasively drawn."

"I should still like to see it," Prue said.

"Joe's got it at the tavern. I'm sure he'll show it off, if you ask."

He did not report any of the Junto's further findings or discussions to her. Prue never saw him reading up on anything, though their own small library might have been of tremendous value to him; and she wondered at times if he'd concocted the idea of a Junto to explain his ever-presence at the Liberty Tavern. She didn't have the heart to ask Israel Horsfield if her father's story was true.

Pearl could do little to escape their house, and Prue could see how much this tried her; but she herself began going down to the distillery earlier in the morning and remaining later in the afternoon, to recheck belts that had already been checked, and to rewrite the inventory logs in a cleaner hand. She also shirked her lessons with Abiah and began to take evening rambles with Ben.

She had no sense if this was truly how she wished to spend her leisure. She worried about leaving Pearl to her devices in so sad a house, and agonized over how it was her fault her sister could not communicate with Abiah except by the grossest signs. Yet she could not force herself to remain at home; and Abiah never reproached her over the missed tutoring. Prue's love for Will Severn meanwhile burned unabated, but Mr. Severn did not go out walking with her, and had none but the most pastorly advice about her mother's ailment. He thought Roxana should repent and pray, and Prue grew uncomfortable trying to convey to him the unlikelihood of such a change of heart. Ben, by contrast, always took Prue's side when she recounted an opinion or disagreement, and registered his views with oaths and exclamations. He still reminded her of a puppy, though of a nearly grown one. His hair had gone light brown, but retained its slight curl; and with his blue eyes, still too large for his pointy face, he continued to regard her as if she were both trustworthy and humorous. Without doubt he was her closest friend, and the only person who heard her current difficulties without offering pious counsel; even Isaiah was apt to mention "duty" when pressed. Both boys had finished school the previous year and were employed in learning the business of their father's small farm, that they might choose to manage it, if so inclined, or else learn through physical labor the value of pitching upon a more learned profession. Both were released from responsibility when the sun went down, but it was always Ben with whom she went out.

Here Prue paused in her writing, out of a native unwillingness both to divulge what had hitherto been private and to fluster Recompense, whom Prue had always found reserved. Yet Prue had already brought her most disgraceful secret into the light; and if she continued her account, she would have eventually to confess her own terrible stupidity, both about Pearl and about the bridge. Either she would drive Recompense away in disgust or the revelations would draw them closer. From her current vantage, she could not say which it would be, but she prayed it would be the latter. She inhaled deeply, then, and resolved to continue her account.

Then she laughed to herself, for what did she know of Recompense's last years at home? She had always struck her mother as prim, but Prue had heard the rumors circulating about her daughter and young Nelson Luquer. She wouldn't put it past her to have had some clandestine sport.

From the start of these peregrinations, Prue knew it was only a matter of time before she and Ben got into mischief. She held few opinions about this, except that it was only the Livingston girls who raised their noses high when boys approached them. Everyone else made trouble sooner or later; it was mostly a matter of waiting one's turn. She and Ben seldom touched except to roughhouse or hold hands, and never discussed the possibility of doing otherwise; simply, when he walked her home one spring night, instead of turning in at her fence, they continued down Joralemon's Lane and went through the distillery gate. It was a waxing moon, but overcast, and she did not fear being seen; the slave quarters were at the far northern edge of the property, and the rest of Brooklyn turned its back on the river at night. The slaves' fires were burning cozily, and there was almost no chance her parents or the Schermerhorns would look out their windows to peer down on the manufactory. A chilly breeze blew in off the river. "I don't have any keys," Prue said.

Ben swung her hand back and forth. "No matter, then."

This was why her father locked the buildings at night in the first place, though it was mostly drunken boys about whom he worried. She knew Scipio Jones, however, sometimes locked his tools in a chest for the night and neglected to latch his shed. She led Ben northward, listening to the river slip by.

"The cooperage," she said, as he could not have seen much in the dark. She lit Scipio's stove—still certain the slaves would not look out and notice, and that no one else would peer down upon the works—and cleared his kettle from the top. He kept a clean pile of straw in the corner, on which he rested when work was slow. Ben led her there, and plumped it up before sitting down in it.

Prue spent little time in the company of girls besides her sisters; but she had heard Annie Luquer recount her clumsiness unlacing and unbuttoning a boy's britches, with whose methods of fastening she'd been unfamiliar. Prue wore britches every day, and had no difficulty with Ben's. What she had not anticipated was the sheer pleasure of lying down with him—the smell and taste of him, made sweeter by proximity, and the soft rasp of his belly against her own. She did not know what she thought of it, and felt embarrassed when, still mostly naked, he kissed her all up and down the side of her throat; but she knew she would take her father's keys the next night, in case some locked building might provide them a better spot.

They neatened up the straw and put out the fire before walking back up the ravine. Her father was at Joe's when she returned to the house, and if Pearl looked at her with irritation, it was the natural expression of someone who'd been left alone with a servant and an ailing mother, and spent the entire evening embroidering a bizarre and gruesome Pietà. Prue skulked off to bed, and only the next morning felt a tug of doubt about her conduct. Before her father and sisters arose, she dressed and went out, telling Abiah (who was already up, and had built the kitchen fire) she would return shortly. This time she took her father's keys from the hook, went down to the stable, and saddled up an old, yellow-white gelding whose disposition was so foul, Tem had—in a bald attempt to even the score with their parents—named him Jolly. He tolerated Prue and never bucked with her; and he made moderate haste to Mrs. Friedlander's that morning.

Prue found her out weeding her garden in a straw hat, though it was not even an hour past dawn. "Mother faring poorly?" Mrs. Friedlander called when she saw Prue approach.

"Neither better nor worse."

"Give it time, give it time. The herbs can't work in an instant."

Prue dismounted and tied Jolly to the fence. He bent down to eat the clover as if it were the worst moldy oats from the cellar. Mrs. Friedlander had tomato vines growing, and their green fruit gave off a peppery scent.

When Prue told her of her worry, Mrs. Friedlander broke into a toothy grin, scanned her up and down, and peered into her eyes. Prue shuddered to think what she was looking for, but stood firm. "I don't think you've much to worry about, but come," Mrs. Friedlander said. She released her sun hat down her back and took off her gardening gloves. "Into the house with you." She herded Prue into her tidy kitchen, put water on for tea, and went to rummage in her storeroom. Prue sat listening to the skittering tick of her mantel clock and to Jolly, complaining to himself in a low voice outdoors. Mrs. Friedlander returned with two paper packets, marked *Tansy* and *Pennyroyal* neatly in pencil. "A dry spoonful of each, morning and night," she counseled, "or steep them in tea, and plenty of fresh air and exercise. Can you ride that horse of yours at a gallop?"

"Only if it's dire; he's old and crotchety."

Mrs. Friedlander laughed and began to pack her teapot with mint leaves. "As fast as you can, then. And I'm sure you do plenty of climbing and jumping in that distillery of yours."

"Yes, ma'am."

"This is the surest way to keep a young creature like you from losing her menses. When you're my age—well, you'll have had your children by then, and if your menses get lost, you won't run looking for 'em. Have you had your breakfast? I've just smoked my first bacon of the season, and it's very good, if I may say so."

Prue was relieved to find her so matter-of-fact, and stayed for a gluttonous breakfast.

When she returned home, she saw that Pearl had made great progress on her Pietà the night before. The dead Christ now had the full regalia of his wounds, upon which, through careful stitching, real blood appeared to have dried. Prue had never seen any such depiction in Protestant Brooklyn or New York; her sister must have seen an engraving in one of Mr. Severn's art books, then brought her imagination to bear on it. Prue wanted to ask why she had fixated on so grisly a subject, but Pearl was making an unusual clamor with the breakfast dishes and Prue held her tongue.

Their mother continued in her state of ill health until winter. Neither Mrs. Friedlander's tisane nor the exhortations of her husband and daughters had improved her spirits, but neither had her health grown worse. As soon as the days began to shorten, however, her condition declined. She still appeared at table, and if she ate with little interest, she continued to eat everything that was placed before her. Even so, she began to waste away. The sharpness of her cheekbones and the thick knuckles on her long fingers grew more pronounced. Her auburn hair was still only streaked with gray, but overnight it lost its luster. After All Hallow's, when the neighborhood children went tearing through the streets shrieking, she took to her bed.

At first, no one worried much; Roxana had done this before, and was sure to come downstairs sooner or later. But after a few days, when Prue went up to visit her, she thought she had never seen her mother look so wan, and was disturbed by the aimless way she stroked the coverlet. "Are you unwell?" Prue asked her. "Should I get Dr. de Bouton?"

Roxana licked her lips and patted the bed beside her for Prue to sit down. "There's nothing he can do. But thank you."

"What ails you?"

She shook her head no. "Nothing that hasn't always. I'll be fine, you'll see."

"Shall I bring you something to read?"

Roxana shook her head again. "Prue?" she said. Prue looked at the skeletal face and reminded herself this was her mother. "You know I have always known?"

Prue said, "Excuse me?"

Roxana reached for her hand; Prue couldn't tell whose was clammy. "You know Johanna told me what you did to Pearl when you were small."

A soft ringing began in Prue's ears, and she reminded herself to keep focused on her mother, that the sound not overwhelm her. "I didn't know." This was not at all how Prue had imagined being revealed; though of course if Johanna had told anyone, it would have been Prue's mother.

Roxana squeezed Prue's hand gently. "Don't look so frightened. I think nothing of it."

Prue prayed her sister wouldn't walk into the room right then. "You must, or you wouldn't have—"

"Shh," Roxana told her. "There's no such thing as a curse; or if there were, I don't think a little mouse such as you could have found out the secret." She licked her lips again. "It only came to mind because I'm thinking of Pearl."

"Thinking what?"

Roxana shrugged her bony shoulders up and down. "Wondering what will become of her. Wondering what misdeed I must have committed, that she should be so punished."

Prue knew only too well whose had been the misdeed, and she thought she knew what would become of Pearl—an old spinster with extraordinary talents in needlework. She knew whose fault this would be. But she did not say so.

"You and Tem will look after her, won't you, when your father and I are gone?"

"Of course," Prue said. "But that's far in the future."

Roxana nodded and said, "I'm going to rest. I'll see if I can gather my strength for supper."

"Very well," Prue said, and kissed her cheek before going down. Her mother's hair had an unpleasant, earthy smell, as if it hadn't been washed in months.

Roxana did not venture downstairs again. She began asking for her meals to be brought up on a tray, and would return them nearly untouched. She refused to go to the outhouse, and instead used the pot all day. The whole upstairs began to smell of urine and feces, and Abiah grumbled when she took the pots out to be emptied. "I didn't realize I'd be caring for a baby," she said to no one in particular one morning, but the whole family heard. One day in January, Roxana turned her face toward the far wall, and would not turn back over, though Pearl later said she'd spent much of the afternoon trying to coax her to do so. Toward teatime, Pearl appeared in the mill yard. Prue came down from the stillhouse to find her out in the yard, writing a note to Owen, the caretaker.

"Pearlie?" she called. Her voice sounded quiet in the stiff wind.

Pearl's small, wind-chapped face flooded with relief. She curtsied to Owen and ran to her sister with her notebook clasped tight in her hand. After reading what she'd written about their mother, Prue hustled her into the office, left her there for the moment with some paper and charcoal, and ran off to find their father.

All three daughters followed him home as he stormed up the hill. "Can we come in with you?" Tem asked, her eyes sparkling.

"No," he said, and took the stairs two at a time as his boots scattered malted barley to the ground.

His daughters waited at the foot of the kitchen stairs. Abiah was out.

"Dammit, Roxy, this will not do," they heard their father say the next moment. "What in Heaven's name are you thinking?"

"Should we leave?" Tem asked, straining her ears upward all the while. Pearl hushed her.

"I will not have this!" Matty shouted. They both had their tempers, and their daughters were used to squabbles and altercations, which flared up and burned down at regular intervals; but this time Roxana did not respond. After a long while, he said more quietly, "Roxy, this is absurd," and a few minutes later came back down. The girls tried to disperse around the kitchen, but it was obvious they'd been listening. He neatened his hair back toward its tail with both hands. "All right, we must do something. You," he said, pointing to Tem, "go upferry and round up de Bouton and Philpot, either or both. Prue, bring Mrs. Friedlander. I'm sure Israel's fine, but I need to get back to the works. There was trouble with the morning's mashing, and I want to be certain it's fixed."

"What of Pearlie?" Tem asked.

"Pearl shall sit home with her mother, of course."

After their father had returned to the brewhouse, Prue saddled up Jolly and sat Pearl on the pommel before her. Pearl kept shifting in discomfort, but Prue gathered she was less anxious than if she'd been left home to wait.

None of the remedies produced a change, and only Dr. Philpot's nostrum did Roxana take with any relish. She gulped it down as if it were a form of sustenance, and began to refuse all food but milk and toast, as if she were indeed an infant.

In February, for all his drinking, Matty Winship realized his wife and family needed some spiritual guidance, as no physical ministrations were helping. He sent first for the young domine, telling Prue he thought it might be easier to confess his troubles to a stranger. When the domine could do nothing either for Matty's sleepless worry or for Roxana, Matty sent for Mr. Severn, who stood in the kitchen with his tattered brown hat in his hands.

"Mr. Winship," he said. His voice was low and comforting. "I have been among the Brooklanders almost three years now. I have made known to you my admiration for your father and his work, and have, I hope, contributed to the moral upbringing of two of your daughters, of whom I am truly fond. I have exhorted you, as neighbor and friend, to come into the church for succor and celebration, but have seen little of you but your money."

"A fair bit of my money," Matty said, without malice.

"Yes."

"Pearl," he said quietly, "take Mr. Severn's coat?"

Pearl did, and he bowed his head to her as she took it from him.

"I am not an old man," their father continued, "but I have been set in my habits of mind since my youth. I am not a churchgoer, nor ever shall be. But if I may speak plain, sir, we are desperate. My wife seems almost beyond help, and if there is, as you say, any succor in your presence, we would be most grateful if you could offer it to her. That is all."

Will Severn's small mouth drew closer in upon itself, as if hearing of Matty's suffering gave him a physical pain. Prue wondered what his temperament had been like before the untimely deaths of his parents. She could imagine them his mooring ropes, and him a rowboat drifting on the open water without them. He did not seem to have any brothers or sisters. "I only wish to say it is never too late to welcome the love of God into your heart," he said simply.

Matty nodded and looked off toward the window. His collar and cuffs—usually so neat, they were the envy of men of leisure—were wilted. "You are kind to come, Mr. Severn, but you are under no obligation to remain."

"I disagree," Prue said. "You must help her, Will."

He said, "Of course I shall do what I can. Where is she?"

Pearl, with her head ducked down, walked toward the stairs and beckoned him to follow. After they'd gone, Matty raised his unshaven chin toward Prue and said, " 'Will'?"

"It's his name, Daddy."

When Pearl returned alone, he poured them each a thimbleful of gin, with which Tem feigned unfamiliarity. They sat down together to wait.

The hall clock—a masterpiece of irregularity the Winships had acquired with the house from the Joralemons—cycled through two quarters of an hour, meaning somewhere between twenty and forty minutes had elapsed when Will Severn returned, with his gray hair disheveled, as if he'd had his hands in it. "Mr. Winship," he said, "should we step into the parlor to speak?"

Matty scratched his fingers through his stubble. "There is nothing you may not say before my daughters. I've more or less raised them to be boys."

Severn looked around at all of them. He had come up behind Pearl's chair, and put one hand gently on her shoulder. "I sat by your wife this while and prayed for her with all my heart. I asked God to have mercy on her and show her the way to salvation. Then I asked if there was aught I could do for her, if I might speak with her or give her the Blessed Sacrament. She did not respond."

"It has been some while since she's spoken," Matty said.

"Not even with a glance," Severn added.

Prue said, "I would take the Sacrament for her."

He patted Pearl's shoulder, since it was the one he could reach. "That's good of you, but I fear it doesn't work that way. We can pray for her, however. Did your wife never pray, Mr. Winship?"

"My daughter seems to be calling you Will," he said, with what sounded like pique; "you might as well call me Matty." Prue's heart jumped when she realized no one would call her father "Reverend" once her mother was gone. "Roxana hasn't prayed in all the years I've known her. Which is twenty-six. No doubt about as long as you've been alive."

He nodded. "Does she yet take sustenance?"

"Of the most meager sort."

Will Severn looked down at the table, as if this required the sum of his concentration. "If the doctors can uncover nothing—"

"Nothing," Matty said. "No physical cause."

"—and if Mrs. Friedlander can do naught to improve her condition, then I can only conclude she suffers from some malady of the spirit. And I am neither wise nor holy enough a man to cure her if she does not desire my intervention. I don't know that any man could, short of a saint." All trace of oratory had deserted him, and he was speaking as quietly as Prue had ever heard him speak. "And if your wife will not accept help," he went on, "then perhaps the kindest thing, the only thing to do is, with as much grace as we can muster, to allow her to resign herself to God." At this, Matty Winship closed his eyes and pressed his thumb and forefinger over them. "I am sorry if I have spoken out of turn."

"No," Matty replied. "It's the trouble that troubles me, not hearing it named."

"May we offer a prayer together?"

"Please," Prue said.

Matty shook his head no.

"Will you send for me if her condition changes, or if she experiences a change of heart?"

"Without fail. Thank you, Reverend," Matty said. "We shall remember your kindness."

"And I shall pray for Mrs. Winship." Mr. Severn took up his coat and hat, looked around at all of them, and said, "God bless you. Any hour of the day or night, you may call on me." He touched Pearl's shoulder one last time, then took his leave.

After he'd left, Pearl wrote, *I believe in God*, on her pad, and put it on the table for all of them to see. *Cannot I have some Infloonse wth Him, on her behaf?*

"Pray, Pearlie," their father said. "By all means, pray. You, too, if you feel inclined," he said to Prue.

Prue went to sit on the retaining wall down by the water to offer her prayers. The current rushed loudly beneath the thin layer of grubby ice nearest the shore, and as the last river commerce of the day concluded, men shouted and hallooed to one another. Prue could not imagine how God could hear her prayers when she could barely hear herself think, and she wondered if the time for intercession might not have been when her mother was still well. But it was no use wondering. This was her holy ground; this the view she had observed while she had both dreamed her fondest dreams and committed her worst transgressions. She could only beg for mercy, and hope the cry of a single human soul might be audible above the water and the ships.

Abiah was usually first up in the morning, but Prue was often second; and in the weeks that followed, she took to stopping in the hallway outside her parents' door to see if she could make out the sound of her mother's quiet breath beneath the louder rising and falling of her father's. Prue could not go downstairs or go on about her tasks until she'd heard that sound. As February wore on, Roxana began refusing food, and then water; until at last she would take nothing but Dr. Philpot's sweet philter on a spoon. She stopped opening her eyes even to see if it was coming, but she must have been able to hear the cork popping out of the bottle, or smell the nostrum's spicy perfume. One evening as she gave her the dose, Prue whispered to her, "Why are you doing this?"

She did not expect a response, but Roxana worked her tongue in her dry mouth a moment, then whispered a reply so quiet, Prue could not hear it.

"What did you say?" she asked.

But Roxana's face had already slackened into sleep. She never spoke again, and Prue wished she had been able to make out those words.

Roxana died one night in early March of 1791. She must not have struggled, for Matty slept peacefully beside her until dawn. Prue awakened that morning to hear him crying quietly in his bedroom and whispering, "No." She felt her heart seize up in her chest, but she could not say anything or even force herself to sit upright. She concentrated on her father's weeping as if she could will it to stop, as if she could will its cause to vanish. She might have remained there an hour had her sisters not rustled in their bed. When Prue rolled over to face them, Tem was sitting up with her palm over Pearl's ear. They both had their dark eyes trained on the bedroom door, but looked immediately to her for succor. Dawn had hardly broken, and the light coming through the window was a pale gray-blue, but she could see the terror on their faces. She stepped across the cold floor to their bed and took both of them in her arms, though she herself was shaking. She wondered how they would approach their father, and if it was possible to prepare herself to see her mother's corpse.

Prue had known her mother's death would come, but this did little to relieve the shock of her passing. All along, the family and neighbors had spoken in low voices of Roxana's illness and declining health, but Prue knew the name for what she'd witnessed, and though she dared not speak it aloud, in her heart she called it *suicide*. She could not reckon how one could call it anything else, when her mother had, after years of unhappiness, simply given up her desire to live and laid herself down to die.

As they lived through the first awful hours of that morning, Prue found herself wondering what her mother had been thinking the night before her death, under the influence of the Eugenic Water. She knew this line of reasoning availed her nothing, yet it was as if she saw her father and sisters through a scrim, so vivid were her imaginings. She wondered if Dr. Philpot's nostrum, or the proximity of death itself, had given her mother new expanses of vision, and if she'd seen Tem and Pearl, incandescent as water nixies, sharing a lukewarm bath in the kitchen, or her husband leafing through one of Pearl's books of art and architecture, the images rebuffing his gray eyes. She wondered if her mother had seen her fear.

As the evening had worn on, Prue imagined the ponderous eaves of the house had gone translucent as glass, the woodwork, masonry, and furniture like so much aspic. Perhaps for the first time in all the years Roxana had lived there, the old Dutch house had been full of evening light. She might have seen every woman passing on the Ferry Road with a baby in her shawl, every bare branch of the Winship cherry trees, and the broad dome of the evening sky, with dark wisps of cloud blowing past overhead. If she had looked out over the shipping lanes and roiling Manhattan, she would have seen the marshes of Jersey beyond.

Prue imagined that as evening fell in the workaday world, the sun grew brighter for the dead and those soon to join them. Roxana's own mother, Susannah Parker—from whom Roxana had not had even a letter since she'd run off with Matty Winship, and whom Prue pictured as no older than thirty and slim as a cattail—had come in with a picnic luncheon. She'd spread a cloth on Roxana's wasted lap, and set out a lard-fried chicken, pork ribs, a crock of potato salad, damson plums, and a jar of homemade cider. After all those weeks starving herself, Prue's mother sat up hungrily. Prue pictured Susannah Parker with a mole on her right cheekbone. Roxana's dead sister, Louisa, had come to sit by her feet, and struggled to keep in check all the wiggling infants who'd never been named. The largest had sucked happily on a rib bone. Other women, whom even Roxana did not recognize, had stood guard around the edges of the room, doing needlework far stranger than Pearl's. All those weeks, Roxana had not realized how famished she was. The day seemed warm, though she knew it was late winter. When she had finished her lunch, she lay back on her pillow and closed her eyes. The sun burned swirling patterns on the backs of her eyelids, and heated her cheeks till she was sure they would freckle. Metal cups clanked around her, and the womenfolk spat plum pits out through the empty walls. After a time, they finished eating and fell silent, but the breeze continued to play among the branches, and out by the river, the gulls began to cry.

Through the fog of all this imagining, Prue saw that Tem had returned to her bed and was bawling there, and that Pearl, in a daze, was drifting around the house, touching things. Prue ran out to the back fence and scrutinized the river, but of course there was no spirit ferry. Her mother had been a dire sinner—a person of no belief; a person whose despair had led her to neglect her family, and to value her own immortal soul as lightly as a cast-off feather—but wherever she had gone, it was not as simple as Manhattan. A passing schooner rang its warning bell, as if to tell Prue her reasoning was correct. The breeze seemed especially salty that day and stung her cheeks. She knew she should not wonder if her mother and Johanna had gone to the same place; she should go back inside, and help her family in whatever way she could.

To Recompense, half a lifetime later, she wrote:

I cannot wish you should die before me as that lies not within the bounds of any mother's heart. But neither do I wish upon you the task I performed that day of washing down my mother's body for the coffin. How many hundreds of times she had bathed me in my infancy, I could'n't say; but it seemed stark wrong to take a cloth & soap to that nude & lifeless form. Her skin had never look'd so pale, nor her hair so dull and orange, & when I held her in my arms, she weighed no more than Pearl. Abiah spent the morning stitching the shroud.

Prue thought her father seemed unnaturally subdued. She had heard him weeping that morning, but by the time he had come to tell his daughters their mother had passed, his eyes had been dry and his face expressionless. He had remained thus ever since. During all the months of her mother's decline, Prue had feared the way her father's floodgates would burst open at the loss of his beloved. She had imagined he would come unhinged, and had brooded over how she and her sisters would help him. Instead, he seemed as if a gun had gone off near his ear and he was momentarily deaf. He went out; Prue thought he'd gone to arrange for a funeral, but was relieved to discover he had been to knock on Israel Horsfield's door. Israel sent Ben and Isaiah down to keep watch over the girls and shepherded his friend to Mr. Severn's home. He left him there and went down to call off all operations at the distillery, except to commission the carpenter to build a coffin.

All that day and night, the people of Brooklyn came and went as Roxana lay, with her eyes closed with coins and her jaws bound shut with a clean strip of linen, on the cooling board—an old wooden door—in the parlor. She had candles around her, and a garland of rosemary, but Prue thought she could already smell the stench of the grave, and wondered others did not comment upon it. Ben wanted to hold her hand and bring her tea cakes and liquor, but she could do nothing but sit in a corner and cry. The wake passed in what seemed rather a jumble of events than a straight line, but she recalled seeing, from time to time, one of her sisters come unraveled and some woman of the town taking her upstairs or into her arms to recover.

Matty Winship stood dry-eyed and unshaven beside Roxana's grave the next morning. Everyone called it a sign that the first crocuses had shot up in the Congregational churchyard; a sign of what, Prue didn't know. All Roxana's lost infants were buried at the Reformed Dutch, but Matty had chosen this spot out of some fondness for or gratitude to Will Severn. Abiah had tried to convince Matty to shave and had laid out a clean shirt, collar, and cuffs for him, but he had put on the same dirty clothes from the night before. His daughters stood by crying—and Prue felt herself part of the chorus in some tragic ancient play—but he did not even shed a tear when he shoveled the first spadeful of dirt onto Roxana's hollow-sounding coffin. It was a terrible sadness to have lost her mother, but to see her sprightly father so evacuated of himself only compounded the loss.

All that day he stood tall, his large, dirty head bowed in deference, as friends, neighbors, customers, employees, slaves, and even his banker, Timothy Stover, came to offer their sympathy. Many brought gifts, as if, Prue thought, one could barter even a peculiar mother's love for some material thing: Peg Dufresne made half a dozen baked pears, and hid them in the cellar to prevent their being eaten by visitors; Ben must have sat up half the night punching holes in a sheet of tin, and presented Prue with a homemade lantern whose punches represented a delicate filigree of vines. Prue stuck a candle into its bottom and set it in the spot where the cooling board had lately lain. Could they have gone out to the shed together, this might have provided some comfort; but she did not long allow herself to consider the possibility. Will Severn took her aside that morning to offer his friendship and any help he might give. She could not bear the cedar scent of his clothes, the weight of his palm on her upper arm, or the aching sympathy his countenance betrayed, and she ducked away from him as soon as possible. She later saw him speaking to Pearl, who looked at him forthrightly, nodded from time to time, and kept turning new leaves of her book in passionate debate. Prue wondered at her self-possession. There stood a girl not even thirteen, blighted since birth and stunted in physical growth, who had recently lost her mother; yet despite all this, and the awkwardness of her method of conversation, she comported herself better than many an adult.

Prue was half frightened and half proud of her father's detachment and fortitude. She imagined he was waiting until he was alone to cry out to the heavens; and she set herself to wrap up her sniveling by day's end, in the event he needed her comfort later on.

He did not, however, appear to desire comfort; only sleep. When at last the house emptied, he sat his daughters and Abiah down at table. "I am sorry, Miss Browne, that your first year with my family should involve so much extra work, resulting from such sad events."

"I, too, am sorry," she said. She looked exhausted.

"I shall remunerate you fairly for your toil. I only wish it could have been in celebration of some happier event. Perhaps next time, it'll be my Prue's wedding."

Prue was too tired to fret about whether this contained a double meaning.

"Girls," he said, addressing Prue and Tem, who was slouched so deeply in her chair Prue thought she might slip out of it, "Mr. Horsfield can manage the distillery for a short while, but it is unfair to leave it under his sole management for long. I'll return to work tomorrow. You may do as you wish, but I'd like you back soon. The work will do you good."

Tem curled even lower into her chair.

What shall I do? Pearl asked. Prue had to crane her neck to read it.

"What do you mean?" their father asked, turning one palm up to face the ceiling.

What shall I do, to eese my Sorrow?

"You'll do as you always do, Pearlie. You'll focus on your reading and your needlework. Perhaps you'll be a good girl and help Abiah; she's quite a lot on her hands." Pearl's face was darkening by the moment, and their father's was following suit. "Do you want me to set you a task, gell? Teach yourself the French language. I'll bring you back a primer from my next trip to New York."

& what shall I do with it? With whm may I speak this French besides the Chardonnen's?

Tem buried her face in both hands, and Prue wanted to do the same; her father and Pearl had only, to her knowledge, had that single altercation three years since, but it had put the fear of God in Prue.

"What are you asking?" Matty demanded. "What is it you're trying to say?"

That I want to work. That I want some Jobb to compleat.

He shook his head and let out a great exhalation. Prue had not realized until then how he stank of liquor. "Pearl," he said. "I may not be a wealthy man, but I am mighty comfortable. None of you *has* to work; Prue and Tem want to, so they can carry on the family business, but if they did not want to, you would all three be women of leisure."

Pearl flipped angrily to a new page to retort, then stopped herself. She closed the book, worked the pencil through its hasp, cast Prue a reproachful glance, and left the table. "Well," their father said. He looked as if he'd been stung.

"I'll be back at work tomorrow," Prue said, and also pushed back from the table. Pearl's expression had made her shiver.

Tem said, "I, as well." They both kissed him on his stubbled, juniper-scented cheek, and went upstairs, Tem with her eyes wide in confusion.

Pearl was sitting on Prue's bed, and had lit a candle in the new lantern. *Damn his eyes,* she wrote when her sisters came in.

"Shh," Prue said. She felt it was she herself had been damned. "This is harder on him than you know."

"D'you think he'll cry now?" Tem asked.

"I do. I hope so."

Yet half an hour later, after they heard his two boots fall to the floor and the bed ropes creak beneath his weight, his room fell silent.

The next day was awkward at the distillery, but Prue would rather have been busy than have all her time to think, as Pearl did.

Thenceforward, their father was a man transformed. His care for the distillery was as meticulous as before, but the animating spirit had left it. He had always taken care of his appearance and worn clothes of good stuffs, although wort or basil oil might spill on them. Now he did not even brush his hair before drawing it back in its tail, and he sported a scrubby, grizzled beard. He no longer bothered to wear a cravat, so the neck of his shirt gaped open, and his coats started to wear thin at the elbows. One afternoon in the brewhouse, Prue overheard John Putnam say to one of his underlings, "Looks like Mr. Winship's out to win a new bride." Prue would have given her teeth to be able to strike him; instead, she stood up to her full height—admittedly, not very impressive, but the best she could muster—and stared him down. He later apologized to her, after the mash room had closed for the night.

Each day, Prue told herself grief took a good while to heal. As that winter blossomed into spring, and as spring passed into summer and summer to fall, she continued to miss her mother—or the mother she remembered from her childhood, who had been half melancholic and half minx. She understood, however, it was the natural order of things to lose one's parents; and she could see how it might be more difficult to lose one's chosen mate. Still, she kept waiting for her father's reserve to crack. All her life, he had been a man of good spirits and occasional temper; but Roxana's death had sucked away all his humor and fire. He no longer seemed to care if a batch of spirit came up proof, or if Tem, on a dare, climbed out onto the sails of the windmill. Surely, Prue thought, some circumstance would arise to raise his hackles, or make him laugh or cry; but whatever that circumstance might have been, it never seemed to come. In the meanwhile, Prue learned from Israel Horsfield that her father had told the truth about the Junto: Those men of even moderate learning were meeting at the Ferry Tavern Wednesday nights, to discuss such topics as whether Brooklyn should incorporate, the likelihood of bridging the East River, the necessity for organized street sweeping, and the practicability of forming a professional watch and a fire company. "Everyone is giving his all—who knew old Simon Dufresne still had so much vinegar in him," Israel told her when she accosted him out smoking a cigar by the retaining wall in the middle of the afternoon. "But your father never seems to do his reading, and contributes little to the discussion, except to second another man's point." He picked a stray fleck of tobacco from his tongue. He was squinting at her, either in response to the water's glare or as if not certain how much he could divulge. "Of course we all have sympathy for him. My children were much younger when my Amy died, and I didn't know if I could last a week without her."

"But you did. You have."

"Not without some heartache, and hard work as well. So we must pray your father turns the bend. We give him every opportunity at the club—offer him the choice of the next week's topic, every week. But he never takes us up on it. I still have my hopes the business'll turn him around."

"I, too," Prue said, then nodded, as if the double affirmative could make it so.

Eight

WINSHIP DAUGHTERS GIN

Matty Winship went on for years in the half-waking state he'd fallen into after Roxana's death. Though his blithe spirits had vanished, he maintained all his faculties, and fulfilled his responsibilities to the letter. Then, one bright morning in November of 1794, he came looking for Prue in the stillhouse, where she was shouting at the men to remove some wood from one of the fires. She had been delayed that morning, as she'd been engrossed in a report in the *New-York Journal* of Mr. John Jay's mission to avert war with England; and now she was in a foul temper. "Miss Prue," Matty said. She looked up and saw him standing there polite as a suitor, with a tasting beaker in his hand. "A word, please."

She had been sharp with the workers a moment before, but softened her tone, and stepped aside to speak with him.

"May I ask you to taste this?" he said, holding it out to her.

She glanced around; the men were all watching, but there was no time to go outside. She sniffed at the beaker. Its aroma was unremarkable, but the liquor had a peculiar harshness as it went down her gullet. She sipped it again, and noticed a distinct burnt flavor.

"Ah," he said. She must have pulled a face. "You notice it, too."

"It's off," she said.

"Five hundred gallons," he said, shaking his head.

"No doubt the next'll be better."

He continued to shake his head no. "I fear I've lost the trick of it," he said, as quietly as he could and still be heard above the room's roaring fires.

"Everyone gets feints every now and again. Even you." She felt odd, offering him comfort—it had always been his job to assure her ruined product was not a personal failing but built into the cost of manufacture. It was his money, after all, about to be dumped into the straits.

He looked preoccupied, and didn't answer her.

"Leave it for now," Prue said. "I'll finish this morning's rectifying, and you'll try again in the afternoon."

He let out a plosive breath and said, "Very well. I'll take over for you here." He put out a hand to touch her shoulder.

When she went to the rectifying house, she feared his feints had been due to some defect in the essences or the stills. But by the time the bell rang announcing lunch, she had made progress toward another five hundred serviceable gallons of Matthias Winship & Daughters gin, and expected it could go down to the casking house by day's end. After the lunch of pottage Abiah brought down from the house, Matty went back to the rectifying room, and ruined a hundred gallons of Prue's batch. Then he disappeared for the remainder of the afternoon. Some of the men said they'd seen him walk south on the Ferry Road. Prue would not have found him had she not borrowed a new English book on the varieties of bridge architecture from Cornelis Luquer and wanted to return it at the end of the day. Dusk was already falling, but when she rounded the bend into the Luquers' mill yard, she spied what she believed was her father's form, squatting on the roof above the trash rack, a few feet out over the straits. He must have had a handful of pebbles, as he was pitching something into the water. Prue wondered if her eyes were deceiving her—the river was flowing briskly and pebbles were unlikely to skip. "Father?" she called out, but he couldn't hear her above the current. "Daddy?" she said, more loudly, and moving closer.

He glanced over his shoulder at her, then settled back facing the water. When she crept onto the small roof behind him and put her hands on his shoulders, he still didn't turn around. "Feints again," he said.

She had difficulty hearing him above the rush of the water and the plash of the Luquers' breast-wheel. "I know. But what of it?"

"I'm turning all the rectifying over to you, beginning tomorrow."

"That isn't necessary. You've always said one day's feints can't ruin us."

"If you do well enough," he said, "I shall turn over the stillhouse also, and back down the line until the whole works is under your control." She sat down as well as she could on the pitched surface, crowding her legs up close to her chest, then pushed on his shoulder to force him to turn toward her. He did not look well even in the pinkish light shining in from across Manhattan. "This is senseless," she said.

"One day, you shall have to run the manufactory without me."

"When you're an old man."

"I'm an old man now. I'm fifty-two years of age, and a number of the friends of my youth are long since in the soil. I want to make sure you're properly trained."

"You've done that, these past dozen years." As he did not respond, she asked, "What responsibilities will you turn over to Tem?"

"None, I think." He smiled, and she could see one of his incisors had gone dark with rot. "Tem will never be your equal. She lacks discipline; she hasn't the knack for it."

"I have six more years' experience than she. She will yet improve."

He put his hand on the book she'd nearly forgotten she was still holding. "What's this?"

"I borrowed it of Cornelis."

"He wouldn't be a bad match. He'll inherit this mill and the property."

"But I'm not talking of marrying him. I'm returning a book."

"Picked the feckless little Horsfield, didn't you? You'd have done better with Izzy. He's the heir to the farm, a valuable piece of land, and he'll make a good foreman, if you have need of him."

Prue was uncertain how the conversation had taken this turn. "I'm not marrying anyone at present, and please don't call my friend feckless."

"I'm sure you're right. He only seems so in comparison with his brother." He patted the book's cover twice. "Return this to Cornelis, then, and we'll walk up together. I'm hungry for supper."

She did as she was told, and did not tell Cornelis about the queer exchange with her father. "That's my girl," her father said, when she returned to give him a hand off the roof onto the soggy bank. The light was fast descending; it would be winter soon enough. "You know I've always felt you're the one most like me: the one with the head for business, and the one who loves a project."

Prue felt a surge of pride tickle up her spine. Her father put his arm around her to warm her as they walked. Before she realized she was thinking it, she said, "I sometimes imagine you love Pearlie best."

"Bah," he said, "a man doesn't love one child more'n the next. Though I suppose he can keep a place in his heart for the one who carries on his trade." He squeezed her toward him. "I do love Pearl differently. If you were a litter of kits, I'd coddle the one that was lame or runted, or blind in one eye. That's the one needs caring most. But it doesn't mean one loves it more or less."

Over the course of that winter and spring, he absented himself from one aspect of the distillery's operation after the next, until at last, by the summer of 1795—when the United States Senate, to Prue's relief, at last ratified the treaty Mr. Jay had so skillfully brokered—Prue found herself in full command of the works, with generous help from Israel. This was the season in which yellow fever raged through New York, and Prue daily prayed it would not cross the water to Olympia or her slaves; and throughout the hot summer, only a few cases were reported in Brooklyn. Prue was twenty-three years old and uncertain of her abilities, but as her responsibilities increased, she rose to meet them, by dint of hard work, careful planning, and sleepless nights from which she rose wishing she could leave her mind in the kitchen when she went up to retire for the night.

One Wednesday evening during the harvest moon, Matty Winship went up to his Junto and did not return by the usual hour. Pearl had already scooped up her cat and gone to bed, and Abiah was asleep in her room off the kitchen, but Tem and Prue sat in the parlor trying to read the shipping news and watching the fire die down. "Must be quite a discussion," Tem said. "Do you know what their subject was this week?"

Prue shook her head no. "He tells me nothing of it. I think he only goes because Mr. Horsfield thinks it's salutary."

"Suppose he's drunk himself senseless."

Prue could picture him sprawled across one of Joe Loosely's tables with his head on his arms. If her father had fallen thus into oblivion, she knew Joe would pile logs on the fire and wrap him in a blanket. "Should we go fetch him?"

Tem looked to the grandfather clock, which had recently wound through its ten o'clock chime. "It is late."

"Come," Prue said, and led her sister to the kitchen to put their boots back on.

The day had been one of the last of Indian summer, but the damp breeze off the river that night spoke November to the marrow of Prue's bones. The Ferry Road was quiet. The Livingston and Cortelyou chimneys were letting off only fine wisps of smoke, and no sound rose from the Winship or Schermerhorn slave quarters down by the river. The Liberty Tavern also sounded quiet as the sisters approached, though Prue could hear some men laughing, a distance up the turnpike. Joe and his wife were eating fish and chips in the barroom; they turned to the door when Tem and Prue entered. "Hello, girls," Joe said. "It's late for you to be about. Annithing the matter?"

"We're looking for our father," Tem said. Prue had immediately seen he wasn't there. "We thought the Junto might yet be in session."

Annetje Loosely rose, wiping her hands on her apron. "No, that nonsense finished hours ago. Though they had a good book tonight—that British lady's *Vindication of the Rights of Woman*. Read it? I've not, but I hear it's sharp; of course, you girls already have some small bit of freedom, don't you? Well, I'm glad enough the men are discussing such things here in Breuckelen. I've some extra fish, if you'd like."

From across the room Prue caught an expression of concern on Joe's broad face. "Was he drunk when he left?" she asked him.

"He'd had his fill. He hasn't been home, you say?"

"No. With whom did he leave? You look anxious, Joe."

"Merely thoughtful." He turned to his wife, as if she might help him remember. "They all left together, 's I recall. Your father, Horsfield, van Vechten, Luquer, De Bouton."

Tem had both lips drawn between her teeth.

"I'll wager he's at the Twin Tankards," Prue said.

"Or he went home with Israel," Tem offered.

This seemed reasonable enough. "Or he's gone down to the works."

Joe wiped his mouth and hung his napkin over the back of his chair. "I'll help you find 'im," he said. "If he tumbled into a ditch, you'll need a man to get him on his feet again."

The night was overcast, and Prue had not thought to peruse the sides of the Ferry Road as they'd walked up; but she thought she would surely have sensed if her father were lying there. She tried to calm her heart, but it seemed it would jump until he was home safe.

Joe took his coat and escorted them out into the road. He would check the Twin Tankards while they knocked up Israel Horsfield. As Joe turned onto the pike, two drunken fellows came laughing and stumbling down toward the Ferry Road, both too slight to be Matty Winship. As they approached the crossroads, Prue saw it was young Jacob Boerum and one of his compatriots, returning no doubt from an evening's whoring at Tony Philpot's. "Lower your voice, there, Jake," Joe said as he passed them. "All the neighborhood's asleep."

"Exactly so, Mr. Loosely," Boerum said, leaning into his friend. A moment later he burst into laughter.

Through the Horsfields' parlor window, Tem and Prue could see a fire burning down, but no one was in the room. Their breath fogged the old, warped panes. "I don't want to wake them," Prue said. She had rather expected to see her father stretched out on the rug.

"I don't see we have any choice."

Israel Horsfield answered the door with a candlestick in his hand. Its flame threw his angular features into sharp relief. His sons were quickly down the stairs behind him. "We're sorry to wake you," Prue said, "but our father hasn't come home from the Junto. We thought you might have him here."

"Prue?" Ben said, pushing past his father.

She reached out to touch his face, and he wrapped his fingers around her own.

"No," Israel said. "No, we left together, but he turned off toward your house."

"He isn't come," Tem said.

"He should have been there more than an hour since." Israel wiped his hand down his jaw as he thought. Prue's heart redoubled its thumping; her own worry was discomfiting enough, but it spooked her to see both Joe and Israel concerned. "Wake Maggie," Israel told Isaiah, "and tell her we're going out to look for him."

By the time they were all dressed, Joe had returned to report no sign of Matty Winship had been seen at the Twin Tankards. "He must be down at the works," Tem mused, though Prue had seldom known him to go there at night.

Isaiah lit two lanterns and gave one to Ben, and they led the small party down to the water, which was a dull black. The wind was fiercer, down beneath the bluffs, and blew both lanterns out almost immediately. As Isaiah took them to the shelter of the brewhouse to relight them, Israel said, "We shan't need them." He cupped his hands around his mouth and shouted, "Matty! Hoy, Matty!" Some of the slaves began to stick their heads out from their quarters.

With the help of the slaves, they searched the entire manufactory in a quarter of an hour, and still no sign of him could be found. Prue could not stop shivering, and Ben stood with his arms around her on the hard-packed sand of the mill yard as they waited for the rest of the group to assemble. Israel and Joe were the last to join the group. "I don't know what to say," Joe said, coming up behind Tem and placing his hand on her shoulder.

"Should we drag the river?" Israel asked.

Prue could not bear to think of this; and as if likewise unwilling to entertain the notion, Tem asked, "Why so?"

Joe drew her closer in to him. "In case he's drowned, gell."

"I see no reason why Father should be in the river," Tem said, angrily pulling away from him. "Far more likely he is stone drunk in one of our own fields."

"She has a point," Isaiah said.

"It's a dark night," Joe said. "Better to drag in the morning."

"He's certain to be found in one of our fields," Tem repeated.

"We should comb the Remsens' and the Joralemons' as well," Isaiah said. "And whoever finds him, shout out for all to hear." He started toward the ravine, with the rest of the search party following behind him.

As they were walking up Joralemon's Lane, Pearl came running down it, and nearly ran headlong into Prue. Her hair was loose, whipping back toward Brooklyn in the stiff breeze. She could say nothing in such darkness. Prue took her by the shoulders and said, "Father hasn't come home. We're going to search the fields."

Abiah also ran up, and said, "The commotion wakened us. We came as quickly as we could."

"He is fine," Tem said, but she was hurrying up the hill.

The various parties walked the fields for hours, during which Prue heard no sounds but the call of her father's name and the crackle of boots over dead maize stalks and trampled wheat. Only the late barley was yet to be mowed, and had to be searched more thoroughly. Had the clouds cleared, it would have been a three-quarters moon, but in the darkness that prevailed, Prue could hardly tell on whose land she was standing. She could hear the river far below her. "It's no use," she said to Israel Horsfield when her party met up with his on the road.

Israel stamped his foot and turned as if he could see more in another direction. He said, "We'll simply have to try again in the morning."

Ben added, "We'll keep watch with you tonight."

Israel instructed one of the slaves, Actæon, to wait for other returning parties and send them home. As he and his sons walked with Abiah and the Winships back to their house, Tem said, "No doubt he is safe home by now, thumbing his nose at our worry."

He was not, however. The fires had burned down, and Pearl and Abiah set to building them back up. Abiah put water on for tea, and Pearl slipped the dough that had been rising by the hearth into the oven adjoining the fireplace. No one spoke, and as the hour progressed, Prue heard the other search parties dispersing and heading home. She curled up on Ben's lap on the divan and tried to take comfort in the smell of his hair and skin. She believed she had sat listening the whole night, but shortly past dawn she awakened to find her head on Ben's bony shoulder, the house perfectly still. A hoarse shriek rose up off the river, soon followed by another. Prue knew this was what had roused her; and soon Ben stirred, as did Israel Horsfield, in her father's chair.

"What is that?" she asked. She had slept with her neck in an odd position, and a sharp pain shot down it.

The shriek gathered into a cry for help. Someone fired a gun twice, and the cry continued. The voice tickled around the edges of her recognition until at last Israel said, "That's Cornelis Luquer."

The house smelled of the bread Pearl had baked. Prue rose from the divan and found one leg too full of pins and needles to support her.

The gun fired again, and Cornelis's shouts died down. As soon as she could walk, Prue went upstairs. Her sisters, who had also slept in their clothes, were rising from their bed; Pearl was tying her hair back into a tail. When Prue opened her father's door, his sheets were not even disarrayed.

Prue went out to the tumbledown fence, and at first could see nothing out of the ordinary. The sky was nearly white, as if it presaged snow. Her father's manufactory and the Schermerhorns' would not commence their workdays for two more hours, and the river was smooth, almost empty of traffic. A few minutes later, however, she saw the grain wagon set out from the Luquer Mill, up the Shore Road. Two men were riding the buckboard seat, and three others walked alongside. As the wagon rolled up the road, people began to join the procession, until at last a clot of a dozen neighbors trailed it toward the Heights. Prue watched it in silence a moment, then turned toward the house and called out, "Temmy? Pearl?" A gust of wind rose off the river and blew away the tarpaulin that had covered the back of the wagon. Two of those following the wagon ran after it and folded it, and one of them tucked it beneath his arm. Even from such a distance, Prue could see there was a body in the wagon bed.

Her sisters came outdoors and crossed to the back fence as slowly as Prue had ever seen them move, Pearl's brown skirt rustling across the dead grass. They stood beside her, and watched the procession up the road. The Luquer Mill was nearly half a mile distant from the Winship property, and Prue still could not make out the faces of the people in and around the wagon, but Pearl bent double and began to make a sound that would have been keening, could she have gotten enough voice behind it. That her cry was soft and raspy as the wind in the marsh rushes made it all the more awful to hear. Prue wanted to go out to the road to greet the wagon—she had no doubt it was coming for them, no doubt what it contained—but she wrapped her arms around Pearl's bent form and tried to make her stand upright. Pearl had wept her fair share over their mother and Johanna, but at that moment she seemed to have snapped in two; and Prue wondered if she herself might have done the same, had she not had her sister to look after.

The wagon cornered awkwardly at the foot of Joralemon's Lane, and Prue could now see Nicolaas Luquer driving and Cornelis beside him. Rem and Jens walked alongside the wagon, and Nicolaas's two blond Clydesdales bobbed their heads low as they drew up the steep lane. None of the men wore a hat. Tem walked back toward the house, muttering,

"No, no, no," and shaking her head, as if someone had incorrectly totted up a bill of sale. Abiah had to steer her back outdoors.

Pearl was still bent double, and Prue could not quit her side. This left Rem Luquer to unlatch the gate, and his father to drive the gentle horses across the yard. Those who'd followed the wagon milled in the road. When the wagon was halfway to the back fence, Nicolaas drew lightly back on the reins and dismounted. He patted himself down as if about to enter a church. "Prue Winship?" he said.

"You have found him," Prue said. Old Mr. Luquer breathed deeply, as if unable to find his voice. "How so?" she asked. She could hardly believe her own composure, or how quiet the day was.

Cornelis climbed down from the wagon seat. His coppery hair, which Prue rarely saw uncovered, seemed impossibly bright. "I heard something smash into the logs of the trash rack this morning," he said. He came up and put his hand on Prue's arm. Neither his voice nor his hand was steady. "When I went out to check it, he was bobbing and turning there, Prue, as would any flotsam intent on breaking the mill wheel."

"Oh," Prue said.

He withdrew his hand, and began picking nervously at the blunt tips of his fingers. Rem and Jens set out for the toolshed, to bring back the cooling board, Prue thought. Cornelis was shaking in earnest now. She remembered that he had seen his own brother drowned, and felt a shiver of empathy for him.

The Horsfields were coming toward them across the yard, and Prue could see how distorted their faces were by grief. "Christ, Matty," Israel said as he walked. Prue now realized she was the only person in this assembly too shocked to have any response but wonder. At that moment Ben grabbed her in so fierce an embrace he knocked her to the ground and stumbled on top of her. They were both startled enough to laugh, and the laughter unleashed Prue's tears. She began to sob, and though she thought at every moment she might manage to contain herself, she cried until her eyes burned and her ribs felt cracked open. Ben remained curled around her.

"Shh, now. You're all right," she heard Isaiah say. When she looked up, she saw Pearl sitting on the dead grass in his embrace. He was stroking the back of her skull as she mouthed an emphatic *No*.

Ben wiped his red nose on his shirt cuff and whispered, "I'm sorry I knocked you over."

She laid her head down on his bent leg, and listened to her own breath as it caught in her throat. Tem was still saying "No," with more and more force. Prue knew she should stand up, but felt she could do nothing but breathe in the smoky, gamy scent of Ben's trouser leg. She wondered why she had wasted so much of her childhood thinking about death, when all the thinking had done nothing to prepare her for the shock of it, no matter how many times it came to her door.

From the corner of her eye she saw Rem and Jens arrive with the cooling board and begin to unload the corpse from the back of the wagon. Prue rose, leaning on Ben for support as she did so, and walked over to meet them. Her father had not been in the water so long, but he had begun to bloat. His skin was mottled blue and green, and his belly pushed against the buttons of his vest. She looked at him only for a moment, but saw that something had already eaten out his gray eyes.

Israel sent one of the onlookers upferry for the doctor. Prue could not think why.

When Dr. de Bouton arrived at the house he wept over his old friend. He had been with Israel and Nicolaas at the Junto the evening before and, like the rest of them, had not remarked where Matty had gone on leaving the company. Not even he would conjecture if Matty Winship had drunk too much and slipped from his own retaining wall or if he'd stepped down with some darker purpose. In his pocket Matty had carried only his keys and Roxana's ring. He'd left his watch on his wife's small desk that afternoon, but had left no instructions about the distribution of his property. Prue found those he'd written years before stashed in one of the desk's cubbies. He had willed Prue the house, distillery, and land entire, with the provision she was to give Tem meaningful employ and the funds necessary to begin a family or business of her own, should she choose to do so; and she was to look after Pearl, to the best of her ability, as long as they both should live. She would gladly have traded all this wealth for her father to bang up from the countinghouse, swearing about some debtor in New York.

The neighbors rallied around the Winship girls and made certain they were well supplied with food. The women brought their needlework and sat by the fire, while the men saw the last of the Winship barley was properly harvested and stored. Patience Livingston—who, being too dull to have a social calendar, had found her niche in taking an overweening interest in the misfortunes of others—began to arrive with baskets of bread and elaborate-looking sweets. Tem refused to eat them, asserting, even in the midst of her grief, that "Patience Livingston's two eyebrows have grown together to avoid the sin of superfluity. I shan't eat anything with her taint on it."

The distillery shut down the day Matty was found; and Prue asked Israel to keep it so long enough for her to gather her wits. She was not, however, truly thinking, at least not about the business, or not in a productive manner. She kept returning to the river, as if it held some secret she might convince it to divulge, as if it might tell her what she had done to have earned such pain. She walked down to the millrace so many times, Cornelis came to tell her he didn't think it wise. He brought her up to his parents' house and coaxed her to eat a sandwich. Having been denied the opportunity to stand staring at the trash rack, she began going down to her own retaining wall instead. She felt certain it was the spot from which her father had embarked on his last journey; it would do as well as the spot at which he'd washed up.

She watched Losee row his ferryboat back and forth across the river as the days passed. The ropewalk belched forth as much smoke as ever, and at regular intervals, the Schermerhorns' men continued to load the vast spools of rope onto barges. Trade with the Continent and the southern and northern states seemed every day increasing, and each day more sloops and packets were moored in the deep water at Brooklyn. Only Prue's own manufactory was quiet, and even it, not completely so. As she stood staring one afternoon, she heard the slaves cleaning their quarters, and heard Owen's barrow squeak and clank across the damp, hard-packed sand. Two slender plovers were hopping at the water's edge a few yards off. Yet as she looked around her, at this view as familiar to her as anything in the world, she felt distant from it, as if she were a traveler newly arrived and too exhausted from her journey to care for the sights.

What a comfort it would have been, had she known where the dead resided. Manhattan was such an easy solution—big enough to hold every sinner in Creation, and with a various terrain of shoreline, creeks, city streets and winding country lanes, rocky precipices and rambling hillsides. In it was a place to suit any individual's preference, and sufficient goods and trade to supply an eternity of afterlife. Had her parents resided there, she would have boarded Losee's ferry right then, or had her men row her across, and besieged them with questions. It seemed tragic to have outgrown her childhood, all woolgathering and fancy, only to have become a sober woman with two sisters to look after and an inactive manufactory, losing money by the hour; because if she thought about her parents from an adult perspective, their fate looked bleak. Will Severn, out of either friendship or ignorance of the true manner in which Matty and Roxana had died, assured Prue and Pearl they were in Heaven, united with God. Even so religiously ill-educated a person as Prue, however, knew suicides had from birth not been among the elect; even she knew their sin was the ultimate sin, and they were damned. Tem argued their mother had taken ill, and their father had suffered an accident; then, too, in the days since their father's death, Tem had begun spending more of her time at the tavern. If Prue had to trust one of them was looking straight in the face of their situation, she would not have chosen Tem.

It was Pearl who suffered most. She spent most of her day weeping, her only solaces spending time in Will Severn's company, helping Abiah with the cooking, and stroking her cat. Prue wanted to tell her she was free now to do as she chose; but had she told her so, it would not have been true. She was free to continue assisting Abiah, and free to join Patience Livingston in her pious knitting, but Prue could think of no other comfort to offer her. Prue resolved that whenever the manufactory came to start up again, and whenever she recommenced making frequent visits to New York for deliveries and banking, she would continue her father's practice of bringing home gifts for Pearl. But Prue could not imagine when that would be, and knew no candied violets or French grammar could supply the want, or ease the sadness, her sister felt.

As for the distillery, a week after Matty's funeral, Israel Horsfield came knocking at the kitchen door. "I don't mean to intrude upon your grief," he said, "but I simply don't think we can leave off production any longer. We feed the slaves and keep them in firewood whether they work or no, and the hired men will leave us if they're too long without pay."

Tem had been out drinking with the Luquer boys the previous evening, and sat at the table holding a cool rag against her occiput. "Can they wait a little longer?" she asked.

Prue watched Israel weigh his response. Tem was only sixteen, but she knew the business better than anyone save Prue and Israel. Her opinion mattered. "A brief while," he said. "But we don't want to lose our men. Perhaps you don't understand how they live, who work for wages." Here he glanced apologetically toward Abiah, who did not seem to have taken offense. Israel looked haggard and let out a slight cough. "They haven't anything laid by. What we give them on a Saturday is gone to feed the children by the Thursday next, and they scrape for sustenance the week after."

Tem said, "Perhaps we're not paying them enough, then."

Both Prue and Pearl cracked smiles for the first time in days. Tem overdrank, and she could be insolent when caught in a mistake, but Prue liked her for considering this possibility.

"No," Israel said. He coughed again. "We pay as well as the ropewalk and better than the Longacre Brewery. The trouble is what they skim off the top in drink."

Here Tem looked at the ceiling, as if she were being lectured.

Pearl opened her book and wrote, *M' H, are you unwell?*

He cleared his throat and said, "No, only a tickle. Thank you for asking."

"Another week," Prue said. "I can't begin yet; but a week hence."

He nodded his acceptance and took his leave. A week thence, however, his cough had begun to rail in his chest, and he was confined to bed with fever. Prue supposed she could run the distillery without his assistance, but felt nervous about doing so; and she resolved to wait until he should recover to open the works.

His respiratory infection had come in off one of the boats and was sweeping through the neighborhoods near the ferry, including the slave quarters and Olympia, where many of the paid workers resided. As the second week passed, those who were well began stopping by the Winship house with gifts of eggs, salt pilchards, and dried apples; Prue tried to refuse these on the premise the givers needed them more than did she, but they entreated her to take them. She knew they were asking to work again, and she began to be anxious for Israel's recuperation. Even if half her men remained abed, she could resume production partway if Israel were well.

In anticipation of his recovery, she called Scipio Jones up to the house and asked him to repaint the side of the storehouse to read *Winship Daughters Gin*. Scipio was an old man, perhaps old enough it was unwise to ask him to climb a ladder, but he had been one of her father's first employees and had worked for him near thirty years. He wept when she asked this of him, but agreed to do it. Abiah sat him down and gave him a good, strong cup of tea; and Pearl went upstairs to get one of her father's silk cravats to give him. Of course, this made him cry the more. When he had settled down and drunk his tea, he told Prue a few of the less rooted men had decamped to the Longacres in Queen's County, and when he left, she resolved the works must reopen as soon as possible.

"The fires have been cold almost three weeks," she told Tem, before her sister went off for her evening's drinking. "Will you help?"

Tem pressed her lips together and made a wan attempt at a smile. "I don't see I have a choice," she replied. "There's a singer down at the Twin Tankards this evening. Would you like to join me?"

Prue shook her head no. She did not think her sixteen-year-old sister should be out carousing like a workingman, and knew the neighbors disapproved; but she said nothing, certain it would pass.

"Pearl?" Tem asked.

She, too, declined. After Tem had left, she wrote to Prue, *I shll help you.*

"Thank you. I'll think on what you might do," she said, but the thought fled her mind the next moment. She resolved to march upferry in the morning and tell Israel to mend himself.

Perhaps an hour after Tem left, however, Ben came to the kitchen door. He was breathing heavily when Prue let him in, and his cheeks were red from the cold. "What's wrong?" she asked.

"Father isn't at all well," he said. "He's asking to see you."

Prue and Pearl put on their coats, hats, and scarves, and followed Ben back up to his house. Maggie and Dr. de Bouton were both seated by Israel's bedside, and the sickroom stank of camphor and mustard plasters. Isaiah had been standing near the door, and retreated to the hallway to allow the others in. "Honey and thyme for the cough," de Bouton was saying. He obviously saw the terror on Prue's face, for he said to her, "He'll recover, Prue. Few of the cases have proven fatal, thank God."

Israel's face was greenish and waxy, however, and his breath was shallow, taken through the mouth.

"If you need me," de Bouton told Ben, "I shall stop in at the Twin Tankards and then return home for the night." His fingers were thick with arthritis, and it took him an age to close up his case. He nodded to Maggie and Pearl as he took his leave.

"Prue," Israel said. He sounded like an old man. "Glad you've come." He fumbled toward the bedstand for water, and Maggie lifted the cup to his mouth for him. "Listen, miss. It's going to be weeks before I'm well, and your father's tossing in his grave to see the distillery dark so long." He stopped for a breath. "You and Tem can manage; or Izzy, will you assist them?"

"Certainly," Isaiah said. Neither of the brothers enjoyed his apprenticeship on the farm, and both had long been considering what professions they might study to slip free.

"Good. Put the word out, start Monday. I'll be in soon 's I can."

"Do you need anything in the meanwhile?" Prue asked.

He shook his head no.

"Maggie?"

"Thank you for offering, no."

"Tell Tem she'll have to do her fair share," Israel said. "No more of this idling about."

Prue nodded, and she and Pearl both kissed his feverish forehead before they left. The next morning Prue wrote two copies of a sheet to hang up in the taverns, advertising the works' reopening the coming Monday; but before she could post the notices, Israel died of his illness.

The Winship and Horsfield houses were now both mad as Bedlam. All six sons and daughters were orphaned now, and Prue, Tem, and Pearl had barely recovered enough from their own loss to provide comfort to their friends. Ben and Isaiah were further in misery about the farm, which neither of them wanted, but which they did not believe they should sell. Prue, meanwhile, had been almost unable to consider running the works with Israel; without him, it seemed impossible, and she could not bring herself to start.

Within days of consigning his father to the ground, Isaiah had proposed marriage to Patience Livingston. When he arrived at the Winship house to tell them, his narrow face looked more pinched and anxious than ever. Prue, Tem, and Pearl were all horrified; Pearl threw up her hands, and Tem and Prue both shouted incoherently at the news.

"What?" Isaiah asked. His furtive misery made Prue wince. "I'm heir to my father's property. I can take a wife."

" 'What'?" Tem asked. "Dear God, you must be starved for comfort to choose such a creature as she."

An uncomfortable silence settled around them. Prue thought something similar, but had the sense not to voice it.

"Really, Isaiah," Tem said. "If you're desperate to marry someone, why not my sister? At least she's pleasant some of the time."

Prue swatted Tem on the head; and of course Tem's statement had offended Isaiah even more. "I should think the reasons I cannot marry Prue would be obvious," he said, but Pearl and Tem were still staring at him. "Indeed the question might rather be why your sister has not married elsewhere by now." Prue wondered if, despite how long she and Ben had carried on, her sisters did not know about him; or if they had divined her attachment to Mr. Severn and therefore thought Ben unimportant. "Besides which, it is Patience I fancy, and I think it stark rude of you, Tem Winship, to speak ill of her."

"I apologize," Tem said in an unconvincing tone.

"I came for your congratulations, you know, and think this a pauper's welcome."

"You have all our apologies," Prue said. "Of course we are glad for you."

But the ditch had been dug. Now, in addition to the potential misery of having Patience in the house every time she went to visit, Prue needed Isaiah for an overseer, and she could not ask when he was angry at her whole family. She began walking upferry with gifts, exactly as her workers had done: a chicken Abiah had roasted, fine bayberry candles from the Chardonnons' shop, a songbook Pearl was done looking at. He took all her gifts as stone-faced as his intended bride, but when at last she arrived with a gallon of gin, he invited her in to make some headway on it. He wasn't much of a drinker, but probably thought Ben would enjoy it, as well as Prue's company.

The liquor gave her boldness. "Isaiah," she said. Before her, beside her gin and in their mother's next-best china, was a cup of the tea the Horsfields all favored, which smelled, for all the world, of smoked bacon. "I need to reopen the works. I want to hire you in your father's place."

Ben, who'd been knocking his spoon around his teacup, stopped and said, "Hey?"

"I don't know," Isaiah said.

Ben repeated, "Hey!" But Prue knew what he thought: that she should have asked him, preferring his companionship; as if the counting-house were her bed.

"Hush," she said to him. "Later. Isaiah, I lose money every day the fires sit cold, and your father himself knew we were losing men to the Longacres. He wanted you to help us. My father thought the same."

Isaiah said, "It seems soon to think about anything."

"Not too soon to think about marrying," Prue retorted. Then to apologize she poured him another drink, though she didn't suppose he'd touch it.

"I don't know what to tell you, Prue. I am not ready. Even if I were, I'm uncertain I'd want to do it."

Prue shook her head no. "What else should you do, mind this farm? Who could be more precise and exacting a foreman than you?"

Ben replaced his cup in his saucer so loudly, Prue was surprised it didn't shatter. "Why do you ignore me?" he asked. "You shall have to coax my brother into this, while I'm eager for the work."

"Ben, we shall speak of it later, without fail. Isaiah, if you say me no, I will advertise for a replacement. But you must choose."

Ben stood, took his coat, and left the house without excusing himself. Maggie said, "Now you've done it," but Prue didn't care what she thought.

Isaiah looked as if Prue had rubbed his fur against the grain. "I know what our fathers wanted, but none of us imagined it would come to pass so soon."

"Exactly so," she said. "And do you want to manage this farm? Or do you think Patience will consent to marry you while you apprentice yourself to some trade? I'll pay you half again more than your father earned. You'll keep the accompts alongside me, so you'll see it plain."

"Christ, Prue, I don't think you'd lie to me." His eyes looked mournful. "I'm sure you're correct, this is what I should do."

She reached across the table for his hand. "Monday week. Take the night to think it through."

He nodded solemnly. "I dislike you all speaking so ill of Patience. Ben as well. I don't take it kindly."

"I'm sorry," Prue said. "We shall find a way to be friends. Where do you suppose I'll find him? I should apologize in that quarter as well."

Maggie said, "I think I heard the barn door open."

Prue could not imagine what the house would be like, with both her and Patience in it. Maggie seemed to hear the thought, and drew herself taller in her chair. As Prue stood, she said, "Tomorrow, Isaiah. I shall entertain high hopes till then." She let herself out their kitchen door and stood in their muddy yard overlooking the Shore Road and the straits. It was a warm, gray November afternoon.

Losee rang his bell below and cried, "Over!"

"Ben Horsfield?" Prue said as she walked over the dead grass toward the barn. She noticed the Horsfields' apple trees had a few last fruits hanging among their shriveled leaves.

The barn door creaked open. Ben stood leaning sullenly against the doorpost. The moment he saw Prue walking toward him, he backed inside.

He'd lit a small oil lantern such as the one he'd given her, and it cast speckled light on the floor. The two horses stamped and burred as she entered, and a rat streaked across the rafters. "I've come to apologize," she said.

He closed the door and latched the hook and eye, which had proven invaluable in their childhood games of war. He took her hand and sat down in the center of the hay-strewn floor. He kissed the side of her face, and a flicker of electrical current traced the path his lips made, as if a storm were brewing over Jersey. He said, "Why does it matter what our fathers wanted? They're both gone."

"But Isaiah has exactly the temperament for the countinghouse. You wouldn't be happy at the 'factory all day."

"I'd rather be with you, at the distillery, than wondering what sort of beetle's got into my damned corn."

Prue laughed and stroked his hair. Her body reached for his like a horseshoe for a magnet, but she held herself in place. The horses, apparently satisfied she wouldn't make any more ruckus, snorted and resettled themselves.

"At all events, I shan't be a farmer," he said. Prue took this for the same sort of posturing that had made him say as a boy he'd be a pirate, and she kept smiling at him. "It's not a joke. Isaiah and I have spoken. He'll hire a man—perhaps one of Patience's cousins from Flatbush— and I shall become a surveyor."

"Oh, come," she said, and tapped lightly at his breastbone. "And survey what? We know the bounds of every holding in Brookland, and it's too late to mark out the plots for Olympia."

"Not here, Prue. Whom could I learn it of here? I shall go to Boston, to apprentice myself to Hiram Bates."

This Mr. Bates was well known, rumored to be a burly, boisterous man. "Surely there's naught left to survey in Boston? Any more than here?"

Ben pushed a loose hair back from her brow. "He lives there. I'll spend three or four months in the workshop, learning the use and calibration of instruments. From there, after the thaw, we journey out past Albany and Troy, and thence westward, into the open territory formerly of the Iroquois Nation. There is a great need for surveying now, as so many wish to settle there. I had planned this before Father died. Before any of this had come to pass."

Prue knew she should congratulate him, exactly as she should have congratulated Isaiah, but could only ask, "Why did you not tell me sooner, then?"

He stroked her temple again. She was irked at him, but she butted up against his hand like a cat. "I was waiting to work up the nerve. Some days I imagined you'd give up your training to come with me, others I knew you never would. Now, of course, you can't." He drew his lower lip between his teeth briefly, as if waiting for Prue to contradict him. "In truth, a surveying expedition is no place for a woman."

"I'm not a rosebush," Prue said. "I needn't be swaddled against the weather."

"But you wouldn't leave your business, either."

Prue was as vexed with him as he had been with her in the kitchen. "I'm not certain I understand. A moment since, you were angered because I choose to employ your brother over yourself; and now I learn you've planned to leave all along. Which is it?"

"A choice. If my life is my own, I shall learn surveying and travel the land. If it is not, I would assist you in your work. But I shall not remain in Brookland tilling a few acres of sandy soil."

"I am bound to my father's business," Prue said. "Shackled, with irons." He tried to stroke her hair again, but she took his hand and held it in her own. "You may decide whether you stay or go, but I should be happier if you remained."

As she said it, however, she wondered if, in fact, she meant it. She would be running the distillery and would have little time for dilly-dallying; and then, too, if he left, she wondered how her relations with Will Severn might progress. She tried to banish the thought.

"If I do leave," Ben said, "I give you my word I'll come home again as soon as I'm able." He kissed her; but she knew Maggie and Isaiah were watching the barn door from the kitchen, and she extracted herself as quickly as she could.

The next day, Isaiah came to the house with his hat in his hand and asked for his father's position. Prue held him close. Abiah clucked at her and said, "Sakes, woman, it's not as if he's asked you to wed him."

"Truly, I think it better," Prue said.

When Prue at last posted her bills that afternoon, they named Isaiah Horsfield as the distillery's new manager, and the date of reopening as the third week of November 1795. Prue knew events of greater moment took place in the world—France had just set up its Directory, for example, and Prue understood that country's tumult in recent years made anything that had gone on at home look like a squabble in a chicken coop—but in Brooklyn, Winship Daughters Gin was all the week's news. Wherever Prue went, men who might once have scoffed at the idea of a girl taking over a manufactory paused to shake her hand. Simon Dufresne stopped her in the street to hug and congratulate her, and when she pulled free of him, she thought she saw his eyes glisten. When she took her first trip to New York—she had a great deal to see to there, in the acquisition of supplies, the appeasement of creditors, and the hiring of men to replace those who'd gone to the brewery—she brought Pearl home a cone of candied violets, then tormented herself with anxiety over what a paltry gift they now seemed, as a reminder of the dead. And a few days before the distillery reopened, Ben lit out for Boston. He kissed her a long good-bye before climbing aboard the ferry, and promised to write as soon as he was settled. She did not have time that week to sit home and brood about his departure, but it was difficult to lose him, no matter how ambivalent her feelings toward him. Late in the winter, one of Patience's cousins would arrive to superintend the farm; and for the nonce, Isaiah thought he could make do with his hired hands.

On the Monday Winship Gin was to begin operating under her official direction, Prue awakened with a hollow feeling in her stomach, deeper than hunger, less desperate than grief. It was as if that morning she possessed, for the first time, a true understanding of the breadth of the world and of her insignificance within it.

Yet it would be no small task to run the distillery. She had been doing so, of course, for years; but while her father lived, she had always known she could turn to him for advice, no matter how sunken his spirits. The emptiness in her stomach reminded her that, for all her years of training, in her heart she had never believed this day would come. Her father had taught her everything from the mathematics of bushels and barrels to the arcana of bouquet; yet the Reverend Mr. Elihu Juster Winship had lived to be seventy, and she'd expected no less from her father. She had always imagined she and Tem would apprentice into their forties, and would together run the business half by instinct—they would, by then, have lived more than half their lives within its enclosure—and half by the freedom granted the old of good standing to quack on about their obsessions without exciting notice. (Her exemplars were the brothers Hicks, who probably dreamed their very dreams in rods and acres, and the irascible old Mr. Patchen, out past the Philpots', who sat each day on his stoop with a loaded musket in his lap, lest a second civic-minded citizen approach to inquire whether a streetlamp and footpath might be erected upon his property for the public weal.) Prue did not really suppose she, Tem, and Isaiah could run the distillery into the ground; but she recognized it was a business with as much worth in its name as in its coffers, and she felt the burden of upholding that reputation.

Prue cracked the thin layer of ice that had formed over their wash-bowl during the night. If she couldn't control her mind's propensity to worry, she could, at least, see to her body.

She and Tem picked at their breakfasts that morning, but as they walked down the lane, the very set of Tem's shoulders—back and down, so her breastbone rode high—expressed her eagerness to face her new responsibilities. "You don't feel ill at ease?" Prue asked her.

"Of course not. You're the one who'll have to make the speech to the workers." She glanced over to her sister, obviously delighted to have discomfited her. "As I see it," she went on, kicking a pebble down the lane, "very little has changed, as far as the distillery is concerned. We shall keep doing the work we've been doing, exactly as before. I think the only difference will be the suitors lined up outside our door."

"Really," Prue said.

Tem shook her head as if Prue were a dour old maid. "You'll see."

If the men doubted the sisters' ability to run the works, they kept mum about it; many of them wore bright expressions when Isaiah rang the bell to gather them in the assembly hall. ("They haven't worked in a month," Tem whispered. "You'd be happy, too.") He had lit a fire in the stove, and the room was cozy.

"Gentlemen," Prue began. Her voice wavered, and someone shifted his weight, causing the floor to creak. "Gentlemen, it has been a trying month for Winship Gin. We have lost both my father and Mr. Horsfield, God rest their souls." She saw Tem pull a face at this. "And I know it has been a month of hardship for those of you who have lived without your wages and meaningful employ. I thank you all for having faith in this distillery, and for being here this morning." Speaking to the men turned out to be less difficult than she had supposed. "Protocol will be chiefly as it has been for the past year. You will refer your inquiries to me as the sole proprietor of this distillery; in my absence, you may consult Miss Temperance. We have also a new foreman for the works. I introduce to you Mr. Isaiah Horsfield, son of our late and most wise manager."

Rather to her surprise, the men began to clap; and Isaiah, who looked as if his stomach had eaten itself out from the inside, removed his hat and made a deep, awkward bow.

"Very well," Prue said. She had no idea how to finish. "We will commence the first mashing in a quarter hour. Those of you who work in the stillhouse, rectifying house, and cooling house should begin to scrub down your places of employ."

Many of them lingered by the stove a moment before heading out. Neither Tem nor Isaiah said anything to her, but Prue felt she had at least not botched her performance. She felt her father's watch ticking in her waistcoat. It was an unfamiliar sensation; it called to mind how it might feel to hold a sparrow to her breast.

By sundown, they'd managed two mashings and gotten the wort safely to the cooling floor and the fermenting-back. Prue had heard of no waste or accidents, and more grain was set to arrive the next morning. Prue knew her father would have counted such a day a success.

After closing, Tem ran up to tell Pearl they'd run the business a day without mishap, and Isaiah stayed behind to tour the works with Prue. He knew nothing about distilling except what he'd gleaned at the supper table, but she could not at present afford the kind of thorough education her father had given her; she would teach him everything she could on the fly, and send him back for his apprenticeship later. He made extensive notations as they inspected the tuns, the cooling floor, and the wort, but he kept glancing at her. At first she ignored him, but when they climbed back aboveground from the fermenting room, she turned to him and asked, "Do you have a question?" Night was coming down quickly, but she could see she'd caught him off his guard.

"No," he said. "That is, I have a thousand, but they'll all be answered in due time. I wonder if you've heard from Ben."

"I don't think there's been time for a letter to arrive from Boston. Do you?"

"No, and he isn't much of a writer. I imagine when you do hear from him, there'll be as many blotches as words." Isaiah nodded. "I miss him," he said. "I've spent every day since he was born in his company." He brushed at his lapel. "Though perhaps it's worse for you."

Prue said, "I wonder what he's told you."

"Oh," Isaiah said, and laughed quietly. His laugh always sounded uncomfortable, as if it grew rusty through infrequent use. "I'm sure it's not to share, what a brother says in confidence to his brother. But I daresay he loves you."

After all the misery that month had brought, Prue's heart warmed to hear him say it.

This intimacy must have discomfited Isaiah, however, for he patted more briskly at his lapel and said, "So how many days will it be before we have the product our sign advertises? Our first batch of Winship Daughters gin?"

The evening wind was picking up, and made a hollow sound as it whistled through the buildings. Prue did not know why his question had driven all their losses home. "By the end of the week. But we age it awhile. We'll be selling Matthias Winship's for some time yet."

"Everyone knows it was yours anyway," Isaiah said. "Or at least, so my father told me."

"Do you think they can see us now?" she asked. She pulled her coat tighter around her. The watch tickled her ribs.

"I have no doubt. They are looking down from Heaven as we speak. They're probably continuing their Junto, still talking about the merits of a bridge, but now with all the great thinkers to assist them. Plato and Aristotle, perhaps even Euclid himself." He put his arm around her shoulders and turned her toward Joralemon's Lane. "Come, it's growing cold. We should both get home to supper."

Prue began to walk but could not help saying, "My father cannot have gone to Heaven. He cursed God and the church all his days, and took his own life."

"You don't know that," Isaiah said.

"I do, though."

He pulled the gate shut behind them and bound it with its rope. "Well, he was a good man, and a winsome conversationalist. He'll have realized his mistake and done his best to remedy it."

If Isaiah Horsfield had never done anything more for her—had he not been her friend and supporter in all the endeavors yet to come, nor proven an even more able manager than his father had been—Prue felt she would have been indebted to him for life for saying that to her, and for walking her to her door that dark November evening.

Nine

THE DREAM

S lightly more than two years after her father's death, on the morning of her twenty-sixth birthday, Prue awakened from a vivid dream in which she'd been the pilot of that same spirit canoe she'd imagined as a child. Like many of her nights of dreaming, her birthday eve had been a whirlpool of images and anxieties—her overseer, someone who both was and wasn't Isaiah, had vanished; an entire shipment had gone down in the straits while she'd stood moored to the retaining wall, unable to dive in or shout for help. But it was the image of the spirit canoe that remained with her when she awakened.

Even twenty-four years later, when she recounted the dream to Recompense, she could recall the sound and feeling of paddling the canoe toward Butcher's Wharf, on which Pearl stood wearing a flimsy white dress of republican cut. Pearl's hair, ordinarily so fine and dark, was a blazing mandorla of fire, and her pale chin and throat glistened pink with blood. Prue pulled the paddle back into the canoe and allowed the boat to drift toward her sister as she watched the blood trickle down the bosom of Pearl's dress and form a spreading stain. When Pearl opened her mouth, Prue could not see her teeth for all the gore; and in a sudden flash of understanding, she knew she herself had cut out Pearl's tongue and thus hastened her on her journey to the beyond.

Prue glanced down in shock, and saw her own knees were draped in a moth-eaten gray cloak and her hands were ashen as the water of the East River. She reeked of kelp and fish. As her canoe drifted toward the landing, it bobbed in the wake of a swift fore-and-aft schooner, gliding out toward Nutten Island and Upper New York Bay. (Here Recompense paused to wonder why her mother did not call the Governor's Island by the name it had been given forty years since; but there were some things, she realized, she would never understand.) As her vaporous craft bumped against the wharf, Prue found herself appalled by what she'd done. Even in the midst of the dream, she recognized the injury she'd given Pearl as bearing a "symbolickal relationship" (as she wrote to Recompense) to the metaphysical crime she'd committed against her in childhood; but though she felt an immediate stab of remorse, she could say nothing to her. When she opened her mouth, nothing came out but wind.

Pearl gathered her skirt awkwardly around her with one bloodstained hand and crouched down with the other extended to offer payment for her passage in cockleshells. Prue opened her mouth wide and lifted her tongue to accept the briny offering. The shells stung the delicate ligaments, as if to remind her how it had pained Pearl to have them severed. Prue spat the shells into her boat's pitched hull, already littered with the fares of the unlucky and taking in water through a leak plugged with an oily rag. In life, Pearl moved with grace, as if the elegance of her carriage could make up for her raspy silence, but in the dream, she wobbled as she settled in the canoe's bow to face her sister. The empty shells cracked beneath her good cloth shoes, which were soon stained dark with water.

Prue pushed off, turned the boat to face westward, and began to paddle. The water offered little resistance. Traffic glided by all around her, fishing boats steering clear of the lumbering square-riggers, and she feared someone would cry out about the hideous work she'd done upon her sister. No one did. It was dusk, and the men loading goods on the docks of Winship Daughters Gin and the Schermerhorn ropewalk were so weary, they paid the straits no mind. Losee van Nostrand rowed toward his landing without seeing her, and wearing a thoughtful expression on his broad, sunburned brow. Prue tried to concentrate on paddling, so the image of her maimed sister would not hew to her memory.

But Pearl's nimbus of fire cast a red glow on her eyes, her bloody face and hands, and the gray water. To an onlooker on either shore, Prue thought her boat would be a shimmering memento mori; but for the first time in her memory, the river was going unremarked. Her sister, having apparently lost her notebook, raised a finger and pointed over Prue's shoulder. Prue kept a steady rhythm with her paddle, to the left and to the right. Pearl continued to point, and after a time, Prue once again drew the paddle in, its blade spraying droplets into the river, and allowed her canoe to drift southward with the tidal current. She looked up to see what had drawn Pearl's attention.

And past her left shoulder, a mighty structure arced over the water. It was a bridge, moored to the rocks of the river's twin towns and traversing the straits in a single span. The shape of the bridge was revolutionary and, even in her role as Charon, brought her breath up short.

To her daughter, she wrote,

By now you know well how I had hoped since childhood to find a way to bridge the roiling straits that separated my home from that nearby city. On a practical level, I wished to do this for Brookland's sake,—to ease the transport of produce & Schermerhorn rope & my gin,—but as time wore on, I began to wish to do so even more for the sake of your grandfather's memory. I imagined he had loved New-York with something like my fervour, and though he'd mentioned it only that once & in passing, I knew he'd loved me because I, like him, had possess'd a head for projects. He had been grateful for the river's transport & the power it supplied to his stills; and whether by his choice or accident, it had taken him. It had *taken him*; I could not bear to think long on how. I wanted a bridge to honour my love for my father, and to honour those terrible phantasies that had so afflicted me as a child; & I wanted a bridge to lay them to rest.

Until that moment, I had not, however, been able to reckon how anything could be built across the broad East River without grossly curtailing the passage of ocean-going ships. I had, a few years previous, read a *Treatise on Bridge Architecture*, and had seen therein, with my own eyes, the aqueducts of Rome side by side with various constructions of timber & iron in Europe & the Americas; I had seen the steeply pointed bridges of the Chinese, drawbridges and rope bridges, & swings made of living vines by the natives of the world's deep jungles. I had read with interest of Pritchard & Darby's iron bridge at Coalbrookdale and of the former's plans for a nearby masonry bridge, with elegant pierced spandrels. Cornelis Luquer & I had debated about a Mr. John Smeaton's invention, while he built a lighthouse at Eddystone, of a sort of mortar of calcified lime that could set underwater & remain impermeable to that corrosive element evermore. Yet nor the wisdom of the ancients nor the great modern thinkers on angles & abutments could tell me how I might hope to span anything broader than Gowanus Creek without letting the weight of the structure rest at intervals on piles driven into the riverbed.

Yet I knew it was possible. The previous summer, Cornelis had constructed a springboard high over the millpond, that his eight younger sibs might avail themselves of some healthful recreation when their work was through, & keep clear of his business in the tidal mill &c. When he boasted to me of it and suggested I might give it a go, I my self rode down with the distillery's wagon next day to drop off the slops for his mother's pigs & to fetch the first load of the day's ground grain. There,—high above that same pond in which the Luquers & Horsfields & my sisters & I had brawled & attempted to drown one another many a happy summer day,—stood a jumble of dripping, laughing Luquer children, their sundry types of carroty hair all wet to a uniform cinnamon brown. Eelkje, the smallest, was at the outside of the group curled picking at her pink foot. The springboard was bent rainbow-wise under their weight, but even when Jens,—who ought to have been on his way to work, and not goading his brothers & sisters into a phrenzy,—jumped lustily to get the thing abouncing, it held; and it pitched them into the air with a satisfying rattle, Eelkje tumbling gleefully off behind. Jens spied me from the water, & wiping the wet hair from his eyes, cried out for me to jump in, too; but though the day was hot and the pond enticing, I had the distillery to 'tend to. I meanwhile also had an inkling the springboard might have aught to do with my idea of building a bridge, but my errand was foremost in my mind.

The dream, however, at once revealed to me, as only a dream can do, that Cornelis's springboard *was the answer*:—for all it required was that a lever projecting over the water be sufficiently anchored & strong enough to bear the weight at its tip. Cornelis's board was perhaps eight foot in length, of a single plank's thickness, and could hold up a whole rowdy clot of Luquers. Could not two boards, placed tip to tip across the breadth of the pond, support every child in Brookland? Could not a similar construction of a number of planks' thickness cross Gowanus Creek solidly enough to let a horse and cart pass over? *This was how my bridge would work*;—two gigantic springboards, end to end. The dream did not spell this out for me in good English prose, but the idea was manifest perfectly. It would be strong & supple enough to support the burthen of traffick, yet soar high enough above the water, the masts of tall ships would not touch the parabola of its backbone. I was well nigh certain no bridge had yet been attempted upon this plan, but this fact excited rather than discouraged me.

Pearl's whole bodice, meanwhile, was stained with streams of red, and the blood trickled down her arms. Prue yearned to ask her sister's forgiveness, but still found herself with no voice. When she tried to speak, she managed only to blow Pearl's flaming hair toward New York. She began to paddle more quickly, steering the boat for the Fly Market wharf, where someone was sure to pounce upon her for her crime. But Fly Market was empty. The only sound Prue heard as she approached the landing was the mournful cry of a gull swooping down over the water. When the airy substance of her boat struck the gray-green pilings of the abandoned wharf, the jolt shook her awake.

She was relieved to find herself in Brooklyn, in the bedroom she'd slept in all her life. Some willow branches she'd tossed on the embers late in the night were crackling. Pearl was asleep on her side in the other bed, under the eaves. She was curled toward the wall as if it afforded her protection, and her long, fine hair spilled back over the sheet and toward the floor. Tem had moved to the room across the hall after their father had died. This suited Pearl and Prue fine, as her restless sleep had often kept them both awake.

It took Prue what seemed an hour to quiet her heart and recover from her guilt over what she'd dreamed of Pearl. It seemed one thing to utter a mindless curse as a child, but quite another to concoct such a gruesome crime in one's sleep. After a time, however, she soothed herself, and found her mind still buzzed with the image of the bridge her dream had brought her. Her practical guides, until then, had been few: the wooden balconies she'd designed for the distillery, the other work she'd engineered and witnessed during the distillery's expansion, and the three stone beaver dams that galumphed across Gowanus Creek. She had known the jumping board contained the key, but had not been able to figure out how. The books she'd inherited from her father contained engravings of the Pantheon at Rome and the Hagia Sophia of Constantinople, which inspired her but did not provide models for what she wished to build. She and Cornelis had acquired every book on the subject they could find, but even the thoroughgoing *Treatise* had not described a bridge that could cross the East River without disrupting it. People in both New York and Brooklyn—with the notable exception of Losee van Nostrand—had griped intermittently about the need for a bridge as long as she could remember, and proposals had been put forth and hotly contested. Telford's drawbridge was the one she recalled most clearly, but she also remembered an eager debate at the Old Stone Tavern in her childhood. She had been standing at her father's elbow, choking in the haze of tobacco smoke, when Joe had produced a newssheet featuring a design by an eminent Frenchman (if memory served), for a bridge modeled after the Ponte Vecchio in far-off Florence. Joe, after traveling around to exhibit it to every man in the barroom, with a particular flourish toward Prue, retired to a table to pore over it and smoke his pipe.

"No," he'd said, shaking his head as if the drawing truly made him sad. "No, I say it is *too damned ugly* for this New World!" And with a comical growl, he'd leapt from his chair and tossed the sheet into the fire, to general applause from the menfolk of Brooklyn.

It was always thus, Prue thought, with a bridge: Its merits might be weighed, but unless it was perfect, it would come to nothing. Every bridge that had yet been proposed for Brooklyn had either been too fanciful or too mundane, too expensive to build or too disruptive.

But as she sat up in her creaking bed that morning, she thought if she could prove her bridge as sound as her dream of it was beautiful; if she could draw it, and build a working model; and if it could be accomplished at reasonable cost, it might be possible to build it. People from Loosely's tavern to Mayor Varick's office across the water would stand behind such a proposition, for everyone knew the East River needed a bridge. Few had believed her father could train up a girl to be a distiller, and it had been done. Why could she not, by dint of research and that same diligence that had brought her all her success thus far, propose a viable plan? She suspected it would be a more complex and finical operation than managing a distillery, but not by an order of magnitude.

Pearl sighed in her sleep and rolled onto her belly. Prue wished she could still gather her up in her arms, as she'd been able to do when Pearl was small. She was sorry to have dreamed of killing her. She'd already in-jured Pearl enough for one lifetime, and brooded on it ever after; her imagination had rehearsed each fashion in which Pearl might come to know of her misdeed, and rejected them all as too awful for further con-sideration. For a moment, she wished she could sweep the dream aside, no matter how beautiful the bridge had been.

The sky beyond the whorled glass of the bedroom window was black. It could only have been three or four in the morning; but though it was January, with a late-rising sun, in a few hours' time Tem and Prue would need to be supervising the distillery. Pearl slept on as Prue sat in bed and watched the dawn steal across her patch of wall. When the fire had died out, she arose and went down to the kitchen, her feet falling into the grooves they'd helped wear in the back stairs.

Tem was at the table, wrapped in the remaining tatters of their fa-ther's red robe and poring over the distillery's account books by the light of a candle. Her dark hair was rumpled, as if she'd worried it while she ciphered. When she looked up, the light cast deep shadows beneath her close-set eyes.

"What are you doing?" Prue asked quietly. Abiah was still sleeping, and deserved another hour's rest.

"The accompts," Tem said. "For your birthday." Beside the book was a paper covered with scribbles, tots, and tallies. "I know what you're thinking," she said, raking her ink-stained fingers along her scalp. "I'm checking my sums."

"It's kind of you to do the books," Prue said, "but Isaiah would have done them in the morning." She reached for the tumbler at Tem's elbow, and though Tem put out her hand to swat her, she did so halfheartedly, or too slowly to effect her desired result. Prue sniffed the glass and took a sip to be sure of its contents. She had guessed she'd find their own gin inside—and it turned out to be a good if unripe batch, redolent of car-damom. She took another sip and felt it shimmer down her pipes.

"I don't want a lecture, Prue," Tem said. She laid her forehead down on her crossed arms. Prue knew she had probably been awake, and cranky about it, for hours; but it still stung to know Tem's first thought was that she would deliver a sermon.

"I won't, Tem. I wouldn't."

"Go," Tem said lazily into the table. "Go back to sleep, or go fish oysters from the millpond, but please don't stand there watching me count."

Prue wanted to put the kettle on, but Tem looked so exhausted, she knew the noise of building a fire would grate on her. Tem's coat was on the chair by the door, where she had probably flung it after a late-night ramble, and her boots lay on their sides nearby. Prue pulled these things on as quietly as she could and went out into the morning—the first day of her twenty-seventh year, and a gray Tuesday dawn, promising what looked to be another year of hard work and unfavorable weather—to gaze out at her beloved East River.

She remained out by the back fence until the day turned brighter and the cock began to crow. When she returned to the kitchen, the sound of the door closing awakened Tem, who had fallen asleep over the ledger. The sound also startled Pearl, who was crouched making a fire in the hearth, wearing a threadbare blue jumper Prue had knit her ten years before. After Tem saw Prue, she saw the blotch her pen had left on the accounts and said, "Shit."

Pearl turned from the hearth and replied with alacrity, *Language!*

"Hoy, who's awake?" Abiah said from her bedroom. She sounded as if she'd still been sleeping.

"All of us," Prue answered. "Sorry to've woken you."

"No matter. I'll be out shortly."

Tem picked sleep from the corner of her eye.

"How much did you drink?" Prue asked. Tem continued to pick her eye. Prue asked, "Will you have one egg or two?"

"Enough to ascertain its quality," Tem said, and it took Prue a moment to realize she'd answered the first question.

Pearl placed the heavy skillet on the hob. She already had a pot on to boil Tem's singular egg. As she was reaching for the butter crock, Abiah came out from her room, braiding her hair as she walked. "Leave it, Pearl, I'll do it. Happy birthday, Prue."

"Thank you," Prue said.

She watched Pearl as they ate breakfast. Pearl could no more intuit the grisly thing Prue had dreamed than prognosticate the next month's weather, but the image of her sister's bleeding mouth filled Prue with shame. Prue knew she must have been staring at her sister, because Pearl opened her eyes wide at her, as if to say, *What, then?* But Prue did not take the invitation. She knew she ought to have confessed the dream right away, and dispelled its hold on her; but because of the bridge, she also wished to remain in its thrall. Coupled with Tem's foul temper, this kept her silent.

The day, however, passed slowly. Isaiah had told the men it was Prue's birthday, so every-odd-where she went there were jibes and congratulations to contend with, when she was half feeling herself a murderess and half nursing an idea that, like a word stuck on the tip of the tongue, might well evaporate if she did not find some opportunity to blurt it out. Pearl brought down sandwiches in a pail for lunch, and stayed for an interminable conversation about the week's groceries, Prue feeling guilty about her dream the whole while. She was almost relieved when the valve controlling the chutes in the brewhouse floor stuck shut. Of course when she'd heard the danger bell, she'd worried someone might be prostrated or dead, but when she arrived and found it a matter for the carpenter, she was glad for the distraction.

Isaiah was unwilling to let the mash room workers go for the day, as he thought it better to pay them for half an hour idling than to lose a whole afternoon. But Tem immediately had the idea to order out a cask of the wares to entertain them, and soon, so many pipes were lit in the mill yard, the smoke rivaled the still fires', and men from elsewhere in the manufactory stepped out to join them when they found leisure to do so. Realizing the afternoon was now certain to slip down the latrine, Prue excused herself and walked all the way past the Luquer Mill to the tannery and back, though her toes were numb in her boots. The exercise felt good, and gave her time to think.

A few workers were still out drinking in the yard when she returned. Dusk was descending, and Isaiah must finally have given in and called off operations for the day. The carpenter would remain until the work was complete, and Prue could see the foremen through the various windows, patiently plucking at belts and lining up paddles. She recognized tall, slim Phineas Bates—no relation to Hiram, she had learned in a rare letter from Ben—moving around the brewhouse. Prue had hired him only a few months before, when her former brewmaster, John Putnam, had abruptly quit, claiming gratitude for all her father had taught him but homesickness for his family on the outskirts of Philadelphia. She'd been shocked by his sudden leave-taking, after all his years in her father's employ; but she was pleased with this new Mr. Bates thus far.

Isaiah came out from the countinghouse, squaring his stooped shoulders in his coat. When he saw her, he waved a weary hello. "It's nearly fixed," he said.

"Good," Prue said. "Thank you."

"Pleasant walk?"

"Yes," Prue said, and again said, "thank you."

He touched the brim of his hat to her and said, "I should be getting home." He trudged off uphill, toward Patience, Maggie, his year-and-a-half-old son, Israel, and his new baby daughter. Prue thought wistfully of Ben, who would have deplored this living arrangement. She had imagined, when he'd left more than two years since, that she might take the opportunity to deepen her connection to Will Severn, but this had never occurred. She continued to enjoy and learn from his sermons, and he continued to welcome her to his home as a friend; but ever since her father's passing, something between them had changed. She could not ask him about it, and had to assume he had either come around to her position on her parents' deaths or learned of her escapades with Ben. Nothing else could explain the subtle coolness she felt from him. Pearl did not seem to notice it and spent as much time as ever in his company, while Prue contented herself corresponding with, and dreaming about, Ben. Tem, after all, had proven the one the neighborhood bachelors had come calling for: She was younger, prettier, lighter of spirit, and good at cards. But thus far she'd turned down both Cornelis Luquer and Anton Remsen, giving no explanation beyond that they did not suit her fancy, and imitating their shock at being refused with a wicked, mirthless accuracy.

Prue loved the mill when it was quiet and she could hear the river rush by. She also loved how the warmth of the fires clung to the buildings even after a day's work had ended. It was a typical, tepid January sunset, but the air felt milder once the wind had died down.

Now, at low tide, the smooth rocks of her father's retaining wall were high above the water, dry and dark. She walked along the strand until she was opposite the stillhouse's huge chimney, then sat down with her back to the river and the last few rosy wisps of cloud. From this vantage, the distillery appeared vast, and the Schermerhorn and Horsfield houses looked like frills, lace collars and cuffs around the edges of the promontory. If she looked toward Buttermilk Channel and Nutten Island ("I tell you, it has been the Governor's Island for decades now!" Recompense exclaimed aloud, though she was alone in the room; her mother's stubbornness about such matters irritated her no end), Prue could imagine how different this land must have looked when her father had first seen it, more than thirty years before. She could imagine the cypress that had grown on the bluffs. She could not quite imagine how her father had built a modern manufactory on a site where previously had stood little more than a two-bit homemade still, with nothing to bank on but his faith he would succeed.

She felt in her bones she could build a bridge. She could not yet know if what she'd imagined would work, but it seemed worth exploring. If her own books and Cornelis's proved inadequate, they had a subscription library in New York; she could join it, and borrow the most up-to-date treatises on engineering. She knew enough about the properties of timber, stone, and iron from her work on the distillery to begin to think about materials, and she could study up on this Mr. Smeaton's miraculous cement. She believed she could correctly calculate the total avoirdupois of whatever materials she chose, and determine if making the bridge both large and sturdy enough would cause it to collapse under its own self-weight. She ran a distillery; she did not doubt she could arrive at efficient methods of construction and organize work crews. What else was there to consider? Money, but she had her fair share of that. The beginnings of what she could not give from her own pocket she believed she could raise among her neighbors and in New York, exactly as Mr. Whitcombe had raised funds for Will Severn's church. The New York State legislature—or, if it came to it, the federal government, far off in Philadelphia—would have to supply the rest. It would be necessary to earn the approval of her neighbors, but Prue did not imagine much difficulty in this quarter, except, perhaps, from Losee and a Mr. Ezra Fischer, a New York gentleman of the Jewish faith who had recently bought up land between the ropewalk and Butcher's Wharf, and who proposed to begin a second ferry service that summer. She felt less certain of the approval of the people of New York, their mayor and their board of aldermen, the assembly, the senate, and the governor; but though what she knew of New York politicians she knew only through hearsay, she thought she might go a good distance with them on money and gin. On the New York side, she would have to purchase land for a footing, at who knew what cost; but on the Brooklyn end, she believed she might use the empty space between her storehouses and the ropewalk without interfering with either manufactory.

She also realized she'd gotten far ahead of herself. If the bridge proved feasible and worthwhile, her ability to worry over every last detail of a plan would be invaluable; but it would not matter how artful a letter she could write Governor Jay if there turned out to be no real grounds for a bridge.

However long she had sat there, evening had settled in, and the wind picked up again at her back. Jens Luquer, who was now the foreman of the stillhouse, came out from the building, turned up his collar, and started down the Shore Road, his form visible against the sand in the dim moonlight, his back canted wearily forward as if he were walking into a gale. He didn't see her, in her dark clothes, on the dark wall.

When she returned home that evening, Prue wished she had a door to shut against her sisters, or that she might, for an hour, borrow Pearl's affliction and sit silent. As was often the case, because she yearned for solitude, her sisters were solicitous of her; it was, after all, her birthday, and Abiah had baked her a rye bread and a pound cake before going off to an evening prayer meeting in Mr. Severn's church.

"Is everything all right down there?" Tem asked, striding in from the parlor in her worn-out house shoes when she heard the door shut.

Prue pulled off her boots; it would be pleasant to warm her feet by the fire. "Isaiah thinks so."

"What took you so long, then?"

"I don't know. I was thinking."

Tem hung, practically swaying, by the door to the hallway, as if it were an affront to nature to be still. "Did you have an enjoyable walk?"

Pearl came gliding up behind her. Snippets of the bright silk threads she'd been working with clung to her sleeves and skirt. Her dark eyes fixed keenly on Prue, who was finding both her sisters irksome. "Yes," she replied. "And I also enjoyed sitting on the retaining wall, regarding the distillery."

Pearl wrinkled her nose and pointed her forefinger toward that corner of the house past which lay the distillery, the East and North Rivers with New York tucked snugly between them, and the vast, woody continent beyond. "It may not sound titillating, but I enjoyed it." Her toes prickled in the cook fire's heat. Pearl began to brush the threads from her clothes, and Tem uncovered the cake and broke off a corner.

Pearl said "Ssst!" and smacked at her while continuing to brush her skirt.

"You know, the distillery really is beautiful when it's quiet and everyone's gone," Prue went on. Pearl flashed her a helpless glance, possibly of solidarity, and went back to her thread-picking.

"It's a manufactory, you know," Tem said, "not an aesthetic object." Apparently tired of breaking off pieces of the cake, she cut a slice and a clean one from behind, and offered the latter to Prue on her open palm.

"No, thank you," Prue said. Though a moment since she'd wished for nothing more than solitude, she now felt nettled that Tem did not share her sentiment.

Pearl opened her notebook and wrote, *For Heavens Sake T we've a perfectly good supper in that clay Pot. All I've to do is serv it.*

Tem offered her the slice of cake in apology, and Pearl rather ostentatiously put it on a plate and set it on the sideboard. Then she took three bowls and a ladle and served up their sweet potato stew. Tem leaned over her shoulder as she did so, and sniffed at the bowls.

"I'm tired of sweet potatoes," she said, and went to bring the pitcher of milk to the table. En route, she drank from its spout. Tem behaved thus a hundred times a day, without any ill intention or causing real harm to anyone, but Pearl looked violated anyway as she sat down. Prue figured it was not so unusual to spend one's adult life with one's sisters, but surely it was among the pleasures of marriage that, when one despised it, it was one's own chosen Hell.

As she had sat on the retaining wall, Prue had prepared herself to begin her great undertaking in secret. It would not do, she had reasoned, to have her sisters or Isaiah prodding her with questions or watching over her shoulder as she worked. But as she settled down for supper and watched Tem and Pearl squabble as they'd done when they were small, she wondered how well such secrecy would serve her. Her first and deepest secret had corroded her heart; and those that came after—her early visits to Will Severn's church, her fondness for him, her goings-on with Ben, the unwelcome intuition that her father's death had not been accidental—remained burdens. Had it been possible to tell her sisters all these things, she would have done so; but that was too much to ask of herself. She had not even fully decided to speak to her sisters of her plan, but found herself saying, "There is something I wish to discuss with you. A matter of some importance."

Pearl looked away from her argument with Tem; her expression, however, showed some eagerness to get back to it.

Prue drew in a breath. Now she had begun, she could think of no way to avert the disclosure. "I'm considering building a bridge," she told them.

Pearl opened her eyes a bit wider, but did not write her a note. Tem said nothing.

Prue said, "I wonder if either of you heard me just now."

"I believe so," Tem said. "Between which buildings?"

"Across the river. A bridge to New York."

"Ha!" Tem said, and slapped the table. This obviously annoyed Pearl, who let her spoon drop in exasperation. Tem dug into her supper. While she chewed, she eyed Prue merrily, as if the revelation had been a scheme to make Pearl forget about the cake and the milk.

"I am quite serious," Prue said.

Tem and Pearl glanced at each other, and Pearl wiped her mouth, took her book from around her neck, and laid it on the table as she ordinarily did at mealtime. *A bridge of what Descrption?* she wrote. She was running low on pages; they would have to cut more.

Prue had not reckoned how difficult it would be to speak of an idea still so nebulous and unformed. Her hand was quivering, and as much as she wished to disclose her secret, she half hated Pearl for making her do so. "A vast bridge," she said quietly. "Simple in form, and tall enough to admit the masts of ships."

But 'tis'n't possible, Pearl wrote. *There have been a doz. such Plans.*

"I believe mine will prove more sound," Prue said. She had no better argument.

Tem shook her head no. "Prue, are you ill? Why should you be thinking of this?"

"I don't know," Prue answered truthfully. "Or perhaps I have simply done so since before you were born." She expected Tem to laugh at her again, but her sister was chewing and listening. "Before you came, Pearl," she went on, "I gazed across the straits every day, with a terrible fear of what went on there, and of what our father's business was with the inhabitants. I suppose I have never quit dreaming on it. And now I feel— the river has taken our father, and I wish to do something to mark that; beyond which, there is a great necessity for a bridge. It would be a boon to ourselves and our neighbors. And such an accomplishment. Far greater than running a distillery."

Why were you afear'd, as a gell? You were so grave, Pearl wrote. She was watching Prue intently.

Prue wondered why she had asked about this and not about some other aspect of her exposition, and saw Pearl trying not to allow her face to show how much the answer interested her. "It doesn't bear repeating," she said, "and I learned soon enough there was nothing to dread there. When Father began allowing me to accompany him on his deliveries, I went so often my boots became permanently salted."

I rmmber.

"So I've been thinking about traversing the distance a long time; and as I say, most everyone believes a bridge would be of service. It's been a matter of arriving at a workable plan. I think I may have done so."

"Damme," Tem said. She poured some milk into her glass.

Pearl, who'd been holding herself up by the collarbones every time Tem's hand approached the pitcher, relaxed. She wrote, *How did you arriv there?*

"I had a dream last night," Prue said. Tem turned her head to one side, preparing to badger her sister; but Prue said, "Hear me out. Hear me out."

Tem exhaled through her nostrils and folded her arms on the table.

Prue was aware of a slight nervous stoop in her own posture. "It wasn't a dream born of fancy. You know I have studied the art of building ever since I could read, and I have been considering some of the laws of natural philosophy since last summer, since I saw the springboard Cornelis built over the millpond. The dream merely showed me the manner in which I might bring these laws to bear on a structure." She blew on a spoonful of her stew as if this gesture could protect her from her sisters' scrutiny. "Or perhaps it did not show me, but I believe it has pointed me in the correct direction."

"No other bridge has met with Brookland's approval," Tem said, her tone still combative. "And the plans have been put forth by some of the great engineers of our time. Why should yours fare differently?"

"Because all the previous proposals would have blocked traffic on the straits. The bridge I envision would cross the East River in a single span."

Tem slapped the table again. "That's impossible."

Prue half wished to yell at her and half to go upstairs and sulk. Instead of either she said, "I haven't worked it out mathematically, but I believe it can be done."

Pearl wrote, *I'm good at Mathematicks. I shall help.* Prue didn't especially want her help.

"No. Prue," Tem said, "you aren't thinking." She drained her glass of milk. "I'm no expert, but I do know that to build an arch requires a latticework, a wooden centering beneath it, to support it while you build. A *centering*, until the keystone is in place. Can you imagine the size of the support you speak of? It's not possible. It would block the entire river for months."

"This bridge wouldn't need a centering. That's much of the beauty of the plan."

Tem looked skeptically at Pearl, who was scrutinizing Prue. Tem said, "Well, I think you're barking mad. That's my opinion."

Pearl put her spoon down, and turned to a new page. *Neither here nor there*, she wrote. *But P, I thnk every Arch in History,—every last Corse of Bricks over a Doorway,—has been built on a wooden Centering, wh^{ch} was dismantl'd when the Mortar was sett.*

"Yes," Prue said, "you are both correct. But simply because something always has been done doesn't mean it must be. I don't believe anyone else has yet arrived at the method I propose; but surely Euclid and Sir Isaac Newton will solve the conundrum, if I put it to them?"

Pearl flared her nostrils, less scornfully than their mother would have done.

Prue had known they would be skeptical; this was why she had hesitated to explain herself. But if the bridge was ever to be built, she would have to learn to steel herself against such doubt. She further recognized that the only evidence against the idea's lunacy was to have witnessed the vision, and she did not yet have means to show it to her sisters. She

would be patient. "Tem," she asked, "do you imagine you could look after things awhile? So I might find out?"

" 'Things.' "

Do'n't be difficult, Pearl wrote. *Ov course she means t^b Distillery.*

Tem exhaled through her nostrils again. "For how long?" she asked.

"I don't know. Not an age."

The fire popped, and outside, some horses walked past at a clop, their
riders singing:

> *Yes, gin's the man,*
> *If any can,*
> *To steal a man from 'is bran-dy!*

The men burst out laughing.

Prue said, "There's no reason you couldn't manage. You know the
works as well as I."

"But I haven't your disposition."

"I always thought you considered that a blessing." Prue also thought,
in passing, her sister hadn't her intelligence, either; which wasn't fair.

Tem cracked a wan smile and said, "Hmm."

"I realize I'm asking a favor of you. But I think it will be worthwhile.
At least I see no other way to prove my idea reasonable. Have we an
agreement? For a few days only, to begin."

Tem took and chewed a mouthful of food, then said, "I shall not be
held responsible if a batch goes feints or the stillhouse catches fire."

"Certainly not, unless it's your fault."

Tem was regarding her with a frank, inquisitive expression that told
Prue her sister found her both pedantic and odd; but this was not news.
"Prue," she said.

"If there was an emergency, of course I'd come see to it."

"Is feints an emergency? Where should I find you?"

"I don't know yet," Prue said. "I can't figure it out unless you give me
leave to do so."

Tem had the fingers of one strong hand splayed on the table. She
touched their tips to the surface, each in turn, then said, "Very well. I
shall never get to be master, otherwise."

Prue leaned over to hug her, and Tem shied away, as if to be caught doing her sister a good deed might sully her reputation.

I wold help you all I can, Pearl repeated. Once again, Prue chose not to respond.

After clearing the dishes, Prue went upstairs, in case its two wide, low-ceilinged rooms might conceal some hitherto undisclosed spot in which she might work out a plan for her bridge. There was, in fact, only Roxana's fold-out desk, in what was now Tem's room. It was no wider than Prue's hips or deeper than her forearm; a piece of furniture Abiah slapped at with a dust rag only when it became so encrusted with soot and spiderweb it made one's teeth shake to look at it. Prue sat down at it anyway, pulled out its desiccated blotter, and tried resting her elbows on it. The wind was now rattling the windowpanes. Prue had seen her mother sit in this spot only to reconcile the household accounts in her haphazard manner; she never wrote a letter, and never received one. Whom did she have to write to, when she had turned on her family and made no friends in her chosen home? Wondering what this desk might have been used for by some more outgoing mother, Prue thought Roxana's life had been sadder than she herself had realized.

She rested her forehead on her palms, the heels of her hands pressing into the sockets of her eyes, and watched the pattern of dim aurora borealis as she thought through the buildings of her distillery. She did not imagine she could plan a bridge in her office, with Tem and Isaiah wandering in and out. The storerooms were quiet, but too dark.

The assembly room would do, however. It was large enough to pace; and Isaiah and Tem might at least think twice before coming to question her. It would be no trouble to have a table and chair brought in, and she could move them to the side when she needed to gather her men.

Tem's bedroom was chilly and dark, and it was time to light the upstairs fires, but Prue felt anchored to the prim desk by iron weights. She heard Tem speaking downstairs; it sounded like a monologue, but one could never tell, from any distance, if Pearl was participating. When Prue sat at this desk, the eaves were so close to her head and shoulders, they almost forced her to duck down. She felt again how strait her mother must have found this house, and wondered if Pearl did as well. No, she knew Pearl did—she was always volunteering for whatever project was at hand, always escaping to the rectory, and Prue thought if she did not keep an eye on her, Pearl would try to go help Tem run the distillery this next short while. But what could be done? It was tragic she'd been born as she had—tragic, and Prue's fault, no matter if their mother had thought otherwise—but Prue had obviously long since lost God's ear. She could not change Pearl's circumstances simply by wishing to do so.

Prue thought if she could bridge the distance between here and the Other Side; if she could build a monument to expiate her sin and her folly, and to embody the love she had borne her parents, who'd crossed over too soon, before she was ripe to understand them; if she might take this wealth of money and skill her father had bequeathed her, and *do* something with it, for the public good and perhaps to the general wonderment—if all, if any, of these circumstances might come to pass, Will Severn could keep to himself, and Ben could remain in the wilderness, and she could never move a hair's breadth closer to knowing where the dead resided, yet she would be happy the rest of her days.

Ten

NATURAL PHILOSOPHY

W ednesday the twenty-fourth of January, 1798, dawned clear. Prue disliked looking around her for signs—it seemed almost as childish as fearing the shades clamored for gin in Manhattan—but she couldn't help seeing the day as auspicious for a new endeavor. She went down Joralemon's Lane before anyone else in her house had even awakened.

She lit the stove in the assembly hall first thing, then went to Owen's shed to retrieve his broom. When Isaiah arrived at seven, he knocked, opened the door, and stood blinking at her, as if he could not understand what he saw. "Prue?" he said. "Is aught amiss?"

"No," she replied, but he was obviously wondering about the broom. "I need a quieter place to work for a spell. I thought I'd set up here."

He removed his hat and pushed the brown hair back from his brow. "Is something wrong with our office?"

"No, but I need a bit of privacy."

"I see," he said. He unbuttoned his coat.

"I shall put up a table and chair, and when we need to use the room, we'll move them aside. I have some reading to do, and then some ciphering and drawing. For a structure."

Without waiting for her to finish, Isaiah said, "I apologize if I'm dull, Prue. Baby Joan has the colic, and we don't get three hours' sleep."

"I'm sorry," Prue said. She had no direct experience of the colic, as Tem had been the last infant she'd known, and she'd been unusually sturdy; but Isaiah did look awful.

Isaiah said, "Do you require my assistance?"

She looked around at the plain walls, and out at the fine view down to the water and up to the cooling house. "Might you take Joe Loosely's shipment to him?"

"Of course, but you know he prefers to receive his goods from you."

"Tell him I'll bring his next myself."

Isaiah nodded. "I'll bring the coffee down, soon 's the stove's lit." He went out, and up the stairs to the office; a moment later she heard him banging the grounds out from the previous evening's pot. Shortly afterward, the mill bell rang, calling everyone to work. Prue found herself imagining Tem, supervising the morning's mashing in her galoshes; and it seemed unwise to leave her in command of anything. Yet Tem was never so foolish as Prue thought her—she was more high-spirited than truly irresponsible—and, Prue reminded herself, a bridge would be worth a great deal of inconvenience.

A quarter hour later she walked north to the carpenter's shed, and found him measuring out boards to replace some worn latticework over the cooling floor. Isaiah had hired the fellow, Jean Boulanger, only a few months before; he still regarded Tem and Prue with some disbelief. She asked how long he would need to build a simple table, as large as the one she shared with Tem and Isaiah, for the assembly room.

Jean frowned at her and checked his measurement.

"It is a matter of some importance, Mr. Boulanger."

"A proper table?" he asked. "If it can be a plank on sawhorses, I can get wood from van Vechten today."

"Good," Prue said. "You finish that work for the cooling floor, and I'll go up to Theunis's this morning. You'll let me know the moment the wood arrives?"

He nodded, but the trace of his frown remained.

Gray-haired Scipio Jones waved to her as she stepped outside. She waved back, elated at the prospect of beginning that afternoon. She began to list the items she would need to borrow or acquire: a chair from the house, compasses and a protractor, a straight edge, a right angle. But it was idiotic to think she'd sit down Thursday morning and begin to plot and draw. She may have had the shape of the thing clearly in mind, but visions didn't tell a person how high an arch would need to soar above high water to admit a tall ship, nor what stone and mortar would serve best for an abutment, nor how wide a roadway must be for two carriages to pass abreast and not mow down the foot traffic.

She had a great deal to learn, and thought she required a collaborator with a thorough understanding of mathematics and the laws governing natural philosophy—in a word, Ben. As she could not, however, separate this practical need from what had grown into almost a full-time longing for his scent and the cowlick at the back of his hair, she tried to put him from her mind. Instead, she went up to the countinghouse, took a nip of Isaiah's strong coffee, and decided to head up to the sawmill.

Isaiah was in the yard ticking off casks against his list, while the blinkered drays stamped and burred in the cold air. "I can take Joe's shipment after all," Prue told him. "I need to go to van Vechten's."

Isaiah held his index finger up, then returned to his list. When he'd finished, he folded the papers into the crook of his arm. "Hang it, it's quiet this morning. Let's both go."

She had known Isaiah most of her twenty-six years; such a glimmer of irresponsibility was rare. "Are you certain?"

"It won't take a minute." He gave her his hand to climb up.

Before she could, however, someone was calling, "Miss Winship?" She turned to see Jens Luquer jogging up behind her. He was blowing steam from his nostrils and over his red mustache. "Sorry to disturb you, Prue," he said, "but it seems a small batch of yesterday's came up feints, and I can't say why."

"Did anyone taste the wort before it went in?" she asked.

"No, but it smelled fine."

She wanted to counsel him always to rely on his tongue; but in the general clamor, she herself often went by the nose. "Worm dirty?"

"Cleaned on schedule on Friday, and the flannel beneath it changed. I suppose I can check it again."

Phineas Bates overheard the conversation, and drew nigh to listen. He stooped down, as if to be a more ordinary height would make him less conspicuous.

"Which batch is it?" Prue asked.

"Four-aught-fourteen."

She had smelled it herself the previous day, and it had seemed normal. Some coal shovelers and horse keepers were now finding pretexts to be nearby, as they sometimes did if Prue idled too long. She fancied they were waiting for her to begin uttering Delphic pronouncements. Feints was always serious, as Prue could see from Isaiah's pinched expression; nevertheless, she looked at the loaded wagon and said, "Isaiah and I are off on business. Phineas, can you lend Jens a hand?"

Phineas nodded, his whole figure stooping into the gesture.

"Mr. Bates will help you, then; and have Miss Tem look into it."

"With all due respect—"

"Have Tem look into it, Jens," she repeated, as she was also trying to convince herself this was a reasonable course of action. "She knows feints as well as anyone." Jens's breath rose around his broad face in plumes, and Isaiah kept holding the near horse by its reins. "You may as well know, I have some work to accomplish outside my ordinary sphere," she went on, directing her voice to everyone around. "If in the next few days you must inquire about foul-smelling spirits or a broken machine, speak with Mr. Horsfield or with Tem."

Jens looked like he had more to say, but Phineas put a hand on his shoulder and steered him back toward the stillhouse. They made a comical pair—the one so solid and Dutch, the other so elongated. The other men were leaning on their shovels and exchanging views. "There'll be plenty of time for opinions at the Twin Tankards this evening," she said. A few shook their heads at her. "Back to work. Mr. Horsfield will return within the half hour."

The crowd dispersed when Isaiah clicked to the drays. As soon as Prue and Isaiah cleared the distillery gate, they passed Nicolaas Luquer heading down the hill for slop exchange. They all waved to one another. As the horses strained uphill, Prue glanced sideways at Isaiah and found him doing the same. "Spooked 'em good," he said.

"Oh," Prue replied. She wasn't certain it was a compliment.

He reached around to pat her far shoulder. "It's just as well the men find you uncanny. I can't see them taking orders from a pretty gell otherwise."

It was pleasant to know he thought her pretty. She looked out over the bluff and toward the river, and saw one of the Schermerhorn barges bobbing toward them, empty except for its tired, half-frozen pilot.

"Can you tell me what sort of a structure you're intending?" Isaiah asked.

The previous evening's difficult conversation with her sisters remained fresh in her memory; but it was difficult to keep a secret from Isaiah, and he had a milder temperament than either of them. "I'm hoping to figure out how to build a bridge," she said, and pointed toward the Fly Market. "To New York, I mean."

For a moment, he kept quiet, and Prue nearly winced each time her watch ticked against her ribs and told her another second had gone by between them, silent. The hooves and wheels clattered on the hardpacked road, and the great engines of the ropewalk thrummed. He said, "Goodness, Prue. That's an undertaking. Have you considered how vast it is?"

Prue nodded and glanced sideways at him again. He wasn't laughing at her; this was a start. "I have an idea," she ventured. "It is yet to be proved. And I do know the rudiments of construction. I shall attempt to learn what I don't know through reading, experimentation, and questioning; and then I'll draw up plans for it and build a small representation, to see if it has the least chance of holding. 'Tis a pity your brother isn't here. I don't think there's anything I want more, in determining if this plan will prove practicable, than a surveyor."

He looked askance at her again. "I've something I'm supposed to keep secret from you," he said. They drove past his house, up on the ridge. There were Maggie and Patience, the latter with the screaming infant on one arm. Both women were taking down their frozen laundry, which had been hanging on the line since Monday.

"Ben's coming home?" Prue asked.

"Well, I'm not to say."

Prue leaned over and kissed his cheek, and the Devil care if his wife saw her. He pushed her off, laughing, as if they were still children. "I could kill 'im," Prue said. "He hasn't written in ages."

Isaiah shook his head. "He's been deep in the wilderness, Prue. I hadn't a letter of him in six months."

"Still."

"But he's—" Isaiah stopped himself, and appeared to weigh the worth of keeping part of his secret. "He's been appointed surveyor for King's County. I believe he'll set up shop within the month."

The day remained frigid, but the warmth in Prue's heart flooded her chest. "I could dearly use his help."

"And nothing more?" Isaiah asked.

"What is it you ask?" Prue said.

"If you require him for aught else than bridge-building."

She itched to push him off the wagon, but they had arrived at the Liberty Tavern, and Joe was out smoking on his stoop and awaiting his delivery. Isaiah pulled twice at the reins, and the horses looked daggers back at him over their withers.

"Both of you?" Joe asked. "Slow day for gin. Come in and have a sup."

Prue thought of Tem down there, battling the feints. There was nothing to be done about it now—the money and labor were already lost—and Tem was no fool; she'd arrive at a solution. "No, Joe," she said. "Isaiah'll stay for a pint, but I've business to conduct this morning."

"Suit yourself, fancy lady," he said, and spat a shred of tobacco to the ground. His boys began with their usual languor to unload the casks onto barrows.

Isaiah hopped down, and said to Prue, "If I can be of further assistance—"

"You've been a great help already," Prue said. "More than you know." Waving good-bye, she set out along the turnpike for the sawmill.

Ten years earlier, she might have felt embarrassed, striding along in a man's coat, knee britches, and tall boots entirely unlike the delicate pumps Pearl wore; but she had grown accustomed to her place in the world, and that day she felt each step over the frozen mud as a promise. She thought she might be the only woman in Brooklyn with a gold watch ticking along against her breast, and she felt proud of the distinction.

The pavement rumbled as heavy carts rolled by, and pedestrians walked on the frozen dirt margins of the road. Five students from Mr. Severn's school, however, tromped up the center of the roadway, with their lunches in buckets. Simon Dufresne nearly ran them down, and swore over his shoulder at them as he swerved past. The boys, of course, laughed, and dared one another to remain in the path of the next carriage. Prue thought they were all lucky it was midwinter; in any other season, they would either have been choked with dust or ankle-deep in mud.

Simon whistled and beckoned Prue in as she walked past his gate. Prue reminded herself van Vechten would still have wood at his sawmill a quarter hour hence, and turned into the yard. Two of Simon's men were unhitching his team, and the barrel-chested old man himself was standing by the empty wash line, talking in icy puffs to Peg as she wiped bird excrement from the rope with a cloth. "Prue," he said, "what're you doing away from the mill? Get back to your gin. Peg, make 'er some coffee."

Peg nodded her head toward the door as she stuck some stray clothespins in her pocket. "Come, I've got honey cake. You can bring some home for little Pearl."

"She's nineteen."

"Pshaw."

"Will you mind if I'm brief? I've an errand at van Vechten's."

"No, no," Peg said, and hustled Prue toward the kitchen. "Into the house with you. You look cold."

Simon followed on their heels. "Don't tell me you left Temmy running that distillery?" he asked.

"Just for an hour or two."

"Oh, she could break a heart in less time than that."

"Mind your business, Simon," Peg said as she ground the coffee. She put cinnamon in the grounds, and its scent made Prue want to settle in for the remainder of the morning.

She sat down on the long bench. "She's grown up a fair bit these past few years."

"Grown pretty, too, 's all I'm saying. I'm surprised she turned down Cornelis. Not as if she could find a decenter fellow."

"No, nor one she's known better nor liked so well."

Simon shook his white head and sat down across from her. "People are saying she's proud."

"Perhaps so." She was still thinking about Ben's return. "She'll have more responsibility in the near future. I have plans to improve access to the distillery."

"Right smart of you," Simon said. "You should rebuild the whole place in stone while you're at it. That's what you need, for real security. I told your father so when you were a pip, and again when you did all that rebuilding a few years back."

"We're heavily insured, and we've been lucky thus far."

"Mmm," Peg said, "but who but God knows how long that will continue?"

Prue said, "I should think whatever curse fell on Mr. Joralemon would have outlived its usefulness."

Simon spat (prophylactically, Prue thought) into the fire, and Peg clicked her tongue. "I'll hope you're correct, Prue," he said.

"Enough on that, now," Peg said.

Simon thumped the table. "She's right, of course. Miss Winship, I've a favor to ask. I've a grandnephew, brother's grandson, out in Midwout. Nineteen years old—"

"Just right for Pearlie," Peg added. "A dear, sweet boy."

"—and a hardworking one, looking for a place. Any chance he might find work with the Winship daughters?"

"Of course," Prue said, relieved it was something so easy. "What are his skills?"

Peg set down a pitcher of milk with the cream floating on top.

"He's not the strongest lad—he had the whooping cough a few years since, and hasn't been the same—but a diligent study, and clever with his hands."

"Send him to me as soon as he can come. I'll see what he can do."

Peg set the coffee down in its steaming tin pot, and Prue warmed herself all the way through with their fire and conversation.

When Prue set out again for the sawmill, her spirits were soaring—she could not say if because of her project, the news of Ben's return, or Peg's coffee. She found Theunis in his office above the whining sawmill. When she arrived, he was sitting with his feet up on his desk and the holes in his boot-soles exposed. He was chewing tobacco, which he removed from his cheek in a hurry, and he beckoned her in with a welcoming hand. "Little Prudie," he shouted over the screech of the saw and the plash of the waterwheel. "What can I do for you?"

"Good morning, Theunis. I need a plank of wood big enough for a desk."

"Does it have to be fancy? Or pine'll do?"

"It hardly matters, so long as it's level and broad."

"That's done," he said. "I'll send one over this afternoon." He noted it down on a sheet of paper. "Something else?"

"Yes, actually. I've also come to ask you about timber."

"Timber," he said, "that's my specialty; but it's been twenty years since we had any round these parts. Do you even remember what a forest looks like?"

"They were still standing when I was a child."

The saw quit whining, and Prue could hear the river and horses going by. "Ah," he said, "isn't it lovely when the machines go off?"

"I know," she said.

"So. What can I tell you about timber?"

"Well," Prue said. In fact, now that she had told Isaiah, it was no use trying to keep it secret. Isaiah was trustworthy, but rumor spread through Brooklyn more quickly than black flies in June; so Prue realized she might as well start the rumor herself. She sat down across Theunis's desk from him. "I have it in mind to build a bridge across the East River."

He widened his rheumy eyes at her.

"I know," Prue said. "I may yet abandon the idea; but not until I'm certain I've proven it impossible."

"We've needed one a long time," Theunis said. "And it'd be a fine thing to have it homegrown."

"Thank you," Prue said.

"But Prue," he continued, "you know well you won't be the first to try. No plan has ever even earned the approval of Joe Loosely, never mind the legislature."

"I know. I shall try not to hope too dearly for it; but I also can't know it's impossible unless I work all the details out.

"At all events, I have a great deal to learn of materials, but from what I know of them, I think it might be best to build such a structure in wood, for its lightness and flexibility." She would tell no one but her sisters she had remarked this in looking at Cornelis's springboard. "I wonder if you've any notion what would bear the most weight without itself being unnecessarily heavy; and what you think would best resist the weather. I shall need to know my material to work the plan according to it." She saw him eyeing his tobacco pouch and said, "It's all right if you want to chew."

"Much obliged," he said, and worked himself another plug. The saw screamed through something below, then fell silent again. "You realize you're speaking of a good deal of wood, and there's little but saplings hereabouts. I sold your father the lumber for his original plant, for pennies. Excellent wood, too—seasoned right. What you can buy nowadays for a shilling isn't good enough for a chicken coop."

"If I were willing to spend more, could I yet buy something fine?" She didn't know if he meant a shilling per plank or per tree.

"Not as good as what built my house, but sure," Theunis answered. He was known in the village for his oaken floor, which hadn't a single knot in it.

"But what kind of timber would it wish to be?"

He rubbed his fingers over his chin. "Fir'd be your man, no doubt: flexible, strong, and sturdy, so far's the rain goes. Often used in bridges, though not, that I know of, in any as large as the one you speak of. You could get some up the Hudson at a fair enough price."

Prue was pleased he had so decisive an answer, though she would also need to see for herself why this was so. Fir it would no doubt be, but she knew she would do best to question its fitness, rather than to rely on his opinion. "I wonder if you can school me in the properties of the wood? Its strength, in tension and compression? Its ability to bear loads?"

"Absolutely. I am sure you know it has always been my chief desire to become a natural philosopher. I run this mill because my father left it to me; that, and it's a good living, of course. You understand. But I've a hundred experiments I can show you, and more still in which your assistance would be a boon."

"That sounds wonderful," Prue said.

"We'll begin as soon as the weather breaks, if you can wait that long. In the meantime, that plank? Give me its dimensions."

"Six feet by four? Doesn't need to be pretty."

"Quite a desk you're after. Shall I send it down this afternoon?"

"Please."

As she stood to take her leave, he said, "I think you'll find the scientifical experiments interesting."

"I sincerely look forward to them."

"The first warm day," he said. "Now off with you."

Ivo Joralemon was out lurching along the road on his crutches, and he beamed at her as she passed.

When the plank arrived that afternoon, Jean Boulanger used the sand of the mill yard to brush it smooth. The next morning, again leaving the distillery under Tem's direction, Prue accompanied one of her shipments to New York, and while there paid down the hefty security required to join the lending library. She brought home a stack of books, and felt her chest constrict when she realized how forbidding were some of their theorems and diagrams. They required her strictest attention and most careful study, along with a willingness to stretch her mind more strenuously than she had done since finishing her apprenticeship to her father. It was not enough to know, as she already did, that the strength of a beam was a function of the area of its cross section, increasing along a parabolic curve relative to that area; she must recognize that the weight of such a member would be a function of its volume—that is, that it would increase along a cubic curve. It would therefore be a challenge to build a structure of such magnitude without having it collapse under the simple strain of supporting its own weight. Likewise, she already understood that a lever relayed a weight at its tip back to its base—if it did not, Cornelis and his siblings would simply have tumbled into the pond. But she did not yet know the function by which that weight was magnified as it approached the ground. She knew her bridge's abutments would have to be mighty to withstand such force, but she did not yet know how to guarantee their strength. Studying these questions consumed her whole attention, and left her spent and bleary-eyed by late afternoon. She remembered her dream of the finished bridge at such moments; only infrequently did she recall its twin dream of a maimed and bleeding Pearl. To relieve these periods of intense concentration, she began to travel on alternate days around Brooklyn, in search of knowledge that could not be found in books. The first few times she went out in this manner, passersby stopped to ask if she was abroad because aught was amiss at the mill; but Prue's neighbors soon grew as accustomed to this peculiarity as to her others, and began to leave her in peace.

On her days out in the world, Prue commandeered Jolly from her stables, as he was unlikely to be missed. Before she would mount him, she'd offer him a lump of table sugar, which he chewed as if it tasted like poison. He'd shake his head in disgust when she prodded him with her heels. But bitter old Jolly also did nothing more than grumble when schoolboys yanked his tail, and he was strong enough to carry Prue on a day-long journey. She began frequenting the shipyard at Wallabout Bay to observe their techniques of building, and to note, of course, the height of a mainmast. The Wallabout was two hours distant by the Shore Road, but

Jolly became so accustomed to the route, he'd walk there if she held the reins slack in her lap. Prue was a stranger in all but reputation to the slaves and free workers of the Wallabout (who seemed pleased the rumors about her britches were true), but when she went, she carried a bottle of gin in each saddlebag, and found the shipwrights willing enough to teach her what she needed to know. She thought she could herself shape the posts and beams to frame a building if she had to, but it was of great use to watch the shipbuilders plank the sides of a schooner, fill the seams with tar-soaked rope, and coat its outside in pitch. Prue remembered that this was precisely the technique Ben and Isaiah had shown her in the book on shipbuilding all those years ago; but not until she saw it in practice did she realize how well it would likely work to prevent rot upon the sides of a bridge. The shipbuilders' lumber was floated rough-cut up the river from van Vechten's, and the saw pit on the site sang each day till dusk.

February brought a false spring, and on its first day, Prue went up to the van Vechten mill, where the sawdust smelled sweet as apple blossoms. Under Theunis's guidance she conducted experiments on such woods as ash, locust, heart pine, and native fir, to discover how much weight they might bear, and what might be the degree of their distortion beneath that weight. Theunis cut her a beam of each type of wood, free of imperfections and a uniform eight feet in length by one and a half in height and six inches in breadth, and securely clamped one end of each to a level platform. His men helped her attach weights from fifty to a thousand pounds to the lever ends of the beams, and Prue measured the angle of their distortion from true and noted when the beam splintered and sent the weight tumbling to the ground. (The ash, the most beautiful of the woods, gave way first.) Her mind already felt stretched by her book learning and what she had acquired in the shipyard; and on some days, she was anxious she would be unable to hold the knowledge Theunis was bequeathing her. On the other hand, the experiments bewitched her; and after a few weeks, she began to feel their import in fleeting moments as part of her bodily understanding, a faint echo of the way she understood gin in her nose, skin, and bones.

Having learned Theunis's methods of testing and notation, she began, with growing confidence, to conduct experiments of her own. She requested beams of differing lengths and breadths and continued to explore their susceptibility to stresses and to shearing along the grain. Prue also took blocks of the various woods, treated some with pitch and allowed others to remain as nature had made them, and left them out to see what the weather would do to them. Theunis, meanwhile, was delighted to have occasion to share his knowledge of timber and of the laws governing the natural world. He rigged up a ramp so a horse could, with some coaxing, walk out onto a long lever. In this way, he and Prue could observe how the various kinds of timber behaved when subjected to unequal stresses, such as a bridge would experience with carriages moving along it ad libitum.

When the library proved insufficient to her burgeoning understanding and the deeper questions it raised, Prue began to purchase more books, many of which her bookseller had to order from England and the Continent. She requested all available treatises on the works of Telford, Pritchard, and Brunel, who were the Old World's most celebrated builders of large-span bridges. She learned with elation that a Philadelphia landscape architect by the name of Thomas Pope had received his state's approval to build a timber and masonry bridge across the Schuylkill, and she wrote to him directly to open a dialogue and ask to see his plans. Her knowledge of mathematics and bridges grew brighter and more thorough by the day, and as Prue traveled back and forth to New York to acquire the fuel for this bonfire, she felt a thrill she had not known since the workings of the distillery had first revealed themselves in their true glory. She felt profound gratitude for this understanding, and for the diligence that underlay it, without which it would never have come to pass. At the same time, she eagerly awaited Ben's return. She no longer had time to attend Will Severn's church, as her every free moment was given to study; but she found she did not miss it overmuch. Pearl went without her, and sometimes as she left or returned cast her sister a sharp glance which Prue could not interpret.

When she did not have a boat of her own going across, Prue had to take the ferry, though she thought the well of Losee's legendary good spirits had at last gone dry. Instead of gossiping or chatting about the news, he now spat venom about Ezra Fischer.

"We've always done fine with one ferry," he said one morning, hunching into his labor.

"But surely, Lo, you can't keep doing this forever," Prue said.

"No, not forever. But a few years more yet. And that damned Fischer—have you met him? Has anyone met him?"

"Not that I know of," she said. She did think Losee old for such back-breaking work.

"No one's even met the *klootzak*, and he proposes to serve our village." He looked out over his shoulder for traffic. "And he's a Jew."

"If it's the slightest consolation, I promise I shall never once use his boat."

"Hmm," Losee said. "It'll be a good deal closer to your property."

"We Winships have walked up to your ferry for decades. I imagine we can continue to do so."

He nodded. "You're a good girl. Your father's girl," he said. "You wouldn't put a man out of business."

She wondered if he'd heard anything from Theunis, as the project upon which she was working could do him in far more swiftly than a second ferry. But she could not guess what he knew, and despite ample opportunity, told him nothing about what she hoped to attempt.

Evenings, she sat at her new desk in the assembly hall, totting up what she'd learned against the questions thereby raised. She was grateful for the rare day on which the accounts came out in her favor; but chiefly, she was aware what a solemn duty it was to propose a bridge. If people chose to travel across it, they would stake their lives on her knowledge of the physical world. She did not, therefore, begin to make any calculations until she had spent more than two months in almost uninterrupted study. In April, she received a warm reply from Mr. Pope, who was only too happy to supply an image of his future bridge and small sketches of the plans on which it would be based. He was treating her, Prue noted with elation, as an equal, a comrade in arms; and she pored over his drawings until she'd nearly memorized them. She also sent a cask of gin for him on her next delivery boat bound for Philadelphia. His bridge was not so revolutionary as the one she proposed—his would rest on pilings, its weight borne by a harmonious string of segmental arches—but he found her idea intriguing. In his letter, he asked her to furnish him with as much detail as she could at this early stage, and to send drawings once she had them. "It would be my Delight," he wrote, "to serve in whatever Wise as *Mentor* to your *Télémache*; & to offer whatever counsel my age & experience may entitle me to give."

Only when Prue trusted her grasp of all her material did she begin to cipher, and to draw ever more detailed diagrams and images in her clumsy hand. Her dream had begun to metamorphose: No longer an airy substance, each day it relied more upon the precision of its angles and the weight of its abutments, the progressive diminution of the levers' size as they approached their zenith, the particular manner in which its every joint would be mortised and reinforced with nails, the exact pitch of the roadway. Prue began to understand that, though money would be an object, the true work would be in the hands of the men who would build it day by day. If they were to be safe, dangling from the sides of the bridge and securing its joists, she would have to devise slings to hold them; if the great timbers were to be hoisted aloft without benefit of a thousand spare hands, she would have to get to work designing movable cranes, which would allow pulleys to bear the brunt of the labor.

And as she sketched and calculated, the bridge seemed to take on life and breath of its own. In her vision, it had arched like a rainbow, like God's promise to man, over the straits; but in the quotidian world, if people were to travel across it without strain, it would have to arc at a gentler inclination, in a flatter parabola. The bridge's shape would, therefore, more closely resemble the trajectory of a bullet, and the anchorages would have to be stronger than at first she'd imagined to withstand that increase in lateral force. This was not within Prue's control; this was the way the bridge itself needed to be. Its twin spandrels had, from the start, sloped gently to convey any weight at the structure's center safely back to the ground; but as she figured and drew, Prue at last uncovered the method for planking them that would both best repel water and please the eye. Here, too, however, she felt the bridge had suggested the plan to her, and not the other way around.

Once she had worked out the size, depth, and weight of the bridge's abutments, she was at leisure to determine their appearance, and here she could give her imagination free rein. At first she'd envisioned the abutments as no more than a pair of bookends, propping the structure up from its two ends. The two sides of the river differed markedly from each other, however—the bridge would originate in Brooklyn at the foot of a cliff, whence it would spring up from between the two manufactories; but in Manhattan, it would alight in the midst of lively urban streets. It was only sensible the abutments should suit their individual environs.

Prue hoped to look across at the New York side of the bridge the rest of her days, and hoped what she gazed upon might stand as fitting testament to her achievement. She arrived at the idea of a simple stone pyramid, with the roadway running in a vaulted tunnel through its middle. For the Brooklyn footing, in its less scenic locale, she imagined a Gothic structure, whose spires would echo those of New York's churches across the water. Neither abutment would be the more grand, but Brooklyn's might be more decorative, to atone for its less aesthetically pleasing location.

When Prue's father had begun training her in the distillery, Prue had been eager to please him and to dispel any lingering doubts he might have about her fitness for the work. She had always lived in terror of failure—close kin to being known for the sinner she was—and had honed her skills and attention in order to stave it off. Now the distillery was hers, she more or less believed its continued success depended upon her industry and vigilance; and though she could rest on the day of rest, she did not allow herself much leisure otherwise. Even she, however, was caught off guard by her dedication to this new project, because her absorption in it was at once so intense and so joyful.

As if her work had a spell on it that might be broken by uttering its name, her sisters at first gave her a wide berth; but Pearl soon gave in to curiosity. She began following Prue down to her workroom, whither she had brought Johanna's rocker in which to read. While Prue worked, Pearl rocked in the creaking chair and bent over her needlework, which at the time was yet another Pietà, this one with a sad, green-faced Virgin bending over her even sadder gray son. When she grew tired, Pearl would retire to the house without so much as meeting Prue's eyes or bidding her good afternoon. The next day, she would be back. At first Prue found her presence irksome, but after a few days, she began to look forward to this silent time in Pearl's company. Prue could hear the rush as Pearl pulled her silk floss through the muslin, and she felt the heat of Pearl's gaze upon her as she figured and sketched. At last, on the evening she'd made her first complete drawing of what she believed would be the actual bridge, Prue pushed abruptly back from the table and met Pearl's dark stare. Pearl whistled a descending scale and drew her palms together in the air to indicate she had been caught.

"Indeed," Prue said. "But I've been watching you, too, when your head's down. May I see?"

Pearl secured her needle in the fabric, unhitched the tambour hoop, and stretched her scene wide for her sister's view. It was broad as her arm span, and half as high; and her hoop had left a large dimple surrounding Mary Magdalene's hand, which was clutched tight around a handkerchief, her very sinews expressing her grief. Pearl was peering at her sister over the top, awaiting her approval.

"It is most affecting," Prue said, "and beautifully composed." Pearl dropped her chin in thanks. "I am not certain I understand where you acquired a taste for such images."

Pearl folded her scene in her lap, opened her pad, and wrote, *I might ask the same of you, in oth' Circumstanses.* She paused to sharpen her pencil against her pocketknife. The shavings curled to the floor. *M' Severn also thinks it most affeckting, & our Catholic Neighbours will almost certenly wish t'exhibit it in thr Church.*

"Should I hire you some minions to execute your designs?"

Pearl's small eyes widened, while she awaited further explanation.

"You could make a tidy business of it. It wouldn't earn so much as a distillery, but I daresay you'd do well."

Pearl smiled and shook her head. *Might earn more'n a Bridge. But t'would'n't work,* she wrote, then tapped her left fingers against her breastbone. *No use unless you feel it Here. Never fear, the Catholics pay me well. I am quite satisfy'd I shll have a new Dress come spring.*

"You needn't save up your shillings for that," Prue said.

I know. I can ask whenever I wish. Now may I see what yr working uppon?

Prue's mouth went dry, but she answered, "Yes."

Pearl watched her a moment, as if to ascertain whether her answer still held true. Then she placed her embroidery on the chair and crossed the few paces to the desk. Prue could not fathom her own nervousness at the prospect of showing her sister this work.

"You will forgive my inexpert drawing," Prue said, and slid before her the most detailed sketch, which showed the whole structure seen from the south, with Winship Gin to its right and, across the river, the Old Market Wharf.

Pearl took it up by its edges, mindful as she was of graphite's impermanence, and let out a breath of surprise or delight. She bent her head down close, as if to smell each detail, and scanned it up and down. After a while, she settled it on the table and reached out her hand for Prue's arm. It was their mother's hand Prue saw—all length and veins. With her free hand, Pearl gestured to the other drawings around the desk.

"Yes, if you like," Prue said, and pulled away from her enough to gather them.

Before Pearl picked them up, she wrote, *Beautiful.*

Pearl scrutinized the cross section of one of the levers, the joists supporting the roadway, the foundations for the abutments, and the abutments themselves. She brought Prue's candles closer to her and arranged the drawings around them. At last she drew one of Prue's clean sheets of paper—a full-sized sheet—toward her, dipped Prue's pen and wrote, *Y^r Mathmaticks are sound?*

"To the best of my knowledge," Prue said. "The model bridge will help show if such a structure can stand at all: if it be a plausible method of construction."

& Yr Materials will hold, over such a Spann?

"Again, it appears so. Once we have the facsimile, I shall test it with weights out of all proportion to its size, in the hopes this will prefigure the weight of the eventual thing itself."

Pearl stepped back from the table and regarded them all once more. Then she returned and dipped the pen again. *In truth I think it magnificent,* she wrote. Prue felt her face light up with pride. *Magnificent. But I could draw it better for you. W. a better draw^{ng} you'd be able to see more clearly, where there are Flaws. May I have a go at it? Even if only for a few Days?*

She was leaning toward Prue, her face eager. Prue could see she had a faint rash at her temples, no doubt from the dry air. "Of course," she said. "I would be most thankful."

Pearl slapped the table as Tem might have done. The inkwell wobbled, and she reached out to steady it before dipping her pen once more. *The Moment I finish my Pieta, then.*

"I cannot thank you enough," Prue said. A moment later the gratitude itself flooded her chest. She was surprised both at how pleasant it felt and at how long it had taken to arrive. "Shall we go up?"

Pearl nodded, and began to blow out the candles.

Prue closed the stove's door. "When do you imagine you'll begin?"

she asked. But as the room was now nearly dark, her sister could not answer her. The date didn't matter, after all; it would be soon.

Prue had never seen her sister so happy as over the next few days. She began arising earlier than Prue; when Prue arrived downstairs for breakfast, there Pearl would be by the kitchen fire, working on her embroidery. She would continue to pore over it long past dark, though her eyes grew red from the strain. Prue thought, watching her, it was as if Pearl had been struck by lightning—she had a current of energy coursing through her where previously only her own mild spirit had appeared to move. She understood the pleasure and satisfaction Pearl anticipated in working out the drawings; and when she thought it had always been possible to bestow such a gift on her sister, and she had only now figured out the way, she felt something very like the silent awe she sometimes glimpsed during Will Severn's sermons. She hoped she would have the opportunity to join her sister at church again soon.

It was also with great joy Prue returned to supervising the distillery. She had never before left it for more than a day. While she had performed her experiments and calculations and worked out her first drawings, she had generally been on or near the premises, and apprised of the business's daily output and events; but for the first time in more than half her lifetime, she had not had her hands regularly in the malt nor the burning fumes of proof spirit in her nostrils. She felt, on returning, she could see Winship Daughters Gin with new eyes; she could appreciate the sheer size of the manufactory, and its gruff, unstudied grandeur. She experienced for the first time an understanding of what her father had meant when he'd likened the process to alchemy. If only he had not been so full of doubt, she thought, he might have likened it to a miracle.

Eleven

BENJAMIN'S RETURN

Ben came home to Brooklyn in mid-April sporting a coonskin cap, its wildness at odds with his pointy Horsfield chin, which was itself incongruously covered in a trim reddish beard when Prue first caught sight of him. She chanced to see him debark from Losee's boat as she looked out the countinghouse window. Although he wore a thick shearling coat, he appeared slighter than she recalled; but there was no mistaking the cock of his head or the exuberance with which he sprang up to the wharf. She was glad Tem and Isaiah were elsewhere, so she could watch him in peace.

He did not call at once. Prue started at every footstep, both at home and at the distillery, but none was his. He could only have gone to stay with Isaiah, but her overseer told her nothing the next morning. Gossip sped around Brooklyn, however, and she learned from Joe Loosely that Ben had gone that very morning to see about buying one of the tidy new houses of Olympia, in Buckbee's Alley. "That'll give 'im a place to hang his shingle," Joe said, serving her a plate of fried fish. "And keep him clear of that colicky whelp of Patience Livingston's." He blew out a whistle of surprise. "Healthy lungs, that one. My wife and I hear her from our bedroom."

Prue had two questions of great importance for Ben: whether he would assist in the design of her bridge, and what he had concluded, during his years away, as regarded their former intimacy. She berated herself for wondering when he would come make love to her, and tried to find comfort in telling herself the bridge was the only important thing.

"Yep, bought that little blue house," Joe told her the next day. The day after that, "My boys carried his trunks over this morning, and he's hiring one of the lads away from me, for an assistant." Prue had never eaten so much fried cod in her life, but vowed she would lunch at the tavern until she received some definitive news. Three days had passed and the man hadn't called. Prue dreaded to know why—perhaps he had taken a wife in the north country, or worse, had simply worn out his fancy for his child-hood friend—but at last she determined to seek him out and learn his reasons. As dusk began to fall, she hung her work clothes on a peg and put on the plain brown dress she still had not bothered to replace. She noticed as if for the first time how awkwardly she moved in it. Abiah stood cutting carrots in her palm with the paring knife. "You look pretty," she said.

Prue could not read Abiah's tone, and took up her coat from the rack without responding.

"Going to see Ben Horsfield, I'll wager."

Prue wondered why anyone in Brooklyn even bothered to have conversations, when everyone knew everything already. Abiah put down her knife, wiped her fingers on her apron, and went over to pinch Prue's cheeks. "Don't," Prue said, but she also could not help feeling flattered.

"That's better," Abiah said. "Shall I expect you back for supper?"

"Yes."

"Hmm," she said, and returned to her work.

The blue house Ben had taken was next to Will Severn's. When Prue arrived, Will was standing at his open door, sweeping dust out into his yard. Prue wondered where his servant was. Though dusk was falling, she saw him suck in his lower lip in what appeared genuine surprise at seeing her in a dress on a workday. "Hello, Prue," he said. He bowed his head, still holding his broom. "No Pearl?"

"No, not tonight. Hello."

"Hello." He blinked at her. "Well, welcome. Ellie has the afternoon off, and I'm nearly done cleaning up after the boys. I don't know where they find so much mud."

"Thank you, Will, but I've come looking for our surveyor."

"Oh." He glanced off toward the fitful smoke rising from Ben's cen-tral chimney and swallowed, his Adam's apple bobbing. "He appears to be at home." Ben had hung a bright placard from the tree by the road; it read *Benj. Horsfield, King's County's Surveyor.* "Another time, then. But I haven't seen you in a while. Is aught amiss?"

"Not at all," Prue said. "Business is fine. Tem grows more capable at the distillery, and I'm working on another project, I believe for the public good." Even in the waning light, however, she could see that he meant between them. "And your school? Does it fare well?"

"Yes, by God's grace. Twelve pupils now, and only eight of them incurable rascals." He began to laugh, but instead cleared his throat. From the corner of her eye, Prue saw Ben draw back the curtain in his nearest window and peer out at her. She felt she might forget to breathe. "Well, I shouldn't keep you. But I've missed your visits. I have told Pearl as much."

"Thank you," Prue said. She wondered Pearl hadn't passed the message on; she was usually so punctilious. "I have been too busy at the works for social calls, but I look forward to visiting again soon. I'll come later in the week."

"I shall anticipate it," Will said.

He stood in the doorway watching as Prue crossed the dry grass to Ben's door. She knocked, as if she had not seen him standing there behind the window. He opened the door and stood aside to let her into his hall, and she raised her hand to Will Severn before she stepped inside. As soon as he'd closed the door, Ben gathered her up in his arms. He was newly shaven and in his shirtsleeves, and he smelled exactly as he always had, and better than Prue had recalled. At one level she was thrilled to be in his embrace; at another, all she could bring herself to say was, "I can hardly believe you didn't come visit."

"My Prue," he said, and kissed her ear. "Hello."

"Hello. Why didn't you come?"

"I wanted to get myself in order," he said. "I wanted a haircut and a shave, and to set up house before I came calling. I've been two years away from home and society; I thought it best to get settled." He pushed her away to arm's distance to examine her. His cowlick was sticking up, as usual. "You're even prettier than I remembered."

"I'm wearing a dress."

"That isn't what I meant."

"You've been here for days," she went on. She would have liked to stop herself, but couldn't seem to. "You might have come. And what of all these months of silence?"

"I was marking roads deep in the wilderness, Prue; there wasn't any post there. Didn't I write you when I could?" He pulled her in close again and leaned down to kiss the side of her neck. "When I could manage a letter, I had time for but one, so I dashed a line off to Isaiah and told him to tell you I was coming. Did he not do so?"

As Prue recalled, Isaiah had told her of Ben's approach as if it were a secret; but she said, "He did."

Ben kissed her once more. "Come in, then. I am making supper, and I shall show you my house." The house was built, like Mr. Severn's, on an English plan, with a neat central hall, the sitting and dining rooms to either side, and a kitchen at the back. Only the cook fire was lit. "Will you let me take your coat?"

When Prue removed it, he draped it over the banister. He untied her hat strings himself and put the hat on top of the coat.

"I saw my neighbor detained you," he said.

"He is my friend, you know."

"And a good man. I think a bit lonely. This shall be the dining room," he said, indicating a room that contained nothing but two crates, "and this the parlor." In that room, his theodolite was set up on its tripod beside a stool with books and a compass stacked on top.

"I hope your brother can spare you some furnishings," Prue said.

"He's given me some plates already. Of course, he's hurt I won't live with him, but I can't abide Patience or that baby." He led her by the hand back into the spacious kitchen. "I'm nearly done cooking. It'll be a bachelor supper, but I'd be delighted if you'd join me."

Prue did not know what waywardness in her character made her want to refuse him, but it prevented her answering.

"I'm sure Abiah's making something better, but stay for the company." His kitchen was spotless, and had nothing going in the fire but a tarnished copper pot of boiling potatoes. One other such pot—an expensive item, Prue noted, and not acquired in Brooklyn—hung from a hook on the wall, and there were two wooden bowls and a few plates on a shelf. Other plates, covered in dishrags, stood on the sideboard. "I'll wager it's better drinking at the Winships', too." He let go her hand to pour her a mug of beer from a covered pitcher on the table.

"I should have brought you some. But then, you should have come to see me."

"What's got in you?" he asked. "You didn't used to be so snappish."

"I haven't heard from you in months!" Prue almost shouted.

"But not from lack of affection," Ben said. "I do apologize, but it's done now. Drink up, eh?"

The beer was cool and mild, and she thought it had come from the Philpots'. "I, too, am sorry," Prue said.

"It's no matter." He refilled his own cup. "D'ye ever pay my brother in gin?"

"Perish the thought," she said, taking the seat he held out for her. The two chairs didn't match, and the other had a hole in its rushing. "I pay the men part of their wages in liquor only because they demand it."

He leaned down to kiss her head. "Prue, I promise I shall never again leave for so much as a week without writing you. I only asked because he hasn't brought me one blessed ounce."

"He takes little for his own consumption. He's the oddest man imaginable for a distillery; or the best."

"I could have told you that. And I think the drink would do him a world of good," he said, going to mind his pot. "As for me, I buy from the alehouse, like any other man."

"There'll be no more of that. Let me leave with an order tonight, and I'll send it up to you tomorrow."

"Now, you see? When the lads suggested I ought not to choose a girl in britches, I knew I'd prove them wrong." He began spearing the potatoes, and deposited them in a wooden bowl to cool. "I do sometimes wish Isaiah were a better drinking companion," he said.

But Prue thought it had very likely been love for the product had done her father in, and she sometimes worried it would level Tem. Ben cut off a chunk from his cake of butter and broke some rosemary from a dried branch on the windowsill. "Milk, Ben," she told him. "Salt," as if she'd mashed a potato in the past fifteen years.

"I can manage it," he said, pointing around with his index finger in his search for the milk, which had no place to hide in the spare kitchen. "Out in camp, we gents cook for ourselves." He pulled a dishrag off a second pitcher, poured some in, added a pinch of salt, and mashed the potatoes. " 'Tain't fancy," he said, serving his handiwork into two cracked blue and

white bowls, which had once been his mother's, and setting one down before Prue. His grin made it clear how little he valued fanciness; and brandishing two forks, he sat down with his leg touching Prue's.

She was surprised to find the potatoes good, and her face must have
shown it.

"Didn't know bachelors cooked, did you?" he said.

"The Philpots cook," she said. "No womenfolk in camp to feed you?"
She heard the faint challenge in her voice, and half wished she could retreat to Will Severn's and begin her visit anew.

Ben stood again and brought back from the sideboard a plate covered
with an old checked cloth; beneath it was half the cold carcass of a
roasted chicken. He ripped off the remaining drumstick and perched it
on the flat edge of her bowl.

"Thank you," Prue said.

"I know you're awaiting your answer. The only women traveling with
a company of surveyors are likely to be whores, if you'll pardon my saying so."

"As I thought."

"One is far better off eating what one can cook oneself." He was
blushing through the freckles on his cheekbones. "I notice you haven't
married anyone since I've been gone."

"Whom would I marry?"

"I can think of a few candidates."

Prue wanted to tell him none of them had come calling but had the
sense to keep this to herself.

Ben said, "Well, eat your supper."

The chicken was as savory as the potatoes; and Prue knew she was be-
having badly, but she couldn't stop herself. "I'm sorry, Ben."

He examined his plate. "I should prefer you quit apologizing, and instead were happier to see me."

"I'm happier to see you than I can express," she said.

An awkward moment looking at each other passed before Ben put his
fork down, and Prue climbed into his lap and wrapped one hand into his
hair. Now when he kissed her, his breath tasted of rosemary. He tucked
her head into his shoulder, as if he could pull her closer than she already
was. She had not forgotten about the electrical charge that passed from
his skin to her own, but her memory of it had been pale indeed beside

the pleasure of the thing itself. "Prue," he said. "What's this about a bridge?"

"Did Isaiah tell you?"

"He did. And that Tem has been running the works. He said you want to bridge the East River."

"I do."

Ben reached around her for his mug and took a long pull from his beer. "You realize it would be a masterpiece—a miracle of engineering?"

Prue nodded her head against his shoulder, then pulled back so she could see his face. He regarded her as if she was ordinary and sane, as had long been his habit, no matter how odd others might have found her. "Yes, I do. But I believe it can be done. I wonder if Isaiah doubts it."

"He does, of course, but also mentioned he knew none of the specifics of your plan." Prue felt stung, and Ben obviously saw it. "Isaiah's not your man for such a thing. He's too fond of order and routine." He waited a moment before going on. "You know he tried to dissuade me from my chosen profession, not because of any inherent danger, but because he disliked the idea of my mucking about through the squelchy bits."

Prue could not help smiling at this. "Isaiah hasn't even seen a sketch of the thing. And I believe it has a chance at working—it seems so, at least, in the calculations and the drawings. I shall build a model and see what I can learn thereby. But I came this evening to ask your assistance."

"And not to kiss me?"

"And also to be kissed by you."

He did so, then said, "I'm not a bridge builder, Prue."

"But you have a theodolite. You can survey the proposed course of the bridge and see if I've projected the angles true. And surely, in your work, you've had some experience preparing the groundwork for large structures?"

He shook his head no. "I do know a thing or two about rock and soil, and I observed some blasting for tunnels as we worked; but what I really know is trigonometry. Of course I can survey the site. I would be delighted. That is, I'm willing to be of service in whatever fashion I may; but I repeat, I am no bridge architect. Can you show me what you have thus far?" He reached to the back of her head and removed the pin that held up her hair.

"I can, indeed." It was difficult to concentrate on what she was saying. "Pearl will check my calculations and see if she can do better with the drawings than I. On such drawings as I imagine she can render, we should be able to build a preliminary representation."

He unwound the hair down her back. "I've good maps as well, which may be of use. I believe, however, we need to discuss my payment for this service."

Prue was surprised at this, but did not wish to say so. "Whatever the going rate is, of course. Whatever you tell me is fair."

"Well, I am paid by the job for surveying. I don't know how men are paid for building bridges."

"Nor do I."

"These will be my terms. First off: I shall have as much gin as I can drink."

"That, of course. We've settled that already."

"Second: If the idea appears unfeasible, I shall be permitted to absent myself from the project without incurring your wrath."

"Naturally," Prue said.

"Third: As I now have a house of my own, with a bed in it, I should like to ask you to stay with me this evening. With the understanding that, on a date of your choosing, I shall make an honest woman of you."

Prue wondered if she had somehow misheard him. She felt sure she would have given up her dreams of Severn years ago, had Ben only asked; though she could not be certain she remembered that passion in all its complexity. She had never doubted Ben loved her, not in her innermost heart, but there was something marvelous in this audible proof. At the same time, she did not see how she could wed him. Winship Daughters Gin was hers in its entirety, but the moment she married, it would become her husband's property. This seemed an intolerable circumstance.

"I don't think it bodes well for me that you haven't answered," he said.

"No." Prue realized this answer was as equivocal as her silence, but he was smiling at her. "That is, it doesn't bode ill."

He kissed her again, and kept his hand on her nape. "Then what do you say?"

"That I don't know if I can be any man's wife." The words sounded harsher than she'd meant them to. "I love you, Ben. I always have. But if I marry, I shall lose control of my distillery; and I don't think I could abide it."

He nodded, and worked his fingers into her hair. "You suppose, however, that this future husband should wish to be a distiller."

"He wouldn't have to," she said. "He'd own the works. That is what affronts me."

"I see." He never once looked away from her eyes. His pupils were wide and black in the firelight. "But this 'he' you speak of is not I. I shall be King's County's surveyor, Prue. You shall make the gin, and it seems only fair that you should therefore own and manage your distillery." He kissed her softly. "The law can say what it will, but that is how I see things standing between us. What do you say, then?"

"That I find your terms agreeable," Prue said. She still felt unsettled, yet could not contain her grin. "But I don't know when we'll find time for a wedding. We've a bridge to plan, and I've my distillery."

"We can bide awhile. Lord knows we've managed all this time; a few months more won't seem long in comparison."

"Then it's settled," she said, and held him close.

"Oh," he said into her hair, "that's my Prue."

"But I don't think it wise to stay the night."

Once again he pushed her away enough to see her. "Why so?" he asked. His face was merry, as if her constant fretting were the very thing he liked in her.

"My sisters will worry."

"They'll figure it out," Ben said.

"And what will Mr. Severn say?"

"That I'm a luckier man than he."

Prue shook her head no.

"Very well," Ben said. "But you will stay another time? When your priggish friend hasn't seen you arrive?"

"He's shy, not priggish."

"Hmm." He kissed her once more and brushed her off his lap. "You should be home for supper. I know Pearlie; she won't let anyone eat until you appear."

"That isn't quite true," Prue said, but she did feel she should return home before she committed some other act of rudeness.

Ben walked her back through his dark hall, and helped her on with her coat and hat. He kissed her in the doorway, about which she felt strange, though the street was dark. As she once again crossed his lawn, Will Severn looked up from his reading to watch her pass; and when she reached the crossroads and turned around, Ben was still standing beside his open door, his arms folded in front of him for warmth. He raised a hand to see Prue off and did not go back in until she'd gone a distance down the turnpike.

The next day, as she walked the boards of the cooling room, feeling the warmth of the wort rising from underfoot, she saw him fix one end of his Gunter's chain at her boundary with the Schermerhorns. His assistant—Adam, the van Suetendaels' youngest son—took up the other end and began to chain off the property's perimeter. She stopped along the open southern wall to observe them.

"Anything wrong?" Mr. van Voorhees asked, behind her.

"No," she said, and watched as Ben picked up his end of the chain to continue the measurement. She knew the rudiments of surveying—that he would next use his transit to determine true north, and then measure angles with the theodilite so he could accurately calculate distance—but could not estimate how long he would be about the property; yet she thought she'd have a fine time looking after business with him wandering the premises.

Ben's first project as county surveyor was to parcel off some land southeast of Brooklyn proper, across Bergen's Hill. Throughout the remainder of April he went down to the distillery just past dawn each day to borrow a horse and cart to drive himself, Adam, and their instruments to the site. He performed his calculations for the bridge while he was there. At first, he took bearings on Prue's land and across the river; after a time, he began to check his angles and distances against hers and Pearl's at the large plank desk in the assembly room. He helped her move the desk aside one morning when the men needed to be paid. Prue took real pleasure in his proximity, and Isaiah in harassing her about it, "as," he said on a few occasions, "you could have had him here every day of the past few years, if you'd only said the word."

"Ah," Prue would answer, "but now I have you both, which is exactly as I please."

Ben's own drawings indicated only the edges of property and the height of the cliffs, but through his measurements he thought he might propose some emendations to the plan. Prue had always had the distillery in common with Tem, but had thought little of her judgment; it was thrilling now to share a project with both Ben and Pearl and to believe each might have something valuable to contribute. Of a Sunday, then, Prue and Pearl began sitting toward the back of the church—which Prue now found herself with the time and inclination to attend—and were among the first to leave. While Will Severn chatted with his parishioners, they would run up Buckbee's Alley, where Ben would be waiting with a pot of coffee and some dried-out baked goods from Thursday's market. There at his table, they argued over the angle of approach vehicles would take and the construction of walkways for pedestrians; the means of bracing the structure against the wind; the merits of moving the Brooklyn abutment ten feet closer to the water's edge, thus decreasing the lateral force by a fraction of its magnitude. Will Severn often took his Sunday dinner with a member of the parish, but when he returned home, Pearl would sneak out the surveyor's door and knock on the minister's; and Ben and Prue would spend the remainder of the afternoon upstairs. Prue did not discuss this arrangement with Pearl, but assumed she found it acceptable. At least, when Prue began taking Mrs. Friedlander's herbs again and jumping around the yard for exercise, Pearl took a mild interest in it but did not question her.

Pearl herself, meanwhile, began to assemble a file of information about the bridge, and made sketches of every slight change they considered. She was waiting to execute her final drawings—a large, detailed view of the structure as a whole, and the plans from which they might construct the various members—until their plan had arrived at relative stasis; but although she could not yet engage in her work, it had already begun to brighten her manner. She was spending less time at home with Abiah poring over her needlework, and more time taking long walks through Brooklyn—a habit into which she had never before fallen, as she had been so discouraged from it as a child. When she wanted a book, instead of asking Prue to fetch it from New York, she began going down to Losee's landing, riding across, and visiting the bookseller herself. Prue thought her sister must have laid a fair sum by from the sales of her needlework, as she never asked another penny for the household expenses, and this was the only other money to which she had access.

When at last the fruit trees were swathed in the pink mist that pre-saged blossoms, Prue, Ben, and Pearl all agreed their plans were as complete as they would be. Prue handed them over to Pearl, along with her key to the assembly hall.

And as she read her mother's letters, Recompense marveled at the bitter-ness of her first upstate winter, and tried to envision that workaday space in her mother's distillery given over to such a use. Like her brother, she had been given free run of the premises when she'd been small; but Rec-ompense had found all the noise and bustle frightening, and had felt she would wilt, surrounded by such heat and such powerful scents. The as-sembly hall, clean and empty most of the time, had been the place that most appealed to her, rather to her mother's disappointment. She en-joyed now imagining it full of bustle, promise, and purpose.

Recompense loved Jonas and enjoyed their evening discussions but, for reasons she could not articulate, had not yet told him of this corre-spondence. The world her mother drew within its pages opened itself for Recompense's eyes alone; and she could not say why she wished it to re-main so. She read this most recent letter through twice, folded it, and tucked it into the bottom of her workbasket. There it was well hidden be-neath the white cotton yarn from which she'd make her baby's things, if ever she quit feeling so low.

Twelve

PEARL'S ELEVATION

Pearl was secretive about her drawings. When she worked in the assembly hall, she locked the door, and took breaks only to eat or visit the privy. She put in as long a day as the foremen, and though she must have been making good progress, she would neither talk to Prue about it nor show her the fruits of her labor thus far. Prue was piqued by this refusal, but also understood her sister's dedication; she herself worked this way, and though her father's humor had been lighter, he had been similarly single-minded when occupied with a task. The assembly room's windows were, however, large and numerous, and allowed Prue to glance in on her, always in passing. In this way Prue saw her sister had purloined some more candle stands from the house and acquired others from the Chardonnons. Prue also discovered, after a few weeks, that Pearl had dismantled the table and stacked its components against the far wall. She was working spread out on the floor, on a great roll of printing paper. This had arrived at the Winship dock one morning and caused speculation among everyone who worked at the distillery, but among no one more than Tem and Prue. They had both been out at the wharf, supervising outgoing shipments, when the log-thick roll of paper had arrived. Prue directed the deliverymen to their destination, and Tem stood watching with her arms akimbo. After a moment, she began to laugh. "Damme if she didn't find a printing press," she said. Prue was likewise amazed. "I do underestimate her," Tem said cheerfully, "don't you?"

"Yes," Prue said. "I suppose."

Pearl, meanwhile, must have caught her sister or others spying, because she'd had the great roll of paper no more than a day before she'd tacked lengths of it over the lower halves of all the windows. Prue thought her canny: She had deflected both the stares of interested parties and the human propensity to gawk out from windows, while still admitting the needed light and her view of the sky through the upper panes. When Prue and Tem needed the assembly room to distribute payroll or make an announcement to the men, Pearl would roll her work up and let it lie unobtrusively against the far wall. The men stood clear of it, as if it were charmed.

When Pearl drew, she drew for hours at a stretch, and would emerge, wan and red-eyed, blinking in the noise and bustle of the yard. Any of the men nearby would say hello to her as easily as they did to Tem or Prue; and Prue saw how taken they were with her thoughtful expression and the sweet manner in which she waved her reply. Prue remarked her forthright gaze in such moments; if she herself had not worked in the distillery so long, she might have wished to bury her head in the sand, but Pearl kept hers up, where it belonged and could be admired. She would stand outside for a few minutes and breathe the salty spring air, then turn back and lock the door behind her. A while after the bell rang for closing, she would plod up the stairs to the countinghouse and either pour herself a drink or sit down in whichever seat was empty and lay her head on her arms; but by the time they sat down to Abiah's supper, she would have left a sheet of questions beside Prue's plate. The questions she asked—about distances and types of materials, about the fir's strength under tension, about the means of constructing the twin voussoirs to either side of the elliptical central arch—all indicated an understanding at least as thorough as Prue's own. On a few occasions, Prue had to hunt down the answer in a book.

While Prue and Pearl discussed the bridge's evolution over supper, Tem and Abiah generally sat across the table, not talking. Abiah might have preferred to gossip or hear the news, as she still could barely read and the balladeers came only from time to time; but the moment the conversation turned to construction, Tem began stabbing at her food and dragging her utensils across her plate. Prue imagined she might be jealous of Pearl's work on the bridge, which was, after all, the most interesting thing occurring on the distillery's premises at that time. Prue also realized she had not consulted Tem on a single question about construction. Though this was reasonable, as Tem could not have much useful knowledge to bestow, she was accustomed to being party to decisions. Not all her annoyance was related to her sisters, however; some stemmed from the attentions of Ezra Fischer. He had recently moved to Brooklyn to begin preparations for his new ferry and had bought the old Pierrepont mansion, which had stood empty since the close of the war. The whole town was abuzz with news of him. Some were in favor of his ferry, and others entrenched against it; some were impressed by the renovations he'd undertaken on the house, while others thought them extravagant; some found his manners refined, others unctuous; and more or less everyone was interested to have a Jew in their midst. Even Prue, who had plenty to occupy her, wondered if until his ferry began operating he would have to take Losee's boat to attend his worship in New York; and if so, what the two men would find to say to each other.

As he was a bachelor, Mr. Fischer took his evening meal at the Twin Tankards. Tony and Tobias Philpot were welcoming and lively conversationalists, and could provide him, in addition to his roast, a friendly introduction to many of the men of the community. Ben had met him right away, and reported him outgoing and intelligent, though Ben had disliked the foppishness of his attire. On perhaps Mr. Fischer's fourth night in Brooklyn, Tem had banged in at the close of the workday, thirsty for her pint, and poor Mr. Fischer had fallen in love with her in an instant. Tem had sat down with Cornelis and Jens, but later told her sisters she'd seen Mr. Fischer making what he must have supposed were discreet inquiries about her.

"No," she heard Tobias answer in his low voice, "she's not taken." He smiled at her, as if this could prevent her knowing it was she of whom they spoke.

"Refused every man who's tried her, and good 'uns, too," Tony added. "Including one of those fellows she's sitting with."

"Well, I've never seen such lovely gams," Ezra Fischer said in a tone of reverence.

"Actually," Tem said loudly, "I'll wager you've never seen any *gams* at all, as women don't *damn well display* them. Unless, of course, you are referring to your taste for whores, quite a pretty few of whom you'll find upstairs."

Cornelis later told Prue he'd never seen such an expression of shock on a man's face. Mr. Fischer said, "I crave your pardon, Miss . . ."

"Temperance Winship," she spat. Cornelis stifled a laugh, as he had never before heard her use her full name; and he was glad, after all, his advances were not alone met with such scorn.

"I ask your pardon, Miss Winship."

"Her sister is Miss Winship," Tony said under his breath. "That one's Miss Tem."

"Miss Tem," Fischer repeated. He stood and approached their table. He was wearing a fine brown silk jacket and cravat, both of which Cornelis reported looked out of place in the barroom. "I spoke out of turn, and I give you my apologies. But please allow me to make your acquaintance. I am Ezra Fischer, lately arrived from New York."

Cornelis said Tem's eyes burned so hot and her nostrils flared so wide, it was as if Roxana had returned from the dead. "Delighted," she said, stood up, and left. The Luquer brothers apologized to Fischer, but followed her, and stood her a drink at the Old Stone.

Tem's report left her sisters galled at Mr. Fischer's behavior, but when Prue later heard a softer version from Cornelis, it roused her interest; and a few nights later, she took Pearl down to the Twin Tankards after supper. Mr. Fischer nearly fell off his stool to see a second woman in britches, accompanied by one who bore such a strong resemblance to the cause of his disgrace. Both sisters laughed at his response, and he appeared further startled by Pearl's weird hiss. But Prue went right up to introduce herself, and invited him to join them for a glass of Madeira wine. Tony brought a whole decanter. Prue was surprised Tem hadn't mentioned the salient fact of Mr. Fischer's appearance: which was, he was extraordinarily good-looking, with dark wavy hair and lovely moss-green eyes. After his initial discomfiture over their arrival and Pearl's unique method of communication had evaporated, Prue questioned him about his history and his prospects in Brooklyn. Both sisters found him cordial and articulate, and Prue, for one, rather liked his fancy coat, as it reminded her of something their father might have worn.

Tem was angry her sisters had gone looking for Mr. Fischer at all, and even more so once she discovered their affability toward him had encouraged him in his suit. He began to appear bearing small gifts—candies, periodicals, and, on one occasion, a delicate painted teapot a person such as

Tem could never have use for—and Tem began spending as little time as possible in the countinghouse, as this was where he would try to apprehend her. That her sisters seemed bent on encouraging her to talk to him galled Tem even further.

"Why should I?" she said at lunch one afternoon. They were gathered around the desk, eating cold smoked ham and pickled cucumbers.

"Because he's a good fellow," Prue said. "Decent. And interesting."

Pearl added, *& wealthy.*

"Pff," Tem said, "I haven't any need of his wealth."

'Twould'n't hurt y, either.

"For crying out loud, he's a Jew," Tem said.

Prue said, "Well, I don't know." She had almost no knowledge of Jews, but thought Mr. Fischer ordinary, except for his fine looks. "You're the one who'll never set foot in church. I can't see why you should mind."

Tem stretched her eyes wide. "I don't understand either of you. Why are you so eager to marry me off?"

"We're not," Prue said, before Pearl could finish writing it. "I simply allow it might be pleasant to be courted by such a man."

"You take him, then," Tem said, and stalked off. For weeks she remained in a foul temper whenever either of her sisters spoke to her. Thus she was doubly disgruntled whenever they began to discuss their bridge.

One evening at the start of June, Pearl wrote to Prue, *I am nearly finish'd my drawings.*

"My," Tem said. She had her elbow on the table, and feigned a gesture of interest with her fork.

"That's wonderful," Prue said. "When do you suppose you'll be done?"

3 or 4 Days? but I want to wash th Floor before I shew it you.

Tem said, "How big is the thing?"

Pearl shrugged her shoulders. *Plans & Sections &c &c moderatly small. Elevation?* She looked around the kitchen. *I did it to Scale, 1/250 of t'actual Bridge' Size. 'Twould'n't fit in this Room.*

"Holy Christ," Tem said.

Prue said, "I am so eager to see what you've done. Later this week, do you say?"

Pearl gave it a moment's thought—perhaps for show—before nodding her assent. *Sunday Morning after church*, she wrote.

Prue said, "The days will drag till Sunday."

Pearl began to clear the dishes with a sudden burst of energy that sent her spotted cat hissing from its place on the edge of the rug.

The days were slow. There was enough to do in distilling grain alcohol to keep Prue busy for all eternity, but she couldn't think of anything but Pearl. When at last Sunday morning arrived, it was bright and clear. Prue could hardly listen to Will Severn, though he preached eloquently; and when he had finished, she took Pearl by the hand to lead her down toward Joralemon's Lane and the distillery.

Pearl shook free of her, took out her pencil, and wrote, *Are'n't you hungry? Abiah bought some Sosages.*

"Afterward," Prue said. It was all she could do not to run down the street.

The rising tide of the East River lapped against the Winships' stretch of shore, and the sails of the windmill twirled in the Sabbath breeze. A cask had burst the previous afternoon while being loaded onto a wagon, and Prue thought the spot still bore a faint odor of juniper. Pearl unlocked the assembly hall, from whose windows she'd removed the paper, and where a tall, bulky scroll was propped into a corner, tied with a thin black ribbon. She unrolled a smaller set of drawings, each perhaps a yard wide, onto the floor.

These were plans for the bridge's foundations, the two abutments, the stacking method Prue had envisioned for constructing the voussoirs, and the ways of facing the bridge's exterior and of trussing and paving the road. At the bottom of the sheaf was a visual depiction of the results of Prue's experiments on the relative strengths of woods under the various kinds of stresses they might endure. These drawings were all executed with a line as fine as that made by an engraver's burin, and shaded with a delicate webwork of crosshatches. If Prue had not known how she intended to build this bridge, she felt she could have learned it from the drawings at hand; and though she had known Pearl had a talent for drawing, she was taken aback by their precision and beauty. "Pearl," she said, "gòod God. Thank you."

Yr welcome, Pearl wrote. *Do you think they'll suffise?*

"Without question." Prue spread them around her on the floor. "I have no doubt we can build a model from these. If the plan proves viable, they'll take us a long way toward an actual bridge."

To build the B. itself, I'd need to draw up a Plan for the Cranes; but I assume these draw^{ngs} too will undergo some Changes before then.

"Yes," Prue said, but the images made her feel as if she were in a trance. She could dive into them and remain there; she could feast on them and not exhaust them. She was awed by Pearl's skill, and amazed to see the thing she had dreamed of translated into concrete terms by the mind of another.

Pearl whistled at her, and she knew she must have gone off wool-gathering. *Do you want to see the big one?* she asked.

"Yes," Prue said. "But first you must tell me how you learned to draw so well."

I've all ways been good at it.

"Yes, but—" Prue cut herself off, as her sister was still writing.

& I have had some Practise. Will study'd you know, in his Youth. He has taught me some Fundamentles.

"I didn't know," Prue said, and thought she would simply have to accept her sister's prowess in this regard. She appraised the scroll propped in the corner. It stood about as high as a horse. "That's the elevation?"

Pearl nodded and stowed her pencil in its hasp. She walked over to the behemoth, reached toward its upper extremity with one hand, and waited for Prue to come to her aid. Prue went over and steadied the bottom end while Pearl coaxed the top down into her hands. Prue was surprised at its weight and unwieldiness, and Pearl hissed at her in laughter as she deftly swung her end down to the level of Prue's. Together they brought it out to the middle of the room. When Prue attempted to lay it down, Pearl freed a hand to make a circle in the air, in sign they must rotate it first. When they placed it on the floor, Pearl whistled again.

Prue said, "I didn't ask you to make it so large."

Pearl patted her breastbone to accept the blame.

They bent over the scroll like reapers, untied the ribbon, and began to pull the ends apart. They had gone no more than a foot when the unfurling image stopped Prue still. There was a schooner tacking into the wind, with her sails as round and full as life and her sailors pulling on her halyards. The water through which the ship plowed was murky and rough, as it often was on the kind of overcast spring day on which Pearl had modeled the drawing. High above arched the most delicate part of the bridge. The round gray clouds overhead seemed as if they could either roil the port with rain or blow off in an instant. It was the very sky of Brooklyn.

"Jesus," Prue said quietly.

She heard Pearl continuing to unroll her half, but had difficulty looking up from what had already been revealed. After a moment she recovered herself and kept going. The bridge continued to soar across its great arc, unfurling until it was half as wide as the broad side of the room. There were the two fanciful abutments, and springing from them were the two levers, faced in clear timber and sweeping up toward their meeting point over the center of the river. Around the feet of the bridge New York and Brooklyn bustled, recognizable in all their particulars. There stood Winship Daughters Gin, the sails of the windmill having been cleaned and the sign repainted for the occasion; and though the rope-walk's workers were too small to be recognizable, Prue made out Tem's figure, in waders, tallying a shipment, while she herself stood in profile, simply gazing at the bridge. The craggy Heights appeared just so; likewise New York's docks and the myriad of boats and ships, all meticulously observed. It was not possible Pearl could have learned the wharves in such detail in only a few weeks; it had to be that she had long been spending a great deal more time in watching, and less in needlework, than Prue had known.

She said, "Pearl."

Pearl paced along the bottom of her work, with her hands clasped behind her. She was appraising her own workmanship, not awaiting Prue's approbation.

1/250th the size, she wrote, the next time she found herself near her sister, *of the finish'd Structure. We shall build the 1st Facksimile to the same Spessifications.*

Prue took her hand and said, "This is the most beautiful thing I have ever beheld." Pearl narrowed her eyes at her. "In all seriousness. I cannot believe how perfect it is. I did not know you possessed quite such a talent."

Buried it in the Yard? she wrote, and returned to examining the bridge. *Mighty thin at ye Keystone; but the Maths seems to support yr nocion.*

Where the two levers met, high over the middle of the river, the bridge appeared thin as air, a bare demarcation of the space above from that below. "A few hundred times larger, it'll have more heft."

& when 'tis an axual Bridge, the guard Rail'll prevent the hapless from pitching off the Side while they Gape. Pearl had drawn the bridge pristine and empty of traffic; but in reality, the heads of horses and the tops of high loads would dot the horizon like so many beads. *If we've done our Calculations correckly,* she wrote on a new sheet, *you'll be able to ship a whole year's worth of Gin over at a go.*

"If ever I can deliver a single cask by such means, I'll be happier than I can describe. And to walk over it, and look down at the straits—it is almost too much to hope for."

Well it's good you've made it solid. A brdg'll have to be strong if in Deed 'tis to reach th. Other Side.

Prue said, "Pardon?"

You herd me plain, Pearl wrote.

"It will stretch from the foot of Clover Hill to the Old Market Wharf," Prue said, as if this were not apparent from the drawing.

Yes. To New-York. Where the Dead do ther Marketting. She flipped to a clean page, stepped back a few paces, and sharpened her pencil against her pocketknife. *Lets roll it up before some Ill befalls it.*

Prue kept an eye on her as she walked to one end. "Pearl, what are you saying?" she asked. Pearl wrote something and held it up, but Prue was too far off to see it. "Well, let's put it away, and then speak." She began to roll in the side of the elevation, but she was preoccupied with what Pearl had written, and could not keep the drawing centered along its own axis. As she rolled it, it stretched into a tube. She started over twice, and when she finally reached the midpoint, found Pearl crouched down waiting, with her pad open on her knee. *Johanna told me. Sometimes I think you & T. think I am deaf.*

"No," Prue said, "you're mistaken." Though even as she said it, she knew she sometimes considered Pearl less perceptive than an ordinary person; when, if anything, the opposite circumstance obtained. "Johanna told you I once thought New York the Land of the Shades?"

Pearl nodded.

Prue could not remember ever having spoken to Johanna of her belief, and a shiver coursed down her spine as she realized Johanna might merely have intuited it. "Why did she tell you this?" she asked, though she wanted badly to drop the subject. This was not how she had imagined Pearl learning of her crime; this would not do. She reached down for the two ends of the black ribbon and tied them around the scroll.

Pearl touched her hand to Prue's arm, then held a note in front of her. *In illustracion of Why you were so Sad a Gell.*

"You'd asked her?"

Pearl nodded. *You worry'd me.*

Prue blew a breath out through her nostrils. As much as she wanted to run from the room, she had to find out how much Pearl knew. "I wonder what other illustrations she may have given you," she prompted. "I don't believe she was fond of me."

O I know she was! Pearl wrote. *She pray'd for you always.* She flipped her page. *She say'd you'd drunk that Fret of our Mother w. her Milk. I did'n't have so much Milk, you see, for some While. Joᵃ thought it spar'd me.*

"I remember." Even after so many years in each other's company, Prue could not always read Pearl's tone in her hasty notes. She believed she could read her sister's eyes, however, with utmost clarity; and she did not sense any hostility behind this, though she was uncertain she understood its import. She found herself longing to tell Pearl of the curse she'd inflicted on her, to be rid of the burden once and for all; but after so many years guarding her secret, she could not bring herself to do so. It mortified Prue—it broke her heart—to think she had ever harbored such resentment against her sister. In defense of her own thoughts and actions, she told herself that before Pearl had been born, she had had no means to know how much she'd value her. It was only now she could not imagine anyone dearer to her than this small-boned person, with such particular curves and angles in her face.

& so I understand, why it's a __Bridge__ you wish to build. I understand the desire to get there & proov yr Self wrong.

Prue said, "It isn't only that. I learned I'd been mistaken, of course, a hundred years ago."

It's for Mother & Father?

"And for myself also. To have done something that wasn't handed down to me." She hadn't known she thought this until she said it. Her breath felt tight in her rib cage, but she continued anyway. "And it's for Brookland." Hearing herself say this, however, she felt foolish.

Pearl wrote, *I think it noble of you. Truly.*

"Thank you."

& I want to help you build it, in what ever way I can.

"You have done much already."

I want to help with the Moddel.

"You don't know anything of construction."

I know more than you think I know. Pearl patted the roll with her pencil hand, then wrote, *& I did this.*

"It's true," Prue said. "We should put it away."

Together they heaved the scroll upright, and it stood tall and broad as a house post between them. They shuffled it over to its corner. Pearl *was* correct, about the drawing and what it showed she knew of the natural world. When it was safely stowed, Prue said, "We must show Ben your work, and I believe Tem will also wish to see it. Perhaps we can begin building after that."

Pearl nodded, and gave her a swift hug before making her way to the door. What an unanticipated delight, Prue thought, to see her sister so full of enthusiasm.

Thirteen

A WORKABLE PLAN

P rue received Recompense's next letter, as she had received all the others, in the countinghouse. The postman knew where her home was, but as everyone excepting Abiah could usually be found below, it was no doubt worth an extra few minutes of his time to descend the ravine; any of them would slip him a gratuity for a letter delivered by hand. Prue thought he seemed a kind boy, not over-rough on the post horses.

Prue had to put the letter aside, however, to see to more pressing business. She was teaching her son, Matty, to rectify, and though he was much older than she had been when she'd begun studying the process, he was not learning well. When her father had told her that to rectify spirits required a gift, she had not truly believed him; but in all her years in the distillery, she had had only one employee who'd shown the slightest aptitude for the process. Prue had always assumed she'd inherited her skill from her father in the same way she'd acquired her mother's kinky hair. She had likewise assumed her son's mind and nose would prove educable, that he would come into the knowledge as a result of his parentage; but she was beginning to despair he'd ever get the knack of it. If he didn't, what then? She could hardly call Recompense home.

At day's end, while Tem stood at the west-facing window and drank her first glass for the evening, Prue read her daughter's letter. She laughed over Recompense's account of a visit from Jonas's cousins, the Starks. (She wrote: "These are: Chas. Wallace Stark, the cousin himself, a good spirited gentleman & farmer of Jonas's age; Charlotte, his wife; and two children, Harry & Lydia, of six or seven years of age. O mother, what *en-ergy* they have! These two are like tops;—set aspinning at sun rise, and not tumbling to ther sides till long past dark. I see they are good children,— they sit quiet at table, & Miss Lydia makes valiant efforts to murder my spinet,—but I cannot recall running so much in my own youth nor Matty doing likewise neither. They have given me a *terrour* of this infant within me, who is already, I think, starting to kick to apprise me she wishes to *get out.*") The rest of the letter troubled her, however, for Recompense was bothered—a state of mind Prue little thought her daughter experienced—by how her mother had treated Pearl. ("Did you really disregard her so?" she asked. "& did you all those years count her talents so cheap?")

Prue read the letter over, then laid it by. "Tem?" she asked.

Tem turned from the window to face her. Her hair was graying in delicate stripes but remained black underneath. Prue thought it becoming in the dusk's soft light.

"D'ye think I treated Pearl unfairly when we were planning the bridge?"

Tem blinked twice. "How so?"

Prue could not answer succinctly; her daughter's question had raised a thousand instances from her memory.

Tem leaned back on the windowsill and finished her drink. "I imagine we all did. Why do you ask?"

"Recompense wondered."

Tem shook her head and walked to the shelf to replenish her cup.

Prue knew they would not discuss the matter at greater length; and she dreaded that same awkwardness if she brought it up at home. Therefore, she told herself Recompense's objection was as to degree. She herself had admitted having rated Pearl's abilities too low; perhaps Recompense wished her to feel greater remorse for the misdeed. This was impossible, however. Prue could not yet explain to her daughter why so.

When she wrote her next letter, later that evening, she began by asking about the cousin's children, and did not respond to Recompense's concern.

It was a lovely late spring day when Prue and Pearl brought their sister down to view the elevation. They waited until the works had gone silent, and led her out to the yard. Then Pearl blindfolded Tem with one of their father's stocks.

"Oh, please," Tem said, although she was smiling. "We are not children."

"But it is a surprise such as you may not have had since you were a child," Prue said. She took her by the hand, and looked out for anything she might trip on.

Tem said, "Then I earnestly hope it's a pony."

Pearl hissed.

Once in the assembly hall, they left Tem in one corner while they went to its opposite and untied the drawing.

"This is stupid," Tem said. "May I take it off?"

"No," Prue replied. She and Pearl unfurled the scroll upright along one of the room's long walls. It made a satisfying rattle as they did so. They kept hold of its ends, and Prue said, "Very well. Now."

Tem pulled her blinder straight off overhead, and it was still in her hand when she covered her mouth with surprise and bent over as if the drawing had punched her in the belly. "Good God," she said, into her hand and the piece of silk. Her dark eyes began to pool. "What a beautiful thing." She took a few steps closer to it. "I had no idea it would be so lovely. Pearl, I had no idea you could draw so well."

Prue felt vindicated. Pearl shrugged her shoulders but looked pleased.

"My God, Prue, it's a much better idea than I thought it would be. Gravity will keep it up, you say?"

"I believe. We're about to commence building a facsimile, on a small scale, to begin to find out."

"Suppose I'll be running the works again, then." Tem did not phrase this as a question.

"If you don't mind."

"No. It's odd; I wouldn't say I enjoyed it during the last spell, but I found it gratifying to know I could." Tem crouched down to peer at the boats. "You got it all, Pearlie, even the bucket on Losee's landing. I am most impressed."

Pearl gave her a small curtsy and nearly lost hold of her end of the drawing.

Prue's head was full of how to construct the model. It seemed clear she should build it of the same wood she proposed to use in the finished structure, and with the individual members cut to the same relative dimensions; but she wondered if she could secure iron nails at a two-hundred-fiftieth their normal size.

"I'd say glue's your man," Theunis van Vechten said, when she went up to order the wood. "Otherwise you'd have to use jeweler's tools to hammer in the little pins. Have to become a watchmaker. A proper mallet'd break 'em." Prue wondered if he'd told anyone of her intentions.

"But glue won't hold if we take it out to see how it fares in the weather."

"I don't know, then," Theunis said. "See what the smiths recommend."

"And what of the stone? I can't ask a quarry for bricks. It wouldn't be worth their time."

Theunis took up his toothpick and, with an expression of satisfaction, worked it between his teeth. "Let me look after that as well. I'll find you a bit—just enough to anchor the thing."

"Thank you," Prue said.

"This time next week."

Waiting was an agony; but she realized if she actually was to build a bridge, this was an agony to which she had best grow accustomed. There would be waiting for the signatories to sign, and waiting for the legislature to approve her plan. If they did approve it, there would likely be a long, long wait for any money to arrive, and another for men and materials. Prue had always known she could be impatient, but she realized now she would have to pluck that quality out of herself by its roots if she was to get anywhere in this work.

After closing one day that week, Tem found Prue in one of the storehouses, where she'd been draining off samples of their three oldest batches. It was not quite time to test them, but she wanted to see how they were faring in the heat. Tem motioned toward the gin in her sister's hand. "How is it?"

"Still good," Prue answered. She held the beaker toward her. "A bit perfumey, to my taste."

Tem rolled it around her palate before swallowing. "I agree. How many are left?"

"Just eleven."

"It sells well, then," Tem said. "So it shan't matter if we think it perfumey." She drained another dram into the receiving vessel, and Prue pulled out the spigot and recorked the cask so she wouldn't take more. "What's that?"

"We've plenty at home. Don't take from the samples."

Tem swallowed her second draught and said, "It tastes better, the more of it I drink."

Prue raised a cloud of dust off the next batch's test cask and turned in the spigot. Their father had designed the mechanism to work like a drill, and had given a similar one to Joe Loosely, who still used it in his tavern. Prue wondered where they would get another if ever it broke.

"I've been thinking," Tem said, "it might be time to quit experimenting on the receipt."

"But the experimentation is my delight," Prue said.

"Yes, and what makes you indispensable to the operation of this distillery." She went over to the water skin on the wall and doused the beaker, splashing her dirty boots as well. "If I'm to manage things without you, it would be better to have a formula I can follow blindly."

"Well, or we need to train up a second rectifier."

Tem looked at Prue expectantly and handed back the beaker.

"Simon Dufresne is sending us a grandnephew. Perhaps he'll show talent for it."

"There's no way to predict that. Furthermore, if we make only a single variety, we'll turn a better profit. We won't always be in search of interesting herbs, or cursing if the deer get them from our garden."

Prue thought the next batch had a faint stink. "Does this smell off to you?" she asked.

Tem bent her head to it, and her short tail slipped forward over her shoulder. "Cherries?" she asked. She flipped through the notes on its distillation.

"No, Tem, it's turned."

"Then let's tell Isaiah to lower its price and have done with it." She reached again for the spigot, then stopped herself.

"I'm not certain I see why we need to turn a better profit," Prue said. "I think we're doing very well as it is."

Tem patted the top of the cask. She wasn't superstitious, but the gesture had a placating air. "We are; but if you intend to build a bridge, we'll need a fair bit of money squirreled away to keep the works off Joe's auction block." She wasn't smiling.

"Joe would never—"

"He'd not have a choice." She tucked the tasting vessel into her belt. Prue plucked it out again and left it on the nearest cask. "Are we done here?" Tem asked. "I am not saying I think the worst will come. Merely that I think it wise to prepare."

"I'm certain you're right," Prue said. "Though I think the project, being for the public good, would be entitled to a certain amount of public money."

"We don't yet know. I think you should consider simplifying what happens in the rectifying house. It's up to you, of course." She blew out the torch on the wall and ducked under the low storeroom door as their father would have done, though she was in no actual danger of banging her head. "Lovely evening."

"Indeed," Prue said. Owen was finishing up, sweeping detritus from the brewhouse into the yard. "And I will think it through."

A swift black boat, manned by a burly oarsman, was skimming across the water toward Butcher's Wharf. Prue said, "I wonder if that's the new ferry."

Tem took a few paces toward the retaining wall and said, "It shan't be my business if it is."

Prue wondered why her sister had to think so ill of Mr. Fischer; but she soon marshaled her mind back around to Tem's suggestion. This would be much of what she needed to consider as she and Pearl began building their representation of the bridge on the assembly hall floor. To change the manner in which she rectified Winship Daughters gin would be to change something fundamental about the business. Her father had taught her to value equally a fine product and her satisfaction in creating it. This was why he had always allowed the ingredients to vary: because he considered creating a balanced, harmonious flavor the crowning joy of making gin, and if he had once settled on a recipe, he would have forfeited that happiness ever after. It was Prue's great pleasure in the work, as well; and her chief pride, as it required her to have both an innate facility for the work and the dedication to cultivate it. Yet Tem was correct about the benefits of simplifying the process. It would save a good deal of worry, but at the expense of such joy, Prue was not certain she thought it advisable.

Though news of yellow fever once again came from Manhattan, and despite her own immediate dilemma of rectifying, Prue became engrossed in building the model. To distill gin and keep the works in good order required her full advertence to detail, yet she could not lose herself in it as she could in chiseling out one side of a piece of wood so it would hold securely to the span's central rails. Such a task required exactness of both mind and hand, and she often found herself surprised, when the noon bell rang, that hours had gone by in what might have been either minutes or weeks. She and Pearl worked well together, in a companionable silence broken by occasional discussions, fits of laughter, or sudden sprints to stretch their legs and shake out their aching hands. Together they built the model's platform base; they mixed pints of mortar to secure shards of stone into the general shape of the abutments, then affixed to these the iron rails to support the roadway. They used a small bow saw, wood file, and plane to shape the six-inch-long "timbers" in the necessary stepped fashion to face the sides of the bridge. They proofed the planks of the roadway against the weather in pine pitch, whose acrid odor sent them both to the door every few minutes. The wood itself smelled wonderful, as if they were working in a heaven of balsam sachets; and though it required care to measure all the angles, lengths, and distances time and again, and precision to drive in the square nails without marring the surrounding wood, both Pearl and Prue took to the work. The days were punctuated only by occasional visits from Tem, Isaiah, and Ben, and sporadic distillery business to which Prue had to see. Only when she left the assembly room did she notice how callused her fingers were.

The bridge's levers began to protrude from their abutments as she had imagined they would. The two main rails stuck almost straight out from the stone to begin with. Upon them Prue and Pearl constructed the well-trussed roadway, and from it hung the facing for the sides of the bridge, which they completed a few inches at a time. Prue's theory had been that the bridge would support itself during construction, as building would begin at the thick, weight-bearing ends of the levers and continue, foot by foot, out toward their graceful tips until they met midstream. As Pearl worked on what represented Brooklyn and Prue on New York, the hypothesis began to seem correct; though had the span been broader, she knew it would have been a delicate business to get the arms to meet exactly as planned. The model's miniature timbers lay back, one atop the other, toward their base, as a fish's scales lie flat toward its tail. She could not yet say, of course, that the principle would hold for something a few hundred times the scale; but that it should suffice for something seventeen feet in length seemed a start. After all, the whole thing might have collapsed immediately, if bridges could not be built upon such a plan. That the model appeared sound was a place to begin. Next she would see how it bore up under weights and stresses, and if necessary, she would emend the thrust of the levers or their thickness at the zenith or base ends. She might well revise the theory of construction before commencing a larger facsimile, which would represent at least a bit more truly the strengths and weaknesses of an actual bridge.

By the time Mr. Fischer opened his ferry that July, the model was complete. Prue was delighted that it appeared to function, but perhaps more thrilled at its beauty. Its shape was simple and pleasing to the eye; the pitch gave a dark cast to the wood, but its natural reddish gold color shone through. Though there was nothing beneath the bridge but the simple base to which it was anchored, she could imagine how lovely it would be soaring above the water.

After pacing around it a moment, Ben said, "It does seem sound." Then he walked to its middle, stepped up onto the most delicate part of the arch, and began to jump up and down.

Pearl sucked her breath in over her teeth, while Prue cried out, "What are you doing?"

"You can't mean to tell me the finished structure won't support the weight of two hundred fifty men?" Ben asked.

"Yes, but it will have proper foundations. And not be held together with pins the size of sewing needles. You can't judge the strength of a bridge by the strength of its model."

Ben continued to jump at the bridge's zenith, a foot and a half off the ground. Prue kept expecting the arc to flatten under the force of his falling weight, but the structure held. "I don't know, love. I'd say it's doing well thus far. Our next task, of course, *must* be to break it."

Pearl took out her pencil and wrote a plaintive *WHY?*

"Because there's no better way to determine how to make it cohere."

Pearl shot her sister a glance of annoyance, indicating, Prue thought, that she understood Ben was correct, and deplored the notion anyway.

"Yes," he said. "We'll stack it with weights; we'll invite the little Luquers to have at it; we'll leave it out for the wind, rain, and birds, and we'll pitch salt water at it, to see how it fares." As they both remained unconvinced, he said, "It'll be a holiday, I promise."

"Perhaps," Prue said, "we might show it to our neighbors before we destroy it. If they have no interest in pursuing the idea, there'll be no need to go on and ruin it."

Ben hopped off to the floor. Pearl wrote, *I agree*. Ben said, "Ah, you only want to save the thing from being jumped upon." He continued to walk around it. "Have I told you, Miss Prue, I think it magnificent? I've seen bridges in my travels, but none so fine as this."

Prue was relieved he hadn't shattered it. "I think we should call a meeting of every landowner in Brooklyn, show them this representation and the drawing, and see if they'd stand behind it if it went any further."

& what of New-Yrk? Pearl wrote.

"No need to address them, if our neighbors say nay. If they approve it, New York will have all the more reason to do so."

"A fine plan," Ben said. "And it'll let your model live another week or two."

Prue could not deny her sentimental attachment to the thing. It was the literal representation of her dream, and she and her sister had built it with their own hands. It was no less natural to wish it to survive than it had been for Patience to hope her baby would outgrow its colic. Prue determined to call the meeting as soon as she could, for it would be agony to wait to hear what her neighbors thought.

Fourteen

THE PETITION

There were two practical matters to attend to, however, before Prue could make a public presentation of the bridge. The first was the unwieldiness of Pearl's elevation, which Prue could not imagine placing on view in its current state. When she and Pearl had attempted to hold it up for Tem, it had been almost impossible to keep upright; and if they were to lay it flat, it would likely be besmirched by a passing boot. Prue therefore asked Jean and Scipio to mount two thick dowels on sturdy wooden bases, crown them with simple finials, and paint them black. Prue and Pearl then glued each short end of the elevation along the shaft of a dowel. The whole drawing could still be rolled in upon itself, like a scroll, but when unfurled, could stand in a great shallow arc on its two feet. They were pleased with this solution for both its practicality and its aesthetics. The black bases and finials anchored the ends of the drawing as surely as the abutments anchored the ends of the bridge; and both sisters thought the drawing appeared more monumental in this fashion than when it had lain on the floor.

The second matter was of greater delicacy: how best to present the plan, particularly in New York and Albany, with regard to its authorship. In Brooklyn, people counted it ordinary enough that Tem and Prue ran their distillery. If, when their father had begun to train Prue, some of the neighbors had sniggered, the quality of the gin Winship Daughters produced had long since put to rest any lingering doubts. When Prue dealt with her customers, suppliers, and Mr. Timothy Stover at the Bank of New-York, she did not feel she could have been treated with greater respect had she been a man. And had she been required to visit Albany with some grievance regarding the distillery, she expected the gentlemen of that august body would receive her petition fairly.

A bridge architect, however, was another thing. Though it had been years since any of the neighbors had twitted her about her britches, she believed some of them might cavil at the prospect. She could only imagine how New York's aldermen, or the state assembly itself, might respond. "Brookland is a backwater; they have their own ways," she could picture them remarking as they puffed on their cigars. She did not think it would stand so singular and expensive a proposition in good stead to be the brainchild of a woman.

Ben, however, had received his commission from the governor's office; he was already known to the senate. Even Prue granted that surveying seemed, on its surface, a line of work more likely than distilling to produce a bridge architect. He could stand in her stead as the author of this plan. He had a pleasing voice and an earnest manner, and could expound passionately and knowledgeably upon the merits of the proposal. Yet Prue could not bear to consider giving him credit for work whose seed had been her own. She herself had performed most of the investigations into the idea's feasibility; she had stretched her faculties to the utmost to propose how such a structure, never before seen, might hold. She would never have been able to express her vision so well without Pearl's assistance, but it was her own imagination on view in the drawing and the wooden model. She knew it would smart to stand in the background and let another—even one so dear to her as Ben—pretend to have been responsible for that dream and that work. Prue recognized this as the ranting of her own *amour propre*, and wished she could shut it up and move on; but it was not so simple. For all Ben's kindness and generosity, it still rankled that he would become the legal proprietor of her distillery; now he would come to own the bridge as well.

Ben gathered she was in a simmer, for which insight he was rewarded with a torrent of pleading and invective. To him, however, the dilemma did not seem so heart-wrenching. He walked her to the retaining wall, sat her down, took both her hands in his own, and said, "It isn't so dire. I think we should present me as the chief author of the plan and say I have developed it in partnership with the owners of Winship Gin, as it is upon their property I must needs erect a footing and accessway."

His idea did sound reasonable.

He said, "It makes perfect sense. In this manner, we can placate the aldermen of New York at least on this front; and should the governor, the senate, or the assembly agree to hear my petition, it will be natural for you to accompany me to Albany. It might even make sense for you to address them."

Prue wanted to disagree, but could arrive at no reasonable objection. It was, therefore, by Benjamin's pen they dispatched letters to Mayor Varick, in New York, and to their assemblyman in Albany, one Garret Willemsen, of an old Bushwick family. They entitled the project *A Proposal for a New-York & Brookland Bridge. Benjamin Horsfield, King's County' Surveyor, Architect.* Both Varick and Willemsen wrote back by return post, expressing their strong interest. Willemsen told Ben that the assembly was then afire with arguments for and against an eventual manumission of all slaves within New York State; but he believed the gentlemen would be willing to pause in their arguments to hear plans for a bridge. He suggested Ben write, with his blessing, both to Governor Jay and to the speaker of the assembly, Hendrik Stryker. Though Prue still felt the indignity, she helped Ben compose letters to both men, under Mr. Willemsen's aegis, to request an audience with the legislators. Together they also wrote up a detailed proposal, explaining the costs of the plan and the methods of construction they intended to use. They gambled that by the time Ben received his replies, they could secure the backing of Brooklyn and New York. (Prue had no idea what would become of Winship Gin if all its slaves were suddenly freed; but as Willemsen had written that the issue was still under debate, she supposed she could save up her fretting for some quieter time.)

Prue therefore scheduled a meeting with the landowners of her neighborhood for the first Sunday in August. She commissioned Cornelis's youngest brother, Claes—a freckly critter, not ten years old—to run from business to business and house to house, bearing a statement of the purpose of the meeting and a paper on which gentlemen might sign their acceptances or regrets. Much of Brooklyn already knew what she'd been scheming, if only because it was a short line from Ben's mouth to the ear of anyone who frequented the Twin Tankards. But people who'd had business on the East River had also seen Ben taking his bearings; and any who'd visited the mill yard had tried to peek into the assembly hall window to see the emerging model bridge, though Prue and Pearl had covered it with tarpaulins when they'd locked up the room for the night or when the distillery workers had assembled. Prue had been in the Liberty Tavern little since Ben's return, but she knew opinions on the bridge were already well formed there; and although Brooklyn did not as yet have any newspapers of its own, the New York sheets ran speculations about what might be transpiring in Winship Daughters Gin's assembly hall. Nevertheless it seemed important to gather the Brooklanders together. Only in this way could they explain the scheme in all its detail, exhibit the lovely model and Pearl's miraculous depiction of the elevation, and gather signatures in favor of the plan. With Brooklyn behind them, she thought she and Ben could earn the support of New York. Remsen, Luquer, Livingston, Schermerhorn, Hicks, and Joralemon were all old, powerful Brooklyn names—much more so than Winship and Horsfield—and they would surely make Mr. Varick take notice. Mr. Varick, in his turn, had been elevated to his position by the legislature's council of appointment; Prue believed the assemblymen would value his signature.

News of the meeting spread through Brooklyn as would fire through a corn crib. Over the following days, a number of those Claes Luquer had not tagged—Mrs. Tilley and her daughter, the women of the old families, the Philpots, the Whitcombes from out past the Cobbleskill Fort, and three of John Boerum's tenants—stopped by with housekeeping gifts for Pearl, and asked her to add them on. Pearl had never been courted, and she loved the attention. When her sisters came home from the distillery, she delighted to show them the squab they would have for supper, or her new sewing scissors, or the peppermint candies they could all share. *Now I really don't know why you're so Rude to Mr Fisch'*, she wrote to Tem when he brought her a rosebush more than half her own size, its roots wrapped snugly in burlap. (This caused Tem to throw up her hands and curse.) Meanwhile, the distillery workers—many of them residents of rented rooms, men who would receive no benefit from a bridge but a straitened view from their place of employ—and the slaves proved the most eager petitioners of all. They came in groups of five or six, their hats in their hands, to ask to be included in the viewing. They came every man and boy of them, all seventy-nine. More than half of them brought a wife or sister as well.

Distillery business went on as usual. Prue ordered her weekly fuel from Queen's County and worked out a better schedule for slop exchange with the Luquers, but she was impatient for the day to come. Pearl and Abiah set themselves to baking armloads of *koekjes* from old Jannetje's recipes. Though many burned, and many more were consumed in a testing of batches as rigorous as any performed down at the manufactory, they managed to lay enough by to sweeten an entire regiment, should the need arise. Each evening, Ben and Prue practiced their presentation on their siblings, accepting their critiques, encouragements, and vacant stares, and the howls of Isaiah's unhappy baby. They practiced each phrase until it fell from their tongues as easily as water fell from a waterwheel.

At last, on the Saturday afternoon before the appointed meeting, Pearl and Abiah scrubbed down the assembly hall floor with soap, shined it with wax, and polished the windows with vinegar. Prue argued she could have had some of the distillery's slaves perform the labor, but Abiah disagreed. "We want it done right," she said as she filled her bucket at the distillery's pump. "And I, for one, take pride in helping you prepare for such a momentous event. I believe Miss Pearl does, too." It was a hot summer day. As the men filed out after work, they all seemed to want to look in on the preparations. A few stopped by the countinghouse to wish Prue courage and good luck, which made her worry she had more to fear than she'd anticipated. She waited until they had all left the premises and the sun was about to go down before setting out the smaller drawings on the table. Then she removed the tarpaulins from the model, on display along one long wall; the scrolled elevation stood propped up against the other.

The next morning, she and Pearl went to church. When Will Severn saw them, his face lit up with excitement; Prue marveled that even his imagination could catch fire, thinking about a bridge. Though she tried to listen to the sermon, she was more aware of the birds twittering outdoors and the way her palms were perspiring than she was of any wisdom Mr. Severn might have to convey. As soon as the service ended, she ducked out of the church, as had become her habit, and she hoped her Sunday dinner might provide some distraction. It did not, however. Abiah was as keyed up as any of them, and looked uncomfortable in her crisp new flowered dress; and although Ben had come to join them, conversation was strained at the Winship table. The quiet in the house was unbearable, and Prue found herself listening anxiously to the erratic ticking of their clock and watching Pearl's old cat lick its dull fur clean.

She considered changing into her dress, and realized she'd want a new one if they were fortunate enough to be called to Albany. She went outdoors to remove the caked mud from her boots, and would have blacked them had Abiah not taken them from her and done so herself, taking care not to sully her skirt. Deprived of her task, Prue went out to the pump and scrubbed her fingernails until her hands were raw. Tem walked out to the back fence and immediately cried, "Christ! Prue, have you seen this crowd?"

From the pump Prue answered, "I'm trying not to look."

"Damme."

"Tem, please."

Tem whistled. "I didn't know there were so many people in Brookland," she said. "We should set out; it's almost time."

Prue knew she was correct. Ben, Pearl, and Abiah all came outdoors, with nervous expressions on their faces; after Abiah had closed the door, she kept smoothing down her dress and touching at her bonnet at intervals. "There's nothing for it but to go," Prue said. Tem led the way out into the road.

From the top of the hill, Prue saw hundreds of people gathered in the mill yard, while still more hurried down Joralemon's Lane and up the Shore Road. She would have stopped and gaped, but Pearl put her fingers on the small of Prue's back and propelled her forward. Tem continued to march in front of them, as if clearing the path for dignitaries. Old Mrs. Livingston, her bonnet trimmed with a garish new green ribbon, fell into step beside Prue and Pearl and exclaimed her excitement, and Ezra Fischer swooped in from the other side to express his eagerness to view the work. "Thank you," Prue said to all their compliments. Her mouth was already solidifying into a painful rictus, but she gathered this was better than wearing no smile at all. She was terrified at the notion of presenting this scheme to her neighbors; but she tried to remind herself they cared little if the bridge came from her, Ben, or the moon. The thing itself was what had piqued their interest, exactly as, when Rem Cortelyou's milk cow had given birth to a two-headed calf, the whole county had gathered to shudder and stare.

There were faces in the yard—whole clans—Prue did not recognize.

They must have come in from Bedford Corners and Midwood. Mad Ivo was waiting for her by the gate, freshly shaven and with a clean white stock around his throat. He leaned into his crutches and reached out to offer her an apple as she passed. "Thank you, Ivo," she said. He wagged his head shyly to reply, and Prue felt blessed by him.

Isaiah was standing atop a stepladder in the middle of the fray, as if he could thus keep order. His narrow face lit up in relief when he saw them all approaching, and he climbed down to meet them.

"I hope Pearl made enough *koekjes*," he said into Prue's ear as they reached out to hug each other. He had removed his hat because of the heat, but now his forehead and cheeks were tinged pink. "Patience and Maggie want to help set up the refreshments. They're over by the brew-house."

"That's good of them," Prue said, handing Ivo's apple to Pearl. Pearl glanced at it, then looked off sourly toward the water.

Isaiah reached over to pat his brother's back. "Are you ready?" he asked.

Ben nodded, but he looked as nervous as Prue felt.

"You've no idea how excited I am to see it," Isaiah said.

Ben and Prue had agreed that as he would make their presentation to Mayor Varick (and to the state assembly, should they have the good fortune to be summoned there), she would do the speaking here at home. She felt now as if her feet were stuck in the sand; and despite their preparations, all memory of her speech had vanished.

"You'll do admirably," Ben said. He steadied the ladder for her as she climbed up. Prue was glad to have worn britches and her distillery boots; the climb would have been unmanageable otherwise.

As soon as Prue ascended the ladder, the crowd around her began to quiet. She was surrounded by a sea of warm bodies, including every last person of her acquaintance and a number of strangers. She imagined she understood how poor, stuttering Moses had felt, charged with addressing the Israelites, then thought if Will Severn knew she'd thought this, he wouldn't be pleased. She opened her mouth but found it thick as a half-dried pot of paste. One of her slaves reached up to offer her a tin cup of water. She drank it, handed it back down, and thanked him. "Hello," she at last managed to say. "Good afternoon. Thank you for coming." She felt her want of confidence idiotic. She addressed her own men thus every week; she tried to tell herself this was not so different.

A hush settled over the crowd, and she could hear the tide lapping along the dry strand. Children, dragged to the gathering heedless of the reason why, continued to race with rocks and sticks around the assembly's periphery.

"I am Prudence Winship, owner of this distillery, and coauthor, with Benjamin Horsfield, King's County's surveyor, of the plan you are invited here today to witness and approve." It was probably unnecessary to introduce herself—no one would mistake her for some other redheaded woman wandering the premises in a man's attire and work boots—but the ruminant gaze directed up at her from those assembled faces had unnerved her. She cleared her throat, resolved to do better, and explained as succinctly as she could her plan for the bridge and the barest outline of its novel method of construction. She then told them of the elevation and model they were about to view.

The sails of the windmill, unhooked from the gear shaft, spun easily in the hot breeze, and the flag of the Republic snapped atop its pole. She caught sight of Will Severn in the crowd, his undershot chin nearly quivering with expectation. He seemed to be looking for someone.

She wished she had more water. "Shall we proceed, then?"

A murmur of assent rippled through the crowd.

Prue saw Tem had stationed herself by the door to the assembly hall. "My sister Temperance Winship stands by the room wherein the materials may be viewed. If you will line up outside the door, everyone will be admitted in turn."

Tem waved a hand in the air, and the crowd began to converge on her.

Prue saw Abiah speaking to Patience, Rachael, and Maggie near the distillery gate. A moment later, they started up the lane. Patience was once again large with child, and she lagged behind the rest of them. When Prue descended the ladder, Ben said, "Well done."

"Thank you."

He said, "It's such a large gathering."

Prue thought he meant to say he was nervous, and she nodded her understanding.

Pearl took her sister's arm as they moved toward the countinghouse.

Those at the front of the line stepped back so Ben and the Winships might enter first. As they passed him, Will Severn raised his hat in greeting, and Pearl waved back with her free hand. Someone unknown to Prue asked his companion if they were likely to be offered samples of the wares later on. She hoped few of these people had come merely to drink.

Pearl walked over to the table of drawings, and Isaiah to the model bridge. Ben and Prue untied the ribbon from the elevation and began to unwind it. He was sweating in his high collar and frills but had somehow managed to grease his cowlick down. They all glanced nervously around between them, and Isaiah said to Tem, "Very well. Let them in."

"No more than twenty shall enter at a go," Tem announced to the crowd. "And we would be most obliged if you'd spit out your tobacky before you step inside." This provoked laughter, but Prue heard people spitting outdoors. Hot, humid air puffed through the windows, and the planks of the floor creaked as the first viewers arrived.

"Oh, good God!" Mrs. Livingston exclaimed on seeing the elevation, and began touching at her hat as if the drawing might cause it to disintegrate. "Impossible!" As the room was still almost empty, it gave back her words with a sharp, metallic echo.

"It'll never do, never do," her husband comforted her.

Of course, the crowd erupted in a volley of speculation and surged toward the door, but Tem held them back. "In due time," she called, and they subsided. But those who had made their way indoors felt free to gesticulate and shout about what they saw. Much of the commentary was incredulous, but much was full of interest and awe.

When Peg Dufresne's turn came, she leaned in to touch Prue's arm and asked, "Pearlie really drew that?"

"She did."

Pearl beamed from the table end of the room. She was flushed, and her delicate collar was wilting with perspiration.

"Bless her," Peg said. "I always knew she was special."

From the door, Tem shouted out, "May I ask for order? My friends, please. If you line up and enter in a systematic fashion, you'll all get in quick enough."

Isaiah called out, "Temmy? Let us trade places," and she seemed relieved to comply. She tugged at her vest as she moved inside.

The line did quiet and grow neater with Isaiah to regulate it. Ben stood by New York's abutment, and Prue by Brooklyn's. In clots and clumps the neighbors, employees, slaves, and numerous strangers filed past the items on display, some taking only a cursory glance around before retreating, others exclaiming, still more crouching down to squint at the layered timbers or at some detail of the drawing, as if it were a queer fish brought up in the day's catch. Not a few kissed Pearl, or bowed to her, which raised a thick bubble of gratitude in Prue's breast. Will Severn happened to be standing by Ezra Fischer when he entered.

"Fancy that," Mr. Fischer said, placing his hand on Will Severn's sleeve. "Her drawing rolls up like the Torah, in which we read the holy Scriptures."

"I have heard," Will Severn said. "Your work is magnificent, Miss Pearl."

She smiled broadly in reply.

Soon afterward, an unfamiliar young man entered and began scribbling furious notes on a folded bill. His whole body hunched around the work, and the underarms of his pale linen jacket were dark with perspiration.

"How's that, sir?" Ben asked him.

"Ah, Mr. Horsfield," the young man said. He stood up sufficiently to remove his hat, and gave a perfunctory bow. "C. Mather Harrison, of the *New-York Daily Argus*. I've been sent to observe this wonder; and a wonder it is."

Prue felt her pulse in her throat, but knew she should allow Ben to speak. He replied, "We have not yet presented this plan to the good people of New York."

Harrison gave a quick, affable smile. "Indeed, sir. That's why I'm sent to write up the report." Like Will Severn, he had a slightly undershot chin, but Prue thought the resemblance ended there.

Ben looked to Prue for guidance, but Pearl stepped over to him and wrote him a note. Ben took a deep breath after reading it, then turned to Harrison and said, "Very well, sir. Present the facts; your fellows will know them soon enough. Mind your pencil, however. I don't want you marking up our elevation."

"Of course not, sir. Much obliged." He returned to his work with a dedication Prue found worrisome.

Jens and Cornelis Luquer let out a whoop of astonishment when they saw what their friends had been working upon. Many of Brooklyn's womenfolk seemed curious how all these things were put together. Mrs. Luquer eyed the way the elevation attached to its poles, and Katrintje Remsen showed an interest in the model's pattern of timber. None of this was as Prue had expected, but it pleased her nonetheless.

The reactions of some of her father's compatriots, however, worried her. Mr. Remsen and Mr. Joralemon hurried by the drawings almost with their eyes averted. Prue feared their displeasure, for it was their names, and their property, that would sway the legislature. She tried to remind herself that if a man had lived twice as long as she, and had land and a family to protect, he would not be likely to jump up shouting for change. It was beginning to seem natural to Prue that her workers loved the bridge—building it would bring good jobs to their sons and brethren.

Though the hottest part of the day soon passed, the room continued to grow hotter with the sour warmth of bodies and breath, and Prue knew her own agitation contributed to her discomfort. Pearl's hair had begun to come undone, and her shoulders were sagging; Isaiah had removed his coat but was still red and perspiring. Prue worried the floor was seeping the scent of stale liquor, though this seemed impossible. The stream of gawkers showed no signs of abating; but at last, when Isaiah let in a group that included Claes and Eelkje Luquer, he said, to no one in particular, "That's it. That's the last of them."

Prue's throat felt dry as a rock in the sun, and she thought she saw Pearl wobbling on her feet, but there could be only a few minutes more of exclamations and sullen stares to live through. Claes and Eelkje were wearing their Sunday clothes and comported themselves better than many of the grown people around them; Prue did not know how they had managed to wait, with such apparent patience, for so many hours together. " 'Tis very beautiful, Miss Winship," Claes said as he came around to her. "I'm glad I could help."

"You were of great assistance," Prue said, and found his bright expression buoyed her up for her last half hour of standing. Before those in the room had departed, Isaiah called out to those still milling in the yard, "Miss Winship and Mr. Horsfield will take questions, as soon as they have had a moment to refresh themselves."

Prue wished she had had the foresight to stow a pot up in the countinghouse; there was no possibility she could get clear up to the privy with such a crowd gathered.

When at last Claes and Eelkje filed out, Pearl sat down on the floor.

"Are you all right?" Prue asked.

She fumbled to remove her pencil, and wrote, *Only the damn'd Heat.* Her finger left a smudge on the page.

Isaiah said, "Abiah brought some cake and lemonade upstairs for us."

Ben took Pearl's hand and drew her upright. She leaned unsteadily into him, and he led her toward the door.

People began clamoring with questions the moment they appeared, but Ben called out, "Fifteen minutes, I beg you. We will give you all evening, if you require it."

Isaiah locked the door to the assembly hall before following them upstairs. Prue felt sick, but once she could force herself to swallow the lemonade, it cooled her. Pearl drank and allowed Abiah to press a cool rag to her neck and forehead, but she looked unwell.

"I'm going to take her back up to the house," Abiah said. "She'll fare better there."

Pearl shook her head no.

"That, or a dunk in the river," Isaiah said. "Your choice."

Pearl wearily opened her book and wrote, *Thank you, I wo'n't be mortify'd befor all theese People. It is my bridge, too. I wish to stay for the Questions.*

"You have done a great deal," Prue said, "but you really should let Abiah take you home. You'll be quite ill otherwise."

Pearl shot her sister a perturbed glance as Abiah helped her to her unsteady feet. Abiah said, "If she seems well enough, I'll come back to help with the refreshments."

"Thank you, Abiah," Isaiah said. "If you do not return, my wife and sisters will manage it." The moment they'd left, he said, "We should go back down. Perhaps we can answer questions from the countinghouse steps; it'll be easier to see into the crowd that way."

Ben removed his jacket and hung it on a peg by the door before they left the room.

Outdoors, Patience, Maggie, and Rachael were manning two tables set out with *koekjes*, cakes, lemonade, and cups for the casks of gin. Patience looked exhausted. She and the refreshments had been an attraction until

Prue and Ben appeared on the stairs, and then most of the crowd turned back to them. Prue did not even feel she had time to straighten her damp cuffs before the questioning began: "You can't really think it'll work?" Mr. Joralemon shot out at them; and someone near him, "How long would it take to build?" Mr. Cortelyou called out, "We don't have enough hands to spare you, not from here to Nassau County. Where will you get the men?" To which young Gregor Joralemon, with one arm draped affably around his brother Ivo's shoulders, replied, "I don't mind saying, if you're going to use explosives to clear the earth for the foundations, I'll be the first to volunteer for the job." The newsman, Mr. Harrison, stood at the outskirts of the crowd and made notes about the questions.

Prue saw Pearl and Abiah go out the gate and leave it swinging open behind them.

Ben had recovered himself sufficiently to start in on the questions, and began to address them, one by one. He detailed the cost of the bridge, which was reckoned in pounds, though the joint houses of the state legislature had the previous year approved the adoption of the federal dollar. (Ben and Prue agreed that as everyone still used pounds and shillings for their daily transactions, to state the cost in dollars would only breed confusion. Neither did it escape Prue's notice that the dollar was valued rather lighter than the pound, so any sum reckoned in that currency sounded greater.) Ben explained the time he believed would be necessary to build the bridge and the number of men it would require. Some of the younger Brooklanders sat down in the sand to listen. John Boerum whispered something to his adult son, who appeared uninterested; Jacob was known for a bounder and probably wanted to get back to the gin.

At last Joe raised his hand to question them, and asked, "Would you stake your life upon this thing's ability to stand?"

Prue glanced at Ben, but he did not even pause before replying. "I shall have no choice, Mr. Loosely," he said with a broad smile, "as I shall be up on it every day, supervising its construction."

This raised a faint wave of laughter, and Prue felt as if a cool breeze had blown through, despite the day's heat. The crowd still did not feel entirely friendly.

"Prue?" she heard someone call from the edge of the gathering. She looked out to see Losee van Nostrand making his way forward through

the crowd. "Please pardon me," he said. Those in his path stepped aside
for him, yet he seemed to be drawing his strong, hunched shoulders inward to take up as little space as possible. He stopped in front of the
staircase and stood with his hat in his hands, his hair tawny white above
his tanned brow. "I am exceedingly proud of you for all this," he said,
"and I wish your father were here to see it. If there is any justice, he's
looking down on us from Heaven right now."

Someone called out, "I wouldn't count on it, Lo."

Again some of the neighbors laughed. Losee turned his hat around by
its brim, and took a full breath before speaking. "I see the beauty of your
proposal, and I see it would serve our port well; but please understand,
my livelihood depends on people needing to be ferried across these
straits. My business will already be harmed by Mr. Fischer's new ferry."
The mill yard fell almost silent. "What do you say to that?"

Prue had felt guilty about the prospect of injuring Losee ever since
she had conceived the idea for the bridge. She was afraid if she did not
speak with care, she would burst out in apology to him, which would not
address the issue at all. "I know Mr. Fischer's ferry has come as a blow to
you," she said, "but I also know how many people in Brookland are loyal
to you, and will continue to ride your boat simply because it is yours."

He shrugged his great shoulders. "Of course I shall carry on. A
bridge, however; that would change things."

"There will always be those who prefer to cross by water," Prue said,
feeling her voice weak.

"During a freeze?" Losee asked.

She almost wished he sounded angrier, so she might be angry in turn.
"I agree there will be competition between ferry and bridge," she responded, doing her best to maintain an even tone, "but I see no reason
there should not be sufficient custom for both."

Losee's kind face darkened. "I am the only man in Brookland must
compete for his business. Think about it, Prue: one alehouse, one tavern;
one rope manufactory; one sawmill, one gristmill; one chandlery. If there
are three smithies, there are enough horses to occupy two more. One surveyor. What would you say if someone proposed to distill gin at Red
Hook?"

"I don't know," she replied. The answer that sprang to mind concerned the relative likelihood of a newcomer being able to produce good

gin on such a scale; and she had the sense to keep this to herself. "Perhaps I should say that after all the kindness you have ever shown me and my family, I would not willingly do anything to harm you." Her throat was dry again, and she didn't know how much longer she could speak. "If the bridge serves its purpose of increasing trade to our port, that will, I hope, redound to your business's good as much as to anyone's."

She felt certain Losee would object, but he only looked at her, his mobile old face hardened and set. "I shall not sign for you," he said. "But neither shall I seek to influence my neighbors. They'll do as they think's best. Good day, Prue." He cupped his hat over his heart and made his way back through the crowd. Someone coughed.

"Are there other questions?" Prue asked, in an attempt to clear the air. Her voice had a break in its middle. She worried that Losee's dilemma might sway the opinions of his friends. The flag continued to crack in the breeze, but no one spoke for what seemed an uncomfortable while.

"Thank you for your time, then," Ben said. "The gin flows freely from those two casks; and should anyone wish to sign our petition, you will find it, along with pens, ink, and a blotter, on the table outside the brewhouse, at the southern end of the property."

There followed some applause, but as the crowd began to open up, Prue could only watch Losee, and a small party with him, departing up the Shore Road.

Most of the listeners remained, however, to drink and discuss; and though Prue tried not to watch, there seemed a steady enough flow of persons to and from the brewhouse. People continued to stand around drinking for hours; and it was well past suppertime when at last Boerum's high-spirited son and his drunken compatriots broke into fisticuffs and removed themselves to the Liberty Tavern. Only the lees were left of the second cask, but Tem proposed they finish them. She looked exhausted.

Ben said, "Before we drink, let us see how our petition fared."

Tem tried to lean against the cask, which creaked and fixed to roll off its sawhorses.

"I'm not certain I can bear to," Prue said.

Tem said, "There's always more gin if the news is bad." She led the way to the brewhouse.

The sunlight shining in across shadowed Manhattan was tinged orange and cast a warm glow on the page on which Ben had written their petition. It was covered in signatures, which ran on to fill six more sheets. There were hundreds of names, some curly as new ferns, others mere X's scratched by hands more used to gruffer labor. "Dear God," Prue said as she shuffled through them. She began to laugh. Ben seized the papers, handed them to Tem, and lifted Prue up to spin her around.

"I knew it," he shouted. "Hoo-hoo!"

Tem was laughing, too. "You'd best make plans for your departure," she said.

"No," Prue said. When Ben put her down, the mill yard continued to spin, and the sweet scent of his sweat clung to her chest and arms. "No, first the mayor and the aldermen. Then Albany."

"Come," Ben said. "I want to read them."

Tem spread them out on the board so they might see.

For all the names she saw there, it hurt Prue that Joe Loosely's familiar scrawl was not to be found. Losee's she did not expect to see, nor Rem Cortelyou's, nor Mr. Livingston's. She tried to concentrate on all those Luquers turning the notion around their practical noggins and pronouncing it worthwhile; but it still pained her, that she could not earn the support of most of her father's friends.

"I feel certain you will go to Albany," Tem said.

Prue said, "Thank you," and gathered the papers to her breast.

"Are you joining us for supper?" Tem asked Ben.

"If I may."

"If there is any," Prue said. "Abiah never came back. I hope Pearl is well."

"If nothing else, there's soup and bread," Tem offered. "And gin, of course."

Ben said, "It will be a fine supper."

Prue let him lead her by the hand up to the house, and could not quit dreaming of how different Brooklyn would be when her bridge leapt out from its soil, a marvel for all the world to admire.

Fifteen

HENRY HUDSON'S RIVER

Secnd April, Winship Gin

Beloved Recompense—

As your mother, I believe I may say you have always thus been sensitive to the travails of others. It is not merely the fault of your condition, & you may believe me it is one of your many qualities I cherish.

You are correct that disappointment is a terrible circumstance,—among the most terrible,—but there are others, more painful still, from which I would rather seek to shield you. Perhaps I should counsel you to keep your dreams of modest size; then you can your self prevent any great disillusionment in that regard, & leave your mother to fret on your behalf about all those affairs no man nor woman may control.

As you see, I survived, so there is naught to worry over on my account. I do appreciate your concern.

Your Aunt Tem, however: Now there was a puzzle. What was I to do with her? So pretty;—moderately good natured;—shewing increasing skill at the distillery;—and yet so *proud*, she would have no man, nor make aught of her life.

The very evening after our petition-signing, Mr. Fischer showed up in the countinghouse. He bore a bouquet of daisies & wore a white weskit to match. —Miss Temperance, he said, bowing, as he knocked and entered, will you do me the honour of accompanying me for a stroll?

She rolled her eyes and would certainly have refused had I not stood at our desk staring her down. —Yes, she said in a tone flat as a griddle cake, a stroll sounds like just the thing.

As they left together he offered her his arm, but she would not take it. I remained another half hour balancing the accompts, & did not expect to see her until supper;—but lo, she came bounding in, and flung the daisies down, shouting, —God damn! The *Insolence!*

—Tem, I said, please.

She stalked directly to our shelf, and took a drink from the bottle. —He *proposed marriage* to me, she said. Had she been a bull I daresay her expression would have caused me to run. —Miss Temperance, she said, folding her hands before her in cruel imitation of her suitor, I realize you may not hold me in the highest possible regard; & yet I believe you will find, on further acquaintance, I am a man of sterling character; and once I am won, I am a friend for life. I hope you will therefore not think me *importunate* if I &c. &c. Christ! (Here, of course, she laid aside his gesture & articulation, and took a swig from the bottle.)

—And what did you say? I ventured.

—*What* did I *say?*

—He is a proper handsome gentleman, I said. Wealthy, & obviously struck with you.

—He is an intolerable bore, Tem said. She took a third long drink. —He spoke of the *advantage* to our *businesses*. He said the family that owned both a ferry and a bridge could comfortably be said to own all Brookland.

—I cannot disagree with him, said I.

—Fine, then, she said. You marry him. Or let him marry Pearl.

I would have objected, but she had already gone out again & slammed the door. I knew not to dwell on't. Temmy was 19 years old,— mistress of her own fate, howsoever she might chuse to squander it, and it was not for me to tell her where lay her happiness,—& furthermore other issues required my attention. The morning had brought a scruffy delivery boy bearing a letter for Ben from New-York's aldermen, who had heard with great interest of our meeting the previous day, and charged us to bring our model & drawings for their perusal at our earliest convenience. This we planned to do the Wednesday morning, & I was full of trepidation about it. The only man I knew who had any connexion with the board of alders was Timothy Stover, my banker;

who had told me (I could not tell if with disdain or relish) they were *drinkers, gamers, theatre-goers,* and in short the kind of *urbane gentlemen* who could eat a country lass like me at teatime and still have appetite for their evening roast.

In a panic, Prue took Pearl to Mrs. Tilley's the next morning, picked out some deep blue yard goods, and left them off with the seamstress, muttering vague instructions for a dress to be made along the same straight, fashionable cut as Pearl's. Of course it could not be done by the morning, despite its simplicity; and Prue did not like the woman's smirk as she wrote down the order.

She thinks you're after a Husband, Pearl wrote as Prue closed the jangling door behind them. Then Pearl clicked her tongue at her sister as one would to a chicken, and butted her forehead against her shoulder.

Pieter Huber, the cobbler, also broke into a waggish grin when Prue requested a pair of black ladies' shoes with pointed toes, delicate heels, and a row of buttons to fasten them. "Won't last a day, Miss Winship," he said, exhibiting the brown stubs of his former teeth. "Not the way you treat your boots."

Not for th. Distillery, Pearl wrote in what Prue thought an unusually prim hand.

"Ah, yes: dancing shoes," he said. "When d'ye need them?"

Prue found the entire situation mortifying. She said, "As soon as possible."

"Yesterday week. Without fail."

When they were back out in the steaming turnpike, Pearl wrote, *What a Donkey. I do hoap you get to wear the shoes to Albany. What a fine Lady you'll seem to those Rubes!*

"Don't fool yourself," Prue replied. She wanted to yell at someone, but reminded herself to take care it not be Pearl. "If they're sophisticated enough to pay for a bridge, their wives have very good shoes."

Prue would go in her old brown dress to Mayor Varick and the aldermen, and beforehand had the sense to load a cask of gin onto the barge with the cumbersome model bridge and the elevation, both of which were wrapped in oilcloth. Before they left she also took Ben aside and offered him $300 in Bank of New-York paper money. His eyes nearly jumped clear of his head, and Prue wondered if he'd never before seen notes in such large denominations. "What on earth is this for?" he asked.

She was still ruffled from her visit to the shops the previous day, as well as nervous about their errand, and she said, "Ben, don't be such an innocent." She did not think they'd get far with the politicians of New York unless he could be more canny; but he continued to look at her with his blue eyes wide and to hold the money in his hand rather than to pocket it. "I don't know to what exact end you might have need of it," she told him in a more careful tone. "Only that it may prove useful to have it on your person."

He shook his head with a rueful smile, folded the thick stack of money, and tucked it into his burgundy waistcoat. (Even as Prue wrote to Recompense more than twenty years later, she did not know with what subtlety Ben had deployed that money. By day's end, it had been gone— taken as tribute, Prue had supposed, along with her gin. She had later asked him what he'd done with it, but he'd refused to answer, saying, "A man must have some secrets from his future wife. Else what will provide the mystery when they have exhausted all other subjects of conversation?" She was pleased this act of bribery was not the only topic left to them.)

The aldermen were a glib and cultured crowd, but they too had long been dreaming of a bridge; and as Ben and Prue hoped to have it financed by the state, some thought it might be possible to get it at very little personal expense. Mr. Harrison had, furthermore, written an article of superlative praise for the plan's ingenuity, and had thus already influenced many of the alders' opinions. They brought the matter straightaway to a vote—*viva voce*, with Ben and Prue standing right there—and a few more than half gave their consent to the proposition. Prue had worried about Mr. Varick's long, sallow face and dyspeptic appearance while Ben spoke; yet he, too, voted in favor of the petition to Albany. He also offered his help in Ben's suit to a Mr. Cornelius Brouwer, who owned the Old Market Wharf, should Ben prove fortunate enough to have reason to approach him.

Mr. Hendrik Stryker's letter arrived a week after the meeting with the mayor and aldermen. Stryker had spoken to the governor and had his permission to second Mr. Willemsen's enthusiasm for a viewing of the entire plan. He requested Ben to bring up his drawings and model bridge for presentation as soon as business would allow. He added a note at bottom about his personal fondness for Matty Winship, which Prue considered a benediction.

Ben would present his proposal at Albany; yet however old-fashioned the men of the legislature might prove, he and Prue both thought they should be able to view her as a participant in the design without suffering bouts of apoplexy. Prue also wanted Pearl to accompany them, as she believed the pathos of her condition should bode well for their suit.

"And she played an important role in bringing the plan to its current state," Ben added.

"Yes," Prue answered. "That is the other reason why she should come."

At a practical level, this meant Tem would be left, with Isaiah, in charge of the works. "For how long a period?" she asked.

"A week, or perhaps a fortnight," Prue said.

"I don't know," she responded, and turned to look out the window toward the loading dock. She was still mightily peeved about Mr. Fischer. Isaiah cast Prue a glance of frustration, but did not speak up.

"You've done it before," Prue said, "and nothing ill befell you."

"You were always nearby," she replied, her back still to them and her arms crossed.

"And you never once sought me out. Isaiah will be here, as well."

Tem said, "I, too, should like to travel."

Isaiah let out an exasperated breath through his nose, and began patting down his pockets for his tobacco.

"It'll hardly be a pleasure tour," Prue said. "Besides, people who have business that depends upon them don't travel. Father left the works only once in thirty years."

"And you went with 'im," Tem muttered.

"Before you were born!"

"You know," Isaiah added, unrolling his pouch, " 'tis said to be a family charm keeps the place from burning to the ground as Joralemon's distillery did. Without one Winship on the premises, I can't say what'd happen."

Tem wheeled back around to face him. "Is that true?" she demanded. "I've not heard it."

Isaiah kept packing his pipe. "Common knowledge."

Tem looked skeptically toward Prue, who nodded. "Hang it all, then," she said. "I'll stay, you superstitious louts. You'll excuse me if I head off to the stillroom and make certain it doesn't burn down." She left the door ajar behind her, and galloped down the open stairs, calling a colorful stream of invective out into the air.

Prue continued to watch Isaiah try to start his unwilling pipe from the tinderbox.

"What?" he asked between puffs.

"Izzy, there's no such tale."

He finally got a good start on the thing and said, "What of it? She's staying. The warehouses call." Chuckling to himself, he went outside.

Prue was both pleased and surprised to find him capable of such humor.

Since that journey overland with her father twenty-odd years previously, she had never been farther than Wallabout Bay or across the river to her New York customers and the bank. Of course, she knew the geography of the region from the map they kept in the countinghouse, and could imagine how long it would take to deliver a shipment of gin to (or receive a shipment of empty casks from) Flatbush, Peekskill, Weehawken, or Trenton. Yet despite her proximity to the water and her absolute dependence upon it as a means of transporting her wares, she had never spent more than half an hour on its surface. "The prospect of sailing up Henry Hudson's River therefore pleased me," she wrote to Recompense:

In my girlhood, my father had read me accounts of th'exploration of this river, with its awesome granite cliffs & clusters of native villages. When your father had gone northwards, I'd imagined him amidst such unspoiled scenery, & in the low, drifting river fog of early morning.

Pearl had the laundress wash their stockings and chemises, and herself starched their collars stiff as plates. Prue left Isaiah detailed notes about the workers' payment and what provisions he should apportion to the slaves; traveled back and forth across the river to settle her accounts, both credit and debt; and did her best to finish training Simon's grand-nephew, Marcel Dufresne, to work the herb press without her supervision. Prue considered him a gift from Heaven—a slight, delicate creature, but unusually smart, and with a sensitive nose and palate. Had he not come, she did not think she would have been able to go to Albany, as rectifying could not have continued during her absence. Prue also spent time contemplating her father's travel box, which still smelled of him, though it had sat empty but for cobwebs and a lone collar stay up under the eaves for decades. She wanted to crawl in and simply breathe that evanescent odor, but instead she placed their folded dresses in along with books, blank paper, and her father's travel desk, knowing these relics of the workaday world would dispel that last trace of his scent. Pearl added sufficient supplies for a few weeks' needlework, extra pencils, and a bar of store-bought soap. The small bridge and drawings would be wrapped twice in oilcloth, as they had been to go to New York, and bound with rawhide thongs. Prue thought she might pray over them as well. She and Ben resolved not to test the model bridge thoroughly until they had used it for show, as they could not take it to Albany if they discovered how much weight could break it, or if weeks out in the elements destroyed its fine color.

As she completed her preparations, Prue could not refrain from walking out to the old stone fence, which had been heaved and tumbled by many winters' frosts. She stood atop its crumbling edge and looked off to the northwest with an intensity of observation she had not mustered in some while. She could recall the heat of her rage at the unborn Pearl, but she could also see how the landscape around her had changed in her lifetime—how her own works and the Schermerhorns' had grown, and how the smokestacks now so clouded the atmosphere, the view was in places even more obscured than it had been in her childhood. North of the ropewalk, Mr. Fischer had built his ferry house, and beyond the water, the city of New York had grown vast and dense; it had spread up past its canal, and what had hitherto been tiny hamlets had been subsumed into the urban bustle. The windows and spires that had once taken her breath in awe were eclipsed now by the sheer magnitude of what had risen around them; and this was to say nothing of the political changes that had occurred,—a federal government come and gone, a mayor and board of alders put in place, the Bank of the United States come to rival the Bank of New-York. A quarter century did not seem time enough for so much to have changed; yet, for all Prue and her sisters had grown, their world had done so even more dramatically.

She could have gone to church to pray, but in her heart she still believed God favored the river. She asked the ordinary things: safety in their
travels, success in their errand, good fortune for Tem at the works. She
also asked permission to assay the bridge; she asked God's blessing on it,
and could not tell if the old man heard her. A few fishermen rode the
tidal current down toward Red Hook, where mussels and scallops could
be plucked aplenty for a poor man's supper once the heat of the year had
passed. Losee drifted in to his landing and rang his bell. Prue saw neither
of these as a sign.

Though Prue and Pearl had long since banished Tem to sleep in their
parents' room across the hall, she wakened them next morning when she
tossed so hard in her sleep, she pitched herself to the floor. The rooster
began almost at once to screak in the yard, and when they all arrived
downstairs, Abiah had for the first time in years managed to burn the
coffee. Pearl was subdued, and Prue wondered if she saw it all as bad
omens and did not want to make her sisters quail by remarking it. Prue's
whole frame flooded with relief when Ben pulled up in one of the distillery's wagons, with yellow Jolly tethered morosely to its front along
with one of his blither brethren. As the scroll and model bridge were
both large and unwieldy, she assumed he had loaded them down directly
from the countinghouse.

"Piss of a horse," he said as he came inside. Jolly burred in evident
disgust. "Don't know if I ever saw four such pretty women look so low."

Pearl attempted a smile for him. Tem said, "I am besieged with nightmare at the thought of her leaving."

& she prevents the rest of us Sleeping, Pearl wrote.

"My brother claims the sincerest belief in your fitness for the task,"
Ben said to Tem, "and as for you, Pearl, the salt breeze will revive you.
Prue is always pensive. Abiah, that leaves you to merit my concern."

Prue said "Hey!" at the same time Abiah said, "I shall not be glad till
you're all home safe again."

"Is this all your things?" Ben asked.

Pearl did not appear convinced by his good spirits, but she nodded toward the trunk, which he hoisted up and placed abaft the wagon's seat.

"Well, your shipment is ready to leave when you are," he said. "Tem,
Abiah, will you see us off?"

Tem made a wavering sound of assent, and Abiah began to stack the plates. They all rode down to the wharf together. One of Prue's own boats would carry them to Mount Pleasant, a port village a short distance up the Hudson, with a shipment of Winship gin. Thence Ben had arranged they would travel with the product of a local textile mill up to Saugerties, and thence on the mail boat to Albany, as at that time, no shipments of their own wares were slated to go any farther north.

Although the distillery would not open for another hour, some of the slaves had arisen early to load up the hoy; and as they rounded the corner from Joralemon's Lane, Prue saw perhaps two dozen men, both slave and free, standing around the yard, fiddling the sand with their bare toes, smoking and talking. Two men were raising the ship's single spritsail on its halyard. Ben urged the horses to halt. Marcel Dufresne, apple-cheeked as a child, reached up for Prue's hand and said, "We wish you great success in your journey."

"Thank you," Prue said. A few hats came off their respective heads. "You'll be careful with the press?"

"I'll treat it like royalty," Marcel said.

Isaiah said, "I'll make certain; and I'll keep my eye on Miss Tem."

As a man loaded the trunk onto the boat, Tem stood with one palm over her chin, her elbow supported on the other arm. She said, "I shall miss you something fierce."

"And I, you," Prue answered. "Trust in Isaiah, should anything go amiss."

"Something surely will."

"No. You'll manage it." She took Tem in her arms. Though at first Tem shied like a frightened horse, she soon softened. It was galling how much Prue loved her; though perhaps somewhat less so than how excited she was to leave all her work and worry in her sister's hands for a fortnight.

When she had let Tem go, Ben handed Prue and Pearl down into the boat and climbed in beside them. "Make us proud, Tem," he said to her as they pushed off.

"Devil take you," she said back.

As they made their way into the current, clumps of observers waved their handkerchiefs from the Schermerhorns', Butcher's Wharf, and Losee's and Fischer's landings. The ordinary folk to whom Prue and Ben shouted their farewells were, she knew, their greatest supporters and those for whose opinion the assemblymen would care least. But she would carry the image of them northward and cherish it in the event all did not go as they hoped. All nine of the Luquer siblings had gathered on their dock and the trash rack roof, and they whistled and hooted to the swift boat as it sailed into the Upper Bay. Pearl waved back so hard Prue thought she might fall overboard. Her throat grew tight at the prospect of leaving Brooklyn.

The delivery boat skirted to the north of the Governor's Island and entered New York Harbor, which to Prue seemed wide as a veritable sea. As she breathed in its familiar salt fragrance, she felt a pang for her father, who had so yearned for the ocean in his youth.

Are you thinking of Daddy? Pearl asked.

Prue did not know how her sister had gleaned this. She nodded.

I can almost smell him.

"I, too."

Shortly, the little hoy tacked to leeward and entered the mouth of the Hudson. To the west clustered the villages of Hoboken, Pavonia, and Weehawken, where poor Mr. Hamilton had been murdered, while to the east spread Manhattan, who appeared unfamiliar seen from her other flank. The North River wharves were not half so busy as their sisters to the east. After the boat sailed past a row of fashionable houses, their backs to the river behind deep, enclosed yards, Prue regarded the district of poor dwellings and eagerly wondered which of them might be those dens of thieves and prostitutes and fences for stolen goods she had heard populated the area. A tannery's stink announced its presence long before the boat drew nigh; and donkeys and goats grazed in ramshackle lots.

" 'Tisn't much to look at, is it?" Ben asked, leaning onto the gunwale on Prue's other side. "Homesick already?"

"No."

He glanced at Pearl and said, "I'm certain it'll go well."

Prue liked the sureness on his bright face. She wished she could lodge it in her own bosom.

"Here," he said. He backed off the gunwale and, pulling his sleeve over the heel of his hand, wiped down the flat tops of two casks. "Seats fit for princesses, and a view as fine as any in Europe, or so I'm told."

As she sat down, Prue fidgeted to make her skirt comfortable. Pearl began to smile. A fine late-summer breeze was licking the river into soft peaks, and northern Manhattan looked like home as they skimmed past it—rolling meadows and stands of birch and elm, punctuated at wide intervals by beetle-browed Dutch houses and the occasional herd of ruddy kine. Jersey was lush with ripe corn and riotous gardens of squash and sunflower. And once they had passed the last of Manhattan's docks, the river was quieter than Prue had known a river could be. The wind cracked in their single spritsail, and the water plashed against their sides; the crew chatted together when there were no orders to convey; and the terns cried before diving for fish or swooping back over land. The hubbub of the docks, which had played as the burden note beneath nearly Prue's every memory, was nowhere to be heard.

Abiah had packed a plentiful lunch of bread, cheese, ham, and a purple-stained cloth full of blueberries, which Prue placed on the barrel to keep its juice off her dress. She could not remember a meal that had tasted so delicious, and she wondered if this was because they were out on the water. As she ate, she thought of her father, eating whatever sailors ate at sea—oatmeal and stale biscuits, she supposed. Ben had fresh water in his leather wineskin, warm from the sun and faintly tinged with grape.

"Perhaps we might skip Albany," Prue said to him, "and keep on the boat a week or two."

"You've caught it of me," he said. "The *wanderlust*."

Prue slapped at his leg, and Pearl wrote, *O! O! Not Dom^ne Syrtis!*

"I believe I caught it of my father," Prue told him. "He was a merchant sailor, before any of us was born."

Ben nodded. "I always had an inkling of that, with him." He squinted at Prue in the noonday light and added, "Mine was born and died in Brookland. I wonder if I'll do the same."

'Tis not the same if you wander off North^wds & return with a coon Cap, Pearl wrote.

"No, I suppose not," he said. "But it's hardly a life of adventure to measure Mr. Whitcombe's holdings so he can build for a new tenant."

"If we succeed," Prue said, "we shall need someone to oversee the daily works of the bridge, you know."

"Is that an invitation?" he asked.

Prue shrugged her shoulders, constricted in the bothersome dress.

"Someone needs to see the voussoirs are built according to plan. I shall do as much as I can, but will perforce wish to keep a hand in the distillery, too."

Ben walked to the other side of the boat and back. "Prudence Winship, do you offer me employ?"

She couldn't tell if laughter lurked behind his stern expression, though it often did. "If you'll take it."

A smile did emerge, as if through a scrim of clouds. "Well, dammit, you're a bit late, woman," he said, and walked off toward the bow.

Pearl's narrow face sparkled with curiosity, but she did not inquire.

"Hush," Prue said to her. To Ben she called out, "We cannot have a stranger." There was, she supposed, no guarantee they would need anyone at all.

The river widened just then into a lovely inland sea, with rolling hills to both sides, the trees showing the first faint tinge of yellow though they would not turn in Brooklyn for another few weeks. The water itself took on a bluer cast, and to the west were two pleasure boats, bearing a party in good clothing who seemed out to enjoy the weather.

Ben came back. "The *Tappan Zee*," he said flatly. "I'll look after your bridgeworks."

Prue beamed at him. Pearl was watching her with some interest.

"How could I go chasing down property lines while I knew there was a task of such magnitude up the way?" He reached for Prue's hand and stroked the backs of her fingers with his papery thumb. Pearl was no idiot; she obviously knew what was in the air. As Ben sat down beside Prue, he folded her arm into the crook of his own. Pearl had her lips pursed tight, as if it was all she could do to keep herself from inquiring about Ben.

They arrived in Mount Pleasant in good order in the afternoon. A man representing the local taverns was there with four empty mule carts to sign for the gin; and when this had been accomplished, Ben hired a wagon for the baggage and a boy to keep watch over the model bridge, as it was too large to transport easily from the docks. Ben, Prue, and Pearl walked to the crossroads, where they secured places at the inn. Ben suggested he might leave them in the women's quarters to wash and nap, but Pearl wanted to explore this new town.

"What's t'explore?" Ben asked as the servants carried the boxes upstairs. "You've seen the whole place."

I've never been so far as Bushwick, Pearl wrote. So of course they agreed.

They spent the afternoon as pleasantly as if they'd magically arrived in London or France without the dangers and discomforts of the crossing. Mount Pleasant may have been little more than a port, but the houses were built of fieldstone, and Pearl and Prue delighted to compare them with those at home. If the women of the town wore wide skirts such as had not been seen in Brooklyn in a decade, these had since become a marvel to look upon. Mrs. Andressen, the wife of the inn's owner, was as friendly as Mrs. Loosely, and Prue suddenly understood this was a characteristic an innkeeper sought in a wife, not some happy accident of Annetje Loosely's birth. Mrs. Andressen gave them a fine supper of salmon in pastry accompanied by their local asparagus—nowhere near as good as Brooklyn's, though Prue could not tell her obliging hostess the ghoulish reason why—and her home-brewed ale. Pearl retired early to the bed the sisters would share, but Ben and Prue sat up with Mrs. Andressen, talking of their journey and the personages who passed through her inn.

When it came time to sleep, Ben took a small oil lamp up the pie-shaped steps, and kissed Prue on each cheek before giving her the lamp and retiring to his room, from which a man down on business from Kingston could already be heard snoring. Pearl was asleep, crowding herself up against the wall in the small bed. She had left her note case open on the blanket beside her. Prue placed the smoking lamp on the nightstand and saw her sister had written, *We all know what you do with him, P. Why do'n't you fr Heaven's Sake marry him? It'd be much simpler.*

Prue was startled by this bluntness, and half wanted to awaken Pearl, but could not bring herself to do so when she slept so peacefully. How long had Pearl known, Prue wondered, and how could she be so matter-of-fact in her assessment of the situation? The drawings had shown Prue how incorrectly she'd rated her sister's powers of observation; the note did so again. Prue did not, however, know what to do with this sentiment but to undress, blow out the lamp, and ease herself into bed around her sister, whose hair smelled of the lavender water in which she'd bathed it and the sunshine on the boat. Her words flopped around Prue's mind like so many fish in a bucket; but after what seemed hours of watching the flickering streetlamp cast shadows across the wall, Prue fell asleep.

Pearl must have climbed stealthily over her in the morning, for she was dressed and writing at the desk when Prue woke. "Good morning," Prue said.

Pearl rested her pen and leaned over to tap her page from the night before.

Prue had not forgotten about the note all the time she slept. "It's too early for such questions," she said.

Why not marry 'im? Father'd jump for Happiness in his Grave.

"I'm not confident of that. And we've been far too busy with the bridge to plan to wed. When we return home, I'm sure. It's more complicated than you know. Besides which, I'm not certain I think any of this your business."

Why've you snuck round with im all this Time? Nor Tem nor I should have judg'd you harshly, you know. 'Tis only what's natural.

Prue felt a flare of anger over this. Ben was private—her love for him was private—and she did not want her sister poking at it with words. The bridge was enough to think about at present.

I see I've fluster'd you, Pearl wrote. She looked toward the ceiling as if in appeal to Heaven, then turned back to take up her pen.

Her calm piqued Prue even more. "To whom are you writing?" she demanded.

Pearl continued to the end of the page, signed her name with a flourish, blotted it with their father's blotter, its handle shaped like a lion, and folded her letter to seal. Then she scribbled an address on its front. When she'd blotted this, she tucked it into her belt, seal-side out. *I'm going for the Post,* she wrote on her silver pad. *See you at Brekfast.* She went down the steep stairs.

Ben was nearly done eating and Pearl just served by the time Prue could master herself enough to go down. The fellow from Kingston might have snored through the night, but his refreshing slumber gave him a stentorian voice with which to tell Ben about the fishing and hunting in the region. He had great, woolly muttonchop whiskers such as were uncommon in Brooklyn, and Prue took a certain unkind pleasure in watching him chew. Pearl made a favorable impression on him; he gestured toward her with his elbow as he cut his steak, and said to Ben, "Lovely sister you've got, sir."

Ben smiled and said, "She's not mine, but thank you."

The fellow shook his head as he chewed, and glanced at both women's hands to determine, Prue supposed, if either of them was Ben's wife. "Is she for sale, then? I've long fancied a wife who wouldn't talk back to me."

Ben said, "Oh, bless you, but she does talk back," while Pearl wrote, *Devill take you, Sir*, held it up to their companion with her left hand, and continued on with her breakfast. Mr. Kingston kept chewing but blushed into his whiskers and hair. As soon as his plate was clear, he excused himself. Ben reached across the table for Pearl's fork hand. "Minx," he said, and her fork clattered to her earthen plate. Prue thought, *Indeed*.

They traveled upriver to Saugerties in the company of bolts of muslin much larger than their rolled-up river view. Prue was glad not to be sharing a boat with Mr. Kingston, though sorry not to visit his city. Prue had heard it had been trammeled during the late war, and much besieged by Indians, but rebuilt with vigor. Saugerties also proved to her liking, but it was the river itself enchanted her. She had read, in the travels of Europeans come to view the fledgling American nation, that the beauty of the North River rivaled that of the Rhine; but living, as she did, by the edge of a grubby (if quite useful) tidal straits, she'd always imagined the continentals had inexplicable ideas of the picturesque. Now she saw what had long been obvious to everyone who'd traveled farther than from Red Hook to the Wallabout: that the East River wasn't much to look at. Her cliffs were gray as the underworld; the Hudson's soared up from the valley and were shot through with rust and white. Behind them, to the west, stretched the jagged peaks of the Catskills, whose trees were beginning to turn color. Pearl and Prue stood side by side at the gunwale, not speaking about the topic of interest to both of them, and entranced by the magnificent scenery streaming by. When Prue began to fret either over the magnitude of her errand or about her sister, the beauty around her soothed her spirit.

Prue had known of the brisk whaling trade out of Hudson, but still thought it miraculous to sail up an inland river and spy those great ships, provisioned for a year and more in the one direction, and heavy laden with whale oil in the other. Prue remarked the mighty port as they passed it, but did not then know she would one day wish to have noted it in greater detail.

When they moored at Albany, Prue thought the city looked as if it had burst forth like a crop of weed. Much of it appeared so recently built the cedar shakes still glowed; but it did have a permanent, roofed market, which promised abundance even when, as on that Wednesday, it sat empty.

"If you require anything," Ben said as he again oversaw the loading of their possessions onto a wagon, "we'd best fetch it now. The assembly's session begins early in the morning. *Marrons?* Sugared violets?"

Pearl's eyes still went wide as coins for sweets, as they had when she'd been little and had ogled the jars on Mrs. Tilley's counter. *I'd love some Marrons*, she wrote.

Once again Ben arranged a man to guard the model bridge, and to transport it to the Stadt Haus in the morning. He had a preference for a Mrs. Finley's establishment—a private house in which the owner let rooms because she'd been widowed. The place had a cheerful aspect, with rough blue linen curtains blowing through the open windows, and boxes of dark chrysanthemums out front. Mrs. Finley herself leaned out the top of her Dutch door to greet the cart as it arrived. The ribbons hung askew from her cap. "Is't rooms ye'll be wanting?" she asked, as if, Prue thought, they might have come in search of lumber.

"Two, for two nights, Mrs. F.," Ben said as he jumped down from the cart.

"Ah, Mr. Horsfield! Lovely to see you 'gain," she said. Her face was broad, and rendered broader by the frill of her cap. She had a comical air, hanging over the door.

"Thank you, Mrs. Finley."

"An' I see you've brought your, what—your sisters?"

Ben helped them down from the cart. "My future wife, and her sister. Miss Winship and Miss Pearl."

Mrs. Finley tapped her middle finger against her teeth. Prue thought she looked displeased to find them not his relations. "As in the gin?" she asked.

"We make the gin," Prue said. "In Brookland. I am Prudence Winship; this is Pearl."

"Winship Daughters gin, yes," Mrs. Finley said. Pearl beamed, as if it was delightful to be mistaken for Tem. "Drink it all the time. Never thought there'd be actual daughters behind it, mind."

"Do you purchase from Elisha Green?" Prue asked. "He is a customer of long standing. We hope to meet him, if our other business allows."

"Heavens, yes, Elisha Green. He's on up the road, I can show you the way."

Ben unpacked Prue's traveling desk in the yard and penned a quick note to Mr. Willemsen to inform him of their arrival and whereabouts. The driver was dispatched with an extra penny in payment for delivering the note.

Mrs. Finley showed Pearl and Prue to a room whose windows were open wide to the breeze and whose plump down quilt was folded back at the foot of the bed. While Ben went out to find the promised sweets, Pearl and Prue unpacked, still not talking about what was between them. Prue was doubly uncomfortable, as she had begun to grow nervous about the presentation before the assembly. On his return, Ben proffered the *marrons*, then led the sisters out for a walk, to see the neat houses with fenced yards. Albany, it seemed, had been built on a plan, unlike Brooklyn, upon whose landscape the homesteads might have been blown in and dropped by violent weather. They found Elisha Green's establishment by happenstance, and stopped in for fish and chips and a sort of gin toddy in which he specialized. Prue thought the sun tarried longer in the sky than it did in Brooklyn, though she knew this was more the product of her leisure to look upward than the truth.

As soon as the last rosy clouds began scudding toward darkness, they returned to Mrs. Finley's, though the streets were still bustling. They would meet the assembly early in the morning, and wanted to rest well beforehand. They found their hostess sitting before her fire with two mousy, round-faced daughters. Both had ribbons in their hair for the benefit of a visiting businessman, who was as dull brown as they—quite possibly, Prue thought, a good match. The moment she spied them, Mrs. Finley stood, spilling her knitting to the floor, and retrieved a letter from the table. "Came for you, Mr. Horsfield, while you were out." She handed it to Ben with a self-important wiggle of her hips and went on, "From an assemblyman, even. Can't say I've received a letter from any of their sort before."

"Thank you," Ben said.

The shy gentleman cast an appraising glance Ben's way, and the eyes of the Finley daughters narrowed as a result. Pearl folded her arms across her; she liked watching the feline behavior of certain women. As Ben read, she raised one hand and spread its fingers sharply away from her lips in sign for him to read aloud what was written.

"Mr. Willemsen sends warm greetings, asks leave to visit before the session opens on the morrow, and invites us to sup at his quarters tomorrow eve."

Pearl opened her book and wrote, *Not bad.*

"Supper with your assemblyman?" Mrs. Finley asked. "My, you Winships do more than brew gin."

Distill, Pearl wrote.

The shy fellow cocked his head to one side. "You're the Winship daughters?" he asked.

She is, Pearl wrote. *I'm extra.*

"A fine product, miss," he said, nodding to Prue.

"Pleased you like it. Before you depart, let us give you a bit. We carry some with us in case of just such a circumstance."

"Delightful. Won't you join us for tea?" he offered.

The Finley sisters scowled at their needlework.

Ben said, "Thank you, but we've a long day ahead tomorrow. We'll bid you goodnight."

Mrs. Finley rose to provide them a lamp, but didn't try to stop them from leaving. "Sleep well," she said.

Pearl was hissing to herself as they went up.

"What?" Prue asked.

You're evil, she wrote at the landing.

Ben cuffed her playfully across the back of the head. Prue said, "What do you mean?"

Gin—Assmblymn Willemsn—those poor Girls!

"Bosh," Prue said, "if 'twasn't me, their mother'd have done all the talking for them. I don't think she even knows you're mute."

"Goodnight," Ben said, and kissed them both. "Rest well."

Prue thought only an hour had passed before the cocks began to crow and the dogs to bark at them. Pearl rolled directly onto her elbows and patted Prue's cheeks with her fingertips.

"That bad?" Prue asked.

She shrugged her shoulders toward her ears, which meant yes. She reached for her pad and pencil from the stand. *I'll pinch y' cheeks agin before we go in.*

Prue reached for her armpits, and Pearl opened her mouth as another would to shout and jumped clear of the bed. After Pearl washed, used the pot, and dressed, she helped Prue into the new blue gown, which closed by a system of hooks and eyes that trailed around Prue's frame like a creeper. Pearl sat her down on the ladder-back chair, spat in her own right hand, and neatened each of Prue's curls. After she'd finished, she secured them loosely to Prue's head with combs, then drew open the curtains and led her to the looking glass. Prue had to duck to see herself in it. The flesh beneath her eyes was puffed and dark, but the brightness of the dress made her skin and hair look less accidental than vivid. She was accustomed to herself in waders; and though she'd long accepted that she'd never be pretty as her sisters, she was surprised and gratified to be pretty at all.

"Sakes," she said. "Thank you, Pearl."

Pearl wrote, *I think we'll win them,* and returned her pencil to its hasp so they might go down for breakfast.

The moment they were downstairs, they unwrapped the drawings from their oilcloths, tied them up in their ribbons, and left the elevation leaning against the parlor wall. Prue worried what might have become of the facsimile overnight, but Pearl said, *It manag'd to get this far.*

Garret Willemsen arrived while everyone but Prue was eating porridge, and they all rose to greet him. He was a tall man, balding and with a slight potbelly that looked official in his silver-buttoned coat. Ben took his hand, and Willemsen regarded all five women around the table, until Prue stepped forth and offered her own hand. "Mr. Willemsen," she said, "this is a true honor."

"Mr. Horsfield, Miss Winship, the honor is mine."

Mrs. Finley offered him breakfast, and it was the other boarder's turn to appear vexed.

Willemsen said, "My carriage waits outside."

Ben took a last spoonful and wiped his mouth on his napkin. "Finish up, then, Prue," he said, passing her a slice of toast and jam. But she'd been unable to eat, and could not begin then.

"I didn't mean to rush you," Willemsen said.

"Not at all." Prue pushed her chair back. Pearl folded her napkin and leaned across to pat Prue's cheeks once more, which made Prue blush with shame. "We have large drawings, sir," she said, "though our model will arrive separately. Has your carriage sufficient room?"

"Tut," he said, and bowed to the Finleys. "Very pleasant to have met you all. Your establishment seems comfortable; I shall recommend it."

"Thank you, sir," said Mrs. Finley.

Ben took the roll of smaller drawings from the front hall, and summoned Willemsen's driver and man for the larger exhibit. Mr. Willemsen's eyes popped when he saw the size of it. "I warn you, Mr. Horsfield," he said, "it shall be quite a session."

The carriage was fine,—all open, & painted black, with bright red wheels,—and hitch'd to a sleek team of dapple-greys. Willemsen's servant also observed our cargo wide-eyed, but said nothing as he and the driver loaded our drawing end-up into the open passenger compartment. I climbed in beside it, and rode with my arm around it the whole way there.

You see, I cannot say I'd loved anything so much till then. My parents, my sisters, your father, the rectifying room,—they all had their hold on me; but that view of a thing sprung of my imagination, leaping as it did from the only home I'd ever known out to the beyond,—it seemed my whole future happiness depended from it.

Matty bids me tell you, he misses you around the house & wishes you were here to learn rectifying for him. I eagerly await your next; & then shall tell you how we fared before the state assembly,—

With abiding love,
Your mother

Sixteen

THE GENTLEMEN OF ALBANY

P rue sometimes reflected on how, during the period the nation's capital had resided in New York City, the most important American business had been conducted in a modest stone building, all but surrounded by pigsties. She herself had seen the Stars and Stripes flying overhead, and had heard rumors of General Washington pacing the balcony (just as she'd heard rumors of him keeping a lookout once on Clover Hill—all unsubstantiated claims, as far as she knew), but beyond that, she'd always thought the seat of government less impressive than her father's manufactory.

When the state capital had moved to Albany just the year before Prue and Ben proposed their bridge, the plan had been to endow the government with a ceremonial home that would give the lie to the notion the city was New York's little sister. Prue had been looking forward to this grandeur; but found, to her dismay, that Governor Jay and the two branches of the legislature were still squabbling over the cost and had done nothing to effect the transformation. (She was disappointed both because she thought that, arriving on an errand of such importance, she should have someplace impressive at which to arrive, and because it boded ill for their willingness to finance something as costly as a bridge.) The assembly and the senate now sat in two large halls in a building still called the Stadt Haus. It was a large wooden structure, not especially impressive though built on an unusual octagonal plan, and surmounted by a bell and weathercock, as if that alone should inform visitors they had arrived at a place of moment. As Mr. Willemsen's carriage pulled up to the front steps, Prue's pulse beat so hard in her throat, she worried she resembled a bullfrog. A huge oxcart had already arrived bearing the model, and its driver was smoking on the steps.

"I shall inform my colleagues of your arrival," Willemsen said, as the bewigged Negro porter helped him down. "It shouldn't take a minute."

After seeing Willemsen into the building, the porter sauntered back down to wait beside the carriage. He pointed with his nose toward the elevation. "Quite a thing you've got there," he said.

Prue was uncertain what the correct response might be. Ben said, "Thank you."

Pearl got down from the carriage and walked forward to admire the horses. Willemsen returned shortly with a score of porters to bear the model and elevation inside. They all flocked to the drawing, as no one wanted to have to carry the bridge on its platform base. Ben took the roll of smaller drawings, then gave Prue his arm and escorted her up the stairs.

The door opened into a small rotunda, such as Prue had seen in etchings of the ancient world, though made of simple wood. The inlaid floor was smooth beneath her thin-soled shoes, and around the gallery, high as a roof, loomed statues of portly men in old Dutch ruffs and tall boots. Prue imagined these must have been left over from the building's former use. There were two sets of oaken double doors, one to Prue's right and one to her left, and behind both sets the rumble of voices rose and fell. The empty-handed porter stopped before the left-hand set of doors, and Prue squeezed Ben's arm and let him go. Two of the other porters had the scroll up on their shoulders as if returning from the hunt. The men bearing the heavy model had already placed it on the floor. They would remain out in the foyer with these objects until called for, as both Ben and Prue imagined they would be unable to speak a word once the representations of the bridge had been seen. Prue nodded to the man at the door, and he lifted the iron latch to usher them in. "Benjamin Horsfield, King's County's surveyor," he announced, "and Prudence and Pearl Winship, distillers, of Brookland."

The gentlemen of the assembly rose and turned toward them as one, their fussy wigs making them resemble grandfathers, though many, Prue saw, had the high color of youth or overindulgence. There were at least a hundred of them. She did not, at first, recognize Willemsen with his bald pate covered, but he nodded to her as they stepped forward. Many of the gentlemen were regarding Prue and Pearl with some interest—as, Prue supposed, "distillers" did not call two young women to mind. The speaker of the assembly, Hendrik Stryker, looked Dutch as the statuary, and stood at a table facing the representatives' desks. Porters were buzzing all over the room like gadflies.

"Mr. Horsfield, Miss Winship," Stryker said. He was a jowly man, but the hand he extended in greeting was long-boned as a lady's. Prue's knees felt gelatinous, but supported her through a curtsy. Pearl remained a step behind her. "When your father applied for a license to distill—which, you may be surprised to hear, was only about fifteen years ago—I was the man to issue it. And glad, indeed; I have long been fond of your product. You know the Joralemons had tried just such a venture on your property before he arrived?"

"Yes, sir. It's how we acquired our windmill."

He nodded. "When your father opened that distillery back in '67, everyone said he'd fail within the year—and I believe he came close on a few occasions. But he persevered, and built an enterprise I count an honor to this state."

"Thank you, sir."

"When he passed on, I did not know how you'd fare." His glance also indicated Pearl.

"That is Pearl, sir, unrelated to the distillery. Temperance is at Brookland, managing the works."

"Ah, yes, Pearl," he said, and winced at her, in what he must have intended as a smile. It was not the first time Pearl had encountered such treatment, and Prue heard her skirt fold as she curtsied. "You've defied everyone's expectations, Miss Winship. The business appears stronger than at your father's passing, and, if I may say so without disrespect to the departed, the quality of your product has even improved."

"Hear," someone said. Another hushed him.

Ben nudged her arm, and though she was uncertain why he'd done so, she said, "We have brought a cask of the wares, sir, for you gentlemen to enjoy; but we did not bring it with us this morning, lest our most honest assemblymen misconstrue a friendly gift as an attempt at bribery."

All around, the legislators laughed, and Stryker bestowed on her an indulgent smile. "Very good, Miss Winship. We look forward to receiving it later. If your father has the good fortune to be watching from Heaven—as I pray he does—I am certain he is most pleased with your work."

Prue said, "Thank you." She did not know why anyone had to bring up her poor, cursed father's whereabouts.

"It was with true curiosity Governor Jay and I greeted the proposal Mr. Horsfield has lately submitted; and the governor has charged this body to determine its worthiness. I confess I relish the opportunity to see the plans you have brought today. Do you wish to address the assembly, Mr. Horsfield?"

"Thank you, I do," Ben said.

"Gentlemen?"

They sat down once more. Before Stryker's table was a half-moon of open space, and handing off the small roll of drawings to another porter, Ben strode forward to stand slightly to Stryker's side and before him. Pearl and Prue remained where they were, in the middle of the aisle; and Prue hoped the nerves that had beset her before her own neighbors would not trouble Ben here.

Ben cleared his throat and began. "Mr. Stryker, Mr. Willemsen, gentlemen of the assembly, I believe you all know the reason for my visit to you today. I have a plan to bridge the East River, which flows between the deepwater ports of Brookland and New York and is one of the busiest waterways in the nation. This bridge will increase commerce to and between the two ports without disrupting traffic upon the water, as it will arch over the straits in a single span. Land values on both sides of the river will rise; shipping in both ports will increase; and the state of New York will gain both in revenue and in prestige. The structure itself will employ the most modern methods of engineering. I humbly believe both bridge architects and sightseers will come from far and wide to study it.

"The bridge I have designed is founded upon the principle of the lever, by which means the very balconies above us are kept from crashing to the floor." Some turned to glance at them, perhaps never before having considered how balconies were tethered. "This principle states that the end of a beam that appears to hang free—*id est*, the edge of the balcony—is not, in truth, unsupported. It may well hold some good amount of weight, so long as it is sufficiently strong to refer that weight back along its length to a perpendicular member—in this case, the wall of this building—that may in its turn carry it down into the ground. No structure of appreciable size has ever before been founded upon this principle; yet all natural philosophy shows clearly it can be done. I have experimented extensively on the properties of timber, stone, and iron, and have brought with me today a model of this bridge, one two-hundred-fiftieth the size of the proposed structure. By means of this fac-simile, you may both appreciate the appearance of the bridge and begin to understand the magnitude of its eventual strength. I have also brought with me a large and detailed drawing of the bridge's elevation as seen from the south, that even those of you who have never had the pleasure of visiting New York and Brookland may yet have the benefit of imagin-ing the work *in situ*."

Prue was impressed by Ben's apparent ease in addressing the assem-bly; yet she disliked listening to him claim credit for a theory she herself had devised. She knew this was the only way to get the bridge built, but it continued to bother her all the same.

"Miss Winship," Ben said, "might you ask the gentlemen to bring in the view?"

Prue went into the entry hall and summoned the two men who still bore the heavy scroll upon their shoulders. They walked ceremoniously to the front of the room and placed it down upon its two flat ends. Ben said to them, "Once we have it set up, ask the others to bring in the model."

"Yessir," one said, and they both retired.

Ben took one end and Prue walked forward to take the other, though her knees still felt curious, no doubt from nerves. Ben nodded to her, and people murmured and shifted in their seats.

They began to draw the bridge open, and as its rainbow span cleared the three masts of the central ship, many of the company's chairs screeched back across the floor, and the gentlemen erupted in a volley of exclamations. Prue saw Pearl close her eyes a moment, perhaps in some private pain or rapture. They kept unwinding the scroll, and the whole crowd drew to their feet. When Ben and Prue stood at its ends, support-ing it like a pair of mismatched caryatids, their assemblymen began to shout. "Good God!" cried one, and *"Jezus Christus!"* another. Someone burst out laughing, and Prue looked around for him, in a panic at the thought of being derided. When she singled him out, three rows back and wearing an odd red wig, he was obviously in a transport of joy. The other porters—nearly twenty of them, carrying the great model aloft by its base as if it were the spoils of war—came in with the representation of the bridge and laid it down at the foot of the elevation; this, too, provoked commentary. Someone was whistling clear down the scale, and Willemsen was gesticulating to his neighbor. Stryker began to rap on the table with a gavel.

"Order!" he called, but no one quieted. "Order!"

"Somebody get the senators!" a voice cried.

The assemblymen continued on volubly until their anger, indignation, delight, or surprise began to abate, and only then did they heed their speaker's repeated smacks upon the table.

"Gentlemen!" Stryker called, his tone indicating good-natured astonishment at their behavior. The legislators did not sit, but most of them quieted, cleared their throats, and straightened their wigs and robes. In the back, a conversation continued in heated whispers. "Please."

"But sir—" someone called out.

"No." Stryker lifted his chest and resettled his ample robe. Prue thought it no wonder he remembered her father fondly—he resembled him, both in girth and in temperament. "You will take your seats, and ask questions according to protocol."

Most of them complied. One who remained standing raised his hand.

"Assemblyman from Westchester County?" Stryker said.

The assemblyman was huffing a bit, as if unable to calm himself down. "Sir, I agree with whoever cried out just now: We should bring in the senators. They will wish to see this."

"The senate has business of its own, Mr. Lancaster."

But Prue could hear a faint knock at the door; and when the porters answered it, some of the senators, curious and bewigged, stood behind it, seeking admission. "Gentlemen," Stryker called to them, "has not the lieutenant governor enough on his agenda to occupy you this morning?"

"Indeed he has, Mr. Speaker," one said. "But when we heard the commotion in the assembly, we gathered your business might be more interesting."

"This is most unusual," Stryker said. "This is entirely out of the ordinary."

The senators, however, did not budge, and some of their peers were lining up behind them.

"Does Lieutenant Governor De Lancey give you permission to leave off your own business?"

"I do, Hendrik," a voice called from out in the hallway. "I'm curious myself."

The assemblymen laughed, and even Prue could not suppress a smile. Stryker shook his great head as if there was nothing he could do to control them. "Very well, then," he said. "File in."

The procession of senators seemed endless; Prue knew there were three score of them. Though they regarded the drawing and the model with as much evident disbelief as had the assemblymen, they chiefly whispered among themselves as they filed in to stand around the perimeter of the hall.

When the porters closed the doors again, a few assemblymen were still standing, one of whom looked familiar to Prue. After searching long through her memory, she thought she knew who it was: Hezekiah Pierrepont, that same staunch Loyalist who, at war's end, had been forced into exile in some godforsaken barrens of New Jersey. Twenty years later, there could be no mistaking the Gallic hook of his nose, nor the slight cross of his dark eyes. He raised his chin.

"Representative from Ulster County?" said Mr. Stryker.

"Sir, what you see before you is no *bridge*," the man said. It had to be Pierrepont—he had the same oleaginous voice. "This is, you will excuse me, a young man's fancy. And in part, I understand, a young *lady's*." There was some quiet laughter among the desks. "In all my travels, and they have been wide, I have never seen any such structure. How would it stand?"

Stryker acknowledged another assemblyman. "Gentleman from Dutchess?"

He cleared his throat. "Bridges have supports in their middles, Mr. Surveyor Horsfield. Of all people, surely you should know it's how they remain steady."

Without waiting for permission, another called out, "And supports would block the free flow of traffic upon the river. So you see, a bridge *won't do.*" Stryker shook his head and banged twice with his gavel, and the representative sat down, saying, "My apologies, sir, for speaking out of turn."

Stryker turned to Ben and said, "Mr. Horsfield, can you allay the representatives' concerns?"

Ben nodded once with his chin. "I can, sir." He put his fingers in his collar and tugged it away from his throat. How Prue envied him his man's figure—his squared shoulders and even his pointy, clean-shaven chin—for how it enabled him to stand up thus before them. She loved him dearly, and at the same time felt what seemed love's opposite: a sickening jealousy.

"Gentlemen," he began. "A simple bridge—say, a log thrown across a rushing stream—works on a simple principle. That is, the weight of a man walking across the log does not fall straight downward (or he would plummet into the current), but is rather distributed along the length of the log, and thence to the ground at both ends. If the log be sturdy enough, he arrives safely at the other side of the stream. If it be too delicate to support his weight, it snaps, and he goes for a swim. For this reason, bridges have hitherto been built with supports, or piers, at close intervals. If they are close enough together, a man's weight need not be carried too far to be relayed safely to the ground; and the spans themselves need not be exquisitely strong to provide safe passage.

"You are correct, my esteemed representatives, that a bridge of this magnitude—its span forty-four hundred feet and its arch, at its center, one hundred fifty feet above high water, high enough to clear the masts of seagoing ships—would obstruct the flow of traffic *intolerably* were it supported by pillars with breakwaters. The piers would fill the entire waterway. This is why, for a river of the East River's importance, a bridge such as that I here propose is not only a fine innovation, but an absolute necessity."

He motioned to the porter who bore the smaller roll of drawings, and the young man approached and handed them to him. Ben drew out the diagram illustrating how a weight was relayed from the tip of a lever back toward its support. "This top diagram shows a man standing at the farthest extremity of a lever—and to be clear, two of them, tip to tip, form the chief structure of my bridge." Pearl had drawn Isaiah—his expression serious, and all his buttons buttoned—bending the lever slightly downward. "If, as I earlier explained, the beam upon which he stands is strong enough, he shall return home this evening with his clothing still dry. For this to happen, his weight must travel back along the beam to here," he said, tapping his finger over the top of the sheet at the lever's support, "the point at which the beam makes contact with the earth. This illustration below"—in which a small circle represented a weight at the tip on which Isaiah stood, and circles of ever greater circumference represented that same weight as it passed down the lever toward the ground—"shows by what proportion that weight seems to increase as it moves along the lever arm. As you can see, any weight placed upon the center of the span is referred to the end of the span and appears to be magnified, thus.

"Therefore, two primary circumstances must obtain for the bridge to hold. First, the center of the bridge, where the levers meet, must be strong enough to support any weight likely to happen upon it—two teams of oxen, to give a simple example, crossing in opposite directions. Second, the abutments shoring up the twin levers must be heavy enough to resist the rotational forces exerted upon them from the intrinsic weight of the lever arms and from any persons or vehicles thereupon. What supports the bridge at the center of its span, I mean to say, is not some prop beneath it—which is rather a primitive solution to the problem—but the increasing bulk of the *structure itself* as it approaches the ground; this, and the solidity of the connection between the base of the structure and the earth. Hence"—he pulled off the next sheet, illustrating various potential types of abutments—"my designs for structures, from the fanciful to the mundane, to keep the ends of the bridge anchored to the ground."

Mr. Stryker asked, "Is your question well answered, Ulster County?"

Pierrepont drew a breath and said, "I am uncertain."

"May I give another example?" Ben said, but did not wait for anyone's approval. "You will excuse me if it is of the grossest nature. How strong would you say this little bridge is before me? How much weight would you suppose it could support?"

"I couldn't say," Pierrepont sneered. "I should think my granddaughter would like to play upon it with her dollies."

"Very well," Ben said. "But this model—an exact representation of the bridge I propose to build—is stronger than it may appear. Now, bear in mind that a model cannot predict the structural integrity of the edifice it represents; the eventual bridge would be both vastly stronger and vastly heavier than this one. But the facsimile does show that the principle behind the bridge is sound." He rolled up the drawings again and with them still in his hand, stepped onto the center of the bridge. Prue winced, but the gasp the representatives let out showed her he had chosen a good course. He took a few small jumps—far less exuberant than those he'd taken in the countinghouse—but the model did not budge. "Miss Pearl, would you join me here?" he asked.

Pearl drew her skirts closer toward her as she walked forward to join him near the center of the span. Her lips were slightly pursed.

"And you, Miss Winship?"

Prue went to stand at Ben's other side. She imagined she felt the bridge give under her weight, though it could not have. Now all three of them were standing on it, and it hadn't even squeaked. She was relieved it hadn't broken; they had, after all, tested it only minimally, and were unsure of its ultimate strength with its abutments thus moored to the platform and not anchored in solid ground.

Now the gentlemen were talking out of turn again. Mr. Stryker was once more asking for order.

"And if half the men in this room wanted to climb on, too," Ben said, "it would support them. Are there any takers?" Not one of the men volunteered, but Ben waved to some of the porters. "Come, might as well. A number of you can fit."

In fact, the bridge held every one of them; Prue imagined they must all resemble rooks lined up along the eaves of a barn. They stood there, some still and some hopping up and down; the fellow beside Prue was chuckling to himself, as was Mr. Stryker. "Have you further questions, Ulster County?" he asked.

"For the nonce, I have none," Mr. Pierrepont said, and sat down.

As they climbed off and returned to their places, Prue felt a moment of exultation that it had held, and another stab of jealousy that it was not she presenting it. Pearl also looked bothered by something; perhaps she, too, who had given so much to the model and elevation, wished she might contribute to Ben's exposition.

"Representative from Chenango?" Stryker said.

"Yes, sir. I seek to know by what method such a structure can even be built."

"A good question," Stryker said, and turned to Ben with an affable expression.

Ben did not appear the least bit nervous. This vexed Prue, though she was delighted he could present their case so eloquently. She recalled her own dry throat when she'd stood before the people of Brooklyn and she fumed at his composure. "A good question, indeed, Mr. Assemblyman," Ben said. "As you perhaps all well know, each arch of a traditional bridge must be built over a wooden centering, which supports it until its keystone is set in place and can bear the weight of its two arms. Such a centering involves great expenditure both in timber and in labor. In a bridge of this size, once it was floated into place it would block off the river and both ports altogether.

"Some of the great bridge builders of our time have built admirable structures upon this plan. Mr. Telford and Mr. Pritchard of Great Britain have constructed numerous arched masonry bridges whose elegant lines bespeak their strength. Almost twenty years ago now, Mr. Pritchard, in connection with a metalsmith named Mr. Abraham Darby, successfully built at Coalbrookdale a similar bridge with its members made up entirely of cast iron—a feat many naysayers had thitherto pronounced impossible. Mr. Thomas Pope of Philadelphia is even now constructing a large-span timber and masonry bridge over the Schuylkill River. Need I ask if, as proud New Yorkers, we should allow Pennsylvania to be the first state to fund such a bold and salutary public works?"

"No, sir," one of the assemblymen cried out, "but we should first bridge the cataract at Niagara Falls! That would put Pennsylvania to shame."

Mr. Stryker hit his gavel on the table once more. "Representative from Niagara County, you will not speak out of turn!"

"Apologies, Mr. Speaker, Mr. Horsfield," the assemblyman said.

Ben gave a gracious nod; Prue once again remarked upon his apparent ease. "Niagara's claim is pressing indeed," Ben said, "but I respectfully argue that the East River's is even more so. The traffic to and from the deepwater ports at Brookland and New York is at present the greatest in the nation; if we can connect them by so magnificent a means, their allure to foreign and domestic shippers will surely increase.

"But I must return to the specifics of my plan, and to the impracticability of building an arch of such size over a wooden centering, thus blocking ingress to both ports. I ask you, esteemed assemblymen, to recall that unlike a traditional arched bridge, the two sides of my bridge do not thrust their weight in toward their central keystone, but *outwards*, toward the anchorages, exactly as a springboard thrusts its weight not toward its tip but toward its support. It should be immediately apparent from this circumstance alone that my bridge will require no centering crutch. Continue along this line of reasoning and you will deduce the method by which I propose to construct this bridge: which is to *begin from* its anchorages and to progress thence from the strongest parts of the levers out to their slender tips. During its construction it will be *entirely self-supporting*, from beginning to end. The two arms will grow out from the banks simultaneously, and one day simply meet in midair, high above the river. Traffic upon the straits will not be disturbed for a single day—unless you count the disturbance caused by the captains of ships pausing to gawp at such an awesome sight."

Some of the gentlemen chuckled again. Prue did not know how Ben had brought them to this point, but knew she could never have done so herself, even had she been a man.

"The timber for each day's work can be floated by barge to its appropriate location and, by means of a crane operated by the strength of one or two men, hoisted to its position." They did not yet have a drawing of the crane; it was their good luck no one asked to see it.

Mr. Pierrepont continued to nod, as if he had been called upon to concede some point. Prue looked around to see if she could intuit the opinions of those around him; and while some still appeared angry or bewildered, many were scanning the drawings with interest. "Mr. Horsfield," Pierrepont said, "has it not occurred to you that were it *possible* to build a bridge upon your plan, the great architects would have done so long ago?"

Prue was glad Pearl was not taking part in this discussion, and equally glad Tem was in Brooklyn.

"Quite the contrary," Ben said with ease. "Had no one ever attempted to build something that had not been built before, there should be no great bridges, nor cathedrals, nor the Pyramids at Giza. It is through experimentation that science progresses; and the same is true for these homely arts that follow in science's wake."

"But it is all well and good to build a doll-model," Mr. Pierrepont said. "How do you know the thing itself would stand?"

Ben paced back and forth before Stryker's desk. Prue thought he must have been catching his breath. "As King's County's surveyor, I believe I have more ability to judge the plan's practicability, if you will excuse my saying so, than any other man present. I have myself surveyed the site, examined the quality of the soil, rock, and sand on which the foundations are to rest, projected the bridge's course, and measured the speed and strength of the winds and currents in the vicinity. I have conducted numerous experiments to determine the relative strengths of timbers in tension and compression, and conclude that my calculations will allow me to build a bridge to withstand any stresses likely to be placed upon it by traffic, the structure's intrinsic weight, or exigencies of weather. The model itself cannot prove that such a bridge would hold; the actual bridge would be two hundred fifty times the length of the one you see before you, but its weight would be exponentially greater. My design accounts for this, of course. I propose that my next step in realizing the bridge should be to build one at a twenty-fifth the size of the eventual structure—ten times as large as the model you see before you. This would allow me to test the methods of construction and to ascertain that the principles hold true at a greater magnitude."

"Further questions?" Stryker asked.

Garret Willemsen stood. "What do you reckon this bridge will cost, sir?"

Ben cleared his throat. "As you know, Mr. Willemsen, most of Brookland's great timber was harvested during the late war by our enemies, for their fortresses and ships. Thus, timber will have to be floated downriver, and the costs in that regard may prove high. But the New York and Brookland Bridge should prove a veritable boon for the timber merchants of northern New York." He smiled around to the assemblymen and senators; he was surely correct in supposing this was how some of those present had made their fortunes. "Assuming the workers to be paid a fair wage for the proposed period of two years, the total sum, in timber, iron, and men, should be in the vicinity of three hundred thousand dollars."

The legislators burst out with more complaints and questions, and Stryker banged his table again. "Order!" he called, more irritably than before. It took a moment, but the representatives complied. "If the men of this assembly agree to pass your request along to the governor, how much of that sum will you ask him to supply?"

"I would ask him to supply it nearly entire, sir." Ben took a deep breath, straining the new buttons of his coat. "It is a public work, for the public weal. It must be funded with public money."

"But sir," Mr. Stryker said, his face showing real concern, "we cannot even agree on an appropriation to build ourselves a state government. And believe me, that would require a far smaller sum than the one you seek."

"I understand," Ben said. "But in truth, a bridge is a matter of pressing importance, and if it is to be built, there is no other way. Miss Winship has graciously agreed to donate land for the bridge's Brookland footing and to assume a share of the costs. I myself shall do the same, though my assets as a private man are perforce smaller than those of Winship Gin. Beyond that, I propose to sell subscriptions in New York and Brookland, that interested parties might contribute to the cost of the works and reap the profits in tolls later on.

"Let me be clear, however, that before we undertake such a vast expenditure, we shall begin with a smaller one: the building of the second model bridge at the aforementioned scale. While this project too will come at its cost—fourteen thousand dollars, if I reckon true—it is only a fraction of the cost of a bridge itself, and I believe the most prudent course of action, as it will allow a more detailed and intricate study of the laws of natural philosophy as they pertain to such a structure. If you gentlemen and Governor Jay would consent to grant me monies sufficient for that endeavor, I would have far more solid evidence of the plan's feasibility when the time comes to request funding for an actual bridge.

"If I may add one thing more: The citizens of Brookland are strongly in favor of this project. When Miss Winship and I presented it to them a few weeks since, they were packed tight as salt cod in a barrel, and offered hundreds of their signatures in testimony, which we have since submitted for your perusal. Mayor Varick and the aldermen of New York

City have likewise written to you of their support. I know that Niagara County and others to our state's far north may wonder why they should allocate such vast sums to a project their constituents will never see. I argue that the New York and Brookland Bridge will redound to the honor of every man in this state; that it will stand as a monument to our fortitude, and that it will increase revenues so greatly, it will improve the fortunes of every New Yorker. That is all I shall say in my own defense, though I shall remain in Albany, should you wish to question me further on any aspect of the proposal. I thank you for taking the time to hear our cause."

"Thank you," Mr. Stryker said. He placed one long hand on a sheaf of papers that looked to be the petition. "Are there further questions?" he asked once more of the room. A younger representative stood and raised his hand. "Representative from Saratoga?"

"I only wish to say, sir, that although I represent the north, I think the bridge beautiful." He nodded and sat back down.

"Thank you, Mr. Gannon." Stryker turned to Ben and said, "We shall begin discussion of this matter this very afternoon. May I ask you to leave this facsimile and these plans here, that we may observe them during our discussion?"

"By all means, sir," Ben answered.

"If that is all, gentlemen?" Stryker said, and people began to rustle and murmur as if it was. "Thank you, Mr. Horsfield, Miss Winship, Miss Pearl. I promise you nothing, but you will have word from us as soon as is feasible."

Pearl and Prue curtsied again, and followed Ben back out to the hall. The senators who stood nearest the door made way for them; and many of them, as well as the assemblymen, grumbled as they passed. Few would meet their eyes. Willemsen, however, nodded to Prue as she walked past him; she wasn't certain she could read his expression, but she thought his acknowledgment a good sign. Willemsen's driver and beautiful horses had gone off to wherever they were stabled, and it seemed to have become an ordinary, sunny day in a busy district.

Ben waited until they were well out into the street to turn to them, grinning, and shout, "It went admirably, do you not think?"

"You did not allow me a word," Prue said, and quickened her stride.

"Prue?"

"And never once mentioned Pearl's contribution. Why in Heaven's name do you suppose they thought she was standing there? For the pathos of it?" She was mortified that this had been her original reason for desiring Pearl's presence.

Ben caught up to them, and interposed himself between them. "I am sorry, Prue, Pearl; but you must agree with me, it went well. They were impressed by the proposal. I should not be at all surprised to find it on Governor Jay's desk in the next few days."

"It is not entirely a question of how the interview went," Prue said, charging ahead into an intersection. A man driving his team swerved to avoid her, and shouted curses at her over his shoulder. "I agree, Ben: You explained my dreams as eloquently as I could hope. The assembly's decision is their own, and depends upon circumstances none of us can envisage, let alone control. I simply hadn't reckoned on feeling such jealousy as you made the presentation."

Ben walked along in silence a moment, which Prue knew did not bode well. "I don't think I understand," he said. "We discussed this long ago, and determined it was the wisest course of action."

"I know, Ben," she said. Her eyes were hot, but she would pitch herself into traffic before she allowed herself to cry. "I still believe it to be so. Yet it is also the idea dearest to my own heart. Can you imagine how it feels to watch another assume credit for it?"

"Your dearest friend," he said, without recrimination. "Your future husband."

She felt nearly as bad for having wounded him as for the wound she herself was nursing, but she could not retract her words. She simply said, "I wish I could have spoken," and remained silent the rest of the way back to Mrs. Finley's. Pearl walked slightly apart from them. Prue wanted to write the morning's news to Tem, so Ben and Pearl agreed to go walking, and to meet her later.

She did write to Tem, but this took only a moment. When she'd finished her letter, she sat at the tidy desk thinking through the events of the day, though the bustle of the household downstairs kept interrupting her thoughts. She wanted to reconcile herself to the present state of affairs; had Mr. Stryker invited her to present her case, the assembly's reception would have been even more equivocal. She knew this should have been some consolation, but couldn't accept it. She decided to write a second letter, which she would send by express boat down to Beacon. A shipment of Winship gin was due to that town that very week, and she wished to divert it to Albany; the small amount of liquor they had brought with them would never do to bribe a hundred assemblymen and sixty-odd senators. She also wrote again to Tem to tell her she'd appropriated the gin, and to ask her to send more to their customers.

When she went downstairs a few hours later, the sun had moved considerably westward in the sky. Prue had not eaten her breakfast and the presentation had lasted through midday, and she was now famished. She heard the rhythmic whirr of eggs being beaten in the kitchen, and the rasp of a knife along the skin of some fruit or vegetable; and she considered asking for some bread and jam, or whatever might have been left over from dinner. But when Mrs. Finley called out, "Miss Winship, is that you?" Prue did not think she could abide her eager questioning or the sullen stare of whichever daughter sat with her. She made her way out the door without stopping to talk.

She walked straight to the docks, which resembled the bustling wharves at home, but she could not grow accustomed to their pond-scum smell. She knew the natives of the place had called their river *Muhheakantuck*, or the river that flowed two ways, as it was half salt water traveled up from New York Bay, and half fresh water from the far north; yet still it seemed uncanny to see little transport smacks and hag boats going about their business and not smell the sea. Prue could not help imagining a bridge of her own design spanning the North River here; and in the next instant felt the pang of knowing that even were it possible, it would never be known as hers.

Well, hang it, she thought. *If two people are said to become one before God and the law, perhaps they have only one set of ideas between them.* Her own parents had done things otherwise, but she and Ben might manage.

Some questioning found her a schooner bound for Beacon en route to New York, and she entrusted her letter to its captain along with a shilling and the widest smile she could muster. Along the river, hawkers with buckets and clam knives sold what looked a fine meal; but much as Prue would have liked to slurp shellfish from her hands, it was easier done in work britches than a dress. Elisha Green's establishment was not far off, and she made her way along the busy wharves as far as possible to reach it. The moment she arrived, she saw Ben and Pearl through the open door. Pearl still looked sullen, but waved her hand as if it was possible Prue might not have seen them. The tavern was full, though who knew how so many Albanians had leisure to drink tea and ale on a weekday afternoon. "Hello, Prue," Ben said, standing and turning to face her as she entered the smoky room. He didn't seem to want to risk his earlier enthusiasm.

Prue kissed his cheek, then Pearl's. She hoped this would stand for an apology. She sat down beside her sister and put her elbows on the sticky table.

"We have some news," Ben said, and Pearl began riffling through her knitting bag. "Not altogether good, I fear."

The proprietor's daughter came to take Prue's order. She was a girl no older than twelve, the spit and image of her father, and crowned with a mop of woolly blond hair that took up more space than she. She told off her menu by heart. Prue's ears must have been ringing, because the child sounded far away. Prue cared only for the news, but she managed to order some smoked sturgeon and a pint of beer. Though she almost couldn't bear to look at Ben, Prue was keenly aware of what was going on outdoors. A milkman drove past with his empty buckets clanging in the back of his wagon, and a child slipped in the road and began to howl. His brother dragged him up to the curb and wiped off his knees. The stage flew by, its driver shouting to clear sluggish pedestrians from his path.

"Hoy, Prue," Ben said. She only then realized her mind had wandered off. "Willemsen sent word to Mrs. Finley's. Pearl has the letter."

Pearl at last extracted the paper. Prue went to break the letter's seal but saw it was, of course, already broken; for who was the bridge architect but Ben? She reminded herself it must have cost them both some effort to hold their peace and allow her to read it for herself.

Mr. Willemsen reported that the gentlemen of the assembly were deeply divided in their initial discussion about the prospects for the bridge. New York County's representative, as well as many others from downstate, wished to approve the $14,000 appropriation; many of the upstate members were vehemently opposed. The senators had, further, been sufficiently riled by the proposal to wish to debate it themselves; and they had voted to make their own suggestion, regardless of the assembly's, to Governor Jay. Willemsen could not conjecture how long it might take to reach a decision on the matter, but he thought there might be some use in Ben remaining in Albany until that time, in case his skills of persuasion might be put to use.

When the girl arrived with Prue's fish, Ben ordered a second pitcher of beer. "You'll have to return to the distillery, will you not?" he asked.

Prue looked blankly at her sturgeon. A moment since, it had interested her—as it was fished from fresh waters, it was a rarity in Brooklyn—but now she wondered if she could eat it. "I promised Tem I'd return in a fortnight at most. I don't know how she will fare without me."

Pearl placed one hand on top of her sister's. Ben said, "As I thought."

"But I cannot leave you here, either. It is my bridge, Ben. I am willing to share the credit with you, but not to turn it over to you entire."

"It is your decision," he said.

Prue did not like the wary look in his eyes. She took a long pull from her beer and tried to settle down to eat.

She did not think she could go back to Brooklyn before the bridge's fate should be decided. If that meant residing in Albany another month, then so be it. The first bite of fish reminded Prue she was ravenous with hunger; she resolved to eat quickly, and to write to Tem and Isaiah as soon as she finished.

The days wore on, and the two houses of the legislature continued to squabble; Prue read both sides of the argument in the Albany papers. Both the assembly and the senate called Ben back on various occasions the next week; and in the evenings, he took Prue and Pearl to the quarters of one assemblyman and the next, where Prue understood she was to make polite conversation with the womenfolk. On one occasion the young representative from Saratoga asked about her contribution to the plan, and listened with interest as she recounted a straitened version thereof. The shipment that had been meant for Beacon arrived early in the week. Prue asked Elisha Green to introduce her to a glassblower, that she might portion the gin out for the various representatives. This occupied at least some of her time. Pearl used up her embroidery silk and, growing restless in the house, set out to wander the city in search of more. Prue fretted about her sister's welfare, out in the streets thus unattended, but knew she could not stop her going. Late in the week a letter from Tem arrived, full of ill-spelled vituperation; another, from Isaiah, told Prue the second shipment had gone off to Beacon and that all else was well.

After two weeks of heated debate—during which Prue came to pity Mrs. Finley's daughters, though she remained grateful for their good cooking—Mr. Willemsen at last wrote to report that the assemblymen had taken a vote, and had come out fifty-seven to fifty-one in favor of funding the model at one twenty-fifth the scale of the eventual bridge. This was a small majority, but sufficient to send their recommendation to Governor Jay. Mr. Willemsen cordially invited Ben, Prue, and Pearl to sup at his quarters that evening.

The letter reached them at Mrs. Finley's, just after the tea dishes had been cleared. Ben began whooping as soon as he read the document, which caused the mousy Finley daughters to retreat to the kitchen. Prue had to read the letter twice to understand its import, and even then was not certain if she should feel disappointment or delight. Ben took her in his arms and kissed her, then pulled back and shook her gently when she did not break into peals of laughter. "Come now, woman," he said, beaming at her. "Fifty-seven to fifty-one. I'd say that's nearly unanimous."

Pearl whistled her disagreement.

"Both of you, dark-minded as your mother," Ben said. He was still smiling, but Prue did not find this amusing. "We shall have our small bridge; and if all goes as well as I wager it will, we'll bridge the East River next. *Oh*, I can just picture Hezekiah Pierrepont's scowl as the ballots were tallied."

I think it fine News, Pearl wrote on her book, *though less ecciting than if the Legislature had simply writ*ⁿ *you a Gigantic Draught.*

"I know you're right, Ben," Prue said, though she considered Willemsen's letter only a halfhearted vote of confidence.

"Write Tem immediately," Ben said. "She'll be eager to know."

Prue did write her, and continued to wonder how she fared at the distillery. She supposed she would have heard had anything gone amiss; then again, letters took days to go up or down the Hudson, and anything might have happened since last Tem had written. Prue had to trust her sister could manage.

In the meanwhile, Garret Willemsen had laid in a prodigious store of Madeira wine, "intending no offense," he said, "to our local geniuses of grain alcohol," and they made their way through bottle after bottle that evening. Prue was not certain they had cause to celebrate in any earnest. Even if Governor Jay approved the plan, it would be a long time in the building, especially with the state overseeing it. Prue reminded herself, however, of the justice of Ben's assessment: It had indeed always been her habit to take the darkest possible view. Perhaps on this occasion, she might persuade herself of the rectitude of what was actually transpiring. She might praise God for what was instead of begging Him, with uncertain result, for something yet to come.

Seventeen

THE WEDDING

W hen the wine was finished and the next day's headache had passed, they boarded another boat to begin their journey home. As Prue watched the lovely mountains roll by, her spirits continued to improve. Their journey had been only a qualified success, and there was no saying what Governor Jay would decide, but overall, they had done well. Pearl sketched the scenery most of the way home, to show Tem and Mr. Severn what she had seen. And when they stopped at Poughkeepsie, Ben and Prue took a short walk out one of the country lanes to discuss standing up in church together.

"You agree with me," he said, swiping idly at the tall brown corn with his stick, "that now our bridge is seen to, we are free to seek your friend's blessing."

"I think we'd best get everyone's," Prue said. "We've traveled all over Creation together, and I've no doubt Mrs. Livingston will make a feast of it otherwise."

"And you're done feeling jealous that I'm the bridge architect?"

"I suppose so. Yes." She didn't know she ever would be, but it seemed wise to assent.

"Then we'll have a wedding straightaway, and you'll come live in my house."

A herd of belted cows was out grazing and napping in the field sloping off to the left, in which white sweet peas ran rampant. "I don't think I can," she said.

"Why not? What is it now?"

"I need to be near the distillery."

Ben continued to swipe good-naturedly at the corn. "Very well, then," he said. "I shall come live in your house."

"With my sisters?"

Ben said, "I could as easily have been living with Isaiah, Patience, and Maggie all this time."

"And been miserable at it."

"Ah, but I like your sisters better than I like Patience," he said.

Prue wasn't convinced, but said, "If you say so."

"I do. And I say we should get back to town as well. There's no use stopping to pay calls on your customers if we ramble all day."

They took two extra days in returning to do just that; she did not know when she would have another opportunity to meet these gentlemen she had known only by name all these years. Most of them seemed as surprised as the hotel guest had been to discover there were actual daughters behind the gin; but they sent her away with larger orders than usual, and those who'd asked to see the drawings for the bridge sent good wishes for its success.

Prue had written to Tem again, directly before they left Albany, to apprise her of their plans for return; and as soon as their boat entered Buttermilk Channel, Prue saw a rider take off up the Shore Road.

Must be for Temmy, Pearl wrote.

As the rider rode past, Prue could see people from the tannery and the Luquer Mill and all the way north coming out to look at them. When they passed their own wharf, perhaps thirty persons were crammed against the retaining wall, and a score more dotted the fences that backed along Clover Hill. Others, including Tem, had clustered around van Nostrand's landing, where Prue, Pearl, and Ben would be dropped off with the mails. Tem waved and shouted as she saw them approach, though over the din of the port, Prue could not hear what she was saying. Pearl waved back. An auction was under way at Joe Loosely's, and a crowd of children was gathered appreciatively around a flock of agitated black-faced sheep.

When they landed, Tem jumped down onto their boat. Losee was sitting on the flat rock north of his landing with his young daughter, Petra, eating a fried chicken. After Prue had exchanged greetings with Tem and Isaiah, and learned no terrible fate had befallen the works in her absence, she tried to forget Losee's words at the petition signing, and went over to the rock. "Losee, Petra, it's good to see you," she said. "Looks like a fine lunch."

He wiped his hands and mouth on his gingham napkin in what seemed an ordinary fashion, but Petra stared at the ground so that her pale blond braids swung down to hide her face, and blushed in a manner that told Prue she'd been the subject of conversation at table. "Indeed," Losee said. "You met with some success, I hear?" He was wearing an old shirt, thin at the elbows, with his deceased wife's signature blue stitching. He surely thought he'd never have another like it, once it wore out.

"Some," Prue said. "Perhaps not as much as we might have hoped."

"Papers said otherwise. Your father would be proud." Had he not looked out across the water, a stranger would never have known he found this troubling. "Very proud."

Prue said, "Thank you." She wanted to tell him that in honor of her father, she would make certain he was never driven out of business—she would employ him to ship her own goods, should it prove necessary—but she knew this would please him no more than anything else she might say.

Losee pointed toward Ben and Pearl. "Was it trouble looking after those two?"

"No trouble," Ben called, but any humor he might have intended was lost between his mouth and the small, lapping waves. "Bit of unloading to see to," he said. "Excuse me."

Losee's broad, wrinkled face unnerved Prue; it gave the impression she was keeping him from a more important task. "I don't want to interrupt your lunch," she said.

He answered, "No, not at all."

"I'll be up to the works, then. I'm sure there's plenty to see to."

"One hears."

"How so?"

He shrugged his shoulders, and took up a new piece of chicken. Petra hadn't looked at her all that time. Loosely's boys had shouldered the scroll and the Winships' trunk and were carrying them down to the Shore

Road. They'd called out a team of horses to move the model bridge; Ben's small trunk had gone on a barrow, and a lone boy had set out to wheel it up toward Olympia. "What kind of a gratuity will you give us, Mr. Horsfield?" one boy asked. "Can you make Miss Winship pay us in gin?"

"I'll pay you all in broken noggins if you don't get everything to the distillery in one piece," he said.

They shouted at him and stuck out their tongues. He capered along in front of them to lead the way.

Tem and Pearl were having what looked to be an animated conversation, but Prue broke into the middle of it and led them both down the open stairs toward the Shore Road. "Losee made me wonder if everything really is all right at the works," she said.

Tem put her strong arm around Prue's shoulders. "Nothing burned down. There was one small accident."

"Of what kind?"

"Nothing, really. I received one of your letters on Saturday," Tem said, letting go of her sister, "and the last just yesterday. Prue, I am so proud of you. This is the best that could have happened."

Prue was still wondering about the accident, but would have to let it be for the moment. Though Tem was no taller, her stride was longer, and it took some effort to keep up with her. "And Ben and I have finally decided to marry. This autumn."

"That's excellent news," Tem said, beaming over her shoulder at her. "Quite a week." They were approaching the ropewalk and the din of its machines. "Where shall you live, by the bye?"

"In the house," Prue said, nearly shouting.

"The lot of us, all together?" She was walking at a brisker pace now. "I hope I shan't grow to be a sour little pippin, like Maggie Horsfield."

"She was born sour, don't you remember? Have no worries; we shall manage it somehow. Both you and I need to live in the house, after all. It isn't practical for either of us to live beyond sight of the works."

Ben had instructed the boys to take the drawings upstairs to the countinghouse. Those bearing the trunk would continue up Clover Hill to the house. "Gratuities!" they were shouting to him. "We want our gratuities!" A few of the men were smoking in the yard, and they waved and called out their greetings.

Pearl tapped Prue on the shoulder and held up a note to her. *I shall go check on Abiah at Home. Come soon*, it said.

"Very well." Prue followed Tem up to their office.

Tem once again smiled over her shoulder at Prue. "I'm not certain I want to live with you and your husband."

Prue wished she could wait until the door was shut behind them. "Why so?" she asked.

Ben was on his way back down, and said, "Off to see how Adam's done without me," as he ran to follow the second set of porters up the hill.

"I'm unsure," Tem said. "Perhaps it's that the house will be so close, for five of us."

"I know you're right," Prue said. The countinghouse smelled good and familiar—juniper, burnt coffee, fire, and dust. It smelled like home. "But what else should we do? If I lived at Ben's I'd have to keep a saddled horse tethered to the porch, that in case of emergency you might blow on a conch shell to hurry me down."

Tem laughed and poured them each a drink.

"Thank you," Prue said, taking hers. She could see that behind Tem's bright expression, this troubled her.

"Well, how shall we manage it? I can't share a room with Pearl. She'll never sleep again."

"We'll build on. It's high time, anyway; Father should have done so himself."

"Father should have leveled the house and built a more modern one," Tem said.

Once again, Prue missed him acutely. It had been almost three years since he'd died, yet he continued to come back to her at these odd intervals. "We could still do that. We could live at Ben's while the work was accomplished."

"No," Tem said. "I would miss the old place too dearly."

"You're not yet twenty, you know," Prue said to her. "You shall yourself yet marry, and be free to leave."

Tem wrinkled her nose at her.

"Why do you show me that countenance?"

"Because I don't think I shall ever marry," Tem said, as if it were the plainest statement possible.

"Just because you don't like Cornelis or Mr. Fischer—"

"It isn't that I don't like them," Tem said. "Or, it *is* that I don't like Mr. Fischer. Cornelis is a fine friend. But look around you, Prue. Who of the married women is as happy as we?"

"Peg Dufresne."

"Granted," Tem said. "But other than her. Mrs. Livingston? Patience? Our mother wasn't happy a day in her life. I prefer to be a distiller."

"You don't see, Tem. You and I shall do both. Mother was constitutionally unhappy; it had naught to do with being Father's wife. Quite the contrary. I think he rather cheered her up."

Tem shook her head but didn't respond, and poured herself a second drink, which she drank quickly. "Well, I left Jens with a thousand gallons of low-wines. I ought to go see to it."

"I'll be down in a moment," Prue said.

Tem stopped at the door and turned around to face her again. "The accident, Prue?" The expression on her face reminded Prue of how a child would look, confessing some unutterable sin, except that Tem had always done her mischief in the open air. "Marcel Dufresne lost two fingers in the press."

Prue's breath hissed in across her teeth, and her own hands flew up instinctively to her mouth. "No," she said. After all her mother's dire predictions, this had been the accident she'd most feared; she had always imagined its victim would be herself. "How did it happen?"

"I don't know. I wasn't there. Inattention, I suppose."

"But I trained him myself." Prue's eyes were full of tears. The press exerted about a thousand pounds of force, and she could only too well imagine how the blow must have felt.

"He was extracting essence of orrisroot and turned to answer a question from someone behind him. The press slammed down on the first two fingers of his left hand."

"This is a 'small accident'?" All Prue's own fingers were throbbing in sympathetic pain. "Oh, God," she said. "He cannot have died of his wound, or you would have told me straightaway."

"No, he lives."

At this moment, Isaiah walked in. Prue could see he immediately read the topic of conversation in their expressions. "Why did no one write me of this?" she demanded.

"We didn't know what it could avail to do so," Isaiah said. Prue thought the vertical crease between his brows had deepened during her absence. "He was maimed, not killed; and there was nothing you could have done from Albany."

"I did not need to tarry on my way home. We could have been here two days since."

"But what good would it have done Marcel?" Isaiah asked, leaving Tem by the door and approaching Prue at the desk.

"I don't know," Prue said. She sat down on the desk's edge. "Were his fingers crushed or severed?" she asked.

"Crushed," Isaiah said. "He fainted on the spot. I was the first to respond to the bell, and I sent for Dr. de Bouton right away. He looked haggard when he saw the injury. He pronounced the fingers beyond repair, and amputated them right there, on the press."

"God," Prue said. "He's only a boy."

"And therefore recovering well," Isaiah said.

"You've been to check on him?"

"Of course," Isaiah said.

"We both have," Tem added. "I feel very bad this happened on my watch, Prue."

Prue shook her head. "It was my fault, not yours. My fault in training him. You couldn't have prevented it."

"Still, it seems—"

"No," Prue said. "You're not a bad steward."

"Thank you," Tem said. "Jens remains on his own in the stillhouse. I should get back."

Both Prue and Isaiah nodded to her. She practically ran down the stairs.

"Will you have a drink?" Prue asked.

"Thank you, no."

"How does Simon take the news?"

"Well enough," Isaiah said. "As you would expect. Peg is nursing the boy back to health; and they both understand it was an accident."

"We are paying him, I hope, while he recovers?"

Isaiah said, "Payroll will be this Saturday; I shall pay him if you wish."

Prue nodded. She could imagine the seeping bandage on Marcel's left hand, and felt it was her personal responsibility. "When he returns, I want him kept out of the rectifying room and brought up to you in the office."

"I don't know, Prue," Isaiah said. "He likes working with you. He has an irreplaceable nose. And has he any aptitude for writing?"

"We shall train him to if he doesn't. Dammit," she said, and slapped the desk. "Simon was one of our strongest supporters for the bridge."

"And surely remains so."

Prue glanced out the window. "You are ever the voice of reason. When did this happen?"

"Tuesday. We shut down the rectifying stills until your return; but we can fire them up this afternoon if you are willing."

"You haven't rectified in nearly a week?"

"What choice had we?" Isaiah asked.

If no one had rectified, the remainder of the manufactory had to have been operating below capacity. The days were still long, and Prue could catch up quickly enough; but her eyes felt sandy, and she rubbed them until they burned.

"Don't worry," Isaiah said. "Both storehouses are full."

"And I shall still sit here on tenterhooks until we hear from Governor Jay."

"But I have wonderful news from my brother," he said. At last his expression softened. "I have anticipated it a long time."

"I, too," Prue said. "I am so glad you're happy."

"The only thing would please me more would be to know the date."

"We haven't one yet. We haven't spoken to Mr. Severn." Prue opened the nearest account ledger, and glanced down at the blotched and X'd-out columns of Tem's entries. Her heart dropped into her stomach.

"It's all right," Isaiah said. "She's slovenly, but her arithmetic is correct. Would you like me to help you man the press?"

Though Tem's crazed handwriting still distressed her, Prue said, "Yes."

"It'll be a long day," Isaiah said. He emptied the dregs from the morning's pot of coffee into a cup of questionable cleanliness and handed it to her. "We shall have to clean the room first. I shut it down on the instant when Marcel was injured; I'm sure the blood is still there, and herbs scattered on the floor."

"We'll manage," Prue said, and drank the cold, bitter coffee to fortify herself.

Without Marcel to assist her, it took more than a week of working from dawn till dusk to catch up to the rest of the manufactory. Before she began her day, Prue would check on how the model was weathering outdoors and record its progress in a ledger; and every evening, she went out the turnpike to Simon Dufresne's, until Peg drew her aside and commanded her to cease her worrying. In this way, almost a fortnight passed without so much as seeing Ben, let alone approaching Mr. Severn; but Prue thought of Ben constantly, and wondered when he would come to inform her of Mr. Jay's decision.

In the last week of September, an unseasonable rain began to fall—not especially heavy, but relentless in a manner more consistent with spring than with autumn. It came down in gray sheets that rendered the landscape soft and gloomy, and in twisting silver ropes that hung like icicles from branches and eaves. Brooklyn's streets were all shin-deep in mud, and after the fourth day, Prue shut down the works and went out with Tem, Isaiah, and all their men to lay sandbags atop the retaining wall. The model bridge weathered the downpour well, which gave Prue some satisfaction. Nothing entered or left the port; Losee stopped running his boat; and even the enterprising Mr. Fischer left off the construction of his ferry house. Prue felt certain everyone but her was bitter about the loss of business the rain caused, their spirits as well as their underclothes dampened; but as miserable as she was, slipping through it with flour sacks on her shoulder, she was delighted at the good it proved a bridge would do them.

"Lord," Abiah said, when she and Tem returned home that evening, "you smell like wet sheep."

As she stripped in the kitchen, Tem said, "That's how we feel, as well."

Pearl went upstairs for towels. As Prue wrung her hair out in the doorway, she saw Ben running up the path, under cover of an umbrella, yet still soaked to the skin. "News!" he hollered.

"Dammit," Tem said, and rushed for the back stairs in her undershirt. She passed Pearl on her way back down, snatched one of the towels she was carrying, and took it up with her.

Ben stuck his head in the doorway to kiss Prue's cheek, but remained on the threshold, dripping. Prue passed him the towel Pearl gave her, and he, in turn, pulled out a letter from deep in his shirt. Even it had gotten wet, but not so thoroughly Prue couldn't read it.

"Good news," Ben said, and turned around to shake his head like a dog out onto the stoop. Pearl returned to the stairs, but more slowly this time.

"What does it say?" Abiah asked.

Prue read it all the way through before answering. "Mr. Jay supports the legislature's proposition." Her heart skipped a beat as she heard herself say it. "He shall send us the fourteen thousand dollars to build a small bridge on the plan we propose; and if it proves sound, both by our reckoning and by that of experts appointed by the state, he will be willing to discuss a larger appropriation."

Ben leaned in to kiss her again, then continued to towel off his head. "At first I thought we should not be able to work on it over the winter, but on reflection I see, if we dig the foundations now, we can use the winter profitably in cutting the timber and stone to size, and assemble it come spring."

"This is excellent news," Abiah said.

Pearl returned with a pile of their father's clothing for Ben, with Tem close behind her in dry work clothes. "Thank you, Pearlie," he said. "Did you hear?"

He might have guessed from her bright expression, but she nodded anyway.

"Change in my room," Abiah said.

Ben left his boots by the door and went inside, then reemerged a few moments later in britches and a shirt that were musty and far too big for him. He had his wet clothes in a dripping bundle before him.

"I'll take those," Abiah said, and hurried them outdoors, along with Tem's.

Pearl scooped up her sleeping cat from the rocking chair and sat down with it in her lap.

"Supper smells delicious, Abiah," Ben said.

"It's only vegetable soup," she said over her shoulder as she wrung out the clothes, "but if you're angling for an invitation, I'm sure there's one to be had. Prue, you go change yourself, too. I can't have those wet clothes in the house; they smell rancid."

By the time Prue returned, in her spare britches and a woolen sweater, Tem had poured five glasses of gin and taken hers to her chair, which she turned around before straddling it. Her short pigtails continued to drip on the floor. "You can't be surveying in this weather?" she asked Ben.

"No, no. I suppose I shall use the time to order some of our materials, assuming the roads to be passable tomorrow." Prue sat down beside him, and he raised his glass to her. "So, Prue, sisters. We have a wedding to plan, and I think we should take advantage of this foul weather to get to work on it."

Tem looked him in the eye and drained her glass, as if this were a toast.

He drank his down as well, but his eyes watered. "A lucky man, who marries a distiller." Pearl shook her head at him. "Very well. As this rain has perforce confined me to my home and near environs, I had no choice but to visit Mr. Severn this afternoon. He was quite affable; rather a change from his usual demeanor. At all events, he proposes to marry us the third Saturday of October, to give us a few weeks to plan. If it suits you, and assuming the weather permits, I'd like to suggest we set up dancing and refreshments in the mill yard."

In Octob'? Pearl wrote. *It may be cold.*

"The twentieth," he said. "It'll likely be warm yet. And in that way, we could ask all of Brookland, your employees, and New York's aldermen to attend without any great bother."

Abiah whistled, closed the door behind her, and wiped her hands on her apron. "That's a lot of people."

"Have you any relatives besides each other?" he asked.

"I believe one of our father's sisters lives in New Bedford; but we've never met her," Prue answered.

Catharine Winship Orr, Pearl wrote.

"And I've only Izzy and Mags, and Izzy's children. So we'll be a dozen for church. It won't matter how many for the celebration."

"I don't mean to disappoint you, Ben," Abiah said, "but the baking we did for your meeting in August nearly killed Miss Pearl and myself." Pearl nodded, with one hand in the cat's fur.

"I wouldn't ask," he said. "Do you suppose Mrs. Loosely is better equipped?"

"Are we in a position to ask anything of the Looselys?" Prue asked. "Perhaps the Philpots will help."

"And lend us musicians," Ben said. "All that's left to settle, then, is how we'll live."

Tem poured herself another cupful and sighed.

Ben reached across the table to have his glass replenished, as well. "Prue tells me," he ventured, Prue thought unwisely, "you have some reservations about the living arrangements we've proposed."

"Why'd you tell him that?" Tem asked Prue. "Not exactly, Ben. It's only I think the house will be rather small with all of us bumping about all winter. There aren't enough bedrooms."

"We could build out from the side wall," Prue said, gesturing to the one opposite Abiah's room. "We could build two more rooms, an upstairs and a downstairs."

"There'll be money when I sell my house," Ben said.

Do'n't you want to save it for yr Bridge? Pearl wrote. The cat, miffed at being used as a lap desk, jumped down and stalked away.

"I believe the price I'll get for my house will go much farther in building rooms. I can easily afford two of them, whereas I can't have more than a foot of bridge."

Tem accidentally clanked her glass against her teeth, then drained it. "We won't be able to do it until spring," she said. "It'll be a crowded house until then."

"Unless we stay in mine," Ben said to Prue.

"I cannot be that far from the works. It won't be so bad, Temmy. It'll only be a season."

Tem leaned forward against the back of her chair and drummed her fingers on it. "You two shall take my room—our parents' room—but we haven't resolved the rest of it. I can't share with poor Pearl."

Ben looked at Prue for an explanation. She said, "Tem's a difficult sleeper."

I shall manage, Pearl wrote. *We all did, all those years before our Parents dy'd.*

"Or you can have my bed," Abiah said to her, serving out the soup into bowls. "And I can sleep with Tem."

'Tis'n't nesesery, Pearl wrote, then shook her head, to be certain Abiah had read her meaning.

It was resolved, then. Although for reasons she could not articulate Prue still had her lingering doubts, the next week she moved her few possessions across the hall into the room that contained the bed large enough for two. In addition, it had a wardrobe, washstand, chest, and Roxana's cramped desk—little to grow accustomed to, but after having awakened facing eastward all her life, Prue wondered what it would be like to wake up here, with a wavy view of the river. Tem took her work clothes from the chest and threw them back on what had formerly been her shelf in the cupboard. Prue felt guilty for what she was doing to Pearl, but reasoned that at least now she and Tem would have their separate beds. The day before the wedding, Ben borrowed Jolly and one of the distillery wagons and brought over the trunks containing his books, instruments, and clothing, except for his best suit of clothes, which remained at his house, with his coffeepot, to serve him the following morning. Prue could not explain why she was touched to see how few possessions he had; it was not as if she herself owned many more, though the house's plates and andirons were, technically, hers. To see his life packed up so small, perhaps, simply reminded her of his innate fragility. Then, too, she reminded herself she was prey to her emotions right then. When Pearl washed her hair later that afternoon, she also felt her throat thicken when she realized this was how her hair would smell on her wedding day. Had one of her sisters reported feeling such emotions, she would have laughed at her; but there it was.

October remained warm that year, as if expressly to allow them their outdoor celebration. The morning of the twentieth, Pearl pinned white chrysanthemum blossoms beneath the collars of their dresses. Tem reluctantly agreed to wear her only remaining gown, moth-eaten as it was from disuse, but she did not want to wear the flower Pearl proffered. The day was warm and bright when the bell rang to summon them all to church; and as Prue walked out in the company of her sisters, the Livingstons and Joralemons, all in their best clothes and hats, stood on their stoops to wish them well.

Ben and his family had reached the church before the Winships. Prue could hear the cries of Isaiah's new infant through the open door; she also saw Ben pacing within. Abiah took Prue's bonnet and laid it on a rear pew as everyone in both families, except Patience, who sat soothing her baby, assembled around Will Severn. "It is a delight to be here to celebrate this occasion," he said to Prue. "I have often prayed for you this day would come."

Prue thought the fervor in his shy gaze must carry some meaning, but she did not feel inclined to inquire into it. Ben, after all, stood before her, holding both her hands firmly in his own. The pleasure on his countenance would suffice.

Ben and Prue had asked Severn for the plainest possible ceremony— the witness of their siblings, an exchange of vows, the bestowal of a ring and a kiss. Though the event moved along swiftly, Isaiah's two older children found it intolerable; the elder sat kicking his feet against a pew, while the younger clutched at her mother's skirt and whimpered. Prue knew Patience could do little to control them, yet she found them distracting and wondered if others did as well. Ben, she noticed, looked at nothing but her; Tem kept glancing out the window, as if this could make the children disappear; and Pearl beamed at Prue whenever they caught each other's eyes, her narrow face unaccountably flush. In what seemed a mere moment, Severn pronounced them man and wife. As Prue reached up to kiss Ben, she felt a stab of remorse at having allowed Isaiah's children to irk her rather than concentrating on the event at hand.

As the church bell tolled out their joy, Prue and Ben led their families down toward the mill yard. Some of Prue's slaves had gathered by the distillery gate in their Sunday clothes, and they clapped to welcome Prue to her celebration. Early in the morning, she, Pearl, and Abiah had gone down to the mill yard to set up planks on trestles. Since then, the neighborhood women had arrived with flowered and checkered cloths to cover the boards and with a variety of delicacies to supplement the Philpots' stew and ribs: roast chickens, deviled eggs, cold cured ham, salads of all descriptions, smoked fish, and pickled peppers and cucumbers dripping in brine. Prue had watered down the gin the night before to prevent such roaring intoxication as had afflicted Boerum's son at the petition-signing; but along with their fiddler and the food, the Philpots had sent down four casks of beer. "Drunkenness is imminent," Ben said to Prue, putting his hand around her arm and giving her a shake for courage. "Oh, a wedding is a fine thing."

The neighbors, down to the smallest children, were clean-scrubbed, and the workers, who were generally coated either in malt dust or sweat, all looked like gentlemen. The last leaves of the neighborhood's small oak trees were beginning to turn brown, but in patches still shone bright yellow against the periwinkle sky. Some people danced, while others stood and ate. After all the worry and tumult of that spring and summer, Prue was happy simply to see people enjoying themselves.

She was relieved Joe Loosely and his wife had come. Joe had not signed their petition out of deference to Losee, but Prue had hoped his memory of her father would prevent him from holding a grudge. He arrived with two large jugs of cider, and his wife with a set of embroidered table napkins; and Prue was thankful her hopes in their quarter had been fulfilled. A few of New York's aldermen also came, though they looked uncomfortable out in the mill yard in their fancy coats. Prue asked Isaiah and Cornelis to look after them, and knew they would do their best to make them welcome. But Prue had also invited Losee and Petra, and she kept looking out to see if they'd arrived. He had stared off toward the water while she spoke to him, and she did not expect him; but in the middle of the afternoon, she saw Petra's white-blond head bobbing along the Shore Road, and behind her, her father, his bandy-legged gait recognizable from any distance. He stood at the outskirts of the gathering awhile, as if he were not certain he saw anyone of his acquaintance. Ben was by then engaged in horseplay with Jens Luquer, and while Prue watched them with half her attention, the remainder wondered what Losee would do.

He took his time meandering through his neighbors, who as they parted seemed to give him the same space and caution they would give an excitable dog. Petra stationed herself before a tray of cinnamon pretzels Peg had baked. Her father came over to Prue, and stood, with his hat in his hands, watching Ben and Jens; they straightened up immediately, as if they were still rowdy boys, and Losee one of the many who might punish them. Ben wiped his hair back from his eyes, and extended his hand without a trace of wariness. "Losee," he said. "We're honored you've come."

Losee also extended his hand and, after replacing his hat on his head, clapped Ben on the shoulder. "I wish your parents were still with us. They would have been so glad."

Ben said, "Thank you, yes." He and Prue had spoken long that morning about missing them. "I'm glad you've come."

Losee said, "I, too." He turned and looked straight at Prue for the first time in months. "No need saying how this would have pleased your father."

"Everyone says that," Prue said, "but he always thought Ben a bit of a monkey."

"Ah," Losee said. "But he meant it out of love." He cleared his throat, reached into the vest pocket of his coat, and said, "I've brought you a wedding gift. Something small."

Prue held out her hand, and Losee pressed it with both of his, engulfing it. What was in his palm tickled against Prue's own. When he took his hands away, Prue saw he'd given her his wife's necklace—a delicate enameled forget-me-not on a fine golden chain. From her earliest childhood, Prue remembered, it had glinted from his wife's throat. "I'm sorry, I cannot accept this," Prue said. She hadn't cried all day, but the necklace choked her with tears. "It should be Petra's."

Losee took it back, but only to unhook the clasp. "Petra has other things from her mother. She wants you to have it." He looked around for her, to corroborate this, but she was eating pretzels and talking to Peg. "Please take it."

Prue bowed her head toward him, and he fastened it around her neck. When she stood again, she felt its cool, rounded petals with her fingers. "I can't thank you enough," she said.

Ben moved her hand so he could see it. "It's beautiful," he said.

Losee said, "Wear it in good health. And accept my apologies for how difficult things have been between us. You know where I stand, but I know you don't mean me any harm. It's a dream of yours, and I cannot fault you for wishing to realize it. And your father would be proud of what you're attempting. You're very like him, you know. He had that same enterprising spirit."

Prue thanked him again. The tears were still thick in her throat, but she laughed all the same. Ben put his arm around her. "It's good to have you talking to me again," she said. "And good, however incorrect you are, to know you think I resemble my father."

"No," Losee said, "I'm right as rain." Petra was beckoning to him across the crowd, and he said, "I should go see what she wants. But again, my congratulations." He shook both their hands. Prue sighed deeply once he had gone.

"It's cause for celebration, not mourning," Ben said to her.

"I know," she answered. "I believe I'm doing both."

The mayor had declined to come, and the aldermen left early—on a boat Mr. Fischer had bedecked with garlands of autumn leaves for the occasion—but the neighbors talked and danced until the last speck and drop were consumed and the sun hung low over Manhattan. Patience had long since gone home with her infant, and Tem and Pearl had gone down to the retaining wall to watch the sun set over the crying gulls and the late-day ships. Isaiah's three- and one-year-olds were scratching with shells in the packed sand in the middle of the mill yard and shouting incoherently at each other as they played. Prue leaned her head against Ben's shoulder.

"It was a good day," Isaiah said. Ben rocked Prue against him, perhaps in answer. "Business as usual Monday?"

"What choice have we?" Prue answered.

Isaiah laughed, one of her favorite sounds. "None."

"None at all," Ben said. "You'll make gin, and I'll start inquiring into materials for our bridge. Business as usual, indeed."

The light was draining from the sky. In a quarter hour it would be dark.

"Well," Isaiah said. He wiped something from his sleeve. "Have a good night, and a good day of rest. Will we see you in church tomorrow?"

Ben said, "Perhaps."

Prue thought of her father, damning it to Hell. She was glad Ben was holding her close, as the wind was picking up from the river.

"Monday, then. Israel! Joan!" he called to his children. They heard him, but affected not to have. He whistled through his teeth. "Come! Your Aunt Maggie's making supper."

Small Israel pocketed his shell and tried to drag his sister toward them by the armpits. She began to cry, squirmed free, and started crawling toward her father across the sand. The wind whipped through her fair hair. Ben bent down to pick her up and kiss her. He passed her off, still screaming, to Isaiah, who stowed her under his arm and carried her along the Shore Road, with Israel capering at his heels. As Isaiah walked, he dusted the sand from the baby's kicking legs.

Prue called out, "Tem?" and when she did not reply, "Pearl?" She drew Ben toward the water to see where they'd gone. In only a few minutes, the river traffic had dropped off for the evening. Tem and Pearl were seated on the retaining wall, two dark forms leaning back to back upon each other, before the dark water. "Hoyay," Prue said, not loudly enough to startle them. The sound of the water purling past must have dampened her voice, but one of them turned as if she might have heard something, and waved her hand when she saw them coming. Prue knew the waver had to be Pearl—Tem would simply have shouted—but in the dim light, and with both of them in women's clothing, they were indistinguishable. "Hello," Prue said. "What are you doing?"

"Watching the water. Beautiful," Tem said. She leaned heavily into Pearl and turned her face toward Prue, who could see she'd been drinking.

"Don't you wish to come in?" Ben asked. "It's grown chilly."

"Your beautiful bridge," Tem said, to no one in particular. Pearl had her book right up near her face, and when she finished writing, she beckoned Prue to her. Prue had to remove the chain from Pearl's neck to get the words close enough to see, and she tilted them back and forth in the moonlight. Pearl had written, *Mess in the Yard,—should'n't we clean it?*

"No, it can wait till tomorrow," Prue said.

Pearl gestured she wanted her book back, and wrote, *I'll fetch Abiah. Yr not thinking about Annimals.*

Ben saw it this time, and said, "Oh, Pearlie, if the coons and coyotes want cheese rinds and beer drippings, we should let them feast."

She put her pencil back in its hasp, strung the chain over her head, and leaned back and whistled at Tem.

"Very well," Tem said. Ben offered her his free hand, and she nearly fell as she stood, but didn't want to be supported as she walked.

Pearl reopened her book and wrote, *Wager she'll have a good Puke befor we get home.*

"Never mind if she does," Ben said. "We'll look after her."

When they arrived at the house, Abiah had a fire going, and some toast and tea. "I assume you ate your fill during the day," she said, in apology for the meager supper.

Tem fell asleep in the chair by the fire, and it was not even eight before Pearl began to yawn. She woke Tem up and coaxed her to go upstairs. "Should we retire, too?" Ben asked.

Abiah prepared a candle for him—as, Prue realized, he did not know his way around their house in the dark.

Prue turned by rote toward her childhood bedroom, then reminded herself to go the other direction, across the hall. Abiah had made them a good bedroom fire, turned back their sheets, and placed her wedding flowers, a bunch of the same white chrysanthemums she and Pearl had worn, in a pitcher on the writing desk. They had a sharp odor, even against the strong scent of the fire, but this didn't bother Prue; the flowers reminded her of the day.

She did not write more of her wedding night to her daughter. She couldn't attribute this to modesty—she had, after all, been frank with Recompense about their escapades in the years before they'd married, and had prepared her for her own wedding night, though the conversation had made Recompense squirm. Yet there was something inalienably private about her memory of her first night with Benjamin Horsfield in their own bed; not so much their physical intimacy as her memory of his puzzlement over how the blue dress unhooked, and of the way the wind had rattled the windowpanes. She remembered taking off the forget-me-not and not knowing where to put it for the night, as she had never had a necklace before. She had never had a ring, either, and had been surprised to see it there when she'd awakened the following morning.

What was private, Prue supposed, was to recall that moment of transition from her life alone to her life with Ben. Of course she had felt herself joined to him a long time already, and there was no real separating their marriage from their friendship from their collaboration on the bridge. Neither was there any way to mark out her love for him from the fruit of it, which was the very person to whom she wrote. Yet she wanted to draw a curtain around them that evening, and keep for herself the way the bed-ropes had creaked when Ben sat down to remove his shoes, and how they had both burst out laughing at what her sisters would think. Perhaps she simply wanted to remember what it was like in those last moments before their hopes began to sour into disappointments. And she did not know why it was so difficult to tell her daughter this, except that Recompense's prospects looked so hopeful still. There is nothing the young like to hear less, she thought, than that those who are old and disillusioned were once as optimistic as they; there is nothing they believe less than that they themselves should someday face those same hardships, or others like them.

She was dramatizing, she knew. Recompense may not have been a particularly reflective person, but she was compassionate, and she seemed to know her parents, not simply to love them blindly. This, Prue reasoned, was precisely the reason her daughter would not fault her for this lacuna in the narrative. She drew the curtain closed across her wedding night, and signed her letter with love.

"But I would have liked to hear the story," Recompense told Jonas in bed the evening she received it. A few weeks previously he had noticed her mother's letters in her workbasket, and she had confessed the correspondence, and conveyed to him the entire long history. She had blushed the whole time, as she had been unable to account for her behavior in hiding the letters from him. Certainly he had listened with interest and respect when she had told him the tale; certainly the letters contained nothing of which she should be ashamed.

"Why should you want to hear it?" he asked, and, gritting his teeth together, shook his head as if he had a chill. "There is nothing I wish less to envision than how my parents fared on their wedding night. The less I know, the better."

"I understand," Recompense said. His parents were more staid than hers; she did not wonder he had no interest in imagining their youth, as they did not appear ever to have had one. She pulled the covers up around her shoulders, and the baby did a flip in her belly, as it always did when she settled down for the night. "Still, I can't help wondering what she might have told me."

"You've a different constitution than have I," he said, and curled up around her.

Recompense fell asleep that night imagining her parents in their youth. No portrait had ever been made of her father as a young man, but she could imagine his face from her cousin Israel's; her mother she had seen both in the painting in the countinghouse and in her own reflection. She could conjure up her parents on their wedding day vividly, even down to that now tattered blue dress, which her mother still kept in her cupboard. Recompense knew both her parents had been buffeted by the life they'd led; so she was more pleased than she could articulate to see them, smooth-skinned and not yet disappointed, fumbling with the complicated hooks on that gown, the night of their marriage.

Eighteen

THE SECOND MODEL

B en soon discovered that to buy timber even for a roof beam was not so easy as when Matty Winship had built his distillery. It had been more than a decade since the depredation of war had ended, but as far as the eye could see, the trees were still at most of middling size. The tall, straight beams for ship masts and keels were difficult to find and commanded a good price; and Theunis van Vechten predicted their second model would be built dear. The newspapers concurred, with the exception of Brooklyn's only sheet, the newly founded *Long-Island Courier*, which did not attempt to hide its partisanship.

Prue thought, however, it was a point in favor of her schema that it did not call for any such rarefied timber as a ship. The structure's stability would depend not upon its members' prodigious length or girth but upon their being free of imperfections and cut to the correct size. They would need to be carefully balanced to relay weight to the ground in the proper fashion, and they would have to be ingeniously secured to the structure, that if any single member were to succumb to rot, it might be removed without danger to its neighbors. What the large model needed was not a few gargantuan trees but a great many, medium in size and uniform in growth pattern; the only problem Prue foresaw was to be able to get enough of them. And fir was not a rare or expensive wood; this was part of the reason she had chosen it.

Theunis knew they would not find sufficient timber to build the model in New York or on Long Island; but he thought if Ben set off up the North River, he would find both wood to his liking and limestone to use for the model's abutments. Prue deposited the governor's money, when it arrived, in the distillery's account and signed Ben permission to draw upon it for his purchases. After tarrying for what he called a "wedding-week," during which he sold his house to a family newly come from Virginia and put that money aside, Ben traveled northward in search of the materials. He was, he reasoned, nearly done with his surveying projects for the year; he believed he could tie them up upon his return and restore Adam van Suetendael to Joe Loosely's employ for the season. Though he supposed he could get a better price if he were buying in the quantities required for an actual bridge, he thought Governor Jay's letter, and the promise of a much larger purchase if the model succeeded, would convince merchants to treat him fairly. He kept his promise and wrote Prue frequently, though he would likely arrive home before the letters did.

She, in the meantime, continued to check on the progress of the first model. It was beginning to look weather-beaten but remained solid, which boded well. She took her daily measurements, and found it had hardly degraded in its weeks outdoors. She also returned to her ordinary business at the distillery—the general management she shared with her sister and Isaiah, and the rectifying of spirits in which she found herself once again alone, now that she had moved Marcel, against his will, to the countinghouse.

"No," he had said, on his first day back. "I shall be more careful, Miss Winship." Most people, she found, still called her Prue Winship, in the same way Patience remained a Livingston, or perhaps even more so because of the gin. Though she didn't want to argue with Marcel, she was glad, for his sake, to see a spark of fire in his eyes.

"I can't risk it," she'd said simply.

"What else can happen? What other ill could befall me? The worst has already occurred and, as you see," he had said with some force, "I am faring well."

"You could have lost a hand or an arm. It might have killed you. And while I dislike depriving you of a vocation for which you feel passion and in which you show obvious promise, I feel I must do so out of regard for your granduncle. You may argue as strenuously as you wish, but I shan't change my mind."

He had continued to stand looking her square in the eye, but the next day had begun to learn bookkeeping.

Prue knew she had acted correctly, but now found herself in an awkward position: When Ben returned, she might have devoted her energy to working on the large model, were she not single-handedly responsible for rectifying the liquor. Her options were either to relent with Marcel Dufresne, which she did not intend to do; to find someone else with his talents, which seemed a remote possibility; or to do as Tem had suggested and pin down the ingredients, in precise amounts and a particular order, now and for all time. She could not effect the first two remedies and could not stomach the third. Therefore, she chose none.

Long ago—before she'd once traveled to Manhattan and before her father had reconciled himself to the fact he would never sire a son—she had thought the distillery would offer her incomparable freedom, a wide-open arena in which to prove her mettle. It had, and continued to do so; and Prue considered herself more in command of her own fate than, say, Patience, tied to a house, a sister-in-law, and three small children. Her freedom was immense, compared to Pearl's. Yet the distillery also circumscribed Prue just as surely; her current dilemma did not seem to leave her any room to move at all. Making no decision was tantamount to deciding things should continue as they always had. Though she knew they would have to change soon enough, she chose the course of inaction.

She received news from Ben only a week after he left, that he had found an adequate quantity of fir, already hewn and cured and suitable for use in the model. He noted, however, that this purchase would tax the timber merchant's capacity, and he wondered how they would procure sufficient materials for the bridge itself, were they fortunate enough eventually to build it. For the nonce, he recognized his concern as mere hope. He would hunt down their limestone, including suitable foundation stones, and return with all due haste.

It was another ten days before he returned, bearing receipts for three acres of timber and a few tons of Hudson Valley limestone. His first task was to finish the surveys he'd contracted to do for Mr. Whitcombe and out past Bergen's Hill; his second was to hire men to dig two foundation holes for the model bridge in the sand of the mill yard before the frost. With this work completed, his small crew could spend the winter cutting the timber and limestone to specifications and building the small cranes they would employ to test their methods of construction; actual building might then commence with the first sign of a thaw. He ordered nails by the cartload from the local smiths.

"Is it not your good fortune," he said over supper a few nights after his return, "to have married a man suited to such work?"

Abiah rolled her eyes, and Tem tossed her napkin at him. "I think it is rather *your* good fortune," Prue said, "to have married a woman with such fine ideas."

Pearl wrote, *I thnk it ill becomes you Boath to speak of't.*

Ben laughed. "Modesty does not serve in all regards," he said. "I think your sisters had best watch out, Pearlie, or I'll start poking my fingers in the distillery's pies as well."

Prue laughed at him, but she did feel blessed to know he could look over the building of the model as well as, or better than, she could do herself.

Later that week, on the same day the first of Ben's newly hired men went looking for lodging in the town, there was an accident in the brewhouse, when one of the great agitating arms broke in the second mash tun. Neither Tem, Prue, nor Isaiah was in the brewhouse that morning—an unfortunate, though not an unusual, circumstance—but by Phineas Bates's report, the agitator broke off with a stupendous crack as if of lightning, then became entangled with the machine's other arms as they continued to turn and strain. The tank held three thousand gallons of water and grain; it was a powerful machine could stir all that, and the noise, by all reports, startled everyone in the mash room. They scuttled down the ramps and ladders from their own tuns, and up to the afflicted one. A worker new to the brewhouse—perhaps thinking the break his own fault—panicked at the racket of the agitators grinding one another to shards, and hurled himself over the side of the tank, no doubt with the intention of trying to fix it. He immediately became ensnared in the mass of splintered wood.

The distillery had a protocol for such circumstances. Every building connected to the power train had its warning bell; anyone could unwrap the rope from its cleat and alert the windmill keeper to disengage the drive shaft from the crown gear. In a heartbeat, the rumble of the whole works could grind down to silence. There was no untangling why some more seasoned hand did not, on that day, pull the bell at once, nor why

they all crowded up that single ramp; but minutes elapsed before someone jumped down to ring for mercy. Before the signal reached the
keeper's ears, the ramp collapsed, taking almost twenty men down with it,
and leaving the hapless worker drowning in the tun.

Prue had been in the stillhouse, where some of the machines ran off
the waterwheel's power and therefore kept humming while everything
else fell quiet. The sound of the alarm bell reached her dimly, however,
and the eerie silence of everything shutting down was unmistakable. She
and Jens Luquer left the worm tub unattended and ran outside, to see the
entire mill sprinting toward the brewhouse. "What happened?" Prue
asked everyone around her. A few turned to her with puzzled expressions—either no one knew or no one could stop to tell her. She joined
the crowd and ran down the yard.

Her elderly fermenting master, Elliott Fortune, was climbing the steep
steps from the cellar. He'd been able to hear the tumult from where he
worked, and as Prue hurried past, he held out a finger and said, "Some
kind of accident, Prue. Don't know what yet."

Isaiah had reached the tun room first and was calling for ladders. The
room was in chaos. Men were shouting, in pain or fear, and others were
helping them from the wreckage of the collapsed ramp. The fall from the
top had been only ten feet, but so many had fallen atop one another, they
had injured those closest to the bottom; and the ancient wood of the
ramp itself had cracked into splinters, full of nails. Prue took the arm of
the person nearest her and, without remarking who he was, sent him for
whichever doctor he could find. The ladders came in directly he left, and
were passed hand to hand to those nearest the tun. Isaiah scrambled up
one and stared down into it with what appeared to be blank horror. Prue
was terrified to think what he might have seen, and quickly prayed that
no one be harmed. The moment she'd thought it, she realized her prayer
was no doubt useless; but she still hoped no ill had befallen anyone.
Phineas, who'd been right beside Isaiah, scaled the other ladder and
stood looking down, also clearly confused.

"What is it?" Prue asked. "Who is it? What happened?"

They didn't notice her, however. They regarded each other a long moment before Phineas dropped his boots to the ground and slid over the
side of the tun.

"Man in the tank, ma'am," said one of the workers nearby.

People hushed each other throughout the room. Phineas held on to the rim of the tun with one hand, all that was visible of him. Prue picked her way nearer, noticing, as she went, that while some of the men were badly cut and in obvious discomfort, they all appeared to move and breathe. "Isaiah?" she said.

"Hold, Prue," he said quietly.

Phineas's hand began to move toward the back of the brewhouse. He stopped at the farthest extremity from where Prue stood. "I have him," he called.

"Do you need help?" Isaiah asked.

Phineas's hand slipped another few inches around. "Yes, sir," came his reply.

Tem came in then, from who knew where, and said, "What's going on?"

The whole room hushed her, as it had done to Prue, who now scaled the other ladder to relieve Isaiah of his watch. Before Isaiah could hand it to her, she looked down into the tun. The water in an active mash tun always bubbled as the sugar was extracted from the grain; but this foam was tinged pink with blood. Phineas was bobbing slightly, at the far side of the tank, with one hand holding the worker's corpse. One arm had been torn off at the shoulder and floated free, near his bare feet; and the man's skull had been crushed. The gray matter of his brain wafted behind him on the murky water.

"Oh, God," Prue said, and felt she would vomit or faint.

"Go down, Prue," Isaiah said. When she did not at once obey, he pressed the watch upon her and said, "Someone take her down."

She felt two hands clasp around her waist, and she followed them back down the ladder, the watch chain dangling from her palm. She felt the watch ticking, but her breath could not penetrate the depths of her chest.

Isaiah dropped his boots to the floor and splashed into the tun. Whoever had helped Prue down the ladder passed her off to Tem, who put her arm around her; and they stood back, Prue with her breath short and her stomach clenched against what she knew to be forthcoming. There were splashing and squelching sounds, of something ripping and shifting underwater. Phineas and Isaiah hoisted themselves out and stood side by side on the ladders, soaked and dripping, with every eye in the room upon them.

"On three," Isaiah said. "One, two—"

And on the third count they heaved up the corpse. Isaiah clutched one naked foot, and Phineas the bloodless arm still attached to the body; the brains spilled out like entrails. Prue could now see it was a Negro worker; she had remarked nothing but the gore when she'd stood atop the ladder. The room erupted in clamor, and someone shouted, "Jim!" Tem, who could take many things lightly, turned aside. Ben and one of his new workers came in; and Prue felt she might cry for joy at seeing him, though there was nothing he could do.

"Make way," Isaiah said as they climbed down. "Someone go to the grain bins and bring flour sacks, to cover 'im." They placed the body gently on the floor.

Prue heard someone run out. "Hoy!" he cried in the yard. "Dr. Philpot!"

She would rather have heard de Bouton's name, but charlatan or no, she was relieved to know Tobias Philpot had arrived. Though his nose was thick from drinking and webbed with fine red blood vessels, his hair was still black as a boot. He entered, as always, at his leisure, and bearing a box containing bottles of his nostrum. Even if it had no medicinal value, it would prove a friend to the injured. His sleepy eyes lit immediately on the dead man's body. Isaiah said to him, "No, it is too late. But there are a number who are hurt."

Prue could not stop looking at the corpse. His face was not crushed past recognition, but she was galled that she would not have known his name had someone not called out, "Jim." Prue had seen her mother waste away, and her father bloated and distended by the river he'd so loved, his eyes eaten out by sea creatures; she had seen Johanna ravaged by her tumor; but this, she knew, was death—this ugly stink and anonymity. The body was pooling sugar water and its own fluids on the earthen floor. Dr. Philpot was scanning through the wounded to help the direst cases first; and Prue thought what a comfort it would be to all of them if some gauzy spirit would cloud up from the dead man's lips and observe the proceedings or waft out toward the straits. She watched the body intently, and if she could have willed this to happen, she would have done so. She would have made there be a spirit ferry and a place for the dead to live across the water; but she knew all the hope and fear in the world could not accomplish this.

"Is it our fault?" Tem whispered, so quietly Prue would not have heard her had Tem not been two feet away.

"I don't know," Prue said aloud. In all the years her father had run the distillery, she could not recall any part of a machine breaking off in use. Whatever had appeared worn during his inspection had been brought up for replacement or repair. She and Tem likewise checked their machinery often, and she wanted to say, *Who can know when Fate might choose to take a man?* Yet even to think this was callous. "We shall do what we can to find out."

"Perhaps those of you who are hale and well can help bring the injured out-of-doors," Dr. Philpot said, his voice deep and slow as molasses. God bless him, he did not ruffle easily. "It would be of great service."

At once the men began to sort themselves, and those who were able, to help their brethren to their feet. The boy with the flour sacks came in, too late to be of much use. Prue thanked him, and covered the man's ruined face and shoulder. She and Isaiah stood back as if to guard him, while Tem and Ben went outside with Dr. Philpot. Prue heard Ben ask her sister what had occurred. Isaiah was dripping on the floor and smelled like small beer. When everyone had left, Prue asked, "Are you cold?"

"It shan't kill me."

"I didn't even know his name."

"James Weatherspoon, late of Suffolk. He's a wife and son, up in Olympia."

"I feel we should pay the call ourselves."

He nodded. "I'll see about a cart."

"First change your clothes." He raised a hand, indicating he could not bother. She handed him his watch.

In the daylight, the men did not appear so badly maimed as they had in the dim brewhouse. They were all still talking about the accident. Isaiah set out at once for the stable, while Prue stood by blinking. Tem had called for gin to be brought out to everyone and was crouched on the ground, holding a worker's hand. Someone had already dropped the flag to half-mast. "Operations will be suspended for the day," Prue called out, though she did not suppose the Schermerhorns would have done the same for a mere worker. "And tomorrow, for Mr. Weatherspoon's funeral. We shall resume production on Thursday." The flag snapped as if for emphasis. "You will be paid your full wages for the missed days' labor." Tem glanced at her, but Prue couldn't tell what she was thinking. "And I require Owen, and anyone else who would help him clean; and Jean Boulanger, Mr. Jones, and Mr. Jones's apprentice. Please gather in the brewhouse at four." She knelt down where she was, beside a fellow named Toonis Hansen, and helped him rebind the makeshift bandage on his right hand.

Isaiah came around, leading two black horses by the reins; they were hitched to a small cart, from the back of which two of the stable hands lifted a long board. The hands picked their way through the crowded yard and into the brewhouse. Ben was coming over to talk to Prue, and she said, "Isaiah and I shall carry the body to his wife. Can you help Tem look after things?"

Ben nodded.

Prue turned Mr. Hansen over to Elliott Fortune and followed the cooling board back to the cart. Isaiah handed her up, climbed up himself, and steered the horses gingerly to turn around. They kept flicking their heads back and forth; they knew something was amiss. Isaiah stank of mashed grain; and she thought how a chill could kill him exactly as it had killed his father. She also thought how her mother had lived in terror of such an event as had occurred that day. As if he could read her thoughts, Isaiah said, "This is what Roxana always feared would happen," as they cleared the gate.

"Exactly as I was thinking. But do you ever recall it happening, in our fathers' time?"

"No," he said. "Never anything so serious."

"Nor do I. The only accident was my father's death." She still did not believe she'd ever know if he'd slipped from the retaining wall or meant to step down; but it was best to maintain the former conjecture.

"God rest his soul," Isaiah said, as he steered them through the afternoon traffic on the Ferry Road. His teeth were chattering.

As they drove, Prue pictured the Luquers driving up the Shore Road with her father in their wagon.

That Prue had been able to imagine Ann Weatherspoon's reaction to their arrival could not lessen the pain of thus witnessing another's distress. She was a slight woman, with a toddler on one hip, and she came undone exactly as Prue and her sisters had three years before. "I am sorry," Prue said, as she climbed down from the cart. "I realize no one desires the ministrations of a stranger at such a moment, but please allow me to offer my condolences."

Ann Weatherspoon simply stood with her mouth open, evidently unable to catch her breath.

Prue felt she herself might begin to cry. "Please, allow me to help," she said. The child reached his fat hands out to her, and Prue lifted him from his mother's arms. He was heavy, as if stuffed with grapeshot, and as soon as Prue had hold of him he kicked to be free. Relieved of his weight, Ann Weatherspoon collapsed forward toward the cart. Prue said to Isaiah, "I think you'd best get Mr. Severn."

"Can you manage?"

Prue widened her eyes at him, and he ran off toward the turnpike, his clothes clinging to his body. Prue could manage because the widow did nothing those next few minutes but lean against the cart and cry out her husband's name. Prue held the struggling child on one hip and stroked the woman's thin back with her other hand. Isaiah had disturbed Mr. Severn at his lessons, but he came right away; and as the neighborhood women began to gather, Mr. Severn released Prue and Isaiah to return to the distillery and the awful business of the afternoon. Prue insisted they stop off at Isaiah's house for a change of clothing.

Pearl must have heard the machinery rumble to a halt, for she was helping the doctors as she could when Prue and Isaiah returned; half the workers from the ropewalk also seemed to be on the premises, some helping, others looking around in a daze. The following day both mills shut down, and the workers gave Jim Weatherspoon—a second-generation freeman, Prue learned, who'd been eager to advance in his chosen profession—a long funeral cortège. By the graveside, Will Severn delivered a moving sermon, in which he expressed his conviction that Jim Weatherspoon had been reborn, whole and at peace, in the Higher Realm. Ann Weatherspoon would not look at him, and simply cried into her handkerchief as her son toddled around, pulling at people's coats and skirts and digging in the dirt. When the service ended and the burial began, the company began to stream toward Olympia, but Peg Dufresne came limping over to Prue to comfort her, as if a member of her own family had been lost. Prue had never noticed the limp before, but supposed it had come on gradually, now Peg was getting to be an old woman. She drew Prue aside, toward the cemetery fence, and said, "It's a terrible shame. I can see by your countenance you feel bereaved."

Ben was standing by, waiting. Prue said to him, "Go on, if you like. We'll catch up."

He touched his hat to Peg and walked out with Tem and Pearl.

Prue said, "Tem keeps saying such things are bound to occur; but I feel the worst of it is that it could have been avoided." There had not yet been a hard frost, but the grass was crunching under their feet. "Perhaps if we'd better inspected the agitator, we would have seen it was cracked or failing. Even if not, the power could have been cut off from the machines in an instant, but by all accounts, he *dove in*."

Peg was scanning Prue's face with her kind, dark eyes. "There's no changing that, however."

"I suppose I lose sleep easily."

"Are you taking care of the widow?"

"We've given her what her husband was owed, and a month's extra wages," Prue said. "I can also employ her, if need be."

"She already works. She takes in laundry."

"I didn't know," Prue said. She herself had been married less than a month, but could well imagine the woman's feelings of helplessness and loss. "Peg, what are the neighbors saying?"

Peg licked her lips but didn't respond.

Prue went on, "I know something's amiss."

Peg said, "Oh, Prue, people will say anything. A few have called it a bad omen about your bridge; Jana Friedlander hopes it isn't the river taking revenge on you for your treatment of Losee, which I told her is absurd. Some say these things happen if you leave a manufactory in the care of a nineteen-year-old woman."

"But the accident happened while I was there," Prue said. Still, she had heard Peg plainly: "These things" included Marcel's accident as well. "Tem can manage without me when the need arises."

Peg laid her dry palm on the side of Prue's face. "I know," she said. "You know Simon and I believe in all of you, don't you?"

Prue did, even without her saying so. "Of course. You're the only people who never treated Pearl as if she were a changeling."

Peg glanced off as if Pearl were still nearby. "Prue, your distillery provides as much work as anything else in this village. You employ more men than farm our fields. So I think it only natural people should worry what would become of them should you fail in your endeavor."

"But we shall not," Prue said. "That's why we're building the new model—to test our methods of construction; to be sure."

"I understand, but I'm not certain everyone does. I don't mean to offend you."

Prue said, "I am merely surprised to hear so many people think that way, when the bridge has already brought employment for a few, and may yet prove a boon to many."

"Prue," Peg answered, "you're ignoring the obvious point: People see omens if they wish to see omens. Everything is a sign, when you're looking for a sign."

Prue shook her head. Peg was no doubt correct. "I think we should go eat Ann Weatherspoon's cake. It doesn't look right to keep away."

Peg inclined slightly toward her. "You'll simply have to prove them wrong."

They walked past the rising heap of the new grave toward the gate. Peg's limp seemed more pronounced, walking uphill.

Winter was drawing nigh, and Brooklyn's scrubby brown hills, black rocks, and gray sky looked bleak as anyplace Prue could imagine. She was grateful to Peg for speaking plain, but troubled that her neighbors could think an accident—brought on in part by its victim's inexperience, and certain not to recur—a sign from above. At the same time, it numbed her to think the life of a husband and father could be undone in an instant, and in service of something as ultimately meaningless as the manufacture of liquor. And she worried about the bridge. Even in building Mr. Severn's church, some had been injured by saws, mallets, and the inevitable slips of attention; a project of the bridge's magnitude could not possibly go forward without some loss of life. Prue also knew that from the ancients forward, people had believed a bridge takes a human life during its building, to propitiate the water spirits against the sin of walking above them. A bridge didn't have to span the divide between the living and the dead to require this sacrifice; to cross a body of water is always, at one level, to bargain with the Devil.

Prue was glad to have Peg beside her when she arrived at the Weatherspoon house. It was low of ceiling and stingy of windows, and had never been meant to hold more than a man and his family, without even the comfort of a fireplace in the second room. Now more than a hundred workingmen, half with their wives and broods in tow, were filing through to pay respects, as were a few of the landowners and businessmen. Prue's own dark thoughts made it difficult to be among her men and her neighbors; but Peg's reassurance kept Ann Weatherspoon's pound cake from turning to ashes on her tongue.

It was necessary to shut the brewhouse the rest of that week, but Tem and Prue employed many of the men in building a tun to replace that which had been marked with Jim Weatherspoon's blood, in constructing new ramps and ladders, and in checking each mortise and tenon in every building, that any man who worked for the Winships might do so in the peace of knowing the platform he stood upon was sound. The men thus had ample opportunity to come into contact with Ben's small crew of six, all of whom were at that time digging foundation holes in the sand of the mill yard. These were aligned parallel to the river—the large model would span nothing but bare strand—and almost sixty yards apart. Soon the men would drive piles into the bottoms of the pits to support foundation stones as large as those Matty Winship had placed under the distillery's buildings. This was not how they would build the actual foundation on the New York side, if the model proved a success: They planned to blast into the perdurable rock of Manhattan Island and build into the resulting hole. Ben and Prue both reasoned, however, that if the model bridge could hold when resting upon two foundations sunk into sand, a real bridge could certainly be built with one end that much more securely anchored. The holes he was digging were only five feet deep, but Ben built picket fences around them, that no one might stumble in. He held out hope he might receive his two great stones before the killing frost; if not, he would not see them until after the thaw. He also began assembling the pieces for the two cranes, each of which would be lifted and lowered by means of a Schermerhorn rope wrapped around a block and tackle and turned by a crank. Two strong chains depending from the crane's far end would hold the timber to be moved, and a single man would work the crank to lift the piece into position. It would be an excellent device for saving men's labor, if Ben could be sure to build it both strong enough to do its appointed work and light enough for men to maneuver it without difficulty.

He set up shop in the assembly hall, and for the remainder of the winter, whenever Prue was upstairs in the countinghouse, she heard his stonemasons' chisels clanking, and the rasp of the carpenters' planes and saws. She would have liked to do some of the work herself—and saw Pearl's longing when she happened by the assembly hall's windows—but it was out of her hands now. Ben was the chief architect, and Ben had a commission from the state. It would be regular work, completed by professional laborers; and with each day that passed, Prue thought the bridge became less a thing of her fancy and more a citizen of the everyday world. The workers' heaps of stones, stacks of wooden beams, and barrels full of wooden dowels grew daily farther toward the rafters, until at last space had to be cleared for them in the storehouses. The cast-iron pulleys for the cranes arrived from the local foundry; and Prue kept up a passionate correspondence with Thomas Pope in Philadelphia, telling him of the model bridge's progress out in the weather and of how Ben's work proceeded. She thought it greatly to the famous bridge architect's credit that he answered her assertions and queries as thoughtfully as he might have done had his interlocutor been a man; and she was glad it was he Governor Jay had chosen to inspect the larger model as it progressed.

Prue, meanwhile, began to suspect a life might be quickening within her. She had no unmistakable signs—or was not certain what those might have been—but after the wedding, she had continued to employ Mrs. Friedlander's preventive methods only sporadically, and she had last caught sight of her menses in the autumn. By the New Year, she felt a fullness in her gut she imagined could be no other thing. At first the prospect of a baby disturbed her—how would she care for it, after all, while they built a bridge?—but as she went about her work at the distillery, she began to feel giddy with the possibility. Ben's birthday arrived before hers, in the dark days of January, along with a heavy snow; and she gave him no gift but her disclosure. He watched her a moment in the dim light of dawn and the bedroom fire he'd just kindled, then asked, "Are you certain?"

"No," she answered. The room was still frigid, and her breath formed plumes in the air. "Come back to bed." He curled up around her under the covers. In the few minutes he'd been out of bed, his feet had grown cold as blocks of ice. "I haven't consulted Mrs. Friedlander, but I believe I know."

He reached around her to put his hand on her belly and said, "I feel foolish for not having noticed. When do you suppose it will come?"

"I don't know," Prue said, feeling no doubt more foolish than he. "I imagine in the summertime." She rolled over to face Ben, and found him smiling at her.

"Perhaps the second model will be complete by then. A perfect play-thing for a little Horsfield."

"Oh, it'll be a long while before the creature can play."

"I know," he said, and wrapped her more snugly in the bedclothes. "When may I tell Isaiah?"

"Why don't we tell everyone at once? Let's have them to dinner after church on Sunday."

"With all their children? Oh, Christ," he said.

"Ours'll be shouting and fighting like that soon enough."

"I know," Ben said, and kissed her before he left the bed. He stopped in at the countinghouse that morning to issue the invitation to Isaiah.

"Happy birthday," Isaiah said. "I hope it augurs well for the year for you."

"I think it does," Ben said. It was a dull winter day, but he looked bright as a blue jay. "Thus far, I'd say it's the best year of my life. Though last year comes close on its heels."

"Don't be so quick to judge," Isaiah called after him as Ben trotted downstairs to his own men. To Prue he said, "He looks like he ate the Christmas pudding."

Prue held both palms up in the air. "Perhaps he did."

"Hmm," Isaiah said. Prue suspected he knew their secret. "Someone has to go to the bank today. You or I?"

"I'll go with the shipment," Prue said. "I'd be glad for the distraction."

He shook his head at her as he took the pile of deposits from the safe. He counted out a hundred federal dollars—the amount they kept in case of emergency, though no emergency of such financial magnitude had ever yet arisen—and replaced it. Then he tallied up the rest for her.

"Is it me," she asked, "or does the week's take look slight?"

"A bit," Isaiah said, "but nothing to worry on. We're often sluggish from Twelfth Night to the thaw."

Prue accepted his answer—she tended to forget, from season to season, that business did not remain the same year-round—and had it corroborated by Mr. Stover at the bank.

Both families were thrilled at the news of the baby's imminence, and Tem and Isaiah made a series of toasts on its behalf. "You shall have to name it Archimedes," Isaiah quipped, raising his glass to Prue.

Or Ptolemy, Pearl wrote.

"Sir Isaac Newton," Isaiah said.

"It may very well be a girl," Patience counseled, "in which case you shall have to call it something ordinary, such as Alice."

"Oh, not Alice," Ben groaned, but he would have done so no matter what Patience had suggested; she had that sort of voice.

The child never lived to be called anything, however. Only a few nights after Ben and Prue made their announcement, Prue awakened with a start from an unpleasant dream she could not quite recall, and did not at once recognize her surroundings. After a moment, the room she still thought of as her parents' sprang into place—the small desk and its uncomfortable chair, the wardrobe, with Ben's britches hanging over the door, a fire screen Pearl had embroidered with flowers, which was tucked into a corner and difficult to make out. Ben lay burrowed under his pillow, and in the starlight, Prue saw it was snowing outside. When she stood to add wood to the fire's embers, a rush of warmth coursed down through her belly. She did not at first think it unpleasant, merely foreign enough to catch her attention. Then she recognized it as pain. When she looked down, a black, shiny pool was blossoming between her legs.

She must have cried out as she sat back down, because Ben recoiled as if he'd been struck, and she heard her sisters stirring across the hall. Ben gathered his wits and said, "Prue?" He sat up with one hand on her back. The other settled gingerly on her leg.

When he touched her, she could feel her heart racing and the ache in her gut. She doubled forward, and her head bowed down toward the space between her calves. She could smell the iron in her own rich blood.

"Prue," he said, "should I get Dr. de Bouton?" He looked around the room and said, more loudly, "Pearl, Tem? Abiah?"

Prue shook her head no, feeling her hair brush against the blanket. "There's nothing they can do," she said. Her breath felt hot upon her own legs and face.

"Surely—"

"Nothing." She sat up, and the blood drained first toward her legs, then out of her. "Please, just get me some water and a cloth. I need to wash." Mrs. van Nostrand's forget-me-not was burning against her chest; she had forgotten to remove it for the night.

Tem and Pearl stumbled in at that moment, and both stood looking at the scene before them. After a moment, Pearl sat down on the bed and put both hands on her sister. Tem stepped into the hall and called out, "Abiah? Quickly."

"Coming," Abiah said from downstairs.

"Bring water and cloths," Ben said, and began to work Prue's nightshirt up over her head.

"Please," Prue said, "it's cold," but she could see the nightshirt was stained dark, as was the sheet and no doubt the mattress.

Abiah said "Mercy," when she arrived, and first thing set to diapering Prue. Then she wiped her with a clean rag, took the nightshirt, and began to strip the bed. Prue huddled on the floor while she did this.

"It's no matter," Ben said.

"They'll be ruined," Prue said, though she could not imagine why she cared.

"I'll take them," Abiah said. She took all the bedding, and the mattress was indeed stained. She laid cleaning cloths on top of it, then remade the bed with fresh sheets. Prue lay down immediately, and drew the covers close around her.

Pearl had neglected to put her book around her neck, and sat by helplessly, stroking Prue's arm and leg. "It'll be all right," Prue told her, but Pearl didn't look convinced, and even Prue didn't believe herself. This was just repayment, she thought, for the curse she had so long ago laid on Pearl and on her own mother; this was a fair bargain. Everyone except Abiah sat with Prue until she fell back asleep, and the last sound she heard was of Abiah working the pump in the cold yard.

When she awoke in the morning, Dr. de Bouton was speaking to Ben at the foot of the bed. Pearl half reclined beside Prue, fingering the frizzy tips of her sister's hair. Prue could not meet her sister's eye, so fresh was her guilt alongside this new pain; and for the first time in her life, Prue thought she understood why their mother had so often looked on them as intruders.

"Good morning, there, miss," Dr. de Bouton said.

Prue looked at his familiar black brows beneath his shock of bright gray hair, but couldn't think of a thing to say.

"Prue?" Ben said gently.

"There's nothing to be done, is there?" she asked.

Dr. de Bouton sat down on the other side of the bed. "Not immediately, no. But you'll recover soon. And there will be another, by and by."

"As I told you," she told Ben, her throat full of accusation, though she didn't know why. She shut her eyes again. A moment later she heard them file out and the latch rattle shut on the door.

As she lay in the bed in which her mother had given birth to three daughters, miscarried an untold number of children, and finally died, Prue thought of the dogged manner in which Roxana had knit that small white jacket for Pearl, when any fool could have told her the baby wouldn't live a week. At the time, her singleness of purpose had frightened Prue, but she now saw her mother had worked the wool as an incantation, as a spell to keep away the encroaching darkness. Roxana would have scoffed at this explanation, but it was the truth; and Prue wished she herself knew a similar charm to ward off disappointment and pain. She feared the only true protection might be a clean conscience, which she would not have until she admitted her crime to Pearl; and she did not believe herself capable of owning up to such treachery.

All she dared hope was that if her bridge meant to take a life, this one she had just lost would suffice. If it could prevent anyone else being killed, she felt she might, in time, reconcile herself to the sacrifice.

Later in the day, Pearl brought her a baked potato, its nether part wrapped in a checkered napkin. The potato looked so odd, and Pearl so strange holding it, Prue laughed despite the unease she'd been feeling about her sister, and Pearl broke into a smile and hissed. Prue had never before eaten a potato without benefit of butter or salt, but she was hungry enough to have eaten it without chewing, had that been possible. Pearl sat down beside her and wrote, *I'm glad yr mending. There're more, dwnstairs, if you like.*

"Perhaps in a while."

You know there will be Another, Pearl wrote, and patted her own belly, perhaps in case Prue thought she was still speaking of potatoes.

"I don't know," Prue said. She did not wish to discuss it, but felt she had to, now Pearl had begun. "Our mother had a rotten time of it."

Yr diffrent, Pearl wrote. *I am certin of it.*

Prue watched her sister closely. How easy it should have been, all these years later, simply to tell Pearl what she had done; but Prue could not. She did not believe she could survive the exposure of such meanness. Meanwhile, she was grateful for her sister's reassurance. "Thank you," she said. "I hope you're correct."

She did differ from Roxana, however. She could remember, from the years before Pearl was born, her mother suffering weeks of illness, which could only have been her loss of the unborn children. She would emerge pale and subdued from her room, and mourn for weeks on end. Prue's father had been unwilling to answer questions, and she had learned only the sketchiest facts from Johanna. But though Prue also felt, as her mother must have, that her heart was broken, the following day she had a strong desire to return to the distillery. Ben and her sisters tried to convince her otherwise, but though her body still ached, she would not be told no. Isaiah's expression of pity when she walked in the counting-house door almost turned her around, but she persevered; and when later she found herself sweating as she worked the lever to express the fragrant essence of juniper, she felt better for the exercise, and glad to have something to distract her from her grief.

And as if as a sign that circumstances were improving, the spring thaw arrived early in 1799, though it brought with it the state legislature's Act for the Gradual Abolition of Slavery. Support for the act was much stronger in Brooklyn than Prue might have supposed. Many of those who rejoiced on the streets or in Loosely's tavern were slave owners themselves, but at most of only one or two domestic servants; only she and Pieter Schermerhorn still kept large numbers of slaves for their manufactories. The act, Prue realized, struck a fine balance between pleasing those who relied upon slave labor to make their living and assuaging those who opposed it on moral grounds: All adult slaves were to remain in bondage for the rest of their lives, though they would henceforward be called "indentured servants," and all children born after the coming Fourth of July would be freed in the 1820s, after having given their best years of service to their masters. As matters stood, then, she was free to retain her current workforce for the distillery; and if she had to man all the stills and tuns with paid workers twenty years hence, she had ample time to determine how she would manage to pay them. She could not purchase slaves for the bridgeworks; but with the fervor for abolition so much in the air, she had never for a moment supposed the state would allow her to buy souls with its money.

The early thaw, meanwhile, meant that by mid-March the mud season had commenced, turning the roads once again to sludge and shoes of all descriptions brown and noisome. The neighborhood children, wild with the pent-up energy of having been trapped indoors all winter, tore stumbling through the streets with mud on their clothes and in their hair. After a few days, one could see even fastidious mothers such as Patience simply brushing the caked dirt from their coats and allowing them back out again. Just as in the autumn, it rained for days on end, clotting the river with brackish debris and making the roads all but impassable.

"But it's good news, overall," Ben told her. "Pearl shall have her jonquils, and we shall begin our model bridge weeks sooner than we anticipated."

Both he and Prue were fascinated by the performance of the first model, and sent tracts of observations to Mr. Pope in Philadelphia. The model now creaked if one stepped on it—Prue thought because its primitive abutments had shifted on their base, Ben because every boy in the neighborhood had done his utmost to break it—and its northern side had acquired a faint patina of moss in its months outside; yet the thing still held. Day after day they tested it under weights of various sizes; and though Prue thought it would soon deflect under such pressure as they placed upon it, it remained solid, exactly as a bridge should. Prue was happier with this than she could explain—though the model was diminutive by real-world standards, it had been their first attempt at bridge building, and they had gotten it fundamentally correct.

"When do you think it'll be complete?" she asked him.

"Sometime this summer, I'll wager. And the moment it's done, I'll build a room onto the house for your sisters."

Pearl had been looking wan from her sleepless nights in Tem's company, but as soon as the weather improved and she could resume going out for her long walks, her color once more brightened. Her interest in her needlework declined as her interest in being outdoors grew, and her fair skin freckled from all the time she spent out tending their vegetable garden and wandering the country lanes a stone's throw from town. All those years later, she was still visiting Will Severn's house at least one evening a week, though she could not have believed she owed him a debt any longer; and when their conversations were heated, she would fill sheet after sheet, later in the evening, in continuing with Prue whatever the original argument had been.

The second model was Ben's project. He had no need of Prue's assistance, while until she did something to change the way they rectified, the distillery did. Ben's six men were eager to begin their real work; and Ben vowed to keep them on as foremen if their current project proved successful and the governor gave permission to attempt to bridge the straits. Though they were only seven people, they worked with tremendous speed and dedication. The two anchorages were complete on their foundations by mid-May, and the levers began to spring from the abutments in June. Once he had proven that the cranes worked to hoist timbers into place, Ben wrote Mr. Pope to inquire when he might come to inspect the miniature bridgeworks and issue his report to the state. Mr. Pope replied that his own work on the Schuylkill detained him at present, but that as he had business of his own to conduct in New York in early September, he would be pleased to view the bridge then.

As Prue watched the progress of this model, she felt doubly joyful: because it appeared to be working according to plan, and because exactly as Pearl and Dr. de Bouton had promised, she had found herself with child again as soon as the weather turned warm. This time she did not tell her family anything until the size of her belly obviated an announcement. Dr. de Bouton told her she could expect the child to come sometime in the Christmas season, by which time, she reflected, the model would be long since complete, and plans might even be under way for the bridge itself. At first Prue did not dare hope this child might survive; but as it grew and stirred within her, she began to think she had at last ridden out the effects of her misdeed. Perhaps she and her sister would live henceforward as two mortals bound by ties of love and convenience, and not by any more sinister thing.

She ceased wearing britches, as they made her growing womb look somehow obscene, but she found all her mother's fears had been unwarranted; she was careful with herself, but her skirt posed no danger near the press or the drive belts. The baby left her tired, and she began stopping work in the late afternoon to go out and take measurements on the small model and inspect progress on the large one. By midsummer, she could walk through the arch in the pyramid and out onto the promenade of the bridge itself. In terms of its height, it was no more impressive than standing on the balcony above any room of her distillery: The model bridge would be, at its zenith, barely fifteen feet from the ground, and the approaches were considerably lower. But when she stood out upon the miniature roadway, watching the ships cruise by on the straits, she could already imagine herself standing far above them and pausing for the view in the middle of the river. Even those newspapers skeptical of the project as a whole reported favorably on the structure's beauty. Though it only spanned the dull brown mill yard, the bridge had clean, delicate lines; it was now clear it would "ornament the river as elegantly as a simple flower behind the ear ornaments a fair woman's nape," C. Mather Harrison wrote—rather poetically, Prue thought—in the *Argus*.

Ben finished the model in August. The workers did not let out a shout when they slipped the last timber into place and nailed it in; Prue simply left the casking room one afternoon and saw one of the men standing on the bridge's very apex, stretching his arms up toward the sky. Ben came toward her, his eyes as bright as on their wedding day. "Will you cross the East River with me?" he asked.

And though Prue was beginning to feel awkward when she walked, she said, "Oh, with pleasure."

Nineteen

A GREATER DISAPPOINTMENT

Thomas Pope arrived on Mr. Fischer's ferry one warm, clear morning in September. The previous afternoon he had sent news of his arrival in New York, and Prue had wanted to hurry across the river and fetch him back for supper; but she told herself such eagerness would not do, and resolved to be patient. Instead she gathered her workers into the assembly hall, where she noticed how scuffed and scarred the floorboards were after Ben's season of indoor work. She exhorted the men to wash themselves that evening and to put on clean work clothes the next morning. "And if you have any lingering doubts about the bridge, I beg you hold your peace this one day," she said.

"We have none of us any doubts, Miss Winship," Elliott Fortune said.

The man behind him said, "I should hope she's 'Mrs. Horsfield,' with that belly." Though some around him laughed, Prue was pleased that one of his neighbors hushed him.

The workers were clean as springtime the next morning. Half of them had even shaved.

Prue stationed a young slave—indentured servant, she reminded herself—at Fischer's landing with Ben's sight glass to look out for Pope's arrival. The moment he'd spied the trim black boat, he came tearing up the Shore Road and into the countinghouse. He was so short of breath he could barely speak, but Prue understood his import; and though she could walk only slowly and with no great ease, she and Ben were on the landing when the boat arrived. In her imagination, Pope had been practically a titan, tall and broad, with a strong jaw and flowing gray hair. The man who sat in the bow of the ferry was a mere human, to Prue's combined relief and disappointment. She could not judge his height from the dock, but she could see that his face was round and merry; he obviously enjoyed both his meat and his port. His woolly hair poked out from beneath his hat in all directions, and his eyes took in the straits with interest. "Mr. and Mrs. Horsfield!" he exclaimed before the ferryman could even hand him out of the boat. "Heavens, it is an honor and a delight."

"The pleasure and the honor are all ours," Ben said, removing his hat and bowing. When he stood again, Prue could see Mr. Pope was a full head shorter than her husband. Prue curtsied, and Mr. Pope reached out and kissed her hand. "You have been of tremendous assistance in our work thus far; and we are most, most grateful that you've come. Have you breakfasted?"

Mr. Pope pushed down his hat as if afraid it might blow away, though the breeze was calm. "Excuse me, but I have no interest in breakfast; it's a bridge I've come to see. Quite a miraculous bridge, if you've told me true. Take me to it. There'll be time for victuals later."

Prue's heart fluttered with expectation, and the baby, who knew everything of her emotions, likewise wriggled and kicked.

Fischer's second ferry docked only a moment later, and C. Mather Harrison and two other young men disembarked. "Good morning, Mr. Harrison," Prue said.

"Good morning," he replied. He had his shoulders drawn awkwardly in, as if he thought the other men were standing too close to him.

"We thank you for the fine notice," Ben said.

He nodded politely.

When the two men shot Harrison disgruntled glances, Prue gathered they had come from other papers. They allowed Prue, Ben, and Mr. Pope a respectful few paces of distance as they walked toward the distillery, but Prue knew they were trailing behind like ducklings.

When first Mr. Pope saw the larger model bridge arching across the mill yard, he raised both arms in the air as if to call down Heaven's witness and cried, "Oh, 'tis true! Bless you both, 'tis true!" He walked out upon it with as much wonder and joy as any neighborhood urchin had shown; but when he was done, stood beside it with his hand on its flank as if it were a horse Prue and Ben meant to sell him. He wore a soberer aspect the rest of the day, which he spent in meticulous study of the structure. He took measurements of both model bridges and observed the straits themselves; he asked for some of the weight tests Ben and Prue had engineered to be duplicated; and he examined each detail of the construction of the abutments and the cranes. He wrote copious notes to himself as he worked. By late afternoon, he claimed to have been convinced that such a bridge could soundly span the East River; but Prue caught something hesitant in his expression.

"Have you any lingering doubts?" she asked him.

Mr. Harrison politely looked off toward the water, but she knew he was taking note of everything they said.

"No," Pope replied, but with a faint rising tone at the end of the word. Prue wondered if he might rue not having himself invented the method of construction. She waited for him to qualify his statement, but he did not. She could hear water rushing into the tuns in the brewhouse.

"Come, Mr. Pope. There is something troubles you about our bridge."

He resettled his hat once more. "Only that I think it will be difficult to sight accurately across a distance of forty-four hundred feet."

Prue saw all three young men scribbling with their pencils.

"But we have oft discussed this, Mr. Pope," Ben said. "I do not deny it will be difficult. I say only that I work with the finest philosophical instruments; and that I have the patience and the training to perform the measurements correctly."

"If anyone can do it, Surveyor Horsfield, I am sure it's you," Mr. Pope said. "I sincerely hope the state permits you to build this bridge. I am more eager than I can say to see the outcome."

There remained something in his tone that dampened Prue's spirits, but she went off to fetch some of her favorite batch of gin for the evening's celebration.

When Pope left later that evening, with the newsmen in his wake, he promised to write for advice to a colleague in Boston, by the name of Michael Avery, on the morrow; if Avery could put his last doubts to rest, Pope would write the governor immediately. Ben thanked him and himself wrote to Mr. Jay to relate the progress of both model bridges, and to indicate his belief they were ready to proceed with building in the spring, if the governor would supply both his permission and the necessary funding. He wrote to Garret Willemsen, whom he believed he would find in Bushwick at that time, overseeing his harvest, and asked him to come view the second model before traveling north to the legislative session; and he wrote Mayor Varick a similar invitation. Both men arrived at their earliest convenience, and proclaimed the small bridge a wonder. Prue could not guess how the proposal would fare in the legislature; but she believed with her whole heart there was nothing more she or Ben might have done to ensure its success. Mr. Harrison continued to write favorably of the bridge; and while the other two writers maintained some reservations, Prue thought their descriptions yet cast the project in a favorable light.

One day late in September, Marcel Dufresne came up to the countinghouse to tell Prue a small group of men had arrived from Bedford Corners, in search of work on the bridge. There was a light rain that day, and when Prue looked out the window, there were six men, dripping in the yard.

"For Heaven's sake, bring them up," she said to Marcel, though she had no idea what to do with them. She understood the project was common knowledge, and ordinary men could not have known Ben and Prue had not yet received even a word of encouragement from the governor. Marcel pressed his maimed hand to his chest and trotted back down the stairs. She and Ben had spoken of ordering huge bolts of oiled canvas and hundreds of tent poles and billeting any workers in her barley fields, if they were lucky enough to require workers, come spring. Meanwhile, these men, whoever they were, had walked miles in the rain to present themselves for work, and she did not want to turn them away, although Ben was not on the premises to see them.

Marcel ushered them up, and Prue remained seated; it was bad enough, she reasoned, to be hired by a woman for a job in construction, but it would be worse to see her far gone with child. They all removed their dripping hats. Four of them were white, and two Negro; two of the whites looked to be related. "Gentlemen," she said. "Mr. Dufresne tells me you've come looking for work; and I wager you wish to volunteer yourselves for the bridgeworks. Am I wrong? Do you come for Winship Daughters Gin?"

"No, ma'am," one said. "That is, we'll take whatever work we can get; but we came looking for work on the bridge."

"I hear you and the t'other Miss Winship run your works with great compassion," another volunteered.

"Thank you," Prue said. "Ah. But Mr. Horsfield, the architect of the project, is not to be found today; besides which, he has not yet received money from the state with which to hire workers. Should all go well, the bridgeworks will commence next spring; but we have no guarantee all shall go well."

One of them let out an audible sigh.

"Please come sit," she said. There were only two chairs across the desk; they all remained still. "I have some coffee on the stove. Would you like some? Marcel?"

Marcel stepped forward and helped himself, and held the pot up inquiringly before the men.

"We're sorry to trouble you, ma'am," one of the Negroes said. "There's little work at present in Bedford, and we heard some might be found here. But we don't mean to importune you."

"Hold, now," Prue said. "What are your names and professions?"

The first fellow who'd spoken glanced to the others, to make certain he wasn't treading on their toes. "George White, ma'am. I was apprenticed to a carpenter, but we didn't get on, and he let me go."

The next, younger than his companions, said, "I've done farmwork, and some odd jobs for our wheelwright."

"And your name is?"

"Ed Domer." He appeared uncomfortable saying it. "This is my brother, Pete."

Pete nodded deferentially.

The next to speak was the one who'd sighed in disappointment; he had a bright face, covered in freckles. "Day laborer, ma'am. Matthias Osier."

"My father was named Matthias," Prue said, then wondered how he could possibly respond to such a remark. "Who are you, gentlemen?"

"Lief van de Walle," said one. "Farrier by trade, but I'll take any work that's open to me."

"Alphonsus Weatherspoon," said the last.

Prue's spine tingled at the name. She had never remarked James Weatherspoon's face sufficiently to know if this man resembled him; she thought he did have a similar shade of medium brown skin. "Any relation to James Weatherspoon?"

"Indeed, ma'am; I am his cousin. He spoke highly of this place while he worked here, and the family says you've treated his widow right fair."

Prue did not know how to respond to this; she might have found it easier, somehow, had he shown a trace of anger. "Gentlemen, if you were given instructions, could you build two rooms onto a house?"

George White and Alphonsus Weatherspoon exchanged glances. White said, "Of course."

"I am Prudence Winship Horsfield, Mr. Horsfield's wife," Prue went on. "We need an addition built onto our house, and have had no time to arrange it with all the clamor about the bridge. But if we could hire you to build it, you'd be doing us a great service; and if we get the state's approval for a bridge, we could keep you on." Marcel had also refilled her cup, while he was there. She said, "Thank you." As none of them answered her, she added, "I realize it is not quite such long-term work as building a bridge. I shall not be offended if you decline."

"No, ma'am," said White. "With harvest in, there's little to be found in Bedford Corners until spring. I'd be obliged for the work."

"As would I," said Ed Domer.

"We'll pay you the same as our workers in the distillery; and Marcel, can you run up to Joe and the Philpots and see who would feed and quarter them at the fairer price?"

Marcel nodded.

"Take my waterproof, please."

He removed it from its peg by the door and went back down the stairs. "Hoy, Mr. Horsfield," he said as he went down, but it was Isaiah came in.

"New workers?" he asked her. To them he said, "Hello."

"They came asking about the bridge, but I shall employ them myself, building onto the house. We'll see what we can figure out for you, then," Prue said to them, and wrote their six names down in her ledger. "We haven't drawn up a plan for the rooms yet, but it shouldn't take long; and I think the sawmill should be able to provide timber almost immediately."

They all thanked her, and after they'd left, she put her head down on the desk. "One of them is Jim Weatherspoon's cousin," she said.

"Sakes."

"And I have no idea what to do with them."

"It's no matter," Isaiah said. "You need that addition, now the baby is coming. It'll all work out. If need be, we can put them to work laying in casks or repairing the back fence of your property, which seems ready to tumble down onto the brewhouse."

"You're right," Prue said, and heaved herself up to go to Theunis van Vechten's. Pearl and Abiah might not like the bustle around the house, but everyone would be pleased with the eventual result.

Garret Willemsen's reports indicated that debates over the bridge in both assembly and senate were bitter. Those who supported the bridge thought its feasibility had been amply proven. Some of those who derided it yet claimed it was a fancy; others that as New York City contained most of the state's wealth, it ought to open its coffers for such a project, especially given that a New York and Brooklyn bridge could not be said to serve upstate in any but the most abstract fashion. But New York City could not afford a public works of such magnitude; Willemsen believed the bridge would live or die by how it fared in the legislature. During the month of October it came to vote after vote in each house, struck down narrowly each time, or sent back to the other house for amendment. But at last, by All Hallows', they reached their decision. Governor Jay wrote that support for the bridge was still far from unanimous, but that he himself was satisfied the experiments in bridge building were sound, and that the project would prove the crowning glory of New York State.

In exchange for an eighty percent ownership in the bridge, the state offered to furnish Ben with two hundred fifty thousand dollars toward its cost—half payable on the first of December, half on the same date in the year 1800. Though Ben himself would be responsible either for contributing or soliciting the remainder of the cost, the state would therewith grant him a twenty percent ownership, which he might retain or divvy up in shares, as he saw fit. In this manner, Governor Jay suggested, the wealthiest men of Brooklyn and New York might partake in the eventual profitability of the project, while sparing the state itself undue burden. They might furthermore prove to the senators and assemblymen from the more northern regions how dearly city and village desired this bridge.

Ben and Prue rejoiced over the news. It would be no small task to raise fifty thousand dollars, but it would be worth any amount of labor and ingenuity to be able to build their bridge. Ben at once wrote to the New York aldermen to request their assistance in soliciting Mr. Cornelius Brouwer, who owned the land on which he hoped to build the New York footing; and he was given an introduction and an address in the country-side north of the canal.

"I wish I could go with you," Prue said in the kitchen the night before he went.

"But you cannot," Ben said. He touched her belly, which was flush up to the table, though she was comfortably seated back in her chair. "Look at you!"

"I can go for you," Tem offered.

Almost before Prue could say, "Thank you, but there's no need," Pearl had written on her slate, *Yr Japery wd ruin evr.thing.*

"I'm pleased you think so well of me," Tem said.

"She teases you," Ben said, and leaned down to kiss Prue's belly. The baby smacked at him, in response.

"You'll provision yourself well?" Prue asked.

"Gin, cigars, and money. Anything else?"

"No," Prue said, "that should suffice."

Will you come to M. Severn's? Pearl asked her.

"Christ, no," Prue said, laughing. "I can hardly walk."

Pearl blew her a kiss while putting on her coat and heading out.

Ben rode over on one of the distillery's barges the next morning, which spared him the trouble of the awkward choice between feeling un-comfortable on Losee's boat and betraying him by riding Mr. Fischer's. He then hired a wagon to carry him and the drawings out to the estate. He later reported Brouwer had regarded him "as if I were a prime pig, just ripe to be strung up as bacon," and responded to his initial offer for the land with a guffaw of disgust; but after a long, coffee-soaked morn-ing, Brouwer at last relented, and shook Ben's hand over an offer five hundred dollars above Ben's original proposition. (Once again, the cigars, gin, and a healthy wad of paper money disappeared without a trace. Prue was rather proud of Ben for his circumspection in this regard; and glad that even the industrious Mr. Harrison saw no trace of bribery in the deal.)

Ben was delighted by his success, and pleased with the men Prue had hired to work on the addition. To them he added his own crew of six, whom he would otherwise have had to dismiss until the materials began to come in; once the house was finished, he would put them to work mending fences. He had realized, however, there would be no more going forward with the bridge while retaining his title as King's County's surveyor. Up until this time, he had managed to supervise the models and complete his own work in fits and starts, but an actual bridge would require his constant vigilance. Prue often took her husband's bright spirits for granted, but on the night he wrote Governor Jay to resign his commission, Ben came upstairs wearing a tight smile and continued to pace the room after Prue had climbed into bed. "Are you troubled about your letter?" she asked him.

"What else should I have to trouble me?" he shot back at her.

"Mind your tone."

He threw both hands up in exasperation, but after pacing back and forth across the room sat down beside her and put his hand on her belly. The baby resettled itself. "I am sorry, Prue," Ben said, though he wasn't looking at her. "I realize my plight is none so terrible. But it was my dream to be the surveyor; my dream, and years of work. It was not easy, putting up with Hiram Bates and being separated from all those I loved. To relinquish it is no small thing."

Prue reached her hand up into his hair. He neither pulled away from her nor warmed to her touch as he might ordinarily have done. Prue said, "We had no surveyor before Mr. Jay named you; they were always brought in from outside. Perhaps you can convince him to revert to that system during the period of the bridge's construction, and allow you to return to your chosen work once it's complete."

"Perhaps," Ben said, but he did not sound convinced.

Prue wondered what he wrote to the governor; for days after he sent the letter of resignation, he remained irritable. His workmen, who had come to rely on his good cheer, were all puzzled by his mood. Though they did not question him, when they could spare a few moments from chiseling out the grooves in the house posts, they would invite him out for a ball toss or a drink at the Twin Tankards.

He soon recovered himself, and set in earnest about seeking donations for the bridge. He and Prue had decided to withhold their own funds until they'd determined how much they could gather from their neighbors; they were willing to make as large a contribution as they could, but as they did not need shares in the bridge as incentive to do this, they both thought it wise to use those shares to lure other investors. Prue had copied out the names of all the signatories to the original petitions before sending them to Mr. Stryker. Many of them were honest workers, whose support meant a great deal in spirit but could bring them no closer to having sufficient funds for construction; but those of greater means Ben copied onto a second list, and he began to solicit them, one by one. At first many were reluctant—as who would not be, when asked to give a great sum of money to an endeavor that could not be proven to have been wise until it had long been paid for—but slowly, one Brooklynite of repute after another began to make his donation. As if to prove he was not angry about Marcel's injury, Simon took out an entire share, in Peg's name; and John Boerum and Mr. Whitcombe, who had given so freely for Mr. Severn's church, also wrote large drafts. There were also myriad smaller contributions. Isaiah gave, though Ben and Prue tried to shout him down, telling him he should keep his money for his soon-to-be-four children; Will Severn bought a tenth of a share. When he had gathered as much money in Brooklyn as he thought possible, Ben began traveling to Manhattan to do the same, though again the boats presented him with a dilemma. (He rode Winship Gin's barges whenever he could, Losee's ferry when that was impossible, and Fischer's as a last resort.) In all, by the beginning of December, he had raised thirty-eight thousand in money and promises, which was not quite enough but would suffice for the time being. They would make up as much as they could from their own funds, when the need arose; and Prue expected her neighbors would be willing to contribute more, once they saw the great Gothic abutment rising from the strand.

Ben did not worry about the iron members the bridge would require—he could order nails locally as the need arose, and even the great rods to support the roadway could be had from Queen's County. But he hoped to have enough stone laid in before the North River froze to begin the abutments come spring. The first work after the thaw would be to dig the foundations, and the foundation stone for the Brooklyn side would take months to quarry; but once it had arrived, he did not want work to be delayed by ice floes on the river, or by the sluggishness of the mails. Ben wrote to the owner of the quarry, to inquire about a foundation stone and to ask him to send a first load of building material before the hard frost. Meanwhile, he took four workers away from the addition to the house and had them hew posts for a gigantic new storehouse, near those for the liquor but closer to the water's edge, so that when the timber arrived, sometime the following year, it would have a dry place to lodge in.

The remainder of the autumn progressed quietly. Prue saw to distillery business as long as she could, but began, by early December, to feel faint much of the time, and the pressure on her spine became unbearable if she sat erect too long. With some regret, then, but also with bright expectation, she turned over the business to Tem and Isaiah, and retired to the house. Pearl and Abiah seemed delighted to have Prue at home. She could not sit reading an hour without one of them bringing her some dried fruit or a cup of tea, or interrupting her to ask something about the construction; and when Pearl was not out wandering, she took to sitting on the divan at her sister's feet, reading or working on the embroidery for which she no longer seemed to have quite such a passion. Having given up his role as county surveyor, Ben had little to do until it came time to hire ditchdiggers come winter, and he spent most of December working with the hired men on raising the new rooms' roof beam and battening the roof before the snow. He, too, stopped in to visit throughout the day, and brought newspapers and books to relieve the tedium of Prue's days—the first she had ever spent inactive.

As the month wore on, Prue began to feel some concern for her infant's welfare. Previously, it had been still whenever she had moved about, and had kicked when she sat at her desk or lay down for the night. Now she was resting, it should have found ample opportunity to exercise its arms and legs, but it did so less and less often, and with what Prue thought markedly decreased force. At last, in the middle of December, it quit moving altogether. Pearl and Abiah were full of reassurances: *Resting*, Pearl wrote, and Abiah said, "It'll wake up before long. You wait—when it comes out, you'll wish it were still sleeping." But after a full day's silence, Prue began to worry in earnest, and Ben brought Mrs. Friedlander to examine her.

Jana Friedlander was an ancient old woman by then, half toothless, and with a slight palsy in her hands. But she felt over Prue's body thoroughly, then sat down beside her and took her hand. She kept quiet a long while, and Prue grew anxious she was not speaking because there

was nothing she could say. At last, looking at her steadily, Mrs. Friedlander said, "We shall wait and see what remedy time brings us." She
brought Prue two spoonfuls of dried herbs to eat, and as she chewed
them, Prue recognized their taste. All that time, she had imagined the
herbs had prevented conception; but she came to understand they had all
along hastened out anything that might have been growing within.

By midafternoon, the baby's waters had broken. Later, Prue vomited
all over her wedding sheets, gripped in a pain that blotted out her sight
and squeezed the breath from her chest.

Here, too, she hesitated in writing to her daughter. She wanted to tell her
everything—both to prepare her for what she herself would soon undergo, and to confide, all these years later, in someone who might understand the suffering she had experienced. At the time, who could have
helped her? She had felt she could manage her labor if only she could
have caught her breath for a moment, but waves of pain had kept crashing down upon her, as if trying to drown her. Even in the midst of her
suffering, she had believed she could keep herself from being overwhelmed had this misery not been the wages of her sin, or if she could
have looked forward to dandling an infant daughter or son. But she had
known, without being told, the child was not to be. Pearl, Abiah, and
Mrs. Friedlander had all ministered to her as best they could, but none of
them had been able to assuage her pain. And although she had known
they were attending her, she had been only dimly aware of anything beyond the purview of her travail; as she paused in writing to Recompense,
she could remember nothing any of them had said to her that night.
How could she tell this to her daughter? She longed to be heard, but
could not burden her own child with such a confession.

Instead, she wrote to her:

A few hours past dawn, I was delivered of a stillborn girl child, in the
saddest moment of my life until that time. How I pray you shall never
see such issue from your womb. She was perfectly formed & of good
size, with a shock of black hair like my sisters', but her skin was blue &
looked as if it had been so a good while. Mrs. Friedlander did her best
to revive the child, slapping & shaking her violently, rubbing her

vigorously with gin, and bundling her near the fire; but though I watched all this with some hope, in my heart I knew naught would avail. I had known this child,—your sister, my love; your own sister,—by her flips & kicks, and I saw she no longer abided in that corpse Mrs. Friedlander held.

I should wonder if it did not break your heart to know of the sadness that overtook your father when at last he was summoned to the room. I shall tell you only that he asked to hold her, and cradled her in his arms as if he had indeed received a daughter and not a mere sack of dust & ashes. How I wished it could be so! And how base & weak it seemed to have a human heart, that could seek to delude itself thus. I envied, in that moment, the stills of my manufactory, that did nothing but their appointed work, & *that* only when we caused them to.

Your Aunt Patience, when she came, removed the small corpse from our sight & then ushered your father from the room. When she had latched the door behind her, I grew angry & inquired to know why she had sought to banish my dearest comfort.

—Because it is not a man's place, she said, with what I thought unnecessary vehemence. Yet when she came to sit beside me, she, too, shed tears for my plight & for the child, and held fast my hand like a true friend. It was the first I ever felt a moment's kinship with her; & although I know you find her trying, I have never forgotten this kindness. When we had cried ourselves out, she removed from her pocket a gift for me. I rather expected some pastry, or perhaps an uplifting treatise, but what she had brought was a bottle of Dr. Philpot's nostrum. To see such a dubious thing in the hand of prim Patience Livingston nearly made me laugh, in spite of everything. —Oh, do'n't take it so serious, she said, obviously annoy'd with me. —I simply thought there are some ailments gin cannot cure.

She was correct, of course; and though I hope you will not think less of me for saying it, I accepted the Eugenic Water's oblivion with relief. Once I had tasted its succour, I believed I came to understand my mother's desire for it.

My dear love: We named your sister *Susannah*, in honour of my mother's mother, and your father & I stared off at the dull grey branches of the churchyard trees as we laid her in the ground. *Susannah*, a name of great beauty, & I thought how glad I should have been to bestow it on a living child and call out —Sukey! into the streets when she was abroad making mischief, as I felt certain she should have done. I remember thinking with great bitterness that all around Olympia lived families far less fortunate than we, whose children nevertheless gamboled while we stood lamenting. I ate myself out with jealousy of them, though I knew this was not right.

Will Severn came often to our home to give comfort. Pearl always had some delicacy prepared for him, & he accepted these eagerly. I asked him one evening if he thought it possible my infants had been taken as sacrifice by the river. I regretted asking the moment I had done so, for the expression of horrour on his visage made his answer clear. He stood, came over to where I sat, and kissed the top of my head. He must have discomfited himself as compleatly as he did me, for when he stood again he was pink to the gills; yet said, —Bless you, Prue, I'll not have you be such a pagan as that. There is nothing so dark in all God's kingdom.

—All right, I told him. I see you are right.

—Take comfort in your faith. Your sister Pearl is full to overflowing with it; can you rely, in part, on hers?

—I do'n't know, I answered truthfully.

& I could not, Recompense. What good did it do me to know another did not doubt the rightness of God's plan? It only made my own doubt the more galling. It was with a heart & body suffused with bile I weathered the next few months. Oh, there was much to see to at the distillery, and every where I went, I was met with expressions of pity, but there was no solace in any of it. Children were all around,— Patience's, in particular,—and every one of them made me mourn; and as winter was the slowest season at the works, I had less than I felt my due to occupy my thoughts. Pearl began to spend as little time as possible in my company;—& I assumed she had chosen to spend it in Will Severn's, who could appreciate her faith, rather than in mine who had once cursed her, & ever since reaped the terrible crop I'd thus sowed. This did not strike me unfair. I, too, would have avoided my own company, had such a feat of personal division been within my powers. Tem did her best to engage me on matters regarding the works; Abiah to cook the foods I most enjoy'd; but none of their ministrations could lighten my grief.

& do you see, love, why it was with such unity of purpose I threw myself into the building of the bridge, come spring? You see why I would have let the distillery founder, had that been necessary, and given my life blood to see that lifeless amalgamation of timber & stone rise from the shores of Brookland?

Dear Recompense, do you forgive me relating you this morbid tale when you are with child; & do you know I pray fervently,—with a faith restored in no small part by you your self,—that you shall know an outcome of naught but happiness.

With enduring love,
PWH

Twenty

THE TRUE BRIDGE'S BEGINNING

Ben and Prue recovered slowly from the shock of their loss. As they did, they set about preparing themselves for the momentous spring. Prue wrote an advertisement for the New York and Albany papers and the *Long-Island Courier*. She described the nature of the project and the work to be had, the wages the workers would be paid, and the dates on which potential laborers might apply. When she distributed the workers' pay that week, she asked them likewise to recommend any friends or relations for the work, and though she had felt no joy in weeks, their enthusiasm stirred her. The first date on which she had invited interested parties to apply for the work came early in March of 1800, and she and Ben were gratified when above thirty men from the near environs presented themselves. The second date, two weeks later, brought forty more, this time from farther afield—two from Baltimore, one from the village of New Hope in Pennsylvania, and a father and son from the wilderness in New Jersey. Others continued to arrive, singly and in small groups, as the weather improved. Most of these had some experience in building, and not one appeared drunk at the time of making his application, which Prue counted a blessing, given the proximity of the gin. A few had newly arrived from England and France; some had lost work or grown weary of their chosen professions; a handful were former sailors, who applied because they could no longer bear to leave home two and three years at a stretch. Ben was keen to hire them, as he felt certain they'd have learned good habits of discipline aboard ship. Men defected from mills up and down the river to volunteer; and a few came, it

seemed, simply to gawk at the models. Ben remained in constant communication with Thomas Pope. He consulted the elder bridge builder
four times on his method for marking out the positions of the two footings across the water from each other, as it remained Ben's chief concern
that he might mismeasure, and the twin levers would not meet precisely
when they reached the middle of the straits. Ben also sent copies of his
receipts for materials and a roster of the men he'd hired to the governor's
office, where an independent auditor would determine whether the
bridge's funds were being properly spent. Work would commence, if
weather permitted, on Monday the twenty-fourth of March—the first
full week of spring—but until then, the men were on holiday part-time,
and Prue imagined Joe Loosely and the Philpots were doing a banner
business.

She was relieved they'd ordered in oilcloth and tent poles, as they had
need of them for all these men. Ben had them dig pits for their cook fires
and a deeper one for their latrine, and provided them ample firewood
and free access to the wells both at the mill and in the Winship dooryard.
As they staked out their quarters, the field in which Matty Winship had
grown barley began to look as if it housed an occupying army; the Hessians and the Fourth Prince of Wales had never seemed so numerous,
nor sung such lewd songs late into the night.

To save time during the workday, Ben and Prue planned to provide
the men a midday meal, exactly as Prue did at the distillery, so they put
out an advertisement for two cooks. This turned up, providentially, a distant cousin of Abiah's, from the village of Midwood. She lodged with the
family until she found a permanent place with the van Suetendaels. Pearl,
meanwhile, had developed a marked preference for the new downstairs
bedroom, claiming she liked to be near the kitchen fire, though Prue suspected she liked it because it was farthest in the house from Tem and
closest to the back door, thus facilitating her late and early rambles. The
upstairs room that might have become Susannah's remained empty.

On the first day of spring, Ben asked Prue, Isaiah, and Adam van
Suetendael to accompany him while he marked out the boundaries for
the bridge's Brooklyn footing, where the work would commence.
"Might's well use these tools for something," he said as he unpacked the
velvet-lined cases in which he now stored them. His tone was wistful.
"Mr. Pope and Mr. Avery assure me I can site the bridge properly if I

take sufficient care." Ben spoke only infrequently of his sadness over losing their daughter and resigning his commission, but seemingly overnight he had developed a fine mesh of wrinkles at the corners of his eyes and a gray streak at the front of his fair hair. He seemed determined to restore his former good cheer, and Prue did not want to brake his progress by reminding him of change and sorrow.

That first chill spring day, she put her hand on his upper arm and said, "We could not ask for a better surveyor."

Adam seemed unaware there could be any cause for sadness on such a momentous day; he clearly preferred the romance of being a surveyor's assistant to the drudgery of hauling loads for Joe Loosely. Prue reminded herself that he was still only a boy, and could not be blamed for his high spirits.

Ben loaded his theodolite, spirit level, Gunter's chain, four iron stakes, and a mallet into a wheelbarrow, and together they bumped it down the rutted lane to the strand. Adam carried the pole aloft as if he were marching in a parade. Work had not yet begun for the day at the distillery, but Isaiah was already on the premises—no doubt, Prue thought, to escape his four children. He and Prue both stood aside while Ben set up his theodolite with care on the site he'd previously marked as the center of the anchorage. He centered the instrument with its plumb bob and checked that it was level. Adam held the pole steady while Ben took bearings on it and on the tall pole they'd fixed across the river, and with these new bearings corroborating the old, he once again computed his distances. Isaiah helped him chain out the distances of the site's four corners. Once they were marked, they measured again, and Ben concluded his calculation was true. Prue felt a lump of tears in her throat—a lump of sheer pride—such as she would not feel again until the day far in the future on which her daughter married; and she herself drove the stake to mark the first corner of the Brooklyn anchorage. "Ah!" she cried when she had finished. The mallet was heavy, and she had enjoyed putting it in motion. An event of such moment should, she thought, have such heft.

"Lucky man," Isaiah said, "to be starting up a bridge and have a wife who relishes manual labor."

When the other three stakes were driven in and flagged, Prue thought they didn't look like much; it seemed one of their rolls of oilcloth could have covered such an area. But when the anchorage stood upon it, she knew it would be majestic indeed—the size of half the buildings of the manufactory lumped together, and stretching up as high as the cliffs of Ihpetonga themselves. All day she saw the distillery workers, out on their breaks, visiting the site as if it were holy ground. She was pleased it was not only to her those four iron stakes seemed imbued with extraordinary meaning.

Will Severn was delighted to have the new workers among the Brooklynites. Though most of them were fond enough of drinking, and for the first time in sixteen years the sounds of late-night dart games echoed out across the quiet streets, many of the workers were family men, and not a few showed up to Severn's church their first Sunday in Brooklyn. To a man they were freshly shaven and in clean collars. "They are far from home," he said, grinning, to Prue and Pearl, when they visited him to ask him to bless the beginning of the work on Monday. "They need shepherding and a sense they belong in this community. I am only too glad to welcome them; Heaven knows we had a few empty pews."

Pearl was beaming. *& it'll be a boon for Rachæl Livingston & Mr Tilleys Daught, as surely there are at least 2 eligible Husbands in the groop?*

"Pearl Winship, you mustn't be so cruel," he said, but he was still smiling.

'Tis in my Blood, she wrote, and cast Prue a glance that Prue didn't know how to interpret.

"Nonsense," he said. "And I shall be honored to bless your endeavor," he told Prue. "Your workers have asked me to come speak to them tonight, in their open field. Perhaps you will join us?"

"If I can," Prue said.

From her own kitchen table that evening, she heard his familiar voice carrying over the barley field. She did not feel inclined to go out, and Tem groaned at the suggestion, but Pearl and Abiah put on their coats when they heard him begin, and returned radiant an hour later.

When the cock crowed on the Monday morning, everyone in the Winship house was already up; from her bedroom, Prue could hear them splashing their faces and setting out plates. From the corner of her window, she could see the workmen stirring about their camp. She turned to Ben, who was giving her the tight-lipped smile that had graced his countenance of late, and nuzzled in against his throat. "Oh, dear," he said, hugging her close before pushing her away to signal the start of the workday. "Are you ready?"

"It's your bridge," Prue said, and felt it to be so for the first time. "Are you?"

"I relish it," he said, and pulled on a knitted jersey over his shirt.

During breakfast, Pearl wore the same dark expression she'd worn the day Tem had gone to join Prue and their father in the distillery. "Are you nervous?" Prue asked her.

Pearl shook her head calmly no.

"What, then?"

Pearl again shook her head. Prue could not stop watching her, though she knew her sister might construe this as a challenge. After a moment Pearl took a perfunctory sip of her coffee and wrote, *I shld like to build a bridge.*

"As should I," Prue said, "but it will chiefly be Ben's work hereafter."

Pearl dropped her head to one side, as if weighing this.

"Come, Pearlie, don't look so glum," Ben said. "You shall see the works daily; and your sister and I will be sure to consider if there's anything more you might contribute."

Pearl did not reply. She brushed her spoon against the hominy in her bowl, but did not move to eat.

Tem said, "So, what'll it be, Prue: two years before you can rectify again? I swear I don't know what shall become of us."

"I imagine I'll be in the countinghouse before the morning is through," Prue said. Pearl continued to play with her spoon. "I won't be much use digging a foundation. And with Marcel to help you with the accompts, I can't see how you could fail at the work."

Tem chewed with one eyebrow skeptically raised. "I'll be damned if we don't change the way we rectify before the year is out."

"I'll be damned if we do," Prue said, though even as she said it, she did not feel convinced.

"And you've nothing to worry about," Ben offered Tem. "A bridge may be an enticing distraction, but I don't think your sister can keep her mind off the distillery eight hours running. She talks about it in her sleep."

"Do I?" Prue asked, but Ben only laughed.

After breakfast, as they set out for the water, Pearl went up the Ferry Road to bring Mr. Severn down; and as on the day on which they'd first offered the drawings to public view, Prue was amazed how many of her neighbors had gathered to witness the sight. All the distillery's workers were out in the mill yard, along with the ninety-odd men who would work on the bridge, and everyone who lived within walking distance of the manufactory was hurrying down the roads to get there before the bell rang to commence the morning's work. Even some of the Red Hook fishing boats had anchored close to shore, and Losee, with an unfamiliar passenger in his boat, had diverted from his normal route and also dropped anchor nearby. All the local newsmen had come, and a ship flying the Union Jack and heading up toward Hell Gate sounded its horn at the gathering. Hats and hands went up in greeting as Ben and Prue walked down the lane. Isaiah, Prue saw, had bought a brand-new shovel for the occasion, and had tied some bunting in the colors of the flag of the Republic around its handle. In his other hand he had a bottle of champagne, which he'd evidently chilled in Joe's icehouse, as it was sweating onto the sand at his feet. The *Long-Island Courier* had sent a writer to witness the occasion; C. Mather Harrison was nowhere in sight.

After what seemed an age, Pearl appeared at the top of Joralemon's Lane, with Will Severn right behind her, and behind him, a devout few of the workers who'd attended his morning services. A gust of wind off the river whipped Pearl's coat open and her dress back against her legs, and her cheeks were bright in the chilly air. Her grim expression was gone, and she waved to her sisters. Severn had his Bible tucked under his arm and, wrapped around his throat, a new blue scarf Pearl had made to replace the decrepit red one. Someone raised his hands and clapped when he saw them coming, and a few more followed suit. Their applause sounded hollow on that windy morning. Pearl kept waving, as if she'd been born to public adulation.

The crowd parted for Severn and Pearl to pass through to the site of the four staves. Prue and Ben took up their places before them, and Tem, Isaiah, and Pearl stood to their sides. Will Severn cleared his throat, and the workers and neighbors hushed each other and drew nearer.

"Ladies and gentlemen," he began, then smiled at Prue. Despite his gray hair, he seemed no older than she at that moment. "I am honored beyond expression to have been asked to bless this momentous occasion.

This morning, the people of the village of Brookland begin a public works on a scale our nation has not yet known; a project that will be an honor to us, to the city and state of New York, and to the Winship and Horsfield families." He licked his chapped lips. "Let us pray." He removed his hat and was about to lay it on the sand when Pearl took it from him. When the men all removed their head coverings, they made a soft rustling sound, as of bird wings. Prue saw the men place their hats over their hearts before she closed her own eyes. "Dear Lord," Severn said, "bless this bridge and the people who toil upon it. May the work progress without hindrance or accident, and may it be as pleasing to Your eyes as to the eyes of man." He paused for a moment before saying, "Amen," and in that moment, Prue prayed that if a sacrifice was necessary, Susannah be allowed to stand for it. She did not think she could bear the grief if one more person should die.

All around voices echoed, "Amen." Prue could imagine her prayer scudding out across the water, as the other had done all those years ago. When she opened her eyes, Isaiah was holding the shovel forth to her. "No," she said, "Ben should take the first spadeful."

Isaiah said, "We both disagree," and continued to hold it toward her.

Her breath caught in her throat as she took it from him; she had never imagined how momentous it could feel to put a shovel to this ordinary stretch of Brooklyn shore. She drove it in with the shank of her boot and, using her foot to guide it, drew up a few pounds of mud-brown sand. Her ears began to ring with excitement, and for a brief moment, her fingers tingled and everything within her field of vision was tinged pale violet. She caught herself in time, however, to pitch the contents of the shovel outside the bounds the stakes described, and the rowdy applause that followed brought her back to herself. Ben uncorked the wine, which gave a thunking sound, and a stream of vapor wafted from the bottle neck. He held it out to Prue, and she took a long draught. She had rarely drunk champagne, and found it dry on her palate and ticklish in her nose; but she drank deeply of it, and the workers whistled and hurrahed. Ben next took a long pull, then passed it to Tem; when Pearl drank from it, it made her sneeze, at which the whole crowd laughed. After Isaiah had had his swallow, he passed it to Will Severn, though everyone knew he didn't drink. His hearty sip made the men holler and cheer. He blinked his eyes rapidly, looking quite pleased with himself, before passing it back into the crowd, where it traveled hand to hand until it was empty.

When the clapping and shouts had died down, Tem cupped her palms around her mouth and called out, "That'll be that, for the holiday. Workers to the brewhouse, stillhouse, and casking room. We commence, as usual, in ten minutes." She said something to Isaiah, who walked off toward the windmill. A few minutes later the sails shuddered as the pinion connected with the drive gear and all around the machinery began to hum. Tem kissed Prue good-bye and set off for the mash room.

"So," Ben said, "shall we?"

Prue nodded, and watched Pearl escort Will Severn back up the hill. They were both still laughing about the champagne.

Ben had determined that to build a strong foundation, the hole on the Brooklyn side would have to reach a depth of more than thirty feet. Even at such a depth, the excavation would not reach bedrock, but it would reach a dense, firm soil into which the piles to support the foundation stone could be driven to refusal. While the idea of digging a pit of this size only to found the structure on sand daunted Prue, she also understood Ben's reasoning was fundamentally sound. For the time being, Ben explained to the men the precautions they'd take for safety; and until the hole reached a depth of a few feet, they would be doing nothing all day but shoveling sand into wheelbarrows and either carting it away or using some of it to erect a barricade against nosy children. This no more required two supervisors than it required Prue to pitch in to the labor; so after she watched the workers begin, she waved Ben good-bye and went to find Tem in the brewhouse. Tem goggled at her as if she'd seen a ghost, but Prue said, "See? It'll be months before you have cause to worry about the flavor of your gin."

"I prefer to worry about it every day. I believe that does the most good," Tem said, and went back to leaning on the side of the tank to watch the hot water pour in.

The new workmen made good progress on the foundation hole. After three days of digging, it became necessary to shore the excavation up from the inside, so Ben ordered the men to construct a cross-braced scaffold within the pit. The vertical and horizontal boards and diagonal rakers laddered down the four sides of the hole and, as a secondary benefit, provided a means for the men to descend once the hole grew too deep to jump. Building at each new level took time, as did erecting a barrier good enough to keep out the naughty, the hapless, and the devil-may-care and removing the sand a sufficient distance from the site. Nevertheless, the excavation proceeded at a rate of about a foot per day, which, though she had little experience against which to judge it, Prue thought excellent fast.

Ben managed everything beautifully, to the point of building a thatched roof to keep rainwater out of the hole. He installed a small hand-powered pump to the same purpose and determined that if necessary, he could run a belt to the waterwheel and operate it continuously, without wasting one man's labor. Prue wished there were some work she might do to further the bridge along; but as long as she continued to be obstinate about the rectifying, the distillery would need her. When it came time to begin digging the foundation on the other side, either she or Ben would have to cross the river every day. Until then, she counted the hours until she could begin dividing her time between the two tasks. She could think of no better way to distract herself from her sorrow— and for such a worthy end.

Only a week passed, with the hole no deeper than a mean bedroom was tall, before it began to fill with groundwater. A man had stood knee-deep in water all morning, operating the pump as quickly as he could, before Ben realized the water level would never decrease at such a rate. Many of the rest stood by, eating sandwiches; a few of the more industrious went looking for extra wages, loading rope at the ropewalk; and the laziest went back to their tents to nap. Ben brought Prue up from the countinghouse to consult upon the issue.

They arrived at the pit to find the thoroughly begrimed fellow at the bottom leaning exhausted against the wall nearest the pump. "Sorry, Mr. Horsfield," he said to Ben, "but I don't see as it's making much difference if I pump or if I don't." The water was creeping upward as he spoke.

"Climb out," Ben told him. The man sloshed up the latticework, his boots releasing torrents of brown water back into the hole, and wiped his hands on his backside once he'd arrived on dry ground. "Foot and a half deep, would you say?"

"Bit more." The man gestured to his britches, which were wet to above the knee.

" 'Tisn't so bad," Ben said to Prue, "except that it isn't going anywhere."

Prue looked to see how far distant the waterwheel actually was. "As you say," she offered, "you can provide it power, and keep it going in perpetuity."

"I think I should order a second pump straightaway," he said. When she nodded, he put his hand to his brow in salute and set off toward the New Ferry—just past the ropewalk, and a far faster journey, with its trim boats, each rowed by a younger man than Losee—to visit the company in New York that could order his second pump from Philadelphia.

During the days they awaited its arrival, Ben loaded all the men on barges and took them to New York to dismantle the rotting woodwork of the Old Market Wharf. As they did so, the poor of the precinct stood by waiting for the boards, which they trucked off either to patch their dwellings or to burn for firewood. Once the area was clear of debris, Ben and Adam took their bearings time and again, as they had done at home, until at last Ben felt secure marking out the perimeter of the foundation. Prue could see little of this from the distillery, but if she climbed Clover Hill and stood atop their newly repaired back fence, she could look across the water. Just as when she'd been a girl, she could observe, through the manufactories' smoke, the tiny shapes of men moving across the ground.

Because the composition of the New York earth differed so from Brooklyn's, so, too, did their method for digging into it: There were no shovels, but two-man teams, one member of which steadied and turned a drill three feet in length and an inch and a half in diameter, while the other drove it in with a sledgehammer. This was grueling and dangerous work, but the men had good eyes, and the sheer repetitiveness of the motion seemed to keep them on their marks and prevent them from shattering one another's hands and forearms. One man had his toes broken and another his thumb crushed the first day, but the New York doctor expected both would recover; Ben reminded the men to redouble their care thenceforward. He also said they worked in what appeared to be a kind of trance, in which they were cognizant of nothing but the swing of the mallet and the turn of the spike; often, they did not hear him when he called them for a break or to move on to the next phase of work.

Ben had, while on his northern surveying expedition, observed in mining operations some of the most modern techniques in blasting, which he put to work in gouging out the New York foundation. When the deep, narrow holes pocked a sufficient area, the men filled them a third full with gunpowder, each charge employing about two pounds. The men then dropped fuses—reeds filled with black powder—into the holes, and tamped the remaining space with clay to contain the explosions. Though Gregor Joralemon had volunteered for the commission of lighting the fuses, it was dangerous work, and Ben did not hire him for it. While most of the crew took cover a good distance away, one division ran through lighting the fuses, then hurried to safety. From across the river, Prue would see the rising cloud of dust and rubble, and a moment later hear the deep rumble of the exploding shots. Each time, she prayed Ben had reached safety and none of the others had been killed or maimed. When the dust settled, the men returned to the site of the explosions, swept out the debris, and recommenced hammering in their drills. In the first days of blasting, a number of the men were injured by the blowback of the exploding charges—they were cut and abraded, and a few temporarily lost their hearing. Such wounds were painful and, in the case of loss of hearing, distressing, but none kept a man from working for more than a few days. The men loaded the scree onto punts and sent it to Manhattan's North River side, where an entrepreneur named Comfort Hull was expanding a broad swath of waterfront. The Brooklyn crew did likewise with their excavated sand.

Such blasting had previously only been employed in tunnels and mines, and never in Manhattan. Ben reported that the children of the neighborhood gathered by the score to watch; and the newssheets, while skeptical of the enterprise's safety, explained it well enough to allay the citizens' fear.

The second pump soon arrived by boat from Philadelphia, and Ben attached both of them by long belts to the waterwheel's crown gear. They whirred and screeched incessantly, but they emptied the hole of water, and half the men could then return to work on the Brooklyn foundation. At last Prue believed she could contribute to the work.

"I don't know," Ben argued. "I don't know how well they'll take orders from a woman. You might remain in the distillery awhile yet. Tem needs you."

Prue stood looking over the edge of the Brooklyn pit. "Surely digging a foundation hole doesn't require constant supervision?" she asked.

He shrugged his shoulders.

"They might grow accustomed to me, if I am with them only a few hours a day. The rest of the time I can spend back in the distillery, where they accept direction from me without difficulty."

Ben must have sensed the pique behind her otherwise calm words, for he relented. While he loaded the New York division onto their barge the next morning, Prue set up the workers on the Brooklyn side. "I like your britches," one of them said to her; a few others sniggered.

Prue had encountered this before, and told herself not to lose her temper as Tem would have done. Nevertheless, she could not ignore it. "Further commentary upon my attire will result in your dismissal," she said, holding her face as placid as she could. "If any of the captains hears of such talk, you will report it to me or to Mr. Horsfield immediately. My apologies for being blunt; I see no other way."

The fellow glowered at her like a child caught out at mischief and unable to admit his wrong. But over the hour she supervised them that morning, and when she came to check on them again in the afternoon, the men respectfully called her either "Mrs. Horsfield" or "Miss Winship," and did not smirk when she made suggestions about the digging.

In the kitchen that evening, Ben asked her how it had gone.

"I suppose there will eventually have to be a proper Brookland supervisor," she said. "I shan't be able to divide myself between the foundation and the distillery and have both come out aright. The captains must have someone to report to."

I cld do it, Pearl wrote.

Prue waved her fork at her. "You can't command fifty men with pencil and paper. It'd take too long to disseminate your orders." Abiah clicked her tongue in sympathy. "Besides, I'm certain not all of them can read."

Thn teech me to Rectify.

When Prue knit her brow over the suggestion, Pearl underlined it and pushed it closer toward her.

Tem said, "It isn't the worst—"

"No," Prue said. "It's too dangerous."

I'm not a Child, Pearl wrote on a new page. *& I'm a good Student.*

"I've not inherited Father's nose, but there's no reason to suppose she hasn't," Tem said. "She certainly hears better than either of us."

Ben said, "I think it sounds a fair solution."

Prue thought she'd simply turned to him, but the way he bent down to study his roast made it clear she'd been glaring. To Pearl she said, "I don't doubt you'd excel at rectifying, as you excel at everything to which you turn your mind. And yet—"

But before she could finish her thought, Pearl had turned the page and written, *Everything to whch you allow me to turn my Mind.*

Prue's breath came up short. At once she recognized the truth of what Pearl had written; but she did not intend to be swayed. "What do you suppose should have happened to Marcel, had he been unable to cry out when the press fell upon his hand?" she asked.

"Might have bled to death," Abiah said.

Before someone notic'd his Distress? Pearl wrote. But she did not wait for Abiah to finish sounding out the letters before she added, *Only a Fool turns is Back on a Machine of that sise.*

Ben was cutting his roast into small pieces with a deliberation he rarely accorded his food.

"It is dangerous work, and I shan't have you do it," Prue said. "I could not bear it if any ill befell you."

Pearl hit the heel of her hand against the table, making the plates and flatware jump and the cider slosh in its cups. Then she went into her room and shut the door. No one said anything for a long moment, until Ben said, "Eventually, you know, someone must be with the Brookland crew full-time, and you'll have a conundrum then."

Prue did not answer him, but later that night, when they were already in bed, she told him she thought the day's experiment had gone well enough to continue. It would be a pleasure beyond words, she told him, to have some share in this work; and he agreed things might go on as they were awhile longer. She could not have anticipated, however, that the memory of Pearl's suggestion, and her shame at having rejected it, would leach the joy from both aspects of her work. Prue returned to the Brooklyn crew the next morning but found, in her sourness, she could think of what they were doing as nothing more than digging a big hole; and when she returned to the rectifying house that afternoon, it was hot and unpleasantly fragrant from herbs. The press's open jaws seemed to taunt her. She had been working them for eighteen years without incident; and all at once, her prided art seemed the worst kind of drudgery.

Despite her ill mood, however, the distillery kept running, and the foundation holes for the bridge progressed in due course; they had reached their appointed depths by the end of May, and the men began the grueling work of driving in the huge timber piles that would support the Brooklyn anchorage. No matter how Pearl's words—never repeated, but inscribed in Prue's memory—rankled, there was satisfaction in bringing the first phase of the work to completion without loss of life. And though it was small solace, Prue looked forward to being able to disconnect the pumps. Their constant whine had kept half of Brooklyn awake at night, and engendered many complaints. Prue hoped Patience's screaming babies would at last allow their parents some rest.

On the New York side, the bridge would be founded in the blasted-out schist, but the Brooklyn footing required a foundation stone so vast, it had taken the quarry the entire spring to mine it. As it had floated down the Hudson on eight tethered barges, there had been rumors it had stopped the flow of traffic in both directions; Prue thought it would be only a matter of time before it appeared in the balladeers' songs. When it arrived at Winship Gin, Jens Luquer saw it from the stillhouse window, and without thinking sounded the warning bell, closing down the works. Though he was later abashed to have been so frightened by the thing, it proved just as well production had ceased, for Ben needed every hale man in the village to attach the ropes to it and lay down the logs along which it would be rolled. He had already sent notice to farmers as far off as Bedford and Midwood that he would need to borrow their teams of oxen when the great stone arrived; now he sent out runners to call the favor due. The next day, twenty-three teams of oxen arrived. Prue had never seen so many of the beasts. She had thrilled at their great size and strength when her father and Ben's had set the foundation stones for the distillery; now they seemed to fill the entire mill yard. Ben strung the lead ropes from the stone over a set of pulleys twenty times larger than those for the cranes; from the pulleys, he attached the ropes to the snorting beasts. And with the distillery's men in the water, fighting to hold the barges steady, and the bridgeworks' men alongside them, trying to coax the stone along, he gave the command to begin heaving it up toward shore.

It took four days to drag it to the brink of the pit, and though no lives were lost in the process, some limbs were broken, and Prue shuddered to think what might go afoul when at last the stone settled into place. As she and Tem watched from the countinghouse, she kept thinking of Susannah, who would have been a fat, six-months baby by then, and was instead all desiccated skin and brittle bone. She continued to pray Susannah's life would prove enough for this monstrosity she'd dreamed. She thought her prayers must have been answered, for when the stone settled into its place on the morning of the fifth day, with a crash that shook the distillery buildings and sent a wave out into the river that slopped onto the wharves of New York, everyone was still safe. She oversaw the payments to the farmers, and ordered out liquor for the men.

Atop the gigantic stone on the Brooklyn side, and within the pit on New York's, Ben and Prue instructed the men in beginning to construct the stone feet of the abutments. This was not quite the method Matty Winship had used to secure the buildings of his distillery against the fluctuations of the sand, but it was similar; Prue hoped it would suffice to steady something as large as the bridge. The evidence suggested it would. As the twin abutments grew, the men filled some of the excavated sand and rubble back in around them, so that the structures seemed to grow from the ground itself.

Prue learned from her men that at the work's commencement, the two teams had laid a wager with each other as to who would finish their foundation first. Everyone suspected the Brooklyn side would take longer under a female supervisor than New York's would under the bridge architect himself, so the New York crew had given Brooklyn's a ten-day handicap. When young Alphonsus Weatherspoon told her of this, realizing only too late it was something he ought not to have related, Prue wished she were Tem, so she might swear about it or drink herself into oblivion at the Twin Tankards. In repeating the story to Ben, she nearly shouted with frustration. But when her team at last lost the bet, she assumed their debt, and out of her own pocket treated the men to a night at the Liberty Tavern. In this way she both filled Joe's coffers—she hoped tempering his opposition to the bridge—and earned the reluctant respect of her men. Weatherspoon, Domer, and Osier had never begrudged her their admiration, as it was she who had originally given them employ; but they were bashful of her in front of the other men, so their support had hitherto done her little good.

It soon became obvious that building the anchorage required constant supervision, and Prue made a deal with Marcel Dufresne: They would trade off days overseeing the Brooklyn work crew, that both might continue to fulfill their duties in the distillery. Ben continued to take the boat each day to Manhattan.

Had Prue never before spent a sleepless night, she felt the Brooklyn anchorage should have caused her to do so. All its crenellations and spires required the genius of a master builder, and who was she but an amateur? New York's pyramid would be equally complex, but she trusted Ben better than she trusted herself. Night after night, she imagined wagons and pedestrians ascending the roadway via the vaulted tunnels in the two structures' middles, then imagined some ill-placed stone plummeting free, or a passing stonemason expressing disgust at the way she had her workmen mix their mortar.

"I don't see why you fret so," Ben said one morning as his barge was about to embark for the New York side. "There shall be no second-rate masonry, no mortar squelching out from between stones. We are building according to the most modern and scientific methods, and those of our men who are not expert craftsmen now shall be so before the frost."

Prue thought it typical he should address her concern with blithe good cheer. She was still too wrought up about the previous evening's dream to answer him.

"Prue, really," he said. "If you're so concerned, have Marcel supervise the men for the day, and come across with me. I'll make sure you know how it should be done."

"You needn't patronize me," Prue said.

Ben shrugged his shoulders. "And you needn't worry over something you understand perfectly well."

Though Prue did not concede his point, she left Marcel in charge of the Brooklyn works and spent the day observing Ben's methods for finishing and laying stones. The experience drove home what she had always known: that it was best to check the plans thrice before making any irrevocable step, and that attention and care could avert most accidents. She could not force herself to love the work as Ben did—she was still sometimes raw with sorrow over Susannah's death, and learning of the men's wager as to her competence rekindled her jealousy of her husband—but she could try to imitate his good cheer with the workmen.

In this manner, and with a building season of unprecedented good weather, the anchorages stood nearly complete on both sides of the river by November of 1800. Before the close of the season, the footings supported the stubs of the iron struts from which the arms would soon spring. Though the blunt-topped pyramid would eventually rise another twenty feet into the air, and though the Brooklyn abutment yet lacked all the distinguishing marks that would make it a fancy, these stone constructions had a gruff beauty all their own, and they dwarfed the landscape from which they sprang. Pearl's original elevation for the bridge had seemed massive when first she'd drawn it, and the second model— still being tested each day for its responses to weight and weather—had been large enough to bridge a body of water in its own right; but nothing had prepared Prue for the sheer size of the emerging structure. In relation to houses, manufactories, the straits, and even the cliffs of Ihpetonga, the footings seemed to have been left behind by a race of giants. They were on the same scale as the mountains Prue had viewed up the Hudson; nothing local could compare to them. As she went about the work of the distillery, Prue sometimes glimpsed the Brooklyn anchorage from the corner of her eye, and she would feel as if she'd suddenly turned a corner in a strange city and come upon it, by accident, for the first time. At such moments she felt an emotion she could only describe as awe—a brightness in the chest; a sense of wonder that such a thing existed in the world, quite apart from her role in creating it. She realized with humility what a marvel it was such a bridge could be built at all, let alone partly by the authorship of her own hand.

Prue further marveled that the first season of building had ended without loss of life. (The newspapers also remarked this. Mr. Harrison attributed it, in the *Argus*, to "Benjamin & Mrs. Horsfield's punctilious care in supervision"; the others, to luck.) There had been numerous injuries— burns, fractures, blows to the head; in the worst thus far, a rope transporting a large stone had broken, and the impact had shattered both feet of unlucky George White, whom Dr. de Bouton believed would never walk again—but none had proven fatal. The men were superstitious enough to spit to protect themselves at the beginning of each day, and religious enough to visit Will Severn's church far more regularly than the locals; but

ancient Elliott Fortune, who'd grown friendly with some of them while
drinking his evening pint, told Prue they all believed, more or less sincerely, she must have done some kind of witchcraft to protect the works.
She had known Fortune all her life, and considered telling him her
thoughts about Susannah and the miscarried child protecting the works;
but she soon thought better of it, and kept silent. If the workers wanted
to think she'd blessed the place, she would accept that benediction.

The laborers could not stay the winter. Though there was a few
weeks' extra pay to be earned laying in stores for the next building season
and securing the building sites against vandalism, there would be no work
thereafter; and no matter how hearty they claimed to be, the men could
not sleep in tents through the frost. Prue and Tem managed to find
places for some in the distillery, and others found positions with the
Luquers and Schermerhorns. A few traveled up the straits to Queen's
County to see if employment might be had at the Longacre Brewery.
Olympia was still growing, so there were floors to lay and laths to plaster;
the same was true in Manhattan, which continued to swallow up her forest in northward expansion, and to replace old farmsteads with city
blocks. The rest of the men would return to their families, some bearing
the fruits of eight months' labor, while those who'd taken advantage of
the proximity of the Liberty Tavern and the Twin Tankards would go
home with lighter pockets. Before leaving, however, many signed contracts to return the following April. Ben and Prue counted this a true success. If any spell had been cast, Prue thought, it was in the care the men
gave their work. She was anxious to retain such meticulous laborers as
long as possible.

The last stragglers had left the encampment by late November. Where
ordinarily would have stood the dry stubs of a year's mown grain, the
ground was pocked as from musket fire from hundreds of tent staves,
and worn bare from the traffic. What dull brown grass remained was
matted down in circles, as if deer had lain there. "Looks like the war all
over again," Mr. Livingston said to Prue in passing.

"I daresay we are less harmed by my bridgeworks than by enemy occupation," she replied.

Mr. Livingston fingered the fine brim of his hat. "I hope you prove
correct. Good day, Mrs. Horsfield." He continued up the Ferry Road toward Joe's tavern.

Prue stalked along her fence. She was riled by his unkindness, but remembered that he had been almost ruined by the quartering of British troops; no doubt the sights and sounds of the war remained fresh in his memory. Furthermore, she knew he was skeptical of the bridge, and supposed she should expect him to lash out against it.

Though the distillery still hummed and the docks still thronged, Brooklyn seemed quiet with the bridgeworks shut down. For eight months, it had kept her and her husband busy from dawn to dusk, six days a week; without its clamor and tumult, even the proprietor of a flourishing manufactory had time to mourn a lost child, and to wonder why no sign of one who might take her place had yet appeared. As Prue paced the length of her back fence, looking northwestward to Manhattan, she could remember the intensity with which she'd believed that city another sphere of existence. She could almost imagine the past twenty years hadn't happened: that her parents and Johanna still lived, Will Severn had never come among them, and Ben and Isaiah were simply her dear friends, the web of obligation that now bound them as far from her imagination as the empire of Japan.

The distillery was preparing to ship large orders to fuel the debaucheries of Christmas and Twelfth Night and to provision the taverns before the waterways froze. This was what Winship Daughters Gin did every year at this time; but of course, a great deal had changed. Each time she looked out to the river, Prue saw the Gothic archway rising from her property and the great pyramid looming on the far horizon. If Susannah had remained with them, she would have been nearly a year old: sitting, perhaps crawling, and with a mouth full of teeth. She might have known how to say a thing or two, "Mama" or "dog." Prue knew it was foolish to imagine she had bartered one for the other—she scoffed at herself for it, much as she derided herself for ever having thought the damned lived in New York City—yet the thought persisted, and with it, its own irrational mathematics. Would she give back this bridge, she asked herself, if she might have her daughter? What galled her more than her propensity to ask was that she didn't know the answer. Prue hoped wherever Susannah Horsfield had gone, she was pleased with the work her parents had done, and did not curse them for having inadvertently traded her for it.

Twenty-one

A LONG WINTER

The river froze again in January of 1801. Pearl had apparently been out walking early in the morning, though the day was dull and white, and she came bounding into the kitchen, her breath labored. "How now?" Ben asked, putting his coffee down and rising to greet her. "We were worried where you might be."

Ice-bridge, she wrote, then dropped her book on its chain to raise her hand to her heart.

They might as well have been a table of children for the way they bolted their food and bundled into their coats and boots. Tem was often sluggish from liquor in the mornings, but she raced down the hill faster than any of them. As they passed the distillery, Prue saw Isaiah, waiting for the workers so he could spring them on holiday. He had already notified the slaves, who were out on the ice. "Come with us," Prue said to him.

"As soon as someone arrives to take over," he said. "Go; I'll be along with the children."

"Cross up by the bridge!" Prue called to Tem. Tem turned to glance at her, then continued to run. Prue felt excited to cross near the footing. The ferries were a scant quarter and half mile upriver, but had never afforded so close an approximation of what it would be like to walk over the bridge.

It seemed every inhabitant of Brooklyn and New York was out to try the ice; and it was clear how much these places had grown in the past nineteen years. In 1782 there had been room to slide and skate, but now the whole river, from Red Hook to the Wallabout, was packed with people in brown and gray coats and fur hats. Where there had been half a dozen mongers, there were scores, selling everything from candy twists to warm cow's milk. Ben took Prue's hand. "You look as if you'd never seen a city before," he said.

"I rather feel that way," she said. She remembered from childhood wondering if the ice would groan underfoot; but how different the river looked now, with the stump of their great pyramid looming into view. Her heart cried out for her parents. She would dearly have liked to show them what she had done; and she thought what a pleasure it would be to share some simple holiday fun with them, such as buying a paper cone of roasted chestnuts from a hawker. She hoped they had, indeed, gone to Heaven and could give her a bit of good luck or outright help. The governor had sent the year's money on time, but Ben had spent it on timber before it arrived. This would not cause undue trouble for the nonce— they still had some of their neighbors' contributions in the bank and had not yet spent any of their own money—but Prue had begun to wonder what might happen come spring. She knew it was only a matter of time before the newssheets learned of the shortfall; and she did not know what would become of her neighbors' support then. As she walked with Ben across the river that day, she asked Matty and Roxana, wherever they were, to send a sign that everything would work out in favor of the bridge.

The temperature rose steeply that night, and the river thawed in a rushing torrent; in the morning, as Tem and Prue prepared to leave for the distillery, the Ferry Road erupted into chaos. A saddled black mare was rearing in the middle of the road. She had already kicked out a few pikes from the Livingstons' fence, and seemed intent on breaking more; she neighed fiercely, and rolled the whites of her eyes at whomever approached. A group of men had surrounded her and were approaching her with gentle words and outstretched hands; but they and the horse kept slipping in the mud that had melted since the night before. As Ben went to offer his assistance, Prue saw Joe Loosely, who was good with horses, jogging toward them down the road. If the mare's owner was anywhere nearby, he was embarrassed by her behavior and had made himself scarce.

Prue was so intent on this spectacle, it was a moment before she realized there was another, farther down the road, where a similarly large crowd had gathered. When Prue craned her neck, she could see a dark-haired man, lying supine and still in the middle of the road. Young Gregor Joralemon was out in the street, directing wagons and riders around the fellow, while the family's two serving women bickered with each other and fanned absently at the man's torso. The man had been thrown, then, by the crazed horse—a common enough circumstance, but people ordinarily stood, wiped down their prats, cursed out their horses, and went on about their business. This man, however, was not moving.

"Someone must have called de Bouton by now?" Abiah asked.

Tem squinted to see better. "Hard to say."

Abiah retied her apron, then set out up the road to get him, skirting the spooked horse as quickly as she could.

Dr. de Bouton had already been called, and met her only a short ways up the street. Even from a distance, Prue thought he looked haggard, from drink or from being too old a man to suffer through another emergency. As Abiah hurried him past the Winship gate, he bowed his head to them all, standing in the dooryard. Prue hoped a new doctor would move to town soon and relieve him of some of his burden.

"Let's follow him," Tem said. Others were already trailing in his wake.

"Vulture," Prue said, but also went out into the street. She added, "Perhaps there's something we can do to help."

But there was nothing they could do. Joe had the mad horse by the reins and was being dragged around the street by her, as in a horse-breaking contest; and de Bouton had to push his way through a crowd of people to reach his patient. Ivo Joralemon was leaning on his crutches at the edge of the crowd, his face drawn with anxiety. One of the serving women shouted at Abiah to back off; Abiah moved a few paces away and spoke to one of the Cortelyous' slaves. After a moment in conversation, she came running back to meet Tem and Prue. She had not bothered to put her coat on and had her arms wrapped around herself for warmth. "The Joralemons' woman shooed me off," she said angrily.

"Why so?" Prue asked.

"She said something about a curse."

"Who was thrown?" Tem asked.

"It's Jacob Boerum."

Prue asked, "Does he live?"

Abiah shrugged her thin shoulders and shivered. "No one's quite sure. The story is, he and his friends were carousing last night in the countryside past Cobbleskill, when they ran out of liquor. There was no aqua vitae to be had between there and the Ferry Tavern; but you see, the haunted fort was on the road in between."

Dr. de Bouton was shouting for the crowd to clear off.

"But it isn't haunted," Tem said. "Ben and Isaiah told us that to frighten us, when we were small."

Abiah's eyes widened. "Well, one of the Joralemons' women said Boerum made a profane statement about the ghost and got on his horse to fetch the liquor. He never returned, and never made it up to Loosely's, for no one there saw him and his flask is still empty. And there he lies, in the road."

"Go in," Prue said, "before you catch your own death."

Abiah nodded and ran back up toward the house.

Some of the Joralemon servants passed a long plank into the crowd, that the young man might be laid upon it and carried out.

Now Prue was shivering, too, despite the mild weather and her coat. The horse certainly seemed to have been driven mad; and if it had happened down by the fort, Jacob had had a long, unpleasant ride to the Joralemons'.

"There's nothing we can do," Tem said, peering to get a better look at the body as it was hoisted aloft. One pale hand dangled from the edge of the board and barely twitched. Blood matted the hair over his brow, but from that distance, Prue couldn't see whence it flowed. "Come on. To work with us."

Dr. de Bouton was issuing orders about the boy's removal to his father's home; and Tem put her pinkies in the corners of her mouth to signal the distillery workers to go. Many startled at the sharp sound, but they began walking down toward the water in a boisterous clump. Up the road, Prue saw Joe had managed to subdue the horse somewhat and was speaking to her in a gentle tone as she jerked her neck sharply to one side. Joe spared a dark glance for Prue as she passed.

"D'ye think it's a hex?" Scipio's young apprentice asked Tem.

Tem answered, "Don't be a child."

But the men were arguing volubly about Jacob Boerum's hubris. The slave Actæon wondered aloud if Boerum's mishap was a portent about the bridge.

"Bite your tongue," Prue instructed him. She tried to force herself to laugh, but it sounded false to her own ear.

"I meant no offense, ma'am. Only that it happened direct across the street from your property."

"Yes, we see," Tem said.

"And it's what folks are saying."

Prue, meanwhile, was horrified. She had asked her parents to send her a sign about the bridge's prospects; and at the same time as she dreaded what Boerum's accident foretold, she derided herself for having the least faith in omens, when she so disdained such belief in others.

All the machinery was up and running only an hour behind schedule, but the mood at the distillery was somber. Anyone who stepped out for a stretch or a smoke was hammered with questions the moment he returned, and Isaiah reported a near accident of inattention in the cooperage. After the previous day's unexpected holiday, the brewhouse, stillhouse, and rectifying room seemed preternaturally loud and thick with smoke. Even Tem, who as far as Prue knew had no room in her heart for spooks or hexes, was distracted all day.

It was little surprise when news went around early the next morning that Jacob Boerum had died of his injuries and that his horse, though mollified, had continued to thrash and foam and had been shot toward evening. The Boerums would hold a funeral late that very afternoon, though the earth of the churchyard was still frozen and the men would have to use picks to dig a grave. It was eight in the morning when the news bearers arrived at the countinghouse, but Prue offered them a dram before sending them on their way.

"We'll close the works for the funeral," she said to Tem.

"I don't know," Tem replied. "We lost the entire day Monday."

"The poor man died a hundred yards from our gate."

Tem blew a breath out through her lips. "You and I should go, but we cannot close for every death in Brookland—we'd never make another ounce of gin."

"Tem," Prue said, trying to control her temper, "the neighbors are saying it's a portent about the bridge. The papers will be close on their heels. We must show our sympathy."

"It's hardly my fault people are foolish," Tem said. As Prue did not reply, Tem took the bottle of gin from her hand and poured a splash into her coffee cup. After she drank it down she set both bottle and cup on the desk and said, "I know you're right, but I shall not be held responsible if this distillery fails." She set out to ring the assembly bell to notify the workers.

In the middle of the afternoon, they returned to the house to change their clothes, and found Pearl with her hair combed back neatly and with a new brown ribbon on her bonnet. Jacob Boerum had never paid her any mind, but Prue felt touched her sister would go to such trouble to pay him her respects.

As they walked together up to Mr. Severn's church, Prue thought how it had been just over two years since they'd laid James Weatherspoon in the churchyard and one since they'd buried her own daughter. One of the Cortelyou women had died in childbed the past summer, and a young Quaker housewife down past the tannery had died of a stomach ailment; and this had been a good year, in which none of the ships docked in the port had brought virulent illness such as had carried off Israel Horsfield. Why did it seem such a tragedy to see a young man laid in his grave? Jacob Boerum hardly deserved lamentation. He had been an only son, and of course his parents were prostrated; but he had also been a profligate and a bounder, who'd done nothing for the improvement of his father's property nor learned any profession but drinking. He'd flirted with Mrs. Tilley's daughter, but advertised around town he would never marry a shopkeeper's child. Prue had imagined Jacob Boerum's death would merit less public grief than the death of someone useful to the community; but this was not so. The young Boerum had been well liked by the Twin Tankards' regular customers, whom he had routinely stood drinks; and many people no doubt attended the funeral because of John Boerum's wealth; but beyond this, there was an intrinsic sadness in a man's untimely death, regardless of what kind of man he'd been. Severn used the opportunity to preach on the mystery of God's plan for us all; and though out of tact he did not speak against drunkenness, he had some words for those who believed in ghosts.

"Do you think, gentlemen," he said, craning his undershot chin upward, "any force in the universe to be stronger than the infinite love and mercy of our Lord, Jesus Christ? Do you think the anger of a soldier, twenty years in Mr. Remsen's asparagus field, can rival the power that made Heaven and earth?"

Someone coughed, and half the eyes in the church were filled with tears, Prue wondered if of sadness or relief.

"There cannot be ghosts, nor omens, for good Christians," he said. Tem yanked at the collar of her dress. "There is only the sorrow of Jacob's unseasonable departure from our midst; and the joy of his return to his Maker."

Mrs. Boerum was sobbing as if nothing could be less certain; and continued to do so while Severn concluded and while some of the prominent young men of the town, Ben among them, surrounded and lifted Jacob's coffin to carry it out to the churchyard. Dusk was already descending, and the church bell sounded small and fragile on the chill air. As they filed out, Prue found herself passing close by Will Severn. Although he appeared occupied with his own thoughts, she reached a hand toward him and said, "Thank you for your sermon."

He nodded, still looking at the ground.

It was too far to walk to the Boerums' in such weather, so everyone would pile into carriages and carts; Ben had asked to have one of the distillery's wagons waiting for them by the gate. But as the crowd dispersed, Will Severn continued to stand at the head of the grave, watching the diggers shovel frozen dirt onto what had been the Boerums' dearest hope. Pearl was intent, watching him. Tem gave a tug at her sleeve, but Pearl held up a finger for them to wait.

"Do you need a moment?" Prue asked.

Pearl nodded, and Tem said, "If you like, we can go with Ben in the wagon, and you can find another ride."

Pearl turned to her sisters with a careworn smile, then approached Mr. Severn. He stepped aside toward the graveyard fence, and Pearl followed him. They were nearly hidden in the shadows of the bare ash trees.

Prue walked over toward Susannah's bright little headstone, and Tem followed her. "Glad to see she's finally got a suitor," Tem said, and pulled at her collar again. She was unused to the dress, and said it itched her.

Prue said, "Excuse me?" She was thinking of Susannah.

"Like to come with us?" Simon Dufresne asked as he walked toward the road.

"No, thank you," Prue answered, and Tem added, "Ben has one of our wagons." Peg raised her hand in greeting, and Simon touched his pale brim to them before walking on. To Prue Tem said, "I believe you heard me."

Prue turned and glanced over her shoulder, to see if she could still make out Will Severn and her sister there under the trees. If Tem was correct, this would explain Pearl's absences, and Will Severn's solicitude toward the family, but Prue wasn't certain she could accept this explanation. "I don't know what I think," she said.

Tem laughed quietly. "But you see, it isn't up to you."

Prue mentally bade her daughter's bones good-bye, and she and Tem walked arm in arm toward the gate.

Ben was waiting on the turnpike with the team, and leaned down to help them both up. "Hello," he said, kissing Prue on the cheek. "Where's Pearl?"

Tem said, "She'll be along."

Ben wrapped his arm around Prue's waist, then took the reins again. Brooklyn's few smoking streetlamps did little to dispel the evening's gloom, and petered out altogether as Ben drove past the Remsens' bare fields toward Boerums' estate. When they arrived, the whole hillside was dotted with the dark forms of horses and carriages, mostly tethered to trees.

"I've eaten enough funeral cake to last me the rest of my days," Tem said.

"I, too," Prue said. "Pray there'll be no more for a good long while." But all she could think of was Pearl.

Prue had made her way through a whole pint of ale before Pearl arrived on the minister's heels. Her cheeks were pink, and Prue immediately jumped to read this as a sign; but it was cold outdoors. Nevertheless, Pearl did not meet her eye.

"Tem?" Prue said, as she watched them help themselves to tea.

Tem said, "You often treat me as if I couldn't lace my own boots, and here you are, doubting what looks you square in the face." She took Prue's empty cup along with her own to the sideboard, which sagged in the middle, it was so heavily laden with food and drink.

Ben was engaged in conversation with Theunis van Vechten, so Prue kept watching Pearl. It was, in fact, clear as day she was in love with Will Severn, and clear he was solicitous of her as well. Prue could see in the way her sister moved that every inch of her knew, at every moment, how close or far Will Severn was. What shocked Prue was that Pearl had never told her; and even more than this, that she herself had neither noticed nor suspected her of the slightest intrigue. Her sister was twenty-two years old, and quite pretty, if small. A man accustomed to her peculiarity might easily fall in love with her; and Pearl had always been the largest-hearted of any of them, having been able to love a difficult old woman like Johanna as much as her own father. Why, Prue asked herself, had she never considered the possibility of Pearl being courted? Before she could work it through, Tem brought her a fresh mug of ale. The distraction ir-ritated her, though at the same time, Prue felt relieved to have some new object upon which to concentrate.

"Are you unwell?" Ben asked her, when Theunis chanced to be drawn into another conversation by Simon Dufresne. "I don't know if I've ever seen you so quiet."

"I'm fine," Prue said, "only thinking."

Ben nodded, as if to say it had been quite a year, all around.

When they left that evening, they rode home in silence, with Pearl stretched out in the back of the wagon and watching the dull black sky go past. As they drove along the dark road, Prue thought it was no won-der her neighbors thought the ruined fort haunted; but she felt no ghostly emanations as they drove past it. "Pearl?" she asked, turning around on the seat. She could barely distinguish her darkly clad sister from the wagon bed.

Pearl reached up to touch Prue's sleeve so she would know she'd heard her.

"Why did you not ride down with us after the funeral?"

Pearl opened her arms wide, her hands the brightest objects in sight. How could she answer, in a moving wagon, in such darkness? Prue had no choice but to sit with her question until they arrived home; and as soon as they did, Pearl scooped up her cat from the hearth, went to her room off the kitchen, and shut the door. She did not offer an explanation the next morning, and Prue felt she could not hound her for one.

Severn's words had done little to comfort the grieving parents, and nothing to assuage the general suspicion Boerum's death had been a sign of worse to come. Everyone but Scipio's apprentice was shrewd enough to avoid saying anything to the Winships or Horsfields, but rumors wafted into the countinghouse, along with the sounds of the port and the odors of fish and smoke. It was a fine bridge, some of the neighbors thought, but it had angered God by its pretension; others seemed to believe, as Prue herself did, to her great shame, that it would not rest until a life had been sacrificed to its construction; one of the New York news sheets ran a column the next day claiming the bridge was a dreadful idea, and any reasonable person had known from the start it would fail—though thus far, excepting its cost, it was going according to plan, and with remarkably little mishap. The sadness of knowing everyone around her had concerns about her bridge yet would not express them to her was nothing compared to the sadness of having lost her daughter; yet the two circumstances were bound up together somehow, and left Prue feeling hollow with grief.

"What I don't understand," Prue told Tem, as they worked together at the hydraulic press, the steam of its operation bathing their already slick faces in a fine warm mist, "is how they could have turned against it so rapidly. They all signed our petition."

"People are fickle, Prue," Tem said, and brought the full weight of her body to bear on the lever. Steam billowed out as the essence of angelica trickled into its bucket. Tem unlocked the lever with an expert swagger.

"But why do they see a connection in the first place?"

"Sorry?"

Prue swept the spent herbs into the slop bucket. "What has Jacob Boerum's death to do with the bridge?"

Tem wiped her sleeve across her brow as Prue laid fresh angelica on the press. "Geographical accident. People can't help looking for a cause."

"I don't understand why it must be this one."

"Because it's a great gamble, and people fear it as much as they desire it." She watched the press grimly as she brought its jaw down. Ever since Marcel's accident, and despite their scorn for the superstitions of others, they'd both been leery of the machine, as if it were hungry for blood. "I wish I had some better explanation, Prue," she said. She stepped back and leaned against the nearest post. "But I don't."

"I think I do," Prue said. She looked around to make certain no one else was within earshot. "Two men of influence have stood against this bridge from the start, and they both believe in omens."

Tem said, "No. You cannot—"

"How difficult would it have been to insinuate some passing words of malice that awful day?"

Tem stepped forward again to unlock the machine. "Why don't you banish that thought from your mind," she said, "because it doesn't do you any good there. Losee and Joe would never—"

"We don't know," Prue said. And she found that the more she tried to relinquish the thought, the firmer became its grip upon her.

There were no stranger happenings in Brooklyn the rest of that winter than the ordinary spate of turned ankles, rotten potatoes, head colds, and damp firewood. The abutments stood grandly above the gray river, and withstood the onslaught of snow and sleet. Their foundations held firm through the rush of spring thaw, and Prue knew she should be satisfied with the work and pleased the workers would be back among them soon. But she was concerned and preoccupied with the opinions of her neighbors; and perhaps even more so with her sister Pearl. Surely, Prue thought, it should have come as no surprise that Pearl had an interior life as rich as any other's; that she should love and be loved, that she should keep secrets. But that her sister should keep secrets from *her* seemed impossible. In whom else might Pearl confide? She was neither close to nor distant from Tem, and Abiah could still barely read to understand her thoughts; to whom should she have spoken of love but to Prue? Yet Pearl had said nothing, and continued to say nothing, though her absences, explained by "walking," kept on. Prue supposed it was possible she and Tem had jumped to conclusions; but she did not think so.

She did not, however, question Pearl. She could not articulate why, except that it seemed more correct—perhaps even nobler—to wait for an admission than to demand one. It seemed what propriety required of her, as, after all, Pearl had not been caught doing anything bad, merely suspected of doing something human. Nevertheless, as she went about her business, Prue ate herself out with care, worrying about Pearl and the bridge and Susannah. March's heavy rains came as an unimaginable relief, for they promised construction would soon recommence and give Prue something singular on which to focus her attention.

Twenty-two

THE SECOND SEASON

In March of 1801, the same month in which Thomas Jefferson began to serve as President of the United States, all of Ben and Prue's captains and two thirds of their laborers from the previous year returned to sign up once more for the construction. Prue could spare little time for news beyond her own mill yard. At first she worried where the remainder of the workers had gone; but the returnees drew along many new recruits in their wake. Ben had employment to offer every qualified man who applied, and they came by the score. Ben hired fifty more than he had the previous year, though it meant they would have to spill over into Isaiah's fallow field, a circumstance bound to make Patience scowl. As there was still a balance to be struck between Prue's desire to have a hand in the construction and the workers' native (and, Ben said, understandable) distrust of a forewoman, she would continue to share her responsibilities with Marcel Dufresne. Marcel was delighted with the arrangement. Though his desire to become a rectifier was still likely to be thwarted, to manage a crew at work on the bridge was a man's job, a far sight better than totting up sums in the ledgers. He spoke nothing of this to Isaiah, only to Ben.

Instead of two divisions, the workers split into four that season, and Matthias Osier and Alphonsus Weatherspoon became foremen to help manage the extra men. Two crews would continue to work on the abutments, jobs that required ever more refined skills as the workers progressed closer to the tops of the structures and needed to begin chiseling out decorative scrolls and vines in the stone. The other two would begin to construct the twin levers on the iron foundation rods that had been set into the faces of the abutments the autumn before. Because there were fewer men on each task, the work seemed to progress more slowly, though with the same care and attention as previously. Ed and Pete Domer proved to have an innate understanding of the method for constructing the levers, so by May, Prue had promoted them to captains of the Brooklyn lever's team. They were both young, and had had little good fortune and less recognition in their lives until that point; when Prue announced their new positions, their boyish faces lit up with pride.

As spring progressed, the levers began to emerge from the abutments, far more slowly than Prue had imagined. The method they'd devised for the second model proved sound at the larger scale; but to move members as heavy as those the bridge required simply took longer than either Prue or Ben had known. For each nascent lever, Ben had built its crane, employing the pulleys to allow one man to do the lifting work of a dozen. No matter how well the men greased the ropes and oiled the machines, these screeched loudly enough to wake the dead, and the harbor seals that had been accustomed to sunning themselves on the wharves moved, barking and snuffling, down to Red Hook. With great care, and with his ears stuffed with cotton wool and his head turned aside to avoid the awful sound, the crane operator would crank to draw a single piece of shaped timber up off the ground or a barge. These pieces of timber were unwieldy, but as the crane man cranked, two other men would guide the crane's tip with ropes, thus swinging the timber close to its proper alignment.

Once the timber was dangling over the water, a yard or so from its final destination, the crane operator would bind off his rope tightly on a cleat, while the two guides did likewise with theirs, holding the timber as steady as possible. Then four more men would sling themselves into leather hammocks, gingerly descend the bridge's face, and ease the great piece of wood into position. These men carried mallets and sharp iron studs in their harnesses, and once the member was locked in place, they would use these to fix it there. Prue thought it would have been difficult to say which job relating to the construction was the most dangerous, but these men who climbed down the face of the bridge in slings appeared both most brazen and most vulnerable; and each time they ascended again to safety, those nearby would swear their delight at their companions' good fortune.

As had been the system in building both the models, Prue and Ben directed their men to affix those timbers closest to the abutments to their framework, then to continue building riverward; and as in the models, the backward slope of the beams allowed them to transfer their weight shoreward into the anchorages, and not out toward their unfinished tips. Once a timber had been secured to one of the downriver spandrels, the operator would swing his crane a hundred eighty degrees northward and complete the same operation for the corresponding position on the upriver face of the lever. When the two sides in concert had traveled toward the center of the river a distance of eight feet, the men would hoist up the pitched planks for the roadbed and build it out; after which they would swivel the crane ninety degrees, to face the center of the river, and drive it out nearly to the lever's edge. Here began the most time-consuming part of the operation: drawing up the thick iron beams that supported the whole endeavor. They were heavy enough that to lift them two men had to work the crank in concert, while four guided the ropes. Once they were in place, men would again lower themselves down in harnesses, this time from the tip of the lever. Here each removed a jug of acid from his sling and poured it into the mortises where the rod would go, taking care not to spill any on their own gloved hands or boots. Then, quickly and in concert, they guided in the iron rod and held it there with all their might until the few drops of pitch released from the wood had set. Each time this operation was completed without anyone being knocked senseless by the rod, released to the water by a shoddy rope, or burned with acid, the nearby men would also cheer.

In this way, day by day, the bridge inched closer to the middle of the river.

Prue believed her years of experience running the distillery helped keep the men safe in their labor. She made certain the cranes were oiled and their ropes checked daily; and if workers were to hang in harnesses a hundred-odd feet above high tide, she'd be damned if their ropes and knots were not scanned before each descent and if other men weren't standing on the roadway above them, holding fast their ropes in case of accident. Each night, when the regular workmen trooped wearily back up to their camp, the crew foremen and the captains—those six who'd built the second model with Ben, and Ed and Pete Domer—remained at the work sites and personally saw that each knife was sharpened, each hammer head firmly attached to its shaft, each jug of acid well stoppered for the night. Before they left the premises, they drew the gates shut across the accessways to remind the foolhardy of their peril. On the New York side, there was hardly a moment of construction Ben did not himself oversee with Alphonsus Weatherspoon to assist him; on the Brooklyn side, either Prue or Marcel was generally available, and if not, Matthias Osier stood in. At times questions went unanswered, supplies ran thin, and arguments erupted and descended to blows; but these occurrences were infrequent, given the size and danger of the bridgeworks. Prue believed all these safeguards were the result of the distillery training she had received under her father's tutelage; and each day that a hundred fifty men returned more or less unharmed to camp to smoke, drink, and bathe their hands and faces in buckets, she wished Matty Winship still lived, so she might thank him for his guidance.

She recognized as well that it was not only her experience that kept the men safe, nor even Ben's and Marcel's fastidiousness: It was some amalgam of good luck and God's will. For this she was thankful. She tried not to dwell on the possibility that luck, or divine favor, could change as quickly as the weather.

For each six days' labor completed without significant mishap, Prue went down on the Saturday afternoon to Loosely's auctions and bought pigs to roast, which Scipio Jones slaughtered. The workers delighted in this Sunday feast; and many of them spent the remainder of the afternoon burying potatoes in the dirt at the edges of the fire, and sitting around talking and waiting for them to blacken.

April slid into May and May into June, all with no incidents more serious than broken bones. Prue began to wonder if it was possible to build a bridge without loss of life. Though neither she nor Ben thought it likely they'd complete construction by the end of the year as they had planned, each lever was coming along well. The only trouble was that by June, Ben had spent all the state's money, along with every penny of the contributions they had raised. He insisted—and Prue knew without his saying anything—that he had mismanaged nothing; but the stone had proven prohibitively expensive, and the extra men and extra time the bridge would need were taking their toll.

He and Prue sat by one balmy spring evening as Marcel and Isaiah pored over the bridge's books. All three men were nursing cigars, and the view from the countinghouse windows was dimmed by the smoke.

"Nothing," Isaiah said at last, and bowed his head down to scratch it with his free hand. "I can see no error or mismanagement, but you are nearly a thousand in debt."

Marcel said, "I don't know, Mr. Horsfield. It might have been possible to acquire the iron beams less expensively farther afield, but you would then have had a greater cost in shipping them."

"I think that's so," Ben said. "I wouldn't choose to have done it otherwise."

Marcel nodded and tapped the ash from the end of his cigar.

Isaiah said, "You don't seem especially concerned about it, Benno. Some action will have to be taken. You owe money to the foundry, and there's nothing with which to pay the workers come Saturday."

"I am concerned," Ben replied, "but uncertain, as yet, how to proceed."

Prue said, "We have always said we'd make up whatever was necessary from our private funds, and I suppose we'll begin to do so today. But if the bridgeworks runs into a third season, as I think we all know it will, we won't be able to finance it on our own."

"I shall write the new governor immediately," Ben said, "and take up another subscription among our neighbors."

Governor Jay's term had expired, and George Clinton, who had served as governor many times before, had come out of retirement to be reelected. Prue hoped he would be as well disposed as his predecessor toward the bridge. "There can't be much more to be had in either of those precincts?" she asked.

Ben said, "Perhaps some."

Isaiah sat up. "You could cut the workers' pay," he suggested. "Here and on the bridge."

"We can't do that," Prue said. "It's skilled and dangerous work in both places. It would be unfair, and they wouldn't stay."

Isaiah's countenance showed he agreed with her; the deep furrow between his brows evinced his worry. "I fear you won't be able to support the venture long from your own funds; perhaps not even so long as you suppose. Business never picked up again after Epiphany. I've no idea why, but receipts remain down."

"We've done nothing to merit it," Prue said, thinking that if she'd changed the method of rectifying, they might well have. What Tem called tergiversation was, in fact, yet another stroke of good fortune. "The quality of our goods is the same, and we continue to ship as promptly as ever."

Isaiah shook his head. "We'll find out what's gone wrong; but in the meanwhile, I think we should discuss how you might decrease expenditures in some other area."

"Such as?" Ben asked. "It's not as if I take wages myself, or I could give them up."

Isaiah said, "Materials."

Ben sucked on his cigar while he thought it through, but he shook his head the whole time. "No," he said. "Marcel is correct about the iron members. As for the timber, if we purchase inferior goods, very soon we'll have nothing but a pile of sticks in the water."

Prue was poised to shout out against this eventuality, but Ben put forth his free hand to comfort her before she could.

"Understood," Isaiah said. "I only wonder if you might bargain your supplier down. If he could ship you your timber at three cents less the foot—"

Ben said, "He has given me a very good price already," and at the same time Prue said, "I don't like this."

"I only think it might render your finances a hair less perilous."

Ben said, "I now know why she offered you your position all those years ago."

Isaiah smiled. His cigar had sat idle awhile, and he took up Ben's to relight it. "For this week," he went on, "I wonder if you might consider taking half my salary, toward paying the workers."

"No," Prue said, and Ben said, "That's impossible."

"It needn't be an outright gift. You may consider it a loan. Heaven knows I could live on half my salary for a month, perhaps even a year."

Ben said, "It could well take longer than that."

"Ben," Prue said, "you can't even entertain the notion. It isn't right." To Isaiah she said, "I will not take bread from your children's mouths when I have not yet put in a penny of my own."

"It isn't as baleful as all that, but very well," Isaiah said. "The offer will stand, however. I don't see how you can get quit of this morass without some sacrifices."

"I could give up part of my salary, too," Marcel chimed in.

"No," Prue said. "Both of you. I should sooner mortgage this distillery."

The room fell silent a moment, in which Prue heard Ben's chair creak and her watch and Isaiah's ticking.

"I don't know if Tem would allow that," Ben said.

"Tem wouldn't like it, but she also doesn't own it," Prue said. "So far as the law is concerned, Tem is an *employée*. As, I suppose, am I." As they were all looking at her uncomfortably, she stood, brought down the bottle and cups from the shelf, and poured out a round of the wares.

"I think you are perhaps oversolicitous of my children," Isaiah said, raising his cup and resolutely ignoring her last statement, "and not solicitous enough of your own sisters."

"I disagree," Prue said. "It's not as if I should ruin anyone by taking out a mortgage. As if Ben should. And there's no guarantee we'll need to. We can meet the payroll from our own pockets for the nonce; and who knows what Governor Clinton may do for us."

Isaiah once again let out a sigh, and leaned toward Prue with both forearms on the table and his delicate cup cradled in both hands. "Prue. Either the bridge is a sound venture or it is not. If you will risk seeing everything your father worked for auctioned off at Loosely's, I conclude it must be sound. If so, and if my small contribution may be of use to you, I will make it gladly."

Prue thought she would sooner die than take his money, but she thanked him anyway.

Ben said, "We have not spent all the proceeds from the sale of my house. We shall use that, Izzy, before coming to you."

Prue was suddenly overwhelmed with exhaustion. "It's been a long day," she said, "and I don't think we can resolve this issue by speaking of it further. Shall I see you in the morning?"

"Of course," Isaiah said, and Marcel said, "Good evening, Miss Winship."

"I'll be home in a moment," Ben added.

Prue went down the open stairs to the deserted mill yard. The air was warm, and the setting sun lit the sky a vivid, darkening blue, almost yellow at the horizon, behind the pyramid and the black spires of Manhattan. The longest days of the year were upon them, with all the extra work they allowed. The breeze from Clover Hill carried down the sweet, rich scent of ripening corn, which revived her. Through the countinghouse window, Prue could see Ben, Isaiah, and Marcel still talking, their cigars puffing smoke. She had excused herself with the intention of going to bed, but she no longer wished to. Instead, she climbed Joralemon's Lane and set out along the Ferry Road toward the churchyard.

Prue visited her family graves only infrequently. She knew Pearl went to visit their parents, but could not imagine what she did there—stare mournfully at their names? Imagine what had become of their dear forms in so many years underground? Prue saw no use in it, nor in spending time at the grave of her daughter. She knew it would only sadden her. She no more believed Matty and Roxana Winship and Susannah Horsfield were contained in those plots of soil than that they were residing in Manhattan. But as she left the countinghouse that evening, she thought the thing she most wished for was to be able to ask her parents for advice; and if she could not do that, she could at least sit by them.

The graveyard's wooden gate lolled open, though there was no one inside. Dandelions had run rampant across the hillside, and Prue wondered if it would be any more morbid than buying the fruit of Mr. Remsen's asparagus field to bring some of the greens home to Abiah. For the moment, however, she simply sat down, and looked at her parents' two engraved names, and at Susannah's, removed a slight distance, as if those names bore any true resemblance to the beings they called to mind. *Sukey*, she thought, and tried to imagine what the child would have looked like if she'd lived, what sort of nature she might have had. Then Prue's mind trailed off into emptiness, she didn't know for how long.

The sun was nearly set, and Prue did not want any of her neighbors—particularly Will Severn—to see her sitting alone in the cemetery, waiting for dark; but she tried not to distract herself worrying about this, and to formulate the question she had come to ask. "Would you think it rash of me . . ." she said, looking down at her father's grave and feeling foolish. "Would you consider it a colossal mistake," she said, "to risk everything you worked for, in service of this bridge?" She cleared her throat as if she might go on; but there was nothing more to say. Her whole head immediately flooded with tears, as she imagined her father raining down blame upon her, though he had not been a reproachful man, or at least not to his eldest daughter. Had he been there to advise her, he would have counseled caution; but he would likely have been tickled at the idea of finding his Prue a bridge architect.

Damn the eyes of every man who said I couldn't train ye, she could almost hear him saying, with a slight chuckle. It would have been like him to forget his own ambivalence.

She sat and watched as the shadows obscured their names, then the very forms of the stones. When it was dark, she picked her way back to the fence and set out along the road toward home. She felt as though she had received an answer, although she knew she had not.

Abiah hadn't held supper for her. Tem was in the midst of gesticulating toward Ben with her fork, but stopped midsentence when Prue shut the door behind her. "Where were you?" Tem asked, without accusation. The small windows were open, and the twitter of insects came in from outdoors.

"I went to the graveyard," Prue said. She couldn't tell from anyone's expression if Ben had told her sisters of their earlier discussion. "I wanted to see Mother and Father." Pearl drew her lips tight together, as if she had already tried this experiment and seen it fail. "I have business to discuss with you."

Ben said, "Why don't you first have some supper. Abiah made pork and salsify."

Abiah immediately stood, fixed her a savory-smelling plate, and brought her a cup of cider. Prue was hungry, and relieved Tem hadn't mocked her for having gone to the graveyard, but she didn't think she could wait until she'd finished eating to speak with them. She took a few bites, then set her fork down and said, "Tem, Pearl. Has Ben spoken to you of the bridge's finances?"

Pearl shook her head, and Tem said, "Only in the most general terms."

His expression was pleading; he must have thought she should wait until they were sure how bad their situation was. But Tem and Pearl were not his sisters. "We have spent all the state's money, and everything we raised; and although I can pay for it from my own funds a brief while, I think we must all consider the possibility of taking out a mortgage on the house, lands, and distillery."

She half expected Tem to swear at her or pick up her flatware and throw it, and half recognized the thought as proof of the way she undervalued this sister, too. Tem brushed absently at the table with her fingers while she appeared to give the matter sincere consideration; Pearl kept her pencil in its hasp and looked off toward the fire. Tem said, "You'll write to Albany before you do any such thing?"

"Of course," Ben said. "Though we can't be certain what he'll say—Jay left office, you know, and we've Mr. Clinton again now."

"I know my politics. Did you vote for him?" Tem asked, her face somber.

"Indeed; I think he did a fine job previously. I shall write him this evening, full of compliments, and post the letter from New York to-morrow."

"We have the money from Ben's house, and we can use our own funds until some word from the state arrives. The mortgage is still only a possibility," Prue said to her, "but I couldn't sleep tonight if I hadn't spoken to you of it."

Tem continued wiping at the table. "I suppose I have no intrinsic disagreement with the notion. My only fear is that, as of today, if your bridge should fail, we would still have our distillery. What if we should lose both?"

Prue said, "Neither Ben nor I believe the bridge is in danger of failing, only of costing more than we'd reckoned and taking longer to build. We would buy shares in it with the money from the mortgage; thus the business would be safe." Prue wished she felt so assured in her own heart.

Tem reached her hand out for Pearl, who was still gazing into the fire. "What do you think?" she asked.

Pearl took out her pencil, and wrote, *It worrys me, but I am sure I do'n't understand such Things as well as the rest of you.*

Tem arched her eyebrows at her, but did not respond. After a long pause, she said, "Well, Pearl will support your decision, and it doesn't really matter what I think. You can mortgage the works without my permission."

Prue would have found the conversation easier had Tem been explicitly angry; her restraint made Prue's heart ache. "But you see we would prefer not to," she said.

Tem nodded. "Perhaps Governor Clinton will choose to spare you the dilemma."

Ben said, "I sincerely hope."

Prue felt a flicker of anger toward him for not helping her to build a stronger case. He watched her warily, as if he knew he'd done something amiss, but wasn't certain what.

Pearl held a note up to Prue that read, *But what if it did fail? What then?*

"It's nearly impossible," Prue said, "but I don't know."

Pearl widened her eyes in surprise.

"How can I say, Pearl? We should have to go elsewhere, I imagine; we could not remain here. But Ben's skills would support us until Tem and I could found another distillery."

Pearl shook her head no and wrote, *It is too horrible to think on. All Father' Dreams lie here;—he work'd his whole Life for it.*

"I know," Prue said. She thought her two sisters appeared as like each other as ever they had. Their narrow faces and close-set eyes might have been a mirror and its twin, both showing Prue a mixture of faith and fear. Their father had left Prue the management of all his estate to look after them. If, due to the accidents of their nature, they could or would not go out into other families, he had assured her the means to keep them properly in the family of their birth. "I assure you I will not dishonor his memory," she said.

Abiah took hold of the conversation and turned it to household affairs. Prue was relieved to let the more difficult topic go, and saddened she had not been able to make peace with it. Though they all retired at the usual hour, Prue lay awake much of the night; and as Ben burrowed beneath his pillow, she listened to Tem thrashing about in her bed across the hall. Prue arose with the sun's first rays, dressed, brushed her hair, and sat down at the desk to read the letter Ben had written Governor Clinton the evening before.

It was long and artful. He gave his warm approval for the governor's performance in his previous terms, and said he had been most impressed by Clinton's actions since once again taking up the mantle of office. He told him the people of Brooklyn were considering naming a street in their new district in his honor—which was, thus far, only the talk of the barroom, though by no means a lie; and he expressed his desire to make the august gentleman's acquaintance. Only after paying such compliments—bald, Prue thought, but serviceable—did he detail the cost of timber, and of having the men work slowly and with care. He stressed that the bridge had not, in a season and a half of building, cost a single life, and that he hoped to continue in the same fashion until New York State had a bridge on its hands; but that he would require more funds before the end of the year, were the bridge to continue. He had promised to post the letter before work even commenced on the New York lever that morning, so it could reach its destination as quickly as possible. There was nothing more she could ask of him.

While the house was still quiet, Prue went downstairs. From the kitchen, she could hear both Pearl and Abiah beginning to stir in their beds. She went out into the yard and heard the chickens gabbling in their coop. It was a fresh, clear morning, and there was as yet little traffic on the river as she walked down Joralemon's Lane to the mill yard and northward to the bridge. Three fishing boats were headed out toward the bay. She slipped the rope from atop the paling fence and drew open the gate.

The ramp leading up to the bridge was not the stately thing it would become, but a utilitarian construction of stone and timber solely for the use of the men, materials, and the crane. It had no guardrails, and neither did the advancing lever. Prue kept well back from the edge as she climbed upward toward the bright blue sky laced with tufted clouds.

The bridge carried the sweet scent of young wood and the sharp odor of pitch; and all the tools were neatly stowed in their crates beside two huge spools of Schermerhorn rope. A red-billed tern sat preening atop the crane, and called "kik-kik-kik" to her, perhaps to see if she might offer food. The bridge seemed broader than the Jamaica Turnpike, especially as the sides of the roadway simply trailed off toward the blue-gray water.

Already the Brooklyn lever extended more than a quarter its proposed distance. It did not yet sweep majestically over the bustling center of the straits, and there were no tall ships to soar over at this hour, but Prue felt happy to be able to walk upon it. When she was up on the bridge during the workday, all her thoughts were for order, accuracy, and the safety of the men. At that moment, she could marvel like a visitor on a grand tour at seeing the land and the water from such a prospect. Modesty prevented her ever outwardly using words such as *magnificent* to describe the work they were accomplishing; but only such a word could convey the sense of awe and grandeur she felt as she stood out in the fresh breeze, watching the tern take flight. The protruding stub of the New York arm beckoned from across the water, anchored in its pyramid. Prue thought it impossible something so beautiful, and so well under way, should ever fail for want of money.

Ben posted his letter that morning, and in the afternoon Prue crossed the river to go to the bank with him, formally to purchase a share in the bridge. With the money, they'd be able to pay the workers for much of the summer and stave off their worries till later. She stopped to visit the New York construction before boarding the ferry home, and as Ben returned to his work, she once more found herself in an attitude of awe as she viewed the pyramid from its base. Its proportions were harmonious with those of the bridge as a whole, but up close it seemed large enough to hold a nation's seat of government. It rose purposefully from the ground and, as it pointed skyward, seemed almost to glow, so well burnished was its surface. The ramp led through the splendid arch in its center, and that afternoon the arch framed some woolly clouds in a bright patch of clear blue sky. From the ground she watched Ben shout to the crane's operators to prepare to turn the hulk ninety degrees, toward the middle of the straits. Rather than disturb him, she continued on to Mr. Fischer's boat.

The weeks waiting for Albany's reply resembled any others, outwardly. The distillery kept on about its business, and on every day free from rain, the bridge's two arms continued to stretch toward each other. The men had been at the work long enough by then to have an easy rhythm with it, and as they moved farther toward the middle of the straits, the work grew less grueling day by day—the bridge was much thinner at its apex than at its two bases, so the timbers the men worked with grew progressively smaller, lighter, and easier to manage. After a time, the cranes nearly began to seem superfluous, given the size of the members they hoisted. Prue could see the bridge's growth from one day to the next. At home, however, she felt ill at ease. Pearl appeared anxious about the family's security; and Tem, Prue thought, was not so much worried about the prospect of a mortgage as angry that the decision was not her own to make. She therefore had little to say, and she began to spend more time at the Liberty Tavern. Ben, who had little tolerance for such disharmony, also began spending more of his evenings out, at the Twin Tankards; and Abiah did not want to insert herself into family difficulties. Prue believed even her relations with Isaiah had gone brittle, as he had spoken to Patience of his intention to help with the bridgeworks and she had opposed him fiercely. She would not exchange a word with Pearl at market or meet Prue's eye at church. As a result, if Prue asked Isaiah about anything but casks, firewood, or barges, he would scratch his wrist or glance down at the floor before he responded. She knew he did not do this on purpose to discomfit her, but each time it happened, a small flare of jealousy and unease shot up in her chest, and only with the fiercest concentration could she squelch it.

At last, in mid-August, Governor Clinton's letter arrived. The postman had brought it to Isaiah in the countinghouse, and Isaiah had shouted to Prue through the stillhouse window as he ran up to the New Ferry to carry it across to Ben. Prue left the stillhouse in Jens Luquer's care and followed Isaiah out to Fischer's landing. "Did you open it?" she asked.

"Of course not," he said. "That's why you keep me on." He smiled at her for what seemed the first time in months.

"We shouldn't both leave the works," she said, though her heart yearned for the letter in the same way it yearned for the bridge.

"Jens will do fine," Isaiah said. He squinted out at the fleet little boat coming toward them. "Tem can manage for an hour." He paid both their fares, and as they sat side by side on the damp wooden seat, he put his arm around her shoulders. "Don't worry so," he said. "I'm certain it's good news."

Prue had seen it only briefly before he'd stowed it in his pocket, but could deduce nothing from its appearance. "I hope you're correct," she said, and rested her head on his shoulder, where she kept it until they landed at Catherine Street.

When Ben saw them both approaching, he whistled to his men and gave them a quarter-hour break. Some of them filed off the bridge toward the market, but others continued to mill around, interested in what might happen. "Is aught amiss?" he asked immediately.

Prue glanced sideways at Isaiah's face and saw his pinched expression; she could easily imagine its mirror on her own.

"Letter from Mr. Clinton," Isaiah said, and handed it over.

Ben's face betrayed no emotion as he opened the letter. He read it through once, then glanced around for something to sit on. A casket of tools stood open nearby, and he closed it and sat down on its lid.

"What does it say?" Prue said.

He read it all the way through again before answering. She could still glean nothing from his expression. "His apologies for the delay, as they had a great many matters to attend to before closing for the summer holiday." He wiped his brow and seemed to read it through again. "They will offer us another twenty-five thousand, but not until next spring. It will be impossible before then."

Prue had hoped for the best and half expected the worst, and could not quite force this information to fit either category.

Isaiah asked, "What will you do, then?"

Ben let out a breath through his nostrils and glanced off toward the river. "Ask for my position back as county surveyor? There's a bit of money, right there."

Prue said, "Ben—"

"It's all right," he said. "I shan't be bitter about it long. We have enough as stands to see us through the month; we could call off construction until next year." Prue's face must have betrayed her heartsickness, because he said to her, "Yes, exactly as I feel. Our other option is to go ahead and mortgage the works; which I do not think will improve our standing in your sisters' esteem."

Prue could see the distillery, humming along and belching smoke across the river. She felt a fondness for it almost as dear as that she felt for Ben and her sisters. "There are still shares to be bought. I think we might yet do so safely."

"I agree," Ben said, but he did not stand up from the tool chest or look any less disconsolate.

Isaiah cleared his throat and said, "If you'll excuse me, I've thought a great deal about this issue since last we spoke of it."

"So has Patience," Ben said.

"As you know, she objects to the notion of my giving up any part of my salary. But I think I should mortgage my house and lands for the bridge."

Prue said, "Isaiah, we won't hear of it."

Isaiah moved past her and crouched down to speak to Ben, and Prue was aware of the workers listening out on the lever. "Ben," he said, "I know our father would have wished it so. I know he would not have stood by, safe and secure, as Matty Winship put his property in peril."

Ben did not at once reply, and Prue tried to remember Israel in this light. He and her father had been greatly devoted to each other, as much as if they had been brothers or partners; and yet he had always remained in her father's employ.

"Ben," Isaiah repeated.

Ben shook his head, as if indicating only God could know the answer. He stood and walked down the ramp toward the pyramid.

Isaiah loosened his cravat with one hand. "Prue?" he asked. "What do you think?"

"I could not ask you to make such a sacrifice," she said. "But I shall stand by whatever Ben decides."

Against her expectations, Ben later accepted his brother's offer. They must have had some further conversation about it, but Ben never told her when it had been or what it had comprised. He simply, the next night, drew her close to him in bed and said, "Isaiah and I have gone over the books again. We have enough to see us through until October—almost till the end of the building season—but next month, we shall go to Mr. Stover and ask his help."

"What convinced you to accept him?" she asked.

"I cannot deny him. He sees the bridge is my dream as much as yours. He wants to make his contribution."

As little as she liked Patience, Prue slept badly, imagining her unhappiness and fear over her husband's decision. The injustice of it, when she had four children to feed; the injustice, when she had married the heir to the property, little expecting him to sacrifice it all to the whims of his younger brother. Prue avoided her sister-in-law as much as possible in the weeks to come, but could not help seeing how hollowed out and taut Isaiah's features appeared. He managed the works as well as ever, but had clearly ceased to take even his usual temperate pleasure in this. Prue felt she could bear her sisters' worry and disapprobation; Isaiah's gloom, however, cast a pall over everything.

And Recompense fretted for all of them—her parents, her uncle, her aunts.

"You needn't, though," Jonas told her as he leaned over the back of her chair to kiss her nape. She was ticklish at that moment, and shied from the touch of his whiskers and lips. "You know they are all hale and well, and survived their difficulties."

"That is not altogether true," she replied.

He came around and sat in the chair beside hers. His dark eyes were twinkling, she supposed with the desire to spar with her. "It is very nearly so."

But Recompense had no wish to argue, and her throat felt thick. She wished he would not tell her how to interpret her own family's history.

"What, love?" he asked, and reached out to touch her hair. Recompense flinched, and he at once withdrew his hand.

"I am sorry," she said. "I suppose I am disturbed by the letter."

Jonas nodded. "It is as my sister says, no doubt: Your condition makes you prey to vicissitudes of feeling."

"Perhaps," she said. The twinkle was gone from his eyes, but she could see him trying to keep an attitude of dejection from his countenance. At moments, she felt she had known him always, and at others— as now—something in his features seemed momentarily unfamiliar. She kissed his whiskered cheek.

"You should take care, for our son's sake, to turn your mind to more salubrious subjects."

"I shall," she said, though she knew her mind would remain with her mother, and though she felt certain the child she carried would be a girl.

Twenty-three

THE MORTGAGE

The morning Ben had chosen to travel to the bank was mild and clear, a warm September day that seemed to deny the possibility summer could ever end or the world contain suffering. Ben preferred to travel by the New Ferry, both because of its speed and "because I don't want to see it, if Losee is pleased we've come to this pass," he said.

"I'm sure he wouldn't be," Prue said.

"Even so."

Prue walked him to the landing. Each side of the bridge was nearly two-thirds complete and soared toward the middle of the river like the golden struts of a partly obscured rainbow.

Ben swung her hand as they walked, and said, "God, what a beauty." Prue had been looking at the bridge, but when she turned to regard him, he was smiling at her, in her britches and work boots.

"Oh, come," she said.

"Courage, Prue." He squeezed her hand.

She told herself to try to hold the bridge in her imagination all morning, to wish him luck. It would not be easy to hear her neighbors say she counted her father's dreams lightly, not when the distillery—her father's legacy—was so dear to her. She would risk it for the bridge, but she still wished she could tie a string around Ben, or chant an incantation, to bless his errand that morning.

She kissed him good-bye on the landing and stood watching as the burly young ferryman, unknown to them by name, shuttled him across.

She might have stood there until he reached the other side, but she reminded herself it was no time to be sentimental, when the bridgeworks and the distillery awaited her.

When he returned a few hours later, Prue was up on the Brooklyn lever, observing the turning of the crane, and had the opportunity to view him as he disembarked with his companions. He helped their banker, Timothy Stover, up out of the boat. Prue realized she had never seen the man outdoors, and had thought of him as belonging to the dusky interior of the bank. She had always known he was thin, but had not noticed quite how frail he'd grown until she saw him leaning heavily into his stick as he walked. The other man accompanying them was a short fellow in a round hat, who lifted a case to the wharf before him that stood nearly as high as his knees. Prue thought this must be the assessor. Though Mr. Stover seemed to be chatting affably with Ben, the assessor appeared to be among strangers.

Prue went down to the landing to greet them. Mr. Stover wore a bright expression Prue thought at odds with the situation, and wondered if he might have been starved for fresh air.

"Miss Winship—Mrs. Horsfield," he said, putting out his hand. "What a pleasure to see you today."

"The pleasure is mine."

"May I introduce Mr. Corey, our assessor?"

Mr. Corey bowed to her but did not extend his hand.

"Pleased to meet you," Prue said.

"Dandy of a bridge," Mr. Stover said, shaking his head. He had an orator's rich voice, which made his every word seem a pronouncement. "I didn't realize quite how grand it was until I saw it from the water."

"Yes," Ben said, "it is a most impressive prospect."

"Will you jest at me, Mrs. Horsfield, if I admit to you I had never been out upon the river before this morning?"

This seemed unlikely, but Prue did not wish to convey her skepticism.

"Mrs. Horsfield?"

"Yes, excuse me. As you were saying?"

"Ah," Mr. Stover said, "perhaps I've alarmed you with my admission; but it's quite true. I was raised on a farm up the Bloomingdale Road, and when I broke with my parents, came to apprentice in the bank. I hadn't been north, south, west, or east of town until today. But it was a fine adventure going out upon the river this morning. Bracing! And Brookland appears to have a most healthful outlook, agreeable to the eye."

The ferryman, behind Mr. Stover, was smirking to himself as he kicked idly at the mooring.

"I'm pleased you're enjoying your visit thus far. If you've time to stay, perhaps you'll join us for tea when your work is through; and one of us could provide you a brief walking tour of Brookland."

"I would enjoy that," he said, looking upward. "Great God, there's no question you must be allowed to finish this work."

Ben smiled uncertainly at Prue and said, "Have no fear, we shall." He cleared his throat and said to her, "I see you sent Marcel over to start the New York crew this morning?"

"Indeed. He can manage until your return."

"Good. Perhaps, then, I can show Mr. Corey and Mr. Stover around the properties, and you may return to your business."

Prue nodded, though she inwardly winced, considering how Patience might react when an assessor was brought to her door. Isaiah had kept to himself all morning; Prue had assumed this was the reason why. She wondered how long it would take the papers to report Mr. Corey's visit.

"So," Ben said, smiling to Mr. Corey, who did not appear at all amused. "Do you know how a distillery operates?"

"In the vaguest terms," Mr. Corey said. He gazed around at the buildings as if Brooklyn were an insufferable backwater.

"Ah," Ben said. "Then I shall lead you through it in the order of production, so you may come to understand; and then I shall show you the houses." Prue thought she had never seen him look so disconsolate since the days he'd spent learning Latin in Mr. Severn's school. As they set out, Mr. Corey leaned sideways to counterbalance the weight of his case.

Prue climbed back up the Brooklyn arm, and watched Ben begin his tour of the properties; but she kept thinking about the expression with which Mr. Corey had looked about him. She had never wondered how her distillery might appear to someone who did not call it home. To her it was solid and utilitarian, a thing of use and therefore of beauty; but as if she could borrow Mr. Corey's eyes, she saw that morning how dense the smoke was, how weathered the shake siding, and how primitive the packed earth floors. She thought back to the first time she'd seen Brooklyn from the water, as a girl, and how arbitrarily the houses had seemed to have been scattered on the cliffs, compared to the relative order of New York's streets. This difference was only the more pronounced now. She hoped Mr. Corey would see through to the value of the place, and not merely consider it squalid. She once again felt a flicker of that same sense of injustice she'd felt watching Ben present the bridge to the assembly. He had not worked a day of his life at Winship Daughters Gin, but it was his to show. She told herself to do her best to stifle this emotion. It was enough—it was more than enough—that he made no claim on the distillery and allowed her to continue to run it.

Ben never came to fetch Prue for tea, though she saw him lead both men up Joralemon's Lane to the house and not reemerge for some time. Prue hoped that if Pearl had been at home, she had mastered her anxiety enough to be a thoughtful hostess. At last, shortly before noon, Ben came up to find Prue on the lever.

"They're gone, I take it?" she asked, wiping sweat from her brow.

Ben handed her a cup of water from the nearby bucket. "You can see them there, on Losee's boat," he said, inclining his head toward the dull green ferry, carrying one eager seer of sights and one prim figure reading.

"Clear!" someone shouted farther out the lever, and the crane's winch began to creak.

"How did you fare?" Prue asked, raising her voice above the screech.

Ben said, "I can't be sure, but I think well enough. They asked for the survey I performed when we were making the proposal for the bridge; and they say we'll hear back from them within the week."

Prue thought it would prove a long week, but said nothing.

The press printed its intimations of doom: The writer for the *New-York Journal* was certain "Winship Gin will pay the price of this folly;—along with New-York and Brookland themselves." As much as such aspersions stung, Prue found Isaiah's evident distress the most painful part of the waiting. She asked him again and again if anything troubled him. He looked her in the eye as he said no, but he appeared distracted. Prue thought once the news had arrived, he might rest easier; but of course it was only for the bridge the news could be bad or good. Patience was angry their house was being mortgaged at all, and it would not matter to her if they secured a larger or smaller loan upon its value.

In the middle of the week, Ben returned from New York at the close of the workday, as Prue oversaw the stowing of her men's tools and equipment for the night. He helped with the cleaning, and once all the men had left, husband and wife began to walk down toward the distillery. As they descended toward the abutment's Gothic spires, he said, "I've an idea what we should do once we have our money in hand." Prue wondered if their course of action had been in question. "We should buy both ferries and, once the bridge is open, shut them down."

Prue glanced sideways at him as they walked, to see if he was joking; but his expression was matter-of-fact. "Why so?" she asked.

"Because we'll earn back our investment more quickly if we've no competition."

Prue walked along for a moment, and watched a packet skim past on a good puff of wind. "You're mad, Ben," she said, and laughed at him.

"No," he said; she could hear she'd injured his pride. "It would be good business."

"Good business at Losee's expense."

"We are already building this bridge at Losee's expense."

The smoke over the distillery was gradually clearing as the fires burned down. While at one level she could not argue with his logic, at another she found it irrational. "No, Ben. A ferry will always be of use."

"Why so?"

"I don't know," Prue said, kicking a pebble out of her way. "The bridge will be convenient for us and the Schermerhorns, but perhaps others will wish to ship and travel the way they always have."

"Perhaps."

"And you cannot discount their sentimental attachment to it."

"No," Ben said, "I suppose not."

She still thought his idea odd, and wondered if the strain of waiting was proving too much for him. She knew she herself was acting strangely: All week she had stashed her receipts in the safe and never once boarded a boat for Manhattan, as she could not bear to enter the bank. She hadn't let Tem take them, either, when she'd offered. She had an order due to a tavern north of the canal—far distant from the bank— yet had made no plans to deliver it, for fear of seeing Mr. Corey walking down the street. She thought there would be no other way about things until their news came.

At the beginning of the next week, a letter from Mr. Stover arrived at the countinghouse, addressed both to Ben and to Prue. Marcel had been there alone, and came to find Prue on the bridge, where the men were pitching the next section's timber. Prue knew from Marcel's expression why he'd come.

"Ben was right there on the New York arm," she said, working the seal open while looking across the water toward his crane. "He might simply have spoken to him."

"Would you like me to go, ma'am?" Marcel asked.

"No," Prue said. "Hold a moment."

Before she read the letter, she steeled herself for what it might contain, and reminded herself that however bad the news might be, she was fortunate her father had chosen to become a distiller. He could as easily have taken up chandlery or screw-cutting, and how little succor his wares could have provided her then.

The letter offered a loan of five thousand on the Winship homestead, thirty-eight hundred on the Horsfield land, and seventeen thousand on the distillery.

"Is the news not good?" Marcel asked.

Prue wanted to swear at Mr. Corey, who, Mr. Stover wrote, had not been convinced the distillery was an altogether wise investment, particularly as regarded its susceptibility to fire. *It's why we're insured to the gills*, Prue thought; but nevertheless she said, "Nor all bad, neither." It was nearly twenty-six thousand, all told; a great deal of money, but less than she had expected. The distillery brought in more than seventeen thousand in an ordinary year.

Ben scoffed at the letter when she showed it to him later that afternoon in the countinghouse. " 'Suitably impressed by your scale of production, but concerned by the hazard of fire the wooden buildings pose'? Then he must think all Manhattan a bad investment."

"It probably is," Prue said, and poured them another round. The cups were, as ever, dirty, but she trusted in the cleansing powers of gin. "I've a mind to tell him we pay four times as much as the Schermerhorns in insurance for exactly that reason; but I'm not positive it would change his assessment."

"No," Ben said. "He must know that without being told." He sipped his drink for a moment, then asked, "What are you thinking?"

Prue looked out the window, over the port. "That my father will roll over in his grave to see for how little I'm mortgaging everything he owned."

Ben said, "I still think he'll be proud."

Prue wished she could believe him. She allowed Ben to tell Isaiah the news and to arrange with him their visit to the bank.

When they arrived to meet him the next morning, Isaiah was out smoking on his steps. "Bad night of it?" Ben asked, as the gravel of the walk crunched under their feet. The morning had been washed clean by an early rain, and the branches of the Horsfield apple trees were pearled as with dew.

Isaiah shook his head and held out a hand in warning. When the sound of their footfalls subsided, Prue could hear Isaiah's youngest wailing indoors.

"You are not obliged to accompany us," Ben said in a low voice.

"No," Isaiah said, "there's no question." He took one last puff of his pipe, then tapped it out into the nearest flower bed. "Let me get my coat." He did not invite them in, but shut the door behind him. Prue heard Patience speaking, though she could not make out the substance of what she said, and the baby began to cry more piteously. Before Isaiah could return, Patience opened the door and stood looking out with her face wan and irritable. The screaming baby had one fat wet hand wound into its mother's dull hair, and the three larger children burst past her into the yard. "Do you seek to ruin us all?" she asked Prue, her tone as level as if they were discussing the weather.

"Patience—" Ben said.

"I ask your wife, Benjamin Horsfield, if she seeks to ruin us."

Young Israel ran up to Ben and began pummeling his thighs. "Not now," Ben said, ruffling the child's hair.

Prue said, "Of course not," but felt foolish doing so.

"But it's what you're doing."

Still trying to pull his nephew off his legs, Ben said, "I think it a matter of opinion."

Mrs. Tilley and her daughter, walking past on their way to the store, turned with unabashed interest to listen to the conversation. "Good day, Mrs. Tilley," Prue called to her, and they hurried down the road. To Patience, she said, "You must trust my husband and I would do nothing to

harm your prospects any more than our own. It will be a sound investment."

The baby opened its glistening mouth and shrieked. Ben finally managed to disentangle himself from Israel, and shunted the boy toward the
open door.

Isaiah came quickly down the stairs with his jacket over his arm, and
took his hat and stick from the peg by the door. "Leave her be, Patience,
we've spoken of it enough already," he said, and leaned down to kiss the
baby's slick face as he passed.

"No," Patience said, "I have not—"

But though she might have continued all morning, Isaiah walked
briskly up the path. Prue could see Patience's face begin to redden, but
when Ben turned to follow his brother, she went with him, walking as
quickly as she could.

"I am so sorry," Isaiah said, looking at neither of them. He was leading them up toward Losee's ferry, instead of toward the faster new one;
but this would be all right. "She knows full well it's not your fault, Prue,
nor Ben's, but my decision alone."

Prue felt Patience's pain keenly, and wondered if she was still standing
in their cheerful blue doorway.

Joe Loosely must have heard their whole conversation, for he was
standing on his steps when they approached the ferry, and offered them
a drink, though it was not yet eight in the morning. Ben and Isaiah
glanced at each other before refusing him. "I'll manage," Ben said.

Joe said, "But it's Isaiah I fear for."

Isaiah looked off toward the water and said, "There's Losee at his
landing. We should go."

Losee grinned at them as they approached. Prue had almost forgotten
how infectious that rotten-toothed smile was, it had been so long since
she'd seen it. "Three Horsfields, is it?" he asked. Prue looked around before realizing he meant her as well. As they were too glum to respond, he
went on, "Will you all take passage this morning?"

"Please," Isaiah said, though he had begun to look peaked. Losee
walked bowlegged down to where his boat was tethered, and Isaiah
added, "You seem in good spirits, Losee."

Losee put one hand on the wharf and hopped down into his rocking boat. Once it was steady, he put out his hand for Prue. "I am, Isaiah. Have you not heard the good news?"

Isaiah shrugged his shoulders. The boat resettled to accommodate his and Ben's weight.

"Sold the business," Losee said.

Ben said, "What?" and Isaiah began patting about his coat as if he'd forgotten something.

"I know," Losee said. " 'Twas just yesterday Ezra Fischer approached me and offered to buy the boat, the landing, and my very house. Wearing quite a fancy suit of clothes, I might add; probably cost more than a decent horse."

"You sold the ferry?" Ben asked. Prue imagined what he was thinking: either that he himself would have liked to buy it, or that Losee loved his business as other men loved drink. It was not obvious what he'd do without it.

Losee reached up to the wharf, rang his bell, and called out, "Over!" Then he pulled them into the current and began to turn the boat alee. "I've agreed to. I'm getting old, Ben. I've arthritis in the shoulders and gout in the feet; I've long said if anyone would offer me a good price, I'd give it over." Prue could not recall his ever having said such a thing. He was on the lookout for oncoming traffic, but most of the other boats were fishermen. "He's not such a bad feller as I thought. He'll manage it all right."

"Where will you live?" Prue asked.

He gestured with his chin back toward Brooklyn, dwarfed by the rising arm of the bridge. "One of the new places on Whitcombe's property. It'll make a nice home for Petra, away from all this bustle." As if to prove his point, the bell rang at the ropewalk, and the great water-powered engines began to churn. The distillery's would follow in a moment.

Ben said, "I congratulate you; it's very good news." Prue and Isaiah chimed in their agreement. Glad as Losee looked, Prue could not imagine him anything but a ferryman; it seemed he might die of inactivity. Who would be his fellows if he sat on a stoop two miles inland? Prue also wondered why Ezra Fischer would risk purchasing a second ferry when the bridge stood so near to completion, and so nearby.

"Won't it be quite a change for you?" she asked.

"From workin' to not workin'? I don't know a man who wouldn't take it."

"I rather like to work," Isaiah said absently.

"When will this occur?" Prue asked.

"End of November," Losee said. "I've a little time to grow accustomed to it."

She had to remind herself not to feel nostalgic for something that had not yet happened. Nostalgia for things already past was consuming enough on its own.

When they landed at Fly Market, Losee helped Prue out of the boat, and Ben once again congratulated him. The waiting passengers pricked up their ears, and Prue thought he'd have a picnic telling everyone of his changed circumstances. The pyramid was a fine sight from where they stood on the wharf. Prue saw a few pedestrians turn to regard it as one might a weathercock.

They did not speak as they walked to the bank. It had never before struck Prue how dismal it appeared, with its small windows covered by iron bars. Two gangling boys—young enough to be in school, had anyone cared for them—sat on old stools to either side of the door, guarding it. They nodded to Ben and Prue, but the nearer one held out his skinny hand to Isaiah and said, "State your business, please, sir?"

"Isaiah Horsfield, manager of the Winship distillery," he said, looking at the ground.

The other boy, who'd held his position longer and knew Isaiah, filliped his companion with his finger. "So sorry, Mr. Horsfield, sir," he said. "You can go in, of course. Mr. Stover expecting you?"

"Most likely," Prue said.

He pulled the door back on its creaking hinges.

The gentlemen of the bank sat at cramped desks in neat rows, and were all in their shirtsleeves, crouched scratching at figures. The younger men had the same hunched posture as their elders. One glanced up from his paperwork, but did not appear to think much of Ben, Isaiah, and Prue. When Mr. Stover noticed them he sat up straight and said, "Ah, good morning. I hope I have not kept you waiting."

"Good morning," Prue replied. "We've only just arrived."

Stover stood to welcome them to his cramped quarters. There were two small chairs across his desk, but his near neighbor immediately shuttled over a third, for which Ben thanked him. "I take it, then, you found the terms of our offer satisfactory?" he asked.

Before answering him, she looked to Ben and Isaiah, but could not read their expressions. "We do not believe the assessment to be quite commensurate with the properties' worth, particularly as regards the risk of fire, against which we are more than adequately insured."

Stover nodded. "Mr. Corey was concerned."

"And we therefore think he has undervalued the property. I have brought our terms of insurance for your perusal," she said, and removed a folded paper from the pocket of her coat. "If you like, you may yourself make inquiries at Associated Underwriters. I believe this would assuage Mr. Corey's doubts." All around, pens continued to scratch, but Prue thought some of those nearest her had slowed as the men listened.

"I am sorry to hear you dissatisfied," Mr. Stover said, and smoothed a hair over his balding crown. "Let me see what we have here." He squinted at the page, but nodded to himself as he read it. Then he reached into the file behind him and extracted a thick sheaf of papers bearing the distillery's name. Prue could see he had already had the scrivener draw up contracts for the three separate properties. "I see," he said after a time. "It appears that Mr. Corey did not account for quite such a thorough policy as you possess; in which case, I should be able to offer you"—he ran his finger down the page to arrive at a number— "thirty-five hundred more than the original estimate."

"It's worth more than that," Prue said. She felt poised either to yell at Mr. Stover or to have her heart break in public. She half wished Ben would offer some assistance; but this was her work, and she knew it.

Stover's face conveyed true sympathy. "I do understand your position," he said. "But that is all I can offer you. Will you accept it?"

Prue looked to her husband and brother-in-law. Isaiah was gazing out one of the grubby windows, but Ben nodded to her slowly.

Prue said, "Yes."

One of the nearby bankers rustled his papers, as if to prove he was returning to his work.

"Good," Mr. Stover said. "The contracts are ready for the two houses; and I shall have the scrivener emend the contract for the works. It shouldn't take long."

"Thank you," Ben said. "We will, of course, appreciate it if we can take care of matters as soon as possible."

"Yes," Stover said, "right away. I shall see to it now." He stood with some difficulty and used his cane to walk to the other end of the bank, where Prue saw him conferring with a younger man, who took out a new sheet of paper to write upon. The wait for the contract seemed interminable; and Prue did not know what to do with her hands or her eyes. As if he read this on her, Ben took her hand in his own as they waited.

Stover returned perhaps a quarter hour later. "Very well, here it is. Read it through, and ask any questions before signing it."

Prue's gaze would not stick to the words, and reading the contract took much longer than it ought to have. The document did, however, appear fair; Ben did not seem displeased with it. They applied the same scrutiny to the paper for the house, and Prue saw Isaiah doing the same for his.

"Have you any questions?" Stover asked.

"None," Ben said.

Isaiah said, "It appears to be in order."

Ben signed the papers first, then handed Stover's pen over to Isaiah. Prue was galled to see that however well Stover understood her to run the distillery, her signature was not required for this transaction. Stover replaced the signed contracts in the distillery's file, and it was done. They could now return home, as if nothing had happened. Prue's head felt light, to realize how much one's circumstances could change yet appear the same.

As they traveled homeward on one of Fischer's boats, Prue still felt disconsolate that Ben might, if he wished, have mortgaged the works without even her permission. Yet she determined that if she had to stand by the millrace that evening and shout out her sadness and rage, she would not mention this to her husband; and in the meanwhile, she was surprised to feel a crashing wave of nostalgia for Losee. Bridge or no bridge, she could not imagine riding back and forth across these straits the rest of her days and not having at least the option of his good company. She recognized as well that it was easier to think about Losee than to think about what she'd just done. She imagined how the reports of the mortgage would read in the various newssheets, then chastised herself for doing so. It was bad enough the newsmen's opinions would come; she had no need to compose them herself.

The nascent bridge truly was magnificent from the water—like a rainbow, indeed. This would have to be some consolation. Beneath the Brooklyn spires, Prue could see a group of workers gathered, bent gesticulating over something, no doubt a dogfight or a game of chance. "Ben, are those our men?" she asked. "What are they doing? Where is Marcel?"

"We'll find out soon enough," he said.

She knew the men gambled, and did not mind so long as they completed their work with accuracy and in reasonable time. Still, she felt Marcel should have had the sense to keep them from mischief on such an important day. "He should know better," she said. As the ferry drew closer to Brooklyn, the gathering dispersed, and the men hustled off toward their various stations.

Isaiah did not even look to see what they were speaking of. He had his arms folded before him and sat staring at his whitewashed house atop the bluff. Prue wanted to offer him comfort, but did not want to embarrass him before the ferryman. "Isaiah," she said, "we can't thank you enough. I know it'll turn out for the best."

He ran his fingers behind his right ear, as if he might find a pencil there. "Yes," he said, "I hope it will," but kept silent the remainder of the trip back.

Twenty-four

MR. SEVERN'S QUESTION

I n October, a man lost his footing off the side of the New York lever and hung dangling by his harness a quarter hour. As his compatriots were reeling him in to safety, his rope must have rubbed against the timbers and begun to fray; for with what Ben reported as a sickening ripping sound, the harness broke free, and the worker plummeted into the straits. As if by miracle, he survived the impact, but he was knocked senseless and would have drowned had not a passing fishing dinghy heeled about; the fisherman dragged him into the boat and pumped his arms until he vomited up the water. Ben arrived down on the wharf with his legs shaking so badly he could hardly stand; and though he knew the worker only by name, he knelt down to embrace him. Operations on the New York side were called off for a few hours while all the ropes and harnesses were checked. When the news reached the Brooklyn side, Prue thought she should ask Mr. Severn to bless the workers for the remainder of their term. When she told Pearl of this at lunchtime, Pearl volunteered to go and ask him later in the day. Her eagerness for the task nettled Prue, but the blessing seemed worth some annoyance.

In one respect, Severn's prayer appeared to work: Prue began to think it possible the second building season might end without loss of life. She did not know if this continued success cheered or frightened her, as she suspected that the longer a fatal accident was averted, the more terrible it would be when it finally came. But in other respects, Severn seemed to have little influence with the Almighty. The man plummeting from the bridge made a fine gloomy story in the newssheets; and then in mid-

November, Ben discovered the New York lever had deviated seven minutes of arc toward the south.

"That cannot be," Prue said. The workday was done, and the men had retired to their tents or the taverns. Ben had rushed to the countinghouse with the news. "We have performed our measurements a hundred times over."

Ben paced the room and would not look at her. "And we should not have commenced building before a hundred and one."

"The men work with great care," Prue said. "We supervise them ourselves." She heard herself pleading, as if a plaintive tone could invalidate what he'd seen.

"It doesn't matter, Prue. Something went wrong—either the measurements or the work. There is no saying which at this point."

It was impossible the bridge should fail; her mind could not encompass such a thought. "Can we determine at what juncture the lever diverged? Can we tear it back to that point and rebuild? Seven minutes is far less than a degree; surely the lever is redeemable."

"I don't know," Ben said. He sank down in the nearest chair and took both hands to his head. "Christ!"

"We must seek counsel. We must write Mr. Pope directly."

"That is the last thing we should do; if we tell Thomas Pope, the governor will know within the week, the *New-York Journal* within the hour. We must find a solution ourselves."

Prue went to the shelf and poured two cups of gin. "Ben," she said as she handed him the fuller one, but she could not think of anything more to say. She trusted in both their abilities, yet felt she understood for the first time how vulnerable their inexperience left them.

He downed his drink and immediately stood to pace again. When he reached the far side of the room, he turned to face her with the china teacup still in his hand. His hair stuck out where he had lifted it with his hands, and his eyes were wide. "It never bodes well when you're silent, Prue, but I feel we must attempt this on our own. We cannot afford to lose everything."

Despite that she'd said she would never do so again, and despite her misgivings, she left the rectifying room under Marcel's command over the next few days as she, Ben, and Adam brought out the instruments and tried to ascertain how to correct their error. At least, she reasoned, the deviation was as small as it was: If the New York lever continued along its current trajectory, the levers would indeed meet midstream, but the New York arm would protrude five feet nine inches on the downriver side and Brooklyn's would do likewise upriver. Ben determined that rather than dismantle the New York lever, they should change the trajectory of each lever by three and a half minutes as it progressed. This was a difference of a fraction of an inch per timber. He believed the correction would be invisible and would little affect the strength of the bridge.

And there was, at least, no doubt they would be able to continue the work for a third season; they had sufficient funds to continue. Once again, most of the men contracted to return the following April, and some found winter work in Brooklyn or its near environs. The money from the shares Ben and Prue had purchased sat safely in the bank, along with the remainder of the mortgage; and though Isaiah thought they might merely scrape by with the assurance of the state's money come spring, it seemed likely the bridge would be completed sometime in 1802. Already each lever covered two thirds of its final span. The bridge gave a clear presentiment of its future appearance, and attracted visitors from far and wide. When Prue gazed out on it from the distillery, she sometimes thought the distance between the ends of the two levers appeared short enough for a man to leap across.

As soon as the last worker had been paid and the tents stored for winter, Ben set out north to see if he could bargain for a better price with the timber merchant. If not, he would search for a new one, if another could be found with a large enough supply. He was willing to admit the quality of the wood at the center of the span could be lower than at the abutments; it would, after all, bear less weight, and such a compromise might ensure their ability to complete the bridge.

"You will still write me?" Prue asked him before he left.

Ben rubbed her upper arms affectionately. "I gave you my word. And I shall not be gone long. You won't have sufficient time to miss me."

Prue raised her eyebrows but didn't respond. She would miss him if he went up to the Wallabout for the day; but there was no need to tell him this.

The day he left, though bright and unseasonably warm, seemed long and gloomy. Except for the discovery of the error, the entire building season had gone well, she told herself as she went back to the ordinary business of the distillery. If mortgaging their property was not what she would have chosen, it had been a reasonable solution to their problems; and if Ben could account for the misalignment between the levers, it would prove the bridge had some kind of blessing upon it. Prue's mind was as dark as it ever had been, but this was neither the fault of the bridge nor of Ben's absence.

"Come," Tem told her as they stood together in the cooling house at the end of that day. The wort had drained to the fermenting-back ten minutes since, and Mr. Fortune gone to work; but the floor was still damp and smelled sweet. "This distillery was ever your heart's desire. Surely it can't be so dull?"

"Not dull at all," Prue said. "I can't say why I feel so low."

"You have to cheer up," Tem said. "Soon enough that bridge'll be finished, and what will you have to do ever after but make gin?"

Prue didn't know, but when Tem asked again at dinner that evening, Abiah and Pearl were quick to reach conclusions.

"You'll find yourself with child before long," Abiah predicted, "and that'll lighten your heart."

You simply miss Ben, Pearl wrote, then put her pencil down to take another forkful of potatoes.

"No," Prue said. "That is, yes, but I wish I could say that was what troubled me. It could be so easily remedied."

What, then?

"Have a drink," Tem said, taking down the decanter and raising it to her. Prue shook her head no, and thought, in passing, Tem was servant to the thing. Tem poured her a dram anyway; and since it was before her, Prue drank it. It was redolent of aniseed and warm in her throat.

"I don't know, Pearl," she said. She could say nothing about the difficulty with the bridge. Pearl was as much its architect as she or Ben, but Prue did not believe news of its ailment should travel any farther than was necessary to heal it. "Orders have been down all year; and the mortgage deprives me of sleep."

"Those things will take care of themselves," Abiah said.

You shall be abel to pay it back, Pearl wrote. Her face was encouraging. In fact, she looked as well as ever she had. She had spent much of the summer in outdoor leisure, and though the freckles across the bridge of her nose had since faded, all the exercise seemed to have made her limbs sturdier.

"I wish I could trust as easily as you," Prue said.

It isn't v. difficult, Pearl wrote.

Prue had sometimes thought her sister's life a form of servitude, but really, it was Pearl who was free to do as she liked. She did not have to worry over their finances except in the most general way; now she was a grown woman, she could wander at will and be courted by Mr. Severn in whatever his odd, shy manner. "Perhaps someday you'll teach me how," she said, doing her best to brighten her own expression. "I shan't take any lessons from you, Tem."

Tem said, "Thank you."

Ben returned in mid-November. "We shall manage it," he told Prue, as soon as he stepped off the boat and into her arms. His scent was familiar and sweet, and she could have cried from the sheer pleasure of his proximity. She held him close a long while before pushing him back to examine his face. He looked healthy—not like a man who'd had to make compromises. His time outdoors and upon the water appeared to have fed his spirit.

"You were pleased with the quality of the materials?" Prue asked.

"They won't be quite so fine as before, but they are solid goods. The timber I've ordered will suffice for the courses closest to the arc's center, and I believe our plan of adjusting the levers will work." He stroked the side of her head. "Believe me, it would be my preference as much as yours to make no such modifications. But we shall have our bridge."

"I can imagine the rumors," Prue said.

"We'll quash them. No one will see the deviation, and even if the new wood appears different from the old—and I suspect it may—time's patina will blur that distinction."

The news did not console Prue, but Ben's presence did. She resolved to spend the winter enjoying Ben's company and solving at last the dilemma of the rectifying. It was a circumscribed sphere of action, but she could make it suffice.

Losee's final crossing was on the last Saturday afternoon of November, and throngs of his neighbors and loyal customers—nearly everyone who lived within walking distance of what was now called the Old

Ferry—gathered on his landing to welcome him home. Though the weather was chilly and damp and night was falling quickly, Joe Loosely had put out torches and three casks of beer, so the mood was festive. Jens Luquer first spied Losee's dull green boat slipping toward them in the dark water, and he began to whistle and clap, along with his brothers and sisters. Mr. Fischer, in a trim, peacock-blue coat, clapped as vigorously as anyone, though Prue saw him, from time to time, turn to see what Tem was doing. Tem didn't meet his eye, but neither did she look cross. One of the men from the *Long-Island Courier* stood at the periphery of the crowd; this, Prue thought, was news. Losee let his boat drift in the current a moment, then worked his left oar to spin himself around. His broad face shone for a moment in the torchlight, his mouth agape with pleasure, before he turned around again and began rowing home with renewed vigor. The crowd cheered when he tossed his rope up, and more loudly still when he hoisted himself onto the wharf. "Well, I'll be damned," he exclaimed as he removed his hat to push the thinning hair back from his brow. He wiped down the sides of his mouth with his fingers, as if his senses might be deceiving him. His flaxen-haired Petra, now grown as high as his shoulder, came out from the crowd bearing a gigantic wreath fashioned of dried Indian corn, which she laid on top of his large head. He stooped to receive it as if it were a military honor, and wobbled under its weight as he stood back up. Everyone laughed—it was an ungainly and odd-looking thing—but as Losee took a slight bow to each direction in it, Prue felt her throat thicken with tears.

"May I have your attention, please?" Joe called from atop one of the pilings, then banged a spoon on a tankard.

Ben wrapped his arm around Prue's waist and saluted Joe with his free hand. Joe raised the spoon in greeting to him, then hit the tankard again. The sound was low and quiet compared to the general din, but it had its desired effect until someone cried "Loseeee!" and another cheer went up.

"Indeed," Joe said, and the cheering quieted. "My good friends. Most of you are too young to remember, but for all the years my father ran the Ferry Tavern, Losee's father, Lo van Nostrand, ran the ferry. Those two were inseparable. They loved their pints, horse racing, and cockfights, and they loved working so close to each other. If they look down on us from Heaven, I think they must be pleased to see us still working in the trades in which they trained us. More importantly, I imagine they're happy to see us such good friends."

"God bless old Henry," Mr. Joralemon said, and Joe paused, a pained smile passing across his face.

"Thank you," he went on. "My father teased Lo constantly. He called him 'Ole Charon' and the water he daily traversed the 'Squalid Styx.'" Prue's nape tingled when she heard this. "But he knew his friend to have a generous heart. It is no easy lot in life, to be a ferryman. On days a farmer might count his stores or sharpen his blades, the boat keeper still goes out to ply the gray waters. On days mothers keep their children indoors, he puts on an extra muffler and heads out to the wet.

"My father left me a business I can enjoy until my dotage. When I'm half deaf with age, a man'll still be able to give me the sign he wants his dram; or if I'm blind, he'll shout his order. Lo van Nostrand left his son a lifetime of toil, which he has performed for more than three decades now, with sometimes not even a rest upon the Sabbath. It's a miracle he's kept at it, so uncomplaining and in such good health. Another man would have collapsed under the strain or given up long ago."

Prue thought of Losee's son, Piers, who'd been much older than Petra—nearly as old as Ben—and had died of diphtheria in early childhood. Prue had never really known him, but knew how much his death had pained Losee and his wife, now so long dead herself. Perhaps if Piers had lived, or if Petra were sufficiently grown to marry off to some strong fellow, Losee would not have had to sell his business, but would have lived out his days in the house in which he'd been born. It wasn't meant to be, Prue told herself. It wasn't meant to be, or it would have been.

Joe went on, "I've never lived a day of my life without Losee as a neighbor; and frankly, I find it difficult to imagine. I know we shall always be friends, but yet I shall miss him. I am glad, however, that he's got a few years of the easy life ahead of him; and if I may say so without offending our Winship and Schermerhorn neighbors, I'm glad for Petra to grow up away from the smoke of the manufactories."

"No offense taken," Pieter Schermerhorn said.

Even in the torchlight, Prue could see such abject love in the way Ezra Fischer watched Tem, she wondered Tem was not moved by it. Though in part she puzzled over what he saw in Tem, she chiefly wished to know why her sister would so adamantly reject the honest suit of so successful and besotted a man.

"Let us raise a toast to him, then," Joe said. Those who held cups raised them; many of the rest removed their hats. "To Losee van Nostrand, Brookland's great ferryman: long life, good health, and rest from labor."

Some said, "Cheers," and others, "Amen," and the cups were passed hand to hand. Prue took her draught before handing it on to Pearl, who drank deeply in honor of the occasion. A passing freighter rang its bell, and a few of the children pushed to the edge to watch its dim form glide past on the dark water.

Mr. Fischer stepped up to Joe, who gave him the tankard. When he touched the spoon upon it, people turned eagerly toward him. No doubt, Prue thought, they wondered what kind of man he was. He seemed mysterious not only because of his faith, but because it was rumored he'd lived all his days in Ulm before immigrating to New York only a decade previously, and yet his command of English was past compare. Furthermore, since Matty Winship had passed on, Brooklyn had lacked a gentleman who cared for his appearance; so Prue felt certain the sheen of Fischer's coat in the flickering torchlight held its fascination for others besides herself.

"Mr. van Nostrand," he said, his voice clear, "you have been a noble competitor, and have given me good reason to understand the loyalty your neighbors feel to you and to your business. Now I hope to be able to earn that loyalty myself, and in doing so I shall always use you for my example. Let me say to you, your fair daughter, and all this assembled company, that I shall do my best to provide your friends and neighbors safe and timely passage; and that if I can do so in even the palest imitation of your good spirits, I will count myself a success."

The cups went up once more, and Losee said, "Thank you, Mr. Fischer."

"Do you see?" Abiah said quietly to Tem. "You're a fool to spurn him. He's a perfect gentleman."

Tem swatted at her, but then laughed.

Ben and Prue took a number of compliments on their bridge—from that vantage, it was a ghostly structure in the distance, already so vast it

made Winship Gin, the Schermerhorn ropewalk, and the houses of
Clover Hill resemble so many outbuildings. She saw Will Severn listening
in at the edge of their conversations, but in his shy fashion, he averted his
gaze whenever Prue chanced to catch his eye.

It was a chilly evening, and Prue thought to be out in gloves must be
a hardship for Pearl, as they dulled her voice as a mouthful of cotton
would an ordinary person's. They therefore said their good-byes while
there was still quite a gathering upon the landing, and made their way
down the open stairs to the Shore Road. In addition to the torches, the
waxing moon shone on the water. They had not ventured far before Prue
heard a voice behind her call out, "Mrs. Horsfield?"

Prue instinctively looked to see if Patience was nearby, then turned to
find Will Severn a few paces behind them, his hat in his hand and his
shock of gray hair bearing its impression. Tem and Abiah kept walking.

"May I have a word with you?" he asked.

Ben swung Prue's hand lightly. "Go on," Prue said, reaching up to
kiss his cheek. "We won't be a minute." To Pearl she said, "You as well,"
and Pearl hissed as she took Ben's arm.

Severn stood with his battered brown hat against his chest.

"You don't really want to stand in the road, do you?" Prue asked him.

"No."

"Come with me to the countinghouse—the stove heats up in an instant. Or have you been out upon the bridge yet? It's a fine view at night,
though it'll be windy there."

"I would be delighted, if it's not too much to ask."

"It would be my pleasure," Prue said.

They kept silent as they walked downriver toward the gate, which was
tied shut with a sturdy knot. It took a moment to work it open with her
cold fingers, and then Prue swung the gate back on its hinges. It moaned
as she pulled it.

As they ascended the ramp, Will Severn's face shone bright as the
evening. Prue enjoyed his expression of delight. "I had no idea," he said,
"how beautiful it would be to stand upon it."

Indeed, the lights of the gathering on the landing, and those of the
visible houses of the ferry district and Olympia, twinkled like fireflies.
The river smelled fresh and clear.

"What a wonder," he went on. "Truly, a miracle."

"Your praise means much to me," Prue said. "Thank you." They continued in silence up as far as possible on the Brooklyn arm. The water glittered like coal beneath them, and Prue wondered if she knew why he wished to speak with her. "If you aren't afraid of heights, we can go closer to the edge," she offered.

He looked taken aback by the suggestion. "I admit to you I've never been higher than my own belfry."

"Then let us stay as we are," Prue said.

The upward slope of the ascending arm felt slight underfoot, but they were now standing high above the water. Though Prue was anxious to hear what she thought would be the good news for which he'd drawn her aside, this was almost secondary to the simple, visceral thrill of standing upon one arm of the bridge she'd dreamed of, and looking out at its dim sister, jutting toward them from Manhattan. The wind had picked up, and whipped against Prue's limbs.

"I am so proud of you, Mrs. Horsfield," he said.

Prue let out an awkward laugh. "Why do you address me so formally? I have ever been Prue to you, and you Will to me."

"But you're not a girl anymore," he said, as if this were an explanation.

"No, and I regret it little, except if it means you shall no longer be my friend." She looked around and said, "If it were still the building season, I could offer you a fancy seat on a spool of rope or a crate of tools, but if you want to sit now, we have only the boards of the roadway."

"I am fine to stand," he said. He stood nodding and looking out at the view. "I'm sure you wonder what has made me seek you out this evening." He looked away toward the water, then back to her, his chin tucked slightly beneath his blue muffler. "I desire to marry your sister."

"Oh, I had hoped it would be so," she said, and reached out to touch his arm.

When he had recovered from the surprise of being touched, he took her hand in both his own. "You give your permission, then?"

"It is not mine to give."

"And you know which sister I mean?"

Now Prue began to laugh in earnest, and pulled back her hand. "Do you imagine I could think you meant Tem? Who has turned away every suitor who's approached her, and would cow you utterly within the week?

No, Will Severn. I know which sister you mean." She was surprised, after all the years in which she had thought little of him, to find her body had been so drawn to his. "You wish to marry my sister Pearl."

"I do," he said. "I love her dearly."

"She has spoken nothing to her sisters about this attachment, but we have both seen the way you look at each other, and I imagine you will be happy together. But are you sure," she went on, "she is the sort of creature of which one makes a wife?"

"In what way do you mean?" he asked. "She has already accepted me, but I come to you, as her guardian, to ask permission."

"I simply want it clear between us, Will, that you understand what you would be doing, marrying such an invalid."

The smile did not fade altogether from his face, but even in the moonlight, she could see it wane. "She is not an invalid," he said. "She is as healthy as you or I."

"But she cannot see to your parishioners as a minister's wife should do."

He shook his head. "I disagree with you. She can do so as well as anyone. Perhaps better, as unlike many of my parishioners, she has a heart full of compassion."

Prue felt a vague discomfort at his words, though she could not have said why.

"Prue Winship, I am not a wealthy man, but I love your sister, and I desire to marry her. Please give us your permission."

"I repeat, I cannot give it. I am not her father. I will speak to my husband and see what he says; and we will bring word to you as soon as possible."

"Yes," he said, and licked his small lower lip. "Perhaps, if I may be frank with you, I should indicate it is a matter of some urgency."

The wind freshened, and the water seemed to be rushing by more quickly. Prue could hear the laughter and the rumble of conversation at van Nostrand's landing, but could not make out its substance.

"Do you hear me plain?" he asked, and reached over to touch her elbow.

Again, she felt the electrical current travel through her, though it felt milder now. "I believe I do," she said. "I will speak to Ben at once."

"Thank you." He brought her hand up to his face and kissed it, then let it go.

They walked back down the bridge in silence, and Prue could not feel her feet on the roadbed. She did not know if this was due to the cold or to the shock of what she believed she'd heard him say. He tied shut the gate inexpertly and asked, "Shall I see you home?"

"Heavens, no," Prue said, thinking all the while she could not make the situation ordinary by pretending it was so. "It's a short distance." As he continued to watch her, she said, "We shall seek you out in the morning, have no fear."

He bowed to her before heading the other way up the Shore Road.

Prue found herself uncertain where to go on the silent road. She had traveled from the works to Joralemon's Lane on so many occasions, she thought her body should be able to walk the route without her mind's intercession; but it was her body, at that juncture, seemed outside her control. Her mind was blank as the water she walked beside.

At home, she found a fire blazing in the kitchen, and Tem and Ben sitting before it, apparently in good spirits, and drinking gin.

"Where is Pearl?" Prue asked the moment she had closed the door behind her.

Ben rose to greet her and said, "Christ, you look ill. What did the minister say?"

"Where's Pearl?"

"She and Abiah are changing her sheets," Tem said, also rising to her feet.

Prue crossed the room to the half-open door, behind which Pearl was folding back an embroidered sheet over her quilt while Abiah had the turnscrew in the bedpost to tighten the ropes. They had a good fire going in the grate. Prue had never understood the rage that had possessed her father the night he'd dragged Pearl practically by the hair to apologize for the theft of the book; but although she could not explain herself, if she'd held a weapon in her hand at that moment, she believed she could have killed her sister.

"What did he want, love?" Ben asked, coming up behind her.

"Pearl," Prue began, in as calm a tone as she could muster, "are you carrying the minister's child?"

Abiah turned dumbstruck to look at Prue, and both Ben and Tem began exclaiming as if she'd gone mad, but Prue hushed them.

"Pearl?" she repeated.

Pearl tentatively raised both palms toward the ceiling, and her eyebrows followed.

Before Prue knew what she was doing, she lunged across the room and slapped her sister's face. Pearl didn't try to fend her off, but Ben was on her in an instant, wrapping one arm across her breastbone to pull her back. "Prue," he said, "what are you thinking?"

"What do you have to say for yourself?" Prue said sharply to Pearl. Pearl recoiled at her tone. Prue had slapped her near her nose, and her left eye began to water, though she wasn't crying. More quietly, Prue said, "Pick up your book."

Pearl reached down and opened it, but stood saying nothing. After what seemed an eternity, she wrote a note, then held it out to Prue. *I am not certin*, it read, *but I believe*.

"Good Lord," Ben said softly, and dropped his arm from across Prue's chest.

Abiah said, "What has she written?" though she must have known the answer.

Tem, who had come into the doorway, said, "She believes herself with child."

Abiah said, "Mercy."

Pearl wrote, *How does one know, without Fail?* and held it out to Prue.

Prue shook her head no and said, "You must have reason to think it might be so?" The idea of Will Severn making sport with her sister was unbearable. She could neither imagine it nor drive it away.

Pearl wiped her nose on her sleeve, wrote, and held the book back up to her. *Who are you to ask?* it read.

Prue felt the embers of her anger continuing to smolder. "Your sister, and your guardian."

She took it back to write, *& when you & Ben had yr Pleasure in the Haystacks all the Yeers before you were wed, to whm did you have to apologize?* No one answered her, and she flipped to a new page and wrote, *I've never once prezum'd to tell you how to manage y^r Affayrs.*

"But you are not responsible for me," Prue nearly spat at her. "You are the one has been marked since birth, and it is my duty to look after your welfare."

Pearl hissed, and wrote, *Mark'd because you mark'd me.*

Prue read the words twice before she understood their import. "Pearl," she said, "you cannot—"

But Pearl gave her a sharp "Ssst," and went back to writing. Prue could not summon the words to object a second time.

Ben asked quietly, "What is this?" but Prue waited for Pearl's response.

It came: *I know you curs'd me in our mothr' Womb. Is it not so?* Her eye was still watering from the blow, and she brushed angrily at it.

As long as Prue had lived, she had striven to keep this knowledge from Pearl and from everyone else. She had regretted it as she regretted no other thing, and kept it locked away where not even her husband might know it. To have Pearl bring it out into the open so matter-of-factly, on a cold November evening, seemed strangely familiar—it was the thing Prue had most dreaded, and she had therefore already drama-tized this scene in her imagination a thousand times—and yet uncanny, like a voice from the grave. She was horrified to know her sister knew of her crime, but Pearl's admission also came as a kind of relief. What could Prue not tell her, if she knew this?

"How long have you known?" Prue asked. Though Ben and Tem were quiet, she could feel their confusion in the air behind her.

Always, Pearl wrote. *Johana told me, when I was small.*

"And all these years, you've said nothing to anyone?"

She shook her head—equivocally, Prue thought—no.

Ben touched the back of Prue's arm and asked again, "Sweet, what is this?"

"Not to Tem? Not to Mother nor Father?"

"I've no idea what you speak of," Tem said.

Pearl shook her head with greater emphasis, and both her eyes filled with tears.

Prue's own smarted, as if she were the one who'd been slapped. She looked at her sister, standing there ready to cry and no doubt pregnant, and Prue loved her more than anything in the world. She loved her more than Ben, more than her lost daughter, the distillery, or the dream of a bridge. "I am so sorry," she said. She longed to pick her up and hold her. "I'm sorry, Pearlie," she said again, and watched Pearl's mouth open exactly as it had in the awful dream, and watched her white teeth shine as she cried.

"But what for?" Ben asked.

"I laid a curse on her when she was in the womb." There was pleasure in saying what all these years she had striven to hide. "You see what was the result."

"I don't understand," Tem said. "Were you five years old when Pearl was born?"

Prue turned and nodded to her. "Six."

"Well, you can't have put a curse on her."

Pearl kept crying.

"Prue, are you listening? You may have wished her ill, but little girls can't curse their sisters. Believe me, it's not possible; had it been, I should have done it to you long ago."

"But you see, it is what happened. I stood at the top of Clover Hill and wished with all my might for the Lord to smite her. And look what came to pass."

"Lord have mercy," Abiah said quietly, and excused herself from the room. A moment later, Prue heard the door to Abiah's bedroom shut behind her. Prue thought she had gone in to pray.

Pearl flipped to a new page and wrote, *Will you let me marry him?*

"I don't see I have any choice," Prue said. "And I wouldn't keep you from him, in any case."

Pearl wiped mucus from her upper lip. *And will you apologize?*

"I have already done so, Pearl. I am sorrier for what I did to you than for any other thing I've done in my life."

"Apologize for slapping her," Ben said.

"Yes," Prue said. "I am sorry. I'm ashamed of myself."

Pearl weighed this a moment, then went to her wardrobe and gruffly unlatched the door.

"What are you doing?" Prue asked, but Pearl simply removed her other dress and a clean chemise, and laid them on the bed for a brisk and sloppy refolding. "Pearl," Prue said. When Pearl did not respond, Prue grabbed for her arm, but Pearl pushed her off. "I am sorry. I've regretted what I did every day of your life."

Tem said, "You've done nothing."

"I love you more than I can say," Prue said, but herself could hear how tinny the words sounded.

Pearl balled up a pair of stockings and threw them on top of her clothes. She wiped her nose again brusquely on her sleeve, and began to write. When she had finished the page, she tore it from the book and would have flung it at Prue, could paper be flung. Instead, it wafted to the floor. She continued to write as Prue bent to pick it up.

It read, *How dare you acuse me of Immorality, when you yrself are the darkest Sinner in the Room? You might have said a Word,—one Word,—of Apology all this Time, & you've skulk'd around, hoping I would'n't take you to Task. I wo'n't,—*

She tore off a second sheet, and this time held it out to Prue. *—accept yr Apology. It is'n't good enough.*

"No," Prue said, "please don't go. I am sorry." She wished there were some other way to phrase it, but it was all she could say. "You don't know how I have suffered over this."

Ben had read the notes over her shoulder and said to Pearl, "Please put that down."

She had bent over for the pillow slip she had not yet worked onto her pillow. It was one she had embroidered herself, with flowers and vines.

Prue said, "I will not have you leave this house," though she heard this ring false as well. How could she prevent her? Who was she to say?

Pearl shoved her clothes in the pillow slip, and took her extra pencils from her table and crammed them in on top. She was still crying, and obviously annoyed at herself for it. She twisted the bundle closed and held it against her chest.

"Put that down," Prue said, and felt a new surge of anger when Pearl did not comply. "I demand that you put it down," she said more forcefully, then grabbed for the bundle.

With one hand Pearl continued to grip tight to her possessions, and with the other she struck out at Prue with the blind viciousness of a cat. Her mouth was wide open, and she let out a rasping cry. When Prue tried to contain her, Pearl kept striking at her until at last she pushed her with enough force to send Prue stumbling a few steps back. Whether from the force of this exertion or simply from rage, she collapsed onto her mattress with her pillow slip in her arms, and continued to make her awful, inarticulate, nearly soundless howl. The fire continued to crackle, and the floorboards creaked as Prue resettled her weight, but a terrible silence seemed to reign in the room as Pearl gave vent to her anger and frustration. Prue did not know what to do or say. She did not want to see Pearl thus, yet could not avert her eyes from the spectacle. When she looked to her husband and to Tem, they appeared equally watchful and uncertain.

After a few minutes, Tem said, "Pearl? It won't be so bad, you know. It isn't so bad." But when she tried to move closer to comfort her, Pearl's hand shot out in warning, and Tem backed away.

Her howling soon subsided into sobs, and Prue longed to gather her into her lap. She knew Pearl would still fit; she knew comfort still resided in such an embrace. But she could not approach her. As the minutes passed, Pearl gradually gained control of herself, and drew her handkerchief from her pocket to blow her nose. Her face was red as blood, her eyes accusing. She took up her pad to write again, and for an agonizing moment everyone in the room was still. Then she returned the pencil to its hasp, stood slowly, and shook her fingers at Tem to ask her to move from the doorway. Without a word, Tem stepped aside.

"Please don't go, Pearl," Prue said, following her into the kitchen. She felt desperate—felt she would grab her and throw her down if she had to; but in the moment, she did not.

Pearl took the tinderbox their father had given her from the mantel and placed it inside her bundle. Then she pulled on her boots, took Tem's coat from its peg, wrapped it over her shoulders, and walked out, leaving the door open behind her.

Abiah came out from her bedroom, and they all stood in the doorway, watching her cross the dead grass in the moonlight. Prue expected her at least to turn back to look at them, but she did not; she walked with a firm stride out into the Ferry Road, and was soon lost to sight.

Ben said, "Should I run after her?"

But Tem answered him, "I don't see what good it would do if she wants to go."

"She won't stay away," Ben said. He shepherded them all back in and shut the door against the November air. As they were all looking at him quizzically, he said, "This is her home."

"I think she'll go to him, Ben," Prue said. "I reckon she'll stay."

"She'll at least return to let us marry her from this house," he said. Prue hoped he was correct.

"Why did she take my coat?" Tem asked. "Her own hangs there beside it."

Prue looked at Pearl's gray coat. She had thought it serviceable, but perhaps, on reflection, it was wearing thin at the seams. "She might have thought yours would be warmer," she said, "or was a better coat," and Tem shook her head.

They sat down to wait, as if there were any real possibility she would turn back. In the worried silence, Tem began pouring out gin; and when they had finished it all, she set out for the storehouse to bring up more. She had been gone only a few minutes, however, before she returned. "What's wrong?" Prue asked. Her heart was in her throat, and though she tried to tell herself there was nothing over which to panic, she couldn't calm herself.

"My keys were in my coat pocket," Tem said. "I can't get into the storehouse."

Prue could not express her gratitude there was no worse news, though she could not imagine what it might have been. "Mine are on the peg," she said, and Tem took them and went back down.

When she returned, they continued drinking; but Prue thought they could never distill a gin strong enough, nor could she drink sufficiently of it, to bring her the oblivion she sought. She wanted to obliterate everything: her queer reaction to Will Severn and his proposition; the way she had slapped Pearl; the curse she'd laid on her in the first place, and the horrible disposition that had led her to do so. She wished she could tear her own personality out by the roots. No liquor could make that possible.

Twenty-five

THE CONFLAGRATION

Thurs^d 13 June 1822

Dear R,—

How I wish I could give you the satisfaction you desire as regards my treatment of your Aunt Pearl; & how I wish even more I could demand you believe me an altogether good woman, whose desire was never to harm anyone, least of all my sister.

I fully comprehended the injustice of the way I'd treated her. That night she left, I felt as if my chest & throat had been scraped raw from within, so profound was my remorse for my misdeeds. Your father, Aunt Tem, & Abiah after a time retired to their beds, but hours passed before I could quit pacing the kitchen & Pearl's small closet. One says, in relating such circumstances, one was *thinking them over*, but I was not thinking; only moving restlessly, in an agony of remorse & self incrimination. I do not know how long I walked the floorboards,—Abiah had forgotten to wind the clock, and it wound down soon after the house went quiet,—but at last the kitchen fire burned out & I realized I was too tired to wish to stoke it. I went upstairs & put down my head, and before I could fall to sleep, the memory of the dream of the *spirit canoo* once more presented it self to my inward eye. Once more I could see Pearl awash in slick, dark gore & hear the sad splash of my paddle in the night-time river; and of a sudden, I believed I understood what the dream had meant to reveal to me all along,—which is very like the thing you your self tell me in your letter. This revelation was not *The Bridge*, nor a dramatization of the ill I had so long ago done Pearl, but a simple sign for the manner in which I had made her suffer daily. In that moment, it was as if the curse I'd laid on my sister were an onion, & though I had sought to peel it all my days, I had only just then gotten past the paper to the luminescent flesh within;—& I saw that the curse lay not in the words I had uttered, which had scudded across to Mannahata never to be recalled; but in the manner in which I'd allowed them to colour my behaviour toward her, ever since. For 23 years I had showered my guilt upon her, thought of protecting her, bought her gifts, worry'd on her behalf; but I had never once simply looked to see in whose interest I had done all this. Had I done so, I might have seen the depth of that streak running through her, or how she felt confined or unhappy. But you see, I did not. You see, my Recompense, you have hit your mark.

More soon,—I cannot bear to write it now,—

Mother

But there it was, clear as day in her memory.

She went downstairs at dawn the next morning when she heard Abiah go into the kitchen to light the fire. "Has Pearl come home?" Prue asked.

Abiah regarded her a moment as if she, too, had slept badly. Then she proceeded to sweep out the grate.

Prue resolved to bring her sister home. She could imagine what she looked like after the night she'd spent, but without stopping to splash her face or smooth her hair, she stood up and put on her coat.

"It won't do you any good," Abiah said.

Prue worked her buttons shut. "No, I imagine it won't, but I shall go anyway."

It had grown colder since the evening before, and as most of her neighbors had been out late drinking on the landing, the Ferry Road was unusually quiet. Prue heard her chickens fussing in their coop and saw wisps of smoke beginning to curl from the Livingston and Cortelyou chimneys, but no one but her was about. Her footfalls seemed to echo against the road. There was no smoke rising from Will Severn's chimney, and Prue hesitated before knocking on the door. As she did, she heard a baby crying from the house that had once been Ben's, and looked over toward that door as if she could will her husband to be standing behind it, offering her courage. She knocked once, and when she heard no stirring within, knocked again, more loudly.

A moment later, Will Severn arrived at the door in his dressing gown. Prue had never seen him unshaven, but he looked as if he, too, had passed a difficult night.

"I'm sorry to disturb you so early," she said.

"No," he said, then cleared his throat, which still sounded thick from sleep. "It's no bother. I trust nothing is amiss."

Prue could not read his expression; perhaps he was merely tired. "Is my sister Pearl here?"

He nodded, but neither said more nor opened the door to her.

"May I see her?" Prue asked, though she felt it demeaning to have to.

"I'll ask," he said, and closed the door gently in her face.

He needn't have done more. Prue knew she should turn and walk up Buckbee's Alley right then, but it was almost as though her pride wished to be wounded by Pearl's response. Some minutes elapsed before he returned wearing the same benevolent expression he offered troubled parishioners.

"Forgive me, Prue," he said, and reached out for her hand. "I cannot make her change her mind."

Prue's face smarted. "It's not your fault," she said. If Pearl had told him everything, she was surprised Will Severn was treating her so civilly. "Please convey my apologies to my sister, and tell her that as happy as we would all be to have her back home, we would be content to be able to speak with her."

He squeezed her hand before letting it go. "I will tell her. She wept all evening."

"As did I," Prue said, and turned back toward the port.

It was with a heavy heart she went back to pressing herbs in the rectifying room that day. Had she not known how to do the work by second nature, she would have spoiled the batch. She could only think how large the distillery was—how great the buildings, how prodigious its noise, bustle, and output of smoke. From the outside, she sometimes imagined it looked as if it might produce something necessary to the sustenance of a nation, not mere liquor. Yet at its center stood nothing more than herself and her sister Tem, both brokenhearted that day, to differing degrees. The manufactory was as fragile as they were.

Isaiah came to find her when the bell rang to return the workers to their posts after the midday break. "Did you eat, Prue?" he asked, coaxing her away from the press.

"I'm not hungry."

"She'll come home," he said.

"No, she won't." Her arms ached from working the press all morning and into the afternoon. "I imagine the news is all over town by now."

He gave her a curt nod, his lips pursed as he glanced toward the window. "I took lunch at Joe Loosely's. One cannot say how gossip travels so quickly, but it was the talk of the barroom. That, and that Joe had a visit this morning from another purveyor of gin."

This was the last thing Prue had expected to hear. "How so?"

"A new operation, called Putnam's, on the Schuylkill."

Had she not been so exhausted and fraught with care, she felt her heart would have jumped out of her body. "Not really?" she said, and to clarify, "John Putnam? The foreman of my father's brewhouse?"

Isaiah shrugged his shoulders defeatedly.

There were herbs lying in the press, but she felt she must go speak to Joe right away, though she knew she would either be subject to questioning about her sister or, worse, catch her neighbors glancing sidelong in her direction. She closed her eyes for a moment.

Isaiah said to her, "If you go talk to him, please eat while you're there."

"Yes," Prue said, and left to walk upferry by the Shore Road. Ezra Fischer was out on his landing with two workmen and seemed not to have heard her news, for he removed his hat and bowed pleasantly to her as she passed. His gallantry only irritated her, and she picked up her pace.

Most of the men of Brooklyn had finished their midday meal and returned to work by the time Prue arrived, but she still felt the barroom hush as she entered. The Hicks brothers turned away, as if they didn't want to see her, and a few others coughed or made extraneous noise with their knives and forks. It had been a while since she'd gone into the Liberty Tavern. She and Joe had both done their best to smooth out the wrinkles between them, but it still made Prue feel awkward that he had not supported the bridge.

"Prue Winship," Joe said from behind the bar. He was depositing dirty cups in a basin of water to soak.

"Is it true what I've heard from Isaiah?" she asked straightaway. "About John Putnam?"

Joe shook his head at her and smiled. "We can't be certain it's him, of course."

"Who else learned the business of distilling from my father? And he had family near Philadelphia. It must be he."

Joe continued to shake his head. "I told Isaiah all I knew of it, which was the representatives of Putnam Gin came by boat to exhibit their wares this morning. Said they'd been doing good business in and around Philadelphia and were looking to expand north and south. Sit down, Prue. We've veal cutlets; would you like one?"

Prue was so upset about her sister and John Putnam, she could not imagine how she'd eat, but she said, "Yes, thank you."

Joe called into the kitchen to convey the order to his wife. "Never fear," he said when he returned. "His product's not so fine as yours."

"You tasted it?" Prue asked.

"You'd rather I hadn't? You wouldn't know a thing about it, then." Prue sat down in front of him at the bar. He drew her a pint and she sipped at it without tasting it. "Nowhere near so fragrant. But he's selling it a good deal cheaper than you, and they claim to be getting a good business, down south." He dried his hands, drew a pint for himself, and came around to sit beside her. "Bad day for business all around, I suppose. Did you see what Fischer was doing?"

"Standing on the landing of the New Ferry. He took off his hat to me."

"He's building an alehouse, right there."

"He cannot—"

"Well, God bless the legislature, they wouldn't grant him a license for hard liquor. But they say we're a big enough town to support three places to drink in." Mrs. Loosely brought out Prue's plate, and as soon as she smelled the cutlet, Prue realized she was ravenous. "Fischer's a weasel. Says he thinks people'll just stop off for a pint and a boiled egg and be on their way, but I don't know who he thinks he's fooling."

"He hasn't your stables," Prue said between bites. "Nor your auction block."

"And he shan't, either. He's boxed in—there's nothing else he can buy in the area, unless Isaiah Horsfield goes under."

Prue scanned Joe's face to see if he meant any malice; but she told herself it was in her imagination.

"Sorry to hear the news about your sister as well," Joe said, lowering his voice. Still, all the other patrons quieted down to listen.

"Thank you, Joe. We hope we shall remedy it soon." She could not taste her lunch, but she ate it all to show she was not troubled by the conversation.

That evening, Tem went up to the minister's to attempt to talk to Pearl, but she, too, was rebuffed, though she had only asked for the return of her coat and keys. To be inside their own house was unbearable—they all sat there gloomily, and Pearl's old cat wandered around, mewling like a lost kitten—yet Prue imagined her sister and husband felt as she did, that it would be even worse to light out for one of the taverns. Prue wished their current difficulties could sit more lightly on Ben's shoulders than on her own, but this was impossible. He loved Pearl as a sister; and his fortunes, and the bridge's, were every bit as much tied up in the distillery as Prue's or Tem's.

The week passed slowly, though there was work to do at the distillery, preparing for the holidays. Each morning and evening, one of them would walk up to Will Severn's house to ask if Pearl would see them. Each day, though Severn offered his apologies, he turned them away.

In the evenings, Prue took to sitting in Pearl's room, as if this itself could explain the pass they had come to, or bring her home. She searched again and again through the few possessions her sister had left behind— some old underclothes, her books, her embroidery, and some knitting pins that had belonged to their mother.

"We should bring them to her," Tem said, "so she'll have aught to do there."

"If she wants them, she'll ask," Prue replied, holding tight to the bundle of ebony pins. "I think it might be better if she grows bored. She'll come back more quickly."

The last thing Pearl had been embroidering was a foldback for a sheet, with a thick, satin-stitched border of jungle plants. Prue could not find the illustrations on which these had been modeled, but their outlines were traced in pencil across the blank part of the landscape. Prue had little facility with the needle, but she worked it out from where her sister had anchored it in the fabric, and began trying to stitch across the outline of a leaf. Her embroidery looked childish by comparison with her sister's; Prue thought that if Pearl saw it, it would surely anger her. Nevertheless, she persevered. Working on this project her sister had abandoned seemed a way of being close to her; or at least, with each stitch, Prue thought she came a stitch's distance closer to understanding the boredom that had afflicted her sister in her days at home, and that same distance closer to repenting for the wrongs she had done her.

Still, she could not sleep, knowing Pearl was abroad. She almost wished Will Severn would tell them he and Pearl had married and invited none of them; it would be better than the silence that then obtained. It would be better than to sit awake each night, once the clamor of the docks and the roads had subsided, and hear the bitter shrilling of a barn owl, and wonder what would become of her sister.

One night perhaps ten days after Pearl's departure, Prue was sitting at the kitchen table with the needlework, and suddenly realized everything around her sounded strange. Usually she heard the rustle, if not the calls, of nocturnal creatures, but they were all quiet; instead, she thought she heard sounds out on the docks. Her first thought was, there were boys enough in Brooklyn to upend every fishing boat in Creation, if they'd set their minds to it; she imagined they had worked open the gate to the bridge and were out drinking upon it, and she only hoped none would fall to his death. She thought she heard something being dragged along either the docks or the bridge's wooden roadway, then stopping; a moment later, it resumed, then again fell silent. Yet though the sound concerned her, she was exhausted deep in her bones; and though she tried to remain awake, she knew she must have drifted off, for she was awakened before dawn by the unmistakable sound of one of the distillery's warning bells ringing agitatedly in the night.

She knew she did not imagine this sound, because she heard the rest of her family sitting up or resettling in their beds. "Prue?" Ben whispered. She could hear him through the floorboards, and walked as softly as she could upstairs.

He was sitting up in bed. The bell pealed thrice, then stopped; thrice again, then stopped again, which was the signal of distress. Whoever was ringing it was upset enough to choke the rope, and was not allowing the clapper to complete its swing before tugging it again. "It must be a fire," Ben said.

Prue strained her nose but could smell nothing. Before she could answer him, he was out of bed and tucking his nightshirt into his britches. Prue went across the hall to rap on Tem's door. "Get up," she said. "Something's amiss at the works."

Tem opened her door quickly; she must have been standing there fully dressed. She had one hand on her forehead. "You're certain it's our bell?"

"Did you drink too much?"

Tem held up her finger and thumb to indicate a small amount.

Prue started down the stairs.

Abiah was already rummaging in the pantry and bringing forth their leather buckets. All four were crazed with a fine lattice of cracks from being stored in the dry kitchen, but they would still hold water. Abiah handed the buckets to Ben and Prue, and went to the peg for her coat. When she opened the kitchen door, Prue smelled the smoke for the first time. It was rising from the waterfront, not so thickly it obscured the view, but enough so she could not determine which building was aflame, though she could see by its proximity it belonged to the distillery.

"Look up," Ben said, as she peered down toward the water. The very tip of the Brooklyn arm was also on fire—though again, from that vantage, she could not determine the extent of the blaze.

Prue let out a deep breath and stood transfixed. Ben went inside for all their coats; Prue put on Pearl's, though it was tight, and let Tem wear her own. "Come, then," Ben said, and they hurried down the hill.

Halfway down Joralemon's Lane, the air began to thicken with smoke. Ben stopped and turned to the three women. "Tie your handkerchiefs over your noses and mouths and crouch down," he said. "When you get to the water, wet the cloth." He kissed Prue's cheek and set off toward the blaze. The warning bell was still tolling, and a crowd had begun to gather, most with buckets, a few gawking.

"I am sure they know, in New York," Tem said, shaking out Prue's handkerchief of pocket lint. The one in the pocket of Pearl's coat was clean. "They must have sent their engine by now."

But beyond the bell, the sounds of people shouting, and the rumble of burning wood, Prue heard nothing from the river.

The southern end of the distillery, including the windmill, appeared safe for the moment, but the end nearest the bridge was clotted with black smoke. Neighbors—not all of whose faces could Prue recognize behind their handkerchiefs—were hauling buckets of water up from the straits and dashing them at the flames, which had thus far engulfed only the rectifying house. Prue feared the machinery within would tumble like boulders if the floor beneath gave way, but her true concern was the possibility, if the casking house caught fire, the warehouses would go next; as she thought this, she noticed the near storehouse's door lolling open. If ignited, the stores would burn with a fierce heat and intensity. "Better to keep it off the storehouses than the other buildings," she said to Tem. Tem said nothing in reply. They tied on their handkerchiefs and ran with their buckets around the fire's periphery to the water. There Prue lost sight of Abiah and Tem but found Isaiah, also with his kerchief over his face like a bandit, looking out at the bridge. Its whole tip was engulfed in flame and burning like a torch.

He put his arm around her and said, "I've spied the engine," directly into her ear. Otherwise she might not have heard him above the din. "God grant they can help us."

"God grant, indeed. I'm afraid for the warehouses," she nearly shouted to him. "I think we should let the rectifying house go, and douse the casking room and the stores instead."

He stepped back and scanned the scene, his blue eyes red with smoke and the reflected firelight. "I don't know what to do."

"Do anything," Prue said. "I deceive myself to think it matters." She left him and dipped her bucket into the frigid water of the straits. She could not see Ben or Tem, but was glad to see ever more people streaming down Joralemon's Lane and the Shore Road to help.

Prue heaved the contents of her bucket at the foot of the casking house, and others followed suit. Soon enough, people were passing buckets along three lines—one for the stores, one for the casking house, and one for the blazing rectifying house. The water hardly affected the fire. When Prue glanced up at the Brooklyn lever, its river end was a ball of blue and yellow flame, surmounted by a storm cloud of acrid smoke. It creaked ominously, and with a crack like thunder, a section of the lever split off and tumbled into the river. People flinched, but continued to pass the buckets along. As she labored, alternately sweating from the fire and chilled from the water as it splashed, Prue remarked the bridge was burning fiercely—the timber had been well cured on installation, and pitch was as combustible as oil—but she had no time to prognosticate how the fire might spread.

No amount of water seemed sufficient to protect the casking house, for the rectifying house was burning like a kiln. Prue felt a moment of nostalgia for the beautiful copper stills and the hulking press—the machines on which her father had made his fortune and taught her his art—and could not bear to think of them melting into the hard Brooklyn sand; but it was no use feeling sentimental over machines. It was fortunate no one had been inside the buildings when the fire began, and Prue would count it a miracle if no one was killed before the fire burned itself out.

It was difficult to hear anything over the roar of the burning rectifying house, but Prue dimly heard bells clanging all over town to call people to the distillery's aid. In addition, a smaller bell was ringing from the river itself, which Prue prayed meant the fire engine was arriving. She thought she heard men shouting from the water, and she so wanted to hear the plash of oars drawing nigh, she easily could have imagined that, too. In the meantime, the heat of the burning building seemed to push against her, and the air was so foul she could barely breathe. No more than half an hour could have passed, but Prue felt she had been engaged in this futile labor for days.

When at last she heard the engine pull abreast of the bridge, the relief that flooded her body was unlike any she had ever experienced, cool and sweet as summer rain. Marcel Dufresne came to spell her in the line, and she ran down to the river, where a scant few—mostly neighborhood children, whom she shooed angrily up to the safety of Clover Hill—were also watching. The engine all but filled a double-sized barge and had been rowed thither by a team of twenty men, some of whom were now dropping anchor to hold the lumbering machine steady. Others were uncoiling the enormous hose. Phineas Bates, standing near Prue on the strand, was calling himself hoarse, shouting, "Weigh anchor! Weigh anchor! Get the buildings first!" but the engine men could not hear him. Four of them began turning the enormous crank wheel, which let out a shrieking whine as it drew water into the belly of the machine, and most of the rest braced the hose as it filled with water and stiffened. Phineas took off his greatcoat and without warning dove into the straits and began to swim.

Prue thought he would die of the cold before he reached the engine, and shouted at him in horror to turn back, but though others around joined in her cry, none would venture in after him. His slick head bobbed above the icy water like a seal's.

Sections of the Brooklyn lever continued to burn, and landed as gigantic flotsam in the river. This debris began to rush downstream, and Prue thought it would batter the Luquers' trash rack and tumble down the millrace to crush their wheel. As Phineas swam upriver toward the barge, those onshore screamed their throats raw trying to tell him to look out for the burning debris. As a spray began to emerge from the tip of the fire engine's hose, the men aimed it toward the lever and slipped and struggled to control the hose's force. It looked as if a giant serpent had risen from the straits. The water fanned out in the air, its arc much lower than that of the bridge, and Prue began to despair of its reaching its intended target. Slowly, however, the men twisted the hose and angled it farther upward; and at last it made contact with the underside of the lever. Phineas reached the barge, and one of the anchormen struggled to help him on board. Prue saw the fireman remove his coat and try to drape it around Phineas's shoulders; the coat was not big enough and hung high above his knees. Phineas hunkered down to be out of the way.

At first the water from the hose appeared to have no more effect upon the bridge fire than that being ferried by bucket to the rectifying house; both fires continued to roar. Prue stood with her eyes watering, still barely able to breathe, praying that some of the arm might be spared and that no one might die in the effort. The engine crew were shouting to one another, but she could no more hear what they were saying than they could hear her.

The men turning the wheel began to spin it harder, and a more forceful stream bathed the bridge's trussing. Only a few moments before, it had seemed foolhardy to hope for a good outcome, but now the dark smoke billowed more copiously and the bright core of the fire began to contract. People whooped their encouragement. Prue understood she would not know until later how much of the Brooklyn lever had been lost, but it did not appear to be half; she tried to contain her worry and tell herself it would not be an entire year's work to rebuild. The charred tip of the lever continued to smolder, and the engine men kept the stream of water upon it. Before the flames could be stanched, however, a shout arose from behind Prue. When she turned, she saw a mass of white flame where the rectifying house had been. The building's very shape had vanished; and it was so hot, no one was trying any longer to douse it, as it would have been too dangerous to approach those jumping, dancing flames. People stood back as if charmed, their buckets dangling from their hands. The horses in the stable, which stood between the warehouses and the abutment of the bridge, were whinnying madly, and someone hacked at the lock with an ax to free them. They bucked and thrashed their heads as they were led out, one by one, to the Shore Road. Prue saw poor Jolly go by, with the fire reflected in his wild eyes, and thought he was looking around for her, the one person who might convince him he was safe.

Suddenly a tendril of fire leapt across toward the casking house, which caught like a tinder stick. Some unlucky man stood in its way, and remained looking around him for a moment, his pants and shirt on fire, until another threw him to the ground and rolled him on the damp sand. They were both screaming. Shouts also came from the river, and the barge at last weighed anchor and began to lumber toward shore. The casking house was engulfed within moments, and the flames immediately began to lick at the near storehouse.

"Stand back!" Prue shouted to those near the building. They could not hear her over the ruckus from the river and the roar of the fire, but still she kept shouting. Those closest by her, realizing the hopelessness of her lone cry, began to echo it until it passed to those nearest the fire. They looked frantically for someplace suitable for retreat, and everyone else made way. As those closest to the storehouses scrambled back, the fire lit on the near one, and in a moment it was burning fast and hot. It was spectacular to see a thing consume itself so quickly; it nearly overwhelmed Prue with its terrible beauty. The flames spread to the other warehouse without pause, and thence to the shed that housed the timber for the bridge.

People continued to stream down to the waterfront, and the engine drew nearer the shore. It landed not far from where Prue stood, and immediately the men dragged the heavy hose up over the retaining wall and onto the strand. "Clear out!" they called, and everyone backed toward the cliffs. Phineas, still wrapped in the fireman's small coat, walked shivering through the shallows to shore. Two other men rushed out to him and led him back by the elbows. The pump men again began turning the wheel, and the spray pushed at the fire. The men still struggled to contain the force of the hose. This fire seemed much hotter than that which smoldered on the bridge. Some noble souls continued to throw their buckets of water at the edges of the conflagration, as if those droplets could tame the raging beast. The firemen kept spraying the hose back and forth across the blaze, daring it to spread beyond its current confines.

Prue expected the whole distillery to go up, followed by the ropewalk, the ferries, her own house, and Isaiah's. If the fire did not then spread to the trees, Brooklyn as a whole would likely be safe, as there was considerable distance between the older houses. If it managed to cross the road from Isaiah's house to Olympia, however, it would devour the entire neighborhood, so tightly were the houses packed together. Prue felt sick with worry and guilt as she thought this, but as she did, the blaze began to succumb to the water. It still burned, but less fiercely, until at last it was chiefly burning embers and clouds of charcoal-black smoke, more foul in scent than anything she had yet known. If there was an Other Side, and if the damned were banished there, this would be their very air.

Prue stood for what seemed an age watching the men contain the fire. As the flames subsided into a quiet hiss, the firemen called out to their compatriots to slacken their pace on the wheel. The pressure in the hose lessened, and it began to drip onto the sand.

Prue could hear her own breathing for the first time since the fire had begun. When she looked around, she felt as if she'd wakened from a nightmare. Everyone was covered in sweat and grime, obscured by a thick haze of smoke, and her knees were shaking. A three-quarters moon hung in the starry sky, and despite the acrid smoke, illuminated the scene sufficiently to see.

"Miss Winship?" one of the firemen said to her, and held out his sooty hand to her through the dark mist.

She took it, though her whole body was trembling. "I can't thank you enough," she said. "We should have lost everything without you."

He glanced up at the ruined, smoking bridge. "You must keep an eye on it yet; but I believe it is contained. I can hardly believe no lives were lost."

All around, people echoed his sentiment. "I can't thank you enough," she repeated. Her throat burned, and she could think of nothing more to say.

He nodded and wiped his dirty brow with the back of his equally dirty hand. "God grant you won't have need of us again."

"I pray so," she said, and others murmured assent. People were beginning to pull their ash-coated kerchiefs down from their sweating red faces and to sit down on the ground to rest, though the fire still smoldered.

The engine men slowly coiled the hose back onto the side of the great machine, and with bodies evidently aching with exhaustion, boarded it to row home. Though there was little light now, Prue saw Tem sitting a short distance off on the retaining wall, her head in her hands. "Who was burned?" Prue asked. "Where is he?"

"Elliott Fortune," Abiah called to her. Prue's heart stopped beating a moment; it might as well have been her own father. "It's Mr. Fortune, Prue. He's here. He lives."

Prue made her way through the crowd to him and, had she not been so shocked by the events of the evening thus far, would have begun to cry the moment she saw him. Abiah was beside him, squeezing well water over him from a bucket, using a piece of cloth torn from her skirt. Prue could not tell if he was wincing or smiling. "Mr. Fortune?" she said.

"No need to look so frightened," he said, looking up at her. His face was unharmed, but even in the dim light she could see his hands were blistered; and where Abiah had unbuttoned his shirt, the skin also appeared raw and slick. "It's not so bad as it looks."

Abiah shook her head as she kept trickling water on him. She said, "Dr. de Bouton will see him once we've got him home. I wanted to cool him off first."

"I cannot abide the notion of your being injured, helping to save this distillery," Prue said.

"No, never fear," Fortune said, and winced over the latest application of water. "If naught else, I owed it to your father's memory."

Prue looked around at the wreckage of so much of her father's dream. "Thank you," she said.

Joe Loosely was at the outskirts of those gathered around. "If I were you," he said, "I'd look into what Fischer had to do with this, is all I'll say."

Others standing around murmured. "Why so?" Prue asked. The thought had not even occurred to her.

Joe snorted and turned his head to the side. "Thirty-four years this distillery has stood on this property, and with all that combustible liquor, not a single blaze."

"Perhaps we were overdue," Prue said. She did not exactly believe this, but had no better theory.

Joe snorted again. "Then what explains the bridge? There wasn't any lightning this evening. I don't know what else could have set it off so hot and fierce."

"I agree," Simon Dufresne said.

Elliott Fortune said, "It's no time to think ill of our neighbors."

Prue said, "Mr. Fischer would never—"

But someone was frantically calling, "Prue? Prue?" from the top of the hill. It was a man's voice, high with distress, and Prue did not at first recognize it. When he hoarsely called out, "Tem Winship?" however, she realized it was Will Severn.

Jens Luquer put his hands around his mouth and shouted, "Mr. Severn? What's the trouble?"

He did not answer, but ran down the hill toward the works. "Tem?" he said, as he began to move through the knot of people. They made way for him. He had not been standing in the smoke all that time; no doubt he could not see through it, despite the moonlight.

Tem rose from her spot on the retaining wall. "Here," she said. She leaned over and spat into the river.

He ran toward her, but encountered Prue first and stopped, panting and leaning on his knees for support. "Heaven be praised," he said, still catching his breath, "there is not so much damage as I'd imagined."

"No thanks to you," someone muttered, and another whistled to quiet him.

Will Severn continued to pant. "Prue. Tem," he said. Tem came up behind her and put her hand on Prue's shoulder. "She's disappeared."

Prue had inhaled the thick smoke for what seemed hours, but only at that moment did she feel herself unable to breathe.

He wiped his mouth with the back of his hand. "She was sitting by the hearth reading when I went up to bed. When I was roused by the bells, I looked all round the house for her, but she was gone. I would have come to your aid, but I had to find her; and I've traveled the whole neighborhood, but she's nowhere. She's nowhere, Prue—her things are gone. Her clothes, Tem's keys—everything."

Until he spoke, Prue had felt she had borne up as well as could be expected of a person. She had just lost a fair portion of the bridge for which she'd mortgaged all her property, and she'd lost every ounce of product her factory had produced in a year. Elliott Fortune might very well die of his burns and Phineas Bates of the influenza. But when Will Severn told her Pearl was missing, she thought she might at last come undone. She stood, aware of nothing but her breath and the sound of the river running, and afraid she might faint. But in a moment, a thought arose in her mind with the vigor of a bubble in the mash tun: Pearl had been responsible for all this. Even to think it felt like blasphemy, but Prue's imagination swiftly sought to connect the open storehouse door and the flaming bridge with the scraping sounds she'd heard earlier. She could not figure how her small sister might have rolled or dragged a cask of gin up the accessway's incline, but the image remained with her. When she tried to drive it from her, it continued to hover nearby.

There had to be another explanation. "This cannot be," she said to Will Severn. To the crowd around her, she asked, "Has anyone seen my sister Pearl?"

People looked around before answering, "No."

"No one?" Prue asked, though she knew the question was redundant.

The river continued to lick past, carrying off pieces of the bridge's debris. She did not think she could voice her suspicion of her own sister. It was bad enough to have thought such a thing, but it would be worse still to give it play in the world. What choice did she have, however? Something must be done: Pearl was unaccounted for, and all the assembled people were waiting for her to speak.

"I wonder . . ." she began, but found her dry, sooty tongue unwilling to complete the work. She cleared her throat, and went on, "I wonder if my sister might have had aught to do with this fire?"

Will Severn said, "No," and around him people called out their confusion and concern.

"Prue," Peg Dufresne said, "that's not possible."

Prue wished with all her heart Peg was correct. She said, "I believe it may be. I believe . . ." she began, but again words failed her, and she lost her train of thought. Though her body felt parched all the way through, there were hot tears behind her eyes and in her throat. "My sister has had some reason for anger toward me of late, and likewise of anger toward the bridge and the distillery." To admit this before all the assembled company mortified Prue, yet the words came out more easily than she might have supposed. "You all know her to be of a kind disposition; but I believe it would be unwise not to consider her disappearance as somehow connected to this evening's terrible events." Pearl had the keys to the buildings; this would account for the open storehouse door. A missing cask of gin would explain the fire on the bridge. These facts were unbearable, given the misery the night had brought, and Prue wondered if she might erase them from her memory.

All around, people were frowning or kicking at the sand as if she'd said something inane. Only Tem answered her. "Very well," she said, "I see your reasons; but what, then? Do you suppose she ran off? Or what do you think? She fell in the river?"

Prue turned to regard her, and saw Pearl's very face, grimy and exhausted, looking back at her in the moonlight. "Perhaps we should . . ." she began, but felt her mind veering toward another, more awful possibility: that Pearl might have jumped. Then she turned from this explanation, as it was too frightful to bear. "Perhaps we should send out riders."

"We should dredge the river, that's what," said Simon Dufresne. "If she's fallen in, there might yet be the chance of saving her, but not for long."

Prue said to Tem, "She must have walked off, or asked a ride of a passing carriage."

Will Severn began to weep.

Simon said, "Reverend, excuse me, it's no time for tears. If Pearl is in Buttermilk Channel, she may yet be alive. We need to drag it now."

Prue's neighbors looked as tired as she felt, and the embers were still smoking all around.

Tem drew herself taller and called out, "Anyone with a boat and nets, we would be greatly obliged if you'd help us." She took a moment to collect her thoughts. "Anyone with a horse who would ride out toward Wallabout or Jamaica, or down toward Red Hook, we would also be thankful. Our own horses . . ." she said, and paused, listening for their anxious neighs, which echoed down from the ridge. "I believe Winship Gin's horses are on the Ferry Road, and may be taken by anyone, if they are calm enough to ride." People began to confer, and split off in groups to saddle their horses or retrieve their boats. Will Severn continued to lean on his knees and weep. Tem walked up to him and said quietly, "You will have Hell to pay, sir, if any ill has befallen my sister."

He did not respond to her.

She turned to Prue. "We should go on a boat. I believe it the more likely means of finding her."

Prue said, "I, too," though it cost her some effort to admit it. She took Tem's elbow, and together they walked down to their landing to climb aboard one of the barges. Ben and Marcel came on, along with two of the distillery workers to row it. Before doing anything, Ben took Prue in his arms and held her close. Over her shoulder he said to Marcel, "We shall need a net."

"I'll go borrow one from the dories on Butcher's Wharf," he said, and set out running upriver.

Cornelis Luquer came down to the water and said, "Jens is going to alert my father. If she's in the water, that's where she'll end up. I'll take a horse and head east out the turnpike. Joe has volunteered to ride up to the Wallabout." Prue saw Jens running past, down the dark Shore Road. Up on the hill, a crowd of boys were whistling and clicking their tongues as they tried to subdue the horses.

Someone—Isaiah, no doubt—had gone back to ring one of the warning bells, and it once more pealed out across the river, calm and clear. They had sent the engine home not half an hour before, and already they were calling for New York's help again. Ben said, "We need torches," to someone on the strand, who ran off shouting, "Torches!" This struck Prue as sorely ironic, given what they'd all just witnessed. "She'll be fine," Ben said into Prue's hair. "You'll see."

Prue prayed he was correct, but was preoccupied with thoughts of Pearl setting the fire. How else could it have occurred? The distillery might have gone up in smoke at any time during its operation, but at night, when the fires were cool, it was safer than a house. Barring lightning, there seemed no way to set it ablaze without a tinderbox. And as for Joe's assertion, Prue thought Ezra Fischer had little reason to start a conflagration. He was still taken with Tem, and even had he been angered by her refusal, his business was in no imminent danger from the bridge. As

Prue stood on the gently rocking barge, however, thinking through Pearl's reasons for discontent, she found herself wondering why it had not occurred to her earlier how much Pearl might resent the bridge. She had devoted as much of herself to its planning as anyone, for the reward of a grimace of pity from Hendrik Stryker and a subsequent return to the house. Perhaps she had always hated the distillery; and if she had long known what Prue had done to her and kept the secret to herself, it would no doubt have festered.

Prue tried to talk herself away from this line of reasoning as Ben tried to coax her from what he must have thought was her sorrow and fear. But the longer she dwelt on the possibility, the surer she became in her conviction. Pearl had taken a cask, lit the rectifying house—as this was the building that mattered most to Prue—lit the bridge, and jumped or fallen into the river. They would find her washed up in the Luquers' trash rack—exactly as their father had been found, but well pummeled by the bridge's debris.

Marcel returned with a torch in his good hand and a fishing net slung over his other arm. Prue stepped clear of Ben's embrace as Marcel climbed aboard and told her, "Everyone is coming. We shall all form a line, and begin to drag as soon as possible."

Tem was pacing the length of the barge. Ben said to her, "Don't worry, we shall find her," but she did not seem at all appeased.

Losee's ferryboat, manned by a stranger, was working its way across the river to enlist the New York fishermen's aid; and meanwhile, everyone from Red Hook to the Old Ferry who owned a rowboat was pulling it down off the docks while a companion held a torch aloft. Some of the Cortelyou boys commandeered Joe's fishing boat, which he'd built for sport and which one hardly ever saw on the water. Prue sat down on the barge's gunwale and watched the smoke clear and boats begin to assemble in a ragged line stretching all the way across the river. It made a far less elegant span than did what was left of the bridge, but as it drifted and broke, it was beautiful all the same.

Prue had never been out on the river at night, and was surprised at the gentleness of its motion. It hardly resembled the bustling daytime river; it was calm and black except for the uneven line of flickering torches stretched like a string of beads to its far shore. Prue could hear every word her neighbors spoke—about the fire, and about the likelihood of

Pearl being found in the river and not in an inn somewhere down the Jamaica road. Then the pilot of the final boat to join the New York side of the line hollered for the dredging to begin. Tem and Prue crouched together at the starboard side of their barge and gripped their net. Rachael Livingston held its other end, and Prue watched her across the six feet of water separating them. She thought Rachael was looking at her kindly for the first time in her life.

The scores of oarsmen began to row. Tem retched over the water.

They had traveled no more than a few minutes before a piece of the bridge's flotsam lodged in a net halfway down the line. Everyone stopped, tense with fear and excitement, until it was drawn in and the trapped wood cast into the water upriver, where it would no doubt knock continually on someone's stern. After the terrible heat of the fire, the cold of the river breeze bit at Prue's fingers and face. A great bass next held up their progress at the New York end; after that, some men drew up a broken lobster trap. At this rate, Prue imagined if her sister had hit the water living, there was no possibility she would still breathe when they found her. Seemingly inch by inch they progressed southward toward Upper New York Bay; and if they did not find her before they reached that open expanse, they would not do so until she washed up, bloated past recognition, eaten by crabs and invaded by eels.

Prue did not realize how spent she was until she found herself staring off in the distance for the spirit canoe. She knew it to be a figment of her own imagination, but she almost expected to see its vaporous form sliding silently toward land. Pearl would ride in the bow, her gray dress black with salt water, her wet hair sticking to her shoulders like kelp. The horrible sliver of boat would appear and publish Prue's shame for the delectation of all her neighbors. But of course, this had already happened; there could be no more dark secrets her neighbors did not know. Prue thought no night could be longer than one spent waiting for news of a beloved person. Neither the spirit boat nor Pearl appeared.

They were still out on the river when dawn broke over Brooklyn's rooftops. The light was pink as springtime in the flat, overcast sky, and empty of consolation. Many of those out on the river had not bothered to grab their coats before heading out to the blaze, and now they were shaking with cold. Tem's lips were blue. Even in Pearl's tight-fitting coat, Prue felt her boots and cuffs were frozen, and each time she thought she might be able to control her shivering, a new paroxysm seized her. Marcel kept freeing his maimed hand from the torch to stretch its remaining fingers.

"Does it pain you?" Prue asked him.

"When it's cold," he replied. "De Bouton says it should mend within a year or two."

Whenever the line of boats halted for someone's cry, Prue feared to look toward their nets, so clearly could she imagine Pearl's appearance, drowned. The nets continued to bring up fish and detritus, and the boats continued to move slowly, blocking all traffic. The captains of the few ships waiting in the bay must have known what they were doing, and Prue hoped they were praying for her sister's safe return.

Buttermilk Channel emptied into the bay just past the Luquer Mill and the tannery, and Prue understood their hopes of finding Pearl would be dashed if they did not turn her up before reaching it. No one dredged a bay.

As the snaking line approached the mill, Prue saw old Nicolaas Luquer standing atop the small, pitched roof protecting his trash rack from airborne debris. The blackened shards of timber that had fallen from the bridge had already been dragged up to shore. One of Nicolaas's feet rested on each slope of the roof, and he faced the boats with his arms folded across his chest and his mouth hanging open. Prue had the impression he was looking straight at her, but he was far enough off, she could not say. His daughter Eelkje, three boats down, called "Father?" and the river, against its habit, was so quiet, her voice resounded off the buildings of the mill and farm.

Only after his daughter had called out to him could Prue see Nicolaas was crying; that was why his mouth hung open. Prue began to shake anew. Tem, still crouched on the deck of the barge, said quietly, "No, no, no," exactly as she had done when their father's body had come up in the wagon. She began patting about the bare, moldy planks as if she'd lost something.

Ben wrapped his arms around Prue from behind. He was as damp and chill as she.

Their end of the net slipped into the water, and Rachael Livingston hurried to gather it up. Prue almost wanted to jump in after it and drown, rather than see what she was about to see.

"Father, did you find her?" Eelkje called as they drew nearer.

Nicolaas's mouth still hung open, revealing his tongue and teeth. Prue expected his "yes" or a nod of his head so completely that at first she could not discern that he was shaking his head no. Once she saw, she disbelieved it.

"You didn't find her?" Eelkje said. They were no more than twenty feet from the small roof.

Nicolaas shook his head more forcefully and continued to cry.

The oarsmen drew Prue's barge up to bump against the trash rack, and it came to a halt. Prue's whole body shook as Nicolaas awkwardly crouched down.

Prue saw Pearl's chain dangling limply from his fist, and when he opened his hand, her notecase was nestled inside, its pages so bloated, those that had not torn away were soft and open as a fan made of feathers. Prue recognized it, yet her mind would not apprehend its import, and she stared at it blankly. Someone nearby began to scream, and it took Prue a moment to realize the voice she heard was her own. As soon as she did, she stopped and stood with her hand over her mouth, shaking and crying. Ben, still behind her, held on to her, and Tem walked unsteadily across the deck to take the ruined book from Nicolaas's hand.

The men drew the barge closer in to shore and unloaded Tem, Ben, and Prue onto the strand. Nicolaas stepped from the trash rack to the ground and placed a hand on Ben's shoulder. The men rowed the barge closer to the next one, and Rachael Livingston tossed one end of her net back to Marcel. "We'll keep going, out to the mouth of the bay," Marcel said to Ben.

Ben said, "Thank you."

Mrs. Luquer was walking down the path, wringing her hands. Prue did not feel herself capable of bearing one more person's grief; it was enough to look after her own. The flotilla set off southward, its pace slow as before. Prue kept turning to watch it over her shoulder as Ben led her up the hill to the Luquers' warm house.

Once they were inside, Mrs. Luquer brought them dry clothing and fed them lentils and hot sweet tea. Neither Prue nor Tem could stop crying, but they were so hungry and cold, they spooned food into their mouths whenever they could quit weeping long enough to do so. When they once caught a glimpse of each other, looking as sorry as either of

them ever had, they could not help laughing despite everything. Before
the meal was through, Prue noticed her sister's lips had returned to their
ordinary color; and the moment they had cleaned their plates, Mrs. Luquer led them up to the one large room all her children shared, and they
lay down on various beds. Prue had not even stretched her body out before she fell asleep. She awoke in a ball in the early afternoon to find Ben
and Tem still sleeping, the dull sky unchanged, and no news of Pearl
downstairs, except that the boats had ceased their search when they'd
reached the mouth of the bay. Most of the riders had returned to Brooklyn for news and, hearing of the notebook, had not gone back out to
search again.

Nicolaas Luquer drove them home in his wagon, as if they were a
load of malted grain to be alchemized to gin. As his bandy-legged horses
clopped up the Shore Road, Prue thought once more of the day her father had died, and of all the times she had made this journey in his company. The familiar houses and wharves looked different beneath the
shadow of a life-rending misery. Nicolaas kept leaning toward them, offering hope that although Pearl had not been found, she might yet live;
but Prue saw Ben did not believe this.

Isaiah had left word with Abiah asking them to find him at the distillery when they returned. Abiah had been weeping alone in the house all
day, and fell onto Prue's shoulder the moment she saw Pearl's water-
logged book hanging from her hand. Prue held her to console her but
could no longer cry herself.

"You should both continue to rest," Ben said, brushing his hair back
from his brow as if what troubled him were only a headache. "I can go to
my brother."

"No," Tem said.

Prue echoed her. "We need to see what damage has been done, and
set the men repairing it."

"I'm sure Isaiah has done so already."

"I need to see it with my own eyes," Prue said quietly.

He nodded his understanding.

Oh, this is grief, Prue thought as she walked down the lane to the distillery—this soft December afternoon, overcast and mild. She had thought
her heart could not bear one more hardship when her mother had died,
and again when she'd lost her father; losing the promise of an infant had

seemed the greatest imaginable sadness, but losing Susannah had proven how thoroughly she'd misunderstood. This emptiness, in its turn, showed her truly what emptiness was. She knew no better than anyone where the dead resided—and reflected she knew much less well than Will Severn. His faith in Heaven was solid as an old Dutch house, while hers blew in the breeze as if it were the trailing leaves of a willow. But even Prue's scant knowledge of the Other Side sufficed to show her the dead were dead, their bodies safe in the churchyard and their souls safe who knew where. But who could say where Pearl had gone? Most likely, she had drowned, and would wash up soon in Upper or Lower New York Bay. Until she did, the possibility remained she was alive. Prue felt Pearl's absence keenly, but could not bring herself to mourn for her until she knew without question what had become of her. This was its own rare grief— to lament her sister so utterly, and yet to hold out to herself the prospect of Pearl's safe return.

As she reached the bottom of the hill, she saw the distillery with fresh sadness. The whole waterfront was covered with soot, and on the smoldering spots where the rectifying, casking, and storehouses had been, fires were burning, dispatching the blackened debris. Some of the workers wheeled barrows of charred wood to the bonfires, while others used the push brooms from the brewhouse to sweep ash into the river. The press appeared to have melted around its edges and now resembled a badly scarred old anvil; pieces of the rectifying stills had survived unscathed, bolts and screws and bits of twisted pipe. Men were picking through the detritus to find any such remains, trucking them down to the water, washing them, and placing them to dry on planks set out in the mill yard. Isaiah was up on the bridge, talking to C. Mather Harrison and directing two men in sweeping ash from the charred sides of the Brooklyn lever. The soot fell like a curtain of rain.

When Isaiah saw Prue, Ben, and Tem approaching, he gave the men some last instructions and hastened down. Harrison followed a respectful distance behind him. Prue noticed Isaiah had washed and shaved since the morning. Compared to the wreckage over which he was seeking to establish dominion, he appeared the picture of order. Ben drew him close in an embrace.

"Well met," Isaiah said. After holding his brother a moment, he reached out for Prue and Tem the same.

Harrison removed his hat and stepped forward to shake Ben's hand. "Mr. and Mrs. Horsfield," he said, "I cannot tell you how grieved I am for your loss."

Prue wanted to thank him, but found herself wondering if his professed grief would prevent him from making hay of their misfortune. He himself had always proven trustworthy, but she did not think she could bear to see the words in which his paper's rival, the *New-York Journal*, would couch the tale.

"I know I am a mere acquaintance," he continued, "but I have ever been a great supporter of this bridge, and I am sorry to see it—and you—brought to such a pass. If there is anything I may do—"

"Write nothing of it," Ben said, no heat in his tone. "Leave us in peace."

Harrison looked up at the ruined tip of the Brooklyn lever. "But anyone can see the damage to the bridge and the distillery. The *Argus* would be irresponsible not to print a report."

"The other papers have sent their men already," Isaiah offered.

Ben nodded. "Then please write nothing of our sister Pearl."

"No, Ben," Tem said. "If he writes a notice, it may well help us find her."

Ben regarded her crossly, but did not respond. Prue could see how tired he was. "Very well, then, Mr. Harrison. I see there is nothing you can do."

Harrison put his hat back on and stowed his pencil in his pocket. "You have my word, Mr. Horsfield, I shall not malign you." Ben nodded his thanks, and Harrison bowed before setting off for the ferry. All three of them watched him go. The rhythmic sweep of the push broom kept slow time.

Isaiah waited until Harrison was well out of earshot before saying, "I have news."

"What, has she been found?" Tem asked.

"No."

"I believe no other news would interest me," she said blandly. She looked over to the nearest bonfire and shook her head. "Have we any idea how much has been lost?"

"I shall take tally once we're finished cleaning. I've already written the underwriters, and shall write both to Philadelphia and to England tomorrow to inquire about the cost of replacing the stills and the press. As for the orders, I have begun to contact our customers, explaining the circumstances and begging their pardon for the delay. I believe they will take pity on us."

"They can get gin from John Putnam at a lesser cost," Prue said.

"But of lesser quality, I'm told. And I believe people are larger than that." He coughed into his handkerchief and pulled it away, smudged black. "But this is not the news of which I spoke. How much money was in the safe yesterday at closing?"

Tem shrugged her shoulders wearily.

"You were the last one out," Prue told him. "You ought to have counted and locked it."

He nodded, and the crease appeared between his brows. "Come with me a moment," he said, and they started toward the countinghouse. He took the open stairs two at a time. As he turned his key in the lock, he said, "I have left all as I found it this morning."

Even the countinghouse, whose windows had been closed, stank of the fire, and all the surfaces were dulled with a fine dusting of pale ash. The stove had not been lit, and the room felt chilly. Prue thought how strange the place seemed, without a pot of Isaiah's good coffee burbling in welcome. "I don't see anything," Tem said.

Prue, however, did. The door to the safe was ajar, and she crouched down to peer inside. When she saw it empty, her heart flickered with anticipation, though her mind tried to quiet it. "You left the usual hundred dollars in last night?"

"Indeed," Isaiah answered. "And I assume neither of you came down to empty it."

Tem was shaking her head as if she'd be pleased to wash her hands of all of them.

Prue was doing her best to remain calm, but she felt she might explode. "It must have been Pearl. She had the key. She would not have taken our money only to jump in the river."

"Exactly as I think," Isaiah said, his face as bright as Prue believed her own must be.

"She may yet have fallen in," Tem said.

"But we should send the riders back out at once," Ben said. He looked too grubby and exhausted to do anything, but he said, "I'll run to

Joe Loosely's and see whom else I can find to go," and set off down the stairs.

Tem went to pour herself a sup of gin. She first wiped the ash from the teacup with her cuff. "Don't look so pleased," she said to Prue before taking her drink. "It's still only a chance."

"A better one than finding her book in the river," Prue said. The joy was still fizzing in her breast like champagne. If Pearl had tried to burn down everything Prue owned, she'd had her reasons, had not succeeded, and could yet be forgiven. If she'd taken the distillery's money, it must have been with the intention to escape, though Prue could not understand why her sister had not taken Will Severn with her, or even told him good-bye. No likeness of Pearl had ever been made, but she could easily be recognized by a stranger provided with her description. Prue thought she would be back among them soon enough. "She's fine, Tem," she said, though she knew how little her sister would count this. "I know it."

Tem offered Prue the empty cup. "You know it," she repeated, her eyes watering.

"I do," Prue said. She did not want a drink at all.

Isaiah began moving papers about the desk. "The other question," he said, looking at his own hands, "is how to proceed until we receive funds from our insurers." He found the paper he was looking for, moved it to the top, and blew on it to clear it of ash.

"We've the money from the mortgage," Prue said. Tem glanced at her sidelong, and in her own defense she said, "We can use it for the manu-factory until we are reimbursed."

Tem poured herself a second dram. "It seems risky," she said.

"Not so much in winter as it would be in spring," Isaiah said. "Ben cannot recommence building before the thaw, and surely the money will come in by then." Tem drank, and Isaiah went on, "We have rather a dire circumstance on our hands, Temmy. We need three new buildings, a press, three stills, and a few hundred thousand gallons of gin, all simply to be back where we were on Monday."

"Then perhaps the bridge should wait," Tem said.

Isaiah said, "No. My brother is deeply indebted to Albany. He cannot abandon it."

Tem set her cup down and shook her head. "I can't think of anything, with Pearl missing," she said. Prue understood, and suspected Isaiah did also. "Perhaps I'll go help with the cleaning, or see if Mr. Jones can start replacing our lost casks."

"That would be of great service," Isaiah said.

"I do suppose it gives me hope, to know about the safe," she said, and went glumly toward the stairs.

"Are you at all nervous?" Prue asked Isaiah, once her sister was gone. "Right now I wish your house were secure, and you not responsible for any of this."

"I should be, either way," he said. "I am tied to this distillery as surely as you, and likewise to the bridge." He must have sensed her skepticism, for he said, "The chief matter is to find out if Pearl yet lives. Beyond that, I believe we can manage everything."

Prue nodded to him and said, "I'll go help Temmy, then. I think it'll do us both good."

As she walked down into the mill yard, she imagined how it would feel to find Ben galloping up the road, bearing news that Pearl had been discovered at Jamaica or Croton Point. Then she imagined their young postman bringing similar news in a day or two. Neither fantasy filled the hollowness in her belly, but each provided a measure of relief.

The grounds already appeared more orderly than when she'd arrived. If dusk was descending, she thought, it was probably good news; the day had gone on a long time already, and she would gladly start anew in the morning.

She had no basis nor history for the glimmer of optimism she felt at that moment, but there it was. She did not know if she could trust it, but she felt it rustling to resettle itself within her, exactly as would a baby. She would cherish it the same way, no matter how ill it had ever availed her to do so before.

And as if in sign she had chosen the right course, Mr. Harrison proved as good as his word. His news article the next morning gave the facts of the disaster, but did not deign to speculate about its causes. A separate item told of Pearl's disappearance, and made an earnest entreaty for her safe return.

Twenty-six

THE MEASURE OF A MAN

Wednesday 19 June '22
The Countinghouse

No, Recompense, my beloved;—my sister never did return. No body nor any more of her possessions washed up at the Luquer Mill, nor was her slender form found by the fishermen downstream. We sent notice of her disappearance to every municipality from Albany to Philadelphia & Suffolk, and offer'd a reward for news of her whereabouts; but all those who came seeking it proved adventurers. So far as I knew, Pearl Winship had never gone farther than Fly Market under her own power, yet she had seduced a man of God, committed arson, and ventured out untraced into the world. I had clearly taken her measure incorrectly. If she had not changed overnight, then she had never been the woman I'd supposed her.

All my years, I'd lived in loathful fear of death. I had eaten my self with worry about how people lived on the Other Side; had kept on in my father's business because it was my debt to the departed; had dreamed up a fitting monument to soar over the water & memorialise my terrour of and curiosity about what might come. Yet to ken the suffering of grieving for the dead could not prepare me for the pain of not knowing if Pearl walked amongst them. At least, I thought, had she managed to burn down both bridge & distillery, I would have been ruined outright, had cause to despise her, & begun my life anew in some other locale. Had she died, your Aunt Tem & I would have laid her in the churchyard, mourned her, & bid her adieu. Had she sent news from Boston that she never desired to see us more, we could likewise have said, *Fare thee well.*

But you see, we could do naught. I challenge any man who claims haunting by the dead to feel the chill of being haunted by uncertainty; & I will shew you a changed man. Her absence asserted it self by degrees, like each day's new dawn; but the moment I began to feel at leisure to wallow in my grief, the chair by the fire, in which she had so liked to sit, would suddenly have a hopeful air of prophecy about it, as if it awaited her return to its lap. Or if a morning came on which I felt a tingling sensation she might be nigh, by day's end I would have seen Mr. Severn,—who knew to the depths of his faith she was dead, and mourned her accordingly, his heart cracked open by pain. I some times thought he had far more knowledge than I, & must surely be correct; & I some times thought, how could he think otherwise? To have lost her to untimely death was tragick, but for him to imagine her purposing to leave him would have been intolerable misery.

I began to treat even Pearl's mottled cat as a potential sign. When, in the first few weeks of its solitude, it would cry for her, I believed its mistress must soon come home; and when, late in winter, it crawled beneath her chair and died, I suffered anew. I had never cared a jot for this critter, but I buried my face in its cold fur and wept for all we both had lost. I tied the small corpse in a pillow slip & buried it in the yard, all around which the crocus were just beginning to push up their shoots. I marked its sepulchre with the rosemary plant Abiah has ever since used to flavour chickens & potatoes, that should my sister ever return, she would be able to find her departed friend. No doubt its cat flesh has nourished you well, just as we have all feasted on British soldiers all the years we've enjoyed asparagus in summer time.

On certain days, I found it unbearable to see to rebuilding the distillery & the bridge, when Pearl occupied my every thought. On others, I counted it a blessing to have such work to distract me from my more intimate cares.

The monies from our ensurance came through soon enough, but were a mixed blessing: Associated Underwriters provided us ample funds to rebuild & to replace the lost machinery, but with a concomitant increase in our rate so steep, I thought it should do us in within the year.

The war for independence had largely been fought over taxation; why, I
wondered then, had no one bothered to cry out against the usury of
ensurance? Nevertheless, there seemed naught to do but proceed.
Winship Daughters Gin ordered timber & lumber almost worthy of a
bridgeworks, all through Theunis van V., whose profit thereby was at
least some consolation. We managed to keep all our indentured servants
and nearly all our hired men employed full-time in the rebuilding; & the
new rectifying stills & press were slated to arrive in spring, so we might
resume production then. The repairs progressed as well as anyone could
hope,—we would have roofs on all our new buildings before the
equipment arrived,—but each morning when I woke, I felt as if the
bank & the ensurance company each held a silken noose about my
throat. I imagined them finely made & gossamer, yet capable of choking
me nonetheless. That the hangman would in truth come not for me but
for your father provided no solace.

Dear God, my daughter, I am glad you were not among us then; you
would have thought you had automata for parents. We had to tread so
carefully;—manage each day's work to perfection, and stretch each
penny to the size of a half dollar. We still could not say if our plan of
adjusting the angles of the bridge's two levers would result in a stable
structure, and this caused us daily anxiety. We renounced meat for our
table, and ate beans & vegetables, like the poor. Your bright-spirited
father grew grim as a shade. For my part, although I suffer'd nightmares
over the twin prospects of failing at the bridge & the distillery, there was
no thought induced more dread than the notion of Patience packing up
her four children & linens in a cart & cursing me as they drove away to
who knew where. For her sake, I had to keep my mind on our eventual
success. & such fancies were yet as nothing compared to my dreams of
Pearl. No matter to what task I attended, images of her accompanied
me. As springtime burgeoned, I marked the time when she might have
given birth to a child, as sloe-eyed as she'd been on emerging from the
womb. As spring turned to summer, and the Brookland lever began to
arc gracefully on its now slightly diverted course out toward the river's
centre, I imagined the baby smiling & drooling, holding up her own
wobbling head,—for although I knew naught of this child, including
that it had not been drowned in the East River & et by sea creatures, I
believed her a girl child. & I sensed that, in direct proportion to the way

I'd theretofore been denied the consolation of the fruits of my womb, this girl would be Pearl's balm of Gilead,—the restitution for all she had suffered, & the emblem of her love.

I believed if my own father had brought me home to meet my Pappy, bearing that old man so little affection as he did, Pearl would one day bring this gell to meet us. I recognised I had done Pearl a grievous wrong,—both in cursing her & in treating her as cursed, the rest of her days,—but I thought she must know I had loved her the more deeply because of it. She had a temper, but she had also a good heart, and I thought the seed of forgiveness must already have taken root there. I imagined various scenarios for her return: a simple arrival, on the ferry or the stage; or a letter written in her energetick hand, containing little news but the name of her daughter & the place of her abode. I almost wished it might be the latter, that I could craft with care my reply to her,—pour out the contents of my heart and the apology I had been wrong never to muster when she walked amongst us. She might write back directly, or hold her peace; but when the weather next turned fair, she'd begin the slow journey home, the child exclaiming on every thing from the back of the mail coach or the side of the boat.

& surely you know this is why your father and I visit the Twin Tankards whenever a roaming balladeer arrives;—because I still hope one may bring a ballad of Pearl, scrubbing floors for a living in some northern town, or married to a wealthy New Bedford seaman. Though she will be a woman of middle years by now, I will recognize her by her silent tongue and her raven-black hair, shot through, like Aunt Tem's, with grey. I will recognize her by her beautiful bastard child. And I will leave the distillery in the capable hands of your aunt and your Uncle Izzy, and travel north, south, east, or west to speak with her or fetch her back home. If ever you & Jonas hear such a tale, I pray you,—report it to me right away.

We resumed production of gin in May of 1802. Many of our customers took pity on our misfortune & doubled their usual orders. A few,—Elisha Green of Albany among them,—sent charitable contributions to help us regain our footing after the disaster. The bridge we had begun to repair & realign as soon as the weather had turned warm and the timber merchant had been able to ship our materials down the North River; there was almost enough delay in this to make me despair of the bridge's eventual completion, as we now needed more than we had supposed, & our demand sorely taxed the new merchant's supply. Your father and his crew traveled to New-York each day to continue work on their realigned lever. Marcel & I did the sadder work of making up lost ground on the Brookland side. For each day's progress, and for each section of the arm compleated without fatal accident, we ought to have given thanks; but I found I could think of nothing but the unlikelihood the two arms should actually meet midstream, & how far behind New-York's side we were, & how we had already once been where then we stood, but in happier circumstances.

By the end of that building season, the bridge stood close to completion. The New-York lever had arrived at its ultimate length, and its course seemed to have been corrected; my own lagged perhaps three months' labour behind. Oh, Recompense, I'd have danced round a fire & called out the names of the native gods could I thus have ensured even another week of clement weather, so anxious was I to see the thing done. I cannot express in words the bittersweet way its grandeur struck me. Not even a drawing as large or lovely as your Aunt Pearl's could begin to approximate its beauty as it arced so much of the way across the straits; & yet, each day it was not finished, its expenses mounted, and I began to think it was worth neither the hundreds of thousands of dollars it had cost nor the trouble it had brought us. I sometimes thought, if we eventually ruined our selves over it, at least it would be a grand thing over which to be ruined. At other times I remembered our unwilling partner, Patience, & knew such thoughts were folly.

That winter,—the same in which you were at last conceived,—proved the bitterest anyone could recall. A person could'n't go outdoors without his eye lashes turning to icicles & the hairs freezing in his nostrils. A number of our chickens lost their combs to the frost bite, despite how well we'd packed their coop with straw; and Ivo Joralemon lost two toes of his remaining foot to exposure when he fell in a snow drift & took three hours to attract the attention of a rescuer.

The frost heave was prodigious come spring, tumbling fences that had withstood twenty winters. The papers predicted a dire fate for the bridge, but your father and I knew it was founded well below the frost line. To our horrour, however, the soil must have shifted deep beneath

the Brookland footing, for it settled by three inches on its downriver
side. You can imagine the panick on your father's countenance as he and
Adam checked and rechecked their measurements, their boots sinking
into the mucky springtime sand.

—It cannot be, he once said, as we sat together in this
countinghouse, poring over his figures a fourth time. —Jesus God! We
drove the piles to refusal; what could have moved? He looked to the
ceiling as if it might answer him. —Some soil we did not account for.
Jesus, Prue! We have only just corrected the misalignment in plan, and
now we've one in elevation.

—The Schermerhorns shore up their buildings each spring, I
answered him. Surely we can do likewise?

He shook his greying head. He could fret and curse until the trumpet
blast, but the numbers kept coming up the same. —I cannot go on
hiding this, he said. I'm certain the worry has cost me my old age. I shall
write to Mr. Clinton.

—And to Mr. Pope, I said.

—And to Mr. Pope.

We anxiously awaited their replies. Mr. Pope's came first, indicating
that he would board the stage as soon as it was practical, & offer
whatever advice he might. The governor's response was slower to arrive.
It did not reach the countinghouse until two weeks after the building
season ought to have commenced. Our workers were camp'd in the yard
with naught to do but drink & gamble, to facilitate which Joe Loosely
set up a regular roster of cock baitings, dogfights, & greased pig
contests to lure the men from Fischer's new alehouse, which stood a
quarter mile closer by. Governor Clinton's letter, when at last it came,
advised us to seek counsel from Mr. Pope, whose age & experience
would guide him in directing us. If he believed the Brookland
foundation could be adequately propped to prevent further sinking,
then we were to proceed with the bridge. If not, Ben was to write Mr.
Clinton at his earliest convenience for further instructions.

There was no longer any need for both of us to continue on the
works, especially while the men idled in anticipation of Pope's
inspection. I returned full-time to my distillery, which had never been a
more welcome refuge from the greater world, though the bridge took
up perhaps more of my thoughts than ever. Your father seemed the

victim of a temporary blindness. As if it were truly a remedy, he began asking his men to cut the timbers for the sides of the lever to account, ever so subtly, for this new divergence from true. To the eye, of course, such trickery would be invisible, but the chisel knew it, & the wood plane; and I thought the abutment was destined to know it, too. Before Mr. Pope's arrival, Ben also organized a second crew to build a structure to shore up the sinking side of the anchorage with stone & iron. Mr. Pope scratched his head over it when he came, as he did not see how anything above ground could compensate for a faulty foundation. Your father unleashed his powers of persuasion, however, and ultimately convinced him to think it a wise addition to the plan. Pope wrote to his colleague Mr. Avery in Massachusetts for corroboration; when it arrived, Ben considered himself to have permission to proceed.

When I had once expressed my concern about his methods, your father ceased to discuss them with me. He was as sweet with me as ever, but it was as if I wore a black veil when I spoke with him; there was something gossamer-thin but noticeable between us.

The bridge's last slightly torqued timber was secured to its position on the fifth of June, 1803. The men let up such a raucous cheer, Elliott Fortune & I heard it in the fermenting room, and hurried above ground to see what was amiss. To see it there, its span compleat, was a joy incomparable, despite all we had endured. (When I crowed my happiness at that moment, you made a flip in my womb to let me know the bridge pleased you as well.) Your father came running off the bridge and down the mill yard, hollering like a wild man, & scooped me up, weeping and laughing. The workers applauded for this, we set them free on the gin for the rest of the day; a public celebration would follow, but that afternoon, those who'd built the bridge reveled. That evening, we roped off the entries to the bridge on both sides of the river and hired guards to watch over it, lest it be swarmed with curious folk. Your father wrote to the governor, the newly appointed mayor of New-York (who was also the governor's nephew;—a circumstance I assumed was no accident), Mr. Willemsen, & Mr. Pope that very afternoon, and the date was set to dedicate the bridge in honour of the Fourth of July.

Had you been a sentient being in those next few weeks, you might have thought your native village was preparing for General Washington to march into town triumphant. Every tavern and shop in Brookland &

New-York had its red, white, & blue bunting over the door and its flag of the Republic flying, and nearly every house sported in at least one of its windows a paper silhouette of the bridge. Hawkers on New-York's streets sold paper fans & woodcuts adorned with what they called the "Rainbow Bridge," and broadsheets with at least a dozen different songs and poems in its honour could be had for a federal penny. Joe, the Philpots, & Mr. Fischer laid in prodigious supplies of ale, and Tem & I stepped up production at the works, for we knew a great deal of gin would be drunk from our storehouses. Peg Dufresne was an old, old woman by then, but she set to candying fruit and baking, lest a good opportunity for profit pass her by.

I went out at dawn to observe the bridge on the morning of the Fourth, & already Brookland and the New-York docks were bustling. All three ferry boats were shuttling across the water, carrying those who wished to assure themselves the best view to station themselves near the abutments. Brookland's roads were usually quiet enough until eight in the morning, but that day, carts were rumbling in on the Ferry Road & the Jamaica Turnpike. Pedestrians streamed up the Shore Road and down Joralemon's Lane, many waving pennants with images of the bridge or patriotic slogans.

By nine, thousands of people must have packed the waterfront, and we could see a similar crowd across the water in Mannahata. Ben & Tem & I stood in our appointed place before the Brookland anchorage; and as I looked round at the cheerful, red-faced throng, I wondered if Pearl or perhaps her shade might be hovering at its periphery. I believe Tem saw me thinking this, as, without explanation, she reached up her palm to cup my cheek & held it there longer than I thought entirely comfortable. When Governor Clinton's boat entered Buttermilk Channel near the Luquer Mill, a huge cheer went up from that quarter & echoed up the straits. On hearing it, the regimental band the Philpots had hired struck up its blaring tune, and thousands of banners of welcome began to wave. The roar of cheering and applause when the governor set foot on Brookland's soil was louder than a thunderstorm. Soon after the governor landed, Mr. DeWitt Clinton, the new mayor of New-York, arrived on a bark of his own, surrounded by every last one of the aldermen. The day already promised to be sultry,—the straits stank of salt & fish,—but all these men wore their finest and most formal attire, and dabbed at their faces with lace-edged handkerchiefs.

—May I have your attention? Governor Clinton called out. The crowd quieted, but his voice could not have carried more than ten or twelve heads deep into the assembly. —Ladies and gentlemen, he went on. Today marks a great occasion for our state, the fair city of New-York, & the village of Brookland. Not only does the day commemorate twenty-seven years of freedom from the tyranny of British rule; but it marks New-York's ascendancy as the foremost city of this nation, & Brookland's as a vibrant port and place of manufacture in her own right.

At this last, the cheers were deafening. He continued:

—No other state has yet financed a public work of such magnitude or importance. If it has been alleged by men of the Old World that the New has no wonders of which to boast, we give them the lie today.

Mr. Clinton acknowledged Ben & the workers; & Mr. Clinton his nephew gave also an eloquent speech; and I thought back ruefully on the simple words Will Severn had spoken when we'd dug up the first spadeful for the Brookland foundation. He stood in the crowd that day,—his head bare,—and although I harboured profound anger against him for his role in my sister's disappearance, his expression tore at me. By then his physiognomy had congealed into an attitude of resignation that could have melted the heart of a much colder woman than I. Within the year he would receive a calling from a church in the Carolinas, and go forth from amongst us.

When the speeches were done, Ben handed our governor a pair of scissors polished to a glinting sheen; & with all due ceremony, Mr. Clinton cut the ribbon stretched across the accessway to the bridge. A great shout went up all round & hats were tossed in the air; a moment later, one could see and hear a similar cheer reverberating across the water. The newsmen scribbled on their books. As the whooping continued, Mr. Clinton & his nephew began to process across. The assemblymen followed, as did we; & behind us, the whole crowd began to surge through the archway in the Gothic abutment. I half feared we should be swarmed & trampled, but for all their excitement & their great numbers, people remained in line. On the New-York side, the crowd jumped, hollered, & waved their flags at us with gusto; they could not cross in the opposite direction until our group arrived and Mr. Clinton cut their ribbon as well.

We spent that hot, bright day reveling among the New-Yorkers; and none could have been more awed than I at how wonderful it was to traverse the East River in so novel a fashion. It took four hours to cross in either direction, so many times was your father stopped for congratulations. When at last we were safe home in Brookland, long past sunset, your father, Aunt Tem, & I were all burned red as sour cherries by the sun. As I rubbed the sliced end of a cucumber over Tem's burned nape, I thought of how freckled Pearl had grown, her last summer among us,—and I prayed to God that if my sister yet lived, she would hear news of the bridge's compleation, forgive me my trespass, & come home.

The New-York & Brookland papers gave varying estimates of the crowds that day, but none less than five thousand souls. Only the *New-York Journal* printed doomful prognostications about the bridge's future; and when I complained of this to Isaiah, he promised me the piece had been written by some foolish old Luddite, & would be little attended to. C. Mather Harrison wrote of nothing but the bridge's beauty.

It was a good year for the bridge. However many thousands of people had crossed it that first day,—and however subtle our adjustments to the structure itself, to make its two levers meet,—it had held true; & henceforward, people seemed to have no fear of it. The charge to cross, after that first day, was but a penny, so th'inhabitants of our village and her sister city used it not just for commerce but for sport; and I wondered if I would have to retire my trusty barges, now it was so easy to load gin onto wagons and whisk it across. Ben & I knew years would elapse before the state recouped her investment, we erased our debts, & anyone saw a dollar in profit; but I felt safe in hoping this would not take too *many* years.

The winter of 1803 and aught four proved milder than the previous one. It began to seem your father's subterfuge, sanctioned by Mr. Pope, had safeguarded the bridge against further settling. You were a sleepy dumpling of a baby, & I strapped you in a shawl to my back so that in all kinds of weather your father and I might travel out to measure the bridge & check its solidity in plan and elevation. We began to think we had been spared the worst possible fate; and the *New-York*

Journal's attacks upon the bridge subsided to mere grumblings & whispers.

Everything proved thus sound until the thaw came in March of 1804 & great cracks began to yawn along the bridge's downriver façade. Your father first hired men to pitch these, then to drive iron tie rods through the bridge as a whole, to embrace it tight with brackets. (You can surely imagine what the newssheets had to say about this.) When he took new measurements of the structure at the beginning of the summer, however, he found it was *warping*: listing so severely to southward on the Brookland end that sooner or later, it seemed, the bridge would snap in two, like a wad of dough one breaks in half by twisting. I had never seen Ben look so ashen. What could we do for it, however, but continue to pitch its cracks and pray? That July, we wrote desperately to Mr. Pope & to his colleague Mr. Avery in Boston, asking their advice; but it was too late. Early one morning in August of 1804, a farmer from Flat Bush travelled over in his ox cart, and in the wake of the conveyance, some three central feet of the roadway plummeted into the river, narrowly missing a wherry headed up toward Hell Gate. The cart slipped back over the precipice a moment & lost its bales of hay, but the driver whipped his beasts into a phrenzy to drive them onward, and two men crossing in the other direction leapt off their horses and helped pull the cart up to safety. At last all three men, the oxen, & the cart were safe, but there was pandemonium on the bridge. Within the quarter hour, both accessways were secured against further traffick; and when your father & I arrived on the scene & could make sense of the accusations & conflicting reports that greeted us, we both suspected it had been nothing less than divine intervention had prevented the farmer & the wherryman on the river being killed. When the debris later jammed in the trash rack without breaking the Luquers' mill, this seemed the working of Providence as well.

I wonder if you can imagine our terrour as we awaited word from Governor Clinton, Mr. Pope, & Mr. Avery. The bridge, to both our minds, had now thoroughly failed, and seemed unlikely to be rebuilt, & although the distillery was thus far successful in battling off John Putnam's incursions, we were mortgaged & ensured to our eyeballs, & did not know how we might pay off the debt. More awful to consider was how your father's heart was bound up in the thing, perhaps even more than mine:—his heart, & his reputation. Mr. Pope never wrote us, though we received a letter from his secretary telling us the great bridge architect was taken ill with nervous exhaustion & the doctor had requested all unfortunate news be kept from him. Mr. Avery, however, arrived at his earliest convenience, and first thing, shook his head in pity to see the beautiful thing so ruined. He wrote his recommendation to the governor that the entire Brookland end of the structure should be torn down & rebuilt upon a deeper & sturdier foundation; the which he himself would help us design, for a moderate fee.

As I'm sure you recall, August in Brookland was always long,— pestilentially hot and foul-smelling. That year the month dragged out even more than usual, as we could do nothing but look at the broken hulk until the legislature reconvened. September, for all its beauty, likewise threatened to last an age; but in the middle of the month Ben received his letter from Governor Clinton. Though that gentleman stood in favour of the bridge & of Mr. Avery's proposal, he reported to his great sadness that the state was already far too deeply in arrears as regarded our bridge, & could not afford to invest a penny more in it. If we could raise the needed funds at home, the governor sent his blessings; if not, it was his suggestion we sell off the bridge's *matériel* & remit whatever price they brought to the state. This, he wrote, would discharge our debt, as the bridge had been a brave & noble effort, & its failure could rightly be blamed only in part upon us.

I thought your father might tear out his own hair in grief; & he boarded a boat to Albany next day to plead with the legislature; but to no avail. We could no longer afford the kinds of bribes had got us our permission in the first place. Mr. Clinton was persuaded to return your father to his post as King's County's surveyor, but no more than that. He came home to me with his hands empty, and I wondered if his misery would at last be the thing to do us all in. With his last vestige of good humour departed, our home seemed a dark, dark place. He hired as many workmen as he could muster for the demolition; but it was nowhere near so enticing or skilled a job as raising a bridge, & there were fewer volunteers.

The sale was set for the fifteenth of October, advertised in every town within a three days' journey; & with the exception of C. Mather Harrison, who remained our supporter to the end, the newssheets were

full of ridicule. Broadsides circulated featuring vitriolic cartoons of your
father as a bumpkin in short pants who traced out the idea for the
bridge in the dirt, and of the men building it drunk on gin, & of me as
an Amazon warrioress, breaking the span with my oversized boot. Joe
Loosely himself volunteered to conduct the auction for the thousands
of tons of timber, iron, & stone.

   —You know I never favoured the bridge, Prue, he told me, as we sat
together at his bar. In my lap, you sucked on the yolk of a boiled egg, &
spat crumbs of it onto my britches, oblivious as you were to the
situation's *gravitas*. —Yet it still pains me to see my friend's daughter
brought so low. It is why I wish to do it myself. Do you unnerstand?

   —I do, I said. My own egg was ashes on my tongue.

   Joe nodded grimly. I thought he looked old all of a sudden; & I
wondered if, despite his protestation, he had felt even the slightest
flicker of cold-blooded joy at our misfortune.

   The auction was held on a lovely harvest moon day, very like that on
which my father had died. I watched from the crowd's periphery as the
Hickses, Sandses, and Whitcombes bought up wood for new houses at a
dime on the dollar, & as ambassadors from New-York & Pavonia &
places even farther afield acquired limestone for city halls, &c &c. No
one of my neighbours would meet my eye;—so grief-filled must have
been my countenance, or so thorough my disgrace. Joe was generally a
lively auctioneer, but though his voice was strong that morning, I could
see the work pained him. He had no smiles nor jibes to offer when his
hammer came down. He would simply move on to the next lot of
timber or iron, & cry it without emotion. For myself, I do not know
how I managed not to weep.

   That day, he sold every thing but a vestige of the Brookland
anchorage, which as well you know, still mars the distillery's landscape.
As, numb with sorrow, your father and I left the scene, our neighbours
gave us a wide berth. I imagined this was how we would be treated if we
harboured typhus in our home. By the next day, however, small gifts had
begun to appear on our *stoep*: a parcel of fresh egg noodles, three
pumpkins, & an apple pie so lovely, it could only have come from Peg
Dufresne. We took these gifts gladly, and counted them & you our only
succour. By the next week, the winning bidders had begun to send their
barges & carts to take the spoils home. Neither of us could watch this. I

kept to the distillery & never once looked out the huge windows of the countinghouse. I thought if I might focus all my efforts on the business my father had left me, this might mitigate my sorrow. Your father sat round the house, wondering when someone would offer him a commission in his old employment.

Even at that sorrowful time, perhaps the oddest thing about the whole affair seemed to me how people on both sides of the river had well nigh forgotten I'd had aught to do with the disastrous bridge. I was still *Prue Winship, Distiller of Gin*; but your father, wherever he went, was the *Architect of the Folly*. Few but Ben, Isaiah, & my own two sisters had ever known that the idea, at its origin, had been mine alone; but it struck me as passing strange how even Simon Dufresne & Theunis van Vechten lamented Ben's misjudgment of the foundations, without once mentioning how I had drawn up the articles of our misfortune. When I gathered the courage to begin venturing out once more with my deliveries, I found the story every where the same: That your father was a good man, but had been deluded; & that I was lucky he had not taken down my business entire. He bore up as well as a person could under this calumny, & urged me not to seek to redress it. —It will all pass in due time, he told me, as every thing does.

You see it was not the first nor the last occasion on which it served me well to follow his advice. I think the bridge lives on in people's memories, but it seldom appears in conversation. (I believe a similar situation obtains about my sister Pearl.) It was best to leave it all unspoken. I hope you do not cast blame on me for all these years of silence, exactly as I hope you do not disapprove of me for thinking, even now, my lost sister might one day return home. But at least, if you do, we may now speak of it. At least it need not stand between us.

Dearest:—tell me of your life. Tell me how your womb grows daily, & what pleasure or trepidation it brings you. I cannot continue to live knowing you so ill.

For the nonce, I send all my love,—

Yr mother, PWH

As she closed the letter, Recompense wondered if it was wrong of her to blame her mother as she did. She had mistreated her sister Pearl, and it was almost as great a transgression to have let her own husband carry the burden of a misfortune that had chiefly been her own doing. Recompense thought her mother had been uncivil and inhumane; and yet, Recompense's own childhood had been, if not entirely happy, then comfortable enough. She could not reconcile these opposing views. She reckoned this had something to do with how she herself could never have dreamed up a bridge.

When at last she confessed to her husband the extent of her concerns, Jonas urged her to forget her mother's errors and remember instead how difficult it must have been to vouchsafe them to her daughter. He reminded her how precious a burden such confessions were to bear. Recompense knew her husband was correct, and did what she could, the remainder of the summer, to engage her mother warmly and not to dwell on the repercussions of her actions. If there was some art, some dishonesty, in her own letters, Recompense preferred this to the possibility of driving her mother off forever. She surprised herself, harboring such a preference.

In early October, Recompense was delivered of a healthy daughter, who did, indeed, have the strange sloe-black eyes. Jonas gave his consent for the child to be named Pearl Horsfield Sutler; but the infant seemed to have little in common with her namesake, and babbled the day long. In the spring of 1823, Prue left the distillery in Tem's care, and she and Ben traveled up the Hudson to meet their granddaughter. By then, Recompense had forgotten much of her righteous anger over her aunt's and her father's mistreatment; or if she had not forgotten, she did when she saw her mother's face light up in happiness upon first holding the baby girl.

Pearl Sutler died of malaria that summer, before learning to walk or talk. Though the disease had been rampant that season, both Recompense and Jonas were shocked numb by the blow, and Recompense could not even bring herself to inform her family of it until well after the funeral. When she did, she considered writing her mother how even she now kept her eyes open for Pearl Winship, a small older woman, her black hair streaked with gray; how whenever she saw a dark-haired woman her own age disembark from the ferry, she wondered if it might not be her lost cousin. Then she thought better of it, and simply sent her mother the news.

ACKNOWLEDGMENTS

I wish to acknowledge the founder and the administrators of the Bard Fiction Prize for their generous financial support, and Ledig House International Writers' Colony and the Vermont Studio Center for time and space in which to write.

Many thanks are due to everyone at Farrar, Straus and Giroux for their fine work on *Brookland*'s behalf, but I particularly wish to express my gratitude to my editor, John Glusman, his assistant, Corinna Barsan, and Jonathan Lippincott, who designed this book so beautifully. I also wish to thank my agent, Eric Simonoff.

I owe especial thanks to Kirsten Bakis, both for being my first reader and for bequeathing Jolly to me from her own novel. I thank Laura Harger, Marshall Curry, and Jack Robbins for their invaluable help in reading later drafts; Michael Bardin and Ken Levenson for their assistance with architecture and engineering; Aoibheann Sweeney, Adam Snyder, Lauren Harrison, Jon Austin, Jeff Dolven, Graham Burnett, Edmond Miller, Philip Gura, Joe Martin, Ben Strauss, Kevin Grau, Bibi Gaston, and Judith Berger for answering questions while I was fact-checking; and Cecile Barendsma for the Dutch swears.

And lastly, dear Chris—I realize I promised you a book about the Brooklyn Bridge, but I hope this will suffice.

Emily Barton
Brooklyn, NY
October 2005

A NOTE ABOUT THE AUTHOR

Emily Barton earned her B.A. in English literature from Harvard University and an M.F.A. from the Iowa Writers' Workshop. Her fiction has appeared in *Story*, *American Short Fiction*, and *Conjunctions*. She is the recipient of a 2006–2007 grant from the National Endowment for the Arts; and her first novel, *The Testament of Yves Gundron* (FSG, 2000)—which won the Bard Fiction Prize and a Michener-Copernicus Fellowship—was named a New York Times Notable Book of the Year and a San Francisco Chronicle Book of the Month, and was nominated for Great Britain's Guardian Fiction Prize. She has taught writing and humanities at Bard College, and is a writer in residence at the New School in 2005/2006. She lives in Brooklyn, New York.